S0-AZI-904

BYGONES

Also by LaVyrle Spencer

FORGIVING

BITTER SWEET

SPRING FANCY

MORNING GLORY

THE HELLION

VOWS

THE GAMBLE

A HEART SPEAKS

YEARS

SEPARATE BEDS

TWICE LOVED

HUMMINGBIRD

THE ENDEARMENT

THE FULFILLMENT

BYGONES

LaVyrle Spencer

G. P. PUTNAM'S SONS NEW YORK

G. P. Putnam's Sons
Publishers Since 1838
200 Madison Avenue
New York, NY 10016

Printed in the United States of America

My most sincere thanks to the following people
for their help during the research of this book:

Brenda Taylor
Katie Holdorph
Jennifer Severson
Gar Johnson
Dr. Don Brandt
LaVonne Engesether
Cheryl at the Stillwater Chamber of Commerce

and a special thanks to the following people for allowing me
to use their beautiful homes as settings for this book:

Ted & Lorraine Glasrud
Tom & Edna Murphy

This book is dedicated with love
to some of my oldest friends
and some of my newest—

Barb & Don Fread
and
Barb & Don Brandt

BYGONES

chapter 1

THE APARTMENT BUILDING resembled thousands of others in the suburban Minneapolis/St. Paul area, a long brick rectangle with three floors, a set of steps on each end and rows of bruised doors lining stuffy, windowless halls. It was the kind of dwelling where young people started out with cast-off furniture and bargain-basement draperies, where toddlers rode their tricycles down the halls and could be heard through the floors when they cried. Now, at 6 P.M. on a cold January night, the smell of cooking meat and vegetables sifted under the doors, mingled with the murmur of televisions tuned to the evening news.

A tall woman walked down the hall. She looked out of place, dressed in a classic winter-white reefer coat bearing the unmistakable cut of a name designer, her accessories—leather gloves, handbag, shoes and scarf—of deep raspberry red. Her clothing was expensive, from the fifty-dollar silk scarf looped casually over her hair to the two-inch high heels combining three textures of leather. She walked with an air of hurried sophistication.

Pulling the scarf from her head, Bess Curran knocked at the door of number 206.

Lisa flung it open and exclaimed, "Oh, Mom, hi. Come on in. I knew I could depend on you to be right on time! Listen, everything's all ready but I forgot the sour cream for the stroganoff, so I have to make a quick run to the store. You don't mind keeping your eye on the meat, do you?" She dove into a closet and came up with a hip-length jean jacket, which she threw on over her dress.

"Stroganoff? For just the two of us? And a dress? What's the occasion?"

Lisa headed back to the door, digging her keys from her purse. "Just give it a stir, okay?" She opened the door halfway and stopped to call, "Oh! And light the candles and put a tape on, will you? That old Eagles one is there that you always liked."

The door slammed and left Bess in a backwash of puzzlement. Stroganoff? Candles? Music? And Lisa in a dress and pumps? Unbuttoning her coat, Bess wandered into the kitchen. Beyond the galley-style work area that divided it from the living room, a table was set for four. She studied it curiously—blue place mats and napkins cinched into white napkin rings; the leftover pieces of her and Michael's first set of dishes, which she'd given Lisa when she left home; four of her own cast-off stem glasses; and two blue candles in holders she'd never seen before, apparently bought specially for the occasion on Lisa's limited budget. What in the world was going on here?

She went to the stove to stir the stroganoff, which smelled so heavenly she couldn't resist sampling it. Delicious—her own recipe, laced with consommé and onions. As she replaced the cover on the pan, she realized she was famished: she'd done three home consultations today plus two hours in the store before it opened, grabbing a hamburger on the run. She promised herself, as she did every January, to limit the home consultations to two a day.

Returning to the front closet, she hung up her coat and straightened a pile of shoes so she could close the bifold door. She found matches and lit the candles on the dinner table and two others in clear, stubby pots on the living-room coffee table. Beside these a plate from her old dinnerware held a cheeseball waiting to be gouged and spread on Ritz crackers.

The match burned low.

She flinched and flapped it out, then stood staring at the cheeseball. What the devil? She glanced around the room and realized the place was clean for a change. Her old brass-and-glass tables had been freshly dusted and the cushions plumped on the hand-me-down family sofa. The tapes were stacked neatly, and the junk on the bookshelves had been neatened. The jet-black Kawaii piano Lisa's father had given her for high-school graduation hadn't a speck of dust on it. Instead, the key cover was neatly closed, and on top of the piano a picture of Lisa's current boyfriend, Mark, shared the space with a struggling philodendron plant and five Stephen King books in a pair of brass bookends Lisa had received from her Grandma Stella for Christmas.

The piano was the only valuable thing in the room. When Michael had given it to Lisa, Bess had accused him of foolish indulgence. It made no sense at all—a girl without a college education or a decent car or furniture owning a five-thousand-dollar piano that would have to be moved professionally—to the tune of about a hundred dollars per move—how many times before she was finally settled down permanently?

Lisa had said, "But, Mom, it's something I'll always keep, and that's what a graduation present should be."

Bess had argued, "Who'll pay when you have to have it moved?"

"I will."

"On a clerk-typist's salary?"

"I'm waitressing, too."

"You should be going on to school, Lisa."

"Dad says there's plenty of time for that."

"Well, your dad could be wrong, you know! If you don't go on to school right away, chances are you never will."

"You did," Lisa had argued.

"Yes, I did but it was damned hard, and look what it cost me. Your father should have more sense than to give you advice like that."

"Mother, just once I wish the two of you would stop haggling and at least pretend to get along, for us kids' sake. We're so sick of this cold war!"

"Well, it's a stupid gift." Bess had gone away grumbling. "Five thousand dollars for a piano that could finance a whole year of college."

The piano had remained a sore spot. Whenever Bess came to Lisa's apartment unannounced, the piano held a film of dust on its gleaming jet finish and seemed to be used merely as the depository for books, scarves, hair bows and all the other flotsam of Lisa's busy two-job life. It was all Bess could do to keep from sniping, "See, I told you!"

Tonight, however, the piano had been dusted and on the music rack was the sheet music for Michael's favorite song, "The Homecoming." In years past, whenever Lisa sat down to play, Michael would say, "Play that one I like," and Lisa would oblige with the beautiful old television-movie theme song.

Bess turned away from the memory of those happier times and put on the *Eagles Greatest Hits* tape. While it played she used Lisa's bathroom, noting that it, too, had been cleaned for the occasion. Washing her hands, she saw that the fixtures were shining, the towels fluffy and freshly laundered. On the corner of the vanity was the apothecary jar of potpourri she'd given Lisa for Christmas.

Bess hung up the towel and glanced in the mirror at her disheveled streaky-blonde hair, gave it a pluck or two: after the day she'd put in she looked undone. She'd been in and out of the wind, the shop, her car, and hadn't taken time since morning to pause for cosmetic repairs. Her forehead looked oily, her lipstick was gone and her brown eyes looked stark with the eyeshadow and mascara worn away. There were lap creases across the skirt of her winter-white wool crepe suit, and a small grease spot stood out prominently on the jabot of her raspberry-colored blouse. She frowned at the spot, wet a corner of a washcloth and made it worse. She cursed softly, then found a lifter-comb in Lisa's vanity drawer. Just as she raised her arms to use it, a knock sounded at the opposite end of the apartment.

She stuck her head around the corner and called down the hall, "Lisa, is that you?"

The knock came again, louder, and she hurried to answer it, leaving the bathroom light on behind her.

"Lisa, did you forget your—?" She pulled the door open and the words died in her throat. A tall man stood in the hall, trim, black-haired, hazel-eyed, dressed in a gray woolen storm coat, holding a brown paper sack containing two wine bottles.

"Oh, Michael . . . it's you."

Her mouth got tight.

Her carriage became stiff.

He gave her a stare, his eyebrows curled in displeasure. "Bess . . . what are you doing here?"

"I was invited for supper. What are you doing here?"

"I was invited, too."

Their face-off continued while she curbed the desire to slam the door in his face.

"Lisa called me last night and said, Dinner at six-fifteen, Dad."

She had called Bess the night before and said, "Dinner at six, Mom." Bess released the doorknob and spun away, muttering, "Cute, Lisa."

Michael followed her inside and shut the door. He set his bottles on the kitchen cupboard and took off his coat while Bess hustled back to the bathroom to put herself as far from him as possible. In the glare of the vanity light she backcombed four chunks of hair hard enough to push them back into her skull root-first. She arranged them with a few chunks and stabs of the wire hair lifter, slashed some of Lisa's grotesque scarlet lipstick on her mouth (the only tube she could find, considering she'd left her purse at the other end of the apartment), glared at the results and at the dark blob on her jabot. Damn it. And damn him for catching me when I look this way. She raised her brown eyes to the mirror and found them flat with fury. And damn me for squandering so much as a second caring what he thinks. After what he did to me, I don't have to pander to that asshole.

She slammed the vanity drawer, rammed her fingers into her forelock and ground it into a satisfying mess.

"What are you doing back there, hiding?" he called irritably.

It had been six years since the divorce, and she still wanted to arrange his penis with a hot curling iron every time she saw him!

"Let's get one thing clear," she bellowed down the hall. "I didn't know a damned thing about this!"

"Let's get two things clear! Neither did I! Where the hell is she anyway?"

Bess whacked the light switch off and marched toward the living room with her head high and her hair looking like a serving of chow mein noodles.

"She went to the store for sour cream, which I'm cheerfully going to stuff up her nostrils when she gets back here."

Michael was standing by the kitchen table, studying it, with his hands in his trouser pockets. He was dressed in a gray business suit, white shirt and blue paisley tie.

"What's all this?" he threw over his shoulder as she passed behind him.

"Your guess is as good as mine."

"Is Randy coming?" Randy was their nineteen-year-old son.

"Not that I know of."

"You don't know who the fourth one is for?"

"No, I don't."

"Or what the occasion is?"

"Obviously, a blind date for her mother and father. Our daughter has a bizarre sense of humor, doesn't she?" Bess opened the refrigerator door, looking for wine. Inside were four individual salads, prettily arranged on plates, a bottle of Perrier water, and sitting on the top shelf in a red-and-white carton, a pint of sour cream. "My, my, if it isn't sour cream." She picked it up and held it on one hand at shoulder level the way Marilyn Monroe would have held a mink. "And four very fancy salads."

He came to have a look, peering over the open refrigerator door.

"What are you looking for, something to drink?"

The smell of his shaving lotion, which in years past had seemed endearingly familiar, now turned her stomach. "I feel as if I need something." She slammed the door.

"I brought some wine," he told her.

"Well, break it out, Michael. We apparently have a long evening ahead."

She took two glasses from the table while he opened the bottle.

"So . . . where's Darla tonight?" She held the glasses while he poured the pale red rosé.

Over the gurgling liquid he answered, "Darla and I are no longer together. She's filed for divorce."

Bess got as rattled as an eighteen wheeler going over a cattle guard. Her head shot up while Michael went on filling the second glass.

She hadn't spent sixteen years with this man not to feel a mindless shaft of elation at the news that he was free again. Or that he had failed again.

Michael set the bottle on the cupboard, took a glass for himself and met Bess's eyes directly. It was a queer, distilled moment in which they both saw their entire history in a pure, refined state, so clear they could see through it, way back to the beginning—the splendid and the sordid, the regards and the regrets that had brought them to this point where they stood in their daughter's kitchen holding drinks that went untasted.

"Well, say it," Michael prodded.

"Good, it serves you both right."

He released a mirthless laugh and shook his head at the floor. "I knew that's what you were thinking. You're one very bitter woman, Bess, you know that?"

"And you're one very contemptible man. What did you do, step out on her, too?"

He walked out of the room replying, "I'm not going to get into it with you, Bess, because I can see all it'll lead to is a rehash of our old recriminations."

"Good." She followed him. "I don't want a rehash, either. So until our daughter gets back we'll pretend we're two polite strangers who just happened to meet here."

They carried their drinks into the living room and dropped to opposite ends of the davenport—the only seating in the room. The Eagles were singing "Take It Easy," which they'd listened to together a thousand times before. The candles were burning on the glass-top table they'd once chosen for their own living room. The davenport they sat on was one upon which they'd occasionally made love and cooed endearments to each other when they were both young and stupid enough to believe marriage lasts forever. They sat upon it now like a pair of church elders, in their respective corners, resenting one another and the intrusion of these memories.

"Looks like you gave Lisa the whole living room after I left," Michael remarked.

"That's right. Down to the pictures and the lamps. I didn't want any bad memories left behind."

"Of course, you had your new *business,* so it was no trouble buying replacements."

"Nope. No trouble at all," she replied smugly. "And of course, I get everything at a discount."

"So how's the business going?"

"Gangbusters! You know how it is after Christmas—everybody looking at those bare walls after they've pulled down all the holiday paraphernalia, and wanting new wallpaper and furniture to chase away the winter doldrums. I swear I could do half a dozen home consultations a day if there were three of me."

He studied her askance, remaining silent. Obviously she was happy with the way things had worked out. She was a certified interior designer now, with a store of her own and a newly redecorated house.

The Eagles switched to "Witchy Woman."

"So how's yours?" she inquired, tossing him an arch glance.

"It's making me rich."

"Don't expect congratulations. I always said it would."

"From you, Bess, I don't expect anything anymore."

"Oh, *that's* funny!" She cocked one wrist and delicately touched her chest. "*You* don't expect anything from *me* anymore." Her tone turned accusing as she dropped the cutesy pose. "When was the last time you saw Randy?"

"Randy doesn't give a damn about seeing me."

"That's not what I asked. When was the last time you made an effort to see him? He's still your son, Michael."

"If Randy wants to see me, he'll give me a call."

"Randy wouldn't give you a call if you were giving away tickets for a Rolling Stones concert and you know it. But that doesn't excuse you for ignoring him. He needs you whether he knows it or not, so it's up to you to keep trying."

"Is he still working in that warehouse?"

"When he bothers."

"Still smoking pot?"

"I think so but he's careful not to do it in the house. I told him if I ever smell it in there again I'll throw him out."

"Maybe you should. Maybe that would straighten him up."

"And then again maybe it wouldn't. He's my son, and I love him, and I'm trying my best to make him see the light but if I give up on him, what hope will he have? He certainly never gets any guidance from his father."

"What do you want me to do, Bess?" Michael spread his arms wide, the glass in one hand. "I've offered him the money to go to college or trade school if he wants but he doesn't want anything to do with school. So what in the hell do you expect me to do? Take him in with me? A pothead who goes to work when he feels like it?"

Bess glared at him. "I expect you to call him, take him out to dinner, take him hunting with you, rebuild a relationship with him, make him realize he still has a father who loves him and cares about what happens to him. But it's easier to slough him off on me, isn't it, Michael? Just like it was when the kids were little and you ran off with your guns and your fishing rods and your . . . your mistress! Well, I can't seem to find the answers for him anymore. Our son is a mess, Michael, and I'm very much afraid of what's going to become of him but I can't straighten him out alone."

Their eyes met and held, each of them aware that their divorce had been the blow from which Randy had never recovered. Until age thirteen he had been a happy kid, a good student, a willing helper around the house, a carefree teenager who brought his friends in to eat them out of house and home, watch football games and roughhouse on the living-room floor. From the day they'd told him they were getting a divorce, he had changed. He had become withdrawn, uncommunicative and increasingly lackadaisical about responsibilities, both in school and at home. He stopped bringing his friends home and eventually found new ones who wore weird hairdos and army jackets and one earring, and dragged their boot heels when they walked. He lay on his bed listening to rap music through his headphones, began smelling like burned garbage and coming home at two in the morning with his pupils dilated. He resented school counseling, ran away from home when Bess tried to ground him and graduated from high school by his cuticles, with the lowest grade-point average allowable.

No, their marriage was certainly not their only failure.

"For your information," Michael said, "I have called him. He called me a son of a bitch and hung up." Michael tipped forward, propping his elbows on his knees, drawing gyroscopic patterns in the air with the bottom of his glass. "I know he's messed up, Bess, and we did it to him, didn't we?" Still hunched forward, he looked over his shoulder at her. On the stereo the song changed to "Lyin' Eyes."

"Not we. You. He's never gotten over you leaving your family for another woman."

"That's right, blame it all on me, just like you always did. What about you leaving your family to go to college?"

"You still begrudge me that, don't you, Michael? And you still can't believe I actually became an interior designer and made a success of it."

Michael slammed down his glass, leapt to his feet and pointed a finger at her from the far side of the coffee table. "You got custody of the kids because you wanted it, but afterwards you were so damned busy at that store of yours that you weren't around to be their parent!"

"How would you know? You weren't around, either!"

"Because you wouldn't let me in the goddamn house! *My* house! The house I paid for and furnished and painted and loved just as much as you did!" He jabbed a finger for emphasis. "Don't tell me I wasn't around when you're the one who refused to speak to me, thereby setting an example for our son to follow. I was willing to be sensible, for the kids' sake, but no, you wanted to *show* me, didn't you? You were going to take those kids and brainwash them and make them believe *I* was the only one in the wrong where our marriage was concerned; and don't lie to me and say different, because I've talked to Lisa and she's told me some of the shit you've told her."

"Like what?"

"Like, our marriage broke up because I had an affair with Darla."

"Well, didn't it?"

He threw up his hands and rolled his eyes to the ceiling. "God, Bess, take off your blinders. Things had soured between us before I even met Darla and you know it."

"If things soured between us it was because—"

The apartment door opened. Bess clapped her mouth shut while she and Michael exchanged a glare of compressed volatility. Her cheeks were bright with anger. His lips were set in a grim line. She rose, donning a veneer of propriety, while he closed a button on his suit jacket and retrieved his glass from the coffee table. As he straightened, Lisa rounded the corner into the living room. Behind her came the young man whose picture stood on the piano.

Had Pablo Picasso painted the scene, he might have entitled it *Still Life with Four Adults and Anger.* The words of the abandoned argument still reverberated in the air.

Finally Lisa moved. "Hello, Mother. Hello, Dad."

She hugged her father first, while he easily closed his arms around her and kissed her cheek. She was nearly his height, dark-haired and pretty, with lovely brown eyes, an attractive combination of the best features of both her parents. She went next to hug Bess, saying, "Missed hugging you the first time around, Mom, glad you could come." Retreating from her mother's arms, she said, "You both remember Mark Padgett, don't you?"

"Mr. and Mrs. Curran," Mark said, shaking hands with each of them. He had a shiny all-American face and naturally curly brown hair, crew-cut on top and trailing in thinned tendrils over his collar. He sported the brawn of a bodybuilder and a hand to match. When he shook their hands, they felt it.

"Mark's going to have supper with us. I hope you stirred the stroganoff, Mom." Lisa headed jauntily for the kitchen, where she went to the sink, turned on the hot water and began filling a saucepan. Right behind her came Bess, snagging Lisa's elbow and forcing her to do an about-face.

"Just what in the world do you think you're doing!" she demanded in a pinched whisper, covered by the sound of the running water and "Desperado" from the other side of the wall.

"Boiling noodles for the stroganoff." Lisa swung the kettle to the stove and switched on a blue flame, with Bess dogging her shoulder.

"Don't be obtuse with me, Lisa. I'm so damned angry I could fling that stroganoff down the disposal and you right along with it." She pointed a finger. "There's a pint of sour cream in that refrigerator and you know it! You set us up!"

Lisa pushed her mother's arm as if it were a turnstile and moved beyond it to open the refrigerator door. "I certainly did. How'd it go?" she asked blithely, removing the carton of sour cream and curling its cover off.

"Lisa Curran, I could dump that sour cream on your head!"

"I really don't care, Mother. *Some*body had to make you come to your senses."

"Your father and I are not a couple of twenty-year-olds you can fix up on a blind date!"

"No, you're not!" Lisa slammed down the carton of sour cream and faced her mother, nose-to-nose, whispering angrily. "You're forty years old but you're acting like a child! For six years you've refused to be in the same room with Dad, refused to treat him civilly, even for your children's sake. Well, I'm putting an end to that if I have to humiliate you to do it. Tonight is important to me and all I'm asking you to do is *grow up, Mother!*"

Bess stared at her daughter, feeling her cheeks flare, stunned into silence. From the countertop Lisa snagged a bag of egg noodles and stuffed them into Bess's hands. "Would you please add these to the water while I finish the stroganoff, then let's go into the living room and join the men as if we all know the meaning of gracious manners."

When they entered the living room it was clear the two men, seated on the sofa, had been doing their best at redeeming a sticky situation in which the tension was as obvious as the cheeseball meant to mitigate it. Lisa picked up the plate from the coffee table.

"Daddy? Mark? Cheeseball anyone?"

Bess stationed a kitchen chair clear across the room, where the living-room carpet met the vinyl kitchen floor, and sat down, full of indignation and the niggling bite of shame at being reprimanded by her own daughter. Mark and Michael each spread a cracker with cheese and ate it. Lisa carried the plate to her mother and stopped beside Bess's rigidly crossed knees.

"Mother?" she said sweetly.

"No, thank you," Bess snapped.

"I see you two have found something to drink," Lisa noted cheerfully. "Mark, would you like something?"

Mark said, "No, I'll wait."

"Mother, do you need a refill?"

Bess flicked a hand in reply.

Lisa took the only free seat, between the two men.

"Well . . ." she said brightly, clasping her crossed knees with twined hands and swinging her foot. She glanced between Michael and Bess. "I haven't seen either one of you since Christmas. What's new?"

They somehow managed to weather the next fifteen minutes. Bess, struggling to lose the ten extra pounds she consistently carried, refused the Ritz crackers with cheese but allowed herself to be socially manipulated by her daughter while trying to avoid Michael's hazel eyes. Once he managed to pin her with them while sinking his even, white teeth into a Ritz. You might at least *try,* he seemed to be admonishing, for Lisa's sake. She glanced away, wishing he'd bite into a rock and break off his damnable perfect incisors at the gums!

They sat down to eat at 7:15 in the chairs Lisa indicated, her mother and dad opposite each other so they could scarcely avoid exchanging glances across the candlelit table and their familiar old blue-and-white dishes.

Setting out the last of the four salad dishes, Lisa requested, "Will you open the Perrier, Mark, while I get the hot foods? Mom, Dad, would you prefer Perrier or wine?"

"Wine," they answered simultaneously.

The older couple sat obediently while the younger one got the bottled water, lime slices, wine, bread basket, noodles, stroganoff and a vegetable casserole, working together until everything was in place. Finally Lisa took her chair while Mark made the rounds, pouring.

When the glasses were filled and Mark, too, was seated, Lisa picked up her glass of Perrier and said, "Happy new year, everyone. And here's to a happier decade ahead."

The glasses touched in every combination but one. After a conspicuous pause, Michael and Bess made a final *tingg* with the rims of their old household stemware, a gift from some friend or family member many years ago. He nodded silently while she dropped her gaze and damned herself for disheveling her hair in an angry fit an hour ago, and for dropping ketchup on her jabot at noon, and for not stopping at home and putting on fresh makeup. She still hated him but that hate stemmed from a fiery pride, bruised at the moment. He had left her for someone ten years younger and ten pounds underweight, who undoubtedly never appeared at social functions with her hair on end, her forehead shiny and lunch on her jabot.

Lisa began passing the serving bowls and the room became filled with the sounds of spoons rapping on glass.

"Mmm . . . stroganoff," Michael noted, pleased, while he loaded his plate.

"Yup," Lisa replied. "Mom's recipe. And your favorite corn pudding, too." She passed him a casserole dish. "I learned to make it just like Mom. Be careful, it's hot." He set the dish beside his plate and took an immense helping. "I figured since you're living alone again you'd appreciate a good home-cooked meal. Mom, pass me the pepper, would you?"

Complying, Bess met Michael's eyes across the table, both of them grossly uncomfortable with Lisa's transparent machinations. It was the first point upon which they'd agreed since this unfortunate encounter began.

Michael tasted his food and said, "You've turned into a good little cook, honey."

"She sure has," put in Mark. "You'd be surprised how many girls today can't even boil water. When I found out she could cook I told my mother, I think I've found the girl of my dreams."

Three people at the table laughed. Bess, discomfited, hid behind a sip of rosé, recalling that one of the things Michael had criticized after she'd returned to college had been her neglecting the chores she'd always done. Cooking was one of them. She had argued, What about you, why can't you take over some of the household chores? But Michael had stubbornly refused to learn. It was one of many small wedges that had insidiously opened a chasm between them.

"How about you, Mark," Bess asked. "Do you cook?"

Lisa answered. "Does he ever! His specialty is steak soup. He takes a big old slab of sirloin and cubes it up and browns it and adds all these big hunks of potatoes and carrots, and what else do you put in it, honey?"

Bess shot a glance at her daugher. *Honey?*

"Garlic, and pearl barley to thicken it."

"Steak soup?" Bess repeated, turning her regard to Mark.

"Mm-hmm," Mark replied. "It's an old family favorite."

Bess stared at the young man who was shaped like Mount Rushmore. His neck was so thick his collar button wouldn't close. His hairdo was moussed on top and girlish on the bottom. And he thickened his steak soup with pearl barley?

Lisa grinned proudly at Mark. "He irons, too."

"Irons?" Michael repeated.

"My mother made me learn when I graduated from high school. She works, and she said she had no intention of doing my laundry till I was twenty-five. I like my sleeves and jeans with nice creases in them, so . . ." Mark raised his hands—his fork in one, a roll in the other—and let them drop. "I'm actually going to make some woman a pretty good housewife." He and Lisa exchanged a smile bearing some ulterior satisfaction, and Bess caught Michael adding it up before he swept his uncertain glance back to her.

Lisa said, "We might as well tell them, Mark." The two exchanged another smile before Lisa wiped her mouth, replaced her napkin on her lap and picked up her glass of sparkling water. "Mom, Dad . . ." With her eyes fixed radiantly on the young man across the table, Lisa announced, "We've invited you here tonight to tell you that Mark and I are going to get married."

In almost comical unison, Bess and Michael set down their forks. They gaped at their daughter. They gaped at each other.

Mark had stopped eating.

The tape player had stopped playing.

From an adjacent apartment the grumble of a TV could be heard through the wall.

"Well," Lisa said, "say something."

Michael and Bess remained speechless. Finally Michael cleared his throat, wiped his mouth on his napkin and said, "Well . . . my goodness."

"Daddy," Lisa chided. "Is that *all* you have to say?"

Michael forced an uncertain smile. "You caught me a little by surprise here, Lisa."

"Aren't you even going to congratulate us?"

"Well . . . yes . . . sure, of course, congratulations, both of you."

"Mother?" Lisa's eyes settled on Bess.

Bess emerged from her stupor. "Married?" she repeated disbelievingly. "But Lisa . . ." *We hardly know this young man. You've only known him for a year, or is it that long? We had no idea you were this serious about him.*

"Smile, Mother, and repeat after me, Congratulations, Lisa and Mark."

"Oh, dear . . ." Bess's gaze fluttered to her ex-husband, back to her daughter.

"Bess," Michael admonished quietly.

"Oh, I'm sorry. Of course, congratulations, Lisa . . . and Mark, but . . . but when did all this happen?"

"This weekend. We're really sold on each other, and we're tired of living apart, so we decided to commit."

"When is the big event?" Michael inquired.

"Soon," Lisa answered. "Very soon. Six weeks, as a matter of fact."

"Six weeks!" Bess yelped.

"I know that doesn't give us much time, but we've got it all figured out."

"What kind of wedding can you plan in six weeks? You can't even find a church in six weeks."

"We can if we're married on a Friday night."

"A Friday night . . . oh, Lisa."

"Now listen, both of you. Mark and I love each other and we want to get married but we want to do it the right way. We both want to have a real church wedding with all the trimmings, so here's what we've arranged. We can be married at St. Mary's on March second, and have the reception at the Riverwood Club. I've already checked and the club's not booked. Mark's aunt is a caterer and she's agreed to do the food. One of the guys I work with plays in a band that'll give us a pretty decent price. We're only going to have one attendant each—by the way, Randy has agreed to be one of them, and he even said he'll cut his hair. With only one attendant there'll be no trouble matching bridesmaids' dresses—Mark's sister can buy one anywhere; and as for the tuxes, we'll rent them. Flowers are no problem. We'll use silk ones and keep them modest. The cake we'll order from Wuollet's on Grand Avenue, and I'm pretty sure we can still find a photographer—having it on a Friday night, we're finding out, makes last-minute arrangements pretty easy. Well?"

Beleaguered, Bess felt her lips hanging open but seemed unable to close them. "What about your dress?"

A meaningful look passed between Lisa and Mark, this one without a smile.

"That's where I'll need your cooperation. I want to wear yours, Mom."

Bess looked dumbfounded. "Mine . . . but . . ."

"I'm pretty sure it'll fit."

"Oh, Lisa." Bess let her face show clear dismay.

"Oh, Lisa, what?"

Michael spoke. "What your mother is trying to say is that she isn't sure it's appropriate under the circumstances, isn't that right, Bess?"

"Because you're divorced?" Lisa looked from one parent to the other.

Michael gestured with his hands: that's how it is.

"I see nothing inappropriate about it at all. You were married once. You loved each other and you had me, and you're still my parents. Why shouldn't I wear the dress?"

"I leave that entirely to your mother." Michael glanced at Bess, who was still laboring under the shock of the news, sitting with her ringless left hand to her lips, her brown eyes very troubled.

"Mother, please. We can do this without your cooperation but we'd rather have it. From both of you." Lisa included Michael in her earnest plea. "And as long as I'm laying out our plans, I may as well tell you the rest. I want to walk down the aisle between you. I want my mom and my dad both there, one on either side of me, without all this animosity you've had for the past six years. I want to have you in the dressing room, Mom, when I'm getting ready; and afterwards, at my reception, I want to dance with you, Dad. But without tension, without . . . well, you know what I mean. It's the only wedding present I want from either one of you."

The room fell into an uneasy silence. Bess and Michael found it impossible to meet each other's eyes.

Finally Bess spoke. "Where will you live?"

"Mark's apartment is nicer than mine, so we'll live over there."

And the piano will need to be moved again. It took great control for Bess to refrain from voicing the thought. "I don't even know where he lives."

Mark said, "In Maplewood, near the hospital."

She studied Mark. He had a pleasant enough face but he looked terribly young. "I must apologize, Mark, I've been so taken off guard here. The truth is, I feel as though I barely know you. You do some kind of factory work, I think."

"Yes, I'm a machinist. But I've been with the same company for three years, and I make good money, and I have good benefits. Lisa and I won't have any problems that way."

"And you met Lisa—?"

"At a pool hall, actually. We were introduced by mutual friends."

At a pool hall. A machinist. A bodybuilder with a neck like a bridge abutment.

"Isn't this awfully sudden? You and Lisa have known each other—what?—less than a year. I mean, couldn't you wait, say a half a year or so and give yourselves time to get to know one another better, and to plan a wedding properly, and us a chance to meet your family?"

Mark's eyes sought Lisa's. His cheeks colored. His forearms rested on the table edge, so muscular they appeared unable to comfortably touch his sides.

"I'm afraid not, Mrs. Curran." Quietly, without challenge, he said, "You see, Lisa and I are going to have a baby."

An invisible mushroom cloud seemed to form over the table.

Michael covered his mouth with a hand and frowned. Bess drew a breath, held her mouth open and slowly closed it, staring at Mark, then at Lisa. Lisa sat quietly, relaxed.

"We're actually quite happy about it," Mark added, "and we hoped you'd be, too."

Bess dropped her forehead onto one hand, the opposite arm propped across her stomach. Her only daughter pregnant and planning a hasty wedding, and she should be happy?

"You're sure about it?" Michael was asking.

"I've already seen a doctor. I'm six weeks along. Actually I thought maybe you'd guess, because I'm drinking the Perrier instead of wine."

Bess lifted her head and encountered Michael, somber, his food forgotten. He met her dismayed eyes, straightened his shoulders and said, "Well . . ." clearing his throat. Obviously, he was at as great a loss as she.

Mark rose and went to stand behind Lisa's chair with his hands on her shoulders. "I think I should say something here, Mr. and Mrs. Curran. I love your daughter very much, and she loves me. We want to get married. We've both got jobs and a decent place to live. This baby could have a lot worse starts than that."

Bess came out of her stupor. "In this day and age, Lisa—"

Michael interrupted. "Bess, come on, not now."

"What do you mean, not now! We live in an enlightened age and—"

"I said, *not now,* Bess! The kids are doing the honorable thing, telling us their plans, asking for our support. I think we should give it to them."

She bit back her retort about birth control and sat simmering while Michael went on, remarkably cool-headed.

"You're sure this is what you want to do, Lisa?" he asked.

"Very sure. Mark and I had talked about getting married even before I got pregnant, and we had agreed that we'd both like to have a family when we were young, and that we wouldn't do like so many yuppies do, and both of us work until we got so independent that *things* began mattering more than having children. So none of this was nearly as much of a shock to us as it is to you. We're happy, Dad, honest we are, and I do love Mark very much."

Lisa sounded wholly convincing.

Michael looked up at Mark, still standing behind Lisa with his hands on her collar. "Have you told your parents yet?"

"Yes, last night."

Michael felt a shaft of disappointment at being last to learn but what could he expect when Mark's family was, apparently, still an intact, happy unit? "What did they say?"

"Well, they were a little surprised at first, naturally, but they know Lisa a lot better than you know me, so they got over it and we had a little celebration."

Lisa leaned forward and covered her mother's hand on the tabletop. "Mark has wonderful parents, Mom. They're anxious to meet you and Dad, and I promised them we'd introduce you all soon. Right away Mark's mother suggested a dinner party at their house. She said if you two are agreeable, I could set a date."

This isn't how it's supposed to be, Bess thought, battling tears, Michael and I practically strangers to our future son-in-law and total strangers to his family. Whatever happened to girls marrying the boy next door? Or the little brat who pulled her pigtails in the third grade? Or the one who did wheelies on his BMX bike in our driveway to impress her in junior high? Those lucky, simpler times were bygone with the era of transient executives and upward mobility, of rising divorce rates and single-parent homes.

Everyone was waiting for Bess to respond to the news but she wasn't ready yet, emotionally. She felt like breaking down and bawling, and had to swallow hard before she could speak at all.

"Your dad and I need to talk about a few things first. Would you give us a day or two to do that?"

"Sure." Lisa withdrew her hand and sat back.

"Would that be okay with you, Michael?" Bess asked him.

"Of course."

Bess deposited her napkin on the table and pushed her chair back. "Then I'll call you, or Dad will."

"Fine. But you aren't leaving yet, are you? I've got dessert."

"It's late. I've got to be at the store early tomorrow. I really should be going."

"But it's not even eight yet."

"I know, but . . ." Bess rose, dusting crumbs from her skirt, anxious to escape and examine her true feelings, to crumple and get angry if she so desired.

"Dad, will you stay and have dessert? I got a French silk pie from Baker's Square."

"I think I'll pass, too, honey. Maybe I can stop by tomorrow night and have some with you."

Michael rose, followed by Lisa, and they all stood awkwardly a moment, politely pretending this was not a scenario in which parents were running, distraught, from the announcement that their daughter was knocked up and planning a shotgun wedding, pretending this was merely a polite, everyday leave-taking.

"Well, I'll get your coats, then," Lisa said with a quavery smile.

"I will, sweetheart," Mark offered, and went to do so. In the crowded entry he politely held Bess's coat, then handed Michael's to him. There was another clumsy moment after Michael slipped his coat on, when the two men confronted each other, wondering what to say or do next. Michael offered his hand and Mark gripped it.

"We'll talk soon," Michael said.

"Thank you, sir."

Even more awkwardly, the young man faced Bess. "Good night, Mrs. Curran," Mark offered.

"Good night, Mark."

Unsure of himself, he hovered, and finally Bess raised her cheek to touch his gingerly. In the cramped space before the entry door Michael gave Lisa a hug, leaving only the mother and daughter to exchange some gesture of good night. Bess found herself unable, so Lisa made the move. Once Bess felt her daughter's arms around her, however, she clung, feeling her emotions billow, her tears come close to exposing themselves. Her precious firstborn, her Lisa, who had learned to drink from a straw before she was one, who had carried a black doll named Gertrude all over the neighborhood until she was five, and, dressed in feet pajamas, had clambered into bed between her mommy and daddy on Saturday mornings when she got old enough to climb out of her crib unaided.

Lisa, whom she and Michael had wanted so badly.

Lisa, the product of those optimistic times.

Lisa, who now carried their grandchild.

Bess clutched Lisa and whispered throatily, "I love you, Lee-lee," the pet name Michael had given her long ago, in a golden time when they'd all believed they'd live happily ever after.

"I love you, too, Mom."

"I just need a little time, please, darling."

"I know."

Michael stood waiting with the door open, touched by Bess's use of the familiar baby name.

Bess drew back, squeezing Lisa's arm. "Get lots of rest. I'll call you."

She passed Michael and headed down the hall, clasping her clutch purse under one arm, pulling on her gloves, her raspberry high heels clicking on the tiled floor. He closed the apartment door and followed, buttoning his coat, turning up its collar, watching her speed along with an air of efficiency, as if she were late for a business appointment.

At the far end of the hall she descended two stairs before her bravado dissolved. Abruptly she stopped, gripped the rail with one hand and listed over it, the other hand to her mouth, her back to him, crying.

He stopped on the step above her with his hands in his coat pockets, watching her shoulders shake. He felt melancholy himself, and witnessing her display of emotions amplified his own. Though she tried to stifle them, tiny mewling sounds escaped her throat. Reluctantly, he touched her shoulder blade. "Aw, Bess . . ."

Her words were muffled behind a gloved hand. "I'm sorry, Michael, I know I should be taking this better . . . but it's such a disappointment."

"Of course it is. For me, too." He returned his hand to his coat pocket.

She sniffed, snapped her purse open and found a tissue inside. Still with her back turned, mopping her face, she said, "I'm appalled at myself for breaking down in front of you this way."

"Oh, hell, Bess, I've seen you cry before."

She blew her nose. "When we were married, yes, but this is different."

With the tissue tucked away and her purse again beneath an arm she turned to face him, touching her lower eyelids with the fingertips of her expensive raspberry leather gloves. "Oh, God," she said, and emptied her lungs in a big gust. She drooped back with her hips against the black metal handrail and fixed her tired stare on the opposite railing.

For a while neither of them spoke, only stood in the murky hallway, helpless to stop their daughter's future from taking a downhill dive. Finally Bess said, "I can't pretend this is anything but terrible, our only daughter and a shotgun wedding."

"I know."

"Do you feel like you've failed again?" She looked up at him with red-rimmed eyes, shiny at the corners with a new batch of tears.

He drew a deep, tired breath and took stock of their surroundings. "I don't think I want to discuss it in the hallway of this apartment building. You want to go to a restaurant, have a cup of coffee or something?"

"Now?"

"Unless you really have to hurry home."

"No, that was just an excuse to escape. My first appointment isn't until ten in the morning."

"All right, then, how about The Ground Round on White Bear Avenue?"

"The Ground Round would be fine."

They turned and continued down the stairs, lagging now, slowed by distress. He opened the plate-glass door for her, experiencing a fleeting sense of déjà vu. How many times in the course of a courtship and marriage had he opened the door for her? There were times during their breakup when he'd angrily walked out before her and let the door close in her face. Tonight, faced with an emotional upheaval, it felt reassuring to perform the small courtesy again.

Outside, their breath hung milky in the cold air, and the snow, compressing beneath their feet, gave off a hard-candy crunch like chewing resounding within one's ear. At the foot of the sidewalk, where it gave onto the parking lot, she paused and half-turned as he caught up with her.

"I'll see you there," she said.

"I'll follow you."

Heading in opposite directions toward their cars, they started the long, rocky journey back toward amity.

chapter 2

THEY MET IN THE LOBBY of the restaurant and followed a glossy-haired, effeminate young man who said, "Right this way." Michael felt the same déjà vu as earlier, trailing Bess as he'd done countless times before, watching the sway of her coat, the movement of her arms as she took off her gloves, inhaling the faint drift of her perfume, the same rosy scent she'd worn for years.

The perfume was the only familiar thing about her. Everything else was new—the professionally streaked blonde hair nearly touching her shoulder, the expensive clothes, the self-assurance, the brittleness. These had all been acquired since their divorce.

They sat at a table beside a window, their faces tinted by an overhead fixture with a bowl-shaped orange globe and the pinkish glow of the phosphorescent lamps reflecting off the snow outside. The supper crowd had gone, and a hockey game was in progress on a TV above the bar somewhere around a corner. It murmured a background descant to the piped-in orchestra music falling from the ceiling.

Michael removed his coat and folded it over an empty chair while Bess left hers over her shoulders.

A teenage waitress with a frizzy hairdo came and asked if they'd like menus.

"No, thank you. Just coffee," Michael answered.

"Two?"

Michael deferred to Bess with a glance. "Yes, two," she answered, with a quick glance at the girl.

When they were alone again, Bess fixed her gaze on Michael's hands, wrapped palm-over-palm above a paper place mat. He had square, shapely hands, with neatly trimmed nails and long fingers. Bess had always loved his hands. They were, she'd said many times, the kind of hands you'd welcome on your dentist. Even in the dead of winter his skin never entirely paled. His wrists held a whisk of dark hair that trailed low and made his white cuffs appear whiter. There was an undeniable appeal about the sight of a man's clean hands foiled by white shirt cuffs and the darker edge of a suit sleeve. Oftentimes after the divorce, at odd, unexpected moments—in a restaurant, or a department store—Bess would find herself staring at the hands of some stranger and remembering Michael's. Then reality would return, and she would damn herself for becoming vulnerable to memory and loneliness.

In a restaurant, six years after their divorce, she drew her gaze from Michael's hands and lifted it to his face, daunted by the admission that she still found him handsome. He had perfect eyebrows above attractive hazel eyes, full lips and a head of gorgeous black hair. For the first time she noticed a few skeins of gray above his ears, discernible only under the direct light.

"Well . . ." she began, "this has been a night of surprises."

He chuckled quietly in reply.

"This is the last place I expected to end up when I told Lisa I'd come for supper," Bess told him.

"Me too."

"I don't think you're as shocked by all this as I am, though."

"I was shocked when you opened that door, I can tell you that."

"I wouldn't have been there if I'd known what Lisa had up her sleeve."

"Neither would I."

Silence for a moment, then, "Listen, Michael, I'm sorry about all that . . . well, Lisa's obvious attempt to revive something between us—our old dishes and the stroganoff and the corn pudding and the candlelight. She should have known better."

"It was damned uncomfortable, wasn't it?"

"Yes, it was. It still is."

"I know."

Their coffee came: something neutral to focus on instead of each other. When the waitress went away Bess asked, "Did you hear what Lisa said to me when we were alone in the kitchen?"

"No. What?"

"The gist of her message was, Grow up, Mother, you've been acting like a child for six years. I had no idea she was so angry about our antagonism, did you?"

"Only in retrospect, when she'd talk about Mark's family and how close and loving they are."

"She's talked to you about that?"

His eyes answered above his cup while he took a sip of coffee.

"When?" Bess demanded.

"I don't know—a couple different times."

"She never told me she talked to you so often."

"You put up barriers, Bess, that's why. You're putting up a new one right now. You should see the expression on your face."

"Well, it hurts to know she's talked to you about these things, and that Mark's family knows her better than we know Mark."

"Sure it hurts, but why wouldn't the two of them gravitate toward the family that stayed together? It's only natural."

"So what do you think of Mark?"

"I don't know him very well. I think I've only talked to him a couple of times before tonight."

"That's my point. How could this have happened when they've been dating such a short time that we've scarcely met the boy?"

"First of all, he's not a boy. You have to admit, he certainly faced the situation like a man. I was impressed with him tonight."

"You were?"

"Well, hell, he was there beside her, facing us head on instead of leaving her to break the news by herself. Doesn't that impress you?"

"I guess so."

"And by the sound of it, he comes from a good family."

Bess had decided something on the way to the restaurant. "I don't want to meet them."

"Aw, come on, Bess, that's silly—why not?"

"I didn't say I *won't* meet them. I will, if I have to, but I don't *want* to."

"Why?"

"Because it's hard to be with happy families. It makes our own failure that much harder to bear. They have what we wanted to have and thought we'd have. Only we don't, and after six years I still haven't gotten over the feeling of failure."

He considered awhile, then admitted, "Yeah, I know what you mean. And now for me, it's twice."

She sipped her coffee, curious and hesitant while meeting his eyes across the table.

"I can't believe I'm asking this, but what happened?"

"Between Darla and me?"

She nodded.

He stared at his cup, toying with its handle. "What happened was that it was the wrong combination from the beginning. We were each unhappy in the marriage we had, and we thought . . . well, hell . . . you know. We married each other on the rebound. We were lonely and, like you said, feeling like failures, and it seemed important to get another relationship going and to succeed at it, to sweeten the bitterness, I guess. What it really turned out to be was five years of coming to terms with the fact that we really never loved each other."

After some time Bess said, "That's what I'm afraid is going to happen to Lisa."

His steady hazel eyes held her brown ones while each of them pondered their daughter's future, longing for it to be happier than their own. From the bar around the corner came the whine of a blender.

When it stopped Michael said, "But the choice isn't ours to make for her."

"Maybe not the choice but isn't it our responsibility to make her consider all the ramifications?"

"Which are?"

"They're so young."

"They're older than we were when we got married, and they both seem to know what they want."

"That's what they told us but what else would you expect them to say, under the circumstances?"

He considered awhile then remarked thoughtfully, "I don't know, Bess, they seemed pretty sure of themselves. Mark made some points that had a lot of merit. If they had already talked about when they wanted to have babies, they were a jump ahead of about ninety percent of the couples who get married. And, frankly, I don't see anything wrong with their thinking. Like Mark said, they have good jobs, a home, the baby would have two willing parents—that's a pretty solid start for a kid. You have your kids when you're young, you have more patience, health, zest—and then when they're gone from home you're still young enough to enjoy your freedom."

"So you don't think we should try to talk them out of it?"

"No, I don't. What would the other options be? Abortion, adoption, or Lisa raising a baby alone. When the two of them love each other and want to get married? Wouldn't make much sense at all."

Bess sighed and crossed her forearms on the table. "I guess I'm just reacting like a mother, wanting a guarantee that her daughter will be happy."

His eyes told her what he thought about hoping for guarantees.

After a moment she said, "Just answer me this—when we got married, didn't you think it would be for life?"

"Of course, but you can't advise your child not to marry because you're afraid she'll make the same mistakes you did. That's not realistic. What you have to do is be truthful with her, but first of all you have to be truthful with yourself. If you—I guess I should be saying *we*—can admit what we did wrong and caution them to avoid the same pitfalls, maybe *that's* how we can redeem ourselves."

While Bess was pondering the point the waitress came and refilled their cups. When she went away, Bess took a sip of her steaming coffee and asked, "So, what do you think about the rest? About us walking down the aisle with her and her wearing my old wedding dress and everything?"

They sat silently awhile, their glances occasionally touching, then dropping as they thought about putting on a show of harmony before a couple hundred guests, some, undoubtedly, who'd been guests at their own wedding. The idea revolted them both.

"What do you think, Bess?"

Bess drew a deep breath and sighed. "It wasn't pleasant, getting chewed out by my own daughter. She said some things that really made me angry. I thought, How dare you preach to me, you young whelp!"

"And now?" Michael prodded.

"Well, we're talking, aren't we?"

The question gave them pause to consider the six years of silence and how it had affected their children.

"Do you think you could go through with it?"

"I don't know. . . ." Bess looked out the window at the cars in the parking lot, imagining herself walking down an aisle with Michael . . . again. Seeing her wedding gown in use . . . again. Sitting beside him at a wedding banquet . . . again. More quietly, she repeated, "I don't know."

"I guess I don't see that we have any other choice."

"So you want me to give her the go-ahead for this dinner at the Padgetts'?"

"I think we can fake our way through it, for her sake."

"All right, but first I want to talk to her, Michael, please allow me that. Just to make sure she isn't marrying him under duress, and to assure her that if she makes some other choice you and I will be supportive. May I do that first?"

"Of course. I think you should."

"And the dress, what should I say about the dress?"

This issue touched closer to home than all the others.

"What harm would it do if she wore it?"

"Oh, Michael—" Her eyes skittered away, suddenly self-conscious.

"You think just because you wore it and the marriage didn't last, the thing is jinxed? Or that somebody in the crowd might recognize it and think it's bad judgment? Be sensible, Bess. Who in that entire church besides you and me and possibly your mother would even know? I say let her wear it. It'll save me five hundred dollars."

"You always were putty in her hands."

"Yup. And I kind of enjoyed it."

"Need I mention that the piano will have to be moved again?"

"I'm aware of that."

"On their limited budget, it'll be a drain."

"I'll pay for it. I told her when I bought it I'd foot the bill for the piano-moving for the life of the instrument, or the life of me, whichever ended first."

"You told her that?" Bess sounded surprised.

"I told her not to tell you. You had such a bug up your ass about the piano anyway."

Bess almost laughed. They eyed each other, repressing grins.

"All right, let's back up, boy, to that remark you made about saving five hundred dollars. I take it from that that you're going to offer to pay for the wedding."

"I thought it was damned noble of the two of them not to ask for any help, but what kind of Scrooge would let his kid lay out money like that when he's earning a hundred thousand a year?"

Bess raised her eyebrows. "Oooo . . . you dropped that in there very neatly, just to make sure I'd know, huh? Well, it just so happens I'm doing quite well myself. Not a hundred grand a year but enough that I insist on paying half of everything."

"Okay, it's a deal." Michael extended his open hand above their coffee cups.

She shook it and they felt the shock of familiarity: the fit hadn't changed. Their expressions grew guilt-tinged and immediately they broke the contact.

"Well," Michael said, expanding his chest and touching his stomach. "I've had enough coffee to keep me awake until three."

"Me too."

"You ready to go then?" She nodded and they hitched their chairs back from the table. While they were donning their coats, he inquired, "How's your mother?"

"Indefatigable as always. Makes me breathless just listening to her."

He smiled and said, "Say hi to the old doll for me, will you? I've missed her."

"I'll do that. But if this wedding comes off, you'll undoubtedly be able to say hello to her yourself."

"And your sister, Joan. She still in Colorado?"

"Yes. Still married to that jerk and refusing to consider divorce because she's Catholic."

"Do you ever see her?"

"Not very often. We just don't have anything in common anymore. By the way, Michael . . ." She paused, her coat on. For the first time her eyes softened as she looked at him. "I was very sorry about your mother."

"And I was sorry about your dad."

They had each lost a parent since the divorce but she still had one left. He now had none.

"I appreciated your coming to the funeral. She always liked you," Michael told Bess. She had attended and had taken the children, of course, but had not spoken to Michael. Likewise, he had attended her father's funeral, but they had remained stubbornly aloof from one another, exchanging only the most perfunctory condolences. They had each liked the other's parents. It had been one of the connections hardest to sever.

"It was damned hard when Mother died," Michael admitted. "I kept wishing I had some brothers and sisters, but . . . aw, hell, what good are wishes? I'm forty-three years old. You'd think I'd have gotten used to it by now."

His whole life he'd hated being an only child and had talked about it often with her. She, too, had missed having a sister she was close to. There was a seven years' age difference between herself and Joan, which left them little in the way of childhood nostalgia regarding play, or friends, or even school. In her memory, Joan seemed more like a third parent than a sister. When she'd married and moved to Denver it had made little difference in Bess's life, and though they occasionally exchanged letters, these were merely duty missives.

It felt odd to both Bess and Michael, standing in the doorway of a restaurant, commiserating with each other about their loneliness and their loss of loved ones. They'd handled bitterness well, knew exactly how to handle it, but this empathy was an imposition. It made them eager to part.

"Well," Bess said. "It's late. I'd better be going."

She left the restaurant ahead of him and at the door felt the brief touch of his hand in the center of her back.

Memories.

In the parking lot at the point of parting, he said, "Chances are we aren't going to get through this whole wedding without having to contact each other. I've moved. . . ." He handed her a business card. "Here's my new address and phone number. If I'm not there, leave a message on the recorder, or call the office."

"All right." She put the card in her coat pocket.

They paused, groping for parting words while this present good-bye melded into a montage of a hundred others from their courting years—New Year's Eves, dances and parties, all followed by long passionate sessions on her doorstep. The flashback lasted only seconds before Michael spoke.

"You'll call Lisa, then?"

"Yes."

"Maybe I'll call her, too, just to let her know we're in agreement."

"All right . . . well, good night."

" 'Night, Bess."

Again came that momentary void, with neither of them moving, then they turned and went to their separate cars.

Bess started her engine and waited while it warmed. He had taught her that long ago: in Minnesota a car lasts longer if you let it warm in winter. That was in their struggling days, when they'd kept cars for five or six years. Now she could afford a new one every two years. Presently she drove a Buick Park Avenue. She waited to see what kind of car he was driving—her curiosity some odd possessive holdover she could not control. She heard the muffled growl of his engine as he passed behind her, and caught a glimpse of a silver roofline in the rearview mirror, turning only as he eased into a pool of illumination from a tall pole light to identify a Cadillac Seville. So it was true—he was doing well. She sat awhile attempting to sort out her feelings about that. Six years ago she would gladly have stuck pins in a voodoo doll of Michael Curran. Tonight, however, she felt an inexplicable touch of pride that once, long ago, she'd chosen a winner, and that now, faced with an impromptu wedding, there would be no need to stint their daughter.

Remembering Michael's card, she snapped on the overhead light and fished it from her pocket.

5011 Lake Avenue, White Bear Lake.

He'd moved to White Bear Lake? Back within ten miles of her? Why, when he'd lived clear over in a western suburb of Minneapolis for the past five years? Too close for comfort, she decided, stuffing the card back into her coat pocket and putting her car in gear.

Twenty minutes later she pulled into the horseshoe-shaped driveway of the house she and Michael had shared in Stillwater, Minnesota. It was a two-story Georgian on Third Avenue, high above the St. Croix River, a beautifully balanced home with a center door and bow windows on either side. The entry was guarded by four fluted round columns supporting a semicircular railed roof. From behind the sturdy railing a great fanlight overlooked the front yard from the second story. The place had a look of permanence, of security, the kind of house pictured in children's readers, Bess had told Michael when they'd found it, the kind of house where only a happy family would live.

They had fallen in love with it on sight; then they'd gone inside and had seen the magnificent view, clear across the St. Croix River to Wisconsin, beyond, and the lot itself, cresting the bluff, with its great, grand maple tree dead center out back, and the sparkling river lying below. They had seen the place and had gasped in mutual delight.

Nothing that had happened since had changed Bess's opinion of the house. She still loved it; enough to be making payments on Michael's legal half of it since Randy had turned eighteen.

She pulled into the double attached garage, lowered the automatic door and entered the service door to the kitchen. She'd redone the room since her business had flourished, had installed matte white Formica cabinets with butcher-block tops, a new vinyl floor in shades of seafoam blue and plush, cream-colored carpeting in the attached family room. The new furniture was a blend of smoky blues and apricots, inspired by the view of the river and the spectacular sunrises that unfolded beyond the tall east windows of the house.

Bess bypassed the U-shaped kitchen and dropped her coat onto a sofa facing the wall of glass. She switched on a shoulder-high floor lamp with a thick, twisted ceramic base and a cymbal-shaped shade and went to the window to draw up the blinds. The window treatments were lavish above, simple below: great billowing valances in a busy blue-and-apricot floral, paired with pleated horizontal blinds of pale apricot. The pattern of the curtains was repeated in two deep, chubby chairs; a coordinating splash of waves appeared on the long sofa with its baker's dozen of loose cushions.

Bess drew up the blinds and stood looking out the window at the winter view—the smooth yard, swathed in snow, sloping down to the sheer bluff covered by scrub brush; the granddaddy maple standing sentinel at the yard's edge; the great pale path of the wide river and, on the Wisconsin side, a half mile away, dots of window light glimmering here and there on the dark, high, wooded bank.

She thought of Michael . . . of Lisa . . . of Michael again . . . and of their unborn grandchild. The word had not been mentioned but it had been there in that restaurant between them as surely as their cups of steaming coffee.

My God, we're going to have a grandchild.

The thought thundered through her, brought her hand to her mouth and a lump to her throat. It was difficult to hate a man with whom you were sharing this milestone.

The lights across the river became starbursts and she realized there were tears in her eyes. Grandparenthood had been something that happened to others. It was symbolized by television commercials with sixty-five-year-old gray-haired couples with round, rosy cheeks baking cookies with youngsters; calling their grandchildren long distance; opening their doors at Christmastime and welcoming two generations with open arms.

This child would have none of that. He would have a handsome young grandfather, recently divorced, living in White Bear Lake, and a business-woman of a grandma too busy for cookie-making, living in Stillwater.

Many times since her divorce Bess had felt regret for the loss of tradition and an unbroken family line but never so powerfully as tonight, when facing the advent of the next generation. She herself had known grandparents, Molly and Ed LeClair, her mother's folks, who'd died when she was in high school. Recalling them brought a wistful expression to her face, for they'd lived right here in Stillwater through her younger years, in a house on North Hill to which she'd ridden her bike whenever she wanted, to raid Grandma Molly's cookie jar or her strawberry patch, or to watch Grandpa Ed paint his birdhouses in his little workshop out back. He'd known the tricks of attracting bluebirds—a house with a slanted roof, no perch and a removable bottom, he'd taught her—and always in the summer their backyard had bluebirds flitting above Grandma Molly's gardens and the open meadow beyond.

Times had changed. Lisa's child would have to visit his grandma in her interior design shop, and his grandfather only after he got old enough to drive a car.

Moreover, the bluebirds had disappeared from Stillwater.

Bess sighed and turned away from the window. She removed her suit and left it on the sofa. Dressed in her blouse, slip and nylons, she built a fire in the family-room fireplace and sat on the floor before it, staring, disconsolate. She wondered what Michael thought about becoming a grandfather, and where Randy was, and what kind of husband Mark

Padgett would make, and if Lisa truly loved him, and how she herself was going to survive this charade Lisa was asking of her. Already, after only one night with Michael, she was bluer than she'd been in months.

The telephone rang and Bess glanced at her watch. It was going on eleven. She picked up the receiver from a glass-top table between the two tub chairs.

"Hello?"

"Hi. Just checking in."

"Oh, hi, Keith." Lifting her face to the ceiling, she scooped her hair back from one temple.

"You got home late."

"Just a few minutes ago."

"So, how was the dinner with Lisa?"

Bess flopped onto one of the chairs with her head caught on the rounded back. "Not so good, I'm afraid."

"Why not?"

"Lisa invited me over for more than just dinner."

"What else?"

"Oh, Keith, I've been sitting here getting a little weepy."

"What is it?"

"Lisa is pregnant."

At the other end of the line Keith released a swoosh of breath.

"She wants to get married in six weeks."

"To the baby's father?"

"Yes, Mark Padgett."

"I remember you mentioning him."

"Mentioning him, that's all. Lord, she's known him less than a year."

"And what about him? Does he want to marry her, too?"

"He says he does. They want a full wedding with all the trimmings."

"Then I don't understand—what's the problem?"

That was one of the troubles with Keith. He often failed to understand her problems. She had been seeing him for three years, yet in all that time he'd never seemed sympathetic at the moments she needed him to. Particularly when it came to her children, he had an intolerant side that often irritated her. He had no children of his own, and sometimes that fact created a gulf between them that Bess wasn't sure could ever be bridged.

"The problem is that I'm her mother. I want her to marry for love, not for expediency."

"Doesn't she love him?"

"She says she does but how—"

"Does he love her?"

"Yes, but—"

"Then what are you so upset about?"

"It's not that cut-and-dried, Keith!"

"What? Are you upset about becoming a grandmother? That's a lot of bunk. I've never been able to understand people getting all freaked out about these things—reaching thirty, or forty, or becoming a grandparent. It's all pretty ridiculous to me. What really matters is keeping busy and healthy and feeling young inside."

"That's not what I'm upset about!"

"Well, what then?"

Reclining in the chair, with her chin on her chest, Bess picked up the soiled jabot and toyed with it.

"Michael was there."

Silence . . . then, "Michael?"

"Lisa set us up, she invited us both, then made an excuse to leave the apartment so we'd be forced to confront each other."

"And?"

"And it was hellish."

Silence again before Keith said, decidedly, "Bess, I want to come over."

"I don't think you should. It's nearly eleven."

"Bess, I don't like this."

"My seeing Michael? For heaven's sake, I haven't spoken a civil word to the man in six years."

"Maybe not, but it only took one night to upset you. I want to come over."

"Keith, please . . . it'll take you half an hour to get here, and I should go into the shop early in the morning to do some bookwork. Believe me, I'm not upset."

"You said you were crying."

"Not about Michael. About Lisa."

From his silence she anticipated his reaction. "You're pushing me away again, Bess. Why do you do that?"

"Please, Keith, not tonight. I'm tired and I expect Randy will be home soon."

"I wasn't asking to stay overnight." Though Bess and Keith were intimate, she had made it understood early in their relationship that as long as Randy lived with her, overnights at her house were out. Randy had been hurt enough by his dad's peccadillo. Though her son might very well guess she was having an affair with Keith, she was never going to verify it.

"Keith, could we just say good night now? I really have had a rough day."

Keith's silence was rife with exasperation before he released a sound resembling escaping steam. "Oh, all right," he said, "I won't *bother* you tonight. What I called for was to see if you wanted to go to dinner on Saturday night." His invitation was issued in an acid tone.

"Are you sure you still want me to?"

"Bess, I swear to God, sometimes I don't know why I keep hanging onto you."

Bess became contrite. "I'm sorry, Keith. Yes, of course, I'd love to go to dinner Saturday night. What time?"

"Seven."

"Shall I drive in?" Keith lived in St. Paul, thirty miles away. His favorite restaurants were over in that direction.

"Come to my place. I'll drive from here."

"All right, I'll see you then. And Keith?"

"What?"

"I really am sorry. I mean it."

Across the wire she could sense him expelling a breath and drooping his shoulders. "I know."

After Bess hung up she sat in her chair a long time, curled forward, elbows to knees, her toes overlapped, staring at the fire. What was she doing with Keith? Merely using him to slake her loneliness? He had walked into her store one day three years ago, when she'd been three years without a man, three years trying occasional dates that turned into sexual embarrassments, three years insisting that all men belonged at the bottom of the ocean. Then in walked Keith, a little on the plain side in the looks department, a little on the thin side in the hair department, but one of the best sales reps she'd ever encountered. Known in the trade as a rag man, he'd wheeled in a big 40 × 20-inch sample case and announced he was from Robert Allen Fabrics and that she had decorated the home of his best friends, Sylvia and Reed Gohrman; he liked the looks of her store; needed a Mother's Day gift for his mother; and if she would look through his samples while he perused her merchandise, they might each find something they liked. If not, he'd be gone and would never darken her door again.

Bess had burst out laughing. So had Keith. He'd bought a forty-dollar vase trimmed with glass roses, and when she was wrapping it she said, "Your mother will be pleased."

He replied, "My mother is never pleased with anything. She'll probably come in here and exchange it for those three frogs that are holding that glass ball."

"You don't like my frogs?"

He glanced at the three ugly brass frogs, covered with green patina, their forefeet raised above their heads, supporting what looked like a large, clear glass marble. He raised one eyebrow and quirked his mouth. "Now, that's a loaded question when you haven't told me what you think of my samples yet."

She had looked, and liked, and been assured by Keith that his company maintained careful quality control of its products, would not keep her on ice for three months then ship flawed fabric, provided *free* samples rather than the "book plan" (which required storeowners to sign a year's contract and agree to pay for all samples), offered delayed billing and followed up every order with a computerized acknowledgment and shipping date. She was impressed, and Keith went away knowing so.

He'd called a week later and asked if she would like to go to Dudley Riggs's Brave New Workshop with him and his friends Sylvia and Reed Gohrman. She liked his style—live comedy for a first date, which she needed at the time, and mutual acquaintances as reassurance that she wouldn't have another wrestling match on her hands at the end of the evening.

He had been impeccably polite—no groping, no sexual innuendos, not even a good night kiss until their second date. They had seen each other for six months before their relationship became intimate. Immediately afterward, he'd asked her to marry him. For two and a half years she'd been saying no. For two and a half years he'd been growing more frustrated by her refusals. She had tried to explain that she wasn't willing to take that risk again, that running her business had become her primary source of fulfillment, that she still had her troubles with Randy and didn't want to impose them on a husband. The truth was, she simply didn't love him enough.

He was nice (an elementary word but true, when describing Keith) but when he walked into her shop she only smiled, never glowed. When he kissed her she only warmed, never heated. When they made love she wanted the light off, not on. And when it was over, she always wanted to go home to her own bed, alone.

And of course there was that thing about her children. He'd been married once, briefly, during his twenties but being childless he had remained marginally jealous of Lisa and Randy and slightly selfish in his approach to many conflicts. If Bess had to say no to him because of a previous commitment with Lisa, he became piqued. He held that her stand on his sleeping at her house was ridiculous, given that Randy was nineteen years old and no dummy.

Another thing—he coveted her house.

He had come into it the first time and stood before the sliding glass doors, looked out over the river valley and breathed, "Wow . . . I could put my recliner right here and never move."

First off, she hated recliners. Secondly, she felt a trickle of irritation at the very suggestion of him moving into *her* house. For the briefest moment she'd even had a flash of defense on Michael's behalf. After all, it was Michael who'd paid for the house and helped her furnish it. How dare this upstart stand there musing about usurping the spot that had always been Michael's favorite?

There were many facets of Keith that displeased her. So the question remained, why did she continue to see him?

The answer was plain: he had become a habit, and without him life would have been infinitely more lonely.

She sighed and went to the fireplace, screaked open the metal screen and turned the logs, watching sparks rise like inverted fireworks. She sat before it, with her arms crossed on her upraised knees. *Oh, Lisa, don't worsen the mistake you've already made. It's no fun watching a fire alone, wishing things had turned out differently.*

Her face grew hot, and the nylon slip covering her thighs seemed to catch the heat and draw it to her skin. She dropped her forehead onto her arms but remained where she was. The house was so silent and bleak. It had never been as satisfying after Michael left. It was home, and she would never give it up. But it was lonely.

Outside, most of the lights across the river had disappeared. She rose and wandered into the dining room—an extension of the family room—running her fingers over the backs of the unused chairs as she passed them, and on through an archway into the formal living room, which stretched across the entire east end of the house, from the river view at the rear to the street view at the front. At the rear corner, where two immense windows met, a grand piano stood in the shadows—black, gleaming, silent since Lisa had grown up and moved away. On it was a gallery of framed family pictures. On Thursdays the cleaning lady moved the pictures and dusted the piano. At Christmastime a huge arrangement of red balls and greenery ousted the five framed portraits. After New Year's the gallery came back and stayed until the following Christmas. It was the only thing the piano was used for anymore.

Bess sat down on the sleek ebony piano bench and slid across it in her nylon slip. She switched on the music lamp. Its rays shone down upon an empty music rest and a closed key cover. She touched the brass pedals, cold and smooth beneath her nylon-bound toes. She folded her hands and rested them between her thighs and wondered why she herself had given up playing. After Michael left she'd shunned the instrument just as she'd shunned him. Because he had liked piano music so much? How childish. Granted, her life had been busy, but there were moments such as these when the sound of the piano would have been comforting, when the feel of the keys would have soothed.

She rose and opened the bench, leafed through the sheet music until she found what she was looking for.

The cover of the bench clacked loudly as it closed. By contrast, the key cover made a soft, velvet thump as it opened. The music rustled, and her raspberry silk sleeves appeared in the thin band of light illuminating the keys.

The first notes shimmered through the shadowy room, harp-like and haunting as she found the familiar combinations and struck them.

"The Homecoming." Lisa's song. Her father's song. Why Bess had chosen it, she neither dissected nor cared. The compulsion had struck and she'd responded, rusty as she was on this instrument. As she played, the tentativeness left her fingers, the tension left her shoulders and soon she began to feel what a runner feels when he hits his stride, the immense sense of well-being at baring one's teeth to the wind and utilizing some capability that has lain dormant too long.

She was unaware of Randy's presence until she ended the song and he spoke out of the shadows.

"Sounding good, Mom."

"Oh!" She gasped and lifted an inch off the piano bench. "Randy, you scared the devil out of me! How long have you been there?"

He smiled, one shoulder propped against the dining-room doorway. "Not long." He sauntered into the room and sat down on the bench beside her, dressed in jeans and a brown leather jacket that looked as though a fleet of Sherman tanks had driven over it. His hair was black, like his father's, and dressed with something sheeny, spiked straight up and finger-long on top, slicked back over the ears and trailing in natural curls below his collar in back. Randy was an eye-catcher—her clerk at the store said he reminded her of a young Robert Urich—with a lopsided, dimpled grin; a way of letting his head dip forward when he approached a woman; a tiny gold loop in his left ear; perfect teeth and brown eyes with glistening black lashes that were longer than some men could grow their beards. He had adopted the rough-cut look of the unshaved young pop singer George Michael, and an unhurried manner.

Sitting beside his mother he played a low-register F, holding the key down until the note diminished into silence. Dropping the hand to his lap, he turned his head infinitesimally—all his motions were understated—and unleashed his lazy quarter-smile.

"Been a long time since you played."

"Mm-hmm."

"Why'd you stop?"

"Why'd you stop talking to your dad?"

"Why did you?"

"I was angry."

"So was I."

Bess paused. "I saw him tonight."

Randy looked away but allowed the grin to remain.

"How is the prick?"

"Randy, you're speaking of your father, and I won't allow that kind of gutter language."

"I've heard you call him worse."

"When?"

Randy worked his head and shoulders in irritation. "Mom, get off it. You hate his guts as much as I do and you haven't made any secret of it. So what's all this about? All of a sudden you're buttering up to him?"

"I'm not buttering up to him. I saw him, that's all. At Lisa's."

"Oh yeah, that's right. . . ." Randy dropped his chin and scratched his head. "I guess she told you, huh?"

"Yes, she did."

He looked at his mother. "So, you bummed out or what?"

"Yeah, I guess you could say that."

"I was, too, at first but now I've had a day to think about it and I think she'll be okay. Hell, she wants the kid and Mark's okay, you know? I mean, he really loves her, I think."

"How do you know so much?"

"I spend time over there." Randy ran his thumbnail into the vertical crack between two piano keys. "She cooks me dinner and we watch videos together, stuff like that. Mark's usually there."

Another surprise. "I didn't know that . . . that you spend time over there."

Randy gave up his preoccupation with the keys and returned his hand to his lap. "Lisa and I get along all right. She helps me get my head on straight."

"She said you've agreed to stand up for them."

Randy shrugged and let his eyes rove indolently his mother's way.

"And to cut your hair."

He made a chucking sound, sucking his cheek against his teeth. "There you go. You're gonna like that, huh, Ma?" His grin was back.

"The hair doesn't bother me as much as the beard."

He rubbed it. It was coarse and black and undoubtedly a turn-on for many nineteen-year-old girls. "Yeah, well, it's probably gonna go, too."

"You got some girl who's going to miss it?" she teased, reaching as if to pinch his cheek.

He reared back and brandished both hands, karate-fashion. "Don't touch the nap, woman!"

They poised as if on the brink of combat, then laughed together and hugged, with her smooth cheek against his prickly one, and the smell of his distressed leather jacket engulfing her. No matter the worries he caused her, moments like this were her recompense. Ah, there was something wonderful about an adult son. His occasional hugs made up for the loss of his father, and his presence in the house gave her someone to listen for, someone else moving about, a reason to keep the refrigerator stocked. It probably was time she booted him out of the nest but she hated losing him, no matter how seldom they exchanged banter such as this. When he left there would be only her in this big house alone, and it would be decision time.

He released her and she smiled affectionately. "You're an incorrigible flirt."

He covered his heart with both hands. "Mother, you wound me."

She let his high jinks pass and said, "About the wedding . . ."

He waited.

"Lisa asked your father and I to walk her down the aisle."

"Yeah, I know."

"And it looks as though there's going to be a dinner at Mark's parents' home to introduce the two families." When Randy made no reply, she asked, "Can you handle that?"

"Lisa and I have already got that covered."

Bess's lips formed a silent *oh.* These children of hers had a relationship that seemed to have left her several years behind.

Randy went on. "Don't worry, I won't embarrass the family." After a brief assessment of his mother's eyes, he asked, "Will you?"

"No. Your father and I had a talk after we left Lisa's. We both agreed to honor her wishes. The olive branch has been passed."

"Well then . . ." Randy raised his palms and let them slap his thighs. "I guess everybody's happy." He began to rise but Bess caught his arm.

"There's one more thing."

He waited, settling back into his customary nonchalance.

"I just thought you should know. Your father and Darla are getting a divorce."

"Yeah, Lisa told me. Big deal . . . old love 'em and leave 'em Curran." He gave a disgusted laugh and added, "I really don't give a shit, Mom."

"All right. I've told you." Bess flipped her hands in the air as if excusing him. "End of parental duty."

He rose from the bench and stood in the shadows nearby. "You better look out, Mom, the next thing you know he'll be knockin' on your door again. That's how guys like him work. . . . They gotta have a woman and by the sound of it he's fresh out of one. He made a fool of you once, and I sure as hell hope you don't let him do it again."

"Randy Curran, what kind of an airhead do you take me for?"

Randy swung away and headed for the dining-room archway. Halfway through it he used it to brake himself and turned back to her.

"Well, you were sitting there playing that song he always liked."

"It happens to be one I always liked, too!"

Leveling his gaze on her, he patted out a bongo rap on either side of the doorframe. "Yeah, sure, Mom," he remarked dryly, then gave himself a two-handed push-off and left.

chapter 3

THE ST. CROIX RIVER valley lay under a cloak of winter haze the following day as Bess left home for her shop. It was a frigid, windless morning. To the south rose an inert white plume from the tall brick smokestack of the Northern States power plant, the immaculate cloud building in a thick, motionless bundle that hovered against a pewter sky. To the north, rime formed a jeweled frosting upon the lacy tie braces of the ancient black steel lift bridge that linked Stillwater with Houlton, Wisconsin, across the water.

Rivertown, Stillwater was called. It snuggled in a bowl of wooded hills, rivers, ravines and limestone bluffs that pressed it close against the placid waters of the river from which the town took its name. It had been a mecca for lumberjacks of the 1800s, who'd worked in the pineries to the north and spent their earnings in the town's fifty watering holes and six bordellos that had long since disappeared. Gone, too, were the great white pines that had once supported the town, yet Stillwater prized its heritage of former sawmills, loggers' rooming houses and Victorian mansions built by the wealthy lumber barons whose names still dotted the pages of the local telephone directory.

It appeared, at first glance, a city of rooftops—steeples, mansards, peaks and turrets of the whimsical structures built in another day—all of them dropping toward the small downtown that rimmed the west bank of the river.

Bess viewed it as she drove down Third Street hill past the old courthouse. A right on Olive and she was at Main: a half-mile strip of commerce stretching from the limestone caves of the old Joseph Wolf Brewery at the south to the limestone walls of the Staples Mill at the north. Main Street's buildings were of another century, ornate, red-brick, with arched second-story windows above, old-fashioned street lamps out front and narrow alleys out back. Steep cobbled sidewalks led down the side streets on their way to the riverfront one block beyond. In summer tourists walked its strand, enjoyed its rose gardens, sat in the shade of the town gazebo at Lowell Park or on the green lawns in the sun while licking ice-cream cones and watching the pleasure crafts nose through the blue water of the St. Croix.

They boarded the stern-wheeler *Andiamo* for scenic rides and sat on the decks of the riverside restaurants sipping tall pastel drinks, eating sandwiches and squinting at the rippling water from the shade of chic terry-cloth visors, musing how great it would be to live here.

That was summer.

This was winter.

Now, in droll January, the roses were gone. The pleasure crafts were dry-docked in the valley's five marinas. The *Andiamo* lay ice-bound at her slip. The popcorn wagon on Main Street was battened down and covered with a dome of snow. The ice sculptures in front of the Grand Garage had lost their fine edges and dwindled into crystal memories of the sailboats and angels they had been during the busy Christmas season.

Bess had her usual English muffin and coffee at the St. Croix Club restaurant beside the cheerful gas fire, took another coffee along in a Styrofoam cup and headed for her shop.

It was on Chestnut Street, two doors off Main, an ancient building with two blue window boxes, a blue door and a sign that said BLUE IRIS, HOMESCAPES, with a likeness of the flower underscoring the words.

Inside it was gloomy but smelled of the potpourri and scented candles she sold. The building was ninety-three years old, scarcely wider than a hospital corridor but deep. The front door faced north, creating a cool, shady aspect in summer. This morning, however, cold drafts filtered in.

The walls of the store were papered in shantung-textured cream to match the painted woodwork, and beneath the cove molding ran a border strip of blue irises the same shade as the carpeting. Blue irises also appeared on the signature art that hung behind the desk on the stair wall, and on the paper bags in which customers' purchases were wrapped.

Grandma Molly had grown blue irises in her yard on North Hill. Even as a child Bess had dreamed of owning her own business and way back then had known what it would be called.

Bess picked her way through the maze of lamps, art prints, easels, brass picture frames, small furniture and dried botanicals to the small checkout counter set midway down the left wall against an ancient, steep stairway that climbed to the tiniest loft imaginable. It was pressed close against the ceiling—so close the top of Bess's hair brushed the embossed tin overhead. In the town's heyday some accountant had spent his days up there, penning numbers in ledgers and taking care of cash receipts. It often occurred to Bess that the man must have been either a midget or a hunchback.

She checked at the cash register and found several messages left by Heather the day before, taking them and her coffee up the creaky steps. Upstairs it was so crowded she was forced to balance on one foot while leaning over the clutter of swatch and wallpaper books to switch on a floor lamp, then the fluorescent one on her desk. As an office, the loft was inadequate by anyone's standards, yet every time she considered giving up the store to get a bigger one, it was the loft that kept her here. Maybe it was mornings like this, when her cramped, high work space collected the rising heat and reflected the light off the cream-painted ceiling, and kept the aroma of her coffee drifting close about her head. Or maybe it was the view of the front window and door over her railing. Or maybe it was simply that the loft had character and history, and both appealed to Bess. The thought of a modern office in a sterile cubicle slightly repulsed her.

It was Bess's habit to come early. The hours between 7 and 10 A.M., when the phones were quiet and no customers around, were the most productive of her day. Once 10 A.M. hit and the front door was unlocked, power paperwork was out.

She uncapped her coffee, read Heather's messages, did paperwork, filing, made phone calls and got some design work done before Heather arrived at 9:30 and called upstairs, " 'Morning, Bess!"

" 'Morning, Heather! How are you?"

"Cold." Bess heard the basement door open and close as Heather hung up her coat. "How was your supper at Lisa's?"

Bess paused with the page of a furniture catalog half-turned. Heather knew enough about her history with Michael that Bess wasn't going to open that can of worms yet.

"Fine," she answered. "She's turning out to be a very decent cook."

Heather's head appeared beyond the railing and her footsteps made the loft stairs creak. She stopped near the top of the stairs—a forty-five-year-old woman with strawberry blonde broom-cut hair glazed into fashionable disarray, stylish tortoiseshell glasses and sculptured garnet fingernails bearing tiny rhinestone nail ornaments that flashed as her hand rested on the railing. She had wide cheekbones, a pretty mouth and dressed with insouciant flair, creating a positive first impression when customers walked into the store.

Bess employed three part-time clerks but Heather was her favorite as well as her most valued.

"You have a ten o'clock appointment, you know."

"Yes, I know." Bess checked her watch and began gathering her materials for the house call.

"And a twelve-thirty and a three."

"I know, I know."

"Orders for today?"

Bess handed Heather various notes, gave her instructions about ordering wallpaper and checking on incoming freight, and left the store confident that things would run smoothly while she was gone.

It was a hectic day, as most were. Three house calls left her little time for lunch. She grabbed a tuna-salad sandwich at a sub shop between house calls and ate it in the car. She drove from Stillwater to Hudson, Wisconsin, to North St. Paul and got back to the Blue Iris just as Heather was locking up for the night.

"You had nine calls," Heather said.

"Nine!"

"Four of them were important."

Bess flopped onto a wicker settee, exhausted.

"Tell me."

"Hirschfields, Sybil Archer, Warner Wallpaper and Lisa."

"What did Sybil Archer want?"

"Her wallpaper."

Bess groaned. Sybil Archer was the wife of a 3M executive who believed Bess had a wallpaper press in her back room and could produce the stuff at the snap of a finger.

"What did Lisa want?"

"She didn't say. Just said you should call her back."

"Thanks, Heather."

"Well, I'm off to the bank before it closes."

"How'd we do today?"

"Terrible. A grand total of eight customers."

Bess made a face. The bulk of her business came from her design work; she kept the store chiefly as a consideration for her design customers. "Did any of them buy anything?"

"A Cobblestone Way calendar, a few greeting cards and a couple of tea towels."

"Hmph. Thank God for summer in a tourist town, huh?"

"Well, I'll see you tomorrow, okay?"

"Thanks, Heather, and good night."

When Heather was gone, Bess pushed herself up, left her coat on the settee and headed for the loft. As usual, she hadn't spent nearly as much time as she had hoped on designing. It took an average of ten hours to design most jobs, and she'd barely put in three today.

Upstairs, she kicked off her high heels and scraped back her hair as she dropped to her desk chair, opened a turkey-and-sprout sandwich she'd picked up at Cub supermarket and popped the top on her Diet Pepsi.

Slowing down for the first time since morning, she realized how tired she was. She took a bite of her sandwich and stared at a stack of replacement pages that had been waiting well over two weeks to be inserted in one of the furniture catalogs.

While she was still staring the phone rang.

"Good evening, Blue Iris."

"Mrs. Curran?"

"Yes?"

"This is Hildy Padgett . . . Mark's mother?" A friendly voice, neither cultured nor crude.

"Oh, yes, hello, Mrs. Padgett. It's so nice to hear from you."

"I understand that Mark and Lisa had supper with you last night and broke the news."

"Yes, they did."

"Well, it seems those two are getting set to make us some kind of shirttail relatives or something."

Bess set down her sandwich. "Yes, it certainly does."

"I want you to know right up front that Jake and I couldn't be happier. We think the sun rises and sets in your daughter. From the first time Mark brought her home we said to each other, Now there's the kind of girl we'd like for a daughter-in-law. When they told us they were getting married we were just delighted."

"Why, thank you. I know Lisa feels the same way about both of you."

"Of course, we were a little surprised about the baby coming but both Jake and I sat down and had a long talk with Mark, just to make sure that he was doing what he wanted to do, and we came away assured that he had every intention of marrying Lisa anyway, and that they both wanted the baby and are quite excited about it."

"Yes, they told us the same thing."

"Well we think it's just wonderful. Both of those kids really seem to have their heads on straight."

Once again Bess felt a twinge of regret, perhaps even jealousy, because she knew Mark and Lisa as a couple so much less intimately than this woman seemed to.

"I have to be honest with you, Mrs. Padgett, I haven't met Mark many times but last night at supper he certainly seemed straightforward and sincere when he told us this marriage is what he wants, what they both want."

"Well, we've given them our blessings and now the two of them want very much for all of us to meet, so I suggested a dinner party here at our house and I was hoping we could get together on Saturday night."

"Saturday night . . ." Her date with Keith; but how could she put one ordinary date before this? "That sounds fine."

"Say seven o'clock?"

"Fine. May I bring something?"

"Lisa's brother, is all. All of our kids will be here, too—we've got five of them—so you'll get a chance to meet them all."

"It's very kind of you to go to all this trouble."

"Kind?" Hildy Padgett laughed. "I'm so excited I've been getting up nights and making lists!"

Bess smiled. The woman sounded so likable and breezy.

"Besides," Hildy went on, "Lisa volunteered to come over and help me. She's going to make the dessert, so all you have to do is be here at seven and we'll get those kids off to a proper start."

When she'd hung up, Bess sat motionless in her swivel chair, melancholy in spite of the plans she'd just made. Outside, dusk had fallen, and in the window downstairs the brass lamps were lit, throwing fern-shadow through a plant that hung above the display. In the loft only the desk lamp shone, spreading a wedge of yellow over her work and her half-finished sandwich on its square of white, waxy paper. Lisa was twenty-one, and pregnant, and getting married. Why did it sadden her so? Why did she find herself longing for the days when the children were small?

Motherlove, she supposed. That mysterious force that could strike at unexpected moments and make nostalgia blossom and fill the heart. She longed, suddenly, to be with Lisa, to touch her, hold her.

Ignoring the work that needed attention, she leaned forward and dialed Lisa's number.

"Hello?"

"Hi, honey, it's Mom."

"Oh, hi, Mom. Something wrong? You sound a little down."

"Oh, just a little nostalgic, that's all. I thought if you weren't busy I might come over for a while and we could talk."

Thirty minutes later Bess had turned her back on her best design time and was entering the setting of last night's confrontation with Michael. When Lisa opened the door Bess hugged her more tightly and a little longer than usual.

"Mom, what's wrong?"

"I guess I'm just being a typical mother, is all. I was sitting there at the store, getting all misty-eyed, remembering when you were little."

Lisa gave a foxy grin. "I was pretty fantastic, wasn't I?"

Lisa had the gift for creating effortless laughter but as Bess released the sound she was wiping a tear from the corner of one eye.

"Oh, Mom . . ." Lisa curved an arm around her mother and led her toward the living room. "I'm getting married, not cloistered."

"I know. I just wasn't prepared for it."

"Dad wasn't either." They sat on the davenport and Lisa put her feet up. "So how did it go when the two of you left here last night? I figured you went off to talk about everything in private."

"We went out and had a cup of coffee and actually managed to be civil to one another for the better part of an hour."

"So what did you decide about Mark and me?"

Bess's expression became wistful. "That you're my only daughter, and you're only getting married once . . . at least I hope it'll only be once."

"That's why you really came over, isn't it, to make sure I'm doing the right thing."

"Your dad and I just wanted you to know that if for any reason you decide marriage to Mark isn't what you want, we'll stand behind you."

It was Lisa's turn to display a wistful expression. "Oh, Mom, I love him so much. When I'm with him I'm more than I was. He makes me want to be better than the me I was before, and so I am. It's as if . . ." Sitting cross-legged, Lisa gazed at the ceiling in her intense search for the proper words, then back at her mother, gesturing with both hands as if she were singing a heartfelt ballad. ". . . As if when we're together all the negative stuff disappears. I see people around me in a more charitable light; I don't criticize, I don't complain. And the funny thing is, the same thing happens to Mark.

"We've talked about it a lot . . . about that night when we met. When he walked into that pool hall and we looked at each other, we suddenly didn't want to be in a pool hall anymore but someplace pure, a woods maybe, or listening to an orchestra someplace. An orchestra! Cripes, Mom!" Lisa threw up her hands. "I like Paula Abdul but there I was, with all my senses open and new avenues looking inviting.

"Something happened . . . I can't explain it. We just . . ." Silence awhile, then Lisa continued, softly. "We just felt different. There we were, living that crazy bar scene, hanging around in noisy, smoky places and swaggering and showing off and being loud and obnoxious at times, and then our two crowds bumped into one another, and he smiled at me and said, 'Hi, I'm Mark,' and from that night on we never felt like we had to be phony with each other. We can admit our weaknesses to one another and that seems to make us stronger. Isn't it weird?"

On her end of the sofa, Bess sat very still, listening to the most stirring description of love she'd ever heard.

"You know what he said to me one day?" Lisa looked radiant as she continued. "He said, 'You're better than any creed I ever learned.' He said it was a line from a poem he read once. I thought about it awhile—actually I've thought about it a lot since he said it—and I realize that's what we are to each other. We're each other's creeds, and *not* to marry someone you feel that way about would be the greatest shame of all."

"Oh, Lisa," Bess whispered, and moved to take Lisa in her arms, this very young woman who had found a love to believe in the way every woman hopes she will one day. It was at once shattering and gratifying to learn that Lisa had grown up in a short span of time while she, Bess, had not been as attentive as she should have been. How humbling it was to realize that Lisa had learned something at age twenty-one that Bess herself had not at age forty. Lisa and Mark had discovered how to communicate, they had found the proper balance between praising each other's virtues and overlooking each other's shortcomings, which translated not only into love but into respect, as well. It was something Bess and Michael had never quite managed.

"Lisa, darling, if you feel that way about him I'm so happy for you."

"Yes, be happy. Because I am." While they were still hugging, Lisa added, "There's just one more thing I want to say." She set Bess away from herself and told her point-blank, "I know you're probably wondering how an educated young woman of the eighties could possibly be so stupid that she got pregnant when there are at least a dozen ways to prevent it. Remember when we went skiing up at Lutsen before Christmas? Well, I forgot my birth control pills that weekend, and we realized we might very well be making a choice if we made love. So we talked about it beforehand. What if we risked it and I got pregnant? He told me then that he wanted to marry me, and that if I got pregnant that weekend, it was fine with him, and I agreed. So, you see, Mom, we're not just handing you a pile of gas when we say we're happy about the baby. What you're worrying about . . . well, you just don't have to. Mark and I are going to be great . . . you'll see."

Bess tenderly touched her daughter's face. "Where have I been while you did all this growing up?"

"You were there."

"Exactly . . . there. Running my business. But I suddenly feel as if I spent too much time at it and not enough with you during the past few years. If I had, I'd have seen this relationship between you and Mark blossoming. I wouldn't have been caught so off guard last night."

"Mom, you handled it okay, believe me."

"No, you handled it okay, and so did Mark. Your dad was totally impressed by him."

"I know. I talked to him today. So did Mark's mother. She said she was going to call you, too. Did she?"

"Yes, she did. She's delightful."

"I knew you'd think so. So everything is set for Saturday night? No objections?"

"Now that I know how you feel, none."

"Whew! That's a relief. So Dad said you two talked about the rest—the dress, and all of us walking down the aisle together, and you'll do it, huh?"

"Yes, we'll do it."

"And I can wear the dress?"

"If it'll fit you, yes."

"Hey, Mom? I know what you're thinking about the dress, that it might put some kind of hex on my wedding or something, but that's really a lot of crap. It isn't dresses that make weddings work, it's people, okay?"

"Okay."

"I just like the dress, that's all. I used to play in it when you weren't home. You never knew that, did you?"

"No, I didn't."

"Well, that's what you get for putting something so irresistible off limits. Someday I'll tell you some of the other stuff that Randy and I used to do when you guys were gone."

Bess's grin became suspicious. "Like what?"

"Remember that sex manual you used to keep hidden between the spare blankets in the linen closet in your bathroom? The one with all the drawings of all the positions? You didn't think we knew it was there, did you?"

"Why, you little devils!"

"Yup, that's us. And remember that vase that disappeared and you could never find it again? That white one with the pink hearts around the top? We broke it one night when we were playing monster in the dark. We used to turn off all the lights and one of us would hide and the other one would walk like Frankenstein, with his arms out, roaring, and one night—

chink!—over went your vase. We knew you'd be royally pissed if we told you, so we hid the pieces in a tomato-juice can we found in the garbage and pretended we didn't know anything about it. But I just knew, Mom, that one day you'd have more vases than the Monticello Flea Market, and sure enough, look at you now. You probably have twenty of them in your store as we speak."

How could Bess resist laughing at such flippancy?

"And all the while I was sending you to catechism classes and teaching you to be good, honest children."

"Well, we were, basically. Look at me today. I'm going to marry the boy I got into trouble and give his baby a name."

When Bess finished laughing, she said, "It's getting late. I should go. It's been a long day."

Rising from the sofa, Lisa said, "You work too hard, Mom. You should take more time to yourself."

"I take all I want."

"Oh, sure you do. But I have a feeling that when Mark and I have this baby we're going to lure you away from your little loft in the sky more often. Just feature that, would y'—my mom a grandma. What do you think about that?"

"I think my hair needs bleaching. The roots are beginning to show."

"You'll get used to the idea. What does Dad think about being a grandpa?"

"We didn't discuss it."

"Oo . . . I hear a cool note."

"You bet you do. Now that the emotional part is over I can tell you that was an underhanded trick you pulled last night."

"It worked though, didn't it?"

"We've drawn a truce for the duration of the wedding festivities, nothing more."

"Oh yeah? Randy said you were playing 'Homecoming' when he got home last night."

"Good heavens, have I no privacy at all?" The two of them moved to the apartment door.

"Think about it, Mom . . . Dad and you together again, coming to visit us and your grandchild. That'd be wild, huh? The two of you wouldn't have to fight about taking care of the housework and kids anymore, because we're all grown up and you have a housekeeper. And you're all done with college so he couldn't be barking at you about that. And he's got his own cabin now so you wouldn't have to stay behind when he goes hunting. And since he's all washed up with Darla—"

"Lisa, you're hallucinating." Bess drew on her coat with an air of finality.

"Yeah, well, think about it, I said." Lisa braced one shoulder against the wall.

"I *will not!* I'll treat him civilly but that's the extent of it. Besides, you're forgetting about Keith."

"Old bald-headed Keith the rag man? Don't make me laugh, Mom. You've been dating him for three years and Randy says you don't even spend nights with him. Take it from me, Bess, the rag man's not for you."

"I don't know what's come over you tonight, Lisa, but you're being intentionally outrageous." Bess opened the apartment door.

"I'm in love. I want the rest of the world to be, too." Lisa popped a kiss on her mother's mouth. "Hey, see you Saturday night, huh? You know how to get there?"

"Yes, Hildy gave me directions."

"Great. And don't forget my little brother."

Heading for her car, Bess had totally lost her melancholy mood of earlier. Lisa truly had a gift for making people laugh at their own foibles. Not that she, Bess, had any intention of reviving anything between herself and Michael. As she'd said, there was Keith to consider. The thought of Keith brought a frown: he wasn't going to be pleased about her breaking their date Saturday night.

She called him from the phone in her bedroom the moment she got her suit and hosiery off.

He answered after the fifth ring.

"Hello?"

"Keith, it's Bess. Did I get you away from something?"

"Just got out of the shower."

There wasn't and never had been any sexual innuendo following convenient lead-ins such as this. It was one of the things Bess missed in their relationship, yet she never felt compelled to start it and since he didn't, humorous and intimate repartee was missing.

"I can call back later."

"No, no it's fine. What's up?"

"Keith, I'm really sorry but I'm going to have to cancel our dinner date Saturday night."

In the pause that followed she imagined he'd stopped drying himself. "Why?"

"The Padgetts are having a dinner at their house so both sides of the family can meet."

"Didn't anyone ask you if you were busy?"

"Everyone else was able to make it. I hardly thought I could ask them to delay it for me alone, and given how short a time there is before the wedding, I thought it best if the two families met right away."

"I suppose your ex will be there?"

Bess massaged her forehead. "Oh, Keith."

"Well, won't he?"

"Yes, he will."

"Oh, fine, just fine!"

"Keith, for heaven's sake, it's our daughter's wedding. I can't very well avoid him."

"No, of course you can't!" Keith snapped. "Well, when you have time for me, Bess, give me a call."

"Keith, wait . . ."

"No . . . no . . ." he said sarcastically, "don't worry about me. Just go ahead and do what you have to do with Michael. I understand."

She detested this brittleness he adopted whenever he became jealous of her time with the children.

"Keith, I don't want you to hang up mad at me."

"I've got to go, Bess. I'm getting the carpet wet."

"All right but call me soon."

"Sure," he replied brusquely.

When she'd hung up, Bess rubbed her eyes. Sometimes Keith could be so insufferably childish. Did he always have to see these conflicts as a choice between her children and him? Once again she wondered why she continued seeing him. It would probably be best for both of them, she thought, if she broke it off entirely.

She dropped her arms and thought wearily of the design work she'd brought home and left downstairs on the dining-room table. She hated designing when she felt this way. Somehow it seemed her moroseness might creep into the design itself.

But she had three jobs waiting after this one, and customers eager to get her phone call setting up their presentations, and more house calls on her calendar in the days ahead.

With a sigh she rose from her desk and went downstairs to put in two more hours.

chapter 4

On Saturday night Bess took pains with her hair. It was nearly shoulder-length, its shades of blonde as varied as an October prairie. She curled it only enough to give it lift, and pouffed it out behind her ears, where it billowed like the sleeves of a choir gown caught in the wind. Her makeup was subtle but applied with extreme care—twelve steps from concealer to mascara. The finished results enlarged her brown eyes and plumped her lips. She stared at her reflection in the mirror, sober, smiling, then sober once again.

Unquestionably she wanted to impress Michael tonight: there was an element of pride involved. Toward the end of their marriage, when she'd been caught up in the rigors of studying for her degree and maintaining a domicile and a family of four, he had said during one of their fights, "Look at you, you don't even take care of yourself anymore. All you ever wear is blue jeans and sweatshirts, and your hair hangs in strings. You didn't look like that when I married you!"

How his accusation had stung. She'd been burning the candle at both ends trying to achieve something for herself, but he'd failed to recognize that her output of time meant some cuts were necessary. So her hair had gone uncurled, her nails unpainted and she had forsaken makeup. Blue jeans and a sweatshirt were the easiest to launder, the quickest to grab, so they became her customary uniform. At the end of a six-hour school day she'd come home to face studying and housework while he'd grow obstinate about helping with the latter. He'd been raised in a traditional household where women's work was exactly that, where men didn't peel potatoes or wash laundry or run a vacuum cleaner. When she'd suggested that he try these, he'd suggested she take a few less credits per quarter and resume the duties she'd agreed to do when they got married.

His narrow-mindedness had enraged her.

Her continued lack of attention to herself and to the house eventually drove him out of it, and he found a woman with beautiful curled tresses, who wore high heels and Pierre Cardin suits to work every day and painted her nails and brought him coffee and dialed his clients for him.

Bess had seen Darla occasionally, most often at the company Christmas parties, where she wore sequined dresses and dyed-to-match satin pumps and lipstick that sparkled nearly as much as her dangly earrings. Had Michael simply left Bess, she might have acceded to maintaining a speaking relationship with him; but he'd left her for another woman, and a stunning beauty at that. The realization had galled Bess ever since.

After she'd gotten her degree, one of the first things she had done was lay out three hundred dollars for a beauty make-over. Under the tutelage of a professional she'd learned what colors suited her best, what clothing silhouettes most flattered her shape, what shades of makeup to wear and how to apply them. She'd even learned what size and shape of handbag and shoes suited her build and what style of earring most flattered her facial features. She'd had her hair color changed from muskrat brown to tawny blonde, its style lightly permed into the bon vivant wind-fluffed look, which she still wore. She'd grown her fingernails and kept them meticulously polished in a hue that matched her lipstick. And over a span of years she'd acquired a new wardrobe to which she added judiciously only those pieces which perfectly matched the color and style guidelines she'd learned from the professionals.

When Michael Curran got a load of her tonight there'd be no ketchup on her jabot, no shine to her makeup and no hair out of place.

She chose a red dinner suit with a straight skirt and an asymmetrical jacket sporting one black triangular-shaped lapel rising from a single black waist-button. With it she wore oversized gold door-knocker earrings that drew attention to her winged hairstyle and her rather dramatic jawline.

When the suit jacket was buttoned she pressed both hands to her abdomen and turned to view herself in profile. She needed to lose ten pounds—it was a constant struggle. But since her mid-thirties the pounds seemed to go on so much faster than they came off. She'd shaved off the four extra pounds she'd gained over the holidays but she had merely to *look* at a dessert to put it back on.

Ah, well—she was satisfied with one full hour's efforts at grooming, anyway. She switched out her bedroom light and went down two flights to Randy's room. When he was sixteen he'd chosen to hole up in an unfinished room on the walkout level because it was twice as large as the upstairs bedrooms and two walls were backfilled with yard so the neighbors wouldn't complain about his drums.

They filled one corner, his prized set of Pearls—twelve pieces of gleaming stainless steel, including his pride and joy, three graduated sizes of rototoms, whose pitch could be changed with a simple twist of the revolving heads. The two concrete-block walls behind the drums were painted black. Fanned on one were posters of his idols, Bon Jovi, Motley Crüe and Cinderella. From an overhead strip a half-dozen canister lights picked out the drums. One of the remaining walls was white, the other covered with cork that gave the room the perennial smell of charcoal. The corkboard was hung with pictures of old girlfriends, beer ads, band schedules and prom garters. Since the room had no closet, Randy's clothes hung on a piece of steel pipe suspended from the ceiling by two chains. The floor was littered with several years' issues of *Car & Driver* magazine, dozens of compact discs, empty fast-food wrappings, shoes and overdue video rentals.

There was a compact disc player, a television, a VCR, a microphone and a fairly sophisticated taping setup. Among all this, the water bed—sporting disheveled leopard sheets—seemed almost incidental.

When Bess came to the door Paula Abdul was blasting "Opposites Attract" from the CD player, and Randy was standing before his dresser adjusting the knot in a skinny gray leather tie. He was dressed in baggy, pleated trousers, a silvery-gray double-breasted sport coat and a plaid shirt in muted shades of purple, gray and white. He'd put something on his hair to make it glossy and though he'd had it cut, as promised, it still hung to his collar in natural ringlets.

Coming upon him this way, while he was engaged in tying his tie, looking spiffy for once, brought a catch to Bess's heart. He was so good-looking, and bright, and charming when he wanted to be, but the path of resistance he'd chosen to take had put so many obstacles between them. Today, however, entering his room Bess felt a shaft of uncomplicated love. He was her son, and he was getting to look more like his father every year, and in spite of her animosity toward Michael, he was undeniably a handsome man. The aroma of masculine toiletries drifted to Bess as she entered Randy's room. She had missed such smells since Michael's departure. For that brief moment it was almost like having a husband and a happy marriage back.

Without glancing his mother's way, Randy said to the mirror, "I promised Lisa I'd have it cut, and I did but this is as short as I go."

She went to the CD player, glanced at the flashing control panel and shouted, "How do I turn this thing down?"

He came and did it for her, dropping one shoulder with unconscious masculine grace. The music ceased. Randy straightened and let a grin lift one side of his mouth while his eyes scanned her outfit and hair. "Lookin' vicious, Mom."

"Thank you, so are you. New clothes?" She touched his tie.

"It's a hot deal—the elder sister tying the big knot."

"Where'd you get the money?"

"I *do* have a job, Mom."

"Yes, of course you do. Listen, I thought we could ride over together."

"Yeah, sure, whatever you say."

"I left my car in the driveway. We may as well take it."

She let him drive, deriving a secret maternal pleasure from being escorted by her full-grown son, something she had fantasized about when he was a young boy, something that happened all too infrequently since he'd become a man. They took highway 96 to White Bear Lake, ten miles due west. The ride led them through snow-covered countryside, past horse ranches and long stretches where no electric lights shone. The lake itself appeared, a blanket of blue-gray in the thin light of an eighth-moon, and rimming it, like a necklace of amber, the lights from lakeshore homes. The lake shared its name with the town that lay on its northwest curve, paling the night sky with its halo.

As they were approaching the city lights, with a bay of the lake on their left, Mark said, "That's where the old man lives."

"Where?"

"In those condos."

Bess looked over her shoulder and caught a glimpse of lights receding behind them, tall skeletal trees and an imposing building she'd often admired when driving past.

"How do you know?"

"Lisa told me."

"Your dad will be there tonight, you know."

Randy glanced her way but said nothing.

"See what you can do to act natural around him, okay?"

"Yes, Mother."

"For Lisa's sake."

"Yes, Mother."

"Randy, if you say yes Mother one more time I'm going to sock you."

"Yes, Mother."

She socked him and they both chuckled.

"You know what I'm saying about your dad."

"I'll try not to punch his lights out."

The Padgetts lived on the west side of town in a middle-class residential neighborhood as flat as an elephant's foot. Randy found the house without a misturn and escorted his mother along the edge of a driveway filled with cars to a sidewalk that curved between snowbanks and led to the front door.

They rang the bell and waited.

Mark and Lisa answered, followed by a short woman shaped like a chest of drawers, in a blue dress with a pleated skirt and a white collar. She had brown hair, frizzled in a bowl-shape, and a smile that put six dimples in her cheeks and made her eyes all but disappear.

Mark said simply, with an arm around her shoulder, "This is my mom, Hildy."

And Lisa said, "This is my mom, Bess, and my brother, Randy."

Hildy Padgett had a grip like a stevedore's and a contralto voice.

"Glad to meet you. Jake, come over here!" she called, and they were joined by Mark's father, straight, tall, thin-haired and smiling, with a hearing aid in his left ear. He was wearing brown trousers and a plaid shirt, open at the throat and rolled up at the cuff. No jacket.

There would be—Bess saw—no dog put on by the Padgetts, not even at a wedding. She liked them immediately.

The living room stretched off to the left, decorated like a country keeping room with blue-and-white plaid wallpaper and a plate rail running the perimeter of the room, a foot below the ceiling. The furniture was thick and comfortable-looking and filled with people. Among them, standing near the archway to the dining room, was Michael Curran.

At the sound of the doorbell Michael turned to watch Bess come in, looking very voguish, followed by Randy, looking surprisingly tall in an outsized overcoat with baggy shoulders and a turned-up collar. The sight of Bess coming in escorted by their son caught Michael in a vulnerable spot. Lord, Randy had grown up! The last time Michael had seen him was nearly three years ago in a busy shopping center. It was Easter, Michael recalled, and the mall had been turned into a miniature farm, with children everywhere, petting baby goats and chickens and ducks. Michael had just bought a spring jacket and come out of J. Riggings to find Randy moving toward him in the foot traffic, talking animatedly with another boy about his age. Michael had smiled and headed toward him but when Randy spied him, he'd halted, sobered, grabbed his friend's arm and done a brusque right-face, disappearing into a convenient women's clothing store.

Now here he was, three years later, taller than his mother and shockingly good-looking. His face had filled out and resembled Michael's own, though Randy was much handsomer. Michael felt a paternal thrill at the sight of that dark hair so much like his; the eyes, mouth and cheeks that had at last taken on the mature planes and curves they would keep into middle age.

He watched Randy shaking hands, giving up his overcoat, and finally Randy's deep brown eyes found Michael's. His hand stopped smoothing down his tie. The smile dropped from his mouth.

Michael felt his chest constrict. His heart flopped crazily. They stood for a light-year, across the room from one another while the past rushed forth to polarize them both. How simple, Michael thought, to cross the room, speak his name, embrace him, this young man who as a boy had idolized his father, had followed like a shadow beside him when he mowed the lawn and shoveled the driveway and changed the oil in the car and said, "Daddy, can I help?"

But Michael could not move. He could only stand across the room with a lump in his throat, trapped by his own mistaken past.

Someone came between them—Jake Padgett, extending his hand in welcome, and Randy's attention swerved to him.

Bess moved into Michael's line of vision. They forced smiles while he committed himself to his spot in the dining-room archway. He might have moved forward to speak to Randy while Bess was near at hand to act as a buffer but the hurt of Randy's last snub returned, sharp and real as if it had happened only yesterday. Bess's admonitions the other night at Lisa's rang clearly in Michael's head—Randy needs a father, be one to him.

But how?

The living room was filled with people—the other four Padgett children, all younger than Mark, as well as a grandmother and grandfather—requiring a round-robin of introductions that seemed to shift people like fog. But Randy made sure he remained far enough from Michael to avoid the risk of having to speak. Bess, however, shook hands with one after another and eventually reached her ex-husband.

"Hello, Michael," she said, remote as if their brief truce had never happened.

"Hello, Bess."

They trained their eyes on the people and lamps across the room, avoiding the risk of lingering glances. They struggled for polite inanities, finding none. Covertly he assessed her clothes, hair, jewelry and nails—mercy, had she changed. As much as Randy, if not more.

Bess clamped a black patent-leather clutch bag beneath one elbow and adjusted an outsized gold earring, looking over the crowd while speaking. "Randy's grown up, hasn't he?"

"Has he ever. I couldn't believe it was him."

"Are you going to talk to him or just stand here as if he's a stranger?"

"You think he'd talk to me?"

"You can give it a try."

A memory flashed past of Randy at two, padding into their bedroom on Saturday mornings and climbing aboard his chest in his feet pajamas. *'Toons, Daddy,* he would say, and Michael would open his bleary eyes and tip him down for a kiss, then the two of them would whisper awhile before sneaking out to turn on cartoons and let Mommy have a morning in bed. He wanted to kiss him now, wanted to pin his arms at his sides and take him in a fatherly embrace and say *I'm sorry I screwed up, forgive me.*

Hildy Padgett came from the kitchen with a tray of canapés. Jake was passing around cups of mulled cider. Lisa was showing the grandparents her small diamond ring, and Mark was with her. Randy stood across the room with his hands in his trouser pockets, knowing no one, glancing occasionally at his father but determinedly keeping his distance.

One of them had to make the move.

It required a heroic effort but Michael took the risk.

He crossed the room and said, "Hello, Randy."

Randy said, "Yeah," his eyes casting about beyond Michael's shoulder.

"I wasn't sure it was you, you got so tall."

"Yeah, well, that happens, you know."

"How have you been?"

Randy shrugged, still avoiding his father's eyes.

"Your mother tells me you're still working in a warehouse."

"So?"

"Do you like it?"

"What's to like? You get up in the morning, you go put in your hours. It's just something to do till I get in with a band."

"A band?"

"Yeah, drums—with a band, you know, like *rrupp pup pup rrr . . .*"

"You pretty good?"

For the first time Randy looked squarely into Michael's eyes. An insolent expression twisted his face, and he released a sarcastic snort. "Spare me," he said and walked away.

Michael's stomach felt as if he'd leapt off a second-story roof. He watched Randy's shiny black curls as the young man moved off, and felt the clench of disappointment and failure. His face grew warm and a fist seemed to be closing over his windpipe.

He glanced over at Bess and found her watching.

She's right. I'm a failure as a father.

Lisa came to rescue him, capturing his elbow and hauling him across the room. "Dad, Grampa Earl was wondering about your cabin. He used to be a big hunter and I was just telling him you got a ten-point buck this fall. He wanted to hear more about it."

Earl Padgett was a big man with three chins and a florid face. He had a voice like a truck collision and endless hunting stories upon which to use it. His gestures were wide and sweeping, and when he pointed an invisible gun he might as well have been wearing a camouflage hunting vest lined with rows of shotgun shells. The hunting stories drew in Jake as well as the Padgett boys, who'd been hunting since they were old enough to take gun-safety classes. Of the men in the room, only Randy remained aloof.

Michael listened and added his own hunting anecdotes, all the time aware of Randy visiting with Bess, his back turned on Michael.

He'd bought Randy a .22 when Randy was twelve, and had dreamed of teaching the boy all about the woods and wildlife, and taking him on hunting trips. But his divorce had quashed that dream. Now he stood among a circle of fathers and sons whose enthusiasm had been passed from generation to generation, and his heart broke for what he and Randy had missed.

Hildy Padgett came in and announced dinner.

In the dining room, Michael and Bess were directed to seat themselves side-by-side at one end of the table, while Hildy and Jake presided at the opposite end. Mark and Lisa took chairs in the center of one long side, and the others were staggered around. Michael automatically pulled out Bess's chair. Her poise faltered momentarily while she shot him a wry glance, then she submitted to propriety and accepted his gesture of courtesy.

While Michael was seating himself he caught Randy watching sourly from diagonally across the table.

In an undertone he said to Bess, "I don't think Randy likes seeing me with you."

"Probably not," she replied, flipping her napkin onto her lap, glancing surreptitiously at Randy. "Did he say something about it?"

"No, just glared at me when I pulled out your chair."

"On the other hand, Lisa seems overjoyed. I've assured them both it's all for appearances. So . . . here we go." She picked up her glass of water and saluted him. "Let's see if we can't keep up the charade for our children's sake." He returned her salute and they sipped their water. A platter of ham was served, followed by bowls of vegetables, warm rolls, butter, bacon-and-lettuce salad and glorified rice, all passed around family-style. Passing a bowl to Bess, on his left, Michael remarked, "If someone had told me a week ago that I'd be sharing a dinner table with you twice in one week I'd have said no way."

"We did this a time or two with our own families, didn't we?" She watched him load his plate with au gratin potatoes and said, "Hildy really hit you in the taste buds, didn't she?"

He took an immense helping and answered, "Mmm . . . I still love 'em."

He always had. Watching him loading up on his old favorites brought back a sharp flash of nostalgia. Her mother had always said, *That Michael is fun to cook for. He knows how to eat.*

Bess glanced away from his plate—damn, she was thinking like a throwback. But it was difficult to sit beside a man with whom you've shared thousands of meals, whose table mannerisms are more familiar to you than your own, without those familiarities imposing themselves. She found herself anticipating his moves before he made them—how he held his fork, where he laid his knife, the order in which he tasted his food, the particular way he stroked one corner of his mouth with the pad of his right thumb after taking a drink, how he rested a wrist on the edge of the table while he chewed. Certain quiet sounds peculiar only to him.

"Did you have that talk with Lisa?"

She turned to find him watching her, chewing, his lips politely closed. There was an intimacy to chewing that had never struck her more profoundly than at that moment. He still had beautiful lips. She looked away. "Yes, I did. I went over to her apartment the next night."

"Do you feel better now?"

"Yes. Infinitely."

"Look at her," Michael said, poising with an elbow on the table, holding a glass of iced tea.

Bess studied their daughter. She appeared jubilant, laughing with her intended, the two of them unquestionably happy.

"Look at *them,*" Bess corrected. "She convinced me he's the right one for her. She almost had me in tears that night."

"And what about your wedding dress?"

"She's going to wear it."

Bess felt Michael's gaze on the side of her face and succumbed to the urge to meet his eyes. Webs of wistfulness drew them.

"It's hard to believe she's old enough, isn't it?" he said quietly.

"Yes. It seems like only yesterday we had her."

"Randy, too."

"I know."

"My guess is, he's watching us right now and wondering what's going on down here."

"Is something going on down here?"

He shocked her by replying, "You look great tonight, Bess."

She flushed and applied herself to cutting a piece of ham. "Oh, for heaven's sake, Michael, that's absurd."

"Well, you do. Is there any harm in my saying so? You've really changed since we divorced."

Her anger flared. "Oh, you're really smooth. You're without a wife—what? A month? Two?—and you're telling *me* how great I look? Don't insult me, Michael."

"I didn't mean to."

At that moment Jake Padgett stood up with a glass of iced tea and interrupted. "I think a toast is in order here. I'm not very good at this so you'll have to bear with me." He rubbed his left eyebrow with the edge of a finger. "Mark's our first to get married, and naturally we hoped he'd pick somebody we liked. Well, we sure got our wish when he brought Lisa home. We just couldn't be happier, and Lisa, honey, I know you're going to make him the happiest man in Minnesota when you marry him. We want to welcome you, and say how nice it is to have you and your family here with us tonight." He saluted Michael and Bess and nodded to Randy. "And so . . ." He raised his glass to the engaged couple. "Here's to a smooth road ahead for Lisa and Mark. We're behind you all the way."

Everyone joined in the toast. Jake resumed his seat and there passed between Michael and Bess a silent message, the kind husbands and wives of long standing can execute merely by the expression in their eyes.

Somebody should make a toast on our side.

You want to do it?

No, you.

Michael rose, pressing his tie to his shirt, lifting his glass.

"Jake, Hildy, all of you, thank you for inviting us. It's the proper way to start a young couple off, with the families united and showing their support. Lisa's mother and I are proud of her, and happy for her, and we welcome Mark as her husband-to-be. Lisa . . . Mark . . . you have our love. Good luck to you."

When the toast was complete, Michael sat down and Bess felt herself in an emotional turmoil. There wasn't a false word in his toast. It *was* the proper way to start the young couple off but how bittersweet, having their own immediate family reassembled for the first time amidst all these undercurrents. Earlier, when she'd watched Michael cross the room and approach Randy, her heart had leaped with hope. When Randy turned away, she had felt bereaved. Sitting beside Michael she'd been wafted first by nostalgia, then by bitterness and now, in the wake of the toasts, she simply felt muddled.

She was divorced and independent. She had proved she could live alone, build a business, keep a house and a car and a lawn and her own tax records. But the truth was, sitting beside Michael again, on this auspicious occasion, felt fitting. Having him stand and make a toast on behalf of them brought both a strong sense of security—imitation though it was—and a longing for what was gone: a father, a mother, their children, united as it had been in the beginning, as they had thought it would always be when they'd conceived those children who were now seated across the table.

Michael sensed himself being observed, turned and caught Bess regarding him.

She glanced away self-consciously.

Coffee and dessert were served—a layered concoction of angel food, strawberries, bananas and something white and fluffy. She watched Michael watching Randy while he ate. Randy ignored his father and visited with the Padgetts' seventeen-year-old daughter on his left.

"That was a nice toast you gave," Bess offered.

Michael took a forkful of dessert, which he held without eating. "This whole thing is turning out to be tougher than I thought."

She resisted the impulse to lay her hand on his sleeve. "Don't give up on him, Michael, please."

Cognizant of social obligation, surrounded as they were by people they'd just met, they assumed untroubled faces and pretended to be politely chitchatting.

"It hurts," he said.

"I know. It hurts him, too. That's why you can't give up."

He laid down his fork, picked up a cup of coffee and held it in both hands, looking beyond it at his son.

"He really hates me."

"I think he wants to but it's costing him."

He sipped his coffee, left his elbows propped on the table. In time he turned to study Bess. "What's your stake in all this? Why all of a sudden the push to see Randy and I reconcile?"

"You're his father, nothing more complicated than that. I'm beginning to see what harm we've done by forcing the kids into this cold war we've waged."

He set down his cup, released a weary sigh and settled his shoulders against the back of the chair.

"All right, Bess, I'll try."

On the way home from White Bear Lake, Randy acted surly.

Bess said, "Do you want to tell me what's on your mind?"

He cast her a glance, returned his eyes to the road and went on driving.

"Randy?" she prodded.

"What's going on with you and the old man?"

"Nothing. And don't call him the old man. He's your father."

Randy tossed a glance out his side window and whispered, "Shit."

"He's trying to make amends to you, can't you see that?"

"Great!" Randy shouted. "All of a sudden he's my father and I'm supposed to kiss his ass when for six years you haven't kept it any secret that you hate his guts."

"Well, maybe I was wrong. Whatever I felt, maybe I shouldn't have imposed those feelings on you."

"I've got a mind of my own, Ma. I didn't need to pick up vibes from you to realize that what he did was shitty. He was screwing another woman and he broke up our home!"

"All right!" Bess shouted and repeated, more calmly, "All right, he was but there's such a thing as forgiveness."

"I can't believe what I'm hearing. He's getting to you, isn't he? Pulling out your chair and making toasts and cozying up to you over the dinner table just as soon as his other wife throws him over. He makes me sick."

Guilt struck Bess for having instilled such hate in her son without a thought for its effect on him. Bitterness such as he felt could stultify his emotions in dozens of other ways.

"Randy, I'm sorry you feel this way."

"Yeah, well, it's a pretty quick switch, isn't it, Mom? Less than a week ago you felt the same way. I'd just hate to see him make a fool of you a second time."

She felt a surge of exasperation with him for voicing what she'd thought, and with herself for being culpable. After all it was true she had felt flashes of cupidity at given moments tonight.

Let this be a lesson, she thought, and if you mend fences between yourself and Michael, keep your distance while doing it.

The following day was Sunday. There was Mass in the morning, prefaced by a battle to make Randy get up and go, followed by a lonely lunch for two—a pair of sad, bald, diet chicken breasts and baked potatoes with no sour cream for Bess and very little table conversation out of Randy. He left immediately afterward, said he was going to his friend Bernie's house to watch the NFC playoff games on TV.

When he was gone the house grew silent. Bess cleaned up the kitchen, changed into a sweat suit and returned downstairs, where the silent, familyless rooms held a gloom that was only amplified by bright day beating at the windows. She did some design work for a while but found concentrating difficult and finally rose from the dining-room table to wander from window to window, staring out at the wintry yard, the frozen river, a squirrel's nest in the neighbor's oak tree, the blue shadows of her own maple branches on the pristine snow. She sat down to resume her work but gave up once more, distracted by thoughts of Michael and their sundered family. She meandered into the living room, played middle C on the piano and held it till it dissolved into silence.

Once more she returned to the window to stare out with her arms folded across her chest.

In a yard several doors down a group of children were sledding.

When Randy and Lisa were little she and Michael had taken them one Sunday afternoon much like this one—a sterling, bright, blinding day—to Theodore Wirth Park in Minneapolis. They'd taken red plastic boat-shaped sleds, sleek and fast, and chosen a hill with fresh, unbroken snow. On their first glissade down the hill Michael's sled had slewed one hundred and eighty degrees and had carried him the remainder of the way backwards. At the bottom he'd hit a slight hummock, gone tail over teakettle and rolled to a stop looking like a snowman. He'd grown a beard and moustache that year; they and his hair were totally covered with snow. His cap was gone. His glasses were miraculously in place but behind them his eyes were completely covered with white.

When he'd finally sat up, looking like Little Orphan Annie, they had all rolled with laughter, collapsing on their backs in the snow and hooting themselves breathless.

Years later, when their marriage was losing its mortar, he'd said disconsolately, "We never do anything fun anymore, Bess. We never laugh."

In the yard next door all the children had run away and left one small bundled-up individual behind, crying.

You and me, Bess thought, left behind to cry.

She turned away from the window and went into the family room, where the fireplace was cold and the Sunday *Pioneer Press Dispatch* was strewn on the sofa. With a sigh she picked up the sections and began aligning them. Disconsolately she abandoned the job and dropped to a chair with the papers forgotten in her hand.

In silence she sat.

Wondering.

Withering.

Wasting.

She was not a tearful person, yet her aloneness had magnitude enough to force a pressure behind her eyes. It drove her in time to pick up the telephone and dial her mother.

Stella Dorner answered in her usual cheerful two-note greeting. "Hello."

"Hello, Mother, it's Bess."

"Well, isn't this nice? I was just thinking of you."

"What were you thinking?"

"That I haven't talked to you since last Monday and it was time I called you."

"Are you busy?"

"Just watching the Minnesota Vikings get whipped."

"Could I come over? I'd like to talk to you."

"Of course. I'd love it. Can you stay for supper? I'll make some of those barbecued pork chops you love with the onion and lemon on them."

"That sounds good."

"Are you coming right away?"

"As soon as I get my shoes on."

"Good. See you soon, dear."

Stella Dorner lived in a townhouse on Oak Glen Golf Course on the western edge of Stillwater. She had bought it within a year after her husband died, and had furnished it with sassy new furniture, declaring she hadn't been buried along with him and wasn't going to act as if she had. She'd continued her job as an on-call operating-room nurse at Lakeview Memorial Hospital, though she was nearly sixty at the time; had taken up golf lessons and joined a ladies' league at Oak Glen, the church choir at St. Mary's and the African Violet Society of America, which met quarterly in various places all over the Twin Cities. She went as often as she pleased to visit her daughter Joan in Denver, and once took a trip to Europe (on a Eurail Pass) with her sisters from Phoenix and Coral Gables; she often went on organized bus tours to places such as the Congden Mansion in Duluth and the University of Minnesota Arboretum in Jonathan; spent time at least once a week visiting the old folks at the Maple Manor nursing home and baking cookies for them. She played bridge on Mondays, watched *thirtysomething* on Tuesdays, went to bargain matinee movies most Wednesdays and got a facial every Friday. She had once signed up with a dating service but claimed all the old farts she'd been paired up with couldn't keep up with her and she didn't want any ball and chain around her foot.

Her townhouse reflected her spirit. It had three levels, long expanses of glass and was decorated in peach, cream and glossy black. Entering it, Bess always felt a shot of vitality. Today was no different. In the ten minutes since Bess's call, Stella had the place smelling like baking pork chops.

She answered the door dressed in a sweat suit the colors of a paint rag—a white background with smears of hot pink, yellow, green and purple, all strung together with black squiggles and dribbles. Over it she wore a disreputable lavender smock. She had coarse salt-and-pepper hair, styled only by gravity. It fell into a crooked center part and dropped in two irregular waves to jaw level. She had a habit of pushing it back by making a caliper of one hand and hooking both temple waves at once. She did so as she greeted her daughter. "Bess . . . darling . . . this is wonderful. I'm so glad you called." She was shorter than Bess and reached up to hug her gingerly. "Careful! I don't want to get any paint on you."

"Paint?"

"I'm taking an oil-painting class. I was working on my first picture." She performed the caliper move on her hair once more while closing the door.

"How in the world do you find time?"

"A person should always find time for the things he likes." Stella led the way inside, where the west window light was strong but unreached yet by the afternoon sun, which lit the snow-laden golf course beyond. Facing the window was a long sofa upholstered in coral calla lilies on a cream background. One wall was filled with an ebony entertainment unit, where the football game was in progress on TV. The tables were ebony frames with glass tops. Before the sliding glass doors stood an easel with a partially finished rendering of an African violet.

"What do you think?" Stella asked.

"Mmm . . ." Removing her jacket, Bess studied the painting. "Looks good to me."

"It probably won't be but what the heck. The class is fun, and that's the object." Stella walked over and turned down the television volume. "Can I get you a Coke?"

"I'll get it. You keep on with your work."

"All right, I will." She pushed back her hair and picked up a paintbrush while Bess went into the kitchen and opened the refrigerator.

"Can I fix you one?"

"No thanks, I'm having tea." Beside Stella, a waist-high folding table held her mug and tubes of paint. She reached for the mug, drank from it while studying her artwork and called, "How are the kids?"

"That's what I came to talk to you about." Bess entered the room sipping her pop, slipped off her black loafers and propped her back against one end of the long sofa, drawing her feet up and resting her glass on her knees. "Well . . . part of what I came to talk to you about."

"Oh-oh. This sounds serious."

"Lisa's getting married . . . and she's expecting a baby."

Stella studied her daughter for several seconds. "Maybe I'd better put these paints away." She reached for a rag and began cleaning her brush.

"No, please don't stop."

"Don't be silly. I can do this any old time." The brush joined some others in a tin can of turpentine before Stella removed her smock and joined Bess on the sofa, bringing her cup of tea and hooking her hair back.

"Well . . . Lisa pregnant, imagine that. That'll make me a great-grandmother, won't it?"

"And me a grandmother."

"Spooky, isn't it?"

"Uh-huh."

"Which is the least important aspect of all this. I imagine you're in shock."

"I was but it's wearing off."

"Does she want the baby?"

"Yes, very much."

"Ah, that's a relief."

"Guess what else."

"There's more?"

"I've seen Michael," Bess told her.

"My goodness, you have had a week, haven't you?"

"Lisa set us up. She invited us both to her apartment to announce the news."

Stella laughed, throwing her chin up. "Good for Lisa. That girl's got style."

"I could have throttled her."

"How is she?"

"Happy and excited and very much in love, she assures us."

"And how is Michael?"

"Detached again, on his way to getting another divorce."

"Oh my."

"He said to tell you hi. His exact words were, 'Say hi to the old doll. I miss her.' "

Stella saluted with her mug—"Hi, Michael"—and sipped from it, studying Bess over the rim. "No wonder you wanted to talk. Where is Randy in all this?"

"Where he's always been, very resentful, shunning his father."

"And you?"

Bess sighed and said, "I don't know, Mother." She shifted her gaze to her knees, where it remained for a long time before she sighed, let her head drop back and spoke to the ceiling. "I've been carrying around all this anger for six years. It's very hard to let it go."

Stella sipped her tea and waited. Nearly a minute of silence passed before Bess looked at Stella.

"Mother, did I . . ." She paused.

"Did you what?"

"When we were getting the divorce you never said much."

"It wasn't my place."

"When I found out that Michael was having an affair, I wanted so badly for you to be angry for me. I wanted you to raise your fist and call him a bastard, take my side, but you never did."

"I liked Michael."

"But I thought you should be indignant on my behalf, and you weren't. There must have been some reason."

"And you're sure you're ready to hear it now?"

"Is it going to make me mad?"

"I don't know. That depends on how much you've grown up in six years."

"It was partly my fault, is that what you're saying?"

"It always takes two, honey, but when a man retaliates by having an affair, he's usually the one who gets all the blame."

"All right, what did I do?" Bess's voice grew defensive. "I went back to college to get my degree! Was that so wrong?"

"Not at all. But while you were doing it you totally forgot about your husband."

"I did not! He wouldn't let me forget about him. I still had to cook and do laundry and keep the house in shape."

"Those are superficialities. I'm talking about your personal relationship."

"Mother, there wasn't time!"

"Now there, I think you've put your finger on it." Stella let that sink in while she went to the kitchen to refresh her tea. When she returned to the living room, Bess was sitting with one elbow on the high sofa arm, her thumbnail between her teeth, staring out the window.

Stella resumed her seat and said, "Remember when you were first married how you used to ask Dad and me to take the kids occasionally so you and Michael could go off camping by yourselves? And the Christmas you bought him that shotgun that he wanted so badly, and hid it over at our place so he wouldn't find out? Remember all the trouble we went to, sneaking that thing into your house and hiding it on Christmas Eve? And then there was the April Fools' Day when you had that Fanny Farmer box delivered to his office and it was full of nuts and bolts."

Bess stared at the snowy golf course, her Coke forgotten.

"Those are the kinds of things that should never stop," her mother said.

"Was I the only one who stopped them?"

"I don't know. Were you?"

"I didn't think so then."

"You got awfully caught up in school, and after it was finished, in opening your store. When you'd stop over to see us you were always alone, never with Michael anymore, always rushing between two places. I know for a fact that you stopped having Dad and me over for meals, and that sometimes the kids would come over and act a little forlorn and abandoned."

Bess looked at her mother and remarked, "That's when Michael accused me of letting myself go."

"As I recall, you did."

"But I asked him for help around the house and he refused to give it. Isn't he partly to blame?"

"Maybe. But those kinds of things are a trade-off. Maybe he'd have helped you around the house if he hadn't fallen to the bottom of your priority list. How was your sex life?"

Bess looked out the window and answered, "Shitty."

"You didn't have time for it, right?"

"I thought once I got through school and had my own business, everything would fall back into place. I could get a housekeeper, maybe, and I'd have more time to relax with him."

"Only he didn't wait."

Bess got up and passed the easel to stand near the window with one hand on her hip. She drank her Coke, then turned to Stella. "Last night he told me I looked great, and do you know how angry it made me?"

"Why?"

"Because!" Bess flung up one hand. "Because . . . hell, I don't know. Because he's just sloughed off another wife and he's probably lonely and I don't want him crawling back to me under those circumstances. I don't want him crawling back to me at all! And Randy was watching us from the other end of the table! And I was upset with myself because I took an hour and fifteen minutes getting ready for that damned supper just to show him I could knock his socks off and . . . and . . . then when I did . . ." Bess covered her eyes with one hand and shook her head vehemently. "Hell, Mom, I don't know. It just seems like all of a sudden I'm so damned lonely and I'm caught in this wedding situation and I'm . . . I'm asking myself questions." She stared unseeingly outside and ended, more quietly, "I don't know."

Stella set her mug on the coffee table and went to her daughter. From behind, she finger-combed Bess's hair back to her nape, then massaged her shoulders.

"You're going through a catharsis that's been six years coming, that's what it is. All that time you've hated him and blamed him, and all of a sudden you're starting to explore your own fault in the matter. That's not easy."

"I don't love him anymore, Mother, I really don't."

"All right, so you don't."

"Then why does it hurt so much to see him?"

"Because he's making you take this second look at yourself. Here." Stella produced a wrinkled Kleenex and handed it to Bess.

It smelled like turpentine when Bess blew her nose in it. "I'm sorry, Mom," she said, drying her eyes.

"Don't be sorry. I'm a big girl. I can handle it."

"But coming here like this, spoiling your day."

"You haven't spoiled my day. Matter of fact, I think you've made it." Walking Bess back to the sofa with one arm around her shoulders Stella asked, "Feel better now?"

"Yes. Sort of."

"Then let me tell you something. It was all right for you to be angry at first, right after the divorce. Your anger is what got you through. Then you got efficient, businesslike, and threw all your energies into showing him you could make it on your own. And you did make it. But now you're going into another stage where you're going to do more questioning, and I suspect you might have a few more days like this. When you do, come over and we'll talk you through it, just as we did today. Now sit down, tell me about the wedding plans, and about Lisa's young man, and about what I have to wear to this shindig and if you think I might meet any interesting men there."

Bess laughed. "Mother, you're incorrigible. I thought you didn't want a ball and chain around your ankle."

"I don't. But you can only stand so much of hearing women's cackly voices before you need to hear a male one, and I've been playing an awful lot of bridge this winter."

Bess gave her mother an impulsive hug. "Mom, maybe I never told you this before, but you're my idol. I wish I could be more like you."

Stella hugged her back and said, "You're a lot like me. I see more of me in you every day."

"But you never get down."

"The heck I don't. But when it happens I just go out and join another club."

"Or look for a man."

"Well . . . there's nothing wrong with that. And speaking of the critters, how are you and Keith getting along?"

"Oh . . . Keith." Bess made a face and shrugged. "He got upset because I had to break a dinner date with him to go to the Padgetts' last night. You know how he is where the kids are concerned."

"I'll tell you something," Stella said, "since we're being honest with each other today. That man is not for you."

"Have you and Lisa been comparing notes or what?"

"Maybe."

Bess laughed. "Why, you two devils. If you think this wedding business is going to get me back together with Michael, you're wrong."

"I didn't say a word."

"No, but you're thinking it, and you can just forget it, Mother."

Stella lifted one eyebrow and asked, "How does he look? He still as handsome as ever?"

"Moth-er!" Bess looked exasperated.

"Just curious."

"It'll never happen, Mother," Bess vowed.

Stella put on a smug expression and said, "How do you know? Stranger things have."

chapter 5

THAT SAME SUNDAY MORNING Michael Curran awakened, stretched and stacked his hands behind his head, loath to stir and rise. His stomach grumbled but he remained, staring at the ceiling, which took on a rosy glow from the bright sunlight bouncing off the carpeting. The bedroom was huge, square, with triple sliding glass doors facing the lake, and a marble fireplace. The room held nothing more than a television set and the pair of mattresses upon which Michael lay. They were pushed against the north wall to keep his pillows from falling off.

The ten o'clock sun, reflecting off the frozen lake, made a nebula of light patterns on the ceiling, broken by strands of shadow from the naked elm trees beyond the deck. The building was absolutely silent; it was designed to be. No children were allowed, and most of the wealthy tenants had gone south for the winter, so he rarely crossed paths with anyone, not even in the elevator.

It was lonely.

He thought about last night, about his encounter with Randy. He closed his eyes and saw his nineteen-year-old son, bearing so much resemblance to himself, and so much animosity. The impact of seeing him came back afresh, bringing a replay of last night's convoluted emotions: love, hope, disappointment and a feeling of failure that made his chest feel heavy.

He opened his eyes to the ceiling designs.

How it hurt, being disowned by one's own child. Perhaps, as Bess had accused, he'd been guilty of withdrawing from Randy's life emotionally as well as physically, but wasn't Randy at fault, too, for refusing to see him? On the other hand, if Bess could have felt the cataclysm he'd experienced when he'd seen Randy walk into that house last night, she would have been forced to reconsider her words.

That boy—that *man*—was his son. His son, whose last six vital growing years had been lost to Michael, largely against his choice. If Bess had encouraged, or if Randy had not been brainwashed, he, Michael, would have been seeing Randy all along. There were things the two of them could have done together, particularly hunting and enjoying the outdoors. Instead, Michael had been excluded from everything, even Randy's high-school graduation. He'd known, of course, that Randy was graduating. When no announcement came he'd called Bess and asked about it, but Bess had replied, "He doesn't want you here."

He'd sent money, five hundred dollars. It was never acknowledged, either by written or spoken word, except for Lisa who, when Michael had asked, told him on the phone some weeks later, "He put it down on a thirteen-hundred-dollar set of drums."

A set of drums.

Why hadn't Bess seen to it that the kid went to college? Or a trade school? Something besides that dead-end job in a warehouse. After the way Bess had fought to complete her own college education he'd have thought she'd have taken a strong stand on the issue with her own kids. Maybe she had, and maybe it simply hadn't worked.

Bess.

Boy-o-boy, how she'd changed. When she'd walked into that room last night the craziest thing had happened! He'd actually felt a little charge. Yeah, it was crazy, all right, because Bess had a sharp edge to her now, a veneer of hardness he found abrasive. But she was his children's mother, and a transformed lady, and in spite of the way she carefully distanced herself from him, they shared a past that would forever intrude upon their lingering dissatisfactions with one another. He'd bet any money she felt it, too, at times.

Sitting next to each other at the dinner table, looking over at Lisa and Randy, how could either of them deny the gravity of memory?

As he lay in his unfurnished condominium with the Sunday sun shifting through the room, recollections of their beginnings played back through his mind—when Bess was in high school, and he, already a sophomore in college, had gone back for homecoming and had discovered her all grown up, an underclassman he didn't even remember. The first time he'd kissed her they were walking back to his car after a University of Minnesota football game in the fall of '66. The first time they'd made love was toward the end of her senior year on a Sunday afternoon when a gang of them had gone to Taylors Falls with picnic food, Frisbees and plenty of blankets. They'd been married a year later, with him fresh out of college and her with three more years to go. They'd spent their wedding night in the bridal suite at the Radisson Hotel in downtown Minneapolis.

Her mom and dad had given them the room as a surprise, and a bunch of her girlfriends had bought her a lacy white nightgown with a thin thing that went over it. He recalled how, when she came out of the bathroom wearing it, he was waiting in his blue pajama bottoms, both of them as hesitant as if it were their first time. He'd thought he'd never forget the details of that night but over time they'd become blurred. What he did remember, clearly, was waking the next morning. It was June and sunny and on the dresser sat a basket of fruit from the hotel management, along with two fluted glasses from the night before, each half-full of bubbleless champagne. He'd opened his eyes to find Bess next to him, with her nightgown back on. He'd lain there wondering when she'd gotten up and put it on, and if she expected him to wear his pajamas all night, too, and if, in spite of their premarital sex, she'd turn out to be a prude. Then she'd awakened and smiled, indulged in a quivering, all-over stretch, lain on her side facing him with her hands joined near her knees, and he'd gotten a hard-on just looking at her.

When the stretch ended she'd said simply, "Hi."

"Hi," he'd answered.

They'd lain a long time, looking at each other, absorbing the novelty and wonder of sanctioned morning bliss. He remembered her cheeks had grown flushed and supposed his had done the same.

In time she'd said, "Just imagine, nobody can ever send you home at one A.M. again. We get to wake up together for the rest of our lives."

"It's wild, isn't it?"

"Yeah," she'd whispered, "pretty wild."

"You put your nightgown back on."

"I can't sleep without something on. I wake up and my arms are stuck to my sides. What about you?" The sheet covered him to his ribs.

"I don't have that problem," he'd answered, "but I've got another one."

She had put her hand on his hip—he remembered so vividly what had followed, for in all of his life to that point nothing had been as incredible as that morning. Sex before marriage had been frequent for them but it had carried restraints, nevertheless. That sunny June morning when she had reached out for him those restraints had dissolved. They *felt* married, they *belonged* to each other and there was a difference. The vows they'd spoken gave them license and they reveled in it.

He had seen her half-naked, nearly naked, had gotten her naked from the waist down a lot of times. They'd made love in the sunlight wrapped in a blanket, in the moonlight wrapped in shadows and in cars beneath streetlamps with their socks still on. Even on their wedding night they'd left only the bathroom light on to shed a dim glow from around a corner. But that morning, the day after their wedding, the east sun had been streaming in a broad, high window, and she'd taken off his sheet and he'd taken off her nightgown and they'd indulged their eyes for the first time. In that regard they'd been virgins, and nothing he'd experienced before or since had been any sweeter.

Their breakfast had been delivered on a rolling cart with white linen and a red rose. Over the meal they had studied each other's eyes and reaffirmed that they'd done the right thing, and that their joy was so intense it eclipsed any other they'd ever felt.

About that day he recalled most vividly the overriding sense of consecration they'd both felt. They had met in an era when more and more young couples were declaring, *Marriage is dead,* and were choosing to set up housekeeping together instead. They'd discussed doing the same thing but had decided no, they loved each other and wanted to commit for life.

After breakfast they'd made love again, then had bathed and dressed and walked to St. Olaf's for Mass.

June 8, 1968, their wedding day.

And now it was January 1990, and he was rolling off his mattresses in an empty condo, dressed in gray sweatpants, aroused once again from his memories.

Forget it, Curran. Horn in. She doesn't want you, you don't really want her and your own kid treats you like a leper. That ought to tell you something.

He shuffled to the bathroom, switched on the light, flattened one palm on the vanity top, examined his face and harvested some sand from his eyes. He swigged a mouthful of cinnamon-flavored Plax, swished it around for the recommended thirty seconds and brushed his teeth with a full one inch of red Close-Up. Bess had always harangued him about using too much toothpaste. *You don't need that much,* she'd told him, *half that much is enough.* Now, damn it, he used as much as he wanted and nobody nagged. He brushed for one whole minute, rinsed, then bared his teeth to the mirror and thought, Look at these, Bess, pretty damned nice for a forty-three-year-old, eh?

His flawless teeth were of curiously little consolation this morning in his big, empty, silent condo.

He wiped his mouth, threw down the towel and went to the kitchen. It was tiled in white, had white Formica cabinets trimmed with blond oak and was connected to a family room with sliding glass doors at its far end, facing a small park with a gazebo. His entire pantry stock, on an oversized island in the middle of the kitchen, looked like a city block from 30,000 feet. Instant coffee, a box of Grape-Nuts, a loaf of Taystee bread, a jar of peanut butter, another of grape jelly, a half-stick of margarine smeared on its gold foil wrapper, a handful of paper sugar packets and a plastic spoon and knife he'd kept from Hardee's.

He stood awhile, staring at the collection.

Two times I've let women clean me out. When am I going to learn?

A quick-flash came along: the four of them—himself, Bess, Randy and Lisa—during those fun years when the kids were old enough to sit at the table and swing their feet without their toes touching the floor. Lisa, fresh from church, with her hair in pigtails and her elbows on the table, picking apart a piece of toast and eating it in tiny increments (all the while with her feet swinging wildly): "I saw Randy pick his nose in church this morning and wipe it on the bottom of the pew. *Yuuuuukkkk!*"

"I dint neither! She's lying!"

"You did, too! I saw you, Randy, you're *so gross!*"

"Mom, she lies all the time." (This with a whine that verified his guilt.)

"I'm *never* sitting in that pew again!"

Bess and Michael exchanging glances with their lips pursed to keep from hooting before Bess remarked, "Randy picks his nose in church, his dad does it when he's sitting at stop lights."

"I do not!" Michael had yelped.

"You do, too!"

Then the whole family breaking into laughter before Bess delivered an admonition about hygiene and handkerchiefs.

Sunday breakfasts were a lot different then.

In his White Bear Lake condominium, Michael poured some Grape-Nuts into a white plastic deli-food container, covered them with milk from the otherwise empty refrigerator, tore open a sugar packet, took his plastic spoon and returned to his mattresses, where he propped his pillows against the wall, turned on the TV and sat down to eat alone.

He wasn't up to either evangelists or cartoons, however, and found his mind returning to the perplexing stringball of family relationships he was trying to unknot. For perhaps the ten thousandth time in his life he wished he had sisters and brothers. What would it be like to pick up the phone and say, "Hi, you got any coffee over there?" and sit down with someone who'd shared your past, and your parents, and some warm memories, and maybe a few scoldings, and the chicken pox, and the same first-grade teacher, and teenage clothing, and double dates and memories of Mom's cooking? Someone who knew all you'd put into your lifetime's struggles, and who cared about your happiness and how you felt today.

How he felt today was lonely. So damned lonely, and hurting some, and wondering where to go next in his life. How to be a father to Randy, and how to make it through this wedding, and what tack to take with Bess, and what to make of these nostalgic thoughts he'd been having about her. Even being a grandfather—he'd like to talk about that.

Alas, there was no brother, no sister, and he felt as cheated and isolated as ever.

He got up, showered, shaved and dressed, then tried working awhile at his desk in one of the other two bedrooms, but the silence and emptiness were so depressing he had to get out.

He decided to go shopping for some furniture. He sure as hell needed it, and at least in the stores there'd be people moving around.

He went to Dayton's Home Store on highway 36, thinking he'd simply pick a living-roomful and have it delivered, but discovered to his dismay that just about everything would have to be ordered and would take from six weeks to six months to arrive. Furthermore, he had no carpet samples, no wallpaper samples and no idea what he really wanted.

He went next to Levitz, where he walked the aisles between assembled rooms and tried to visualize pieces in his condo but found he had no concept of what would look good. Color, in particular, threw him, and size, of course, became a factor. He realized that all the places he'd ever lived in had been decorated primarily by women and that he had no eye for it whatsoever.

He went next to Byerly's grocery store, where he stared at the fresh chickens a long time, wondering how Darla had made that stuff called fricassee. He passed the pork chops—Stella was the one who knew how to make pork chops. They had onions on top, he recalled, and lemon slices, but how she got them red and barbecuey, he had no idea. Ham? Ham sounded simpler, though his foremost craving was not for it but for the mashed potatoes and ham gravy that went along with it, the way Bess used to fix it.

Aw, hell . . . he turned away and went back to the delicatessen, where he fixed a salad at the open salad bar and bought some wild-rice soup for his supper.

It was twilight when he headed home, a melancholy time of day with the sun setting in his rearview mirror and the empty condo ahead. He parked in the underground garage, took the elevator up and went straight to the kitchen, where he warmed his soup in the microwave and ate it seated on the cold tiles of the countertop.

The idea hit him while he was sitting there with his feet dangling a foot above the floor, eating soup out of a cardboard carton with a plastic spoon.

You need a decorator, Curran.

He knew one, too; knew a damned good one.

'Course, this could be nothing but an excuse to call her. He looked around, reconfirming that he hadn't so much as a kitchen table to eat at. Fat chance she'd believe he really needed his place furnished; she'd think he was nosing around for something else.

He could call another one. Yes, he could, he certainly could. But it was Sunday: you can't call an interior decorator on Sunday.

He stared at the view of the gloaming out the sliding glass door, picturing Bess. If he called her he'd look like a jerk. So he sat on the cold counter, beside the white telephone, tapping the plastic spoon on his knee.

It took him until eight o'clock to work up the courage to dial his old number. In six years it hadn't changed, and he remembered it by heart.

Bess answered on the third ring.

"Hi, Bess, it's Michael."

A long silence passed before she said, "Well . . . Michael."

"Surprised, huh?"

"Yes."

"Yeah, me too." He was sitting on the edge of his mattress with its messy blankets, fiddling with the material covering his right knee, wondering what to say next. "It was a nice supper last night."

"Yes, it was."

"The Padgetts seem like likable people."

"I thought so, too."

"Lisa could do worse."

"She's very happy, and after seeing Mark with his family I have no objection whatsoever to their marriage."

Each ensuing silence became more awkward. "So, how's Randy today?" Michael asked.

"I haven't seen much of him. We went to church and he left right afterwards to watch the game with his friend."

"Did he say anything last night?"

"About what?"

"About us."

"Yes he did, as a matter of fact. He said he hoped you wouldn't make a fool out of me again. Listen, Michael, is there something in particular you wanted, because I brought some work home to do this evening and I'd like to get back to it."

"I thought you wanted us to be civil to each other for the kids' sake."

"I did. I do but—"

"Then give me a minute here, will you, Bess! I'm making the effort to call you and you start slinging insults!"

"You *asked* me what Randy said and I told you!"

"All right . . ." He calmed himself. "All right, let's just forget it. I'm sorry I asked about him, and besides I called for something else."

"What?"

"I want to hire you."

"To do what?"

"To decorate my condo."

She paused a beat, then burst out laughing. "Oh, Michael, that's so funny!"

"What's so funny about it?"

"You want to hire *me* to decorate your condo?"

His mouth got tight. "Yes, I do."

"Are you forgetting how you railed against my going to school to get my degree?"

"That was then, this is now. I need a decorator. Do you want the job or not?"

"First of all, let's get one thing straight, something you apparently never caught the first time around. I'm not a decorator, I'm an interior designer."

"There's a difference?"

"Anybody who owns a paint store can call himself a decorator. I'm a U of M graduate with a four-year degree and I'm accredited by the FIDER. Yes, there's a difference."

"All right, I apologize. I won't make that mistake again. Madame Interior Designer, would you care to design the interior of my condo?" he asked snidely.

"I'm no fool, Michael. I'm a businesswoman. I'll be happy to set up a house call. There's a one-time forty-dollar trip charge for that, which I'll apply to the cost of any furniture you might order."

"I think I can handle that."

"Very well, my calendar is at the store but I know I have next Friday morning open. How does that sound?"

"Fine."

"Just so you'll know what to expect, the house call is primarily a question-and-answer period so that I can get to know your tastes, budget, life-style, things like that. I won't be bringing any samples or catalogs with me at this time. That'll all come later. During this initial visit we'll just talk and I'll take notes. Will there be anyone else living in the condo with you?"

"For God's sake, Bess—"

"It's part of my job as a professional to ask, because if there will be, it's best to have everybody present at this first consultation and get everybody's input at the start. It eliminates problems later when the one who wasn't there says, 'Wait a minute! You know how I hate blue!' Or yellow, or African masks or glass-top tables. Sometimes we hear things like, 'What happened to Great-Aunt Myrtle's lamp made out of the shrunken head?' You'd be surprised what rhubarbs can come up over taste."

"No, there won't be anyone else living here with me."

"Good, that simplifies matters. We'll make it Friday morning at nine, then, if that's agreeable."

"Nine is good. I'll tell you how to get here."

"I already know."

"You do?"

"Randy pointed it out to me."

"Oh." For a moment he'd flattered himself thinking she'd taken the trouble to look it up after he gave her his card. "There's a security system, so just call up from the lobby."

"I will."

"Well, I'll see you Friday, then."

"Yes." She ended the conversation without either stumble or halt. "Good-bye, Michael."

"Good-bye."

When he'd hung up Michael sat on the edge of his mattress, scowling. "Whoa! Madame Businesswoman!" he said aloud, eyeing the phone.

The place seemed quiet after his outburst. The furnace clicked on and started the fan quietly wheezing through the vents. The night pressed black against his curtainless windows. The ceiling fixture sent harsh light over the room. He fell back with his hands behind his neck. A knot of jumbled bedding created an uncomfortable lump beneath him. He moved off it, still scowling.

This is probably a mistake, he thought.

When Bess hung up, she thought about the infamous decorating Doris Day had perpetrated on Rock Hudson's apartment in *Pillow Talk.* Ah, those red-velour tassles, those chartreuse draperies, that moose head, the orange player piano, beaded curtains, fertility gods, potbellied stove and the chair made of antlers . . .

It was tempting.

Definitely tempting.

The following evening Lisa went home to Stillwater to try on her mother's wedding dress. It was stored in the basement in a windowless space beside the laundry room, inside a plastic bag hanging from the ceiling joists. They went down together. Bess pulled the chain on a light switch and a bare 40-watt bulb smeared murky yellow smudge over the crowded cubicle. Its walls were the backside of the adjacent rooms, giving a view of two-by-fours and untaped Sheetrock. It smelled like fresh mushrooms.

Bess glanced around and shivered, then looked up at the row of shrouded garments.

"I don't think either one of us can reach. There's a step stool in the laundry room, Lisa, would you get it?"

While Lisa went to find the stool, Bess began moving aside boxes and baby furniture, a badminton net, a case holding a twenty-five-dollar guitar they'd bought for Randy when he was twelve, before he'd discovered his true love was drumming. Some of the cardboard boxes were labeled—*Baby Clothes, Lisa's Dolls, Games, School Papers*—representing many years' accumulation of memories.

Lisa returned and while Bess forced the legs of the stool into the tight space among the boxes, Lisa opened one of them.

"Oh, Mom, look . . ." Lisa took out a cigar box and from it drew a school picture of herself. In it she was missing both incisors and her hair was parted on one side, slicked to the opposite side and held in place with a barrette. "Second grade, Miss Peal. Donny Carry said he loved me and put those little heart-shaped candies on my desk every morning, with a different message on every one. *Be mine. Cool babe.* I was a real heartbreaker, wasn't I?"

Bess viewed the picture. "Oh, I remember that dress. Grandma Dorner gave it to you for Christmas and you always wore it with red tights and patent-leather shoes."

"Dad used to call me his little elf whenever I wore it."

Bess said, "It's cold down here. Let's get the dress and go upstairs."

Bess carried the bridal gown and Lisa took the cigar box, glancing through report cards, old, curled pictures and notes from her childhood friends as the two women climbed the stairs. Bess went outside on the front stoop, stripped the dusty plastic bag off the wedding dress and gave it a shake. She carried it upstairs to find Lisa in her old room, sitting cross-legged on the bed.

"Look at this one," Lisa said, and Bess sank down beside her with the gown doubled over on her lap. "It's a note from Patty Larson. 'Dear Lisa, Meet me in the empty lot after lunch and bring your Melody doll and all your Barbies and we'll put on a concert.' Remember how Patty and I used to do that all the time? We had these little penlights and we'd pretend they were microphones, and we'd set up all our dolls as our audience and sing our lungs out." Lisa extended her arms, clicked her fingers and sang a couple of lines from "Don't Go Breaking My Heart." She ended with a laugh that softened to a nostalgic note. "I remember once when we put on a show for you and Dad wearing some of her sister's dance costumes. We made up little tickets and charged you admission."

Bess remembered, too. Sitting beside Lisa, freeing the buttons on the back of her wedding dress, she remembered altogether too well those happier days, before her and Michael's troubles had begun. Though she could feel nostalgic at moments such as this, she was a realist who knew these flashes were momentary. She and Michael would never be husband and wife again, much as Lisa wished it.

"Why don't you try the dress on, honey?" she said gently.

Lisa set aside the cigar box and got off the bed. Bess stood behind her and forced twenty satin loops around twenty pearl buttons up the back of the dress while Lisa studied the results in the dresser mirror.

"It's going to fit," Lisa said.

"I was a size ten back then. You're a size eight. Even if you get a little tummy in the next few weeks there shouldn't be any problem."

Both of them studied Lisa's reflection. The dress had a beaded stand-up collar above a V-shaped lace bodice that ended with a point on the stomach. It had elbow-length pouf sleeves, a full satin skirt and train trimmed with beadwork and sequins. Though it was wrinkled, it hadn't discolored. "It's still beautiful, isn't it, Mom?"

"Yes, it is. I remember the day my mother said I could buy it, how excited I was. Naturally, it was one of the most expensive ones in the store, and I thought she'd say no but you know Grandma. She was always so crazy about your dad she'd have said yes to anything once she heard the news that I was going to marry him."

Without warning Lisa spun from the mirror and headed for the door. "Wait a minute!" she called as she disappeared.

"Where are you going?"

"Be right back. Stay there!"

Lisa thumped downstairs in her stocking feet and returned in a minute making a high-energy entrance, then dropping to the bed in a swish of wrinkled satin with a photo album on her lap.

"It was right where it always used to be in the bookshelves in the living room," she said breathlessly.

"Oh, Lisa, not those old things." Lisa had brought Bess and Michael's wedding album.

"Why not these old things? I want to see them."

"Lisa, that's wishful thinking."

"I want to see how you looked in the dress."

"You want to see things the way they used to be but that part of our lives is over. Dad and I are divorced and we're staying that way."

"Oh, look . . ." Lisa opened the album. There were Michael and Bess, close up, with their cheeks touching and her bouquet and veil forming an aureole around them. "Gol, Mom, you were just beautiful, and Dad . . . wow, look at him."

The photo caught at Bess's heart while she sat beside her daughter searching for the perfect balance in her response to Lisa. She had been bitter too long and was learning the hurt it had caused her children. At this turning point in her life, Lisa needed this foray into the past. To deny her the freedom of exploring it was to deny a certain part of her heritage. At the same time, allowing her to believe there was a chance of reconciliation between her parents was sheer folly.

"Lisa, dear . . ." Bess took her hand. Lisa looked into Bess's eyes. "Your dad and I had some wonderful years."

"I know. I remember a lot of them."

"I wish we could have made a happier ending for you but it didn't work out that way. I want you to know, though, that I'm glad you forced us to confront each other. It's making me take a second look at myself, which I needed, and even though your dad and I aren't getting back together, it feels much better to be his ex-wife without so much animosity between us."

"But Dad said you looked great the night of the dinner."

"Lisa, darling . . . don't. You're pinning your hopes on nothing."

"Well, what are you going to do, marry *Keith?* Mom, he's such a dork."

"Who said anything about marrying anybody? I'm happy as I am. I'm healthy, the business is going good, I keep busy, I have you and Randy—"

"And what about when Randy decides to grow up? What about when he moves out?" Lisa gestured at the walls. "You going to stay in this big old empty house alone?"

"I'll decide that when the time comes."

"Mom, just promise me one thing—if Dad makes a play for you, or if he asks you out or something, you won't get all pissed off and slug him or anything, will you? Because I think he's going to do it. I saw how he looked at you the other night, while you two were sitting down there at your end of the table—"

"Lisa—"

"—and you're still quite a looker, Ma—"

"Lisa!"

"—and as for Dad, he's one of the truly excellent men around. Even when he was married to that dumb Darla I thought so. You know, Ma, you could do worse."

"I'm not going to talk about it, and I wish you wouldn't."

Lisa left soon thereafter, taking the dress with her to drop at the dry cleaner's. After seeing her out, Bess returned upstairs to turn out the light in Lisa's old room. There on the bed lay the wedding album, bound in white leather and stamped in gold: BESS & MICHAEL CURRAN, JUNE 8, 1968.

The room still seemed to retain the musty smell of the bridal gown and the cigar box, which Lisa had left behind. A fitting smell, Bess thought, for the marriage that had turned to must.

She dropped to the bed, braced a hand beside the album and slowly flipped its pages.

Thoughtful.

Nostalgic.

Alternately relishing and ruing while the diametrically opposed wishes of her two children tugged her in opposite directions—Randy, the bitter; Lisa, the romantic.

She closed the book and fell back on the bed with one wrist across her waist. Outside somebody's dog yapped to be let in. Down in the kitchen the automatic icemaker switched on and sent the hiss of moving water up the pipes in the wall. Out in the world all around her men and women moved through life two-by-two while she lay on her daughter's bed alone.

This is silly. I have tears in my eyes and a pain in my heart that wasn't there before I entered this room. I've let Lisa put ideas into my head that are based on nothing but her sentimentality. Whatever she thought she detected between Michael and me the other night was strictly her imagination.

She rolled her head and reached out to touch the wedding album.

Or was it?

chapter 6

SHE WENT TO THE BEAUTY SHOP on Thursday and had her roots bleached, her ends trimmed and her hair styled. She painted her nails that night and spent nearly fifteen minutes deciding what to wear the next morning, choosing a wool crepe dress in squash gold with a tucked waist, tulip-shaped skirt and a wide belt with an oversized gold buckle. In the morning she finished it off with a variegated scarf, gold earrings and a spritz of perfume, then shot a critical glance at the mirror.

You're still quite a looker, Ma.

If, at given moments in her life, Bess Curran had considered herself a *looker,* she had not done so in the six years since Michael had put her down on that score. The insult lived on each time she looked in a mirror, and no matter what efforts she put into her grooming, at the final moment she always found some detail less than perfect. Usually it was her weight.

Ten pounds, she thought today. Only ten and I'd be where I want to be.

Aggravated with Michael for creating this perennial dissatisfaction and with herself for perpetuating it, she slammed off the light switch and left the room.

She arrived in White Bear Lake with five minutes to spare and approached Michael's condominium doubly impressed, observing it at close range in broad daylight. The sign said CHATEAUGUET. The driveway curved between two giant elms and led through grounds dotted with mature oaks. Closer to the building, a pair of venerable spruce trees stood sentinel beside the doors, taller than the four stories they guarded. The structure itself was V-shaped and sprawling, of white brick and gray siding, studded with royal-blue awnings. It had underground garages, white balconies, brass carriage lanterns and a lot of glass. On the uppermost floor, the decks and patio doors were topped by roof gables inset with sunburst designs.

But more, it had the lake.

One was conscious of it even from the landward side, and Bess found herself speculating on the view she'd discover when she got inside.

The foyer smelled like scented carpet cleaner, had tastefully papered walls, an elevator and a small bank of mailboxes along with a security phone. She picked it up and rang Michael's unit.

He answered immediately, " 'Morning, Bess, is that you?"

"Good morning, yes it is."

"I'll be right down."

She heard the elevator hum before its doors split soundlessly and Michael stepped out, wearing gray/black pleated trousers with needle-fine teal stripes, a teal polo shirt with its collar turned up and a finely knit double-breasted sweater in white. His trousers had the gloss of costly fabric, and the polo shirt picked up the exact hue of the stripes. Since becoming an interior designer, Bess noticed things like that. She could spot cheap fabric at twenty paces and clashing colors at fifty. Michael's clothes were well chosen, even the tassled loafers of soft black leather. She wondered who'd chosen them, since Michael was all but color-blind and had always had difficulty coordinating his wardrobe.

"Thanks for coming, Bess," he said, holding the elevator doors open. "We're going up."

She stepped aboard and was closed into the four-by-six-foot space with him and the familiar smell of his British Sterling. To dispel the sense of déjà vu she asked, "How do you pronounce the name of this place?"

"Chateau-gay," he replied. "Back in the 1900s there was a big hotel here by that name, and it was also the name of a racehorse that won the Kentucky Derby years ago."

"Chateauguet," she repeated. "I like it."

They arrived at an upper hall shaped like the one below, and he waved her ahead of himself into the condominium whose door stood open to their right.

She wasn't three feet inside before exhilaration struck. Space! Enough space to make a designer drool! The entry hall was as wide as most bedrooms, carpeted in a grayed mauve. It was totally bare but for a large, contemporary chandelier of smoked glass and brass. Ahead, the foyer widened into a space where a second, matching chandelier created a rich corridor effect.

Michael took her coat, hung it behind a louvered door and turned back to her. "Well, this is it." He spread his hands. "These are guest bedrooms. . . ." Light came through two doors to their right. "Each one has its own bath." They were identical in size and had generous windows. One bedroom was empty, the other held a drafting table and chair. She glanced over the rooms as she followed Michael, carrying a clipboard, measuring tape and pen, leaving her purse on the floor in the foyer.

"Do these windows face due north?"

"More like northwest," he replied.

She decided to put off her note-taking and measuring until she'd moved through the entire place, to get a sense of each of its rooms in relationship to the whole. They advanced beyond the entry to an interior octagonal space in the center of which the second chandelier hung. It appeared to be the hub of the apartment, created of four flat walls and four doorways.

"The architect calls this a gallery," Michael said, stopping dead center in the middle of the octagon.

Bess turned in a circle and looked up at the chandelier. "It's very dramatic . . . or can be."

They had entered the gallery from the hall door. Michael indicated the others. "Kitchen, combination living room/dining room, and utility area and powder room off this small hall. Which would you like to see first?"

"Let's see the living room." She stepped into it to be washed in light and delight. The room faced south-by-southeast, had a marble fireplace on the northerly wall, another chandelier at the south end and two sets of sliding glass doors—a triple and a double—that gave onto a deck overlooking the frozen lake. Between the two doors the wall took a turn at an obtuse angle.

"It's just struck me, Michael, this place isn't rectangular, is it?"

"No, it's not. The entire building is arrow-shaped, and this unit is at the point of the arrow, so I guess you'd call it oblique."

"Oh, how marvelous. If you knew how many rectangular rooms I've designed you'd know how exciting this is." Though the two guest bedrooms were rectangular, this room was a modified wedge. "Show me the rest."

The kitchen was done in white tile and Formica with blond oak woodwork. It was combined with an informal family room, which had sliding doors giving onto the same deck that wrapped around the entire apartment on the lake side. The laundry area was in a wedge-shaped space beside a powder room, both leading off the gallery. The master bedroom led off the living room and shared its fireplace flue. Besides the fireplace, the bedroom had yet another set of glass doors leading onto the deck, a walk-in closet and a bathroom big enough to host a basketball game.

In the bathroom, the smell of Michael's cosmetics was as evocative as that of fresh-cut grass. A rechargeable razor sat on the vanity with its tiny red light glowing. Beside it lay his toothbrush and a tube of Close-Up. The shower door was wet and on a towel bar hung a horrendous beach towel with fireworks designs in gaudy colors on a black background. No washcloth. He'd always used his hands.

Shame on you, Bess, you're regressing.

In the bedroom her glance slid over his mattresses and returned for a second take, then moved on as if the sight of them lumped on the floor had not stirred old memories. He must have left Darla taking nothing. Even his blankets were new; the fold lines still showed. How ironic, Bess thought, I'll probably end up choosing his bedspread again. Already she was envisioning the room with the bed and window treatment matching.

"Well, that's it," Michael said.

"I must say, Michael, I'm impressed."

"Thank you."

They returned to the living room with its magnificent scope. "The way the building blends with the land, and how the architect utilized the mature trees, the contour of the lakeshore and even the little park next door—it all becomes a part of the interior design as well as the exterior. The outdoors is actually taken inside through these magnificent stretches of glass, while at the same time the trees lend privacy." Bess strode the length of the room, admiring the view through the windows while Michael stood near the fireplace with his hands in his trouser pockets. "It's interesting," Bess mused aloud, "clients are often surprised to learn that architects and interior designers rarely get along well at all. The reason is because very few architects design from the outside in the way this one did, consequently we're often called in to analyze the space use and handle the problems the architect left behind. In this case, that's not so. This guy really knew what he was doing."

Michael smiled. "I'll tell him you said so. He works for me."

From the opposite end of the room she faced him.

"You built this building?"

"Not exactly. I developed the property and arranged to have it built. The city of White Bear Lake came to me and asked me to do it."

"Ah . . ." Bess's eyebrows rose in approval. "I had no idea your projects had grown to this size. Congratulations."

Michael dipped his head, displaying an appealing mix of humility and pride.

She was no appraiser but the building had to be worth several million dollars, and if the city came to him and invited him to do the job, he must have established a sterling reputation. So both of them—Michael and she—had made great strides since their breakup. "Do you mind if we continue moving from room to room while we talk?"

"Not at all."

"It helps me recall where I've been and familiarize myself with the psychological impact of each room, how the light falls, the space there is to be filled and the space that should remain unfilled. It's kind of like kicking the tires on a car before you buy it."

They gave each other glancing grins and moved into the gallery, where they stopped directly beneath the chandelier. Bess braced her clipboard against her hip and said, "On with the questions. I've been doing all the talking and it's supposed to be the other way around during a house call. I'm here to listen to you."

"Ask away."

"Did you choose the carpet?"

She'd noted that the same carpet was used throughout, with the exception of the kitchen and baths. It wasn't a color she'd have expected him to like. From the gallery she could glance to the sunny or shadowed side of the condo and observe its subtleties change.

"No, it was here when I took over the place. Actually what happened was that this unit was sold to someone else, a couple named Sawyer, who intended it to be their retirement home. Mrs. Sawyer picked out the carpet and had it laid but before she and her husband could close on the place, he died. She decided to stay put, so I inherited the carpet."

"It's staying?"

"It should. It's brand-new and I'm the first tenant."

"You say that as if you have reservations."

He pursed his lips and studied the carpeting. "I can live with it."

"Make sure before we plan a whole interior around it, and be aware that color affects your energy, your productivity, your ability to relax, many things. You're as affected by color as you are by texture and light and space. You should surround yourself with colors you're comfortable with."

"I can live with it," he repeated.

"And I can tone it down, make it more masculine by bringing out its gray rather than its rose, perhaps using a deep gray and a pastel lavender as an accent, maybe bringing in some black pieces. How does that sound?"

"All right."

"Do you have a carpet sample I can take along?"

"In the entry closet on the shelf. I'll give you a piece before you leave."

"What are your thoughts on mirrored walls?"

"In here?" Michael looked up. They were still standing in the octagonal gallery.

"An interior space like this would benefit from them. It could be dramatic to relight the chandelier in four mirror panels."

"It *sounds* dramatic. Let me think about it."

They moved into the room with the drafting table. "Do you work here?"

"Yes."

"How much?"

"Primarily in the evenings. Daytime I'm in the office."

Bess wandered nearer the drafting table. "Do you work—" she began but the question died on her lips. Taped onto an extension lamp over the drafting table was a picture of their two children, taken when they were about seven and nine, in the backyard after a water fight. They were freckled and smiling and squinting into the hard summer sun. Randy was missing a front tooth and Lisa's hair was sticking up in a messy swirl where the force of the hose had shot it.

"Do I work . . . ?" Michael repeated.

She knew full well he'd seen her reaction to the picture, but she was a businesswoman now and personal byplay had no place in this house call. Bess regrouped her emotions and went on.

"Do you work every evening?"

"I have been lately." He didn't add, Since Darla and I broke up, but he didn't have to. It was obvious he sat here in this room regretting some things.

"Would you ever be needing a desk in this room?"

"That might be nice."

"File cabinets?"

"Probably not."

"Shelving?"

He wobbled a hand like a plane dipping its wings.

"In order of preference, would you place this room high or low in the decorating order?"

"Low."

"All right . . . let's move on."

They meandered to the other guest bedroom, and from there to the powder room, the gallery, the kitchen, ending up in the living room.

"Tell me, Michael, what's your opinion of art deco?"

"It can be a little stark but I've seen some I like."

"And glass—glass tabletops, for instance, as opposed to wood."

"Either is fine."

"Would you be entertaining in this room?"

"Maybe."

"How many might you want to seat at one time?"

"I don't know."

"A dozen maybe?"

"Probably not."

"Six?"

"I suppose so."

"Would that entertaining be formal or informal?"

"Informal, probably."

"Meals . . ." She moved to the end of the room where the chandelier hung, studying the change of light on the carpet, imagining it on furniture as she moved from the light-realm of one window to another. "Would you ever entertain at sit-down meals?"

"I have in the past."

"Will you use the fireplace or not?"

"Yes."

"Will you ever watch television in this room?"

"No."

"How about a tape player or CD player?"

"Probably I'd want that in the family room off the kitchen."

"Which do you prefer, vertical or horizontal lines?"

"What?"

She looked up at him and smiled. "That one usually throws people. Vertical or horizontal? One is restful, the other energetic."

"Vertical."

"Ah . . . energetic. Are you an early riser or a late riser?"

"Early." He always had been but she had to ask.

"And how about the tail end of the day? Do you watch the David Letterman show?"

"Do I what?"

"Are you a night person, Michael?"

He scratched his neck and grinned crookedly at the floor. "I remember a time when I was but it's funny how nature takes care of that for you when you reach middle age."

She smiled and went on to her next subject. "Give me your opinion of this chandelier." She looked up at the ceiling.

He wandered nearer and looked up, too. "It reminds me of grapefruit sections," he said.

She laughed. "Grapefruit sections?"

"Yeah, those pieces of smoky glass all standing on end like that. Aren't they shaped like grapefruit sections?"

"Skinny ones, maybe. Do you like it?"

"Mmm . . ." He studied it pensively. "Yeah, I like it a lot."

"Good. So do I."

She made a note about repeating smoked glass in the tables and another about café doors as she moved through a wide doorway into the family room/kitchen. In this room the view had curved away from the lake and focused instead on a tall stand of cottonwood trees—naked now in winter—and a small town park with a white gazebo. Thankfully there were no swing sets or playground equipment, which would be desirable for a young family, not for a building that catered to older, wealthier people.

"What happens in the park?" she asked.

"Picnics in the summer, I guess. That's about all."

"No band concerts, no boat launching?"

"No. Boats are launched over at the county beach or at the White Bear Yacht Club."

"Will you launch one?"

"Maybe. I've thought about it."

"A lot of sailboats on the lake, aren't there?"

"Yes."

"I imagine you're looking forward to watching them from both inside and out on the deck."

"Sure."

She made a note about vertical blinds and sauntered toward the kitchen island, where a jar of peanut butter, a loaf of bread and some throw-away containers created his bachelor's pantry. She glanced over the pitiful collection, then looked away because it brought a sharp desire to play housewife, and neither of them needed that.

"Will this be a working kitchen?" she asked, her back to Michael as she waited for an answer.

It took some time before he replied, "No."

She gathered her composure and turned to rest her clipboard on the island. "Are there any hobbies of yours I should know about?"

"They haven't changed since six years ago. Hunting and the outdoors but I go up to my cabin for that."

"Have you developed any allergies?"

His eyebrows puckered. "Allergies?"

"It has to do with fabrics and fibers," she explained.

"No allergies."

"Then I guess all that's left to ask about is the budget. Have you thought about a range you want me to work within?"

"Just do it the way you'd do it for yourself. You were always good at it, and I trust you."

"All of it?"

"Well . . ." He glanced around uncertainly. "I guess so."

"The guest bedroom, too?"

His eyes came back to her. "I hate empty rooms," he said.

"Yes . . ." she agreed, "and it is the first room a visitor sees when he steps into the foyer."

She had the illogical impulse to go to him, take him in her arms for a moment, pat his back and say, It'll be all right, Michael, I'll fill it with things so it isn't so lonely, though she knew perfectly well a home full of things could not substitute for a home full of people.

She looked down at her clipboard. "I'll need to take some measurements. Would you mind helping me?"

"Not at all."

"I've tried to sketch the layout of the unit but it's unusual enough to be difficult."

"I have some floor plans at the office that were done for the sales people. I'll send you one."

"Oh, that would be helpful. Meanwhile, shall we measure?"

They spent the next twenty minutes at opposite ends of a surveyor's tape, getting room and window dimensions. When they were all tidily written on her rough floor plan, she cradled the clipboard against her arm and reeled in the tape.

"What happens next?" he asked as they returned to the foyer, where he retrieved her coat and held it for her.

"I'll take all these dimensions and transfer them onto graph paper, room by room. Then I'll go 'shopping' through my catalogs and come up with a furniture plan, window treatments, fabric and wallpaper samples. I'll also have all the suggested furniture cut out to scale on magnetic plastic so they can be arranged on the floor plan. When all that is done I'll give you a call and we'll get together for the presentation. I usually do that at my store after hours because all my books and samples are there and it makes it easier without customers interrupting. Then, too, if you don't like something I've suggested we can go into other books and look for something else."

"So when will I hear from you?"

Her coat was buttoned and she drew on her gloves. "I'll try to get on it right away and get back to you within a week, since you're living in rather Spartan conditions. I don't see anything wrong with playing favorites and putting you ahead of some of my other clients, do you?"

She flashed him a professional smile and extended her gloved hand. "Thank you, Michael."

He took it, squeezing hard. "Aren't you forgetting something?"

"What?"

"Your forty-dollar trip charge."

"Oh, that. I initiated the trip charge merely to dissuade lonely people who only want company for an afternoon—and you'd be amazed how many of them there are. But it's obvious you need furniture, and you're not some stranger whose intentions I question."

"Business is business, Bess, and if there's a trip charge, I'll pay it."

"All right, but why don't I bill you for it?"

"Absolutely not. Wait here."

He went into the room with the drafting table, leaving her in the empty foyer. She watched him through the doorway, stretching her gloves on tighter. She picked up her clipboard, her purse, and watched him some more, then followed him into the room, where he was making out the check with one hand flat on the drafting table, his elbow jutting.

The photo was still there, compelling. She studied it over his angled shoulders and said quietly, "They were adorable when they were that age, weren't they?"

He stopped writing, looked at the picture awhile and tore out the check before turning to Bess. His gaze lingered on her, then traveled once more to the picture.

"Yes, they were."

The room remained silent while the two of them studied their son and daughter caught in a carefree day from their past. His gaze returned to Bess and she felt it on her cheek as one feels heat from a nearby fire, while she continued studying the picture.

"Michael, I . . . ." Struggling for words, she met his eyes and felt a burning sense of imminence in the admission she was about to make. "I went to visit my mother on Sunday and we had a talk." She paused but he said nothing. "I told her how difficult it's been seeing you again, and she said that the reason is because you're making me take a second look at myself and my fault in the divorce."

Still he waited while she clung to her clipboard and willed the words forth.

"I think I owe you an apology, Michael, for turning the kids against you."

Something changed in his eyes—a quick transport of repressed anger, perhaps. Though he moved not a muscle he seemed more rigid, while his hazel eyes remained steady upon hers.

She looked down at her glove. "I swore I wouldn't do this—mix business with anything personal but it's been bothering me, and today when I saw their picture here I realized that . . . well, that you loved them, too, and how it must have hurt you, losing them." She met his eyes once more. "I'm sorry, Michael."

He thought about it for passing seconds before speaking in a low, throaty tone. "I hated you for it, you know."

She shifted her gaze to the drafting table. "Yes, I know," she said quietly.

"Why did you do it?"

"Because I felt hurt, and wronged."

"But that was another matter entirely, what was between us."

"I know that now."

They stared at each other until the silence in the room seemed to be compressing them.

"Mother said something else." Again Michael waited for her to go on while she struggled for courage to do so. "She said that when I went back to college you fell to the bottom of my priority list and that's why you found another woman." Nothing changed on his face so she asked, "Is that true, Michael?"

"What do you think?"

"I'm asking you."

"Well, I'm not going to answer. I don't see any point, not at this late date."

"So it is true."

He handed her the check. "Thanks for coming, Bess. I really should get down to my office now."

Her cheeks were hot as she accepted his check and said, "I'm sorry, Michael. I shouldn't have brought it up today. It's not the appropriate time."

She preceded him into the foyer, where he opened the door for her then changed his mind and held it closed for a moment.

"Why did you bring it up at all, Bess?"

"I don't know. I don't understand myself lately. It seems as if there were so many things between us that were never settled, all these . . . these ugly emotions that kept roiling around inside me. I guess I just need to deal with them once and for all and put them behind me. That's what apologies are all about, right?"

His eyes lit on hers, hard as chips of resin. He nodded stiffly. "All right, fair enough. Apology accepted."

She didn't smile; she couldn't. Neither could he.

He found her a carpet sample and ushered her out, at a respectable distance, and pushed the elevator button. The door opened instantly, while he was still speaking.

"Thanks for coming."

She stepped on, turned to offer a conciliatory smile and found him already stalking back into his condo. The elevator door closed and she rode downstairs, wondering if by her apology she'd made things better or worse between them.

chapter 7

RANDY CURRAN DROPPED INTO a lopsided upholstered rocker and reached into his jacket pocket for his bag of pot. It was almost 11 P.M. and Bernie's mom was out, as usual. She was a cocktail waitress so most nights they had the place to themselves. The radio was tuned to Cities 97 and they were waiting for "The Grateful Dead Hour." Bernie sat on the floor with an electric guitar on his lap, the amp turned off as he picked along with a Guns N' Roses song. Randy had known Bernie Bertelli since the eighth grade, when he'd moved to town right after his parents got divorced, too. They'd smoked a lot of dope together since then.

Bernie's place was a dump. The floors were crooked, and the walls had a lot of plastic knickknacks hanging on them. The shag carpeting was the color of baby shit and matted worse than the hair of the two old Heinz 57 dogs, Skipper and Bean, who were allowed to do pretty much anything they wanted anywhere in the house. Skipper and Bean were presently stretched out on the davenport, which in its younger days had been upholstered in some cheap nylon plaid but now was covered with a flowered throw with soiled spots the shapes of the dogs at either end. The coffee tables and end tables had screw-on legs and the drapery pleats sagged between all the hooks. Against one wall a pyramid of beer cans reached the ceiling, the top can wedged against the water-stained tile. Bernie's mom had put the top one there herself.

Randy never sat on the davenport, not even when he was high or drunk.

He never got *that* high or *that* drunk! He always took the green rocker, a decrepit thing that looked as if it had had a stroke, because everything on it sagged to one side. The broken springs in the seat were covered with a folded rag rug to keep them from poking your ass, and the upholstered arms were covered with cigarette burns.

Randy fished out the Ziploc bag and his bat, a miniature pipe big enough for a single hit. Gone were the days of rolling smokes. Who could afford that anymore?

"This shit is getting expensive, man," he said.

"Yeah, what'd you pay?"

"Sixty bucks."

"For a quarter?"

Randy rearranged his expression and shrugged.

Bernie whistled. "Better be good shit, man."

"The best. Lookit here . . ." Randy opened the bag. "Buds."

Bernie leaned over, took a closer look and said, "Buds . . . wow, how'd you score that?" Everybody knew that buds gave you the most for your money—better than leaves or sticks or seeds. You could pack it tighter and get really loaded off a couple of hits.

Randy packed his pipe, missing the days when he'd tear off a Zigzag paper and roll a joint big enough to pass around. He'd seen a guy one time who could roll one with one hand. He'd practiced it himself at home a few times over a sheet of paper, but he'd dropped more than he'd rolled, so he'd settled for doing it deftly with two hands, which in itself was considered a mark of prowess among pot smokers.

Randy struck a match. The bat held less than a thimbleful. He lit up, took a deep drag and held it in his lungs until they burned. He exhaled, coughed and refilled the bat.

"Want a hit, Bernie?"

Bernie took a turn, coughing, too, while a scent like burning oregano filled the room.

It took two hits before Randy got the rush—the sweet chill that riffled through him and left him with a slow-growing euphoria. Everything became so exquisitely distorted. Bernie looked as though he was on the opposite side of a fishbowl, and the lights on the component set shimmered like a meteor shower that was taking ten years to fall. Someplace in the distance men coughed occasionally but the sound filtered down a long corridor, like shouting through a concrete culvert. The music from the radio became a major sensation that expanded his pores, his hair follicles, his fingers and his ability to perceive.

Words came to him and swirled through his vision as if they had mass and form—graceful, beckoning words.

"I met this girl," Randy said. "Did I say that already?" Seemed like he'd said it about one hour ago and it had taken till now for the words to drift down, landing on the dog Bean, bouncing off his red fur in slow motion, disturbing him so he rolled over onto his back with his paws up and his eyes closed.

"What girl?"

"Maryann. Some name, huh? . . . Maryann. Who names their kids Maryann anymore?"

"Who's Maryann?"

"Maryann Padgett. I had dinner at her house. Lisa is marrying her brother."

On the davenport Bean was snoring and his lip was fluttering. Randy became transfixed by the sight, which took on kaleidoscopic beauty, that dog lip, black on the outside, pink on the inside, flap-flapping in rhythm with his gentle snores.

"She scares the shit out of me."

"Why?"

" 'Cause she's a good girl."

Thirst came, exaggerated like everything else. "Hey, Bern, I got the dry mouth. You got some beer?"

The beer tasted like magic elixir, every sip a thousand times better than orgasm.

"We don't mess with good girls, do we, Bern?"

"Shit no, man . . . why should we?"

"Screw 'em and strew 'em, hey, Bern?"

"That's right. . . ." Two minutes later Bernie repeated, "That's right."

Ten minutes after that Bernie said, "Shit, man, I'm really fucked up."

"Me too," Randy said. "I'm so fucked up your nose even looks good. You got a nose like a goddamned anteater and I'm so fucked up your nose looks cute."

Bernie laughed and scattered sound down a jeweled corridor.

Many minutes later Randy said, "You can't get serious about girls, you know what I mean, man? I mean . . . hell . . . next thing you know you're marryin' 'em and you got kids and you're screwin' somebody else's old lady and walkin' out and your kids are bawlin'."

Bernie digested that a long time before he asked, "You bawl when your old man left?"

"Sometimes. Not where anybody could see me, though."

"Yeah, me too."

A while later Randy felt the lethargy lifting and the munchies coming on. He pitched forward in his chair and counted seven beer cans around him. He belched and Bean woke up, stretched and quivered, jumped off the couch and shook a fresh layer of dog hair onto the matted carpet. Pretty soon Skipper did the same. The two of them nosed at Bernie, whose eyes were as red as if he'd been fighting fires.

Randy gave himself some time, coming down. It was after midnight and the deadhead hour was in progress on Cities 97 and he had to be up at six. Actually, he was getting pretty tired of the Grateful Dead and of that stinking job at the warehouse. And of this pigsty of Bernie's and of the rising cost of marijuana. And of Bernie, who never could afford to buy his own. What the hell was he doing here in this lopsided rocking chair with the cigarette burns on its arms, looking at Bernie's big nose and counting the beer cans?

Who was he getting even with?

His father, that's who.

Problem was, the old man didn't really give a damn.

Bess received the floor plan from Michael on the Monday after she'd seen his condo. He'd mailed it, along with a note in his familiar handwriting, on a piece of notepaper with his company logo in blue at the top.

> *Bess, Here's the floor plan for the condo, as promised. I've thought about the mirrors for the gallery. Go ahead and plan them in. I think I'll like them. I've been thinking about what you said just before you left and it makes me realize there were areas where I needed to change and didn't. Maybe we can talk about it some more. It was nice seeing you again. Michael.*

She got a queer flutter at the sight of his handwriting. Funny about a thing like that, it was like studying his wet toothbrush and his damp towel, things he'd touched, held, worked with. She reread the entire message four times, imagining his beautifully shaped hand holding the pen as he wrote it. *Maybe we can talk about it some more.* Now that was a loaded suggestion, was it not? And had it really been nice for him, seeing her again? Didn't he feel the same tension she felt whenever they stood in the same room? Didn't he feel eager to escape, as she did?

Michael received a call from Lisa.

"Hey, Dad, how's it going?"

"All right. How's it going with you?"

"Busy. Cripes, I didn't dream there was this much stuff you had to do to plan a wedding. You free on Saturday afternoon?"

"I can be."

"Good, 'cause you men have to meet at Gingiss Formal Wear and pick out your tuxedos."

"Tuxedos, wow."

"You're gonna be a knockout, Dad."

Michael smiled. "You think so, huh? What time and where?"

"Two o'clock at Maplewood."

"I'll be there."

Randy hadn't thought about his dad being there. He walked into Gingiss Formal Wear at two o'clock the following Saturday afternoon, and there stood Michael, talking with Mark and Jake Padgett. Randy came up short. Mark spied him and came forward, extending his hand. "Here's our last guy. Hey, Randy, thanks for coming."

"Sure, no problem."

Jake shook his hand. "Hello, Randy."

"Mr. Padgett."

That left only Michael, who offered his hand, too. "Randy."

Randy looked into his father's somber eyes and felt a sick longing to go into his arms and hug him and say, "Hi, Dad." But he had not called Michael *Dad* in a long time. The word welled up and seemed to fill his throat, needing to be spoken, needing to be repressed. Michael's eyes so resembled his own it seemed like looking in a mirror while his father's hand waited.

At last he put his hand in Michael's and said, "Hello."

Michael flushed and gripped Randy's hand hard. Long after the contact ended Randy felt the imprint of his father's palm on his own.

A young blond clerk intruded. "Everybody here now, gentlemen? If you'll step this way."

They followed him into a rear room, carpeted and mirrored. Mark and his father went first, leaving Michael and Randy to exchange uncertain glances before Michael politely waved Randy through the doorway before him. The room held tuxedos in every conceivable color from black to pink, and smelled of a hot iron from a tailor's adjacent workroom. The clerk told Mark, "Sometimes the bride is in on this, too. Since yours isn't, I presume you've talked about colors."

"The bridesmaid's dress is coral. She said I could decide what color the tuxes should be."

"Ah, good. Then might I suggest ivory with coral cummerbunds—ivory is always tasteful, always elegant, and seems to be the trendy choice right now. We have several styles, the most popular are probably the Christian Dior and After Six."

The clerk prattled on while Michael and Randy remained intensely aware of each other, electrified by their encounter. With their emotions in turmoil they missed much of what was being said. They assessed jackets with satin lapels, pleated shirts, bow ties, cummerbunds and patent-leather shoes.

They removed their jackets, faced a wall of mirrors and had their measurements taken—neck, sleeve, chest, overarm, waist and outseam. They shucked off their pants and donned trousers with satin stripes up the sides, stood stocking-footed before a wall of mirrors and zipped up their flies, trading glances in the mirror before looking discreetly away.

They buttoned on pleated shirts, ruffled shirts, experimented with bow ties and thought about when they were a boy and a young father and Randy had put shaving cream on his face and shaved with a bladeless razor while his dad stood beside him and shaved with a real one; and times when they'd stood side-by-side and Randy had asked, wishfully, "Do you think I'll ever be taller than you, Dad?" And now he was, by a good inch—all grown up and capable of holding grudges.

"A forty-two long, sir," the clerk said. Michael slipped into a tuxedo jacket that smelled of dry-cleaning fluid, tugged the sleeves and collar into place while the clerk circled him, assessing the fit. Mark made some joke and Randy laughed. Jake said, "Never been in one of these monkey suits before, how 'bout you, Michael?"

"Just once." At his own wedding.

When the fitting was done they put on their street clothes again, zipping winter jackets as they shuffled from the store into the mall. Saturday shoppers moved past in twos and threes. The smell of baking cookies drifted through the hall from Mrs. Field's across the way. Mark and Jake headed straight toward the exit, leaving Michael and Randy to follow. Every step of the way Michael felt his chest contract as his chance slipped away. A question danced on his tongue while he feared Randy's rebuff.

Just before they reached the plate-glass doors, Michael spoke. "Listen, I haven't had lunch yet, have you?" He strove for an offhand tone in spite of the fact that his heart was in his throat.

"Yeah, I grabbed a burger earlier," Randy lied.

"You sure? I'm buying."

For a moment their gazes locked. Hope took on new meaning as Michael sensed Randy vacillating about changing his mind.

"No thanks. I'm meeting some friends."

Michael gave away none of the crushing disappointment he felt. "Well, maybe some other time."

"Yeah, sure . . ."

The gravity remained in both of them, exerting a force that distorted their heartbeats. But six years is a long time and some sins go beyond forgiving. So they left the shopping center by separate doors, went their separate ways and clung to their separate hurts.

Like a penitent toward Mecca, Randy drove straight into downtown Stillwater to his mother's store. He had no meeting with friends. He quite nearly had no friends. He had only a deep need to be in his mother's presence after dashing aside his father's halting offer of conciliation.

Heather was at the counter when he walked in, and there were customers browsing.

"Hi, Heather, is Mom here?"

"Up here, darlin'," Bess called. "Come on up."

He shuffled upstairs, dipping his head to avoid bumping the ceiling when he reached the top, and found her among the jumble that looked capable of eating her alive.

"Well, this is a surprise." She swiveled to face him, sitting in a wooden captain's chair with her legs crossed and a black high heel dangling from her toes.

He scratched his head. "Yeah, I guess it is."

She studied him more closely. "Is something wrong?"

He shrugged.

She bent forward and began thrusting books aside, flopping heavy binders of fabric samples off the top of a heap, eventually unearthing a chair of sorts.

"Here . . . sit down."

He sat.

"What's wrong?"

He slouched back in the chair, crossed an ankle over a knee and poked at the blue rubber edge of his Reebok.

"I just saw Dad."

"Oh . . ." Her eyebrows arched. The word escaped her in an extended syllable as she, too, sat back in her chair, studying Randy. Her forearms rested along the worn wooden arms and in one hand she held a yellow pencil with her thumb folded over the red eraser. "Where?"

"We tried on tuxedos together."

"Did you talk?"

Randy spit on one finger and rubbed some dirt off the edge of his shoe sole. "Not really." He rubbed some more. "He wanted to buy me lunch but I said no."

"Why?"

Randy forgot his shoe and looked up. "Why! Shit, Mom, you know why!"

"No I don't. Tell me. If you said no and it's bothering you so much, why didn't you go with him?"

"Because I hate him."

"Do you?"

Their eyes locked in silence.

"Why should I go with him?"

"Because it's the adult thing to do. It's how relationships are handled, it's how wrongs are righted, and because I think you want to. But after six years it takes a little swallowing of pride, and that's hard."

Randy's anger flared. "Yeah, well, why should I swallow my pride when I never did anything to him. He's the one who did it to me!"

"Hold your voice down, Randy," she said calmly. "There are customers downstairs."

Randy whispered, "He walked out on me, I didn't walk out on him!"

"You're wrong, Randy. He walked out on me, not on you."

"It's the same thing, isn't it?"

"No, it's not. It hurt him very much to leave you and Lisa. He made many efforts to see you over the years but I made sure that didn't happen."

"But—"

"And in all these years I wonder if you've ever asked yourself why he walked out on me."

"What do you mean why? For Darla."

"Darla was the symptom, not the disease."

Disgusted, Randy said, "Aw, come on, Mom, who put that idea in your head? Him?"

"I've had a long examination of conscience lately, and I've discovered that your dad wasn't the only one at fault in the divorce. We were very much in love once, you know. When we were first married, when we had you kids—why, there was no family that was happier. Do you remember those times?"

Randy was sitting the way losers sit on the sidelines during the last thirty seconds of a championship basketball game. He stared at the floor between his Reeboks and made no reply.

"Do you remember exactly when it started to change?"

Randy said nothing.

"Do you?" she repeated softly.

He lifted his head. "No."

"It started when I went back to college. And do you know why?"

Randy waited, looking disconsolate, studying his mother.

"Because I didn't have time for your dad anymore. I came home at the end of the day and there was a family to take care of and housework to do, besides studying, and I was so set on doing it all that I let the most important thing go—my relationship with your dad. I'd get upset with him because he wouldn't help me around the house, and, yes, he was at fault for that but I never *asked* him nicely, we never sat down and talked about it. Instead, I made cutting remarks occasionally, and the rest of the time I zoomed around the house with my mouth tight, feeling like a martyr. Then it became a bone of contention between us. He refused to help me and I refused to ask him to, and pretty soon it was left up to you kids, and you weren't old enough to do it well, so most of the time things were in a mess. Now, if all that was going on in the rest of the house, what do you think was going on in the bedroom?"

Randy only stared at his mother.

"Nothing. And when nothing goes on in the bedroom it sounds the death knell to a relationship between a man and a wife. And that was my fault, not your dad's. . . . That's why he found Darla."

Randy's cheeks grew pink. Bess tipped her chair forward and rested her elbows on her lap.

"You're old enough to hear this, Randy. You're old enough to learn from it. Someday you'll be married, and at first it'll be a bed of roses, and then the humdrum starts in and you forget to do the small things that made that person fall in love with you in the first place. You stop saying good morning, and picking up his shoes when he forgets to take them to his closet, and bringing home the one special kind of Dairy Queen he likes. After all, it's out of your way and you're in a hurry. When he says, Do you want to take a bike ride after supper? you say no because you've had a rough day, so he goes alone and you don't stop to realize that if you'd gone with him it would have made your day a little better. And when he takes a shower before bed, you roll over and pretend to be asleep already because, believe it or not, you begin to consider sex work. You stop doing these things, and then the other one stops doing them, and pretty soon you're substituting criticism for praise, and giving orders instead of making requests, and letting sex fall by the wayside, and in no time at all the whole marriage falls apart."

A long silence passed before Bess sat back in her chair and went on ruminating quietly.

"I remember once, just before we broke up, your dad said to me, We never laugh anymore, Bess. And I realized it was true. You've got to keep laughing, no matter how hard times seem to be. It's what gets you through, and if you really stop to analyze it, one person trying to make another one laugh is a way of showing love, isn't it? It says, I care about you. I want to see you happy. Your dad was right. We had stopped laughing."

Bess set her chair in motion. The spring beneath the seat made a tick with each slight undulation while Randy studied her crossed legs. From downstairs came the *tt-tt-tt-tt* of Heather closing out the cash register for the day; then she turned on the lamps in the front window and called, "I'm going now. I'll lock the front door on my way out."

"Thanks, Heather. Have a nice weekend."

"You, too. 'Bye, Randy."

" 'Bye, Heather," he called.

When she was gone, the sense of intimacy doubled with all quiet below, and the overhead lights darkened. Only the dim light from Bess's desk lamp spread a brandy-colored glow on her abandoned work. She went on speaking in the same quiet tone as before. "I had a talk with Grandma Dorner a while back. It was after I saw your dad at Lisa's. I asked her to tell me, after all these years, why she'd never taken my side during the divorce. She verified all these things I've just told you and more."

Randy met his mother's eyes again as her tone took on sudden passion. Once more she leaned toward him earnestly.

"Listen to me, Randy. I've spent six years telling you all the reasons you should blame your dad, and now I've spent a few minutes telling you why you should blame me. But the truth is, you shouldn't blame anyone. Your dad and I both had a part in the breakup of our marriage. Each of us made mistakes. Each of us got hurt some. Each of us retaliated. You got hurt, too, and you retaliated. . . ." She took his hand. "I understand that . . . but it's time to reassess, dear."

He fixed his eyes on their joined hands, rubbing his thumb over hers. He appeared sheer miserable. "I don't know, Mom."

"If I can, you can." She squeezed his hand in encouragement.

He remained passive, disconsolate, answering nothing.

After some time, Bess swiveled toward her desk and began clustering her work, though she had little spirit for it. She scooped together a few papers, then swung back to Randy.

"You get to look more like him every day. It really does things to my insides sometimes when I turn and catch a glimpse of you standing the way he used to, or grinning the way he used to." She reached out and took both his hands loosely, turning them palms up within her own. "You got his hands," she said. "And his eyes." She looked into them and let a moment of silence pass before smiling gently. "Try as you might to deny you're his, you can't. And that's what hurts most, isn't it, honey?"

He made no reply but the expression in his eyes told her this day had made a deep impression on him.

"Well!" With forced brightness she sat back and checked her watch. "It's getting late and I have a little more work to do here while it's quiet."

"You going home then?"

"In about an hour."

"What's so important that it keeps you here on a Saturday night?"

"Actually, it's some work for your dad. I'm doing the interior design work for his new condo."

"When did all this happen?"

"I went to see it this week."

"Are you two getting back together or something?"

"No, we're not getting back together. He hired me to decorate his place, is all."

"Do you *want* to get back together?"

"No, but it feels better treating him civilly than it did being enemies. There's something about being hateful that deteriorates a person. Well, listen, honey, I really should get back to work, okay?"

"Yeah, sure. . . ." Randy rose and went down one step so he could stand erect. He turned back to his mother. "I'll see you at home, then. You fixing supper when you get there?"

A shaft of guilt struck Bess deep. "I'm afraid not. I have a date with Keith."

"Oh . . . well . . ."

"If I'd known you wanted to, I would have—"

"No, no . . . hell, I'm no baby. I can find supper by myself."

"What will you do tonight, then?"

"I'll probably go up to Popeye's. There's a new band playing there."

"See you at home in an hour or so."

When Randy was gone Bess turned back to her graph paper but sat staring at it with the pencil idle in her hands. Tonight was one of those rare nights when Randy truly wanted to be with her, and she felt devastated for having turned him down. But how was a mother to know? He was nineteen, she forty. They lived in the same house but went their separate ways. Most Saturday nights he wouldn't have stayed home if she'd cooked a five-course meal.

But all the commonsense self-rebuttal in the world would not assuage her guilt. A thought came to accompany it, to add weight to the burden she already carried: if Michael and I had never divorced, we'd be there together on nights like this when Randy needs us. If we had never divorced, he wouldn't be going through this pain in the first place.

On the street a short distance from the Blue Iris, Randy slammed his car door, started the engine and sat staring at the windshield while it collected his breath and turned it to frost. The streets of Stillwater were deserted, the ice along the curbs was too dirty and pitted to reflect the red stoplights. Dark had fallen. By 6:30 the streets would be strung with cars as diners came out to enjoy the restaurants, but now at the close of the business day the whole town looked like the aftermath of a nuclear power leak—not a moving soul about. A semi lumbered up Main Street from the south. He could hear it coming, downshifting, rumbling. He watched it appear at the corner ahead and make a right-hand turn toward the lift bridge, heading east into Wisconsin.

He didn't want to go home.

He didn't want to go to Bernie's.

He didn't want to be with any girls.

He didn't want any fast food.

He decided to drive over to Grandma Dorner's. She was always cheery, and there was always something to eat over there, plus he liked her new place.

Stella Dorner answered his knock and swept him into her arms for a hug. "Well, Randy Curran, you handsome thing, what are you doing here on a Saturday night?"

She smelled like ritzy perfume when he hugged her. Her hair was combed fluffy and she had on a fancy blue dress. "Just came to see my best girl." When he released her she laughed and lifted her hands to her left ear to fit it with a pierced earring.

"You're a doggone liar but I love it." She turned a circle and her skirt flared. "There, how do I look?"

"You're a killer, Gram."

"I hope he thinks so. I've got a date."

"A date!"

"And he's darned good-looking, too. He's got all his hair, all his teeth *and* his gallbladder! A darned nice set of pecs, too, if I do say so myself."

Randy laughed.

"I met him at my exercise class. He's taking me dancing to the Bel Rae Ballroom."

Randy scooped her close and executed an Arthur Murray–style turn. "Stand him up and go with me instead."

She laughed and pushed him away. "Go find your own girlfriend. Have you got one, by the way?"

"Mmm . . . got my eye on one."

"What's the matter with *her?"* She gave his arm a love pat as she swung away, crescendoing as she walked toward her bedroom. "So how's everything with you?"

"Fine," he called, ambling into the living room. There were lights on all over the condo, with music playing on a component set and a painting on an easel by the sliding glass doors.

"I hear you're going to be in a wedding," Stella called from the far end of the place.

"How about that."

"And I also hear you're going to be an uncle."

"Can you believe it?"

"Do I look like a great-grandma to you?"

"Are you kidding? Hey, Gram, did you paint these violets?"

"Yes, how do you like them?"

"Jeez, they're good, Gram! I didn't know you could paint!"

"Neither did I! It's fun." The lights went off in the far bedroom, the bathroom, the hall, and Stella breezed into the living room, wearing a necklace that matched her earrings. "Did you find a band to play with yet?"

"Nope."

"Are you trying?"

"Well . . . not lately."

"How do you expect to find a band if you don't keep trying?" The doorbell rang and Stella said, "Oh, there he is!" She skipped once on her way to answer. Randy followed, feeling like the old one there.

The man who came in had wavy silver hair, shaggy eyebrows, a firm chin and a nice cut on his suit. His pecs didn't look too bad, either.

"Gil," she said. "This is my grandson, Randy. He just dropped in to say hello. Randy, this is Gilbert Harwood." The two shook hands, and Gil's grip was hearty. They made small talk but Randy could see the pair was eager to be going.

Minutes later he found himself back in his car, watching his grandma drive off with her date. Hungrier. Lonelier.

He headed back down McKusick Lane to the stop sign at Owens Street, where he sat observing the collection of cars around The Harbor across the street. He parked and went into the crowded beer joint, slid onto a bar stool and ordered a glass of tap beer. The place was smoky and smelled like the grill was in use. The customers were potbellied, gruff-voiced and had a lot of broken capillaries in their faces.

The guy beside Randy wore a Minnesota Twins billcap, blue jeans and an underwear shirt beneath a soiled, quilted vest. His forearms rested on the bar while he turned his head and glanced at Randy from beneath puffy eyelids. "How's it goin'?" he said.

"Good . . . good," Randy replied and took a swig from his glass.

They sat with their elbows two inches apart, sipping beer, listening to Randy Travis sing a two-year-old song on the jukebox, and the sizzle of cold meat hitting a hot grill in the kitchen, and occasional loud bursts of laughter. Somebody came in and the cold air momentarily chilled the backs of their legs before the door thumped closed. Randy watched eight faces above eight bar stools turn and check out the new arrivals before returning indifferently to their beers. He finished his own, got off the stool, fished a quarter from his pocket and used the pay phone to dial Lisa's number.

Her voice sounded hurried when she answered.

"Hey, Lisa, it's Randy. You busy?"

"Yeah, sort of. Mark is here and we're making spanakopita to take to an all-Greek supper over at some friends' of ours. We're in butter and filo to our elbows!"

"Oh, well, listen, it's no big deal. I was just gonna see if you wanted to watch a video or something. Thought I could pick one up and come over."

"Gosh, Rand, sorry. Not tonight. Tomorrow night, though. I'll be around then."

"Yeah, well maybe I'll stop over then. Listen, have a good time tonight and say hi to Mark."

"Will do. Call me tomorrow, then."

"Yeah, sure. 'Bye."

Back in his car, Randy started the engine, turned on the radio and sat awhile with his hands hanging loosely on the wheel. He hiccuped once, then belched and studied the lights of the houses on either side of the Owens Street hill. What were they all doing in there? Little kids having supper with their folks. Young married couples having supper with each other. What would Maryann Padgett say if he called her up and asked her out? Hell, he didn't have enough money to take her anyplace decent. He'd spent that sixty bucks on pot earlier this week, and his gas tank was nearly empty, and the payment on his drum set was due, and payday wasn't until next Friday.

Shit.

He rested his forehead on the wheel. It was icy and brought a sharp stab of cold that concentrated in the back of his neck.

He lifted his head and pictured his dad's reflection in the mirror today beside his own while they'd zipped up their flies and experimented with tying bow ties. He wondered where they'd have gone if he'd said yes to lunch, what they'd have talked about, if they'd be together now.

He checked his watch. Not even seven yet. His mother would still be home, getting ready for her date with Keith, and he'd just be in their way if he got there before they left; and his mother would get that guilty look on her face for leaving him after he'd opened his big mouth at the store and asked if she was making supper.

Everybody had somebody. Everybody but him.

He reached into his pocket, found his bat and the Ziploc bag of marijuana and decided, To hell with it all.

chapter 8

BESS AND KEITH ATE AT LIDO'S at a table beneath a potted tree trimmed with miniature lights. The minestrone was thick and spicy, the pasta homemade and the chicken parmigiana exquisite. When their plates had been removed they sat over wine and spumoni.

"So . . ." Keith said, fixing his stare on Bess. He wore glasses thick enough to magnify his eyes. His face was round, his sandy hair thinning, allowing the tree lights to reflect from his skull between the strands. "I've been waiting all evening for you to mention Michael."

"Why?"

"Isn't it obvious?"

"No, it's not. Why should I mention Michael?"

"Well, you've been seeing him lately, haven't you?"

"I've seen him three times but not in the way you infer."

"*Three* times?"

"I hardly thought I'd get through Lisa's wedding with*out* seeing him."

"The night Lisa set you up, and the night of the dinner at the in-laws." Keith ticked them off on his fingers. "When was the third time?"

"Keith, I don't appreciate being grilled like this."

"Can you blame me? This is the first time I've seen you since he came back on the scene."

Bess pressed a hand to her chest. "I divorced the man, are you forgetting?"

Keith took a sip of wine, lowered the glass and remarked, "You're the one who seems to be forgetting. I'm still waiting to hear about the third time you saw him."

"If I tell you, will you stop haranguing me?"

He stared at her awhile before nodding stiffly and picking up his spoon.

"I went to see his condo. I'm going to decorate it for him. Now could we just finish our spumoni and go?"

With his spoon poised over his ice cream, Keith asked, "Are you coming over tonight?"

Bess felt him watching her minutely. She ate some spumoni, met his eyes and replied, "I don't think so."

"Why?"

"I have a lot of work to do at home tomorrow. I want to get up early for church. And something's come up with Randy that's on my mind. I think I should be there tonight."

"You put everything and everybody else before me."

"I'm sorry, Keith, but I . . ."

"Your kids, your work, your ex-husband, they all come before me."

She said gently, "You demand a lot."

He leaned closer to her and whispered fiercely, "I'm sleeping with you, don't I have a right?"

He was so close she could detect the subtle color shadings in his green-brown eyes. She found herself unmoved by his resentment, grown very tired of fighting this fight. "No. I'm sorry, but no."

He pulled back and his lips thinned.

"I've asked you so many times to marry me."

"I've been married, Keith, and I never want to go through that again."

"Then why do you keep seeing me?"

She considered carefully before answering. "I thought we were friends."

"And if that's not enough for me?"

"You'll have to decide."

His spumoni had melted into a sickly green puddle. He pushed it aside, took a deep breath and said, "I think we'd better go."

They rose and left the restaurant politely. At the coat check, he held her coat. At the entry, he held the door. At his car, he unlocked the passenger door and waited while she got in. Inside his car they buckled their seat belts and headed for his place in silence. She had left her car parked at the foot of his driveway. He passed it and stopped before the garage door, which he got out to open. When he'd pulled inside, when the headlights were off and the engine silenced, Bess unsnapped her seat belt but neither of them moved. The beam from the streetlight stopped short of the car, leaving them in blackness. Beneath the hood the engine ticked as it cooled.

The absence of warmth from the heater chilled Bess's legs. The absence of warmth in her heart chilled much more.

She turned to Keith and laid her hand on the seat between them. "Keith, I think maybe we should break it off."

"No!" he cried. "I knew this was coming but it's not what I want. Please, Bess . . ." He took her in his arms. Hampered by their heavy winter outerwear, the embrace was bulky. ". . . You've never given us a real chance. You've always held yourself aloof from me. Maybe it's something I've done and if it is I'll try to change. We could work things out, we could have a nice life together, I just know we could. Please, Bess . . ."

He kissed her heavily, wetting her mouth and spreading the taste of wine into it. She found herself slightly revolted and eager to be away from him. He released her mouth but held her head in both hands with his forehead against hers. "Please, Bess," he whispered. "We've been together for three years. I'm forty-four years old and I don't want to start looking for someone else."

"Keith, stop it."

"No . . . please, don't go. Please come inside. Come to bed with me . . . Bess, please."

"Keith, don't you see? We're a convenience for each other."

"No. I love you. I want to marry you."

"I can't marry you, Keith."

"Why? Why can't you?"

She had no desire to hurt him further. "Please don't make me say it."

As he grew desperate his voice became pleading. "I know why, I've known all along, but I can make you love me if you just give me the chance. I'll be anything you want . . . anything, if only you won't leave me."

"Keith, stop it! You're abasing yourself."

"I don't care. I'll even abase myself for you."

"But I don't want you to. You have a lot to offer a woman. I'm just not the right one."

"Bess, please . . ." He tried to kiss her again, groping for her breast.

"Keith, stop it. . . ." Their struggle became ferocious and she shoved him back, hard. *"Stop it!"*

His head struck the window. Their breathing beat heavily in the confined space.

"Bess, I'm sorry."

She grabbed her purse and opened her door.

"Bess!" he pleaded, "I said I'm sorry."

"I have to go," she said, scrambling from the car with her heart clubbing and her limbs trembling, welcoming the rush of cold air and the sight of her own car in the nearby shadows. She hurried toward it, running the last several yards after she heard his car door opening.

"Bess, wait! I'd never hurt you, Bess!" he called. Her car door cut off his last word as she slammed and locked it, then rummaged in her purse for her keys. The sound of all four automatic locks clacking down should have calmed her but she found herself shuddering and digging frantically, then peeling out of his driveway in reverse.

A quarter mile up the street she realized her hands were gripping the wheel, her back was rigid and tears were running down her cheeks.

She pulled to the curb, dropped her forehead to the steering wheel and waited for the tears and shakes to dissolve.

What had happened to her back there? She knew full well Keith would not hurt her, yet her revulsion and fear had been genuine. Was he right? Did his being her lover give him the right to expect more from her? She *had* always held herself aloof from him: this much was true. Her children *had* often come first, and she *had* frequently put him off in favor of business that could have been delayed.

Furthermore, she was beginning to suspect perhaps Michael did play a part in her rather sudden severing of ties with Keith. He had been the one calling out apologies as she'd run away, but perhaps it was she who owed them.

She thought of Michael too much during the week that followed. While she leafed through wallpaper and furniture catalogs she pictured his empty rooms and recalled their voices echoing off the white ceramic tiles of the empty kitchen. She saw his damp towel, his toothbrush, his mattresses on the floor—most often his mattresses on the floor. Though she was divorced from him it was impossible to divorce herself from the knowledge of him, and sometimes she pictured him moving about the rooms, in intimate disarray, the kind only a wife or lover can know, or in an equally intimate freshly dressed state, with his skin still flushed from a shave and his lips still shiny from the shower. She saw him in a suit with his tie in a Windsor knot, still in his stocking feet, picking up his change, money clip and flat, flat billfold that held little more than his driver's license and two credit cards (he hated bulging out his rear pocket). And last, before he donned his shoes, she saw him opening the penknife he always carried, standing in the bedroom beside the dresser and cleaning his fingernails. He did it every morning without fail; in all the years she'd known him she'd rarely seen him with dirt beneath his nails. It was part of the reason she so loved his hands.

She unconscionably worked on Michael's designs before seven others that had been in her files longer. She knew things he liked: long davenports a man could stretch out on, chairs with thick arms and matching ottomans, the *USA Today* with his breakfast, fires at suppertime, schefflera plants, things with rounded corners rather than squared, real leather, diffused lighting.

She knew things he disliked: scatter rugs, doilies, hanging plants, clutter, busy florals, the colors yellow and orange, twelve-foot telephone cords that got stretched out and testy, television playing at mealtimes.

It was hard to remember a job she'd enjoyed more or had designed with as much confidence. How ironic that she knew his tastes better now than she had when planning the house in which the two of them had lived together. Having carte blanche with his budget didn't hurt, either.

She called him on Thursday.

"Hi, Michael, it's Bess. I've got your design all worked up and wondered when you can come to the store and go over it with me."

"When would you like?"

"As I said before, I try to make the appointments at the end of the day so that we won't be interrupted. How's five o'clock tomorrow?"

"Fine. I'll be there."

The following day, a Friday, she went home at 3:30, washed her face, put on fresh makeup, touched up her hair, changed into a freshly pressed suit and returned to the store in time to lay out the materials for her presentation and dismiss Heather with ten minutes to spare.

When Michael came in the window lamps were lit, the place smelled like fresh coffee and at the rear of the store around the grouping of wicker furniture, the materials for Bess's presentation stood at the ready, fabrics draped, wallpaper books standing; textures, colors and photographs overlapped.

She heard the door open and he came in bringing the smell of winter and the sound of the five o'clock traffic moving on the street behind him. When the door sealed it off Bess went forward, smiling.

"Hello, Michael, how are you? I'll lock that now and turn over the sign." She had to shinny past him in the limited space between her floor stock. The profusion of tables, baskets and glassware filled up all but the most meager traffic paths. She locked the door, reversed the OPEN sign and turned to find him perusing the walls, which were hung with framed prints and wall decor clear up to the blue iris border strip just below the cove molding. He turned her way, still looking up, unbuttoning his coat and blocking the aisle. The store seemed suddenly crowded with his presence, its proportions so much better suited to women.

"You've done a lot with this place," he said.

"It's crowded, and the loft is unbearable in the summer, but when I think of getting rid of it I always seem to get nostalgic and change my mind. Something keeps me here."

His eyes stopped when they reached her and she became aware that he, too, had freshly groomed for this meeting: she could tell by the absence of four-o'clock shadow and the faint scent of British Sterling.

"May I take your coat?"

It was gray wool and heavy in her hands when he shrugged it off along with a soft plaid scarf. She had to say excuse me to get around him once more. Hanging the coat on the back of the basement door, she caught a whiff of scent from it, not simply a bottled scent but a combination of cosmetics and fresh air and his car and himself—one of those olfactory legacies a man leaves on a woman's memory.

She drew a deep breath and turned to conduct business. "I've got everything laid out here at the back of the store," she said, leading the way to the wicker seats. "May I get you a cup of coffee?"

"Sounds good. It's cold out there."

He waited, standing before the settee, until she set the cup and saucer on the coffee table and took an armchair to his right.

"Thanks," he said, freeing a button on his suit jacket as he sat. The furniture was low and his knees stuck up like a cricket's. He took a sip of coffee while she opened a manila folder and extracted the scale drawings of his rooms.

"We'll start with the living/dining room. Let me show you the wallpaper first so you can be picturing it as a backdrop for the furnishings as I describe them." Surrounded by samples, she presented his living room the way she envisioned it—subtle wallpaper of cream, mauve and gray; vertical blinds; upholstered grouping facing the fireplace; smoked-glass tables; potted plants.

"I seem to remember you liked our schefflera plant and watered it when I forgot to, so I thought it was safe to plan live plants into your furniturescape."

She glanced at him and found him considering the collected samples. He shifted his regard to her and said, "I think I like it. Actually, I like the sound of everything so far."

She smiled and went on, laying out her suggestions.

For the formal dining area a smoked-glass Swaim table on a brass base, surrounded by fully upholstered chairs.

For the foyer, a large mirror sculpture above a sassy Jay Spectre console table, flanked by a pair of elegant LaBarge side chairs upholstered in tapestry.

For the gallery, mirrored walls and a single faux pedestal directly beneath the chandelier, highlighting the sculpture of his choice.

A desk, chair, credenza, feather lamp and bookshelves for his drafting room.

For the guest bedroom, an art deco bed and dresser in cream lacquer, and a heavier concentration of lavender in the fabrics.

For the master bedroom, art deco once again—a three-piece suite in black lacquer from Formations, along with torchères and an upholstered chair. She suggested that the bedspread, wallpaper and vertical blinds all match.

She'd saved the coup d'état for last. For the family room, sumptuous Natuzzi Italian leather on a loose-cushioned sofa of cream that stretched out into forever and turned two corners before it got there.

"Italian leather is the finest money can buy, and Natuzzi is the best in the industry," she told him. "It's expensive but worth it, and since you gave me carte blanche on the budget, I thought you might enjoy the sheer luxury."

"Mm, I would." Michael studied the colored brochure of the curved sofa. She recognized the look of covetousness on his face.

"Exactly how much is 'expensive'?"

"I'll tell you later but for now submerge yourself in fantasy. The sticker shock will come at the end of the presentation, so if you don't mind waiting . . ."

"All right, whatever you say."

"The sofa is available in cream or black, and either color would fit but I thought we'd go with cream in the family room. Besides, black shows dust. Here, let me show you the entertainment unit I think would be really wonderful."

It was double wide and could be completely closed to reveal a solid, sleek surface of whitewashed oak.

"Whitewashing is being used a lot. It's rich yet casual, and I've repeated it in this ice-cream table and bentwood chairs for the adjacent informal eating area."

There were more wallpapers, fabric samples, wood swatches and photographs to be considered, as well as furniture layout. By the time she'd covered the highlights it was 7:30 and she'd lost his eye contact and could see that he was suffering data saturation.

"I know I've given you a lot to consider but believe it or not, there's still more. We've barely touched on the accent pieces—floor urns, wall decor, lamps and smaller case goods, but I think we've covered enough tonight. Most people do a room at a time. Doing an entire home is Olympian."

He leaned back, flexed his shoulders and sighed.

She laid a paper-clipped sheaf of papers on the table before him.

"Here's the bad news you've been waiting for. A breakdown, room-by-room and item-by-item with an allowance for additional small decor, which I'll select as I go—always with your approval, of course. The grand total is $76,300."

Michael looked as if he'd been poleaxed. "Holy old nuts!"

Bess threw back her head and laughed.

"You think it's funny!" He scowled.

"I haven't heard that expression in years. You're the only one I ever knew who said it."

Michael ran a hand over his hair and puffed out his cheeks. "Seventy-six thousand . . . Crimeny, Bess, I said I trusted you."

"That's including the Natuzzi sofa, which by itself is eight thousand, and a custom-made five-by-seven rug for in front of the living-room fireplace. We could drop those two items and save you almost ten thousand. Also the mirrored walls in the gallery are fifteen hundred. I went with some pretty classy designers, too—Jay Spectre, LaBarge, Henredon—these are makers who set standards in the industry."

"And how much am I paying you?"

"It's all there." She pointed at the sheaf of papers. "A straight ten percent. Most independents will charge you the wholesale price plus ten percent freight, and seventy-five dollars an hour for their design and consultation time. And believe me, those hours can mount up. It's also important to realize that the term 'wholesale price' is arbitrary, since they can say it's whatever they want it to be. My price includes freight and delivery, and my one-time trip charge, you'll remember, was only forty dollars, which I'll apply toward the cost of the job if you decide to go with me. You're welcome to compare, if you wish."

She sat back, collected, with her eyes leveled on Michael while he looked over the list. He studied it in detail, only the rustle of the turning pages marking the passing minutes. She rose, refilled his coffee cup and returned to her chair, crossing her legs and waiting in silence until he finished reading and closed the sheets.

"The price of furniture has gone up, hasn't it?" he asked.

"Yes, it has. But so has your own social status. You own your own firm now, you're very successful. It's only right that your home should reflect that success. I should think that in time you'll have more and more clients into your home. Decorated as I've suggested, it will make a strong statement about you."

He studied her without blinking until she wanted to look away but resisted. The light from the floor lamp on his far side put a luster of silver on the hair above his left ear. It painted his cheek gold and put a shadow in the relaxed smile line connecting his nose and mouth. He was an unnervingly handsome man, so handsome, in fact, that she had associated that handsomeness with unfaithfulness, so had intentionally chosen an unhandsome one in Keith. She realized that now.

"How much did you say that leather sofa's going to cost?"

"Eight thousand."

He considered awhile longer. "How long before I get this stuff?"

"The standard wait for custom orders is twelve weeks. Natuzzi takes sixteen because it's shipped directly from Italy and it comes over by boat, which takes four weeks by itself. I'll be frank with you and admit there's been some trouble over there lately with dock strikes, which could delay it even longer. But on the brighter side, sometimes we call the manufacturer and find out they have a piece already made up in the fabric we want and out it comes in six weeks. But figure twelve, on the average."

"And what about guarantees?"

"Against defects and workmanship? We're dealing with quality names here, not flea-market peddlers. They stand behind everything, and if they don't, I do."

"And what about the wallpaper and curtains? How long do I have to wait for them?"

"I'll place an order with the workroom immediately, and window treatments should be installed within six weeks. Wallpaper, much sooner. It's possible I could have paper hangers in here within two weeks, depending on their work schedule and the paper availability."

"You take care of all that?"

"Absolutely. I have several paper hangers who do my work. I contract them directly, so you never have to do any of that. All you have to do is make arrangements to have the door unlocked when they come to do the job."

Her estimate still lay on his lap. He glanced at the top sheet and his lower lip protruded.

She said, "I should warn you, I'll be in and out of your place a lot. I make it a point to check the wallpapering immediately after it's done, and I also accompany my installers when they come to put up window treatments. If there's something wrong, I want to find it myself instead of having you find it later. I also come out to see the furniture on site once it's been delivered, to make sure the color match is right. Do you have any problem with that?"

"No."

Bess began gathering up the floor plans and putting them into the manila folder. "It's a lot of money, Michael, there's no question about that. But any interior designer you hire is going to cost a lot, and I think I have one advantage any other wouldn't have. I know you better."

Their gazes met as she sat forward in her chair, with a stack of things on her knees, steadying them with both hands.

"You're probably right," he conceded.

"I know I'm right. The way you've always loved leather, you'll go crazy over that Italian sofa, and the rich rug in front of the fireplace, and the mirrors in the gallery. You'd love it all."

So would you, he thought, because he knew her well, too, knew these were colors, styles and designs she liked. For a moment he indulged in the fantasy that she had planned the place for both of them, as she had once before.

"May I have a while to think about it?"

"Of course."

She stood and he did likewise, while she bent to collect his cup and saucer.

Michael checked his watch.

"It's almost eight o'clock and I'm starved. How about you?"

"Haven't you heard my stomach growling?"

"Would you want to . . ." He cut himself off and weighed the invitation before issuing it in full. "Would you want to grab a bite with me?"

She could have said no, she should put away all these books and samples, but in truth she'd need them for ordering if he decided to sign with her. She could have said she'd better get home to Randy, but at eight o'clock on a Friday night Randy would be anywhere but at home. She could have simply used good judgment and said no, without qualifying it. But the truth was she enjoyed his company and wouldn't mind spending another hour or so in it.

"We could go to the Freight House," she suggested.

He smiled. "They still make that dynamite seafood chowder?"

She smiled. "Absolutely."

"Then let's go."

She locked up and they left the Blue Iris with the lamps softly illuminating the window display. Outside the wind was biting, swaying the streetlights on their posts, whipping the electrical wires like jump ropes.

"Should we drive?" he asked.

"Parking is always horrendous there on weekends. We might as well walk, if you don't mind."

It was only two blocks but the wind bulldozed them from behind, sending their coattails skipping and Bess hotfooting it to keep from toppling on her face in her high-heeled pumps.

Michael took her elbow and held it hard against his ribs while they hurried along with their shoulders hunched. They crossed Main Street against a red light and as they turned onto Water Street the wind shifted and eddied as it stole between the buildings and formed whirlpools.

His hand and his ribs felt both familiar and welcome against her elbow.

The Freight House was exactly what its name implied, a red-brick relic from the past, facing the river and the railroad tracks, backing against Water Street with six wagon-high, arch-top doors through which freight had been loaded and unloaded in the days when both rail and river commerce flourished. Inside, high, wide windows and doors faced the river and gave onto an immense wooden deck, which in summer sported colorful umbrella tables for outside wining and dining. Now, in bitter February the corners of the windows held ice, and the yellow umbrellas were furled fast, like a flotilla of quayside sails. It smelled wonderful and felt better, being in out of the chill.

Unbuttoning his overcoat, Michael spoke to the hostess, who consulted an open book on her lectern.

"It'll be about fifteen minutes. You can have a seat in the bar if you'd like, and I'll call you."

They kept their coats on and perched on hip-high stools on opposite sides of a tiny square table.

"It's been a long time since I've been here," Michael remarked.

"I don't come here often, either. Occasionally for lunch."

"If I remember right, this is where we came to celebrate our tenth anniversary."

"No, our tenth we celebrated down in the Amana colonies, remember?"

"Oh, that's right."

"Mother took care of the kids and we went down for a long weekend."

"Then which one did we celebrate here?"

"Eleventh, maybe? I don't know, they sort of all run together, don't they?"

"We always did something special though, didn't we?"

She smiled in reply.

A waitress came and laid two cocktail napkins on the table. "What would you like?" she asked.

"I'll have a bottled Michelob," Michael answered.

"I'll have the same."

When the girl went away Michael asked, "You still like beer, huh?"

"Why should I have changed?"

"Oh, I don't know, new business, new image. You look like somebody who'd drink something in a tall stem glass."

"Sorry to disappoint you."

"It's not a disappointment at all. We drank a lot of beer together over the years. It's familiar."

"Mmm . . . yeah, a lot of hot summer evenings when we'd sit on the deck and watch the boats on the river."

Their beers arrived and after a skirmish about who would pay, they each paid for their own, then eschewed glasses in favor of drinking straight from the bottle.

When they'd each taken a deep swallow, Michael fixed his eyes on her and asked, "What do you do now on hot summer evenings, Bess?"

"I'm usually busy doing design work at home. What do you do?"

He thought awhile. "With Darla, nothing memorable. We both worked long hours and afterwards just sort of occupied the same lodge. She'd be gone, grocery shopping or having her hair done. Sometimes, when Mom was still alive, I'd go over to her house and mow her lawn. It's funny, because I had a yard service that took care of my own but after she had her stroke she couldn't handle the mower anymore, so I'd go over once a week or so and do it."

"Didn't Darla go with you?"

Michael scratched the edge of his beer label with a thumbnail. He worked up a little flap that was sticky on the backside. "It's a funny thing about second wives. That extended family bonding never seems to happen."

He took another swig of beer and met her eyes over the bottle. She dropped her gaze while he studied the way her lipstick held a tiny circle of wetness after she drank from her own bottle. Beneath the table she had one high heel hooked over the brass ring on the bar stool and her knees crossed. It made a pleasant shadow in her lap where her skirt dipped. Man-oh-man, she looked good.

"You know how it is," Michael continued. "A good Catholic mother doesn't believe in divorce so she never actually recognized my second marriage. She treated Darla civilly but even that took an effort."

Bess lifted her eyes. Michael was still studying her.

"I imagine that was hard for Darla."

"Yup," he said, and snapped out of his regardful pose as if nudged on the shoulder by an elder. "Aw, hell . . . water over the dam, right?"

The hostess came and said, "We have a booth ready for you now, Mr. Curran."

The backs of the booths went clear up to the ceiling, sealing them into a three-sided box which was lit by a single hanging fixture. While Bess spent some time perusing the oversized menu, Michael only flipped his open, glanced for five seconds and closed it again. She sat across from him, feeling his eyes come and go while he finished his beer and waited.

She closed her menu and looked up.

"What?" she said.

"You look good."

"Oh, Michael, cut it out." She felt a blush start.

"All right, you look bad."

She laughed self-consciously and said, "You've been staring at me ever since we came in here."

"Sorry," he said but went on staring. "At least you didn't get mad this time when I told you."

"I will if you don't stop it."

A waitress came to take their orders.

Michael said, "I'll have a grilled chicken sandwich and a bowl of seafood chowder."

Bess's eyes flashed up: she'd decided on the same thing. This used to happen often when they were married, and they would laugh at how their tastes had become so alike, then speculate on when they might start looking alike, the way people said old married couples did. For a moment Bess considered changing her choice but in the end stubbornly refused to be cowed by the coincidence.

"I'll have the same thing."

Michael looked at her suspiciously.

"You won't believe it but I'd made up my mind before you ordered."

"Oh," he replied.

Their seafood chowder came and they dipped into it in unison, then Michael said, "I saw Randy last Saturday. I asked if I could take him to lunch but he said no."

"Yes, he told me."

"I just wanted you to know I'm trying."

She finished her chowder and pushed the bowl back with two thumbs. He finished his and the waitress came and took away their bowls. When she was gone Michael said, "I've been doing some thinking since the last time we talked."

Bess was afraid to ask. This was too intimate already.

"About fault—both of ours. I suppose you were right about me helping around the house. After you started college I should have done more to help you. I can see now that it wasn't fair to expect you to do it all."

She waited for him to add *but,* and offer excuses. When he didn't she was pleasantly surprised.

"May I ask you something, Michael?"

"Of course."

"If I'm out of line just say so. Did you ever help Darla with the housework?"

"No."

She studied him quizzically awhile, then said, "Statistics show that most second marriages don't last as long as first ones, primarily because people go into them making the same mistakes."

Michael's cheeks turned ruddy. He made no remark but they both thought about their conversation throughout the rest of the dinner.

Afterward they divided the check.

When they reached the door of the restaurant, Michael pushed it open and held it while Bess passed before him into the cold. To her back he said, "I've decided to give you the job decorating my condo."

She came up short and turned to face him while behind him the door swung shut.

"Why?" she said.

"Because you're the best woman for the job. What do I do, sign a contract or something like that?"

"Yes, something like that."

"Then let's do it."

"Tonight?"

"Judging from how you handle yourself as a businesswoman, you've got a contract all made up back at the shop, right?"

"Actually, I do."

"Then let's go." He took her arm quite commandingly and they headed up the street. At the corner, when they turned into the wind it whistled in their ears and almost knocked them off their feet.

"Why are you doing this?" she shouted.

"Maybe I like having you poke around my house," he shouted back.

She balked. "Michael, if that's the only reason . . ."

He forced her to keep walking. "Just a joke, Bess."

As she unlocked the door of the Blue Iris, she hoped it was.

chapter 9

FEBRUARY SPED ALONG. Lisa's wedding was fast approaching. The telephone calls from her to Bess came daily.

"Mom, do you have one of those pens with a feather at your store? You know . . . the kind for the guest book?"

"Mom, where do I buy a garter?"

"Mom, do you think I have to get plain white cake or can I have marzipan?"

"Mom, they need the money for the flowers before they make them up."

"Mom, I gained another two pounds! What if I can't get into the dress?"

"Mom, I bought the most beautiful unity candle!"

"Mom, Mark thinks we should have special champagne glasses engraved with our name and date but I think it's silly since I'm pregnant and can't even drink champagne anyway!"

"Mom, have you bought your dress yet?"

Since she hadn't, Bess set aside an afternoon on her calendar and called Stella to say, "The wedding is only two weeks away and Lisa threw a fit when she found out I don't have a dress yet. How about you? Have you got one?"

"Not yet."

"Do you want to go shopping?"

"I guess we'd better."

They drove into downtown Minneapolis, browsing their way from the Conservatory to Dayton's to Gavidae Commons, where they struck it lucky at Lillie Rubin. Stella, turning up her nose at the grandma image, found a hot little silvery white number with a three-tiered gathered skirt and perky sleeves to match, while Bess chose a much more sedate raw silk sarong suit in palest peach with a flattering tulip-shaped skirt. When they stepped out of their adjacent dressing rooms Bess gave Stella the once-over and said, "Wait a minute, who's the grandma here?"

"You," Stella replied, "I'm the great-grandma." Perusing her reflection in the mirror, she went on, "I'll be darned if I've ever been able to understand why the mothers of brides go to such great lengths to add fifteen years onto their age by buying those god-awful dowdy dresses that look like Mamie Eisenhower's curtains. Now *this* is how I feel!"

"It's very jaunty."

"Y' darned right it is. I'm bringing Gil Harwood along."

"Gil Harwood?"

"Do I look like a dancing girl?"

"Who's Gil Harwood?"

"A man who makes my nipples stand at attention."

"Mother!"

"I'm thinking of having an affair with him. What do you think?"

"Mother!"

"I haven't done any of that sort of thing since your father died, and I think I should before all my ports dry up. I did a little experimenting the last time Gil took me out, and it's definitely not his arteries that are hardening."

Bess released a gust of laughter. "Mother, you're outrageous."

"Better outrageous than senile. Do you think I'd have to worry about AIDS?"

"You're the outrageous one. Ask him."

"Good idea. How are things between you and Michael?"

Bess was saved from answering by the clerk, who approached and inquired, "How are you doing, ladies?" But she felt a flurry of reaction at the mention of his name and caught Stella's sly glance that said very clearly she knew something was stirring.

They bought the dresses and went on to search out matching shoes. When they were in Bess's car, heading east toward home, Stella resumed their interrupted conversation.

"You never answered me. How are things between you and Michael?"

"Very businesslike."

"Oh, what a disappointment."

"I told you, Mother, I'm not interested in getting tangled up with him again, but we did straighten out some leftover feelings that have been lingering since before we got the divorce."

"Such as . . ."

"We both admitted we could have worked a little harder at holding things together."

"He's a good man, Bess."

"Yes, I know."

Bess had little occasion to run into the good man between then and the wedding. The paper was hung in Michael's condo and though Bess went over to check it when the paperhangers were just finishing up, Michael wasn't there. She called him the next day to ask if he was satisfied.

"More than satisfied. It looks perfect."

"Ah, good."

"Smells like squaw piss, though."

Bess burst out laughing and even across the telephone wire felt a thrill of attraction that she'd been staving off ever since her last meeting with him. She had forgotten how genuinely funny Michael could be and how effortlessly he'd always been able to make her laugh.

"But you like it?"

"Yes, I do."

"Good. Listen, the invoices are starting to come in now on your furniture. So far it looks as though most things will be arriving in mid-May. No word yet on the Natuzzi from Italy but I'm sure that'll take longer. I'll let you know as soon as I hear."

"All right."

Bess paused before changing the subject. "Michael, I need to talk to you about the bills for Lisa's wedding. Some of them have already been paid and others are coming in, so how do you want to handle it? I've paid out eight hundred dollars already, so why don't you match it and add two thousand, and I'll add the same and Lisa can put it into her savings account and draw on it as she needs it? Then what's left over—if any is—we can split."

"Fine."

"I have the receipts for everything, and I'll be more than happy to send them to you if—"

"Heaven's sake, Bess, I trust you."

"Oh . . . well . . . thanks, Michael. Just send the check to Lisa, then."

"You really think we'll see any leftover money?"

Bess chuckled. "Probably not."

"Now you're thinking like a realist."

"But I don't mind spending it, do you?"

"Not at all. She's our only daughter."

The chance remark left the phone line silent while they reached back to their beginnings, wishing they could undo the negative part of their past and recapture what they'd once had. Bess felt an undeniable stirring, the urge to ask him what he'd been doing, where he was, what he was wearing, the kind of questions that signal infatuation. She quelled her foolhardiness and said instead, "I guess I'll see you at the rehearsal, then."

Michael cleared his throat and said in a curiously flat voice, "Yeah . . . sure."

When Bess hung up she tipped her desk chair back to its limit, drove both hands into her hair and blew an enormous breath at her loft ceiling.

Randy kept his car like the bottom of a bird cage. Whatever fell, stayed. The day of the groom's dinner and rehearsal he took the battered '84 Chevy Nova to the car wash and mucked 'er out. Fast-food containers, dirty sweat socks, empty condom packages, crumpled *Twin Cities' Readers*, unopened mail, unmailed mail, parking-lot receipts, a dried-up doughnut, empty pop cans, a curled-up Adidas, unpaid parking tickets—all got relegated to the bottom of a fifty-gallon garbage drum.

He vacuumed the floor, ran the mats through the washer, Armor Alled the vinyl, emptied the ashtrays, washed the windows, washed and dried the outside and bought a blue Christmas tree to hang from the dash and make the inside smell like a girl's neck.

Then he drove to Maplewood Mall and bought a new pair of trousers at Hal's, and a sweater at The Gap, and went home to put on his headset and play Foreigner's "I Want to Know What Love Is" and beat his drums and dream about Maryann Padgett.

The rehearsal was scheduled for six o'clock. At quarter to, when his mother asked if he wanted to ride to the church with her, he answered, "Sorry, Mom, but I've got plans for afterwards." His plan was to ask Maryann Padgett if he could drive her home.

When he walked into St. Mary's and saw Maryann, the oxygen supply in the vestibule seemed to disappear. He felt the way he had when he was nine years old and used to hang upside down on the monkey bars for five minutes, then try to walk straight. She was wearing a prim little navy-blue coat, and prim little navy-blue shoes with short, prim heels, and probably a prim little Sunday dress with a prim little collar, and talking to Lisa in prim, proper terms. She probably went to Bible camp in the summer and edited the school newspaper in the winter.

He'd never wanted to impress anyone so badly in his life.

Lisa saw him and said, "Oh, hi, Randy."

"Hi, Lisa." He nodded to Maryann, hoping his eyes wouldn't pop out of their sockets and bounce on the vestibule floor.

"Where's Mom?" Lisa asked.

"She's coming. We drove in separate cars."

"You and Maryann are going to be first up the aisle."

"Yeah? Oh, well, hey . . . how about that." *Bravo, Curran, you glib rascal, you. Really knocked her prim little socks off with that one.*

Maryann said, "I was just telling Lisa that I've never been in a wedding before."

"Me either."

"It's exciting, isn't it?"

"Yes, it is."

Inside his new acrylic sweater he was warm and quivering. She had this little pixie face with blue eyes about the size of Lake Superior; and pretty puffed lips and the teeniest, tiniest mole above the upper one but close enough that if you kissed her properly you'd kiss it, too; and not a fleck of makeup ruining any of it.

"Dressing up for first Communion is about as close as I've come to this," she remarked. The vestibule was crowded, and Lisa spied someone else she needed to talk to.

Left in a lull, Randy searched for something to talk about. "Have you always lived in White Bear Lake?"

"Born and raised there."

"I used to go to the street dances there in the summer during Manitou Days. They'd get some good bands."

"You like music?"

"Music is what drives me. I want to play in a band."

"Play what?"

"Drums."

"Oh." She thought awhile and said, "It's kind of a tough life-style, isn't it?"

"I don't know. I never had the chance to find out."

Father Moore came in and started getting things organized, and they all went inside the church and laid their coats in the rear pews, and sure enough, Maryann Padgett was wearing her Marion-the-librarian dress, some little dark-colored thing with a dinky white collar made of lace. Without mousse or squiggly waves in her hair, she was a throwback, and he was captivated.

Randy was standing in the aisle continuing to be dumbstruck by her when someone rested a hand on his shoulder blade.

"Hi, Randy, how's it going?"

Randy turned to encounter his father. He removed all expression from his face and said, "Okay."

Michael dropped his hand and nodded to the girl. "Hello, Maryann."

She smiled. "Hi. I was just saying, this is the first wedding I've ever been in, and Randy said it is for him, too."

"I guess it is for me, too, other than my own." Michael waited, letting his eyes shift to Randy but when no response came, he drifted away, saying, "Well . . . I'll be seeing you."

As Randy's expressionless gaze followed Michael, he repeated sarcastically, "Except for his own . . . both of them."

Maryann whispered, "Randy, that was your father!"

"Don't remind me."

"How could you treat him that way?"

"The old man and I don't talk."

"Don't talk! Why, that's awful! How can you not talk to your father?"

"I haven't talked to him since I was thirteen."

She stared at Randy as if he'd just tripped an old lady.

Father Moore asked for silence and the practice began. Randy remained put out with Michael for intruding on what had begun as a conversation with some possibilities. After the whole day of thinking about Maryann Padgett, cleaning up his car for her, dressing in new clothes for her, wanting to impress her, the whole thing had been shot by the old man's appearance.

Why can't he just lay off me? Why does he have to touch me, talk to me, make me look like a jerk in front of this girl when he's the one who's a jerk? I walked in here, I was ready to show Maryann I could be a gentleman, make small talk with her, get to know her a little and lead up to asking her out. The old man comes over and screws up the whole deal.

During the practice Randy was forced to observe his mother and father walking down the aisle on either side of Lisa, then sitting together in the front pew. There were times when he himself had to stand up front and face the congregation and could hardly avoid seeing them, side-by-side, as if everything was just peachy. Well, that was bullshit! How could she sit there beside him as if they'd never split up, as if it wasn't his fault the family broke up? She might say she had faults, too, but they were minor compared to his, and nobody was going to convince Randy differently.

When the business at the church ended they all went to a restaurant called Finnegan's, where the Padgetts had reserved a private room for the groom's dinner. Randy drove alone, arrived before Maryann and waited for her in the lobby. The door opened and she stepped inside, speaking with her father and mother, a smile on her face.

She saw him and the smile thinned, her speech faltered.

"Hello again," he said, feeling self-conscious waiting there with such obvious intent.

"Hello."

"Do you mind if I sit with you?"

She looked straight at him and said, "You'd do better to sit with your father but I don't mind."

He felt himself blushing—blushing, for Christ's sake—and said, "Here, I'll help you with that," as she began removing her coat.

He hung it up along with his own and they followed her parents into the reserved room, where a long table waited to accommodate the entire wedding party. Walking behind her, he studied her round white collar, which reminded him of something a Mennonite would wear, and her hair, dark as ink and falling in tiers to her shoulders, the tips upturned like dry oak leaves. He thought about writing a song about her hair, something slow and evocative, with the drums quiet at the beginning and building toward a climax, then ending with sheepskin mallets doing a cymbal roll that faded into silence.

He pulled out her chair and sat down beside her, at the opposite end of the table from his parents.

While they ate, Maryann sometimes talked and laughed with her father, on her right. Sometimes she did the same with Lisa or Mark, across the table, or bent forward to say something to her mother or one of her sisters, down the line. She said nothing to Randy.

Finally he asked, "Would you please pass the salt?"

She did, and flashed him a polite smile that was worse than none at all.

"Good food, huh?" he said.

"Mm-hmm." She had a mouthful of chicken and her lips were shiny. She wiped them with her napkin and said, "My folks wanted something fancier for the groom's dinner but this was all they could afford, and Mark said it was fine, as long as Mom didn't have to do all the cooking herself."

"You all get along really well, I guess . . . your family, I mean."

"Yes, we do."

He tried to think of something more to say but nothing came to mind. He grinned and glanced at her plate.

"You like chicken, huh?" She had eaten all of it and little else.

She laughed and nodded while their eyes met again.

"Listen," he said, his stomach in knots. "I was wondering if I could drive you home."

"I'll have to ask my dad."

He hadn't heard that answer since he was in the tenth grade and had just gotten his driver's license.

"You mean you want to?" he asked, amazed.

"I kind of suspected you'd ask me." She turned to her father, sitting back in her chair so Randy could hear their exchange. "Daddy, Randy wants to drive me home, okay?"

Jake touched his hearing aid and asked, "What?"

"Randy wants to drive me home."

Jake leaned forward, peered around Maryann to study Randy a moment and said, "I guess that would be all right but you have things to do early tomorrow, don't you?"

"Yes, Daddy, I'll get in early." She turned to Randy and said, "Okay?"

He raised his right hand like a Boy Scout. "Straight home."

When the meal was over there was a jumble of good-byes at the door. He held Maryann's coat, then the heavy plate-glass door, and they walked across the snowy parking lot together.

"This one's mine," he said, reaching his Nova and walking around to open the passenger door for her, waiting until she was seated, then slamming it, feeling gallant and eager to extend every courtesy ever invented by men for women.

When he was sitting behind the wheel, putting his keys in the ignition, she remarked, "Boys don't do that much anymore . . . open car doors."

He knew. He was one of them.

"Some girls don't want a guy to open doors for them. It's got something to do with women's lib hang-ups." He started the engine.

"That's the silliest thing I ever heard. I love it."

He felt all glowy inside and decided if she could be honest, so could he. "It felt good doing it, too, and you know what? Other than for my mother, I don't do it much, either, but I will from now on."

She buckled her seat belt, something else he rarely did, but he fished around and found his buried buckle and engaged it. He adjusted the heater, stalling for time, judging he'd have her at her doorstep in less than ten minutes. The floor fan came on and twisted the blue Christmas tree around and around on its string.

"It smells good in here," she said. "What is it?"

"This thing." He poked the tree and put the car into reverse and headed toward White Bear Avenue. It would have been more direct to take I-95 to 61 and go around the west side of the lake but he headed around the east side instead, driving twenty miles an hour in the thirty-mile zone through the residential district.

When they were halfway to her house he said, "Could I ask you something?"

"What?"

"How old are you?"

"I'm a senior. Seventeen."

"Are you going with anybody?"

"I don't have time. I'm in girls' basketball and track, and I work on the school paper and I spend a lot of time studying. I want to do something in either medicine or law, and I've applied to Hamline University. My folks can't afford to pay their tuition fees so I'll need a scholarship if I'm going to go there, which means I have to keep my grades up."

If he told her how he'd skated through high school she'd ask him to stop the car and let her out right here.

"How about you?" she asked.

"Me? Nope, don't go with anybody."

"College?"

"Nope, just high school."

"But you want to be a drummer."

"Yes."

"In a rock band?"

"Yes."

"And meanwhile?"

"Meanwhile, I work in a nut house."

"A what!" She was already amused.

"It's a warehouse, actually. I package fresh roasted nuts—peanuts, pistachios, cashews—it's a big wholesale house. Custom orders that go out to places all over America. Christmas is our biggest season. It really gets crazy in a nut house at Christmas."

She laughed, as people always did, but the comparison between their ambitions was pointed enough to sound ludicrous, even to him.

They rode in silence awhile before Randy said, "Jesus, I really sound like a loser, don't I?"

"Randy, I need to say something right up front."

"Say it."

"I'd just as soon you didn't say 'Jesus' that way. It offends me."

That was the last thing he'd expected. He hadn't even realized he'd said it. "Okay," he replied, "you got it."

"And as far as being a loser—well, that's all just a state of mind. I guess I've always thought if a person feels like a loser he ought to do something about it. Go to school, get a different job, do something to boost your self-esteem. That's the first step."

They reached her house and he parked on the street, leaving the engin running. There was a bunch of cars in the driveway—her parents', Lisa's Mark's. The lights were on throughout the house. The living-room draperies were open and they could see people moving through the room.

Randy hunched his shoulders toward the steering wheel, joined his hands between his knees and looked straight out the windshield at a streetlight twenty feet away.

"Listen, I know you think I'm a jerk because I don't get along with my dad but maybe you'd like to hear why."

"Sure. I'm a good listener."

"When I was thirteen he had an affair and divorced my mother and married somebody else. Everything just sort of fell apart after that. Home, school. Especially school. I kind of drifted through."

"And you're still feeling sorry for yourself."

He turned his head, studied her awhile and said, "He screwed up our whole family."

"You think so?" He waited, eyeing her warily. "You aren't going to like what I have to say but the truth is, each of us is responsible for ourself. If you started sloughing off in school, you can't blame him for that. It's just easier if you do, that's all."

"Jesus, aren't we smug?" he replied.

"You said 'Jesus' again. Do it once more and I'm leaving."

"All right, I'm sorry!"

"I said you weren't going to like what I had to say. Your sister made it through. Your mother seems to have done all right. Why didn't you?"

He threw himself back into the corner of the seat and pinched the bridge of his nose. "Christ, I don't know!"

She was out of the car like a shot, slamming the door, leaping over the snowbank onto the sidewalk and heading for the house before he realized what he'd said. He opened his door and shouted, "Maryann, I'm sorry! It just slipped out!" When the house door slammed, he slugged the car roof with both fists and railed aloud, "Jesus Christ, Curran, what are you doing chasing this uptight broad!"

He flung his body behind the wheel, gunned the engine with the ear splitting thunder of an Indy-500 ignition, peeled down the street fishtailing for a quarter of a block, rolled down the window, yanked the smelly Christmas tree off the radio knob, cutting his finger before the string broke, and hurled the thing into the street, cursing a blue streak.

He slewed around a corner at twenty-five miles an hour, came within inches of wiping out a fire hydrant, ran two stop signs and shouted at the top of his lungs, "Well, fuck you, Maryann Padgett! Get that? Fuck you!"

He braked beside some strange house, got out his marijuana, had a couple good hits and waited for the euphoria to drift in and calm him.

He was smiling the last time he either said or didn't say, Yeah, fuck you, Maryann Padgett . . .

While Randy was escorting Maryann from the restaurant, Lisa was saying good night to her mother and father.

She gave Michael a hug first.

"See you tomorrow, Dad."

"Absolutely." He felt unusually sentimental and held her extra long, one of the last times he'd do so before she took another man's name. "I understand you're staying at the house tonight with Mom."

"Uh-huh. We moved all my stuff over to Mark's today."

"I'm glad. I like to think of you there with her tonight."

"Hey, Dad?" At his ear she whispered, "Keep up the good work. I think you're makin' points with Mom." She broke away and smiled. "See you at home, Mom. Good night, everyone!"

Michael hid his surprise while Lisa went out the door with Mark, leaving various stragglers behind. While helping Bess with her coat he remarked, "Lisa seems absolutely happy."

"I believe she is."

The rest of the Padgetts said good night and left. Michael and Bess were the last two in the place, standing near the plate-glass door, dawdling, putting on their gloves, buttoning their coats.

"It looks to me like something is cooking between Randy and Maryann," Michael remarked.

"They were together all night."

"I noticed."

"She's a pretty girl, isn't she?"

"I'll say."

"Why do mothers always make that remark first?" Bess said.

"Because they want pretty girls for their handsome sons, I guess. Fathers are no different. Hell, I'd just as soon see my kids end up with foxes instead of dogs."

Bess chuckled, meeting Michael's eyes while an unsettling quiet fell between them. They should go, should follow the others outside and say good night.

"She's very young, still in high school," Bess said.

"I noticed she asked her father's permission to go with Randy."

"Nice old-fashioned thing to see, isn't it?"

"Yes, it is."

A soft expression came into Bess's eyes. "They're a wonderful family, aren't they?"

"I thought it bothered you to be around wonderful families."

"Not as much as it used to."

"Why's that?"

She gave no answer. The restaurant was closing up. Someone was running a vacuum cleaner and their waitress came through, dressed in her winter coat, on her way home. They should walk out, too, sensibly, and end this cat-and-mouse game they were playing with their own emotions. Still, they stayed.

"You know what?" Michael said.

"What?" Bess said the word so softly it could scarcely be heard above the whining vacuum cleaner.

He'd intended to say, I wish I was going home with you, too, but thought better of it.

"I've planned a surprise for Lisa and Mark. I've ordered a limousine to pick them up tomorrow."

Bess's eyes widened. "You didn't!"

"Why? What's—"

"So did I!"

"Are you serious?"

"Not only that, I had to pay in advance for five hours, and it's non-refundable!"

"So did I."

They began laughing. When they stopped they were smiling into each other's eyes. The restaurant manager came along and said, "Excuse me, we're closing."

Michael stepped back guiltily.

"Oh, I'm sorry."

They went out into the chill night air at last and heard a key turn in the lock behind them.

"Well," Michael said, his breath a white puff in the frigid air, "what are we going to do about that extra limo?"

Bess shrugged. "I don't know. Split the loss, I guess."

"Or treat ourselves. What do you say—wanna go to the wedding in a white limo?"

"Oh, Michael, what will people say?"

"People? What people? Want me to take a guess what Lisa would say? Or what your mother would say? Matter of fact, we could give the old doll a thrill and swing by her place on the way and pick her up, too."

"She's already got a date. He's picking her up."

"She does! Well, good for her. Anyone I know?"

"No. Somebody named Gil Harwood. Claims she's going to have an affair with him."

Michael reared back and laughed. "Oh, Stella, you're a real piss cutter." When his laughter subsided, he angled Bess a flirtatious grin. "Now, what about you?"

She grinned. "Do *I* want to have an affair? Michael, hardly."

"Do you want to ride in a limo?"

"Ohhhh . . ." She drew out the word coquettishly, as if to say, Oh, that's what you meant. "Do I want to ride in a limo? Certainly. Only a dummy would say no to an invitation like that, especially since the thing is paid for with her own money."

"Good." He grinned, pleased. "We'll let yours take Lisa and mine will come and pick you up. Four forty-five. We'll get there in time for pictures."

"Fine. I'll be ready."

They started toward the parking lot.

"My car's this way," he said.

"Mine's that way."

"See you tomorrow, then."

"Yup."

They turned and walked at a forty-five-degree angle away from one another. The night was so cold it made their teeth hurt. Neither of them cared. Reaching their cars, they unlocked their doors and opened them, then stood looking at each other across the nearly empty parking lot while the halogen lights turned everything the color of pink champagne.

"Hey, Bess?"

"What?"

It was a moment as sterling and clear as the silent city night around them, the kind of moment lovers remember years after it happens, for no particular reason except that in the midst of it Cupid seemed to have released his arrow and watched to see what mischief it might arouse.

"Would you call tomorrow a date?" Michael called.

The arrow hit Bess smack in the heart. She smiled and replied, "No, but Lisa would. Good night, Michael."

chapter 10

To Lisa, spending her wedding eve in her childhood home seemed meet. Shortly after eleven, when she dropped her overnight bag on her bed, things were much as they'd been when she was a teenager. Randy was down in his room with his radio tuned low. Mom was in her bathroom cleansing off her makeup. It almost seemed as if Dad would shut off the hall light, stop in the doorway and say, "G'night, honey."

She dropped to the bed and sat looking at the room.

Same pale-blue flowered wallpaper. Same tiered bedspread. Same criss-cross curtains. Same . . .

Lisa dumped her purse off her lap and radiated to the dresser. Into the mirror frame her mother had wedged her school pictures. Not just the second-grade one they'd laughed at the day she'd tried on the wedding dress but all thirteen of them, from kindergarten through twelfth. With her hands flat on the dresser and a smile on her face, Lisa studied them before turning to find, on the rocking chair in the corner, her Melody doll, and propped against its pink vinyl hand, the note from Patty Larson.

She picked up Melody, sat down with the doll on her lap and faced her closet doorway, where her wedding gown hung between the open bifold doors.

She was totally ready for this marriage. Nostalgia was fun but it failed to beckon her into those bygone days. She was happy to be altar-bound, happy to be pregnant, happy to be in love and happy she'd never taken up lodging with Mark.

Bess appeared in the doorway, dressed in a pretty peach nightgown and peignoir, rubbing lotion on her face and hands.

"You look all grown up, sitting there," she said.

"I feel all grown up. I was just thinking how absolutely ready I am for marriage. It's a wonderful feeling. And remember years ago when I asked you what you thought of girls moving in with guys, you said just try it and watch the shit hit the fan? Thanks for that."

Bess walked into the room, leaned over Lisa and kissed the top of her head, carrying with her the scent of roses. "I don't think I said it exactly like that but if the message stuck, I'm glad."

Lisa hugged her mother, her head nestled against Bess's breasts.

"I'm glad I'm here tonight. This is the way it should be."

When the hug ended Bess sat on the bed.

Lisa asked, "You know what I'm happiest about, though?"

"What?"

"You and Dad. It's so great to see you two sitting side-by-side again."

"We're getting along remarkably well."

"Any, ah . . ." Lisa made a hanky-panky gesture with a widespread hand.

Bess laughed quietly. "No. No *ah* anything. But we're becoming friends again."

"Well, hey, that's a start, isn't it?"

"Is there anything you want me to do for you tomorrow? I'm taking the whole day off so I've got time."

"I don't think so. It's hair in the morning and be at the church by five for pictures."

"Speaking of that, your father asked if he could drive you to the church. He said he'd pick you up here at quarter to five."

"Will you be here, too? And Randy? So we could all go to the church together?"

"I don't see why not."

"Wow, won't that be something . . . after six years. I can't wait."

"Well . . ." Bess said, rising. "It's early, and isn't that a miracle? I'm going to get a full night's rest and wake up bright and early with the whole morning to myself." She kissed Lisa's cheek. "Good night, dear." She looked into her happy eyes. "Sweet dreams, little bride. I love you."

"Love you, too, Mom."

The light over the kitchen stove was still on. Bess went down to turn it off. It was a rare occasion when Randy was home at this hour, so she indulged herself and continued down to the walkout level, where she knocked softly on his door. Music played low but no answer came. She opened the door and peeked inside. Randy lay on his side, facing the wall, both arms outflung, still dressed in the new clothes he'd worn earlier. On the opposite side of the room one dim lamp lit the top of his chest of drawers, and the ever-present lights on his component set spiked and fell like electronic graphs.

He always slept with the radio on. She'd never understood why or how he did so but no amount of nagging had changed his habit.

She approached the bed and braced a hand behind Randy while leaning over to kiss the crest of his cheek. So like his father he looked, young and innocent in slumber. She touched his hair; it even felt like Michael's, was the same dark color, the curl more pronounced.

Her son—so proud, so hurt, so unwilling to bend. She had seen Randy snub Michael tonight and thought him wrong. Her heart had gone out to Michael, and in that moment she'd felt a flash of bitterness toward Randy. Mothering was so complex: she didn't know how to handle this young man who hovered on a brink where an influence in either direction might decide his fate for years to come, possibly for life. She saw very clearly that Randy could be a failure in many regards. In human relations, in business and in that most important aspect of life, personal happiness.

If he fails, I'll be part of the reason.

She straightened, studied him a moment more, turned out the lamp and quietly slipped from the room, leaving the radio playing softly behind her.

When the door closed, Randy's eyes snapped open and he twisted to look back over his shoulder.

Whew, that was a close one.

He let his head drop to the pillow and rolled onto his back. He thought she'd come in to ask him some question, and all the while she'd been touching his hair he'd expected her to shake him and make him turn over. She'd have taken one look at his eyes and known, then he'd be out on his ass. He had no doubt she meant it the last time she'd warned him.

He was still loaded, the lights on the component set seemed threatening, as if they were attacking from the corner of his eye, and he was getting dry mouth and the munchies.

The munchies—God, they always got him, hard. And food never tasted so good as when he was high. He had to have something. He rolled from the bed and walked the mile and a half toward the door. Upstairs all was black. He felt his way to the kitchen, turned on the stove light and found a bag of Fritos. He searched the refrigerator for beer but found only orange juice and a covered jar of iced tea.

He drank some tea straight from the jar. It tasted like ambrosia.

Somebody whispered, "Hey, Randy, is that you down there?"

He nudged himself away from the cabinet and shuffled stocking-footed down the hall. Above him Lisa leaned over the rail.

"Hiya, sis."

"Whatcha got?"

"Fritos . . ." A long while later he added, "and iced tea."

"I can't sleep. Bring 'em up."

Climbing the stairs he mumbled, "Jesus, I hate iced tea."

Lisa was sitting Indian-fashion against her pillows, dressed in a gray jogging suit. "Come on in and shut the door."

He did as ordered and dropped to the foot of her bed, where he bounced forever, as if on a trampoline.

"Here, give me some," Lisa said, rolling onto her knees, reaching for the Frito bag. "Randy!" She dropped the bag and grabbed his face, pointing it toward herself. "Oh, Randy, you stupid ass, you've been smoking pot again, haven't you!"

"No," he whined. "Come on, sis—"

"Your eyes look like abortions! Gol, you're so damned dumb! What if Mom caught you? She'd throw you out."

"Are you going to tell her?"

"I should, you know." She looked as if she were considering it. "But I don't want to spoil my wedding day tomorrow. You *promised* me you weren't going to smoke that shit anymore!"

"I know but I just had a couple o' hits."

"Why?"

"I don't know." Randy fell to his back across the foot of Lisa's bed, one arm upflung. "I don't know."

She took the iced tea out of his hand, helped herself to a swig and stretched to set it on her bedside stand, then resumed her Indian pose and wondered how to help him.

"Man, do you know what you're doing to your life?"

"It's just pot; hey, I don't do coke."

"Just pot." She shook her head and sat awhile, watching him stare at the ceiling.

"How much you spend on it a week?"

He shrugged and flopped his head once.

"How much?"

"It's none of your goddamn business."

She stretched out a foot and rocked him. "Look at you. You're nineteen years old and you got a set of Pearls. Big deal. What else have you got? A decent job? A stick of furniture? A car anybody besides your mother paid for? A friend who's worth anything? Bernie, that anal aperture. God, I can't figure out for the life of me why you hang around with him."

"Aw, Bernie's all right."

"Bernie's a loser. When are you going to see it?"

Randy rolled his head and looked at her. She ate three Fritos. She leaned forward and put one in his mouth. She ate another one, then said, "You know what I think is wrong with you? You don't like yourself very much."

"Oh, listen to her, Lisa Freud."

She fed him another Frito. "You don't, you know. That's why you hang around with losers, too. Let's face it, Randy, you've dated some real pus bugs. Some of the girls you've brought over to my apartment, I mean I wanted to stretch a condom over my hand before I shook with them."

"Thanks."

She fed him two Fritos this time, then set the sack aside and brushed off her hands.

"You treated Dad like shit tonight."

"Yeah, well, you treat shit like shit."

"Oh, come off it, Randy, he's doing his damnedest to mend things between you. When are you going to be a big man and get past it? Don't you know it's eating you?"

"He's not what's bothering me tonight."

"Oh, yeah? Then what is?"

"Maryann."

"Struck out with her, too, huh? Good."

"Listen, I was trying. I was really trying!"

"Trying what? To get in her pants? You leave her alone, Randy, she's a nice girl."

"Boy, you really think a lot of me, don't you?"

"I love you, little brother, but I have to overlook a lot to do it. I'd love you more if you'd get your act together and give up that weed and get a job."

"I've got a job."

"Oh yeah, working in that nut house. What're you scared of, huh? That you're not good enough on those Pearls?" She stretched out one leg, put her foot on his ribs and wriggled her toes.

He rolled his head and looked at her.

"You gonna remember this in the morning?" she asked.

"Yeah, I'm all right now. I'm coming down."

"Okay then, listen, and listen good. You're the best drummer I've ever heard. If you want to drum, then by God, drum. But realize this—it's a high-risk job, especially when you go into it smoking grass. The next thing you know they'll have you on coke, then on crack, and before you know it you're dead. So if you're gonna be a musician, you get in with a straight band."

He stared at her a long time, then sat up. He drew one knee onto the bed. "You really think I'm good?"

"The best."

He grinned crookedly. "Really?"

She answered with a quirk of her head.

In time she said, "Okay, so what happened with Maryann? She didn't look too happy when she came charging into the house."

"Nothing happened." He dropped his gaze to the bedspread and ran a hand through his hair. "I cussed, that's all."

"I told you she was a good girl."

"And I apologized but she was already beatin' it inside."

"Next time watch your mouth around her. It won't hurt you, anyway."

"And I no sooner got inside the restaurant than she yelled at me for how I treated Dad."

"So other people notice it, too."

"I don't even know why I should like the girl!"

"Why do you?"

"I just said, I don't know."

"I'll bet I do."

"Yeah? . . . So tell me."

"She's no pus bag, that's why."

Randy chortled deep in his throat. He sat silently for some time before telling his sister, "The first time I saw her it was like wham! You know? Right there." He socked his chest. "Felt like I couldn't breathe."

Lisa gave a crooked grin. "Sometimes it happens that way."

"I put on my best manners tonight, honest, I did." He plucked at his sweater. "Even got these new clothes, and mucked out my car, and pulled out her chair at the table, and opened the car door for her but she's tough, you know?"

"Sometimes a tough woman is best. Same goes for friends. If you had tougher ones who demanded more of you maybe you'd be right for Maryann."

"You don't think I am?"

Lisa studied him awhile, then shrugged and reached for the nightstand.

"I think you could be but it'll take some work." She handed him the Fritos and the iced tea. "Go get some sleep, and your eyes better not look like guts when you walk down that aisle tomorrow, okay?"

He smiled sheepishly. "Okay." He rose from the bed and shuffled toward the door.

"Hey," she said quietly, "c'mere." She raised her arms. He came around the bed and plopped into them. They rocked and hugged a moment with the crackly Fritos bag and the cold tea jar against her back.

"I love you, little brother."

Randy squeezed his eyes shut hard against the sting. He really believed her and wished himself more worthy.

"I love you, too."

"You've got to end this thing with Dad."

"I know," he admitted.

"Tomorrow would be a good time."

He had to get out of there or he'd be bawling. "Yeah," he muttered and fled the room.

The day Bess had predicted would be relaxed was anything but. There was her own hair appointment in the morning, followed by nails. There were two calls from Heather with questions from the store. There were the white satin bows to be hung on the pews at St. Mary's, and the caterers to be contacted with notice of three late RSVPs, and a slotted box to be prepared for guests to drop their wedding cards into, and some odds and ends to be carted over to the reception hall, and the hall itself needed checking to make sure the cake had arrived and the table arrangements were the right color, and the guest register was set up and—how had she forgotten!—a wedding card to buy! And nylons—lord, why hadn't she thought to check her nylons earlier in the week?

By quarter to four Bess was frazzled. Lisa wasn't home yet and she was worried about the limo. Randy kept asking for things—an emery board, some mouthwash, a clean handkerchief, a shoehorn.

"A shoehorn!" she shouted over the railing. "Use a knife!"

Lisa returned, the calmest one of the trio, and hummed while putting on her makeup and donning her gown. She dropped her shoes and makeup into her overnight bag, collected her veil and arranged everything in the front hall for removal to the car when her father came.

He rang the bell at precisely 4:45.

Upstairs, Bess was crossing her bedroom and inserting a pierced earring when she heard it ring. Her footsteps halted. Her stomach went fluttery. She hurried to a window and held back the curtain. There in the street were two white limousines, and downstairs, Michael was entering the house for the first time since he'd collected his power tools and left for good.

Bess dropped the curtain, pressed a hand to her rib cage and forced herself to take one deep breath, then collected her purse and hurried out. At the top of the stairs her footsteps were arrested by the sight below. Michael, smiling, handsome, dressed in an ivory tuxedo and apricot bow tie, was hugging Lisa in the front entry, his trouser legs lost in the billows of her white lace. The door was open; the late afternoon sun slanted across the two of them and for that moment, it seemed Bess was looking down at herself. The familiar dress, the handsome man, the two of them smiling and elated as his hug curled Lisa's feet off the floor.

"Oh, Daddy, *really?"* she was squealing. "Are you serious?"

Michael was laughing. "Of course. You didn't think we'd let you ride to church in a pumpkin, did you?"

"But two of them!" Lisa wriggled from his embrace and danced outside, beyond Bess's sight.

"Your mother had the same idea, so they're really from both of us." Through the open door and the fanlight above it, the westering sun spread gold radiance into the house and upon Michael as he watched his daughter, then turned to look back inside at the place he'd once called home. From overhead, Bess watched his gaze take in the familiar terrain—the potted palm in the corner beside the door, the mirror and credenza, the limited view of the living room to the left of the entry, partially obscured by Lisa's bridal veil, which hung on the doorframe, and the family room straight ahead. He took three steps farther inside and stopped almost directly below Bess. She remained motionless, gazing at his wide shoulders in the exquisitely tailored tuxedo, at his thick hair, the tops of his dark eyebrows, his nose, the silk stripe down his right trouser leg, his cream-colored patent-leather shoes. He, too, stood motionless, taking in his surroundings like a man who's missed them very much. What memories called to him while he stood there so still? What pictures of his children returned? Of her? Himself? In those few moments while she observed him she felt his yearning for this place as keenly as she had many times felt his kiss.

Two things happened at once: Lisa came in from outside and Randy arrived from downstairs, coming to an abrupt halt at the sight of his father standing in the front hall.

Michael spoke first. "Hello, Randy."

"Hi."

Neither of them moved toward the other. Lisa stood watching, just inside the front door. Bess remained where she was. After a pause, Michael said, "You're looking pretty sharp."

"Thanks. So are you."

An awkward pause ensued and Lisa stepped in to breach it. "Hey, Randy, look what Mom and Dad ordered—two limos!"

Bess continued down the stairs and Lisa smiled up at her. "Mom, this is just great! Does Mark know?"

"Not yet," Bess answered. "And he won't till he gets to the church. Grooms aren't supposed to see their brides before the service."

Michael looked up and followed Bess's descent, taking in her pale peach suit and matching silk pumps, the pearls gleaming at her ears and throat, her hair flaring back and touching her collar, the soft smile on her lips. She stopped on the second to the last step, her hand on the newel post. The town idiot could have detected the magnetism between them. Their gazes met and riveted while Michael touched his apricot cummerbund in the unconscious preening gesture men make at such times.

"Hello, Michael," Bess said quietly.

"Bess . . . you look sensational."

"I was thinking the same thing about you."

He smiled at her for interminable seconds before becoming aware that his children were observing. "Well, I'd say we all look great." He stepped back to include the two. "Randy . . . and Lisa, our beautiful bride."

"Absolutely beautiful," Bess agreed, moving toward her. Lisa's hair was drawn back by two combs and fell in glossy ringlets behind. Bess turned her by an arm. "Your hair turned out just lovely. Do you like it?"

"Yes, miracle of miracles, I do."

"Good. Well, we should go. Pictures at five on the dot."

Michael said, "May I get your coat, Bess?"

"Yes, it's in the closet behind you, and Lisa's, too."

Lisa said, "No, I'm not going to wear mine. It'll only wrinkle my dress. Besides, it feels like spring out there."

Michael opened the closet door as he'd done hundreds of times, got out Bess's coat while Lisa took her veil from the living-room doorway and Randy picked up her overnight bag.

"How are we doing this?" Randy asked as they headed outside toward the two waiting cars with their liveried drivers standing beside them.

Michael was the last one out of the house and closed the front door. "Your mother and I thought we'd ride in one, and Randy, you can escort Lisa . . . if that's okay with you."

The limousine drivers smiled, and one tipped his visored hat and extended his hand as Lisa approached.

"Right this way, miss, and congratulations. You've got a beautiful day for a wedding."

Lisa put one foot into the car, then changed her mind and leaned back out as Bess was preparing to step into the second car.

"Hey, Mom and Dad," she called. Bess and Michael both looked over. "Tell Randy not to pick his nose while we're in church. This time the whole congregation will be watching."

Everyone laughed while Randy threatened to push Lisa face-first into the limo as he would have when they were children.

The limo doors closed everyone inside and in the lead car, Lisa reached over and patted Randy's cheek. "Nice job back there, little brother. And your eyes look better today, too."

He said, "Something's going on between those two."

Lisa said, "Oh, I hope so."

In the trailing car, Michael and Bess sat on the white leather seat a careful space apart, employing discipline to keep their eyes off each other. They felt resplendent, wondrous, radiant! Not only in solo but in duet, down to their color-coordinated clothing.

When the temptation became too great, he turned his gaze on her and said, "That felt just like when we used to leave for church on Sunday mornings."

She allowed herself to look at him, too. "I know what you mean."

The limo pulled away from the curb while their eyes lingered. It turned a corner and the driver said, "The bride is your daughter?"

"Yes, she is," Michael answered, glancing up front.

"Happy day, then," the driver ventured.

"Very happy," Michael replied, returning his gaze to Bess while the day became charged with possibilities. The driver closed a glass partition and they were alone. The climate was right, seductive even, and the trappings romantic. Neither of them denied that the past and the present were both at work, wooing and weakening them.

In a while Michael said, "You changed the carpet in the entry hall."

"Yes."

"And the wallpaper."

"Yes."

"I like it."

She looked away in a vain attempt to recall common sense. His image remained in her mind's eye, alluring in his wedding finery of apricot and cream.

"Bess?" Michael covered her hand on the seat between them. It took a great deal of self-restraint for her to withdraw it.

"Let's be sensible, Michael. We're going to be bumping up against nostalgic feelings all day long but that doesn't change what is."

"What is?" he asked.

"Michael, don't. It's just not smart."

He studied her awhile, with a pleasant expression on his face. "All right," he decided. "If that's the way you want it."

They rode the remainder of the distance without speaking but she felt his eyes on her a lot and her own pulse so close to the surface of her throat she thought it must show. It felt exhilarating, and bewildering, and oh so threatening.

At the church the Padgett family had already arrived. The appearance of the limousines set off an excited reaction. Mark, dressed in a tux identical to Michael's and Randy's, saw his bride arriving and smiled disbelievingly as he opened the back door and stuck his head inside.

"*Where* did you get this?"

"Mom and Dad rented it for us. Isn't it great?"

There were hugs and thanks and exuberations exchanged on the church steps before the entire party went inside, where the photographer was setting up his equipment and the personal flowers were waiting in flat white boxes in the bride's changing room. A full-length mirror hung on the wall there, too, and before it, Bess helped Lisa don her veil while the Padgett ladies fussed with their own last-minute adjustments. Bess secured the hidden combs in Lisa's hair and added two bobby pins for good measure.

"Is it straight?" Bess asked.

"It's straight," Lisa approved. "Now my bouquet. Would you get it, Mom?"

Bess opened one of the boxes. The green tissue paper whispered back and her hands became still. There, nestled in the waxy green nest was a bouquet of apricot roses and creamy white freesias that exactly duplicated the one Bess had carried at her wedding in 1968.

She turned to Lisa, who stood with her back to the mirror, watching Bess.

"No fair, darling," Bess said emotionally.

"All's fair in love and war, and I believe this is both."

Bess looked down at the flowers and felt her composure giving way, along with her will to keep things sensible between herself and Michael.

"What a cunning young woman you've become."

"Thank you."

Sentiment welled up within Bess, bringing the faint blur of tears.

"And if you make me cry and ruin my makeup before the ceremony even begins I'll never forgive you." She lifted the bouquet from the waxy green paper. "You took our wedding pictures to the florist, of course."

"Of course." Lisa approached her mother and lifted Bess's chin, smiling into her glistening eyes. "It's working, I think."

Bess said with a quavery smile, "You naughty, conniving, conscienceless girl."

Lisa laughed and said, "There's one in there for Daddy, too. Go pin it on him, will you?" To the other women in the room, she said, "Everybody, take the men's boutonnieres out and make them stand still while you pin them on, will you? Maryann, would you do Randy's?"

Randy saw Maryann walking toward him dressed like some celestial being. Her black hair hung in a cloud against a dress the color of a half-ripe peach. It had short sleeves as big as basketballs, which caught on the tips of her shoulders and seemed to be held there by a sorcerer's spell. Her collarbones showed, and her throat, and the entire sweep of her shoulders above a very demure V-neck.

Maryann walked toward Randy, thinking that in her entire life she'd never met anyone as handsome. His cream-colored tuxedo and apricot bow tie were created to be modeled against his dark skin, hair and eyes. She'd never cared much for boys who wore their hair past their collars but his was beautiful. She'd never cared much for swarthy coloring but his was appealing. She'd never hung around with underachievers but Lisa said he was bright. She'd certainly never gone with wild boys but he represented an element of risk toward which she gravitated as all habitually good girls will at least once in their lives.

"Hi," she said quietly, stopping before him.

"Hi."

His lips were full and beautifully shaped and had a lot of natural pigment. Of the few boys she'd kissed, none had been endowed with a mouth as inviting. She liked the way his lips remained parted while he stared at her, and the faint flare of pink that tinged his cheeks beneath his natural dark skin, and his long, black, spiky eyelashes framing deep brown eyes that seemed unable to look away.

"They sent me with your flower. I'm supposed to pin it on you."

"Okay," he said.

She pulled the pearl-headed pin from an apricot rose and slipped her fingers beneath his left lapel. They stood so close she caught the scent of his after-shave, and whatever he put on his hair to hold it in place and make it so shiny, and the new-linen smell of his freshly cleaned tuxedo.

"Maryann?"

She looked up with her fingertips still close to his heart.

"I'm really sorry about last night."

Was his heart racing like hers? "I'm sorry, too." She returned to her occupation with his boutonniere.

"No girl ever made me watch my mouth before."

"I probably could have been a little more tactful about it."

"No. You were right and I was wrong, and I'll try to watch it today."

She finished pinning on his flower and stepped back. When she looked into his face again a picture flashed across her mind, of him with drumsticks in his hands, and sweatbands on his wrists, and a bandanna tied around his forehead to catch the perspiration while he beat the drums to some outrageously loud and raucous song.

The image fit as surely as Mendelssohn and Brahms fit into her life.

Still, he was so handsome he was beautiful, and his obvious infatuation with her resounded within some depth of womanliness that had lain dormant in Maryann until now.

Today, she thought, for just one day I will bend my own rules.

Bess, too, had taken a boutonniere from the box and gone out in the vestibule to find Michael. Approaching him, she thought how some things never change. Males and females were made to move through the world two-by-two, and in spite of the Women's Movement, there would be tasks that remained eternally appropriate for one sex to do for the other. At Thanksgivings, men carved turkeys. At weddings, women pinned on corsages.

"Michael?" she said.

He turned from conversation with Jake Padgett and she experienced a fresh zing of reaction at his uncommon pulchritude. It happened much as it had when they were dating years ago. The moment his dark eyes settled on hers, embers were stirred.

"I have your boutonniere."

"Would you mind pinning it on for me?"

"Not at all." Performing the small favor for him brought back the many times she'd brushed a piece of lint off his shoulder, or closed a collar button, or any one of the dozens of niceties exchanged by husbands and wives. It brought her, too, the smell of his British Sterling at closer range, and the warmth of his body emanating from beneath his crisp lapel as she slipped her hand beneath it.

"Hey, Bess?" he said softly. She glanced up, then back at the stubborn stickpin that refused to pierce the wrapping around the flower stem. "Do you feel old enough to have a daughter getting married?"

The pin did its job and the boutonniere was anchored. She corrected its angle, smoothed his lapel and looked into Michael's eyes. "No."

"Can you believe it? We're forty."

"No, I'm forty. You're forty-three."

"Cruel woman," he said, with a grin in his eyes.

She backed up a step and said, "I suppose you noticed Lisa picked the same colors we had in our wedding."

"I wondered if it was just a coincidence."

"It isn't. Get ready for another one—she took our wedding pictures to the florist and got a bouquet just like mine."

"Did she really?"

Bess nodded.

"This girl is serious about her matchmaking, isn't she?"

"I have to admit, it did things to me when I saw it."

"Oh yeah?" He dipped his knees to bring his eyes level with hers, still grinning.

"Oh yeah, and don't get so smug. She looks absolutely radiant, and if you can look at her without getting misty I'll pay you ten bucks."

"Ten bucks I got. If we're going to bet, let's at least pick something that—"

Someone interrupted. "Is this the fellow who's been sending me Mother's Day cards for six years?" It was Stella, in her bright silvery tiers, coming at Michael with her arms spread.

"Stella!" he exclaimed. "You beautiful dame!"

They hugged with true affection. "Ah, Michael," she said, cheek-to-cheek with him, "if you aren't a sight for sore eyes." She backed up, commandeering both his hands. "Lord in heaven, you get better-looking every six years!"

He laughed and kept her hands in his larger, darker ones, then clicked his tongue against his cheek. "You, too." He looked down at her delicate satin pumps. "But is this any way for a grandma to dress?"

She kicked up one foot. "Orthopedic high heels," she said, "if it'll make you feel any better. Come on. You, too, Bess, I want you to meet my main man."

They had barely shaken hands with Gil Harwood when the bride appeared in full regalia. She stepped into the vestibule and both Michael and Bess lost communion with everything but her. They turned to her as one, and as she began moving toward them Michael's hand found Bess's and gripped it tightly.

"Oh, my God," he whispered, for both of them.

She was a pretty young woman, the synthesis of her mother and father, and as she moved toward them they were aware of many things—how nature had amalgamated the best features of both of them into her face and frame; how happy she was, smiling and eager for this wedding and her future life with her chosen; that she carried their first grandchild. But mostly they were aware of how carefully she had recreated aspects of their own wedding.

The dress rustled just as it had when Bess wore it.

The veil was a close match to Bess's own.

The bouquet might have been preserved intact from that day.

"Mom, Dad . . ." she said, reaching them, resting a hand on each of their shoulders and raising her face for a touch of cheeks. "I'm so happy."

"And we're happy for you," Bess said.

Michael added, "Honey, you look absolutely beautiful."

"Yes, she does," Mark spoke, coming to claim her.

The photographer interrupted. "Everyone, please! I need the wedding party at the front of the church right now. We're behind schedule!"

As Lisa moved away and the mélange of shifting began toward the front of the church, Michael's eyes found Bess's.

"Even though you warned me, it's still a shock. I thought for a second it was you."

"I know. It's very disconcerting, isn't it?"

During the next hour, while the photographer set up pose after pose, Michael and Bess seemed to be always together, whether in the picture or watching from the sidelines, intensely aware of each other's presence while recounting scenes from their own wedding.

Late in the photo session the photographer turned and called, "Now the members of the bride's family. Immediate family only, please."

There was a moment of hesitation on Michael's part before Lisa motioned him forward and said, "You too, Dad. Come on."

Moments later there they were—Michael, Bess, Lisa and Randy—on two steps in the sacristy of St. Mary's, the church where Michael and Bess had been married, where Lisa and Randy had been baptized, confirmed and received their first Communion, where they had gone as a family during all those happy years.

"Let's have Mom and Dad stand on the top step, and you two just in front of them," the photographer said, motioning them into position. "A little to your left . . ." He pointed to Randy. "And Dad, put your hand on his shoulder."

Michael placed his hand on Randy's shoulder and felt his own heart swell at touching him again.

"That's good. Now everybody squeeze in just a little tighter. . . ."

The photographer peered through his viewfinder while they stood close enough to feel one another's body warmth, touching where they were ordered.

And Lisa thought, Please let this work.

And Bess thought, Hurry or I'll cry.

And Randy thought, Dad's hand feels good.

And Michael thought, Keep me here forever.

chapter 11

DURING THE FINAL MINUTES while guests milled in the vestibule and the bride and her mother were having their photo taken in the dressing room, Michael turned and saw two familiar faces coming toward him.

"Barb and Don!" he exclaimed, breaking into a huge smile. The surprise stunned him even as he hugged the couple, who had been best man and maid of honor at his own wedding. During his years with Bess they had been dear friends but in the years since the divorce, some queer misplaced sense of unworthiness had prompted him to let their friendship flag. He had not seen them in over five years. Hugging Barb, he felt his emotions billow, and shaking Don's hand brought such a sharp pang of fraternity, it simply wasn't enough: he caught him in a quick embrace that was returned with equal heartiness.

"We've missed you," Don said at Michael's ear, squeezing so hard Michael's bow tie compressed his windpipe.

"I missed you, too . . . both of you."

The words brought a shaft of regret for the years lost, of pleasure for the friends retouched.

"What happened? How come we never heard from you?"

"You know how it is . . . hell, I don't know."

"Well, this segregation is going to end."

There wasn't time for more. Others found Michael—former neighbors, aunts and uncles from both sides, some of Lisa's old high-school friends and Bess's sister Joan and her husband, Clark, who had flown in from Denver.

Soon the ushers seated the last of the guests. The vestibule quieted. The bride prepared to make her entrance. While Maryann arranged Lisa's train, Michael found a moment to whisper to Bess, "Don and Barb are here."

Surprise and delight lit her expression. She quickly scanned the heads of the seated guests but of course, they were facing front, and furthermore, it was time for the ceremony to begin. The ushers unfurled the white runner. The priest and servers waited up front. The organ rumbled. The strains of *Lohengrin* filled the nave. Bess and Michael took their positions on either side of Lisa and watched Randy head up the aisle with Maryann on his elbow.

When their turn came, they stepped out onto the white runner with their emotions running as close to the surface as at any time since the plans for this day had begun. Bess's knees shook. Michael's insides trembled. They passed the sea of faces turned toward them without singling out any. They gave up their daughter to the waiting groom, then stood side-by-side until the traditional question was asked: "Who gives this woman?"

Michael answered, "Her mother and I do," then escorted Bess to the front pew, where they took their places side-by-side.

In a day laden with emotional impact, this hour was the worst. Michael and Bess felt themselves moved by it from the time Father Moore smiled benignly on the bride and groom and told the gathered witnesses, "I've known Lisa since the night she came into this world. I baptized her when she was two weeks old, gave her her first Communion when she was seven and confirmed her when she was twelve, so it feels quite fitting that I should be the one conducting this ceremony today." Father Moore's gaze encompassed the assembled as he went on. "I know many of you who have come as guests today to witness these vows." His eyes touched Bess and Michael and moved on to others. "I welcome you on behalf of Lisa and Mark, and thank you for coming. How wonderful that by your presence you do honor not only to this young couple who are about to embark on a lifetime of love and faithfulness to one another, but you express your own faith in the very institution of marriage and family, and the time-enriched tradition of one man, one woman, promising their fidelity and love to one another till death do them part.

"Till death do them part . . . that's a long, long time." The soliloquy went on, while Michael and Bess sat inches apart and took in every word. The priest told a lovely story about a very rich man who, upon the occasion of his wedding, so wanted to show his love for his bride that he imported a hundred thousand silk worms and upon the eve of his wedding had them released in a mulberry grove. In the pre-dawn hours the grove was laced with the efforts of their night's spinning, and before the dew had dried on the silken threads the groom ordered that gold dust be sprinkled over the entire grove. There, in this gilded bower by which the rich man attempted to manifest his love, he and his bride spoke their vows just as the sun smiled over the horizon, lighting the entire scene to a splendiferous, glittering display.

To the nuptial couple the priest said, "A fitting gift, most certainly, this gift the rich man gave his new bride. But the richest gold a husband can bring to his wife, and a wife to her husband, is not that which can be sprinkled on silk threads, or bought in a jewelry store, or placed on a hand. It is the love and faithfulness they bring to one another in the ongoing years as they grow old together."

From the corner of her eye Bess saw Michael turn his head to look at her. The seconds stretched on until she finally looked up at him. His expression was solemn, his gaze steady. She felt it as one feels a change of season on a particular morning when a door is flung open to reveal that winter is gone. She dropped her gaze to her lap. Still he continued watching her. Her concentration was besieged, and the words of the priest became lost on her.

She tried letting her gaze wander but always it returned to Michael, to the fringes of his clothing, which was all she'd allow herself to watch . . . to his knees . . . to the side seam of his tuxedo, which touched the edge of her skirt . . . to his cuffs, his elegant hands resting in his lap, the hands that had touched her so many times, that had held their newborn babies, and provided a living for them, and had rung the doorbell earlier today and had hugged Lisa and touched Randy so tentatively several times that she'd seen. Oh, how she still loved Michael's hands.

She emerged from her preoccupation to find everyone getting to their feet, and she followed suit, bumping elbows with Michael as he rose and jiggled his right knee to drop his pantleg into place. It was one of those little things that got her: Michael jiggling his pantleg down the way she remembered from a past when such a simple action meant nothing. Now it took on undue significance simply because it was happening beside her again.

They sat once more and Bess felt Michael's upper arm flush against hers. Neither of them drew away.

Father Moore spoke again, letting his eyes communicate with the congregation. "During the exchange of vows, the bride and groom invite all of you who are married to join hands and reaffirm your own wedding vows along with them." Lisa and Mark faced each other and joined hands.

Mark spoke clearly, for all to hear.

"I, Mark, take thee, Lisa . . ."

Tears rolled down Bess's cheeks and darkened two spots on her suit jacket. Michael found a handkerchief and put it in her hand, then, in the valley between them, where no one else could see, he found her free hand, squeezed it hard, and she squeezed back.

"I, Lisa, take thee, Mark . . ."

Lisa, their firstborn, in whom so many hopes had been realized, during whose reign as the center of their world they had been so unutterably happy. Lisa had them holding hands again.

"By the power invested in me by God the father, the son and the holy spirit, I now pronounce you man and wife. You may kiss the bride."

While Lisa raised her happy face for Mark's kiss, Michael's hand squeezed Bess's so hard she feared the bones might snap.

In consolation?

Regret?

Affection?

It mattered not, for she was squeezing his right back, needing that link with him, needing the firm pressure of their entwined fingers and their locked palms. She studied the back of Randy's head and said a silent prayer that his antipathy with Michael would end. She watched Lisa's train slide up three steps as she and Mark approached the altar to light the unity candle. A clear soprano voice sang "He has chosen you for me . . ." and still Michael's hand gripped hers, his thumb now drawing the pattern of an angel's wing across the base of her own.

The song ended and the organ played quietly as Lisa and Mark came toward their mothers, each carrying a long red rose. Mark approached Bess and Michael released her hand.

Over the pew, Mark kissed her cheek and said, "Thank you for being here together. You've really made Lisa happy." Shaking Michael's hand, he said, "I'll keep her happy, I promise."

Lisa came next, kissing each of them on the cheek. "I love you, Mom. I love you, Dad. Watch Mark and me and we'll show you how it's done."

When she was gone Bess had to use Michael's hanky once more. A moment later, as they were kneeling, he nudged her elbow and reached out a hand, palm-up. She placed the hanky in it and concentrated on the proceedings while he wiped his eyes and blew his nose, then tucked the handkerchief away in his rear pocket.

They celebrated the remainder of the Mass together, received Communion as they had in the past and tried to figure out what it had meant when they'd held hands during the vows while for the rest of the service they maintained a careful distance, touching no longer. When the organ burst forth with the recessional they were smiling, following their children from the church, Michael's hand holding Bess's elbow.

Lisa had insisted there be no receiving line at the church: it put a crimp in the festivities and made some people uncomfortable. So when the bridal party burst from the double doors of St. Mary's, their guests burst right behind them. The hugs and felicitations that happened on the church steps were spontaneous, accompanied by a quick shower of wheat and a retreat to the waiting limousines.

The bride and groom piled into the first car, the photographer snapped some pictures and Michael called, "Randy and Maryann, you can ride with us!"

Regretfully, Maryann replied, "I'd like to but I brought my own car."

Randy said, "I guess I'll ride with Maryann, then. See you there."

Bess touched Michael's arm. "I have to get Lisa's things from the changing room. I told her I'd bring them to the reception."

"I'll come with you."

They reentered the church and went to the brightly lit room where it was quiet and they were alone. Bess began collecting Lisa's street shoes, makeup, overnight bag. She was putting the smaller bag into the larger one when a great wave of melancholy struck. She released the handles of the duffel bag, covered her eyes and dropped her chin. Standing with her back to Michael she fished in the duffel bag for Kleenex while she felt a first sob building.

"Hey . . . hey . . . what's this?" Michael turned her around and took her gently in his arms.

"I don't know," she sniffled, with her hand between them, covering her nose with the tissue. "I just feel like crying."

"Ah, well, I guess it's allowed. You're her mother."

"But I feel like such a jerk."

"Doesn't matter. You're still her mother."

"Oh, Michael, she's all married."

"I know. She was our baby and now she doesn't belong to us anymore."

Bess gave in to the awful need to let the tears go. She put both arms around his shoulders and bawled. He held her loosely and rubbed her back. In his arms she felt less like a jerk. When her tears had stopped she remained against him. "Remember when she was little, how she used to put on shows for us?"

"And we thought for sure she was going to be the next Barbra Streisand."

"And how she always had to sit up on the cupboard when I was baking cookies and try to help me stir. Her head would always be in my way."

"And the time she tied her doll blanket around the light bulb in her playhouse and nearly burned the house down?"

"And the time she fractured her arm when she was ice skating and the doctor had to break it completely before he could put it in a cast? Oh, Michael, I'd sooner have had him break my own arm than hers."

"I know. Me, too."

They grew quiet, reminiscing. In time they became aware that they stood quite comfortably in a full-length embrace.

Bess drew back and said, "I've probably ruined your tuxedo." She brushed at his shoulder while his hands rested at her waist.

"We did all right by her, Bess." Michael's voice was quiet and sincere. "She's turned into a real winner."

Bess looked into his eyes. "I know. And I know she'll be happy with Mark, too, so I promise I'm done with these tears."

They remained awhile longer, enjoying the closeness, until she forced herself to step back. "I promised Lisa we'd make sure this room was cleaned up. Would you mind closing up the flower boxes while I fix my face?"

He dropped his hands from her and said, "Don't mind a bit."

When she got a load of herself in the mirror, Bess said, "Mercy, what a mess."

Michael looked back over his shoulder while packing up the floral tailings. Bess opened her purse and began repairing her makeup. Michael put the box on a chair by the door, zipped up Lisa's duffel bag and added it to the collection, then ambled back to Bess and stood behind her, watching in the mirror as she did mysterious things to her eyes.

"Don't watch me," she said, tipping her head to catch the light properly.

"Why?"

"It makes me nervous."

"Why?"

"It's personal."

"I've watched you do other things that were a lot more personal."

Her hand paused as she glanced at him in the mirror. He was exactly half a head taller than she. His bow tie and white winged collar showed above her shoulder, setting off his dark features and black hair to best advantage.

She went back to work, dotting green kohl beneath her eyes, smudging it with a fingertip, while he stood with his hands strung into his trouser pockets, defying her order and studying each move she made as though he enjoyed every minute of it. She tipped her head back and put mascara on her upper lashes, tipped it down to do the lower.

"I don't remember you going to all this fuss before."

"I took a class."

"In what?"

"Not a class, exactly. I had a beauty make-over."

"When?"

"Right after our divorce. Soon as I started earning money."

"You know what?" He let his lips hint at a grin and said quietly, "It worked, Bess." Their eyes met in the mirror while she made a grand effort to appear unruffled. When the effort failed, she dropped her mascara wand into her purse and snapped it shut.

"Michael, are you flirting with me?" She lifted her chin and fluffed at the hair behind her left ear.

He let the grin grow and took her elbow. "Come on, Bess, let's go celebrate our daughter's wedding."

The reception and dance were held at the Riverwood Club overlooking the St. Croix, out in the country on the Wisconsin side of the river. They rode there in the leather-wrapped privacy of the limousine, each on his own half of the seat, with not so much as their hems touching. Dark had fallen but as they descended the hill toward downtown Stillwater streetlights glanced into the car and swept across their shoulders, sometimes the sides of their faces. Occasionally they would let their eyes drift over one another, waiting for the sweep of lights to illuminate the other's face, and after it did, would turn their gazes out the windows with studied nonchalance.

They crossed the bridge to a whining note of tires on textured metal and left Minnesota behind as the car climbed the steep grade toward Houlton.

Finally Michael turned, letting his knee cross the halfway point on the seat.

"Bess?" he said.

She searched out his face on the other side of the seat. They had left the streetlights behind now and traveled through upland farm country.

"What, Michael," she said at last.

He drew a breath and hesitated, as if what he was about to say had taken great mulling.

"Nothing," he said at last, and she released her disappointment in a careful breath.

The Riverwood Club sprawled high above the banks of the river in a stand of knotty oaks. On the landward side it was approached by a horseshoe-shaped drive leading to an open-arms style entry reminiscent of a seventeenth-century Charlestonian mansion. The two arcs of its sweeping front stairs embraced a heart-shaped shrubbery garden filled with evergreens, trimmed at an angle to follow the descending steps. Above, six white fluted columns rose two floors, setting off the club's grand front veranda.

Michael helped Bess alight from the limo, took her elbow as they mounted the left stairway, opened the heavy front door, took her coat, checked it with his own and pocketed the number.

The entry held a chandelier the size of Maryland and a magnificent, free-flying staircase that led to the ballroom above.

"So this is what we're paying for," Michael remarked as they mounted the stairs, his knees lifting in perfect rhythm with Bess's. "Well, I don't know about you, but I intend to get my money's worth."

He started with the champagne. A fountain of it flowed just inside the entry to the ballroom, and beside it a cloth-covered table held a pyramid of stem glasses that a juggler would think twice about disturbing. Michael plucked one from the top and asked Bess, "How about you? Champagne?"

"Since we're paying for it, why not?"

With their glasses in hand they headed into the crowd to mingle. Bess found herself trailing Michael, stopping when he stopped, visiting with whom he visited, as if they were still married. When she realized what she was doing she drifted off in another direction, only to find herself searching him out across the room. Round tables with apricot-colored cloths circled a parquet dance floor. Above it, the mate to the entry chandelier hung in splendor, shedding whiskey-hued light over the gathering. Every table held a candle, their dozens of flames reflected in one entire wall of glass that looked out over the river, where the lights of Stillwater lit the sky to the northwest. It was a huge room, yet she could pick Michael out among the crowd within seconds of trying, his pale tuxedo and dark hair beckoning from wherever he stood.

She was studying him from clear across the room when Stella came up behind her shoulder and said, "He's easily the best-looking man in the place. Gil thinks so, too."

"Mother, you're incorrigible."

"Were you two holding hands during those vows?"

"Don't be absurd."

Heather came along with her husband in tow and said, "I loved the ceremony, and I *love* this room! I'm so glad you invited us."

They moved on and Hildy Padgett was there, saying, "Thank heavens I don't have to go through *that* every day."

Jake, beside her, said, "She cried all through the ceremony."

"So did I," Bess admitted.

Randy and Maryann showed up and began visiting with the group. Lisa and Mark appeared, holding hands, being hugged and kissed by everyone. Bess hadn't realized Michael had drifted up behind her until Lisa hugged him and said, "Wow, Daddy, you look good enough to be dessert. Speaking of which, I think they're ready to start serving dinner now. Mom and Dad, you're at the head table with us."

Once again Bess and Michael found themselves seated together while their food was served and Father Moore stood to say grace.

They dined on beef tips in wine sauce, wild rice and broccoli, relaxing even more with each other. The servers came around to refill their champagne glasses for the official toast.

Randy, as best man, stood to make it.

"Attention! Attention, everyone!" he said, buttoning his tuxedo jacket and waiting for the rustle of conversation to die. Several people clinked their glasses with spoons and the room quieted.

"Well, today I watched my big sister get married." Randy paused and scratched his head. "Boy, am I glad. She always used up the last of the hot water and left me with . . ." Laughter drowned out the rest of his recollection. He picked up again when he could be heard. "No, really, Lisa, I couldn't be happier for you. And you, too, Mark. Now you get to share the bathroom with her and fight for mirror time." Laughter again before Randy got sentimental. "Seriously, Lisa . . . Mark . . . I think you're both pretty great." He saluted them with his glass. "So here's to love and happiness, on your wedding day and for the rest of your lives. We hope you have plenty of both."

Everyone sipped and applauded, and Randy resumed his place beside Maryann.

She smiled at him and said, "That seems to come naturally to you."

He shrugged and said, "I suppose so."

"So you'll love it on stage when you get there."

He drank some champagne and grinned. "What, you don't think I'll get there?"

"How can I know? I've never even heard you play."

They ate awhile, then he said, "So tell me about these sports you're in. I suppose you've lettered."

"All three years."

"And you get straight A's."

"Of course."

"And you edit your yearbook."

"School paper."

"Oh . . . school paper, sorry." He studied her and asked, "So what do you do for fun?"

"What do you mean? All that is fun. I *love* school."

"Besides school."

"I do a lot with my church group. I'm thinking of going to Mexico this summer to help the hurricane victims there. It's all being arranged by the church. Fifty of us can go but we all have to raise our own money to pay our way."

"Doing what?"

"We raise pledges."

The concept boggled him. Church group? Hurricane victims? Pledges?

"So what'll you do there?"

"A lot of very hard work. Mix concrete, put roofs back on, sleep in hammocks and go without baths for a week."

"Pardon me, but if you go without baths those Mexicans are going to want you out of there long before a week is up."

She laughed, covering her mouth with a napkin.

"You smell good tonight, though," he said in his flirtiest fashion, and her laughter died. She lowered the napkin, blushed and transferred her attention to her plate.

"Is that the line you use on all the girls?"

"All what girls?"

"I figure there must be plenty of them. After all, you aren't exactly Elephant Man."

He told her the truth. "The last girl I dated seriously was Carla Utley and we were in the tenth grade."

"Oh, come on. You don't expect me to believe that."

"It's true."

"The tenth grade?"

"I've taken girls out since then, but none of them were serious."

"So what else? You do a lot of one-night stands?"

He leveled his dark, long-lashed eyes on hers and said, "For a beautiful girl you sure are vicious."

She blushed again, which pleased him.

She was the prettiest, freshest, most inviolable creature he'd ever had the pleasure of spending an evening with, and he thought with some astonishment that it was going to be the first time in years he kissed a girl without thumping her into bed.

Someone started tapping a champagne glass with a spoon, and the entire phalanx of wedding guests caught the cue and filled the ballroom with chiming.

Mark and Lisa rose to their feet and performed the ritual with gusto. They gave their guests a good one—a lusty French kiss that lasted five seconds.

While Maryann watched the proceedings, Randy watched her. She appeared transported while she took in the kiss with her own lips slightly parted.

When the bride and groom sat down the crowd burst into applause. All but Maryann. She dropped her eyes self-consciously, then, sensing Randy's unbroken regard, flashed a quick, embarrassed glance his way. It lasted only long enough for Maryann to grow more flustered but as her glance fled away, for the merest fraction of a second her eyes detoured to his lips.

The meal ended. Milling began and a band started setting up. Michael pushed back his chair and said to Bess, "Let's go mingle."

They did so together, catching up with relatives they'd each lost through divorce, with old friends, new friends, neighbors whose children had played with Lisa and Randy in their elementary-school days—a hall full of familiar people who politely refrained from asking their status as a couple.

They came at last to Barb and Don Maholic, who saw them approaching and rose from their chairs. The men clasped hands. The women hugged.

"Oh, Barb, it's good to see you," Bess said emotionally.

"It's been too darn long."

"It must be five years."

"At least. We were so happy to get the wedding invitation, and what a beautiful bride Lisa is. Congratulations."

"She is, isn't she? It's hard not to get teary-eyed when you watch one of your kids get married. So tell me about yours."

"Come on. Sit down and let's catch up."

The men brought drinks and the four of them sipped and talked. About their kids. About their businesses. About trips and mutual acquaintances and their parents. The band started up and they talked a little louder, leaning closer to be heard.

In the background, the bandleader called the bridal couple onto the floor as the group struck into "Could I Have This Dance." Lisa and Mark walked out beneath the chandelier and as they danced, captured the attention of everyone in the room, including Bess and Michael.

The bandleader called, "Let's have the other members of the wedding party join them."

Across the hall, Randy turned to Maryann and said, "I guess that means us."

Jake Padgett stood and said to his wife, "Mother?"

Over Mark's shoulder, Lisa pointed and gestured to Michael: *ask Mother!*

He glanced at Bess. She had her forearms crossed on the table and was watching Lisa with a wistful smile on her lips. At the turn of Michael's head, she turned her own.

"Dance, Bess?" he asked.

"I think we should," she answered.

He pulled out her chair and followed her onto the dance floor, conscious of Lisa's wide smile as she watched. He winked at the bride and turned to open his arms to Bess.

She stepped into them wearing a smile, wholly glad to be with him again. They had danced together for sixteen years, in a fashion that attracted the admiring gazes of onlookers, which happened once again as they struck the waltz position, waited out the measure and stepped into the three-quarter rhythm with flawless grace. There might have been no lapse, so at ease were they together. They danced awhile, smiling, making wide sweeping turns, before Bess said, "We always did this well, didn't we, Michael?"

"And we haven't lost it."

"Isn't it great to do this with somebody who knows how?"

"Boy, you said it. I swear, *no*body knows how to waltz anymore."

"Keith surely doesn't."

"Neither does Darla."

They did it properly, with the accent on the first beat. If there'd been sawdust on the floor they'd have scraped a wreath of neat little triangles through it.

"Feels good, huh?"

"Mmm . . . comfortable."

When they'd danced for some time, Michael asked, "Who's Keith?"

"This man I've been seeing."

"Is it serious?"

"No. As a matter of fact, it's over." They went on waltzing, separated by a goodly space, happy and smiling at each other without any undercurrents. What each of them said, the other took at face value.

Bess inquired, "How are things between you and Darla?"

"Uncontested divorces go through the courts quite fast."

"Are the two of you talking?"

"Absolutely. We never stopped. We never cared enough to end it with a war."

"Like we did?"

"Mm."

"We were so bitter because we still cared, is that what you're saying?"

"I've thought about it. It's possible."

"Funny, my mother said essentially the same thing."

"Your mother looks great. What a pistol she is."

They chuckled and danced in silence until the song ended, then remained on the floor for another song, then another and another. Finally walking her off the floor after four numbers, Michael said at her ear, "Don't go far. I want to dance some more."

The music got louder and faster as the night wore on. There was a predominance of young people present, and more drifted in as the night got older. The band catered to their wishes. The slower ballads—"Wind Beneath My Wings," "Lady in Red"—gave way to the kind of songs that lured even doubtful middle-agers out onto the floor: "La Bamba" and "Johnny B. Goode." When the crowd had caught the fire and were heating up, the band threw in "The Twist," followed by "I Knew the Bride," which filled the dance floor and got everybody sweaty, including Michael and Bess, who'd been partners the entire night.

Moods were high. Michael said, "You mind if I dance one with Stella?"

"Heavens no," Bess replied. "She'd love it."

To Stella he said, "Come here, you painted hussy. I want to dance one with you."

Gil Harwood snared Bess, and at the end of the song the foursome switched partners.

"You having fun?" Michael asked as he reclaimed Bess.

"I'm having a ball!" she exclaimed.

They danced another fast, hot one and when it ended, Michael had curled Bess up against his side, puffing. "Come on, I gotta get rid of this jacket." He hauled her by the hand to the table where they'd left their drinks and draped his jacket over the back of a chair. They were taking quick gulps of their cocktails when the band struck up "Old Time Rock and Roll." Michael slammed his glass down on the table, said, "Come on!" and towed her back toward the dance floor. Behind him, she snapped his suspenders against his damp shirt and shouted above the music, "Hey, Curran!"

He turned and dipped his ear to catch what she was shouting in the din. "What?"

"You look pretty sexy in that tuxedo."

He laughed and said, "Yeah, well, try and control yourself, honey!" They elbowed their way into the crowd and launched themselves into the joie de vivre of the music once again.

It was easy to forget they were divorced, to join in the merriment, raising their hands above their heads and clapping while beside them old friends and family did the same thing and sang along with the familiar words. . . .

I like that old time rock and roll . . .

When the song ended they were flushed and exuberant. Michael stuck two fingers between his teeth and whistled. Bess clapped and thrust a fist in the air, shouting, "More! More!" But the set was over and they returned to Barb and Don's table, where all four of them collapsed into their chairs at the same time.

Sapped, exhilarated, wiping their brows, reaching for their glasses, they slipped back into the familiarity of their long-standing friendship.

"What a band."

"Aren't they great?"

"I haven't danced like this in years."

Barb's eyes glowed. "Gosh, it's good to see you two together again. Is this . . . I mean, are you two seeing each other?"

Michael glanced at Bess.

Bess glanced at Michael.

"No, not really," she said.

"Too bad. On the dance floor you look like you've never been apart."

"We're having a good time, anyway."

"So are we. How many times do you think the four of us went out dancing?"

"Who knows?"

"What happened anyway? Why did we all stop seeing each other?" Barb asked.

They all studied one another, recalling the fondness of the past and those awful months when the marriage was breaking up.

Bess spoke up. "I know one reason I stopped calling you. I didn't want you to have to take sides or choose between us."

"But that's silly."

"Is it? You were friends to both of us. I was afraid that anything I said to you might have been misconstrued as a bid for sympathy. And in a way, it probably would have been."

"I suppose you're right but we missed you, we wanted to help."

Michael said, "I felt pretty much the same as Bess, afraid to look as if I wanted you to take my side, so I just backed off."

Don had been sitting silently, listening. He sat forward, working the bottom of his glass against the tabletop as if it were a rubber stamp.

"Can I be honest here?"

Every eye turned to him. "Of course," Michael replied.

"When you two broke up, you want to know what I felt?" He waited but no one said a word. "I felt betrayed. We knew you two were having your differences but you never let on exactly how bad they were. Then one day you called and said, 'We're getting a divorce,' and selfish as it sounds now, I actually got angry. We had all these years invested in a four-way friendship, and all of a sudden—poufff!—you guys were dissolving it. The absolute truth of it is, I never blamed either one of you more than the other. Both Barb and I looked at your relationship through pretty clear eyes, and we were probably closer to you than anyone else at that time. Anyway, when you said you were getting divorced from each other it felt as if you were getting divorced from us."

Bess reached over and covered his hand. "Oh, Don . . ."

Now that he'd said his piece, he looked sheepish. "I know I sound like a selfish pig."

"No, you don't."

"I probably never would have said that if I hadn't had a couple of drinks."

Michael said, "I think it's good that the four of us can talk this way. We always could, that's why we were such good friends."

Bess added, "I never really looked at our breakup from your viewpoint before. I suppose I might have felt the same way if you'd been the ones divorcing."

Barb spoke in a caring tone. "I know you said you haven't been seeing each other but is there any chance you two might get back together? If I'm speaking out of line, tell me to shut up."

Silence fell over the group before Bess said, in the kindest tone possible, "Shut up, Barb."

Randy and Maryann had danced the entire night long, talking little in the raucousness, playing eye games. When the second set ended she fanned herself with a hand while he freed his bow tie and collar button and said, "Hey, it's hot in here. Want to go outside and cool off?"

"Sure."

They left the ballroom, walked down the grand staircase and collected her coat.

Outside, stars shone. The fecund smell of thawing earth lifted from the surrounding grounds and farmlands. Someplace nearby, rivulets of melted snow could be heard gurgling toward lower terrain. The air was heavy with damp that had left the painted floor of the veranda slippery.

Randy took Maryann's arm and walked her to the far end, where they stood looking out over the driveway while the evergreens below them threw out a pungent scent like gin.

Now don't say Jesus, he thought.

"You're a good dancer," Maryann said as he released her arm and braced his shoulder against a fluted pillar.

"So are you."

"No, I'm not. I'm just average but an average dancer looks better when she dances with a good one."

"Maybe it's you making me look good."

"No, I don't think so. You must get it from your mom and dad. They look great out there on the dance floor together."

"Yeah, I guess so."

"Besides, you're a drummer. It makes sense—good rhythm, good dancer."

"I never really danced much."

"Neither did I."

"Too busy getting straight A's?"

"You don't like that, do you?"

He shrugged.

"Why?"

"It scares me."

"Scares you! You?"

"Don't look so surprised. Things scare guys, you know."

"Why should my straight A's scare you?"

"It's not just them, it's the kind of girl you are."

"What kind am I?"

"Goody two-shoes. Church group. National Honor Society, I bet."

She made no reply.

"Right?" he asked.

"Yes."

"I haven't been around many girls like you."

"What kind have you been around?"

He chuckled and looked away. "You don't want to know."

"No, I guess I don't."

They stood awhile, looking out over the horseshoe-shaped drive, surrounded by the burgeoning spring night, a moon as thin and white as a daisy petal, and tree shadows like black lace upon the lawns. Once he looked over at her and she met his gaze, Randy with his ivory tuxedo sleeve braced upon the pale pillar, Maryann with her hands joined primly on the veranda railing.

"So a guy like me just doesn't . . . you know . . . make a play for a girl like you."

"Not even if you asked first and she said yes?"

Miss Maryann Padgett, in her proper little navy-blue coat, stood with her shoes perched neatly side-by-side, her hands on that railing, waiting. Randy drew his shoulder from the pillar and turned toward her, standing close without touching. She, too, turned to him.

"I've been thinking about you a lot since I met you."

"Have you?"

"Yeah."

"Well, then . . . ?" Her invitation was just reserved enough to make it acceptable.

He lowered his head and kissed her the way he used to kiss girls when he was in the seventh grade. Lips only, nothing wet, nothing else touching. She put her hands on his shoulders but kept her distance. He embraced her cautiously, letting her make the choice about the proximity of bodies. Close but not too close, she chose, resting against him the way chalk rests on a blackboard: a touch and it'll disappear. He offered his tongue and she accepted shyly, tasting the way she smelled—fresh, flowery, no alcohol or smoke. As kisses went, it remained chaste, but all the while sweetness coursed through him and he experienced a return to the innocent emotions of first kisses, knowing he wanted more of this girl than he either deserved or probably ought to dream about.

He lifted his head and kept a little space between them. Their fingertips were joined at arm's length.

"Pretty wild, huh?" He smiled, lopsided. "You and me, and Lisa and Mark?"

"Yeah, pretty wild."

"I wish I had my car tonight so I could drive you home."

"I have mine. Maybe I can drive you home."

"Is that an invitation?"

"It is."

"Then I accept."

She started to turn away but he stopped her. "One other thing."

"What?"

"Would you go out with me next Saturday? We could go to a movie or something."

"Let me think about it."

"All right."

He took a turn at turning away but she kept his hand and stood where she'd been. "I've thought about it." She smiled. "Yes."

"Yes?"

"Yes. With my parents' approval."

"Oh, of course." As if a parent had approved of him since he'd turned thirteen. "So what do you say we go dance some more?"

Smiling, they returned inside.

The band was blasting out "Good Lovin' " and the dancers were getting into it. His mom and dad were still on the floor, having a grand old time with their friends the Maholics and Grandma Stella and her date, who'd turned out to be a neat guy after all. Stella and the old dude were dancing the way old people do, looking ridiculous but enjoying it anyway. Randy and Maryann melded into the edge of the crowd and picked up the beat.

When the song ended, Randy heard Lisa's voice over the amplifiers and turned in surprise to see her standing on stage with a microphone.

"Hey, everybody, listen up!" When the crowd noise abated she said, "It's my special night so I get what I want, right? Well, I want my little brother up here—Randy, where are you?" She shaded her eyes and scanned the room. "Randy come up here, will you?"

Randy suffered some friendly nudging while panic sluiced through him. *Jesus, no, not without getting wrecked first!* But everyone was looking at him and there was no way he could slip outside and sneak a hit.

"A lot of you don't know it but my little brother is one of the better drummers around. Matter of fact, he's the best." She turned to the lead guitar man. "You don't mind if Randy sits in on one, do you, Jay?" And to the crowd, "I've been listening to him pounding his drums in his bedroom since he was three months old—well, that might possibly have been his heels on the wall beside his crib but you know what I mean. He hasn't done a lot of this in public, and he's a little shy about it, so after you hog-tie him and carry him up here, give him a hand, okay?"

Randy, genuinely embarrassed, was being encouraged to go onstage by a throng of his peers who circled him and Maryann.

"Yeah, Randy, do it!"

"Come on, man, hammer those skins!"

Maryann took his hand and said, "Go ahead, Randy, please."

With his palms sweating, he removed his tuxedo jacket and handed it to her. "Okay, but don't run away."

The drummer backed off his stool and stood as Randy leaped onto the stage and picked his way around the bass drum and cymbals. They did a little talking about sticks and Randy selected a pair from a quiver hanging on a drum. He straddled the revolving stool, gave the bass drum a few fast thumps, did a riff from high to low across the five drums circling him, tested the height of the cymbals and said to the lead guitar man, "How 'bout a little George Michael? You guys know 'Faith'?"

"Yo! 'Faith' we got." And to the band, "Give him a little 'Faith,' on his beat."

Randy gave them a lead-in on the rim and struck into the driving, syncopated beat of the song.

On the dance floor, Michael forgot to start dancing with Bess. She nudged him and he made a halfhearted attempt to do justice to both but the drumming won out. He bobbed absently while watching, entranced, as his son became immersed in the music, his attention shifting from drum to drum, to cymbal to drum, now bending, now reaching, now twirling a stick till it blurred. Some silent signal was exchanged and the band dropped off, giving Randy a solo. His intensity was total, his immersion complete. There were he and the drums and the rhythm running from his brain to his limbs.

Most of the crowd had stopped dancing and stood entranced, clapping to the rhythm. Those who continued dancing did so facing the stage.

At Michael's side Bess said, "He's good, isn't he?"

"My God, when did this happen?"

"It's been happening since he was thirteen. It's the only thing he really cares about."

"What the hell's he doing working in that nut house?"

"He's scared."

"Of what? Success?"

"Possibly. More probably of failure."

"Has he auditioned anywhere?"

"Not that I know of."

"He's got to, Bess. Tell him he's got to."

"You tell him."

The drum solo ended and the band picked up the last verse while on the floor Bess and Michael danced it out, reading messages in each other's eyes.

A roar of applause went up as Randy struck the cymbals for the last time and the song ended. He rested his hands on his thighs, smiled shyly and let the drumsticks slip back into the quiver.

"Good job, Randy," the band's drummer said, returning to the stage, shaking Randy's hand. "Who did you say you play with again?"

"I don't."

The drummer stopped cold, stared at Randy a moment and straddling his seat, said, "You ought to get yourself an agent, man."

"Thanks. Maybe I will."

On his way back to Maryann, he felt like Charlie Watts. She was smiling, holding his jacket while he slipped it on, then taking his arm, unconsciously resting her breast against it.

"You even look like George Michael," she said, still smiling proudly. "But I suppose all the girls tell you that."

"Now if I could only sing like him."

"You don't have to sing. You can play drums. You're really good, Randy."

None of the applause counted as much as her approval. "Thanks," he said, and wondered if it would still feel like this after twenty-five years of performing—the way Watts had been performing with the Stones all these years—the rush, the exhilaration, the high!

Suddenly his mother was there, kissing his cheek. "Sounds much better in a club than coming up the stairs." And his father, clapping his shoulder and squeezing hard, with a glint of immense pride in his smile.

"You've got to get out of that nut house, Randy. You're too good to squander all that talent."

If he moved, Randy knew, even half-moved toward his Dad he'd be in his arms and this stellar moment would be complete. But how could he do that with Maryann looking on? And his mother? And half the wedding guests? And Lisa coming at him with a big smile on her face, trailed by Mark? Then she was there and the moment was lost.

Jamming in somebody's basement had never been like this. By the time his praises had been sung by everyone who knew him and some who didn't, he still felt like a zinging neon comet and thought if he didn't smoke some grass to celebrate, he'd never have another chance to get the high-on-high. Christ, it'd be wild!

He looked around and Maryann was gone.

"Where's Maryann?" he asked.

"She went to the ladies' room. Said she'd be right back."

"Listen, Lisa, I'm kind of warm. I gotta go outside and cool off some, okay?"

Lisa mock-punched his arm. "Yeah, sure, little bro. And thanks again for playing."

He slumped his shoulders, gave her a crooked smile and saluted himself away.

"Any time."

Outside, he returned to the shadows at the far end of the veranda. The earth still smelled musty, and the runnels were still running, and the thump of the drums could be registered through the soles of his shoes. He packed his bat, lit it, took the hit and held it deep in his lungs, his eyes closed, blocking out the stars and the cars and the naked trees. It didn't take long. By the time he left the veranda he believed he *was* Charlie Watts.

He went inside to find Maryann. She was sitting at a table with her parents and some of her aunts and uncles.

"Hey, Maryann," he said, "let's dance."

Her eyes were like ice picks as she turned and took a chunk out of him. "No, thank you."

If he hadn't been stoned he might have done the sensible thing and backed off. Instead, he gripped her arm. "Hey, what do you mean?"

She jerked her arm free. "I think you know what I mean."

"What'd I do?"

Everyone at the table was watching. Maryann looked as if she hated him as she jumped to her feet. He smiled blearily at the group and mumbled, "Sorry . . ." then followed her out into the hall. They stood at the top of the elegant stairway down which they'd walked together such a short time earlier.

"I don't hang around with potheads, Randy," she said.

"Hey, wait, I don't—"

"Don't lie. I came outside looking for you and I saw you and I know what was in that little pipe! You can find your own way home, and as far as Saturday night goes, it's off. Go smoke your pot and be a loser. I don't care."

She picked up her skirts, turned and hurried away.

chapter 12

BESS AND MICHAEL RECLINED in the backseat of the limousine, a faint sense of motion scuttling up from the trunk and massaging the backs of their heads through the supple leather. Michael was laughing, deep in his throat. His eyes were closed.

"What are you laughing about?"

"This car feels like a Ferris wheel."

She rolled her head to look at him. "Michael, you're drunk."

"Yes, I am. First time for months and it feels spectacular. How 'bout you?" He rolled his head to look at her.

"A little, maybe."

"How does it feel?"

She faced upward again, closed her eyes and laughed deep in her throat. They enjoyed some silence, and the purring, easy-chair ride, the subtle euphoria created by the dancing and drinking and the presence of each other. In time, he spoke.

"You know what?"

"What?"

"I don't feel much like a grandpa."

"You don't dance much like a grandpa."

"Do you feel like a grandma?"

"Mm-mm."

"I don't remember *my* grandpa and grandma dancing like that when I was young."

"Me either. Mine raised irises and built birdhouses."

"Hey, Bess, come here." He clamped her wrist, tipped her his way and put an arm around her.

"Just what do you think you're doing, Michael Curran?"

"I'm feelin' *good!*" he said, exaggerating an accent. "And I'm feelin' *baaad!*"

She laughed, rolling her face against his lapel. "This is ridiculous. You and I are divorced. What are we doing snuggling in the backseat of a limo?"

"We bein' *bad!* And it feel so good we gonna keep right on doin' it!" He leaned forward and asked the driver, "How much time have we got?"

"As much as you want, sir."

"Then keep driving till I tell you to head back to Stillwater. Drive to Hudson! Drive to Eau Claire! Hell, drive to Chicago if you want to!"

"Whatever you say, sir." The driver laughed and faced full front again.

"Now where were we?" Michael settled back and reclaimed Bess, nestling her close.

"You were drunk and being foolish."

"Oh, that's right." He threw up his arms and started singing a chorus of "Good Lovin'," adding a few hip thrusts for good measure.

". . . gimme that good, good lovin' . . ."

She tried to pull away but he was too quick. "Oh no you don't. You're staying right here. We gotta talk about this now."

"Talk about what?" She couldn't resist smiling.

"This. Our firstborn, all married up and off someplace to spend her wedding night, and you and me only months away from becoming grandparents, dancin' our butts off while our secondborn plays the drums. I think there's some significance here."

"You do?"

"I think so but I haven't figured it out yet."

She settled beneath his arm and decided to enjoy being there. He kept on singing "Good Lovin' " very softly, mumbling the words so they barely moved his lips. Pretty soon she was mumbling softly in counterpoint.

He'd mumble, "Good lovin' . . ."

And she'd mumble, "Gimme that mmm-mmm-mmm . . ."

"Good lovin' . . ."

"Mm-mm-mm mm-mm-mmm-mmm . . ."

"Mm-mmm . . ."

"Mm-mm mm-mm-mm-mmm-mmm . . ."

He tapped out the drum rhythm on his left thigh and her right arm, then found her free hand and fit his fingers between hers, closed them and bent their elbows in lazy unison. She could feel his heartbeat beneath her jaw, could hear his humming resonate beneath her ear, could smell the diluted remnants of his cologne mingled with smoke on his jacket.

So quietly the sound of her own breathing nearly covered it up, he sang: "Good lovin' . . ."

"Mm-mm-mm mm-mm-mmm-mmm . . ."

Then nothing. Only the two of them, reclining on his half of the seat, holding hands and fitting their thumbs together and feeling and smelling one another while their arms wagged slowly down and up, and down and up . . .

He didn't say a word, just leaned forward, curled his hand around her far arm and kissed her. Her lips opened and his tongue came inside while she thought of the dozens of arguments she ought to voice. Instead she kissed him back, the leather seat soft against her head, his breath warm against her cheek, his taste as familiar as that of chocolate, or strawberry, or any of the flavors she had relished often in her life. And, my, it felt good. It was the familiarity of that first step on the dance floor magnified a thousandfold. It was each of them fitting into the right niche, melding to the right place, tasting the right way.

They kept it friendly, passionless almost, engaging themselves solely in the pleasure one mouth can give another.

When he drew away she kept her eyes closed, murmuring, "Mmm . . ."

He studied her face for a long moment, then reclined, removing his arm from around her, though she remained snug against his side with her cheek on his sleeve. They rode along in silence, thinking about what they'd just done, neither of them surprised it had happened, only wondering what it portended. Michael reached over and touched a button, lowering his window a couple of inches. The cool night air whisked in, scented by fertile fields and moisture. It threaded across their hair, their lips, bringing a near taste of thawing earth.

Bess interrupted their idyll as if rebutting thoughts they'd both been having. "The trouble is," she said quietly, "you fit in so remarkably well."

"I do, don't I?"

"Mother loves you. All the shirttail family thinks I was crazy to get rid of you in the first place. Lisa would sell her soul to get us back together. Randy's even coming around little by little. And Barb and Don—it felt like slipping into an old, comfortable easy chair to be with them again."

"Boy, didn't it."

"Isn't it strange, how we both gave them up? I thought you were probably seeing them all along."

"I thought *you* were."

"With the possible exception of Heather down at the store, I really don't have any friends anymore. I seem to have forsaken them since we got divorced—don't ask me why."

"That's not healthy."

"I know."

"Why do you suppose you did that?"

"Because when you're divorced you always end up feeling like the odd man out. Everyone else has a partner to be with and there you are trailing along like a kid sister."

"I thought you had that boyfriend."

"Keith? Mmmm . . . no, Keith wasn't one I took around and introduced to many people. When I did, most of them looked at me funny and got me in a corner and whispered, 'What in the world are you doing with *him?*' "

"How long did you go with him?"

"Three years."

They rode awhile before Michael asked, "Did you sleep with him?"

She gave him a mock slap on the arm and put distance between them. "Michael Curran, what business is it of yours?"

"Sorry."

Away from him, she felt chilled. She snuggled back against his arm and said, "Close the window, will you? It's cold."

The window made a whirr and thump and the chill breeze disappeared.

"Yes," Bess said after some time. "I slept with Keith. But never at home and never overnight so the kids would know."

It took some time before Michael said, "You want to know something funny? I'm jealous."

"Oh, that's rich. *You're* jealous?"

"I knew you'd say that."

"When I found out about Darla I wanted to scratch her eyes out, and yours, too."

"You should have. Maybe things would have ended up differently."

They spent time with their private thoughts before Bess told Michael, "My mother asked me if we were holding hands in church today and I lied."

"You *lied?* But you never lie!"

"I know but I did this time."

"Why?"

"I don't know. Yes, I do." She pondered a while and admitted, "No, I don't. Why were we?" She tilted her head to look up at him.

"It seemed like the right thing to do. It was a sentimental moment."

"But it had nothing to do with renewing vows, did it?"

"No."

Bess felt simultaneously relieved and disappointed.

Soon, she yawned and snuggled against his arm once more.

"Tired?"

"Mmm . . . it's catching up at last."

Michael raised his voice and told the driver, "You can head back to Stillwater now."

"Very good, sir."

On the way Bess fell asleep. Michael stared out the window at the blur of snowless, grassless land lit by the perimeter of the headlights. The wheels dipped into a low spot in the road and Michael swayed in his seat, Bess along with him, her weight heavy against his arm.

When they reached the house on Third Avenue, he touched her face.

"Hey, Bess, we're home."

She had trouble lifting her head, as much trouble opening her eyes.

"Oh . . . mmm . . . Michael . . . ?"

"You're home."

She forced herself upright as the driver opened the door on Michael's side. He stepped out and offered his hand, helping her out. The driver stood beside the open trunk.

"Shall I help you carry the gifts inside, sir?"

"I'd appreciate that."

Bess led the way, unlocking the door, turning on a hall light and a table lamp in the family room. The two men carried the gifts inside and stacked them in the family room on the floor and the sofa. The front door stood wide open. Michael followed the driver to it and said, "Thanks for your help. I'll be out in just a minute."

He closed the door and slowly walked the length of the hall to the family room, where he stopped with the sofa and a long table separating him from Bess, who stood among the packages.

Michael's glance swept the room.

"The house looks nice. I like what you've done with this room."

"Thanks."

"Nice colors." His glance returned to her. "I never was much good with colors."

She took two precariously perched boxes off the sofa and put them on the floor.

"Are you coming over tomorrow?"

"Am I invited?"

"Well, of course you are. You're Lisa's father, and she'll want you here when she opens her gifts."

"Then I'll be here. What time?"

"Two o'clock. There was food left over so don't eat lunch."

"You need any help? You want me to come early?"

"No, all I have to do is make coffee but thanks for offering. Just be here at two."

"It's a deal."

A lull fell. They weren't sure if Randy was home or not. If so, he was down in his room asleep. From outside came the faint note of the limousine engine. Inside, the room was dim, the window coverings drawn high, the night beyond the sliding glass door absorbing much of the light cast by the single burning lamp. Michael's tie was in his pocket, his collar button open, his cummerbund a splash of color as he stood on the opposite side of the furniture from Bess, with his hands in his pockets.

"Walk me to the door," he said.

She came around the sofa at a pace suggesting reluctance to see the evening end. Their arms slipped around each other as they sauntered, hip-to-hip, to the door.

Reaching it, he said, "I had fun."

"So did I."

She turned to face him. He linked his hands on her spine and rested his hips lightly against hers.

"Well . . . congratulations, Mom." He gave a smile of boyish allure.

She returned it, accompanied by a throaty chuckle. "Congratulations, Dad. We got us a son-in-law, didn't we?"

"A good one, I think."

"Mm-hmm."

Would they or wouldn't they? The questions glimmered between them as they stood together with every outward sign indicating they wanted to, and every inward voice warning it was unwise: that once in the limousine had been dangerous enough. He ignored the voice, dipped his head and kissed her, open-mouthed, tasting her fully and without restraint. Where his tongue went, hers followed, into all the familiar sleek caverns they'd learned during long-ago kisses. She tasted as he remembered, felt the same, the contours of her lips, teeth and tongue as familiar as during the uncountable kisses of their younger years. Their lips grew wet and he could tell by her breathing she was as turned on as he.

When he lifted his head she whispered, "Michael, we shouldn't."

"Yeah, I know," he replied, stepping away from her against all his basic instincts. "See you tomorrow."

When he was gone she shut off the downstairs lights and climbed the stairs in the dark. Halfway up she paused, realizing he had offered to help her in the kitchen. She was smiling as she continued toward her bedroom.

At 1:30 P.M. the following day Randy found Bess in the kitchen. He was dressed in jeans and a distressed leather bomber jacket. She, dressed in green wool slacks with a matching sweater, was arranging cold turkey and raw vegetables on a two-tiered platter. The room smelled strongly of perking coffee.

"I don't think I can make it today, Mom."

She glanced up sharply. "What do you mean, you can't?"

"I mean, I can't. I gotta meet some guys."

"You're a member of the wedding party. What *guys* are more important than your sister on her wedding weekend?"

"Mom, I'd stay if I could, but—"

"You'll stay, mister, and call your *guys* and tell them you'll make it another time!"

"Mom, goddamnit, why do you have to pick today to become Mussolini?" He thumped a fist on the cabinet top.

"First of all, stop your cursing. Second, stop rapping your fist on the counter. And third, grow up! You're Lisa and Mark's best man. As such you have social obligations that aren't done yet. This gift-opening today is as much a part of the wedding festivities as last night was, and she'll expect you to be here."

"She won't care," he jeered. "Hell, she won't even miss me."

"She won't, because you won't *be* missing!"

"What's got into you all of a sudden, Ma? Did the old man tell you you ought to get tougher on me?"

Bess flung a handful of raw cauliflower into a bowl of ice water. It splashed onto her sleeve as she spun to face him.

"I've had just about all the smart remarks about him I'm going to take from you, young man. He's making an effort, a real effort where you're concerned. And if he *did* tell me to get tough on you, and if that *were* the reason I am—which I'm not saying is true—maybe he'd be right! Now I want you back downstairs, out of that leather jacket and into some kind of respectable shirt. And when our guests get here I'd like you to answer the door, if that wouldn't be too much trouble," she ended mordantly, turning back to the raw vegetables.

He went downstairs, leaving her facing the kitchen sink with her face burning and her pulse elevated.

Mothering! Whoever said it got easier as they got older was a damned liar! She hated the indecisiveness—should she have lashed out or not?

Should she have given orders or not? He was an adult, so he deserved being treated like an adult. But he lived in her house, lived in it virtually scot-free at nineteen, when most boys his age were either attending college, paying rent or both. So she had a right to have expectations and make demands now and then. But did she have to take him on today of all days? Thirty minutes before a houseful of guests arrived?

She dried her hands, swiped the droplets of water off her sleeve and followed him downstairs. In his room the stereo was playing quietly and he was standing with his back to the door, facing the chain-and-metal bar that held his clothes, yanking off his shirt as if someone had called him a sissy. She went up behind him and touched his back. He got absolutely still, his wrists still caught in his inverted sleeves.

"I'm sorry I shouted. Please stay home this afternoon. You were wonderful on the drums last night. Dad and I were so proud of you." She slipped her arms around his trunk, gave him a swift kiss between the shoulder blades and left him standing there, his chin on his chest, his shirt still dangling from one wrist.

When the doorbell rang for the first time, Randy was there to answer it, dressed in a pressed cotton shirt and creased pants. It was Aunt Joan, Uncle Clark and Grandma Dorner, probably the easiest person to hug of all Randy knew, because with Grandma Dorner nothing was calamitous. She had a way of bringing everything into perspective. She hugged him in passing, said, "Nice job with those drumsticks," gave him her coat and continued toward the kitchen, asking what she could do to help.

Lisa and Mark came next, arriving at the same time as Michael, all of them swiftly followed by the Padgetts, who descended en masse. Randy's heart gave a little surge as he took Maryann's coat, but he might have been a hired doorman for all the truck she gave him. She handed him her coat, making sure it was off her shoulders so he need not touch her, turning away in conversation with her mother as they moved toward the family room, where a fire was burning in the fireplace and food was spread on the adjacent dining-room table.

He remained on the perimeter of the activity the entire afternoon, feeling like an outsider in his own home, standing back, watching and listening as gifts were opened and *oohed* over, studying Maryann, who never so much as glanced at him, watching his mother and dad, who remained carefully remote from each other at all times but whose eyes occasionally met and exchanged covert messages.

Damn weddings, he thought. If this is what they do to people, I'm never going to get married. Everybody goes crazy, they do things they wouldn't do for a thousand bucks on a normal day. Shit, who needs it?

When the giftwrap was shaped like a mountain and the table looked as though a grasshopper plague had just passed, the carry-through of weariness from three days of activity began to dull and slow everyone. Michael asked Lisa to play "The Homecoming" on the piano and she obliged. Half the guests left; half trailed into the formal living room while some of the women began repacking the gifts into their boxes and making neat stacks of them.

The music ended and the group thinned more. Randy caught Maryann just as she was about to leave and said, "Could I talk to you a minute?"

She found someplace to occupy her eyes: on her purse handle, untwisting it before threading it over her shoulder with a toss of her head. "No, I don't think so."

"Maryann, please. Just come in the living room a minute." He caught her sleeve and tugged.

Reluctantly she followed, refusing to meet his eyes. Outside, twilight had arrived. The room was dusky at the west end, where no lamps were lit. At the east end, the lamp on the abandoned piano made a small puddle of light. Randy led Maryann around a corner, away from the prying eyes of the departing guests, and stopped beside an upholstered wing chair with a matching ottoman.

"Maryann, I'm sorry about last night," Randy said.

She ran a thumbnail along the welting on the high back of the chair. "Last night was a mistake, all right? I never should have gone outside with you in the first place."

"But you did."

She gave up her preoccupation with the chair and flung him a reprimanding glare. "You're a talented person. It's obvious you come from a home with a lot of love, in spite of the fact that your parents are divorced. I mean, look at this!" She waved a hand at the room. "Look at them, and how they've made a solid show of support throughout this wedding. I know a lot more about you than you think I do—from Lisa. What are you fighting against?" When he made no reply she said, "I don't want to see you, Randy, so please don't call or anything."

She left to join her parents on their way out the door. He dropped onto the ottoman and sat staring at the bookshelves in the far corner, where the gloaming was so deep he could not discern the spines of the volumes.

People were making trips out to Mark's van, carrying the wedding gifts. Lisa and Mark were leaving. He heard her ask, "Where's Randy? I haven't said good-bye to him." He hid silently, waiting out the moments until she gave up calling down to his room and left the house without a good-bye. He heard Grandma Dorner say, "Joan and I will help you clean up this mess, Bess." And his father, "I'll help her, Stella. I've got nothing waiting at home but an empty condo." And Stella again, "All right, Michael, I'll take you up on that. It's just about time for *Murder, She Wrote* and that's one show I don't like to miss." There were more sounds of farewell, and cold air circling Randy's ankles, then the door closed a last time and he listened.

His mother said, "You didn't have to stay."

"I wanted to."

"What's this, a new side to Michael Curran, volunteering for KP?"

"You said it yourself. She's my daughter, too. What do you want me to do?"

"Well, you can carry in the dishes from the dining room, then burn the wrapping paper in the fireplace."

Dishes clinked and footsteps moved between the kitchen and dining room. The water ran, and the dishwasher door opened, something was put away in the refrigerator.

Michael called, "What do you want me to do with this tablecloth?"

"Shake it out and drop it down the clothes chute."

The sliding glass door rolled open and, a few seconds later, shut. Other sounds continued—Michael whistling softly, more footsteps, more running water, then the sound of the fire screen sliding open, the rustle of paper and the roar of it catching flame; in the kitchen the clink of glassware.

"Hey, Bess, this carpet is a mess. Scraps of paper everywhere. You want me to vacuum it?"

"If you want to."

"Is the vacuum cleaner still in the same place?"

"Yup."

Randy heard his father's footsteps head toward the back closet, the door opening, and in moments, the whine of the machine. While the two of them were distracted and the place was noisy, he retreated from his hiding spot and slipped down to his bedroom, where he put on his headphones and flopped onto his water bed to try to decide what to do about his life.

Michael finished vacuuming, put away the machine, went into the living room to turn off the piano light and, returning through the dining room, called, "Bess, how about this table? You want to take a leaf out of it?"

She came from the kitchen with one dishtowel tied backwards around her waist, drying her hands on another.

"I guess so. The catch is at that end."

He found the catch and together they pulled the table apart.

"Same table, I see."

"It was too good to get rid of."

"I'm glad you didn't. I always liked it." He swung a leaf into the air, narrowly missing the chandelier.

"Ooo, luck-y," she said, low-voiced, waiting while he braced the leaf against the wall.

"Not lucky at all, just careful." He grinned while they put their thighs against the table and clacked it back together.

"Oh, sure. And who used to break bulbs in the chandelier at least once a year?"

"I seem to remember you broke a couple yourself." He hefted the table leaf.

She was grinning as she headed back to the kitchen. "Under the family-room sofa, same place as always."

He put the table leaf away, snapped off the dining-room light and returned to her side by the kitchen sink. She had kicked off her shoes someplace and wore only nylons on her feet; he'd always liked the air-brushed appearance of a woman's feet in nylons. He took the dishtowel from her shoulder and began wiping an oversized salad bowl.

"It feels good to be back here," he said. "Like I never left."

"Don't go getting ideas," she said.

"Just an innocent remark, Bess. Can't a man make an innocent remark?"

"That depends." She squeezed out the dishcloth and began energetically wiping off the countertop while he watched her spine—decorated by the knotted white dishtowel—bob in rhythm with each swipe she made.

"On what?"

"What went on the night before."

"Oh, that." She turned and he shifted his gaze to the bowl he was supposed to be drying.

"That was Jose Cuervo talking, I think." She rinsed out her cloth and wiped off the top of the stove. "People do dumb things at weddings."

"Yeah, I know. Wasn't this bowl one of our wedding gifts?" He studied it while she went to the sink to release the water.

"Yes." She began spraying the suds down the drain. "From Jerry and Holly Shipman."

"Jerry and Holly . . ." He stared at the bowl. "I haven't thought about them in years. Do you ever see them anymore?"

"I think they live in Sacramento now. Last time I heard from them they'd opened a nursery."

"Still married, though?"

"As far as I know. Here, I'll take that." While she carried the bowl away to the dark dining room he took a stab at a cupboard door, opened the right one and began putting away some glasses. She returned, took off her dishtowel and began polishing the kitchen faucet with it. He finished putting away the glasses; she hung up her towel, dispensed some hand lotion into her palm and they both turned at the same time, relaxing against the kitchen cupboards while she massaged the lotion into her hands.

"You still like anything that smells like roses."

She made no reply, only continued working her hands together until the lotion disappeared and she tugged her sleeves down into place. They stood a space apart, watching each other while the dishwasher played its song of rush and thump, sending out faint vibrations against their spines.

"Thanks for helping me clean up."

"You're welcome."

"If you'd done it six years ago things might have turned out differently."

"People can change, Bess."

"Don't, Michael. It's too scary to even think about."

"Okay." He pushed away from the cabinet edge and held up his hands, surrendering to her wishes. "Not another word. It's been fun. I've enjoyed it. When is my furniture coming?"

He moved toward the front hall and she trailed him. "Soon. I'll call you as soon as anything arrives."

"Okay." He opened the entry coat closet and found his jacket, a puffy brown thing made of leather with raglan sleeves that smelled like penicillin.

"New jacket?" she asked.

Zipping it, he held out an elbow and looked down. "Yes."

"Did you stink up my closet with it?"

He laughed as the zipper hit the two-thirds mark and he tugged the ribbed waist down into place. "Cripes, a man just can't do anything right with you, can he?" His remark was made in the best of humor and they both chuckled afterward.

He reached for the doorknob, paused and turned back. "I don't suppose we ought to kiss good-bye, huh?"

She crossed her arms and leaned back against the newel post, amused. "No, I don't suppose we ought to."

"Yeah . . . I guess you're right." He considered her a moment, then opened the door. "Well, good night, Bess. Let me know if you change your mind. This single life can leave a man a little hard up now and then."

If she'd have had their glass wedding bowl, she'd have lobbed it at his head. "Jeez, thanks, Curran!" she yelled just as the door closed.

chapter 13

THE LAST OF THE MARCH snows had come and gone, late blizzards battering Minnesota with fury, followed by the sleety, steely days of early April. The buds on the trees were swollen, awaiting only sun to set them free. The lakes were regaining their normal water level, lost through the past two years of drought, and the ducks were returning, occasionally even some Canadian honkers. Michael Curran stood at the window of his sixth-floor St. Paul office building watching a wedge of them setting their wings for a landing on the Mississippi River. A gust of wind blew the leader and several followers slightly out of formation before they corrected their course with a rocking of wings and disappeared behind one of the lower buildings.

He'd called Bess, of course, twice in the past month, and asked her out but she'd said she didn't think it was wise. In his saner moments he agreed with her. Still, he thought about her a lot.

His secretary, Nina, poked her head into his office and said, "I'm on my way out. Mr. Stringer called and said he won't make it back in before the meeting tonight but he'd see you there." Stringer was the architect of the firm.

Michael swung around. "Oh, thanks, Nina." She was forty-eight, a hundred and sixty pounds, with a nose shaped like a toggle switch and glasses so thick he teased her she'd set the place on fire if she ever laid them in the sun on top of any papers. She kept her hair dyed as black as a grand piano and her nails painted red even though arthritis had begun shaping her fingers like ginseng roots. She came in and poked one into the soil of the schefflera plant beside his desk, found it moist enough and said, "Well, I'm off, then. Good luck at the meeting."

"Thanks. Good night."

" 'Night."

When she was gone the place grew quiet. He sat down at a drafting table, perused Jim Stringer's drawings of the proposed two-story brick structure and wondered if it would ever get built. Four years ago he had purchased a prime lot on the corner of Victoria and Grand, an upscale, yuppie, commercial intersection flanked by upscale, yuppie residential streets lined with Victorian mansions that had regained fashionable status during the last decade. Victoria and Grand—known familiarly throughout the Twin Cities as Victoria Crossing—had in the late seventies sported no less than three vacant corner buildings, each of them formerly a car dealership. The Minnesota Opera Company had rented one old relic nearby for its practice studio and had spread the lonely sound of operatic voices up and down Grand Avenue for a while.

Eventually Grand had been rediscovered, redone, revitalized. Now, its turn-of-the-century flavor was back in the form of Victorian streetlights, red-brick storefronts and flower boxes, three charming malls at the major intersection, along with variety shops that stretched along Grand Avenue itself.

And one vacant parking lot owned by Michael Curran.

Victoria Crossing had everything—ambience, an established reputation as one of the premiere shopping areas in St. Paul, even buses coming off the nearby Summit Avenue Historic Mansion Tours, disgorging tourists by the dozens. Women had discovered its gift shops and restaurants, and met there to shop and eat. Students from nearby William Mitchell Law School had discovered its fine bookstores and came there to buy books. Businessmen from downtown, and politicians from the State Capitol, found it an easy ride up the hill for lunch. Local residents walked to it pushing their baby carriages—baby carriages, no less! Michael had been down there last summer and had actually seen two old-fashioned baby buggies being perambulated by two young mothers. At Christmastime the storekeepers brought in English carolers, served wassail, sponsored a Santa Claus and called it a Victorian Walk. In June they organized a parade, street bands and ethnic food stalls and called it The Grand Old Days, attracting 300,000 people a year.

And all that clientele needed parking space.

Michael offset the edges of his teeth, leaned on the drafting table with both elbows and stared at the revised blueprints—including an enlarged parking ramp—remembering the brouhaha at last month's Concerned Citizens' Meeting.

Our streets are not our own! was the hue and cry of the nearby homeowners, whose boulevards were constantly lined with vehicles.

People can't shop if they can't park! complained the businesspeople till the issue ended in a standoff.

So the meeting had adjourned and Michael had hired a public relations firm to create a friendly letter of intent, including an architect's concept of the building blending with its surroundings; the results of the market analysis with demographics clearly indicating the area could bear the additional upscale businesses; additional demographics showing that the proposed parking ramp would hold more cars than the flat lot presently there; and assurance that Michael himself, as the developer, would remain a joint owner of the building, thus retaining an avid interest in its aesthetic, business and demographic impact not only now but in the future as well. Nearly two hundred copies of the letter had been distributed to business owners and homeowners in the vicinity of the proposed building.

Tonight they'd hash it over again and see if any minds had changed.

The meeting was held in an elementary-school lunchroom that smelled like leftover Hungarian goulash. Jim Stringer was there along with Peter Olson, the project manager from Welty-Norton Construction Company, who was slated to do the building.

The St. Paul city planning director called the meeting to order and allowed Michael to speak first. Michael rose, arbitrarily fixed his eyes on a middle-aged woman in the second row, and said, "The letter with the drawing of the proposed building that you got this past month was from me. This is my architect, Jim Stringer, who'll be co-owner of the building. And this is Pete Olson, the project manager from Welty-Norton. What we want all of you to think about is this. We've already had soil borings done on the lot and the land meets EPA standards—in other words, no contamination. With that obstacle aside, the truth is, that lot is going to be built on eventually, whether you like it or not. Now you can wait for some shyster to come along, who's going to build today and be gone tomorrow, or you can go with Jim and me. He designed it, I'm going to manage it, we'll both own it. Would we put up something unsightly or poorly constructed, or anything that would clash with the aesthetics of Victoria Crossing? Hardly. We want to keep the same flavor that's been so carefully preserved because, after all, that's what makes the Crossing thrive. Jim will answer any questions about building design, and Pete Olson will answer those about actual construction. Now, since our last meeting, we've scaled down the number of square feet in the commercial building and increased the area for parking, and Jim's got the new blueprints here. That's our bid toward compromise but you people have to bend a little, too."

Someone stood up and said, "I live in the apartment building next door. What about my view?"

Someone else demanded to know, "What kind of shops will be in there? If we say yes to the building, we invite our own competition to put a dent in our business."

Another person claimed, "The construction mess will be bad for business."

Someone else said, "Sure, there'll be more parking spots but the extra businesses will bring in extra people and that means more cars on our side streets."

The discussions went on; most of the locals were outraged until after some forty-five minutes a woman stood up at the rear.

"My name is Sylvia Radway and I own The Cooks of Crocus Hill, the cooking school and kitchenwares shop right across the street from that lot. I was at the first meeting and never said a word. I received Mr. Curran's letter and did a lot of thinking about it, and tonight I've been listening to everything that's been said here, and I believe some of you are being unreasonable. I think Mr. Curran is right. That piece of land is too valuable and in too desirable a location to remain a parking lot forever. I happen to like the looks of the building he's proposing, and I think a half-dozen more tasteful specialty shops will be good for business all around. Another thing a lot of you haven't admitted is that when you moved here, you all knew Grand Avenue was a business street, whether you're a local resident or you own a business. If you wanted vacant lots, you should have been here in 1977. I say let him put up his building—it's darned nice-looking—and watch our property values rise."

Sylvia Radway sat down, leaving a lull followed by a murmur of low exchanges.

When the meeting ended, the concerned citizens had not yet voted to allow Michael's building but the tide of objection had clearly moderated.

Michael caught up with Ms. Radway in the school lobby just short of the door.

"Ms. Radway?" he called from behind her.

She turned, paused and waited as he approached. She was perhaps fifty-five, with beautiful naturally wavy hair of silver white, cropped in a soft pouf. Her face was gently grooved, roundish and attractive. The smile upon it looked habitual.

"Ms. Radway . . ." He extended his hand. "I want to thank you for what you said in there."

They shook hands and she told him, "I only said what I believe."

"I think it made a difference. They know you—they don't know me."

"Some people are against change, doesn't matter what it is."

"Boy, don't I know that. I run into them all the time in my business. Well, thanks again. And if there's anything I can ever do for you . . ."

She made her eyes wider and said, "If you take any cooking classes just make sure they're from The Cooks of Crocus Hill."

He thought about her on his way home, the surprise of her standing up in the meeting and speaking up on his behalf. You never know about people, he thought; there are a lot of good ones out there. He smiled, recalling her remark about cooking classes. Well, that was going a little far, but the next time he was up at the Crossing he'd stop in her store and buy something, by way of showing his appreciation.

That happened a week later. He had to meet a fellow from a land surveyor's office for lunch, and suggested Café Latte, which was just across the street from The Cooks of Crocus Hill. After lunch he wandered over to the shop. It was pleasant, with two levels and an open stairway, southern window exposure, hardwood floors and Formica display fixtures of clean, modern lines, everything done in blue and white. It smelled of flavored coffee, herbal teas and exotic spices. The shelves were loaded with everything for the gourmet kitchen—spatulas, soufflé dishes, popover pans, aprons, nutmeg graters, cookbooks and more. He passed some hanging omelette pans and approached the counter. Sylvia Radway stood behind it, reading a computer printout through half-glasses perched on the tip of her nose.

"Hello," he said.

She looked up and smiled like Betty Crocker's grandmother.

"Well, look who's here. Come to sign up for cooking class, did you, Mr. Curran?"

He scratched his head and winced. "Not exactly."

She picked up a jar off the counter and tipped her head back to read its label.

"Some pickled fiddlehead fern, then?"

He laughed and said, "You're kidding." She handed him the jar. "Pickled fiddlehead fern," he read. "You mean people actually eat this stuff?"

"Absolutely."

He glanced at the assortment of jars and read their labels. "Chutney—what in the world is chutney? And pecan praline mustard glaze?"

"Delicious on a baked ham. Just smear it on and bake."

"Oh yeah?" he said, taking a second look at the glaze.

"Steam a few fresh asparagus spears with it, a couple new potatoes with the skins on, and you have a meal fit for a visiting dignitary."

She made it sound so easy.

"Trouble is, I don't have anything to steam them in."

She turned with a flourish of the palm, presenting the whole of her shop. "Take your pick. Metal or bamboo."

He perused the store and felt out of his league. Pots and pans and brushes and squeezers and things that looked as if they belonged in a doctor's office. "I don't cook," he admitted, and for the first time ever, felt foolish saying so.

"Probably because nobody's ever turned you on to it. We have a lot of men in our basics classes. When they start they don't know which end of a spatula goes up, but by the time they finish they're making omelettes and quick breads and poached chickens and bragging to their mothers about it."

"Yeah?" He cocked his head and turned back to her, genuinely interested. "You mean anybody can learn to cook, even a dodo who's never fried an egg?"

"The name of our beginners' class is 'How to Boil Water 101.' Maybe that answers your question."

When they'd both chuckled, she went on. "Cooking has become a unisexual skill. I'd say we probably have an even mix of men and women in our classes now. People are marrying later in life, men leave home, get apartments of their own and get tired of eating out all the time. Some get divorced. Some have wives who work full-time and don't want to do the cooking. Voilà!" She threw up her hands and snapped her fingers. "The Cooks of Crocus Hill! The answer to the yuppie quandary at mealtime."

She was such an excellent saleswoman, he didn't even realize he was being pitched until she asked, "Would you like to see our kitchen? It's right upstairs."

She led the way past a tall, fragrant display of coffee beans in clear plastic dispensers to an open stairway of smooth, blond varnished oak. On the second floor more stock was arranged on neat white Formica cubes. Beyond it, at one end of the building, they emerged into a gleaming stainless-steel and white-tiled kitchen. A long counter with blue upholstered stools faced the cooking area. Above it hung a long mirror angled so that any demonstrations in progress could be viewed from the retail sales floor. When Michael hesitated she waved him in. "Come on . . . have a look." He meandered farther inside and perched on one of the blue stools.

"We teach you everything from basic equipment to how to stock your kitchen with staples, to the proper way of measuring liquid and dry ingredients. Our instructors demonstrate, then you actually prepare foods yourself. I take it you're single, Mr. Curran."

"Ah . . . yes."

"We have a lot of single men registering for classes. College graduates, widowers, divorcees. Most of them feel like fish out of water when they first come in here. Some are genuinely sad, especially the widowers, and act as if they need . . . well, nurturing, I guess. But do you know what? I've never seen one leave unhappy that he took the class."

Michael looked around, trying to imagine himself struggling with wire whips and spatulas while a bunch of people looked on.

"Do you have an equipped kitchen?" Sylvia Radway asked.

"No, nothing. I just moved into a condo a few months ago and I don't even have dishes."

"I'll tell you what," she said. "Since you and I are going to be neighbors, I'll make you a deal. I'll give you your first cooking class free if you buy whatever kitchenwares you need from the shop. I won't sell you a thing that's unnecessary. If you enjoy it—and I have a hunch you will—you'll pay for any extra classes you want to take. How does that sound?"

"How long do classes last?"

"Three weeks. One night a week, or afternoon, if you prefer, three hours each class. If you enjoy them, the second series continues for an additional three weeks."

It was tempting. He hated that empty kitchen at home, and eating out all the time had long ago lost its appeal. His evenings were lonely and he often filled them by working late.

"One other thing, Mr. Curran . . . speaking from a purely objective point of view, just in case you're interested, today's women love men who cook for them. That old stereotype has definitely done a turnaround. It is often the men who woo the women with their culinary expertise."

He thought about Bess and imagined the surprise on her face if he sat her at a table and pulled a gourmet supper out of the kitchen. She'd get up and search the broom closet for the cook!

"All I have to do is buy a couple kettles, huh?"

"Well . . . I'll be honest. It'll take more than a couple kettles. You'll need a wooden spoon or two and some staples at the grocery store. What do you say?"

He smiled. She smiled. And the pact was made.

* * *

On the night of his first class, Michael stood in his walk-in closet wondering what a person wore to cooking school. He owned no chef's hat or butcher's apron. His mother had always worn housedresses around the kitchen, and often had a dishtowel slung over her shoulder.

He chose creased blue jeans and a stylized blue-and-white sweatshirt with a ribbed collar.

At The Cooks of Crocus Hill, the class numbered eight, and five of them were men. He felt less stupid to find the other four men present, even less when one leaned close and quietly confided to him, "I can't even make Kool-Aid."

Their teacher was not Sylvia Radway herself but a plain-faced Scandinavian-looking woman around forty-five, portly, named Betty McGrath. She had a cheerful attitude and a knack for teasing in exactly the right way that made them laugh at their own clumsiness and revel in each small success. After a brief lecture they were given a list of recommended kitchen supplies, then they made applesauce muffins and omelettes. They learned how to measure flour and milk, crack and whip eggs, mix with a spoon—"Muffins should look lumpy"—grease a muffin tin, fill it two-thirds full, dice ham and onions, slice mushrooms uniformly, shred cheese, preheat an omelette pan, test it for readiness, fold the omelette and get the whole works cooking at the proper time. They learned how to test the muffins for doneness, remove them from the tin and serve them attractively in a basket lined with a cloth napkin, along with their nicely plumped omelette, all timed to end up on the table together—hot and pretty and perfect.

When he sat down to taste the fruits of his labor, Michael Curran felt as proud as the day he'd received his college diploma.

He furnished his kitchen with Calphalon cookware, oversized spoons and rubber scrapers. He bought himself some blue-and-white dishes and a set of silverware. He found to his delight that he enjoyed poking around Sylvia Radway's shop, buying a lemon squeezer for Caesar salad dressing, a French chef's knife for dicing onions, a potato peeler for cleaning vegetables, a wire whip for making gravy.

Gravy.

Holy old nuts, he learned how to make gravy! And cheese sauce on broccoli!

They did it the night of the second class, along with roasted chicken, mashed potatoes and salad. That night when the meal was done, the man who'd whispered he couldn't make Kool-Aid—his name turned out to be Brad Wilchefski—sat down at the table grinning and saying, "I don't believe this, I just damn well don't believe this." Wilchefski was built like a Harley biker and came close to dressing like one. He had frizzy red hair and a beard to match and wore John Lennon glasses. He looked like a man who'd be at ease walking around a campfire gnawing on a turkey drumstick and wiping his hands on his thighs.

"My old lady'd shit if she could see what I done," he said.

"Mine, too," Michael said.

"You divorced?"

"Yes. You?"

"Naw. She just took off and left me with the kid. Figured, what the hell, she was dumber'n a stump. If she could cook, I can cook."

"My wife always did all the cooking when we were first married, then she went back to college and wanted me to help around the house but I refused. I thought it was woman's work but you know something? It's kind of fun." It didn't occur to Michael that he hadn't even referred to his second wife, only his first.

Wilchefski chewed some chicken, tried some potatoes and gravy and said, "Any of the guys tease me and I'll serve 'em up their own gonads in cheese sauce."

Michael was amazed at how cooking had changed his outlook. Evenings, he left the office when everyone else did. He stopped at Byerly's and bought fresh meat and vegetables and hurried home to prepare them in his new cookware. One night he dumped some wine from his goblet into the pan when he was sautéing beef and mushrooms, delighting himself with the results. Another night he sliced an orange and laid it on a chicken breast. He discovered the wonders of fresh garlic, and the immediacy of stir-frying, and the old-fashioned delectation of meat loaf. More important, he discovered within himself a growing satisfaction with his life as it was and a broadening approval for himself as a person. His singleness took on a quality of peace rather than loneliness, and he began to explore other lone occupations that brought their own satisfaction: reading, sailing, even doing his own laundry instead of taking it to the cleaners.

The first time he took a load of clothes out of the dryer and folded them, he thought, Why, hell, that was simple! The realization made him laugh at himself for all the months he'd stubbornly refused to use the washer and dryer simply because he "didn't know how."

He hadn't seen Bess since the wedding but in mid-May she called to say the first of his furniture had arrived.

"What exactly?"

"Living-room sofa and chairs."

"The leather ones?"

"No, those are for the family room. These are the cloth-covered ones for the formal living room."

"Oh."

"Also, the workroom called to say the window treatments are all done and ready to install. Can we set up a date for my installer to come out and do that?"

"Sure. When?"

"I'll have to check with him but give me a couple of dates and I'll get back to you."

"Do I have to be there?"

"Not necessarily."

"Then any day is okay. I can leave the key with the caretaker."

"Fine . . ." A pause followed, then, in a more intimate voice, "How have you been, Michael?"

"Okay. Busy."

"Me too."

He wanted to say, I'm learning to cook, but to what avail? She had made it clear the kisses they'd shared had been ill-advised; she wanted no more of them or of him on a personal level.

They spoke briefly of the children, comparing notes on when they'd last visited Lisa, and how Randy was doing. There seemed little else to say.

Bess put a postscript on the conversation by ending, "Well, I'll get back to you about when to leave the key."

Michael hung up disappointed. What had he wanted of her? To see her again? Her approval of the strides he was making in his life? No. Simply to be in the condo when she came by with her workmen to bring furniture or trim windows. He realized he had been subconsciously planning to see her repeatedly during those times but apparently that was not to be the case.

On the day of the installation, Michael arrived home in the evening to find his living-room sofa and chairs sitting like boulders in a wide river, looking a little forlorn before the fireplace, but his windows sporting new coverings: vertical blinds and welted, padded cornice boards in the living room, dining room, family room and bedrooms; unfussy little things he immediately liked in the bathrooms and the laundry room.

On the kitchen counter was a note in Bess's handwriting.

Michael,

I hope you like the living-room furniture and the window treatments. I hung the custom bedspreads in your entry closet until your beds arrive. I think they're really going to look classy. The upholsterer who's covering the matching pair of chairs for your bedroom says those should be done next week. One of the vertical vanes in the living room (south window) had a smudge on it so I took it along and will return it as soon as the shop replaces it. I have shipping invoices on your guest-bedroom furniture and the family-room entertainment unit, which means they should be coming in next week, so I'll probably have to bug you to let me in again soon. It'll be exciting to watch it all come together. Talk to you soon. Bess.

He stood with his thumb touching her signature, befuddled by the emptiness created within him by her familiar hand.

He went to the entry closet and found the thick, quilted spreads folded over two giant hangers and got a queer feeling in his chest, realizing she'd been here, putting his house in order, hanging things in his closet. How welcome the idea of her in his personal space, as if she belonged there, where she'd been years ago. How unwelcome the thought of being no more to her than a client.

In those moments he missed her with a desolate longing like that following a lovers' quarrel.

He telephoned her, striving to keep his voice casual.

"Hi, Bess, it's Michael."

"Michael, hi! How do you like the window treatments?"

"I like them a lot."

"And the furniture?"

"Furniture looks great."

"Really?"

"I like it."

"So do I. Listen, things are going to be coming in hot-and-heavy now. I got some more invoices today from Swaim. All of your living-room tables have been shipped. Would you like me to hold them and bring them out all at once or keep bringing them out as they arrive?"

As they arrive, so I have more chances to bump into you. "Whatever's more convenient for you."

"No, I want to do whatever is more convenient for you. You're the customer."

"It's no bother to me. I can just leave word with the caretaker to let you in whenever you need to, and you can go ahead and do your thing."

"Great. Actually that does work out best for me because my storage space is really limited and at this time of year, after the post-Christmas rush, everything seems to be coming in at once."

"Bring it over, then. I'm only too glad to see the place fill up. Any sign of my leather sofa yet?"

"Sorry, no. I'd guess it'll be at least another month or more."

"Well . . . let me know."

"I will."

"Ah, Michael, one other thing. I can begin bringing in small accessories anytime. I just need to know if you want me to choose them or if you want to help. Some clients like to be in on these choices and others simply don't want to be bothered."

"Well . . . hell, Bess, I don't know."

"Why don't I do this. When I spot accessory pieces I think would fit, I'll bring them in and leave them. If there's anything you don't like just let me know and we'll try something else. How does that sound?"

"Great."

He grew accustomed after that to coming home and finding another item or two in place—the entry console, the living-room tables, a giant ceramic fish beside the living-room fireplace, a pair of framed prints above it (he loved how the snow geese on the right print became a continuation of the flock on the left), a floor lamp, three huge potted plants in containers shaped like seashells that suddenly made the living room look complete.

His divorce became final in late May and he received the papers feeling much as he did when a business deal was concluded. He put them away in a file drawer, thought, *Good, that's final,* and made out one last check for his lawyer.

He signed up for his third series of cooking classes and learned to plan menus and make a chocolate cake roll with fudge sauce. He met a woman in class named Jennifer Ayles, who was fortyish and divorced and relatively attractive, and who was looking for ways to alleviate her loneliness so had joined the class to fill her evenings. He took her to a Barry Manilow concert, and she talked him into using her son's golf clubs and trying golf for the first time in his life. Afterward at her house he tried to kiss her and she burst into tears and said she still loved her husband, who had left her for another woman. They ended up talking about their exes, and he admitted he still had feelings for Bess but that she didn't return them, or, maybe more accurately, wouldn't *let* herself return them and had warned him to stay away.

He bought a patio table and ate his evening meals on the deck overlooking the lake.

A torchère appeared in his bedroom and a faux pedestal in the center of his gallery with a note: *You sure you want me to pick out this piece of sculpture? I think this one should be strictly your choice. Let me know.*

He left a message with Heather at the Blue Iris: "Tell Bess okay, I'll look for the piece of sculpture myself."

Another time a message was left on his answering machine: "Get yourself some new sheets, Michael. Your bed is here! We'll deliver it tomorrow." He bought designer sheets that looked like blue-and-lavender rain had splashed across them driven by a hard wind, and slept in a fully decorated bedroom suite for the first time since separating from Darla.

And finally, in late June, the message he'd been waiting for: "Michael, it's Bess, Monday morning, eight forty-five. Just called to say your dining-room table is here and your leather sofa is on its way by truck from the port of entry on the east coast. Should be here any day. Talk to you soon."

He came home the following day at 4 P.M. and found her in his dining room removing the heavy plastic factory wrapping from his six fully upholstered dining-room chairs. A new smoked-glass table was centered beneath the chandelier, which was lit, even in the bright summer afternoon.

He stopped in the doorway and said, "Well . . . hello." It was the first time he'd seen her since Lisa's wedding.

She was on her knees beside an upturned chair, pulling oversized staples out of its four feet with a screwdriver and a pair of needle-nosed pliers. She lifted her head, used one whole arm to knock her hair out of her eyes and said, "Michael, I didn't think you came home this early."

He ambled inside and dropped his keys onto the glass top sofa table beside something that hadn't been there that morning—an arrangement of cream silk flowers stuck in a snifter full of clear marbles.

"I don't usually but I was clear up in Marine so I decided not to go back downtown to the office. How do they look?" he said of the chairs.

"So far so good." Only two chairs were unwrapped.

He removed his suit coat, tossed it onto the sofa and crossed to one of the sliding glass doors. "It's hot in here. Why didn't you open the doors?"

"I didn't think I should."

He opened the vertical blinds and both sets of wide doors, at the living and dining ends of the room. The summer air bellied in, then receded to a faint breeze that trembled the leaves of the new green plants and toyed with the vanes of the blinds.

He went to Bess. "Here, let me help you with that."

"Oh, no, this is my job. Besides, you're all dressed in your good clothes."

"Well, so are you." She was wearing a classy yellow sundress, its matching jacket draped over the back of the sofa beside his jacket.

"Here, give me those." He took the tools out of her hand, knelt and began pulling the remaining staples.

Still kneeling beside him, she looked at her hands and brushed them together with three soft claps. "Well . . . thanks."

"Something new over there." He nodded backwards at the silk bouquet.

She got to her feet, revealing black patent-leather pumps and giving off her customary aura of roses. "I kept it simple, only one kind of flower and very small, which tends to be a little more masculine."

"Looks nice. And if I get bored I can lay a string in a circle on the carpet and shoot marbles."

She laughed and began examining one of the unwrapped chairs. It was armless, with a solid upholstered back shaped like a cowboy's gravestone, covered in a subtle design of mauves and grays that reminded him of the seashore after waves have receded.

"Now these are smart. Michael, this place is coming together so beautifully! Are you pleased, or is there anything you don't like? Because the final okay has to be yours."

"No! No, I like it all. I have to hand it to you, Bess, you really know your business."

"Well, I'd better, or I won't have it long."

He finished with the chair and righted it, and she slid over another to be unwrapped while he reached up and loosened the knot in his tie and freed his collar button.

Setting back to work, he said, "You've got a suntan."

She lifted one elbow, glanced at it. "Mmm . . . a little."

"How did that happen?" He let his eyes flick to her, then back to his work. In all the years they'd been married she'd never taken time to lie in the sun.

"Heather's been scolding me for working too hard, so I've been knocking off a couple hours early once or twice a week and lying in the backyard. I have to admit, it's felt heavenly. It's made me realize that in all the years we've . . . I've lived in that house I never utilized the backyard the way I should have. The view from there is magnificent, especially with the boats out on the water."

"I've been doing the same thing from my deck." He nodded toward one of the sets of sliding glass doors. "I got myself that patio table and I sit out there in the evening and enjoy the water when I'm not on it."

"You're sailing?"

"A little. Fishing a little, too."

"We're slowing down some, aren't we, Michael?"

He lifted his gaze to find her studying him with a soft expression in her eyes.

"We deserve it, at our age."

He had stopped working. Their gazes remained twined while seconds tiptoed past and the screwdriver hung forgotten in his hand. Outside, a lawn mower droned, and the scent of fresh-cut grass came in, along with a faint breeze that ruffled the pages of a newspaper lying on the sofa. In the park next door children called, at play.

Bess studied Michael and recognized not age but a rekindling of feelings she had experienced years ago. In her imagination it was Lisa and Randy outside, and she and Michael thinking, *Hurry, while the kids are busy playing.* Sometimes it had happened that way—the rare hot summer day, the rare hot summer urge, the mad scramble with their clothing, the quickie with shirttails getting in the way, sometimes the two of them giggling, and the mad rush if the kids slammed the kitchen screen door before they had finished.

The memory hit like a broadside, while she became conscious of his attractiveness as he knelt beside the overturned chair, with his open collar casting shadows on his throat, and the breast pocket of his shirt flattened against his chest, and his trousers taut around the hips and his steady hazel eyes hinting he might be having much the same thoughts as she.

Bess's eyes dropped first. "I talked to Lisa yesterday," she said, breaking the spell and prattling on while they busied their eyes with more sensible pursuits.

He finished unwrapping the chairs while she folded and stacked the bulky packing material. When the entire dining-room set was in place, they stood at opposite ends of the table, admiring it in spite of the many blotchy fingerprints on the edge of the glass.

"Do you have any glass cleaner?" she inquired.

"No."

"I suppose it's futile to ask if you have any vinegar?"

"That I have."

She looked properly surprised, which pleased Michael as he went off to the kitchen to find it as well as a brand-new blue-and-white checked dishcloth and a roll of paper towels.

When he returned to Bess, she said, "You have to mix it with water, Michael."

"Oh."

He went away once more and returned in a minute with a blue bowl full of vinegar water. When she reached for it, he said, "I'll do it."

She watched him clean his new tabletop, watched him bend down at times while working at a stubborn smudge, catching a reflection across the glass. Sometimes his shirt would be stretched across his shoulder blades in a way that tightened her groin muscles. Sometimes the light from the chandelier would play across his hair and make her hands feel empty.

When he finished he returned the bowl to the kitchen while she went to the sofa table, confiscated the cream silk flowers and set them in the middle of the larger table. Once more they studied it, exchanging glances of approval.

"A raffia mat is all we need," she said.

"Mm . . ."

"Do you like raffia mats?"

"What's raffia?"

"Dried palm . . . you know, Oriental-looking."

"Oh, sure."

"I'll pick one up at the store and bring it out next time I come."

"Fine."

The table was polished, the chairs in place, the centerpiece centered; nothing more needed doing; they had no excuse to linger.

"Well . . ." Bess lifted her shoulders, let them drop and headed for her jacket. "I guess that's it, then. I'd better get home."

He was closer to the jacket and was holding it for her before she could reach it. She slipped it on and fluffed her hair free from the neck of the garment, picked up a black patent handbag and looped it over her shoulder. When she turned he was standing very near with his hands in his trouser pockets.

"How about having dinner with me on Saturday night?" he asked.

"Me?" she asked, her eyes wide, a hand at her chest.

"Yes, you."

"Why?"

"Why not?"

"I don't think so, Michael. I told you the other two times you called that I don't think it's wise."

"What were you thinking about a minute ago?"

"When?"

"You know when."

"Michael, you're so vague."

"And you're a damned liar."

"I've got to go."

"Running away?"

"Don't be ridiculous."

"What about Saturday night?"

"I said I don't think so."

He grinned. "You'll miss the chance of a lifetime. I'm cookin'."

"You!" Her expression of surprise lit him up inside.

He shrugged and raised his palms to hip level. "I took it up."

She had lost the ability to speak, giving him a distinct advantage.

"Dinner here, we'll christen my new table. What do you say?"

She seemed to realize her mouth was hanging open and shut it. "I'll have to hand it to you, Michael, you still have the ability to shock me."

"Six-thirty?" he asked.

"All right," she replied cockily. "This I've got to see."

"You'll drive over?"

"Sure. If you can cook, I can drive."

"Good. I'll see you then."

He walked her to the door, opened it and leaned one shoulder against the doorframe, watching her as she pushed the button for the elevator. When it arrived she began to step aboard, changed her mind and held the door open with one hand while turning to Michael. "Are you putting me on? Do you really know how to cook?"

He laughed and replied, "Wait till Saturday night and see," then went into his condo and closed the door.

chapter 14

MICHAEL'S CREAM LEATHER SOFA arrived on Friday and Bess moved heaven and earth to find a transport service to deliver it to his place Saturday morning. She wanted it there, wanted to walk in and see it in place that evening, wanted to sit on it herself with Michael in the room and rejoice with him over its sumptuousness. She was as giddy as if it were her own.

She was bound and determined that dressing for dinner with him was *not* going to take on the importance of a State visit. She wore white slacks and a short-sleeved cotton sweater of periwinkle blue with an unornamented gold chain at her neck and tiny gold loops in her ears. She'd had her hair cut and styled but that appointment had been made before Michael's invitation had been issued. She polished her nails but that happened twice a week. She wore perfume but it, too, was as routine as checking a watch. She shaved her legs but they needed it.

The only thing she couldn't dismiss was the new lacy underwear she'd splurged on yesterday, when she'd *just happened to be passing* Victoria's Secret. They were powder blue, with a deep plunge on the bra and plenty of hip showing inside the panties, and they'd set her back thirty-four dollars.

She put them on, looked in the mirror, thought, *How silly,* and took them off. Replaced them with plain white. Cursed and put on the sexy ones again. Grimaced at her reflection. *You want to get tangled up with a man you've already failed with once?* On, off, on, off, three times before defiantly putting the blue ones on and leaving them.

* * *

Michael had thrown himself upon the mercy of Sylvia Radway and admitted, "I want to impress a woman. I'm cooking for her for the first time and I want everything to be the way women like it. What should I do?"

The result was a pair of candle holders with blue tapers, a bowl of fresh white roses and blue irises, real cloth place mats and napkins, stem glasses and chilled Pouilly-Fuissé, a detailed menu plan and Michael's nervous stomach.

At ten to six on Saturday evening he paced around the table he'd just finished setting, surveying the results.

Obvious, Curran, disgustingly obvious.

But he wanted to knock her socks off. Well, hell, he admitted, he wanted to knock off a lot more than her socks. So what was wrong with that? They were both single and uninvolved with anyone else. Still, roses. Lord, roses. And he'd tied the napkins around the foot of the stemglasses just the way Sylvia had shown him. Sylvia said women most certainly appreciated details like that, but now that he'd set the stage Michael studied this invitation to thump and figured Bess would be back in her car before he could say Casanova.

He checked his watch, panicked and hit for the bathroom to shower and change.

Because the table suddenly looked so obviously overdone, he himself purposely set out to look underdone. White pleated jeans, a polo shirt in big blocks of primary colors and bare feet in a pair of white moccasins. A gold chain around his wrist. A little mousse in his hair. A splash of cologne. Nothing out of the ordinary.

So he told himself while he meticulously combed his eyebrows, wiped every water spot off the bathroom vanity, put away every piece of discarded clothing from his bedroom, smoothed the bedspread, dusted the furniture tops with his hands, closed the vertical blinds and left the torchère on beside the bed when he left the room.

She called from the lobby at precisely 6:30.

"That you, Bess?"

"It's me."

"Be right down."

He left his condo door open and rode the elevator down. She was waiting on the other side of the door when it opened, looking as studiedly casual as he.

"You didn't need to come down. I know the way up."

He smiled. "Blame it on good breeding." She stepped aboard and he stole a glance at her, remarking, "Nice evening, huh?"

Her return glance was as cautious as his. "Beautiful."

In his condo a strong draft from all the open patio doors made a wind tunnel of the foyer. It wafted the smell of Bess's rosy perfume into his nostrils as she entered ahead of him. He closed the door and the wind immediately ceased. Bess preceded him through the foyer toward the gallery, where she paused.

"Nothing for the pedestal yet?" she asked.

"I haven't had time to look."

"There's a wonderful gallery in Minneapolis on France Avenue, called Estelle's. I was looking at some Lalique glass pieces there and also some interesting hammered brass. Might be something you'd like."

"I'll remember that. Come on in." He passed her and led the way toward the kitchen and the adjoining family room, stopping in the doorway and deliberately blocking her view. "You ready for this sofa?" he teased, looking back over his shoulder.

"Let me see!" she said impatiently, nudging him on the back.

With his hands on the doorframe he barricaded the way. "Aw, you don't really want to see it, do you?"

"Michael!" she exclaimed, giving his shoulder blades a pair of good-natured clunks with both fists. "I've been waiting four months for this! I can smell it clear from here!"

"I thought you hated the smell of leather."

"I do but this is different." She pushed again and he let himself get thrust forward out of her way. She headed straight for the Natuzzi, five pieces of swank off-white leather that took two turns on its way around the perimeter of the room, dividing it from the kitchen and facing the new entertainment unit. She dropped onto the sofa dead center and snuggled deep. The supple cushions rose to envelop her like a caress.

"Ah . . . luxury. Sheer luxury. Do you like it?"

He sat down at a right angle to her. "Are you kidding? Does a man like a Porsche? A World Series ticket on the first-base line? A cold Coors on a ninety-degree day?"

"Mmm . . ." She nestled down deeper and closed her eyes. Momentarily they opened and she said, "I'll confess something. I've never sold a Natuzzi before."

"Why, you phony. Here all the time I thought you knew what you were talking about."

"I did. I just hadn't *experienced* it." Abruptly she popped up and began examining the sofa, working her way along its length. "I didn't get a chance to look at it before it was delivered. Is everything all right? No tears? No marks? Anything?"

"Nothing as far as I could see. Of course, I haven't had much time to look." She reached his knees and detoured around them as she prowled the sofa, eyeing its stitching and curves and welting. When she'd finished she stood with hands akimbo, looking at the thing. "It really does stink, doesn't it?"

He burst out laughing, sitting with his arms stretched out at shoulder level along the tops of the cushions, feeling the soft leather. "How can you say that about an eight-thousand-dollar sofa?"

"I'm just being realistic. Leather stinks. It's as simple as that. So how do you like the dining-room furniture by now?" She walked toward the doorway leading from the family room into the dining room while he remained where he was, waiting for her reaction.

The sight of the table stopped her the way the ground stops a thrown bronc rider. "Why, Michael!" She stared at his handiwork while he studied her back. "My goodness . . ."

He got himself out of the sofa and went up behind her. "I did invite you for supper, remember?"

"Yes, but . . . what an elegant table," she said in disbelief. "Did you do all this?"

"Not without a little advice."

"From whom?" She ventured closer to the table but not too close, still caught in the throes of disbelief.

"A lady who owns a cooking school."

She gaped at him in amazement. "You went to cooking school?"

"Yes, actually, I did."

"Why, Michael, I'm stunned." Half-turning, she swept a hand toward the centerpiece. "All this . . . roses, blue irises . . ." He could tell she was surprised by his sentimentalism, but he recalled very clearly how she associated blue irises with her grandmother. Her lips closed and her expression became wistful as she continued admiring the flowers, then the matching linens, the stemware.

"Would you like a glass of wine, Bess?"

"Yes, I . . ." She looked back at him but seemed unable to put coherent thoughts together. "Please," she finished.

"Be right back."

In the kitchen he checked the glazed ham in the oven, turned on the burner under the tiny red potatoes, checked to make sure his fresh asparagus was still waiting beneath a lid, centered the cheese sauce recipe directly beneath the microwave, consulted his careful list of starting times and finally opened the wine.

Returning to the living room, he found Bess standing before the sliding door, enjoying the view, with the breeze riffling the hair at her temples. She turned her head at his approach and he handed her a goblet.

"Thanks."

"Shall we go out?" he suggested.

"Mmm . . ." She was sipping as she answered. He slid the screen open, waiting while she stepped onto the deck before him.

They sat on either side of a small white patio table, angled toward the lake in cushioned chairs that bounced at the smallest provocation. The setting was lovely, the evening jewel-clear, their surroundings those of evocative movies, but suddenly they found themselves tongue-tied. Everything had changed with that dining-room table: there was no question anymore, this was a stab at a new beginning. Subjects of conversation were strangely elusive after their easy-fire repartee upon her arrival. They watched some sails on the water, the rim of trees outlining Manitou Island, waves washing up at the feet of some nearby cottonwoods. They listened to the soft slap of water meeting shore, the particular click of the cottonwood leaves against one another, the sound of themselves drinking, the metallic *bing* of their gently bouncing chairs. They felt the warmth of summer press their skins and smelled the aroma of someone lighting a barbecue grill nearby, and that of their own supper stealing outside.

But everything had changed and they understood this, so they sat unnaturally hushed, experiencing the uncertainties of forging into that second-time-around.

Finally Bess broke the silence, turning to look at him as she spoke.

"So when did you take this cooking course?"

"I started in April and took nine classes."

"Where?"

"Over at Victoria Crossing, place called The Cooks of Crocus Hill. I'm doing some developing over there, and I just happened to meet the woman who owns the cooking school."

"It's funny Lisa didn't mention it."

"I didn't tell Lisa." From the first, if only subconsciously, he'd been planning this day, planning to shock Bess. Funny, though, now that tonight was here all sense of smugness had fled. He felt nervous and afraid of failure.

"This woman . . ." Bess looked into her wine. ". . . is she someone important?"

"No, not at all."

His answer wrought only the subtlest change in Bess, but he detected it in the faint relaxing of her shoulders, of her lips just before she sipped her wine, of her eyes as she lifted them to the distant sails on the water. Too, she set her chair barely bouncing again, sending up a rhythmic *bing, bing, bing* that eased some tension in his belly.

He crossed his feet on the handrail and said, "I've been trying to do more things for myself lately."

"Like the cooking?"

"Yes. And reading and sailing, and I've even gone to a couple of movies. I guess I just came to the realization that you can't always rely on somebody else to take away your loneliness. You've got to do something about it yourself."

"Is it working?" She looked over at him.

"Yes. I'm happier than I've been in years."

She watched him study the wine in his glass while a slow grin stole over his lips. "You probably won't believe it, Bess, but . . ." His gaze shifted over to her. "I'm even doing my own laundry." She didn't tease as he'd expected.

"That's wonderful, Michael. That's growth, it really is."

"Yes, well . . . times change. A person's got to change with them."

"It's hard for men, especially men like you, whose mothers filled those traditional roles. You're in the generation that got caught in the cross fire. For the young guys like Mark it's easier. They grew up taking home ec class, with working mothers and a more blurred line between the obligations of the sexes, if you will."

"I never expected to like any of these domestic jobs but they're not bad at all, especially the cooking. I really enjoy it. Speaking of which . . ." He checked his watch and dropped his feet off the rail. "I've got some last-minute things to do. Why don't you just sit here and relax? More wine?"

"No, thanks. I'm going to be more sensible tonight. Besides, the view is heady enough."

He smiled at her and left.

She remained inert, listening to sounds drifting out from the kitchen—the clack of kettle covers, the bell on the microwave, running water—and wondered what he was making. The sun lowered and the lake looked bluer. The eastern sky became purple around the edges. Over on the public beach people began rolling up their towels and heading home. One-by-one the sails began disappearing from the water. The pastoral coming of evening, coupled with the wine and the sense of dissolving friction between herself and Michael, brought on a welcome serenity in Bess. She dropped her head back against the wall and basked in it.

After a full five minutes she took her empty wineglass and went inside, past the dining-room table to the kitchen doorway, against which she lounged with one shoulder. Michael had put on an audiotape of something New Age and keyboardish, and was measuring Parmesan cheese into a bowl, a blue-and-white dishtowel over his left shoulder. The picture he made was still so unexpected she felt a momentary thrill, as if she'd met this attractive stranger only tonight.

"Anything I can do to help?"

He looked around and smiled. "Nope, not a thing. Everything's under control . . ." He laughed nervously. ". . . I think." With a wire whisk he whipped an egg, then opened the refrigerator and took out a salad bowl filled with romaine.

"Caesar?" she inquired.

"Class number two." He grinned.

She raised one eyebrow and teased, "Do you trade recipes?"

"Listen, you're making me nervous, standing there watching me. If you want to do something, go light the candles."

"Matches?" she asked, boosting off the doorway.

"Oh, hell." He searched four kitchen drawers, came up with none, pawed through another and frantically lifted a lid off a simmering kettle before stalking toward his office. Finding none there, either, he hurried back to the kitchen. "Will you do me a favor? Check the pockets of my suitcoats. Sometimes I pick them up at restaurants. I've got to get these vegetables off the stove."

"Where are your suitcoats?"

"Master-bedroom closet."

She walked into his bedroom to find it impeccably clean, the torchère softly glowing, the bed neatly made. The room itself was engaging. All the decor items she'd chosen blended together in a wholly pleasing way: wallpaper, blinds, bedspread, matching chairs, art prints, a floor urn. The gleaming black bedroom furniture had a rich sheen, even in the reduced lighting. She particularly liked a unique, masculine piece called a dressing chest, and the headboard, shaped like a theater marquee from the thirties. Beside the bed the cover of a *Hunting* magazine displayed a stag with its rack in velvet. Michael's pocket tailings lay atop the chest of drawers—billfold, coins, somebody's business card, a ballpoint pen but no matches. Though she had planned the room and been in it countless times while decor items were being delivered, now that it was in use and occupied by his personal items, she felt like a window peeper in it.

She opened his closet door, searched for the interior light and switched it on. The closet smelled like British Sterling and him, a mixture so potent with nostalgia she felt her face heat. His shirts hung on one rack, jeans on another, suits on the third. A row of shoes toed the mopboard, one pair of Reeboks with worn white sweat socks poked inside. A rack of ties hung to the left of the door; one had slipped off and lay on the floor. She picked it up and hung it with the others, an insidiously wifely reaction that struck her only after the deed was done, and she whipped around to make sure he wasn't standing there watching her. He wasn't, of course, and she felt foolish.

Searching his jacket pockets proved nearly as personal as frisking the man himself. In one she found half of a theater ticket—*Pretty*, it said; presumably he'd seen the current hit *Pretty Woman.* In another was a used toothpick, in another an ad he'd torn out advertising a piece of land for sale.

She found some matches at last and scurried from the closet as if she'd just watched a porn movie in it.

The wine glasses were filled and their salad bowls on the table when she returned to it. She lit the blue candles while he came in with two loaded plates.

"Sit down," he said, motioning with a plate, "there." When she was seated, he placed before her a plate of steaming, savory food—glazed ham, tiny red potatoes in parsley butter and asparagus with cheese sauce. She stared at it, dumbfounded, while he seated himself at the opposite end of the table and watched for her reaction.

"Holy cow," she said, still staring at his accomplishment. "Holy old cow."

He laughed and said, "Could you be more specific?"

She looked up to find two candles and an iris directly in her line of vision, cutting his face in half. She craned to one side to see around them. "Who really cooked this?" she asked.

"I knew you'd say that."

"Well, Michael, can you blame me? In the days when I knew you your idea of a three-course meal was chips, dip and a Coke, if you were doing the cooking." She looked down at her plate. "This is incredible."

"Well, taste it, go ahead."

She untied her napkin from around the stem of the wineglass, spread it on her lap and sampled the asparagus first while he held his fork and knife and forgot to use them, watching closely again for her reaction.

She shut her eyes, chewed, swallowed, licked her lips and murmured, "Mmm, fantastic."

He felt as if he'd just landed a job as head chef at the Four Seasons. He put his knife and fork to use as she spoke again.

"Whatever have you done to this ham? It's incredible."

He peered around the centerpiece and abruptly clacked down his silverware on his plate. "Aw, hell, Bess, I feel like I'm on *Dallas.* I'm coming down there." He picked up his wineglass and slid his place mat down to her end of the table, taking a chair at a right angle to hers. "There, that's better. Now let's get this meal off to a proper start." He lifted his wineglass and she followed suit. "To . . ." He thought a while, their glasses poised. "To bygones," he said, "and letting them be."

"To bygones," she seconded as their glasses chimed. They drank with their gazes fused and afterward, with their lips still wet, lingered in their absorption with one another until Michael wisely broke it.

"Well, try the salad," he said, and did so himself.

She was filled with praise, and he with pride. They spoke of cheese sauce, and real estate ventures, and pecan praline mustard glaze, and the smoothness of the wine, and the film *Pretty Woman,* which they'd both seen. He told her about the Concerned Citizens' Meeting and his hopes for the corner of Victoria and Grand. She told him about the American Society of Interior Designers and her hopes that they would get legislation passed to require licensing, thereby prohibiting the unschooled interlopers of the industry from calling themselves interior designers.

He said, "Hear, hear! You've made me a firm believer in interior designers."

"You're pleased, then?"

"Absolutely."

"So am I." She proposed a toast. "To our amicable business association, and its most successful outcome."

"And to the condo . . ." he added, toasting the newly decorated room, ". . . a much brighter place to come home to."

They drank and relaxed over their empty plates. Dusk had fallen and the candlelight created a halo. The scent of the roses seemed to intensify in the damper air of evening. Outside, the calls of the gulls hushed while those of the crickets commenced. Beneath the table Bess removed her shoes. Above it both she and Michael toyed lazily with their wineglasses.

"You want to know something?" he said. "Ever since I divorced you I've longed to live back in our house in Stillwater. Now, for the first time, that's not true anymore, and it feels great. This place suits me. I walk in here and I have no desire to leave." He looked very self-satisfied as he continued in a quiet tone. "Want to know something else?"

She sat with one fist propping up her jaw. "Hm?"

"Since I've bought this place I've finally managed to get over the feeling that I was ripped off when you ended up with the house."

"You felt that way all these years?"

"Well, yeah, sort of. Wouldn't you?"

She pondered a while. "I suppose I would have."

"With Darla it was different. I moved into her place so it never really felt like *ours.* All of her stuff was in it, and when I left it I felt as if I was only letting her have what was rightfully hers all along. I just sort of . . ." He shrugged. ". . . walked out and felt relieved."

"It really was that simple, leaving her?"

"Absolutely."

"And she honestly felt the same?"

"I think so."

"Hm . . ."

In silence they compared that scenario to their own upon divorcing, all the bitterness and anger.

"Sure different from you and me," Bess said.

He stared at his wineglass and rotated it on the place mat, finally lifting his eyes to hers. "Feels good to leave all that behind us, doesn't it?"

"Why do you suppose we were both so hateful?" she asked, recalling her mother's words.

"I don't know."

"It would be interesting to hear what a psychologist would have to say on that subject."

"All I know is, this time when I got my divorce papers, I just put them away in a drawer and thought, So be it, another item of business closed."

Bess felt a pleasant shock. Her eyes widened. "You've got them? I mean, it's final?"

"Yup."

"That was fast."

"That's how it is when it's uncontested."

For a minute they studied each other, trying not to let their total freedom cloud judgment.

"Well!" he said, breaking the spell, pushing back from the table. "I wish I could say I prepared a breathtaking dessert but I didn't. I thought I was pushing my luck to make as much as I did, so Byerly's is responsible for the chocolate-mint creme cake." He picked up their plates and said, "I'll be right back. Coffee?"

"I'd love some but I don't think I have room for dessert."

"Oh, come on, Bess." He disappeared into the kitchen and called from there, "Indulge with me. Can't be more than . . . oh, hell, eight hundred calories in one piece of this stuff."

He returned with two plates of the most sinful-looking green-and-brown concoction this side of Julia Child's kitchen. Bess stared at it with her mouth watering while he went off after the coffeepot.

When he was seated again he dug in and she continued vacillating.

"Damn you, Michael," she said.

"Oh, come on, enjoy yourself."

"May I tell you something?"

She was glowering at him less than affectionately.

"What?"

"Something that's been aggravating me for six, closer to seven, years now? Something you said to me just before we got divorced that's burned me up ever since?"

He set down his fork carefully, disturbed by her quick change of mood. "What did I say?"

"You said I'd stopped taking care of myself. You implied that I'd gotten fat and seedy, and all I wore were jeans and sweatshirts anymore; and see what it's done to me? I'm ten pounds overweight and it might as well be fifty. I look at a dessert and feel like a glutton if I eat it, and no matter what I put on or how my hair looks, I'm still critical of myself; and in all these years I've never stooped to putting on a pair of jeans again, no matter how badly I've wanted to. There, now I've gotten it off my chest, and I'm going to see if it feels better!"

He stared at her in astonishment.

"I said that?"

"You mean you don't remember?"

"No."

"Oh God!" She covered her face, threw back her head, then pretended to pound on the table with both fists. "I go through six years of obsessive self-improvement and you don't even remember the remarks?"

"No, Bess, I don't. But if I made them, I'm sorry."

"Oh, shit," she said gloomily, dropping her jaw to a fist and eyeing her dessert. "Now what am I going to do with this?"

"Eat it," he said. "Then tomorrow, go buy yourself a pair of jeans."

She looked across the corner of the table at him and put on her puckered, disgruntled mouth, lips all turned inside like a stripped-off sock. "Michael Curran, if you knew all the misery you've caused me!"

"I said I was sorry. And there's nothing wrong with your shape, Bess, believe me. Eat the damned cake."

She glanced at the cake. Glanced at him. Felt one corner of her mouth threaten to grin. Saw both corners of his do the same. Felt her grin break, and then they were both laughing and gobbling dessert and it felt so damned comfortable at one point she actually reached across the table and wiped one corner of his mouth with her own napkin.

They finished, leaned back and rubbed their bellies and sipped coffee.

At her first taste she looked with surprise into her cup. "What next? Is this raspberry-flavored?"

"Chocolate-raspberry. Sylvia sells it at the shop, fresh-ground. She said it goes well with dessert and that it would be bound to impress a woman."

"Oh, so you set out to impress me, did you, Michael?"

"Isn't that obvious?" he said, rising with their dessert plates, escaping to the kitchen. She stared at the empty doorway for some time, then finished her coffee and followed him. He was rinsing plates and putting them in the dishwasher when she entered the room. She set their cups and saucers down beside him and remarked quietly, "We've covered a lot of ground tonight."

He continued his task without looking at her. "You named it earlier. Growth."

She rinsed their cups and handed them to him. He put them in the dishwasher. She wiped off a cabinet top and he ran water into the roaster in which he'd baked the ham.

"Tell you what . . ." He closed the dishwasher door. "Let's lighten up a little bit. Let's go out and take a walk along the lakeshore. What do you say?"

Leaning his hips against the cabinet, he dried his hands on a towel then handed it to her. She wiped hers, too, then folded the towel over the edge of the sink.

"All right," she said.

Neither of them moved. They stood side-by-side, studying each other, their backsides braced against the edge of the countertop. They were doing a mating dance and both knew it. They might very well suspect the outcome but when it came to stepping close and bringing the dance to its logical conclusion, both backed off. They had loved and lost once before and were terrified of the same thing happening twice; it was as simple as that.

They walked over to the public beach, speaking little. They stared at the path of the moon on the water. He sidearmed a rock into it, distorting the moon's reflection, then watched it reform. They listened to the soft lick of the waves on the shore, and smelled the tang of wet wood from a nearby dock, and felt the sand close in around their shoes and hold them rooted.

They looked at each other, standing a goodly distance apart, uncertain, desirous and fearing. Then back at the lake again, knowing relationships did not come with guarantees.

In time they turned and walked back, entered the lobby and rode the elevator to the second floor in silence. Back in his condo, Michael stopped off at the bathroom while Bess continued to the family room and flopped onto her back on the leather sofa, staring at the ceiling, one leg stretched out, the other foot on the floor.

I can stay or go, risk it or risk nothing. The choice is mine.

The bathroom door opened and he entered the family room, crossed it and stopped several feet from her, his hands in his rear pockets. For moments he remained so, in the pose of deep reflection and indecision, concentrating on her without moving.

Cautiously she sat up and dropped her other foot to the floor in a last-ditch decision for common sense.

Taking his hands from his pockets, he moved toward her smilelessly, as if his decision had been made. "I liked you better lying down," he said, grasping her shoulders and pressing her against the pliant cream leather as she had been. In one fluid motion he stretched half-beside, half-upon her and kissed her, a soft, lingering question after which he searched her eyes and held her rounded shoulder in the cup of his hand.

"I'm not at all sure this is the right thing to do," he said, his voice gruff with emotion.

"Neither am I."

"But I've been thinking about it all night."

"Only tonight? I've been thinking of it for weeks."

He kissed her a second time, as if convincing them both it was the right thing to do, taking a long, sweet time while temptation began its work. They let it build slowly, opening their mouths to each other, touching and holding one another tentatively, finally ending the kiss to embrace full-length, the way old friends do, needing time before taking one more step.

"What do you think?" he asked.

"You feel good."

"Ahh, so do you."

"Familiar."

"Yes." Familiarity had caught him, too, bringing with it a rightness he welcomed. When he kissed her again the friendliness had fled, replaced by a first show of fire and demand. She returned both and they held strong, heart-to-heart, with their legs plaited and urgency beginning. With their caress gone full-length, the kiss became lush and stormy, wholly immodest as the best of kisses are, with arousal at last admitted and moderation denied. They hove together, searching for a dearer fit, tasting coffee and concupiscence upon one another's tongues, reveling in it while past and present welled up and became enmeshed in this embrace—desire, hope, amity, past failures and fear of repeating those failures.

Their breakdown marked the end of a long abstinence for both of them; passion was swift and complete. He found her breast, cupped and caressed it briefly through her clothing before delving beneath. He shinnied down her body, pushed her sweater up and kissed her through her brassiere and pressed his face between her breasts while pinning her hips flat with his chest. She arched, and cradled his head as a murmur of delight slid from her throat.

He shot up, sitting on one heel, and made short work of her clothing, then his own. Down he flung her again, and she was eager to receive his open mouth upon her naked breasts and belly. He uttered a single word while working his way down her body, to her midriff, stomach, and the warm familiar flesh below.

"Remember?"

She remembered—ah, she remembered—the shyness the first time they had done these things, the years it had taken to perfect them, to feel comfortable doing them. She closed her eyes as his mouth touched her intimately. Her nostrils dilated as he nuzzled her, calling back other nights, other times when, with hearts hammering as now, they'd explored these primal forces and allowed themselves to enjoy them. In three years of intimacy with another man she had allowed no such license. But this was Michael, whose bride she'd been, whose children she'd borne, with whom such intimacies had once been learned.

In time she returned the favor while he lay back with his head against the soft leather cushions as she knelt on the floor in the wishbone of his legs.

"Oh, Michael," she said, "it's so easy with you. It feels so right."

"Do you remember the first time we did this?"

"We'd been married two years before we dared."

"And even then I was scared. I thought you'd smack me and go sleep in the spare room."

"I didn't, though, did I?"

He smiled down at her as she resumed her ardent ministrations. Moments later he reached down to touch her head. "Stop." He groped for his white trousers, which lay on the floor, drawing a foil packet from his pocket. "Do we need this?" he asked.

Smiling, she stroked him and said, "So you planned on this."

"Let's just say I was hoping."

"Yes, we need that. Unless we want to risk having a baby who's younger than our own grandchild." She watched him put on the condom as she had uncountable times before, hoping for a thousand future times.

"Wouldn't the kids have something to say about that?"

"Lisa would be overjoyed."

"She'd be overjoyed anyway. This is what she was scheming for all along." The tone of his voice became sultry. His hair was messed and his grin was teasing as he reached for her. "Come here, Grandma." He laid her where he wanted her and arranged her limbs to best advantage. "Let's christen this Italian leather properly."

She lifted her arms in welcome and they ended six—nearly seven—years of separation.

She looked up at his face as he entered her, and touched his temples where the silver hairs gilded the black, and drew him down flush upon her.

He made a sound, "Ahhh . . ." the way some men would after pushing back their plate after a satisfying meal. She'd been expecting it and it brought a smile. They held one another for a while without moving, letting familiarity and relief overtake them.

"It's wonderful," she said, "doing this with someone you know so well, isn't it?"

He pressed back to see her face and smiled softly. "Yes, it's wonderful."

"I knew you'd make that sound just now."

"What sound?"

"Ahh, you said, 'Ahh,' the way you always did."

"Did I always?"

"Always. At that moment."

He grinned as if this was news to him and kissed her lightly on the upper lip. Then her lower one. Then her full mouth while he began moving.

Her eyes closed, the better to enjoy what followed, and her hands rode low upon his hips.

Sometimes they kissed, softly, in keeping with veneration.

Sometimes they smiled for no single reason.

Sometimes he voiced questions, throaty and thick.

Sometimes she whispered a reply, gazing up into his eyes.

And once they laughed, and thought how grand they could do so in the midst of lovemaking.

When they reached their climaxes, Bess called out and Michael groaned, their mingled voices shimmering through the dimly lit rooms she had so newly trimmed for him. Ah, the dazzling disquiet of those few trembling seconds while they lost touch with all but sensation.

In the afterglow they lay on their sides, sealed to each other and the warmed leather. The welcome breath of early night drifted in to cool their skins. Moths beat against the screen. Through the archway the forgotten dinner candles washed the walls with amber light.

Bess's hair trailed over Michael's arm while his free hand idled over her breasts in a soothing, endless rhythm. She heaved a sigh of repletion and let her eyes close for a while. He knew these were the moments she savored best, afterward, when the souls took over where the bodies left off. Always she'd whispered, "Don't leave . . . not yet." He remained now, studying the faint tracery of creases at the corners of her eyes, the rim of her lips, which were so at rest they revealed a glimpse of teeth inside, the place on her throat where her pulse billowed and ebbed like the wings of a sitting butterfly.

She opened her eyes and found him studying her without the smile she'd expected.

"Just what do we think we're going to do about this?" he asked quietly.

"I don't know."

"Did you have any ideas before you came here?"

She wagged her head faintly.

"We could just keep having a torrid affair."

"A torrid affair? Michael, what have you been reading?"

He put his thumb beneath her lower lip and pulled down until her bottom teeth appeared.

"We're awfully darn good together, Bess."

"Yes, I know but be serious."

He gave up his preoccupation with her mouth and laid his arm along his hip. "All right, I will. How much do you think we've changed since our divorce?"

"That's a loaded question if I ever heard one."

"Answer it."

"I'm scared to." After a long pause she asked, "Aren't you?"

He studied her eyes for some time before answering, "Yes."

"Then I think what I'll do is just get up and put my clothes on and go home and pretend this never happened."

She rolled over and off him.

"Good luck," he said, watching her pick up her clothing and go. She used the guest bathroom off the gallery and felt reality return with every minute while she donned the brief blue underwear that had certainly done its job. Reality was the two of them, failures the first time around, starting up a carnal relationship again without rationalizing where it might lead. Dressed once more, she returned to the doorway to find him standing at the far end of the family room before the sliding glass door, barefooted, bare-chested, wearing only his white jeans.

"May I borrow a brush?" she asked.

He turned and looked back at her, silent for a stretch.

"In my bathroom."

Once again she went away, into his private domain, where she had probed once before. This time was worse—opening his vanity drawers and finding an ace bandage, dental floss, some foil packets of Alka-Seltzer and an entire box of condoms.

An entire box!

Looking at them, she found herself blush with anger. All right, so he was single, and single guys probably bought condoms by the dozen. But she didn't like being duped into believing this was an uncommon occurrence in his life!

She slammed that drawer and opened another to find his hairbrush at last. Some of his dark hairs were stuck in the bristles. The sight of them, and the feel of his brush being drawn through her hair, dulled her anger and brought a sense of grave emptiness, a reluctance to return to her lone life, where there was no sharing of brushes or of bathrooms or dinner tables or beds.

She did what she could with her hair, searched out mouthwash and used it, refreshed her lipstick and returned to the family room once more. He was still staring out at the darkness, obviously troubled by the same misgivings as she, now that the easy part was over.

"Well, Michael, I think I'll go."

He swung to face her.

"Yeah, fine," he answered.

"Thank you for supper. It was wonderful."

"Sure."

A void passed, a great terrifying void that reared up before both of them.

"Listen, Michael, I've been thinking. There are a few more empty walls in here, and you could use some more small items on the mantels and the tables but I think it's best if you find them on your own."

His expression grew stormy. "Bess, why are you blaming me? You wanted it, too. Don't tell me you didn't, not after those underclothes you were wearing. You were planning on it just as much as I was!"

"Yes, I was. But I'm not blaming you. I just think that we . . . that it's . . ." She ran out of words.

"What? A mistake?"

She remembered the condoms. "I don't know. Maybe."

He stared at her with a hurt look around his eyes and an angry one around his mouth.

"Should I call you?"

"I don't know, Michael. Maybe it's not such a good idea."

He dropped his chin to his chest and whispered, "Shit."

She stood across the room, her heart racing with fear because of what he had almost suggested. It was too terrifying to ponder, too impossible to consider, too risky to let it be put into words. They had changed a lot but what assurance was there? What fool would put his hand in the mill wheel after his finger had been cut off?

She said, "Thanks again, Michael," and he made no reply as she saw herself out and ran from the idea of starting again.

chapter 15

When Bess got home the lights were on all over the house, even in her bedroom. Frowning, she parked in the driveway rather than waste time pulling into the garage, and had barely put foot inside the front door when Randy came charging down two steps at a time from the second story. "Ma, where you been? I thought you'd never get home!"

Terror struck. "What's wrong?"

"Nothing. I got an audition! Grandma's old dude, Gilbert, got me one with this band called The Edge!"

Bess released a breath and let her shoulders slump. "Thank heavens. I thought it was some catastrophe."

"Turns out old Gilbert used to own the Withrow Ballroom and he knows everybody—bands, agents, club owners. He's been talking to guys about me since Lisa's wedding. Pretty great, huh?"

"That's wonderful, Randy. When's the audition?"

"I don't know yet. The band's playing a gig out in Bismarck, North Dakota, but they're due back tomorrow. I've got to call them sometime in the afternoon. God, where were you, Mom? I've been hangin' around here all night, waiting to tell you."

"I was with your dad."

"With Dad?" Randy's ebullience fizzled. "You mean, on business?"

"No, not this time. He cooked dinner for me."

"*Dad* cooked dinner?"

"Yes. And a very good one at that. Come on upstairs with me and tell me about this band." She led the way to her bedroom, where the television was on and she could tell Randy had been lying on her bed. He must have been anxious, to have invaded her room. She snagged a robe and went into her bathroom, calling through the door as she changed into it, "So what kind of music does this band play?"

"Rock, basically. A mix of old and new, Gilbert said."

They went on talking until Bess came out of the bathroom with her face scrubbed, rubbing lotion on it while a headband held her hair out of the way. Randy was sitting on the bed, Indian-fashion, looking out of place in her boudoir, with its pastel stripes and cabbage roses, bishop sleeve curtains and chintz-covered chairs. Bess sat down in one and propped her bare feet on the mattress, crossing her terrycloth robe over her knees.

"Did you know about this?" Randy asked. "I mean, did Grandma tell you?"

"No. It's as much of a surprise to me as it is to you." From a skirted table Bess took a remote control and lowered the volume of the television, then pulled the band from her hair.

"Old Gilbert . . . can you believe that?" Randy wobbled his head in amazement.

"Yes, I can, the way he dances."

"And all because I played at that wedding."

"You see? Just a little courage and look what happens."

Randy grinned and slapped out a rhythm on his thighs.

"You scared?" his mother asked.

His hands stopped tapping. "Well . . ." He shrugged. "Yeah, I guess so, a little."

"I was scared when I started my store, too. Turned out good, though."

Randy sat looking at her. "Yeah, I guess it did." He fell pensive for some time, then seemed to draw himself from his thoughts. "So what's this between you and the old man?"

"Your dad, you mean."

"Yeah . . . sorry . . . Dad. What's going on between you two?"

Bess got up and walked to the dresser, where she dropped the headband and fiddled with some bottles and tubes before picking one up and uncapping it. "We're just friends." She squeezed some skin mask on her finger and put her face close to the mirror while touching selected spots.

"You're a lousy liar, you know that, Mom? You've been to bed with him, haven't you?"

"Randy, that's none of your business!" She slammed down the tube.

"I can see in that mirror and you're blushing."

She glared at his reflection. "It's still none of your business, and I'm appalled at your lack of manners."

"Okay! Okay!" He threw back his hands and clambered off the bed. "I just don't understand you, that's all. First you divorce him, and then you decorate his place, and now . . ." He gestured lamely as his words died.

She turned to face him. "And now, you will kindly give me the same respect I give you in personal matters. I've never asked about your sex life, and I don't expect you to ask about mine, okay? We're both adults. We both know the risks and rewards of certain choices we might make. Let's leave it at that."

He stared at her, torn by ambivalence about his father, one facet of him leavened by the possibility of her getting back together with him permanently; the other facet curdled by the idea of having to make peace with Michael at last.

"You know what, Mom?" Randy said, just before leaving the room, "You were never this touchy about Keith."

She studied the empty doorway when he was gone, realizing he was right. She dropped down and sat on the edge of the bed with her inner wrists together between her knees, trying to make sense of things. In time she flopped to her back, arms outflung, wondering what the outcome of tonight would be. She was being protective of herself because she was scared. That's why she had walked out on Michael, and why she had snapped at Randy. The risk of becoming involved was so great—hell, what was she saying? She was already involved again with Michael; to think anything else was self-delusion. *They* were involved, and more than likely falling in love again, and what was the logical conclusion of falling in love if not marriage?

Bess rolled to her side, drew up her knees, crossed her bare feet and closed her eyes.

I, Bess, take thee, Michael, for better or for worse, till death do us part.

They had believed it once and look what their gullibility had cost. All the anguish of breaking up a family, a home, joint finances, two hearts. The idea of risking it again seemed immensely foolhardly.

The audition was scheduled for Monday afternoon at two, at a club called Stonewings. The band had their equipment set up for their evening gig and were working on balancing sound when Randy walked in with a pair of drumsticks in his hand. The place was dark but for the stage, lit by canister lights from a ceiling strip. One guitarist was repeating into a mike, "Check, one, two," while another squatted at the rear of the stage, peering at the orange screen of an electronic guitar tuner.

Randy approached out of the darkness. "Hullo," he said, reaching the rim of light.

All sound ceased. The lead guitarist looked over, an emaciated man who resembled Jesus Christ as depicted on Catholic holy cards. He held a royal blue Fender Stratocaster with a burning cigarette stuck behind the strings near the tuning pegs. "Hey, guys," he said, "our man is here. You Curran?"

"That's right." Randy reached up, extending his hand. "Randy."

The man pushed his guitar against his belly and leaned over it to shake hands. "Pike Watson," he said, then turned to introduce the bassist. "Danny Scarfelli."

The keyboard man came over and shook hands, too. "Tom Little."

The rhythm guitarist followed suit. "Mitch Yost."

There was a sound-and-light man, too, moving around in the shadows, adjusting canisters from a stepladder.

Watson told Randy, "That's Lee out there, doing lights." He shaded his eyes and called, "Yo, Lee!"

Out of the darkness came a voice like a bastard file on babbitt. "Hey!"

"This is Randy Curran."

"Let's hear his stuff!" came the reply.

While the others drifted back to tuning and balancing, Watson asked Randy, "So what do you know?"

Randy's gesture flipped his drumsticks once, like windshield washers. "Anything. You name it—something with a shuffle beat or straight rock—doesn't matter."

"Okay, how about a little of 'Blue Suede Shoes'?"

"Great."

He had expected the simplest of songs, something everybody knew as well as they knew every nick and scratch on their own instruments. Simple songs were the best gauge of true talent.

The trap set was simple, five pieces—bass, snare, a floor tom, two ride toms and assorted cymbals, one, of course, a high hat. Randy settled himself behind them, found the foot pedals of the bass and a ride, rattled a quick riff across the skins and adjusted the height of a cymbal. He put both sticks in his left hand, drew the stool an inch forward, tested the distance again, looked up and said, "All set. I'll count it out, give you three for nothing and then we'll go into it on four."

Pike Watson blew smoke toward the ceiling, replaced the cigarette next to a tuning peg and replied, "Beat me, Sticks."

Randy tapped out the pickup beat on the rim of the snare and the band struck into the song with Watson singing lead.

For Randy, playing was therapy. Playing was forgetting anyone else existed. Playing was living in total harmony with two sticks of wood and a set of percussion instruments over which he seemed to have some sort of mystic control. It felt to Randy as if they put out sound at the command of his mere thought waves rather than his hands and feet. When the song ended, Randy was surprised, having little recall of playing it, measure-for-measure. It seemed, instead, to have played him.

He pinched the cymbals quiet, rested his hands on his thighs and looked up.

Pike Watson appeared pleased. "You got your chops down, man."

Randy smiled.

"How about another one?"

They played a little twelve-bar blues, then three more, typical musicians who, like the alcoholic, can never stop with just one.

"Nice licks," Scarfelli offered when they broke.

"Thanks."

Watson asked, "Do you sing?"

"A little."

"Harmony?"

"Yeah."

"Lead?"

"If you want."

"Well, shit, man, let's hear you."

Randy asked for the new Elton John hit, "The Club at the End of the Street," and although the band hadn't worked it up they ad-libbed expertly.

When the song ended, Watson asked, "Who have you played with?"

"Nobody. This is my first audition."

Watson raised one eyebrow, rubbed his beard and glanced at the others.

"What have you got for drums?"

"A full set of Pearls, rototoms and all."

"You must be into heavy metal."

"Some."

"We don't do much of that."

"I'm versatile."

"A lot of the club stages are smaller than this. Any objection to leaving a few of your Pearls at home?"

"No."

"Are you married?"

"No."

"Planning on it?"

"No."

"Got any kids?" Randy grinned and Watson added, "Well, hell, you never know anymore."

"No kids."

"So you can travel?"

"Yes."

"No other jobs?"

Randy chuckled and scratched the back of his head. "If you can call it that. I pack nuts in a warehouse." The whole band laughed. "If you guys take me on I'll be kissing that job good-bye."

"What have you got for wheels?"

"That's no problem." It was, but he'd face it if and when.

"You union?"

"No, but I will be if you say so."

"Whoever we hire will have to sit in on about six solid days of practices 'cause our drummer's leaving at the end of the week."

"No problem. I can blow off that pistachio palace in one phone call."

Pike Watson consulted the others with a glance, returned his gaze to Randy and said, "Okay, listen . . . we'll let you know, okay?"

"Okay." Randy lifted his hands, let them fall to his thighs, backed off the stool and shook hands all around. "Thanks for letting me sit in. You guys are great. I'd sell my left nut to play with you."

He left them laughing and stepped out into the midafternoon sun, longing for a hit of something to relax the tension. He tipped back at the waist, closed his eyes and sucked in half the blue sky; he jived toward his car, rapping out a rhythm against his thighs with one palm and the paired sticks. Sweet, the very sweetest—playing with real musicians. Hope pressed up against his throat and made his head buzz. He thought about spending the rest of his life playing music instead of weighing and packing nuts. The comparison was ludicrous. But it was a long shot; he realized that. The Edge had undoubtedly auditioned other guys with plenty of experience, guys who'd played with well-known bands from around the Twin Cities or beyond. What were his chances of competing with them?

He unlocked his car, slid in and rolled down the windows. No air-conditioning, so the interior was like a sauna, the vinyl seatcovers radiant, even through his jeans. Somewhere under the seat he'd left a fast-food container with part of an uneaten bun, and it smelled as yeasty as working beer.

He started the engine, turned the fan on, then off again when the blast of engine heat proved hotter than the motionless air had been. He put in a tape of Mike and the Mechanics and began pulling out of the parking lot.

Something hit the car like a falling rock.

Jesus, what was that?

He braked and craned around to find Pike Watson had thumped on the trunk to stop him. His bearded face appeared at the open window.

"Hey, Curran, not so fast."

"Was that you? I thought I ran over a kid or something." Randy turned down the stereo.

"It was me. Listen, we want you to be our rimshot."

Shock suffused Randy. It went through his body faster than a hit of marijuana. Felt better, too.

"You serious?"

"We knew before you went out the door. We just have this policy, we all talk it over, no one person decides. Wanna come back inside and get in a couple hours of practice?"

Randy stared, dumbfounded. He whispered, "Jesus . . ." and after a pause, "I don't believe this."

Watson wagged his head. "You're good, man. Believe it. But we've got only six days to work you into four hours' worth of music, so what do you say?"

Randy smiled. "Let me park this thing."

He parked the car and stepped onto the blacktop, wondering how he'd operate the foot pedals with his knees this weak, how he could do licks with his body trembling so. Pike Watson shook his hand as they headed back inside the club.

"You get that union card as quick as you can."

"Anything you say," Randy replied, matching him pace for pace as he headed toward paradise.

It had been three days since Michael's evening with Bess. At work, he had been withdrawn. In his car, he had ridden with the radio off. At home, he'd spent a lot of time sitting on the deck with his feet on the railing, staring at the sails on the water.

That's where he was on Tuesday evening when his phone rang.

He answered and heard Lisa's voice.

"Hi, Dad. I'm down in the lobby. Let me in."

He was waiting in his open door when she stepped off the elevator, looking quite ballooned, in blue shorts and a white maternity blouse.

"Well, look at you," he said, opening his arms as she hove up against him. "Getting rounder every day."

She rested a hand on her stomach. "Yup. Not unlike the St. Paul Cathedral." The church had a dome that could be seen for miles.

"This is a nice surprise. Come on in."

They sat on deck chairs, sipping root beer, watching evening slant in behind them and tint the tips of the trees golden. The water was jeweled and the smell of wild sweet clover drifted from nearby roadsides.

"How've you been, Daddy?"

"Okay."

"I haven't heard from you in a while."

"Been busy." He told her about the Victoria and Grand plans and the attendant hassle with the locals. He told her he'd been sailing some and had seen the new movie *Dick Tracy,* and asked if she and Mark had seen it. He mentioned his cooking classes and how he was enjoying his new skills.

"I hear you made dinner for Mother Saturday night."

"How did you hear that?"

"Randy called, about something else, actually, but he mentioned it."

"I suppose Randy wasn't too pleased."

"Randy's got other things on his mind right now. He auditioned for a band called The Edge, and they hired him."

Michael's face brightened. "Great!"

"He's blown away, rehearsing all morning with tapes and all afternoon with the band."

"When did all this happen?"

"Yesterday. Didn't Mother call you and tell you?"

"No, she didn't."

"But if the two of you were together on Saturday night . . ." Lisa let the suggestion hang.

"Things didn't go too well between us."

Lisa got up and went to the railing. "Damn."

Michael studied her back, her hair knotted in a loose French braid and tied off with a puckered circle of blue cloth.

"Honey, you've got to stop dreaming that Mom and I will get back together. I don't think that's ever going to happen."

Lisa flounced around to face him and rested her backside on the railing. "But why? You're divorced, she's free, you're both lonely. Why?"

He rose and caught her around the neck with one arm, turning her to face the lake. "It's not that simple. There's history between us that's got to be considered."

"What? Your affair? Mother can't honestly be hung up on that anymore, can she?"

Lisa had never used the word before. Hearing her speak it now, forthrightly, throwing it out for honest examination, Michael discovered the two of them crossing some new plateau as a father and a daughter.

"We've never talked about it before, you and I."

She shrugged. "I knew about it all along."

"But you never held it against me the way the others did."

"I figured you had your reasons." He wasn't going to delineate them at this late date. Lisa added, "All I ever heard was Mom's side of the story but I remember things weren't so super around our house at that time, and part of it was her fault."

"Well, thanks for the benefit of the doubt."

"Dad?" Lisa looked up at him. "Will you tell me something?"

"Depends on what the question is." She bore so much resemblance to Bess as she looked straight into Michael's eyes.

"Do you still love Mom—I mean, even a little bit?" she finished hopefully.

He dropped his arm from around her and sighed. "Oh, Lisa . . ."

"Do you? Because the way you were acting at my wedding, it seemed like both of you had some feelings for each other."

"Maybe we do, but—"

"Then, please don't give up."

"You didn't let me finish. Maybe we do but we're both a lot more cautious now, especially your mother."

"I think she loves you. A lot. But I can understand why she'd be scared to let you know. Heck, who wouldn't be when a guy has left you for another woman? Now, don't get upset that I said that. I *didn't* take sides when you left Mom but now I am. I'm taking both of your sides, because I want you back together again so badly, I just . . . I just don't even know how to say it." She turned to him with tears magnifying her eyes. "Give me your hand, Daddy."

He knew what she would do even as he complied. She placed his palm against her stomach and said, "This is your grandchild in here, some little thing who's probably going to come out looking like you and Mom in some way, right? I want him to have all the best advantages a child can have, and that includes a grandpa and grandma's house to go to at Christmastime, and the two of you together picking him up sometime and taking him to the circus, or to Valley Fair, or going to his school programs, or . . . or . . . oh, you know what I mean. Please, Daddy, don't give up on Mother. You're the one who left her; you've got to be the one to go back and convince her it was a mistake in the first place. Will you try?"

Michael took Lisa in his arms and held her loosely.

"It's dangerous to idealize things so."

"Will you?"

He didn't answer.

"I'm not idealizing. I saw you two together. I know there was something between you the night of my wedding, I just know it. Please, Daddy?"

It had been far easier to promise her he'd have her piano moved forever.

"Lisa, I can't promise such a thing. If things had gone better between us the other night . . ."

The note upon which the night had ended had made mockery of his and Bess's sexual encounter. Since then Michael had viewed his actions as foolish and willful. Lisa's remarks only ripened his disillusionment into confusion. If Bess loved him as Lisa suspected, she had a strange way of showing it. If she didn't, her way was stranger yet.

Lisa drew herself out of his arms, looking forlorn.

"Well, I thought I'd try," she said. "Guess I better go."

He walked her to the door and rode the elevator with her down to the lobby, where she stopped and turned to him.

"There's something else I'd like to ask you, Dad."

"Ask away."

"It's about when the baby's born. I wondered if you'd like to be there during the delivery. We're inviting Mark's folks, too."

"And your mother, too, no doubt."

"Of course."

"Another attempt to work us back together, Lisa?"

Lisa shrugged. "Sure. Why not? But it might be the only chance you get to witness the awesome spectacle. I know you weren't there when Randy and I were born, so I thought . . ." She shrugged again.

"Thanks for asking. I'll think about it."

When Lisa was gone, Michael's thoughts returned to Bess, plunging him into a limbo of indecisiveness.

Ever since Saturday night he'd passed telephones the way sinners pass confessionals, wanting to reach out and dial Bess's number and say he was sorry, he needed absolution. But to call her was to place himself in a position of even greater vulnerability, so he resisted the urge once again.

The following day, however, he dialed the house at eleven o'clock in the morning, expecting Randy to answer.

To his surprise, Bess did.

"Bess!" he exclaimed, lunging forward in his desk chair and feeling his face ignite. "What are you doing home!"

"Grabbing a sandwich and picking up some catalogs I forgot before I head out for a noon appointment."

"I didn't expect you to be there. I called for Randy."

"He's not here, sorry."

"I wanted to congratulate him. I hear he's found a job with a band."

"That's right."

"I suppose he's really excited, huh?"

"Is he ever. He's quit his job at the nut house and he's practicing here every morning and with the band every afternoon. Today, though, he's out shopping for a used van. Says he's got to have one to haul his drums in."

"Has he got any money?"

"Probably not but I didn't volunteer any."

"What do you think? Should I?"

"That's up to you."

"I'm asking your advice, Bess. He's our son and I want to do what you think will be best for him."

"All right, then, I think it's best to let him struggle and find his own way to get a van. If he wants the job badly enough—and of course he does—he'll work it out."

"All right, I won't offer."

A lull fell. End of one subject, opening for another . . .

Michael picked up a stapler, moved it to a different spot on his desktop, moved it back where it had been. "Bess, about Saturday night . . ." She said nothing. He depressed the head of the stapler four times, not quite hard enough to release staples. "All week long I've been thinking I should call you and apologize."

Neither of them spoke for a long time. His fingertips lingered over the stapler, polishing it as if it were dusty.

"Bess, I think you were right. That wasn't a very smart thing we did."

"No. It only complicates matters."

"So I guess we shouldn't see each other anymore, should we?"

Again, no answer.

"We're only getting Lisa's hopes up for nothing. I mean, it isn't going to lead to anything, so why do we put ourselves through it?"

His heart was drumming hard enough to loosen the stitches on his shirt pocket. Sweet Jesus, it was just like when they used to talk this way on the phone in college, longing to be together yet summoning willpower to do the right thing, which they inevitably failed to do once they were together.

When he spoke again the words emerged in a ragged whisper. "Bess, are you there?"

Her voice, too, sounded strained. "The damned awful truth is that it's the best piece of sex I've had since the last good one you and I had together when we were still married. I've thought about it so much since Saturday night, about all those years of learning it took to get it right together, and how comfortable and easy it felt with you. Did it feel that way for you, too?"

"Yes," he whispered hoarsely while beneath the desk he felt himself grow priapic.

"And that's important, isn't it?"

"Of course."

"But it isn't enough. It's the kind of reasoning teenagers use, and we're not teenagers any longer."

"What are you saying, Bess?"

"I'm saying I'm scared. I'm saying I've been walking around thinking of nothing but you since Saturday night and it scares the living hell out of me. I'm scared of getting hurt again, Michael."

"And you think I'm not?"

"I think it's different for a man."

"Oh, Bess, come on, don't give me that double-standard crap. My feelings are involved here just like yours are."

"Michael, when I went into your bathroom to look for a brush I found a whole box of condoms in the drawer. *A whole box!*"

"So that's why you got all huffy and walked out?"

"Well, what would you have done?" She sounded very angry.

"Did you notice how many were used?" When she made no reply he said, "One! Go back and count them. One, which was in my pocket before you got there that night. Bess, I don't fuck around."

"Oh, that word is so offensive."

"All right then, screw. I don't and you know it."

"How can I know it, when six years ago—seven—it's a good part of what broke up our marriage."

"I thought we'd been through all that and agreed that it was both our faults. Now here we go again; we get together, we make love once and you're already slinging accusations at me. Hell, I can't fight this for the rest of my life."

"Nobody asked you to."

After a broad silence he responded in a sound of pinched anger, "All right. That's certainly clear enough. Tell Randy I called, will you? Tell him I'll try him again later."

"I'll tell him."

He hung up without a good-bye. "Shit!" He made a fist and banged the stapler. "Shit! Shit! Shit!" He banged it three more times, pumping out staples and jamming the contraption. He sat staring at it, scowling, his lips as straight and thin as a welt pocket. "Shit," he said again, quieter, spreading his elbows on the desk, joining his hands with the thumbs extended and pressed to his eyeballs.

What did she want of him? Why should he feel like the guilty one when she'd been as willing and eager as he last Saturday night? He hadn't done a damned thing wrong! Not one! He'd seduced his ex-wife with her total compliance, and now she was putting the screws to him for it. Damn women, anyway! And damn this one in particular.

He went up to his cabin the next weekend, got eaten up by mosquitoes, wished it were hunting season; got eaten up by deerflies, wished there were someone with him; got eaten up by wood ticks, wished he had a phone up there so he could call Bess and tell her what he thought of her accusations.

He returned to the city still fuming, picked up the phone on Sunday night and slammed it back into the cradle without dialing her number.

On Tuesday night he attended another "unreasonable citizens" meeting on the Victoria and Grand issue, came out of it angrier than ever because they wanted him to plant twenty-four good-sized boulevard trees all up and down Grand Avenue at a cost of probably a thousand dollars per tree (including concrete ironwork), which had nothing whatever to do with the building he wanted to put up but it appeared he was being legally extorted and would go along with it: twenty-four thousand dollars' worth of trees for his building permit and an end to their squawking.

He had tried to call and congratulate Randy three additional times, always without getting an answer, and that irritated him, too.

Every time he passed through the gallery, with its empty faux pedestal still waiting for a piece of sculpture, he railed against Bess for writing him off with the job unfinished.

She was at the root of his dissatisfaction with life in general, and he realized it.

Two weeks had passed and his disposition hadn't improved. Finally, one night in late July, when he'd overbroiled some fresh scallops for himself and gotten them rubbery, and had listened to roaring speedboats until he'd been forced to close the deck doors, and had picked up the television guide to find nothing but junk scheduled, and had sat at his drafting table for two hours without accomplishing a thing, he went into his bathroom, got the box of condoms, stormed down to his car, drove to her house, rang the bell and stood on her doorstep, waiting to tie into her.

After a delay the hall light came on, the door opened and there she stood, barefoot, wearing a thigh-length thing made of white terrycloth with an elastic neck hole and a tie at the waist. Her hair was wet and she smelled good enough to bottle and sell, which further piqued him.

"Michael, what in the world are you doing here?"

"I came to talk and I'm going to." He burst his way inside and closed the door.

She attempted to check her watch but her wrist was empty. Obviously she was fresh out of the shower. "It's got to be ten-thirty at night!"

"I really don't give a damn, Bess. Are you alone?"

"Yes. Randy's out playing."

"Good. Let's go into the family room." He headed that way.

"You go straight to hell, Michael Curran!" she shouted. "You come bursting into my house giving orders and bossing me around. Well, I don't have to put up with it. You can just get out and lock the door when you go!"

She caught her short skirt in her fingertips and headed up the stairs.

"Wait just a minute there, missus!" He charged after her, taking the steps two at a time, and caught her halfway up. "You're not going anywhere until you—"

"I'm not a missus, and take your hands off me!"

"That's not what you said that night in my apartment, is it? My hands were just fine on you then, weren't they?"

"Oh, so you came to throw that up in my face, did you?"

"No. I came to tell you that ever since that night everything's been horseshit. I walk around with a wad of anger in my throat, and I snap at people who don't deserve it, and I can't even get my own damn son to answer the phone so I can congratulate him!"

"And that's *my* fault?" She opened a hand on her chest.

"Yes!"

"What'd I do?"

"You accused me of screwing around, and I didn't!" He grabbed her hand and slapped the box of condoms into it. "Here, count 'em!"

She gaped at the box, dumbstruck.

"Count 'em! One missing, and that's all. I bought them that day! Count 'em, I said!"

She tried to give the box back to him. "Don't be absurd, I'm not going to count them!"

"Then how will you know I'm telling the truth?"

"It doesn't matter, Michael, because it's not going to happen again."

"The hell it isn't! I'm hornier than a two-peckered goat just standing here smelling you, and either you're by God going to count those rubbers or I will. You're not going to? All right, give them to me!" He grabbed the box and sat down on a step at her feet, opened it and started pulling them out. "One. Two. Three." He slapped them down on the carpet, counting clear to eleven, until they were scattered like petals at her feet. "There, you see?" He looked up at her, high above him. "One missing. Now do you believe me?"

She was leaning against the wall, covering her mouth with a hand, laughing. "You should just see yourself; you look absolutely ridiculous, sitting there counting those things."

"That's what you damn women do to us men, you play around with us until we do things that make us look like blithering idiots. Do you believe me now, Bess?"

"Yes, I believe you but for heaven's sake, pick them up. What if Randy happened to come home early?"

He grabbed her bare ankle. "Come on down here and help me."

"Michael, let go."

He gripped harder and with his free hand lifted her hem. "What have you got on under there?"

She slapped her skirt to her thighs. "Michael, you damned fool, stop it."

"My God, Bess, you're naked under that thing."

"Let my ankle go!"

"You horny, too, Bess? I'll bet you are. Why don't you invite me up to our old bedroom and we'll take one of these things and put it to good use?"

"Michael, don't." He was rising to his feet, one condom in his hand, climbing the two steps to reach her, then flattening her against the handrail, to which she clung with both hands.

"Bess, there's a lot of sex between you and me just waiting to be made. I think we found that out that night at my place, so let's get started."

She was trying hard not to be swayed by him. He looked devastating with his hazel eyes snapping and his hair in need of cutting, and he felt inviting, too, so near and warm and seductive. "You get out of here. You're plum crazy."

He kissed her neck and ground himself against her, breast to hips. "I'm crazy all right, crazy about you, missus. Come on, what do you say?"

"And what then? A replay of the last two weeks? Because it hasn't been any more fun for me than it's been for you."

He kissed her on the mouth once, more the strike of a wet tongue than an actual kiss, and whispered a suggestion in her ear.

She giggled. "Oh for shame, you dirty old man."

"Come on, you'll like it."

He was still grinding, and she was still amused but weakening.

"You're going to crush my pelvis on this handrail."

"But you'll be moaning so loud you won't even hear it crack."

"Michael Curran, your ego exceeds anything known to woman."

"Doesn't it, though." He had her skirt up and a two-handed grip on her buttocks. Then he had his lips on hers, and his tongue in her mouth, and her arms went around his shoulders and he was touching her inside where she was all liquid heat. The kiss grew rampant. Their breathing grew stressed.

Against his lips she mumbled, "All right, you devil, you win."

He hauled her by the hand, up the steps, along the hall, leaving the foil packets scattered on the stairs, into their bedroom, strewing flotsam as they went—his shirt, her belt, his shoes, her white cover-up—and hit the bed naked, already tangled.

They were laughing as they bounced onto the mattress on their sides. Abruptly the laughter fled, replaced by a gaze of pure passion.

"Bess . . ." Michael whispered, "Bess . . ." rolling with her, wanting his mouth everywhere at once. "I missed you."

"I missed you, too, and I thought about this. I wanted it . . ." She sucked in a quick breath and exclaimed, "Oh!"

They were giving and greedy, tender and tensile by turns. With hands and mouths they savored one another's bodies, each the perfect recipient of the other. The bedspread grew mussed, two pillows fell to the floor, several others bolstered them randomly, and in time not so randomly.

He told her, "You smell the way I remember."

She said, "So do you . . ."

Ah, the smells, the tastes.

"Your hands," she said once, examining them. "How I've always loved your hands. Here . . . they belong here . . ."

Later, he murmured, "You still like this, don't you?"

"Ohhh . . ." she crooned, her eyes closing, ending on a whisper, ". . . yes."

What they shared was universal. Why, then, did it feel unique? Triumphant? As if no one before them or after them would share these same feelings? They answered these questions themselves, when he entered her, levered her as close as possible with one heel and clasped her against his breast with her face in the cay of his neck.

"I think I've fallen in love with you again, Bess," he whispered against her damp hair.

She went still, all but her heart, whose beat seemed to suddenly fill her entire body, the entire room, the entire world.

"I think I've fallen in love with you, too."

For that trembling, precious moment each was afraid to speak further, to move. His eyes were closed, his wide hand cradling the back of her head where her hair felt cool. Her mouth had made a damp spot just below his whisker line.

Finally he drew back, tenderly brushing the hair from her face.

"Really?" His smile was delicate, surprised.

"Really."

They kissed with exquisite tenderness, touching each other in places that mattered as much as those joined below—napes, faces, temples, throats—each touch a reiteration of the words they'd spoken.

"These last two weeks apart were horrible. Let's not ever do that to each other again," he whispered.

"No," she agreed, so softly the word drifted back into her throat.

Then all that had begun so ribaldly ended in beauty, a man and a woman, cleaving, rhythmic, then gasping at the moment of cataclysm and smiling when it was over.

Afterward, she whispered, "Stay," and found a place for his hand, and another where her sole seemed to belong.

Later, they lay back-to-belly. The bedside lamp was on and an insect worried the shade with a *tick-tick* of wings. Bess's hair had dried and spread a floral scent upon their shared pillow. The bedspread, now snarled beneath them, rode up in rills here and there, creating a barrier between their legs. Michael flattened it with his calf and found Bess's bare toes with his own, invited hers to curl around his and closed his eyes.

He sighed.

She studied his left arm, stretching forth from beneath her ear; his hand hanging limply over the edge of the mattress; the pattern of dark hair ending along the soft inner arm, where white skin began; his gold watch-band; the inside of his relaxed palm; ringless fingers.

She felt his lips on her hair, his breath warming it. She closed her eyes to enjoy the wondrous impuissance, the sense of well-being.

After many minutes he said quietly, "Bess?"

She opened her eyes. "Hm?"

"Are you ready to hear that M word yet?"

She thought for some time before answering. "I don't know."

He curled his arm toward her face and she turned to look back at him behind her.

"I think we'd better talk about it, don't you?" he said.

"I suppose so."

They settled on their backs. He removed his arm from beneath her.

"Okay," he said, "let's get it out in the open instead of dancing around it the way we have been. Do you think we could make it if we married again?"

Even forewarned, Bess was startled by the word. She said, "I've been spending a lot of time lately wondering. In bed we could."

"And out of it?"

"What do you think?"

"I think our biggest problem would be trust, because each of us has had others and . . ."

"Other. Just one, for me, anyway."

"Yeah, for me, too. But trust will still be a big factor."

"I suppose so."

"We'll each be meeting people, doing business with people, sometimes even in the evenings. If I tell you I'm going to a city council meeting, will you believe me?"

He picked up her near hand and placed it atop his, matching the curl of her fingers to his knuckles.

"I don't know," she answered honestly. "When I found that box of condoms, I really thought . . ." They both studied their hands, fitting and refitting them together. "Well, you know what I thought."

"Yeah, I know what you thought." He deserted her hand to double both his behind his head. "But we can't always be counting condoms, Bess."

She chuckled and turned on her side to study him, laying one hand on the hollow beneath his ribs.

"I know. I'm just being honest, Michael."

"You don't think you can ever trust me again?"

She only studied him, wondering herself. Soon he spoke again.

"I've been thinking about a lot of other things. The fact that both of us are working now—I think I've come to terms with that, and I'd be willing to share the housework, and not even fifty-fifty. Sometimes it might be sixty-forty, other times forty-sixty. I realize now that when both people are working it's got to be a cooperative effort that way."

She smiled. "I have a housekeeper now."

"Does she cook for you, too?"

"No."

"Well, there, you see? We can take turns cooking."

Bess was getting sleepy. "Know what?"

"What?"

"I like being convinced. Go on."

"I've even given some thought to my hunting. I know you used to get upset when I'd leave you to go hunting but now I have the cabin and you can come along . . . light a fire in the fireplace, bring a good book . . . how does that sound?"

"Mmm . . ."

"It'd be good for you to get away from the store, relax a little more . . ."

"Mmm . . ."

Her hand below his ribs lay heavy and motionless.

"Bess, are you sleeping?"

Her breathing was regular, her eyelashes at rest upon her cheek. He braced up on one elbow and reached beyond her, caught the side of the bedspread and flipped it over her, then did the same on his side. She murmured and snuggled deeper. He put a hand on her waist, drew a knee up against her belly, nestled on his side with his forehead near hers and thought, I'll only stay for a half hour or so . . . it's so nice here beside her . . . if I leave the light on it'll wake me up again in a while.

chapter 16

RANDY GOT HOME AT 2:15, pulled into the driveway and sat staring at the silver Cadillac Seville. *What the hell is he doing here?* He glanced up at his mother's bedroom window, found the light on, shook his head in disgust and slammed the van door behind himself.

Inside, the entry chandelier was aglow, as well as the lights in the upstairs hall. Something was scattered on the steps. He went up to get a closer look and discovered an empty box of condoms, along with its contents lying strewn all over two steps. He picked one up, studied it as it lay in his palm and glanced at the head of the stairs. He started up cautiously, passing a piece of clothing, and when he reached the top, peered around the corner along the hall. More clothing left a trail—a man's trousers, shoes, his mother's little white thing that she wore after her bath. At the far end of the hall her bedroom door was wide open and the light was on.

"Mom?" he called.

No answer.

He proceeded to the doorway, stopped just outside and called, "Mom, you all right?"

Again, no answer, so he stepped inside.

His mother and father were lying curled up together spoon-fashion, naked, with the bedspread haphazardly covering them to the hips. Michael's arm was looped over Bess's waist, his hand near her breast. From the looks of the room they'd had a wild one. Pillows lay scattered on the floor around the bed, which itself looked as though a twister had struck it. The empty packet from a condom lay on his father's side of the bed beside a soiled handkerchief.

Randy felt his face flame but just as he made a move to retreat, Michael came awake, lifted his head and discovered Randy in the doorway. He glanced sharply at Bess, still asleep, caught the edge of the bedspread and drew it up to cover her naked breasts. Once more he looked across the room at his son.

"Randy?"

"You got balls, man," Randy sneered, "coming here like this."

"Hey, Randy, just a min—"

But Randy was gone, his footfalls thundering angrily down the hall, down the steps.

Bess squinted awake and mumbled, "Michael? What time is it?"

"Two-fifteen. Go back to sleep."

She clambered onto her knees and began scraping the spread back. "Let's get under."

"Bess, Randy's home."

"Oh so what. So now he knows. Shut off the lamp and get under."

Michael shut off the lamp and got under.

In the morning he awakened to the sensation of being watched. He was. When he opened his eyes he found Bess with her head on the only pillow still remaining on the bed, her face turned his way, studying him.

"Hi," she said, looking quite pleased with herself.

"Hi."

"Where's your pillow?" His head was flat on the mattress.

"I seem to remember we threw it on the floor."

She smiled and said, "So we got caught, huh?"

"Did we ever."

"Did he come in here?"

"Uh-huh."

"Did he say anything?"

"He said, 'You got balls, man.' "

Her smile turned lurid. "Yeah, you do. Mind if I fondle them a little bit?"

He grinned, pushed her hand away and regretfully told her, "Listen, missus, our son's in the house, and he's royally pissed."

She gave up her pursuit and said, "So what are we going to tell him?"

"Hell, I don't know. You got any ideas?"

"How about, 'Forty-year-olds get horny, too'?"

"Cute. Very cute." Michael sat up on the edge of the bed, flexed his arms and stretched.

Bess braced her jaw on one hand and reached up to ruffle his tousled hair.

"He probably won't get up till nine or so."

"Then I'll stay till nine or so."

"You don't have to. I can talk to him."

"You're not the one he'll be angry with. It'll be me. I'm not leaving you here to do my dirty work while I slink off with my tail between my legs."

She let her palm ride down the center of his back. It was a good, straight back, still firm and tapered.

Michael looked back over his shoulder at her. "Did you ever think when we had him that we'd end up making excuses for something like this?"

She smiled.

He rose, fully naked, and she watched him move around the foot of her bed through the bathroom doorway on her left. He left the door open, which brought a smile to her lips and some pleasant memories of married life. After taking care of morning necessities, he leaned against the vanity top, inspecting his face, rubbing sandmen out of his eyes.

"You know how I knew you were having an affair?" she asked.

He said, "How?" opened a drawer, found her hairbrush and started using it.

"You started closing the bathroom door."

From her vantage point she saw the rear half of him, the front half cut off by the doorway. He stopped brushing, tipped back at the waist, peered into the bedroom and said, "Really?"

"Mm-hm." She was lying on her side, with her head cradled on a folded arm, wearing a soft smile. He left the bathroom and walked toward her, undeterred by his nakedness, dropped down to sit on the bed at her hip.

"There . . . you see?" He touched her nose with the back of the brush. "I left it open. Now doesn't that prove something?"

They smiled at each other a long time while he sat with one hand braced on either side of her, their bare hips separated by a single layer of sheet. It had rained during the night. The morning-cool air came through the open window bringing a faintly dank smell resembling mushrooms. Somewhere in a metal downspout droplets of water made a modulated *blip, blip, blip.* It was one of those sterling stretches of minutes that come along rarely in a relationship, certainly the most idyllic for Michael and Bess since their divorce. She hated to tarnish it.

"Michael, listen . . ." She rubbed her palms lightly up and down his arms. "I'm not going to lie to Randy and tell him you and I are getting married again, because it's just not true. I need some time to think things through. This . . . this affair we've started . . . well, it's just that, an affair, nothing more. If Randy has trouble adjusting to that, then so be it but I won't vindicate myself with a lie. Do you understand what I'm saying?"

He withdrew to the edge of the bed, turning his back on her. "Sure. You're saying I'm good enough for you in bed but not out of it."

She sat up, touched his back. "No, Michael."

He rose and found his underwear, stepped into it and followed the trail of clothing still decorating the hall and steps. When he returned he was half-dressed, carrying her white cover-up and a handful of condoms. He tossed them on the bed along with the empty box. "There." He buttoned his shirt and began stuffing it into his trousers with angry shoves. "Keep them handy, then, because I can promise you I'll be back. I won't be able to resist it but we'll be setting one hell of an example for our kids, won't we, Bess?"

"Michael, you came here! I didn't come to you, so don't blame me for what happened!"

"I want to marry you, damn it, and you're saying no, you'd rather have an affair; well what kind of—"

"That's not what I'm saying." She jumped up and grabbed her cover-up from the foot of the bed, flung it over her head. "I don't want to make the same mistake again, that's all."

"I can see the writing on the wall. We'll get together once, maybe twice a week, we'll make love, and afterwards we'll go through this same scene, me saying 'Let's make it honest' and you getting angry, and then both of us getting angry. Well, that's not what I want, Bess. I want what Lisa wants—the two of us back together for good."

She stood before him, a little angry, a little repentant, a lot afraid. No matter what they'd agreed about shared guilt during their first breakup, he'd been the philanderer and the hurt still clung.

"Michael," she said calmly, "I don't want to fight with you."

His shirt was on, his pants were zipped, his belt was buckled.

"Okay," he said. "I've called you twice. It's your turn next time. See how it feels to be the one who comes begging."

He strode toward the door.

"Michael . . ." The tone of her voice was tantamount to a reaching hand but he'd already disappeared around the door. She hurried to it and yelled down the hall, "Michael!"

He called back as he reached the top of the stairs, "Tell Randy I'll call him and explain."

Randy's voice came from below.

"You don't have to call him, he's here."

Michael's footsteps faltered, then continued more slowly to the bottom of the steps, where Randy stood, bare but for his blue jeans, which were zipped but unbuttoned. It startled Michael to see for the first time the dense pattern of hair on Randy's chest and around his navel, proof that he was as fully mature as Michael himself.

"Randy . . . I'm sorry we woke you."

"I'll just bet you are."

"I didn't mean it that way. I had every intention of talking to you about this. I wasn't going to skip out and leave it to your mother."

"Oh yeah? Well, that's the way it looked to me. Why don't you just leave her alone?"

"Because I love her, that's why."

"Love—Christ, don't make me laugh. I suppose you loved her then, too, when you had an affair with another woman and walked out on her. I suppose you loved me, and Lisa, too!"

Michael knew it would do no good to declare he did. He stood in silence. Randy replied as if Michael had answered.

"Well, that's some way to show your kids you love 'em. You want to know how it feels to have your father write you off? It hurts, that's how it feels!"

"I didn't write you off."

"Aw, fuck that, man, you left her, you left us! I was thirteen years old. You know how a thirteen-year-old thinks? I figured it must've been my fault, I must've done something wrong to make you leave but I didn't know what; then Mom finally tells me you had another woman and I wanted to find you and smash your face, only I was too little and skinny. Now here you are, crawling out of her bed—well maybe I should smash it now, huh?"

From the top of the stairs, Bess reprimanded, "Randy!"

His icy eyes looked up. "This is between him and me, Ma."

"You will apologize to him at once if for nothing more than your offensive language!"

"Like hell I will!"

"Randy!" She started down the stairs.

Randy's face wizened with disbelief. "Why are you taking his side? Can't you see he's just using you again? Comes down here saying he loves you—man, that's just bullshit! He probably said the same thing to that other floozy he married but he couldn't make that marriage stick, either! He's a loser, Ma, and he doesn't deserve you and you're a damn fool for letting him in here!"

She slapped Randy's face.

He stared at her in shock. Tears spurted into his eyes.

"I'm very sorry I had to do that. I've never done it before and I want you to know I hated it. But I cannot allow you to stand there berating your father and I. Neither one of us are blameless but there are proper, respectful ways in which to talk these things out. Now, I think, Randy," she said quietly, "that you owe us both an apology."

Randy stared at her. At Michael. Back at her before spinning and hitting for his downstairs bedroom without another word.

When he was gone Bess put her hands to her cheeks and felt them burning. She turned to Michael, who stood forlornly, studying the toes of his shoes. She put her arms around him. "Michael, I'm sorry," she whispered in a shaken voice.

"It's been coming for a long time."

"Yes, I suppose so but that doesn't make it hurt any less."

She held him awhile. Though his arms automatically went around her, they applied no pressure, only hung there like limp ropes.

Finally he pulled back and said in a strange, choked voice, "I'd better go."

"I'll talk to him when he's settled down."

Michael nodded at the floor. "I'll . . ." He didn't know what he'd do. Take another cooking course. Buy another piece of land to develop. Choose a sculpture for his gallery. Pointless, senseless, frantic scrambling by a man seeking to fill his life with meaning when the only meaning in life can come from people, not things.

"I'll see you, Bess," he said, and left, closing the door quietly behind him.

In his room, Randy sat on the edge of his water bed, doubled forward, holding his head in both hands.

Crying.

He wanted a dad, wanted a mom, wanted love like other kids. But why did it have to be so painful, getting it? He'd been hurt so much by their divorce. Why shouldn't he be allowed to vent this fury that had been building in him since the eighth grade, when they'd split? Couldn't they see what jerks they were making of themselves, falling back together this way for convenience? It wasn't as if they talked about getting married again—the word hadn't been mentioned. No, it was just plain lust, which made his mother as guilty as his father, and he didn't want her to be. Damn Lisa for stirring this all up. She was the one—Lisa!—who insisted they end the cold war. Now this.

It had been bad holding things inside all these years but letting them out hadn't felt much good, either. Seeing the look of pain on his dad's face when he had yelled, "It hurts!"—that was what he'd wanted, wasn't it? To hurt his old man for once the way the old man had hurt him. Wasn't that what he wanted? So why was he doubled over here, bawling like a baby?

Goddamn you, Dad, why did you leave us? Why didn't you stick with Mom and work it out?

I'm so confused. I wish I had somebody to talk to, somebody who'd listen and make me understand who I'm angry at and why. Maryann. Oh God, Maryann, I respected you so much. I was going to show you I could be different than my old man, I could treat you like some princess and never lay a hand on you, and show you I was worthy of you.

But I'm not. I talk like a gutter rat, and smoke pot, and drink plenty, and screw any girl who comes along, and my own father doesn't love me enough to stick around, and my own mother slaps me.

Somebody help me understand!

Shortly, Randy's mother came to his door. She knocked softly. He swiped his eyes with the bedsheet, hopped up and pretended to be busy at the controls of the CD player.

"Randy?" she called quietly.

"Yeah, it's open." He heard her come in.

"Randy?"

He waited.

"I'm sorry."

He watched the knobs on the control panel blur as his eyes refilled with tears. "Yeah . . . well . . ." His voice sounded high, like when he was going through puberty and it was changing.

"Slapping you was wrong. I shouldn't have done it. Randy?"

He wouldn't answer.

She had come up silently and touched his shoulder before he realized she was there. "Randy, I just want you to know something. Your dad asked me to marry him again but I'm the one who said no."

Randy blinked and the tears dropped to his bare stomach, clearing his vision somewhat. He remained with his back to Bess, his chin on his chest.

"Why?"

"Because I'm afraid of getting hurt again, the same as you."

"I'm never apologizing to him. Never."

Her hand went away from his shoulder. She sighed. Time passed. Her hand returned, warm and flat on his bare skin.

"Randy, he loves you very much."

Randy said nothing. The damn tears plumped up again.

"I know you don't believe that but he does. And whether you believe it or not, you love him. That's why you're hurting so badly right now." Another pause before she continued. "The two of you will have to talk someday—I mean, really talk, without anger, about all your feelings. Please, Randy . . . don't wait too long, dear."

She kissed his shoulder and silently left.

He remained in his windowless room, willing away tears that refused his bidding. He touched a silver knob on his CD player, let his hand fall to his side. He imagined going to his father's place and knocking on his door and simply walking into his arms and hugging him hard enough to snap their bones. How did people manage to do that after they'd been hurt this bad?

The tape of The Edge was in the deck, the one he practiced with. He knelt down and replaced it with the rock group Mike and the Mechanics, fast-forwarded it to the song he wanted. Forward, back, forward again to the band between songs. The intro came on and he plugged in his earphones, put them on and sat at his drums, holding both sticks in his one hand, too bummed out to use them.

The words started.

Every generation
Blames the one
before . . .

It was a song written by someone after his father had died. "The Living Years." A rueful, wrenching song.

And all of their frustrations, come beating on your door . . .
I know that I'm a prisoner to all my father held so dear
I know that I'm a hostage to all his hopes and fears
I just wish I could have told him
In the living years.

Randy sat through it all, listening to the plaintive call of a son who waited until it was too late to make his peace with his father. He sat with his eyes closed, his drumsticks forgotten in his hand, tears leaking from the corners of his eyes.

That evening, The Edge was playing at a club called The Green Light. Randy was unusually quiet while they were setting up. Through the cacophony of tuning and balancing he let the others go about their BS'ing without him. There was always a lot of give-and-take at this time, part of the ritual of getting up for a performance.

When the lights were set and the instruments ready, the filler tape playing for the crowd and the amplifiers humming softly, the guys put their guitars in their stands and went off toward the bar to get drinks. All but Pike Watson, who stopped by Randy, still sitting behind his drums. "Heya, Rimshot, you're a little low tonight."

"I'll be okay once we start playing."

"Got trouble with some of the songs? Hey, it takes time."

"No, it's not that."

"Trouble with your girl?"

"What girl?"

"Trouble at home, then."

"Yeah, I guess you could say that."

"Well, hell . . ." Pike let his thought trail away, standing with his hands caught on his bony hips. Brightening, he asked, "You need something to pick you up?"

"I got something."

"What, that jimmy dog you smoke? I mean something to really pick you up."

Randy came from behind the drums, heading for the bar. "I don't do that shit, man."

"Yeah, well, I just thought I'd offer." Pike sniffed. "Those drumsticks can get mighty heavy at times."

Randy had two beers and a hit of marijuana before they started the first set but the combination only seemed to make him lethargic and tired tonight. They played to a desultory audience, who acted as if the dance floor was off limits, and after the second set he tried more marijuana but it failed to do the trick. Even the music failed to lift Randy. The drumsticks felt very heavy, indeed. During the third break he went into the men's room and found Pike there, the only one in the room, sniffing a hit of cocaine off a tiny mirror through a rolled-up dollar bill.

"You really ought to try it." Pike grinned. "It'll cure whatever ails you."

"Yeah?" Randy watched as Pike wet his finger, picked up any stray powder and rubbed it on his gums.

"How much?"

"First hit is on me," Pike said, holding out a tiny plastic bag of white powder.

Randy looked at it, tempted not only to get out of this low but to spite his mother and father. Pike wiggled the bag a little bit as if to say, Go on, give it a try. Randy was reaching for it when the door burst open and two men came in, talking and laughing, and Pike swiftly hid the bag and mirror in his pocket.

* * *

After the night Randy discovered them in bed, Michael quit calling Bess, and though she missed him horribly, she, too, refused to call him. Deep summer came on: in Stillwater a time for lovers. They came by the hundreds, teenagers over from Minneapolis and St. Paul, flooding the town in their souped-up sports cars; the town's own teenagers, cruising the length of the quay on Friday nights; college kids off for the summer, dancing to the canned music at Steamers; boaters down for the weekends, setting the river agleam with the reflection of their running lights; sightseers out for an evening, walking the riverbank, holding hands.

At night, the volleyball court in front of the Freight House was a maze of tan, young arms and legs. The riverside restaurant decks were crowded. The old lift bridge backed up traffic several times an hour letting boats beneath it. The antique stores did a landmark business. The popcorn wagon put out its irresistible smell. The wind socks in front of Brick Alley Books waved a welcome to the cars streaming down the hill into town.

One hot Saturday Bess was invited to a pool party at Barb and Don's house. She bought a new bathing suit, expecting Michael to be there. He wasn't; he'd been invited but had declined when he'd learned Bess was coming.

A man named Alan Petrosky, who introduced himself as a horse rancher from over by Lake Elmo, kept up an irksome pursuit until she wanted to dump him into the pool, cowboy boots and all.

Don and Barb noticed what was going on and came to rescue her. Don gave her a brotherly hug and asked simply, "How have you been?" She found tears in her eyes as she replied, "Very mixed up and lonely."

Barb caught her by a hand and said, "Come up to the bedroom for a minute where we won't be disturbed." In the cool green bedroom with the curtains drawn and the party sounds distant, Barb asked, "So how are things between you and Michael?" and Bess burst into tears.

She broke down and called him in early August on the pretext of advising him about some nice pieces of sculpture on display at a gallery in Minneapolis. He was brusque, almost rude, declining to ask anything personal or to thank her for recommending the gallery.

She submerged herself in work; it helped little. She told Randy she wanted to come out some night and hear him play; he said no, he didn't think the kind of bars he played in would be her style. She attended a shower for Lisa, given by Mark's sisters; it only reminded her she would soon be a grandmother facing old age alone. Keith called and said he missed her, wanted to see her again; she told him no, smitten by a wave of mild revulsion.

Life felt humdrum to Bess while, by comparison, it seemed everyone around her was living it to the fullest, having the gayest summer of their lives. She found a batik piece depicting sandpipers that would have been stunning in Michael's dining room, but she stubbornly refused to call him for fear he'd again treat her as if she'd just peed on his shoe. Worse, what if she herself broke down and suggested their getting together for an evening?

Sexuality—damn the stuff. Bess would have thought, considering impending grandparenthood, that she'd be immune. She was not. She thought of Michael in a sexual regard as often as in a nonsexual. She fully admitted the reason she'd been repulsed by the idea of reviving anything with Keith was because, by comparison to Michael, he was a vacant lot. Michael, on the other hand, was a lush orchard—but hardly enough reason for a woman of forty to make a fool of herself gorging on ripe fruit. As she'd told him the night they'd last made love, they weren't teenagers anymore. Still, all the platitudes in the world couldn't prevent her from missing him immensely.

On August ninth Bess turned forty-one. Randy forgot all about it, didn't even give her a card before he left for a three-day gig in South Dakota. Lisa called and wished her a happy birthday but said she'd ordered something that hadn't arrived yet; it should be here by the weekend and they'd get together then. Stella was gone with three of her ladyfriends on a two-week vacation in the San Juan islands north of Seattle and had sent a birthday card that had arrived the day before, along with a postcard from the Burchart Gardens in Victoria, British Columbia: wish you were here.

Bess's birthday fell on a Thursday; she had appointments all afternoon long but rushed back to the store before Heather left for the day, asking if she'd had any calls.

"Four," Heather answered. But none were from Michael, and Bess climbed the stairs to her stifling loft telling herself she had no right to be disappointed. She was responsible for her own happiness, it was not the duty of others to create it for her.

Still . . . birthdays.

She found herself remembering certain ones while she'd still been married to Michael. The first one after they got married, when he'd taken her tubing on the Apple River and had pulled a Pepperidge Farm cake out of a floating cooler tied between them while they were bobbing down the stream on inner tubes, scraping their hinders on rocks and burning the tops of their knees and loving every minute of it.

The year she turned thirty, when he'd arranged a surprise party at Barb and Don's house and she'd sulked all the way there, thinking she was going to a birthday party for their daughter, Rainy, who was turning four the next day.

Another one—she'd forgotten exactly which. Thirty-two? Thirty-three?—when Michael had given her a particular bracelet she'd admired and had pulled it out of his vest pocket on their way out to dinner, the way rich men did in movies. It had been in a black velvet box, a simple gold serpentine chain, and she had it still.

No bracelets today, though. No black velvet boxes, no cards in the mailbox at home, nobody to float down a river with, or go out to dinner with, or surprise her with balloons and cheers.

She stopped at Colonel Sanders's on her way home and picked up two pieces of fattening chicken and some fattening potatoes and gravy and a cob of fattening corn and one of those little fattening lemon desserts, which she ate on the deck while watching the boats on the river and wishing she was on one of them.

Birthdays . . . oh, birthdays.

If there was any day when a lonely person felt more lonely, when a single person felt more single, when a neglected person felt more neglected, she wanted to know what it was.

With dusk approaching she puttered around the yard, plucking weeds in the rock-lined perennial beds she'd once tended meticulously but which had fallen into a state of neglect after she'd gone back to college. She broke a fingernail and got disgusted, went inside and took a long bath and gave herself a facial, examining her skin critically after washing the mask from it.

Forty-one—lord. And her skin getting a little droopy and soft like a maiden aunt's.

Forty-one and no gifts, no calls.

Tiny lines lurking at the corners of the eyes. A faint jowl beginning to show if she forgot to keep her chin high.

At 11 P.M. she turned off the television and lamp in her bedroom and lay with the windows open, listening to a thousand crickets and the bishop sleeves fluttering faintly against the sill, smelling the dampness of deep summer thread in from the yard, recalling nights like this when she was sixteen and went with mobs of kids to the drive-in theater. Always, there was company then.

The neighbors across the street came home, Elaine and Craig Mason, married probably forty years or more, slamming their car doors and talking quietly on their way into the house. Their metal screen door slammed and all grew quiet. Bess had stacked up her pillows as if knowing sleep would be reluctant, and reclined with her eyes wide open, intent upon the fretwork of shadows on the opposite wall, cast through the maples by the night light in the yard.

When the phone rang her body seemed to do an electric leap that shot her heart into fast time. The red light on the digital clock said 11:07 as she rolled over and grabbed the receiver in the dark, thinking, *Let it be Michael.*

"Hello, Bess," he said, his familiar voice at once raising a sting in her eyes.

"Hello." She went back against the pillows, touching the receiver with her free hand as if it were his jaw.

Outside, the crickets kept sawing away, their song throbbing in the summer night while on the telephone a lengthy silence hummed. She knew it meant he was not entirely pleased with himself for having broken down and called her after vowing he would not do so again.

"It's your birthday, huh?"

"Yes." She pointed one elbow to the ceiling, covering her eyes to stop them from stinging.

"Well, happy birthday."

"Thanks."

They remained silent for so long her throat began to ache. The crickets continued their rasping.

Finally Michael asked, "Did you do anything special?"

"No."

"Nothing with the kids?"

"No."

"Didn't Lisa come over or anything?"

"No. She said we'll get together soon, maybe this weekend. And Randy's playing out in South Dakota, so he's not around."

"Damn those kids. They should have done something for you."

She dried her nose on the sheet and forced her voice to sound normal. "Oh, what the heck. It's just one birthday. There'll be lots of others."

Please come over, Michael. Please come over and just hold me.

"I suppose so but they still should have remembered."

Another silence came and gripped them, and beat across the telephone wire. She wondered if he was in his bedroom, what he was wearing, if the light was on. She pictured him in his underwear, lying in the dark on top of the covers with one knee up and the balcony doors open.

"I ah . . . I got that mess straightened out down on Victoria and Grand." She formed an image of him watching his own fingernail scratching a groove into a sheet while he spoke. "Building's going to get under way soon."

"Oh, good!" she said, with false brightness. "That's . . ." Softer, she ended, ". . . that's good."

Why are we in separate bedrooms, Michael?

If she didn't invent some perky conversation soon, he'd surely hang up. She stared at the indigo leaf shadows on the opposite wall and searched for some clever dialogue to keep him on the line.

"Mom's gone on a trip to Seattle."

"Seattle . . . well." After a pause, "So she wasn't around today, either."

"No, but she sent a card. She's having a grand time with all her friends."

"She always seems to manage that, doesn't she?"

Bess turned on her side with the receiver pressed against the pillow, her position going slightly fetal while she coiled the phone cord around the tip of her index finger. Her chest felt ready to splinter into fragments. Oh God, she missed him so much.

"Bess, are you still there?"

"Yes."

"Well, listen, I . . ." He cleared his throat. "I just thought I'd call. Force of habit on this day every year, you know." He laughed. Oh, such a melancholy laugh. "I was just thinking about you."

"I was thinking about you, too."

He fell silent and she knew he was waiting for her to say, *I want to see you, please come over.* But the words stuck in her throat because she was afraid all she wanted to see him for were sexual reasons, and because she was so utterly lonely and it was her birthday, and she was forty-one and dreading the possibility of spending the rest of her life alone; and if he came over and they made love she'd be using him, and nice women weren't supposed to use men that way, not even ex-husbands, and then what would she say afterward, if he asked her again to marry him?

"Well, listen . . . it's late. I should go."

"Yes, me too."

She covered her whole face with one hand, her eyes squeezed shut, her lips bitten to keep the sobs from falling out, the telephone a hard knob between her ear and the pillow.

"Well, 'bye, Bess."

" 'Bye, Michael . . . Michael, wait!" She was up on one elbow, frantic, her tears at last running. But he'd hung up, leaving only the throb of the crickets to keep her company while she wept.

chapter 17

LISA CALLED THE BLUE IRIS at 11 A.M. on August sixteenth and said she had gone into labor. Her water hadn't broken but she was spotting and cramping and had contacted the doctor. There was no reason for Bess to come to the hospital yet; they'd call when she should.

Bess canceled two afternoon appointments and stayed in the store near the phone.

Heather said, "It brings back the days when you were waiting for your own kids to be born, doesn't it?"

"It really does," Bess replied. "Lisa took thirteen hours but Randy took only five. Oh, I must call him and tell him the news!" She checked her watch and picked up the phone. Her relationship with Randy had been bumping along since the day she'd slapped him. She talked, he grunted. She made an effort, he made none.

He answered on the third ring.

"Randy, I'm so glad you're still home. I just wanted you to know that Lisa's gone into labor. She's still at home but it looks as though this is the real thing."

"Yeah? Well, tell her good luck."

"Can't you tell her yourself?"

"The band's heading out for Bemidji at one o'clock."

"Bemidji . . ." Her voice registered dismay.

"It's not the end of the world, Ma."

"No, I suppose not, but I hate your having to travel so much."

"It's only five hours."

"Well, be careful, dear, and be sure you get some sleep before you head back."

"Yeah."

"And no drinking and driving."

"Aw, come on, Ma, jeez . . ."

"Well, I worry about you."

"Worry about yourself. I'm a big boy now."

"When will you be back?"

"Sometime tomorrow morning. We're playing in White Bear Lake tomorrow afternoon."

"I'll leave a note at home if the baby is here. Otherwise call me at the store."

"Okay. Ma, I gotta go."

"All right, but listen . . . I love you."

He paused too long before replying, "Yeah, same here," as if pronouncing the actual words was more than he could manage.

Hanging up, Bess felt forlorn. She remained with her hand on the phone, staring out the front window, feeling like a failure as a mother, understanding how Michael had felt all these years, wondering how to mend these fences between herself and Randy.

"Something wrong?" Heather asked. She was dusting the shelving and glassware, working her way along the west wall of the shop.

"Ohhh . . ." Bess released a deep sigh. "I don't know." After a while she turned to Heather and asked, "Do you have one child who's harder to love than the others? Or is it just me? Because I feel very guilty sometimes but I swear, that younger one of mine is so distant."

"It's not just you. I've got one who's the same way. My middle one, Kim. She doesn't like being hugged—never mind kissed—never wanted to do anything with the family after she reached age thirteen, disregards Mother's Day and Father's Day, criticizes the radio station I listen to and the car I drive and the movies I like and the clothes I wear and only comes home when she needs something. Sometimes it's really hard to keep on loving a kid like that."

"Do you think they eventually grow out of it?"

Heather replaced a bowl on the shelf and said, "Oh, I hope so. So, what's wrong between you and Randy?"

Bess shot Heather a glance. "The truth?"

Heather continued her dusting indifferently. "If you want to tell me."

"He caught me in bed with his father."

Heather started laughing silently, her mouth open wide, the sound at first only a tick in her throat until it crescendoed and resounded through the store. When the laugh ended she twirled the dustrag through the air above her head. "Hooray!"

Bess looked a little pink around the edges. "You're spreading dust all over the stuff you just cleaned."

"Oh, big deal. So fire me." Heather returned to her task, smiling. "I figured it was getting serious between you two. I knew you weren't spending all that time on business, and I for one am glad to hear it."

"Well, don't be, because it's only caused problems. Randy's been bitter about the divorce ever since it happened, and he finally told his father so but I stepped in and things got out of hand. I slapped Randy and he's been withdrawn and unaffectionate ever since. Oh, I don't know, Heather, sometimes I hate being a mother."

"Sometimes we all do."

"So what did I do wrong? His whole life long I loved him, I told him so, I kissed and hugged him, I went to school conferences, I did everything the books said I should but somewhere along the line I lost him. He just pulls farther and farther away. I know he's drinking, and I think he's smoking pot but I can't get him to admit it or to stop."

Heather left her dustrag on the shelf and went around behind the counter. She took Bess in her arms and held her caringly. "It's not always us doing something wrong. Sometimes it's them, and we just have to wait for them to grow out of it, or confide in us, or hit bottom."

"He loves this job so. His whole life long he's wanted to play with a band but I'm so afraid for him. It's a destructive way of life."

"You can't make his choices for him, Bess, not anymore."

"I know . . ." Bess held Heather tighter for a second. "I know." She drew away with glistening eyes. "Thanks. You're a dear friend."

"I'm a mother who's tried her damnedest, just like you but . . ." Heather raised her palms and let them drop. ". . . all we can do is love 'em and hope for the best."

It was hard to concentrate on work knowing Lisa was in labor. There were designs to be finished in the loft but Bess felt too restless to be confined upstairs. She waited on customers instead, tagged some newly arrived linens and hung them on an old-fashioned wooden clothes rack for display. She went outside and watered the geraniums in the window box. She unpacked a new shipment of wallpaper. She checked her watch at least a dozen times an hour.

Mark called shortly before 3 P.M. and said, "We're at the hospital. Can you come now?"

Bess barely took time to say good-bye before hanging up, grabbing her purse and running.

Lakeview Hospital was less than two miles from her store, up to the top of Myrtle Street hill and south on Greeley Street to the high ground overlooking Lily Lake. Though there were other hospitals closer to Lisa and Mark's apartment, her pregnancy had been confirmed by the physicians she'd known all her life, so she'd stayed with the familiar names and faces who practiced right here in town. Bess found it comforting to be approaching the hospital where Lisa and Randy had been born, where Lisa's broken arm had been set, where both of them had been given their preschool physicals, and countless throat cultures, and where their height and weight and periodic infirmities had been recorded and were still safely filed away in metal drawers. Here, too, the whole family had seen Grandpa Dorner for the last time.

The OB wing of the hospital was so new it still smelled of carpet fiber and wallpaper. The hall was indirectly lit, quiet, and led to a hexagonal nurses' station surrounded by a circle of rooms.

"I'm Lisa Padgett's mother," Bess announced to the nurse on duty.

The young woman led the way to a birthing room, where both the labor and birth would be carried out. Lisa and Mark were there, along with a smiley nurse wearing blue scrubs, whose nametag read JAN MEERS, R.N. Lisa was lying on the bed holding up a wrinkled patient's gown while Jan Meers adjusted something that looked like a white tube top around her belly. She picked up two sensors, slipped them beneath the bellyband, patted them and said, "There. That'll hold them." Their leads dropped to a machine beside the bed, which she rolled nearer.

Lisa saw Bess and said, "Hi, Mom."

Bess went to the bed, leaned over and kissed her. "Hi, honey, hi, Mark, how's everything going?"

"Pretty good. Getting me all hog-tied to this machine so we can tell if the baby changes his mind or something." To the nurse, Lisa said, "This is my mom, Bess." To Bess, "This is the lady who's going to put me through the seven tortures."

Ms. Meers laughed. "Oh, I hope not. I don't think it'll be so bad. Look here now . . ." She moved aside and rested a hand on the machine where an orange digital number glowed beside a tiny orange heart that flashed in rhythm with a sound like a scratchy phonograph record. "This is the fetal monitor. That's the baby's heartbeat you hear."

Everyone's eyes fixed upon the beating orange heart while beside it a white graph paper began to creep into sight, bearing a printout of the proceedings.

"And this one"—Ms. Meers indicated a green number beside the orange one—"shows your contractions, Lisa. Mark, one of your jobs will be to watch it. Between contractions it'll read around thirteen or fourteen. The instant you see it rising you should remind Lisa to start breathing. It'll take about thirty seconds for the contraction to reach its peak, and by forty-five seconds it'll be tapering off. The whole thing will last about one minute. Believe it or not, Mark, you'll often know there's a contraction starting before she will."

Ms. Meers had scarcely finished her instructions before Mark said, "It's going up!" He moved closer to Lisa, his eyes on the monitor. Lisa stiffened and he reminded her, "Okay, relax. Here we go now, remember, three pants and one blow. Pant, pant, pant, blow . . . pant, pant, pant, blow . . . okay, we're fifteen seconds into it . . . thirty . . . hang on, honey . . . forty-five now and nearly over . . . good job."

Bess stood by uselessly, watching Lisa ride out the pain, feeling her own innards seizing up while Mark remained a bastion of strength. He leaned over Lisa, rubbed the hair back from her forehead and smiled into her eyes. He whispered something and she nodded, then closed her eyes.

Bess checked the clock. It was 3:19 P.M.

The next contraction came fifteen minutes later and by the time it arrived, so had Mark's mother. She greeted everyone, giving Mark a quick squeeze.

"Is Dad coming?" Mark asked her.

"He's at work. I left a note on the kitchen table for him. Hi, Lisa-honey. Today's the day you get your waistline back. I'll bet you're happy." She kissed Lisa's cheek and said, "I think it's going to be a boy. I don't know why but I have the strongest feeling."

"If it is we're going to be in trouble because we haven't thought of a boy's name yet. But if it's a girl it'll be Natalie."

The contractions came and went. It was hard for Bess to watch Lisa suffer. Her child. Her precious firstborn, who had, as a youngster of five, six, seven, mothered her baby brother the way little girls do: held his hand when they crossed the street together; lifted him up to reach the drinking fountain; soothed and cooed when he fell down and scraped a knee. And now she was a grown woman and would soon have a baby of her own. No matter that the pain was the means to eventual happiness and fulfillment, watching one's own child bear it was terrible.

At moments Bess wished she'd decided to delay coming here until the baby was safely born, then felt guilty for her selfishness. She wished she were needed more, then felt grateful that Mark was the one Lisa needed most. She wished Lisa were a little girl again, then thought, No, how foolish; I really wish no such thing. She was enjoying having an adult daughter. Nevertheless, often during those minutes of travail, she pictured Lisa as a kindergartner, walking bravely up the street alone for the first time—absurd, how fragments of those bygone years kept insinuating themselves into this hour that was so far removed from the days of Lisa's childhood. Perhaps it was peculiar to the stepping-stones of life that at those times an underlying sadness was rekindled.

Sometimes when the contractions ended, both Bess and Hildy released their breaths and let their shoulders slump, then glanced furtively at each other, realizing they'd been copying Lisa's breathing pattern as if doing so could make it easier on her.

At 6:30 Jake Padgett arrived, and Bess left the birthing room for a while because it was getting too crowded. She walked down to the pop machine by the cafeteria, got a can of Coke and took it to the family room, adjacent to Lisa's birthing room, a spacious, restful place with comfortable chairs and an L-shaped sofa long enough to stretch out and nap on. It had a refrigerator, coffeepot, snacks, bathroom, television, toys and books.

Bess found her mind too preoccupied to be interested in amusements.

She returned to the birthing room at five to seven and watched two more contractions, before rubbing Mark's shoulder and suggesting, "Why don't you sit down awhile. I think I can do this."

Mark sank gratefully into a recliner and Bess took his place beside the bed.

Lisa opened her eyes and smiled weakly. Her hair was stringy and flat, her face looked slightly puffy. "I guess Dad's not coming, huh?"

Bess took her hand. "I don't know, sweetheart."

From his chair, Mark murmured sleepily, "I called his office a long time ago. They said they'd give him the message."

Lisa said, "I want him here."

"Yes, I know," Bess whispered. "So do I."

It was true. While she had watched Lisa laboring she'd wanted Michael beside her as strongly as ever in her life. It appeared, however, that he was avoiding the hospital, knowing she was there, just as he had the pool party at Barb and Don's.

By ten o'clock there'd been no change, and the anesthesiologist was called in to administer an epidural, which made Lisa woozy and a slight bit giddy. The baby was big, probably close to ten pounds, and Lisa was narrow across the pelvis. The epidural, it was explained, would not stop the contractions, only make Lisa unaware she was having them.

Mark was napping. The Padgetts had their eyes closed in front of the TV, and Bess went out to find a pay phone and call Stella, who said she wouldn't clutter up the proceedings but wanted to know the minute the baby was born, even if it was the middle of the night. After the phone call, Bess returned to the obstetrics wing and ambled around the circular hall. On the far side she wandered into the solarium, an arc-shaped room with a curved bank of windows overlooking the treetops and Lily Lake across the street. Only a glimpse of the night-dark water was visible and from inside, where climate was carefully controlled and trees were potted, it was impossible to tell if the night was warm or cool, still or noisy, if crickets were chirping, water lapping or mosquitoes buzzing.

The thought of mosquitoes brought the memories of warm summer nights when Lisa and Randy were little and the whole neighborhood resounded with the sounds of squeals from a dozen children playing starlight-moonlight and kick the can. When they were called for bedtime, the kids would whine, "Come on, Mom, just a little while longer, pleeeeze!" When they were finally coerced inside, their bare legs would be welted with bites, their hair sweaty, their feet dirty. Then she and Michael would bathe and dry them and put them in clean pajamas. How good they would smell then, with their faces shiny and their pajamas crisp. They would sit at the kitchen table and gobble cookies and milk and scratch their mosquito bites and protest that they weren't a bit tired.

But once in bed they'd be asleep in sixty seconds, with their precious mouths open and their sunburned limbs half above, half under the sheets. She and Michael would study them in the wedge of light from the hall as it picked out their lips and noses and eyelashes, and often their bare toes protruding from pajama legs rucked up about their knees.

Remembering, Bess felt her eyes grow misty.

She'd been standing a long time, staring out the window, weighted by the bittersweet tug of nostalgia, too weary to uncross her arms, when someone touched her shoulder.

"Bess."

She turned at the sound of Michael's voice and felt an overwhelming sense of relief and the awful threat of full-fledged tears.

"Oh, you're here," she said, as if he had materialized from her fantasy. She stepped into the calm harbor of his arms as she had longed to step into that shadowy bedroom where her younglings slept. The pressure of his embrace was firm and reassuring, the smell of his clothing and skin familiar, and for a minute she pretended the children were young again, they had tucked them into bed together and at last were stealing a moment for each other.

"I'm sorry," he said against her temple. "I'd flown to Milwaukee. I just got back and my answering service gave me the message." The strength of Bess's embrace surprised Michael. "Bess, what's wrong?"

"Nothing, really. I'm just so glad you're here."

His arms tightened and he let out a ragged breath against her hair. They had the solarium to themselves. The indirect lighting created a soft glow above the black windows. At the nurses' station beyond the door, all was quiet. For a while time seemed abstract, no rush nor reason to refrain from embracing, only the utter rightness of being together again, bolstering each other through this next stepping-stone in their daughter's life and their own.

Against Michael's shoulder Bess confessed, "I've been thinking about when the children were little, how simple everything was then, how they'd play games after dark with all the neighborhood kids and come in all full of mosquito bites. And how they looked in bed when they fell asleep. Oh, Michael, those were wonderful days, weren't they?"

"Yes, they were."

They were rocking gently. She felt his hand pet her hair, her shoulder.

"And now Randy is out on the road somewhere with some band, probably high on pot, and Lisa is in there going through all this."

Michael drew back but held Bess by the upper arms while looking into her eyes. "That's how it is, Bess. They grow up."

For a moment the expression in her eyes said she wasn't ready to accept it. Then she said, "I don't know what's come over me tonight. I'm usually not so silly and sentimental."

"It's not silly," he replied, "it's understandable on this particular night, and you know something else? Nostalgia looks good on you."

"Oh, Michael . . ." She drew away self-consciously and dropped into a chair beside a potted palm. "Did you stop by Lisa's room?"

"Yes. The nurse explained they gave her something to help her rest for a little while. She's been here since three, they said."

Bess nodded.

He looked at his watch. "Well, that's only seven hours. If I remember right she took thirteen getting here." He smiled at Bess. "Thirteen of the longest hours of my life."

"And mine," Bess added.

He sat down in a chair beside her, found her hand and held it on the hard wooden arms between them, rubbing her thumb absently with his own. They thought about their time apart, their stubbornness that had brought them both nothing but loneliness. They studied their joined hands, each of them grateful that some force outside themselves had brought them here and thrust them back together.

After a while Bess said quietly, "They said the baby is really large, and Lisa might be in for a hard time."

"So we'll stay, for as long as it takes. How about Stella? Does she know?"

"I called her but she decided to stay home and wait for the news."

"And Randy?"

"He knew she was in labor before he left. He'll be home tomorrow."

They waited in the solarium, alternately dozing and waking. Around midnight they went for a walk around the wing, discovering a new shift had come on, gazing into the empty nursery, passing the family lounge, where Jake Padgett was stretched out on the sofa, sound asleep. In the birthing room Hildy was the only one awake. She was sitting in the wooden rocking chair doing cross-stitch and waved at them silently as they paused in the doorway.

Lisa's new nurse came by and introduced herself. Marcie Unger was her name. She went into Lisa's room to check the digital readings, came back out and said, "No change."

By two o'clock things had picked up. Lisa's contractions were coming every five minutes and the anesthesiologist was called to cut off the epidural.

"Why?" Lisa asked.

"Because if we don't, you won't know when to push."

The birthing room came to life after that. Those who wanted to witness the birth were asked to don blue scrubs. Marcie Unger stayed beside Lisa every moment and Mark, too, holding Lisa's hand, guiding her through her breathing.

Jake Padgett decided to wait in the family lounge but Hildy, Bess and Michael donned sterile blue scrubs.

For Bess it was a curious sensation, looking up to find only Michael's attractive hazel eyes showing above his blue mask. She felt a momentary current the way she had when she was first falling in love with him. His eyes—stunning beyond all others she'd ever known—still had the power to kick up a reaction deep within her.

His mask billowed as he spoke. "How do you feel?"

"Scared, and not at all sure I want to go in there. How about you?"

"The same."

"We're just being typical parents. Everything will go fine. I'm sure of it."

"If I don't faint on the delivery-room floor," Michael said.

Her eyes crinkled. "Birthing room, and I'm sure you'll do just great."

"If we don't want to go in there, why are we doing it?" Michael said.

"For Lisa."

"Oh, that's right. That darned kid asked us to, didn't she?"

The interchange took the edge off their nervousness and left them smiling above their masks. Bess could not resist telling him, "If we're lucky, Michael, this baby will have your eyes."

He winked one of them and said, "Something tells me everything's going to be lucky from here on out."

When they entered the birthing room again, Lisa's knees created twin peaks beneath the sheet. The head of her bed was elevated at a 45-degree angle but her eyes were closed as she panted and labored through a contraction, her face glistening with sweat and her cheeks puffing as she breathed.

"I've g . . . got to p . . . push," she got out between breaths.

"No, not yet," Marcie Unger said soothingly. "Save your strength."

"But it's time . . . it's . . . I know it's . . . oh . . . oh . . . oh . . ."

"Keep breathing the way Mark tells you."

Beside her, Mark said, "Deeply this time, in and out, slow."

Bess's eyes sought Michael's and saw reflected there the same touch of anguish and helplessness she herself felt.

When the contraction ended, Lisa's eyes opened and found her father's, above the blue mask. "Dad?" she said with a weak smile.

"Hi, honey." His eyes crinkled with a smile as he moved to her side to squeeze her hand. "I made it."

"And Mom," she added in a whisper, searching for and finding her mother's eyes. "You're both here?" She gave a tired smile and closed her eyes while Bess and Michael exchanged another glance that said, This is what she wanted, this is what she set out to do. They took their places on Lisa's left while Mark and his mother stood on her right.

A second nurse appeared, all sterile and masked. "The doctor will be here in a minute," she said. She looked down into Lisa's face and said, "Hi, Lisa, I'm Ann, and I'm here to take care of the baby as soon as it arrives. I'll measure him, weigh him and bathe him."

Lisa nodded and Marcie Unger moved to the foot of the bed, where she removed the sheet from Lisa, then the end cushion of the bed itself, before tipping up a pair of footrests. She told Lisa, "These are for your feet if you want them. If not, fine." On the side rails she adjusted two pieces that looked like bicycle handles with plastic grips, and placed Lisa's left hand on one. "And these are for you to hang onto when you feel like pushing."

Mark said, "Here comes another one . . . come on, honey, show me that beautiful breathing. Pant, pant, pant, blow . . ."

Lisa moaned with each blow. In the middle of the contraction the doctor swept in, dressed like all the others in blue scrubs and skull cap. She spoke in a feminine voice. "Well, how are things going with Lisa?" Her eyes darted to the vital signs, then she smiled down at her patient.

"Hello, Doctor Lewis," Lisa said with as much enthusiasm as she could muster. Her voice sounded weak. "Where've you been so long?"

"I've been in touch. Let's see if we can't get this baby into the world and have a look at him. I'm going to break your water, Lisa. After that, everything will happen pretty fast."

Lisa nodded and rolled a glance at Mark, who held her hand folded over his own, smoothing her fingers.

While Dr. Lewis broke Lisa's water, Michael glanced away. The doctor was giving Lisa a monologue on what she was doing but Lisa made small sounds of distress. Under cover of the doctor's voice, Bess whispered to Michael, "Are you all right?"

He met her eyes and nodded but she could tell he was not, especially when he observed the faint pinkish fluid that ran from Lisa and stained the sheets beneath her. She found his arm and rubbed it lightly while from across the room she caught Hildy watching. Hildy's eyes smiled and the two women, who'd both borne children of their own, exchanged a moment of silent communion.

Lisa's next pushing contraction brought even greater sounds of distress. She cried out, and her body and face quaked as she clasped the handles and tried mightily to push the baby from herself.

The contraction ended with no results, and when it ebbed Bess bent over Lisa and said, "You're doing fine, honey," worried herself but hiding it. She lovingly wiped Lisa's stringy, wet bangs back from her brow and thought, *Never again, I'll never watch this again!*

She straightened to find Michael's eyebrows furrowed with concern, his breath coming fast, luffing his mask in and out.

The next contraction seemed worse than the last and racked Lisa even harder. Her head lifted from the bed, and Bess bolstered her from behind while Michael stared at the swollen shape of the baby's head engaged in the birth canal and repeated along with Mark, "Pant, pant, pant . . . push."

Still the baby refused to emerge, and Bess glanced at Michael's eyes to find them bright with tears. His tears prompted some of her own and she glanced away, wanting to be strong for Lisa's sake.

The doctor ordered, "Get the mighty vac."

Marcie Unger produced it: a tiny cone-shaped device at the end of a rubber tube and hand pump.

"Lisa," the doctor said, "we're going to give you a little help here. This is just a miniature suction cup we're going to put on the baby's head so the next time you push, we can pull a little, too, all right?"

"Will it hurt him?" Lisa asked, attempting to lift her head and see what was going on below.

"No," the doctor replied while Mark pressed his wife back against the bed, leaning over her, soothing her, urging her to rest as much as possible between pains. Bess did likewise from the opposite side of the bed, cooing comforting words, softly rubbing the inside of Lisa's knee.

Lisa murmured, "I'm so hot . . . don't touch me . . ."

Bess dropped her hand and felt Michael secretly grope for it in the folds of their blue scrubs. She gripped his hand and squeezed it all the while the tiny cone was inserted, and the hand pump worked by Marcie Unger, all the while Lisa moaned and wagged her head deliriously against the mattress.

With the next contraction the mighty vac began helping but midway through the suction broke and the cup flew free, spraying blood across six sets of scrubs and striking terror into the eyes of Mark, Hildy, Bess and Michael.

"It's okay," Marcie Unger reassured. "No harm done."

It seemed to take hours for them to get the suction cup reapplied.

But with the next pain, it worked.

Dr. Lewis said, "Here it comes . . ." and all eyes were fixed upon Lisa's dilated body. She pushed and the doctor pulled, and out of her swollen flesh emerged a tiny head with bloody, black hair.

Bess gripped Michael's hand and stared through her tears while he did likewise, both of them wonder-struck by what was happening before their eyes.

Between breaths Lisa managed to ask Mark, "Is it born yet?"

Dr. Lewis answered. "Halfway but one more push and it'll be here. Okay, Mark, help her through it."

The next pain did, indeed, bring the full birth. Michael and Bess watched it happen, still clinging to each other's hands, smiling behind their masks.

"It's a girl!" the doctor announced, catching the infant as it slipped forth.

Lisa smiled.

Mark cried, "Yahoo!"

Hildy rubbed Mark's back.

Bess and Michael looked at each other and found telltale dark splotches on their blue masks. Michael shrugged a shoulder to an eye and left another dark spot, and Bess felt her heart go light with joy.

The nurse named Ann came immediately with a soft blue towel, scooped the infant into it and laid her on Lisa's stomach. The doctor clamped the cord in two places and handed a pair of scissors to Mark.

"How about it, Daddy, do you want to cut the cord?"

The baby was wriggling, testing out its arms in the confines of the towel while Bess bolstered Lisa up so she could see the baby's head and touch it.

"Wow . . ." Lisa breathed, ". . . she's really here. Hey, Natalie, how you doing?" Then to the doctor, "Isn't she supposed to cry?"

"Not as long as she's breathing, and she's doing that just fine."

Lisa sank back and discovered there was more work to do—afterbirth to be delivered, and stitches to be tolerated.

Meanwhile, Natalie Padgett was being passed around from hand to hand—to her father, her grandmothers, her grandfather, whose dark eyes beamed above his mask while he, too, welcomed her with "Hi, Natalie." She was about as pretty as a baby bird, still plastered with afterbirth and working her head and arms with the diminutive motions of a slow-motion film, trying to keep her eyes open while her fists remained tightly shut.

Hildy said, "I'd better go tell the news to Jake." While she was gone Bess and Michael had one lavish minute to appreciate their grandchild themselves. She lay in the soft blue towel, squirming, held in Michael's wide hands, with Bess cupping the warm flannel around her tiny, smeared head.

The instinct to kiss her was irrepressible.

Tears kept welling in their eyes and blurring her image while a wellspring of love encompassed them both.

Michael said, "How awful that I missed this when our own were born. I'm so glad I was here this time." He passed the baby to Bess, who held her far too short a time before she was claimed by her father, then by Ann, for weighing and measuring. Hildy returned with Jake in tow, and the birthing room became crowded, so Bess and Michael left for a while, repairing to the family room next door. There, all was quiet and they were alone. They turned to each other, pulled down their masks and embraced, wordless for a long time, the birth they'd just witnessed melding with the birth of Lisa in their memories.

When Michael spoke his voice was gruff with emotion.

"I never thought I'd feel like this."

"How?" she whispered.

"Complete."

"Yes, that's it, isn't it?"

"A part of us, coming into the world again. My God, it does something to you, doesn't it, Bess?"

It did. It brought a lump to her throat and a yearning to her heart as she simply stood in Michael's arms, softly rubbing his shoulders through the ugly blue scrubs, disinclined to ever leave him again.

"Oh, Michael . . ."

"I'm so glad we're together for this."

"Oh, me too. It was awful before you got here. I kept thinking you weren't coming, and I didn't know how I'd get through it without you."

"Now that I've been through it, I wouldn't have missed it for the world."

They remained locked in an embrace until their emotions calmed and weariness made itself known, then Michael asked, against her hair, "Tired?"

"Yes. You?"

"Exhausted."

He set her away and looked into her face. "Well, I guess there's no reason for us to stay. Let's go see the baby once more and say good-bye to Lisa."

In the room next door the new parents created a heartwarming tableau with their clean, red-faced infant between them, wrapped now in a pink blanket, Lisa and Mark radiant with love and happiness. So radiant, it seemed a transgression to interrupt and bid them good-bye.

Bess did so first, leaning over Lisa as she rested in bed, touching her hair and kissing her cheek, then the baby's head. "Good night, dear. I'll see you later on this afternoon. Thank you so much for letting us be a part of this."

Michael went next, kissing them, too, deluged with the same emotions as Bess. "I didn't really want to come in here tonight but I'm so glad I did. Thank you, honey."

They congratulated and hugged Mark and left the hospital together.

Outside it was nearly dawn. Sparrows were beginning to cheep from the nearby trees. The sky had begun its fade from deep blue to lavender. The night dew seemed to have lifted into the air and hung damp all around. The visitors' parking lot was nearly empty as Bess and Michael walked across it with lagging footsteps.

As they approached Bess's car, Michael took her hand.

"That was really something to go through, wasn't it?" he said.

"I feel as if I had the baby myself."

"I bet you do. I never had one, and *I* feel like I just did!"

"The funny thing is when I was the one giving birth I don't think the wonder of it struck me so hard. I suppose I was too busy to dwell on that part of it."

"Same for me. Waiting in another room—I wish things had been different in those days and I could have been in the delivery room like Mark was."

They reached her car and stopped but Michael kept her hand. "Can you believe it, Bess? We're a grandpa and grandma."

She smiled up at him wearily and said, "A couple of very tired ones. Do you have to work today?"

"I'm not going to. How about you?"

"I was supposed to but I think I'll let Heather handle it alone. I'll probably sleep for a few hours then come back up to see Lisa and the baby again."

"Yeah, me too."

There seemed little else to say. It was time to part, time for him to go to his condominium and for her to go to her house on Third Avenue.

They had been through an exhausting night. Their eyes hurt. Their backs hurt. But they stood in the parking lot, holding hands until it made no sense anymore. One of them had to move.

"Well . . ." she said, "see y'."

"Yeah," he repeated, "see y'."

She pulled free as if someone were dragging her against her wishes, from the opposite direction. She got into her car while he stood with both hands crooked over the open door, watching as she put her keys in the ignition and started the engine. He slammed the door. She shifted into reverse and waggled two fingers at him through the window, wearing a sad expression on her face.

He stepped back as the car began to roll, slipped his hands into his trouser pockets and remained behind feeling empty and lost as he watched her drive away.

When she was gone, he sighed deeply, tipped his face to the sky and tried to gulp down the lump in his throat. He went to his own car, got in and stuck his keys into the ignition, then sat motionless with the engine unstarted and his hands hanging limply on the wheel.

Thinking. Thinking. About himself, his future and how empty it would remain without Bess.

It began deep down within him, a bubbling rebellion that said, Why? Why must it be that way? We've both changed. We both want, need, love each other. We both want this family back together. What the hell are we waiting for?

He started his engine and tore out of the parking lot doing a rolling stop at the stop sign, then wheeled out onto Greeley Street on Bess's trail, doing a good fifteen miles an hour above the speed limit.

At the house on Third Avenue he screeched to a halt and opened the car door even before the engine stopped running. Her car was already put away in the garage, the door was down. He jogged up the sidewalk to the front door, rang the bell, thumped on the door with his fist several times, then stood waiting with one hand braced on the doorframe at shoulder level. She must have gone upstairs already. It took her some time to get back down and answer.

When she did, surprise dropped her jaw.

"Why, Michael, what's wrong?"

He burst inside, slammed the door and scooped her into his arms. "You *know* what's wrong, Bess. You and me, living in two separate houses, being divorced from each other when we love each other the way we do. That's no way for us to act, not when we could be together and happy. I want that . . ." He gripped her harder. ". . . oh God, I want that so much." He interrupted himself to kiss her—hard, brief, possessive—before wrapping his arms around her firmly and holding her to his breast. "I want Lisa and Mark to bring that baby to our house and the two of us waiting with outstretched arms, and keeping her overnight sometimes, and all of us together on Christmas mornings after Santa Claus comes. And I want us to try to make up for what we did to Randy. Maybe if we start now we can turn him around." He drew back, holding her face in both hands, pleading, "Please, Bess, marry me again. I love you. We'll try harder this time, and we'll compromise, for both us and the kids. Can't you see, Lisa was right? This is the way it should be!"

She was crying long before he finished, the tears coursing down her cheeks. "Aw, don't cry, Bess . . . don't . . ."

She dove against him and threw her arms around his neck. "Oh, Michael, yes. I love you, too, and I want all those things, and I don't know what's going to become of Randy but we've got to try. He still needs us so much."

They kissed the way they'd wanted to in the hospital parking lot, sealed together full-length, earnest with passion while at the same time too tired to know if they were standing on their own power or supporting one another. Their lips parted, their gazes locked but even so, they floundered in their attempt to impart the depth of emotions coursing through them.

He kissed the crests of her cheeks, sipping up her salty tears, then her mouth, softly this time. "Let's get married right away. As soon as possible."

She smiled through her tears. "All right. Whatever you say."

"And we'll tell the kids today. And Stella, too," he added. "We're going to make her the second happiest woman in the whole USA."

Bess kept smiling. "The third, maybe . . . behind me and Lisa."

"All right, third. But she'll be smiling."

"She'll be doing cartwheels."

"I feel like I could do a few myself."

"You do? I'm falling off my feet."

"On second thought, so am I. Should we go to bed?"

"And do what? Get caught again by Randy? He's due home, you know."

Michael took her breasts in both hands and went on convincing her. "You'll sleep better afterwards, you always do."

"I won't have any trouble sleeping at all."

"Cruel woman."

She drew back and smiled lovingly. "Michael, we'll have plenty of time for that, and I really am tired, and I don't want to antagonize Randy any more. Let's do the sensible thing."

He caught her hands and stepped back. "All right, I'll go home like a good boy. Will I see you at the hospital later?"

"Around two or so, I thought."

"Okay. Walk me to my car?"

She smiled and walked with him, holding his hand, outside into the yard, where full dawn was staining the sky a spectrum of purples and golds and a faint breeze was stirring the tips of the maple leaves. The hydrangeas in front of the garage were heavy with great white blooms and the scent of heavy summer was rising from the warming earth.

At his car, Michael got in, closed the door and rolled down the window.

She leaned inside and kissed him. "I love you, Michael," she said.

"I love you, too, and I really think we can make it this time."

"So do I." He started the engine, still looking up into her eyes.

She grinned. "It's hell being mature and having to make sensible decisions. For two cents I'd drag you up to our bedroom and ravish you right now."

He laughed and said, "We'll make up for it, just wait and see."

She stood back, crossed her arms and watched him back out of the driveway.

chapter 18

THE BAND QUIT PLAYING at 12:30 A.M. It took them one hour to load up and over five hours to drive back from Bemidji. Randy got home at seven to find his mother still asleep and a note on his bed.

Lisa had a girl, Natalie, 9 lbs. 12 oz, at five this morning. Everybody's doing fine. I'm not going into the store but hope to see you at the hospital later. Love, Mom.

But the way it worked out he was unable to make it to the hospital that afternoon. He was still asleep when his mother got up, and she was gone from the house by the time he rose, groggy, at 12:15 to get ready for his afternoon gig, which started at two in White Bear Lake.

These town celebrations paid well. Every little suburb around the Twin Cities had them at some time during the summer: the Raspberry Festival in Hopkins, Whiz-Bang Days in Robbinsdale, Tater Days in Brooklyn Park, Manitou Days in White Bear Lake. They were all the same: carnivals, parades, bingo, beard-growing contests and street dances. Some of the dances took place at night but many, like today's, were scheduled for the afternoon. Bands liked the bookings not only because they paid well but also because the afternoon scheduling gave them a rare Saturday night off to catch a decent stretch of sleep or to go hear some other band play, which every professional musician loved to do.

White Bear Lake had a pretty little downtown—shady, with trees springing out of openings in the brick sidewalks; fancy, old-fashioned storefronts painted candy colors; flags hanging from the sides of buildings; a little town square.

The entire length of Washington Street was barricaded off, and a bandstand was set up at the south end, facing a turn-of-the century post office building with its surrounding green grass and flower beds. While the band set up, little girls sat on the curb and watched, licking ice-cream cones or chewing licorice sticks. Pint-sized boys wearing chartreuse billcaps and hot-pink shorts maneuvered their skateboards back and forth, deftly jumping the thick electrical cables that snaked across the blacktop. From several blocks away the sounds of a carnival drifted over on the whims of the wind—an occasional tinkle of calliope music, the revving engines from the amusement rides. From nearer wafted the smell of bratwursts roasting on a pushcart in front of a ladies' wear shop midway along the block.

Randy stacked a pair of drums and lifted them from the rear of the van. He turned to find a boy of perhaps twelve years old watching. The kid was wearing sunglasses with pink frames and black strings. His hair was jelled up into a flattop, and his high-top tennis shoes had tongues nearly as big as the skateboard on his hip.

"Hey, you play those things?" the kid asked in a gruff, cocky voice.

"Yup."

"Cool."

Randy smiled at the kid and took the load up the back steps onto the stage. The boy was still there when he returned.

"I play drums, too."

"Yeah?"

"In the band at school."

"That's a good way to learn."

"Ain't got any of my own yet. But I will have someday though, and then look out."

Randy smiled and pulled another load of equipment to the rear of the van.

The kid offered, "Want me to help you carry some of that stuff?" Randy turned and looked the kid over. He was a tough-looking little punk, as tough-looking as it's possible to be at a hundred pounds, without much for muscles or whiskers or body hair. His Dick Tracy T-shirt would have fit Mike Tyson, and he had an I-don't-care way of standing inside it that reminded Randy of himself at that age, about the time his father had left: *Screw the world. Who needs it?*

"Yeah. Here, take this stool, then you can come back for the cymbals. What's your name, kid?"

"Trotter." He had a voice like sand in ball bearings.

"That's all? Just Trotter?"

"That's enough."

"Well, Trotter, see what you think about being a roadie."

Trotter was as good as his name, trotting up and down the steps, hauling anything Randy would hand him. Actually the kid was a godsend. Randy was zoned, operating on four hours of sleep and too much pot last night. God, how he needed to chill out for a solid sixteen hours but that hadn't been possible all week. Their traveling schedule had been horrendous, and they'd been rehearsing a lot, too. All that on top of setup and breakdown—which totaled two and a half, three hours a gig—left damned little time for Z'ing out. Now he faced four hours of playing when his feet would scarcely lift to carry him up the steps and his head felt like a bowling ball balanced on a toothpick.

With the help of the tough little groupie, the last of the equipment got to the stage.

"Hey, thanks, Trotter. You're okay." He handed the kid a pair of royal-blue drumsticks. "Here. Go for it."

The kid took the sticks, his eyes huge and filled with worship behind his shades.

"For me?"

Randy nodded.

"Bitchin'," the kid marveled softly and moved off, already jiving to some silent beat.

"Hey, kid," Randy called after him.

Trotter turned, one of the sticks whirling like a propeller through his fingers. "Stick around. We'll send one out specially for you this afternoon."

Trotter saluted with one drumstick and disappeared.

Pike Watson came around the back of the stage carrying a guitar case.

"Who's the punk?"

"Name's Trotter. Just a kid with big dreams, wants to be a drummer someday."

"You give him the sticks?"

Randy shrugged. "What the hell, keep his dreams alive, you know?"

"That's all right."

"I didn't tell him he'd have to learn to sleep and drive at the same time if he wanted to play with a band."

"You droned, man?"

Randy shook his head as if to wake himself up. "Yeah. Major droned."

"Hey, listen, I'll do you a solid. I got some really good shit here." Pike tapped his guitar case.

"Cocaine, you mean? Naw. That stuff freaks me."

"How do you know? One little snort and you're goddamned Batman. You can stop trains and start revolutions. What do you say?"

Randy looked skeptical. "Naw, I don't think so."

Pike gave a mischievous grin. "I guarantee you'll forget you're tired." He spread his fingers and fanned them in slow motion through the air. "You'll play like freakin' Charlie Watts."

"How much?"

"Your first hit's on me."

Randy rubbed his sternum and tipped his head to one side. "I don't know, man."

"Well . . ." Pike threw his hands up and bounced a couple times at the knee. "If you're scared of flyin' . . ."

"What's it do to you—bad, I mean?"

"Nothin', man, *nothiiin'!* You get a little zingy at first—anxious, you know—but then it's strictly superfly!"

Randy rubbed his face with both hands and flexed his shoulders. He blew out a blast of breath that made his lips flop and said, "What the hell . . . I always wanted to play like Charlie Watts."

He snorted the cocaine off a mirror in the back of Pike's van just before they started playing. It made his nose sting and he rubbed it as he headed onto the stage. He felt wildly exhilarated and invincible.

They started the first set and Randy played with his eyes closed. When he opened them a moment later, he saw Trotter out in front of all the others on the street, sitting on his skateboard with his eyes riveted on Randy, playing along on his knees with the blue drumsticks. Yeah, it was hero worship, all right, and it felt sensational. Nearly as sensational as the high that was coming on. Some teenage girls stood at the front of the crowd, too, dressed in shiny biking tights with an inch of their tan, flat stomachs showing below their itty-bitty crop tops. One of them, a blonde with a spectacular mop of curly hair that exploded clear down past her shoulder blades, kept her eye on him without letup. He could spot them every time, the ones who were easy marks. All he had to do was return her gaze a few times, give the little hint of a smile she waited for and at break time stand nearby—not too close, just close enough for her to know he knew—and wait for her to sidle over. The conversations always went the same.

"Hi."

"Hi."

"You're good."

He'd let his eyes overtly explore her breasts and hips. "So are you. What's your name?"

After he'd learn it, he'd make sure he dedicated one song to her and that's all it took to get in her pants.

Today, however, the dedication was for Trotter. Randy put his lips to the mike and said, "I'd like to send this song out to one terrific little roadie. Trotter, this one's for you, kid." Trotter actually smiled, and while Randy rapped out the pickup beat to *Pretty Woman,* he truly forgot about the pretty woman standing behind the kid, and reveled in the genuine admiration he saw beaming up at him from the boy's face.

It happened as they began the second song. One minute Randy was watching the kid idolize him, and the next he was struck by an illogical shock of apprehension. His heart started racing and the apprehension became fear. He turned as if to seek help from Pike but all he saw was Pike's back, in a loose black shirt, diagonally bisected by a wide guitar strap as he stood with his feet widespread, playing.

Sweet Jesus, his heart! What was happening with his heart? It was pounding so hard it seemed to be lifting the hair from his skull. The kid was watching . . . no breath . . . hard to keep playing . . . people everywhere . . . had to make it to the end of the song . . . dizzying anxiety . . . oh-oh, pretty woman!

The song ending . . . "Pike!" . . . everything inside him vibrating . . . "Pike!" . . . and pushing outward . . . Pike's face, leaning close, coming between him and the crowd . . .

"It's all right, man. It always happens at first, you get a little uptight, scared-like. Give it a minute. It'll go away."

Clutching Pike's hand . . . "No, no! This'z bad, man . . . my heart . . ."

Pike, angry, ordering in a fierce whisper, "Let it ride, man. There's a couple hundred people out there watching us right now. It'll be better in a minute! Now give us a goddamn lead-in!"

Tick, tick, tick . . . the sticks on the rim of his Pearls . . . the kid watching from down on the pavement, playing along with the blue sticks . . . dizzy . . . so dizzy . . . kid, get outa here . . . don't want you to see this . . . Maryann, I wanted to change for you . . . his heart fluttering fast as a drumroll . . . everything tipping . . . tipping . . . the floor coming up to meet him . . . the crack of his head as he landed . . . the stool still tangled in his legs . . . looking straight up at the blue sky . . .

The band continued playing for several measures until they realized there was no more drumbeat. As the music dribbled into silence the crowd pressed forward, lifted up on tiptoe and murmured a chorus of concern.

Danny Scarfelli reached Randy first, leaned over him with his bass guitar still strapped over his shoulder.

"Jesus, Randy, what's wrong, man?"

"Get Pike . . . where's Pike?" Danny caught two of his guitar keys on the edge of a drum as he shot to his feet.

Randy lay in a haze of fear with the sound of his own heart gurgling in his ears.

Pike's face appeared above Randy's, framed by the blue sky.

"Pike, my heart . . . I think I'm dying . . . help me . . ."

A jumble of voices.

"What's wrong with him?"

"Has he got epilepsy?"

"Call 911!"

"Hang on, Randy."

Pike leaped off the front of the stage and took off at a run. "Where's a phone? Anybody! Where's a phone!" Before the frantic question left his lips he saw a policeman coming toward him at a run, his silver badge bouncing on his blue shirt.

"Officer . . ."

The policeman ran right past him on his way to the stage, and Pike did an about-face to follow.

"Anybody know what's wrong with him?" the policeman asked, bending over Randy.

Pike said nothing.

The others said no.

Randy mumbled, "My heart . . ."

The man in blue grabbed the radio off his belt and called for help.

Randy lay ringed by faces, looking up at them, terror in his eyes. He grabbed a shirtfront: Danny's. "Call my mom," he whispered.

Blissfully unaware of the events happening at White Bear Lake ten miles away, Bess and Michael met at the hospital, stole one brief kiss in the hall, smiled into one another's eyes and entered Lisa's room together, holding hands. She and Natalie were there alone, the new mother asleep in her hospital bed, and the new baby making mewling sounds in a glass bassinet. The room was filled with flowers and smelled like oniony beef from the remains of Lisa's lunch, which was waiting to be collected.

Bess and Michael scanned the room from the doorway, then tiptoed to the bassinet and stood on either side of it, looking down at their new granddaughter.

They spoke in whispers.

"Oh, just look at her, Michael, isn't she beautiful?" And to the baby, Bess said, "Hello, precious, how are you today? You look a lot prettier than you did last night."

They both reached down and touched the baby's blankets, her downy cheek, rapt in her presence. Michael whispered, "Hi there, little lady. Grandma and Grandpa came to see you."

"Michael, look . . . her mouth is just like your mother's."

"Wouldn't my mother have loved her."

"So would my dad."

"She's got more hair than I thought. Last night it seemed as if she didn't have hardly any but today it looks quite dark."

"Do you think it would be okay if we picked her up?" Bess looked up into Michael's eyes. He smiled conspiratorially, and she slipped her hands beneath the soft pink flannel blanket and lifted Natalie from the bassinet. They stood shoulder-to-shoulder, inundated by love as pure and exquisite as any they had ever felt, stunned once again by a sense of completeness, by the idea of leaving their mark on the future through this child.

"Isn't it something, how she makes us feel?"

Michael kissed the baby's forehead, then straightened and smiled at her. "Wait till you're one or two or so. You'll come to our house to stay and we'll spoil you plenty, won't we, Grandma?"

"You bet we will. And someday when you're old enough, we'll tell you all about how your birth made your grandpa propose to me and brought us back together again. Of course we'll have to edit out the part about the condoms and how your grandpa threw them all over the steps but . . ."

Michael smothered his laughter. "Bess, these are delicate ears!"

"Well, she comes from a randy lot, and if—"

From behind them, Lisa spoke. "What are you two whispering about over there?"

They looked back over their shoulders. Lisa looked sleepy but wore a soft smile.

"Actually, your mother was talking about condoms."

"Michael!" Bess shouted.

"Well, she was. I told her Natalie was too young to hear such things but she wouldn't listen to me."

Lisa boosted herself up. "All right, what's going on between you two? I wake up and you're whispering and giggling . . ." She reached with both hands. "And bring my baby here, will you?"

Lisa pressed a button that raised the head of the bed, and they went to take her the baby, then sit one on each side of her and lean over simultaneously to kiss her cheeks.

"She was awake so we didn't think we'd get in trouble for picking her up."

"She's been a good girl . . . haven't you, Natalie?" Lisa fingered the baby's hair. "She slept five hours between feedings."

They talked about how Lisa was feeling, whom she'd called, who'd sent flowers (she thanked them for theirs), when Mark was expected to return, the fact that Randy hadn't called or stopped by, the probability of his visiting that evening, and Grandma Dorner, too. They admired the baby, and Bess offered reminiscences about Lisa's birth, and what a good sleeper she'd been, and what a lusty set of lungs she'd had when she decided not to sleep.

After all that, while they still sat one on either side of Lisa, Bess glanced at Michael and sent him a silent message. He captured her hand and, resting it on the bedspread covering Lisa's stomach, said, "Your mother and I have something to tell you, Lisa." He let Bess speak the words.

"We're going to get married again."

A radiant smile lit Lisa's face as she lunged forward, the baby still on her right arm, clasping Michael with her left as Bess, too, bent into the awkward, three-way embrace. The baby started complaining at being squashed between two bodies but they ignored her, allowing the moment its due, cleaving to one another, their throats thick with emotion.

Against Lisa's hair, Bess whispered simply, "Thank you, darling, for forcing two stubborn people back together."

Lisa kissed her mother's mouth, her father's mouth. "You've made me so happy."

"We've made *us* so happy." Michael chuckled, drawing a like response from the others as they drew back, all of them a little glisteny-eyed and flushed. They all laughed self-consciously. Lisa sniffed, and Bess ran the edge of a hand under her eye.

"When?"

"Right away."

"As soon as we can get it arranged."

"Oh, you guys, I'm *so* happy!" This hug was one of hallelujah, a near banging together of cheeks before Lisa held Natalie straight out and rejoiced, "We did it, kiddo, we did it!"

Stella spoke from the doorway. "May I get in on this celebration?"

"Grandma! Come in, quick! Mom and Dad have some great news! Tell her, Mom!"

Stella approached the bed. "Don't tell me. You're going to get married again." Bess nodded, smiling widely. Stella made a victor's fist. "I knew it! I knew it!" She kissed Bess first, because she was closer, then went at

Michael with her arms up. "Come here, you handsome, wonderful hunk of a son-in-law, you!" She met him at the foot of the bed as he came around to scoop her up. "I thought that daughter of mine was crazy to divorce you in the first place." Released, she fanned her face and turned toward the bed. "Whoo! How much excitement can a woman stand in one day? All this and a great-grandchild, too! Let me see the new arrival—and Lisa, you little matchmaking mother, don't you look happy enough to float?"

It was an afternoon of celebration. Mark arrived, followed by the rest of the Padgetts as well as two women Lisa worked with, and one of her high-school friends. Bess and Michael's news was received with as much excitement as was their new granddaughter.

At one point Lisa asked, "Where are you going to live?"

They gaped at each other and shrugged.

Bess replied, "We don't know. We haven't talked about it yet."

Leaving the hospital at 4:15 P.M., Bess said, "Where *are* we going to live?"

"I don't know."

"I suppose we should talk about it. Want to come over to the house?"

Michael affected a salacious grin and said, "Of course I want to come over to the house."

They were driving separate cars but arrived at the house simultaneously. Bess parked in the garage and Michael pulled up behind her, went into the garage and waited beside her car while she switched off the radio and collected her purse and turned up the visor. As he opened her door and stood waiting, he found himself happier than he could recall being in years, for simply being with her, feeling certain that the last half of his life was going to be less tumultuous than the first. Everything seemed near perfect—the new baby, the marriage plans, the children all grown up, happiness, wealth and health; he found himself tempted toward smugness as he stood beside Bess's car.

From behind the wheel she looked up at him and said, "You know what?"

She could have announced that she'd taken a job as a palm reader and was going to travel the country with a carnival, and he wouldn't have objected at that moment, as long as he could tag along. Her face looked young and glad, her eyes content. "I couldn't guess."

She got out of the car. He slammed the door but they remained beside it, in the concrete coolness of the garage with its peculiar mixture of scents—mower gas and rubber hoses and garden chemicals. "I've discovered something about myself that surprises me," Bess told him.

"What?"

"That I really don't care about this house as much as I used to. As a matter of fact, I absolutely love your condo."

He couldn't have been more surprised. "Are you saying you want to live there?"

"Where do *you* want to live?"

"In my condo, but I thought for sure you'd have a fit if I said so."

She burst out laughing, draped her arms around his neck and dropped back against the side of her car, taking him with her. With his body fit to hers she smiled up into his eyes. "Oh, Michael, isn't it wonderful, getting older? Learning to sort out what's really important from what's petty and superficial?" She kissed him briefly and told him, "I'd love to live in your condo. But if you'd said you wanted to move back into the house, that would have been all right, too, because it's not so important *where* we live as that we live there together from now on."

He rested his hands on the sides of her breasts and said, "I've been thinking about that same thing, too. Are you sure you aren't saying you like the condo better just because you think it's what I want?"

"I'm sure. In more ways than one we sort of outgrew this house. It was grand while the kids were little but now it's—I don't know—a new phase of life, time to move on. There are a lot of sad memories here, as well as happy ones. The condo is a fresh start . . . and after all, we did decorate it together, to both of our tastes. Why, it makes perfect sense to live there! It's newer, it's got as wonderful a view as this does, nobody has to take care of the yard, it's still close enough for me to get to my store in fifteen minutes and for you to get to downtown St. Paul fast, and there's the beach and the parks, and—"

"Listen, Bess, you don't have to convince me. I'll be overjoyed to stay there. There's only one question."

"Which is?"

"What about Randy?"

She put her hands on his collarbone and absently smoothed his shirt. She let her hands fall still on his chest, lifted her gaze and said calmly, "It's time to cut Randy loose, don't you think?"

Michael made no reply. He had told her essentially the same thing that first night Lisa had tricked them into facing each other at her apartment.

"He has a job now," she went on. "Friends. It's time he got out on his own."

"You're sure?"

"I'm sure."

"Because it strikes me that even though parents think they ought to treat all their kids equally, it's not always possible. Some of them need us more than others, and I think Randy will always need more of our help than Lisa ever did."

"That may be true but it's still time for him to live in his own place."

They let a kiss seal their decision, sharing it leaning against the car with the late afternoon sunlight flooding in, and the sound of condensation dripping off the auto air conditioner, and the smell of gasoline coming from the nearby lawn mower.

When Michael lifted his head he looked serene. "This time I'm staying with you till he gets home, and we'll tell him together."

"Agreed." She smiled and threaded one arm around his waist, turning him toward the kitchen door.

They entered the house to find the phone ringing. Bess answered, unprepared in her radiant state for the voice at the other end of the line.

"Mrs. Curran?"

"Yes."

"This is Danny Scarfelli. I'm one of the guys in Randy's band. Listen, I don't mean to scare you but something's happened to him and he's not . . . well, I think it's pretty serious, and they're taking him by ambulance to the hospital."

"What? A car accident, you mean?" Bess's terrified eyes locked on Michael's.

"No. We were just playing, you know, and all of a sudden he's laying on the floor. He says it's something with his heart is all I know. He asked me to call you."

"Which hospital?"

"Stillwater. They've already left."

"Thank you." She hung up. "It's Randy. Something's wrong with his heart and they're taking him to the hospital in an ambulance."

"Let's go."

He grabbed her hand and they ran out the way they'd entered, to his car. "I'll drive."

All the way to Lakeview Hospital, they sat stiff-spined, fearful, thinking, Why now? Why now? It's taken us all this time to get our lives back on track, and we deserve some unconfounded happiness. Michael ignored stop signs and broke speed limits. Gripping the steering wheel with both hands, he thought, There must be something I should be saying to Bess. I should touch her shoulder, squeeze her hand. But he drove in his own insular parcel of dread, as silent as she, inexplicably reft from her by this threat to their child.

His heart? What could be wrong with the heart of a nineteen-year-old boy?

They reached the emergency room of Lakeview at the same time as the ambulance, catching a mere glimpse of Randy as they ran behind the gurney bearing him along a short hall to a curtained section of the area. An alarming number of medical staff materialized at once, speaking in brusque spurts, in their own indigenous lexicon, focused on the patient with unquestionable life-and-death intensity, ignoring Michael and Bess, who hovered on the sidelines, gripping each other's hands now as they had not in the car.

"Got a sinus tach here."

"What's his blood pressure?"

"One eighty over one hundred."

"Respiration?"

"Poor."

"How bad are the arrhythmias?"

"Bad. Heart is moving like a bag of worms in there. Very irregular and rapid. We put him on D5W."

Three patches were already pasted on Randy's chest, and a blood pressure cuff ringed his arm. Someone snapped leads to them, connected to monitors on the wall. Intermittent beeps sounded. Randy's eyes were wide open as a doctor in white leaned over him. "Randy, can you hear me? Can you hear me, Randy? Did you take anything?"

The doc pulled back Randy's eyelids one at a time and studied the periphery of his eyes. A woman in blue scrubs said, "His parents are here."

The doctor caught sight of Bess and Michael, standing to one side, supporting each other. "You're his parents?"

"Yes," Michael answered.

"Are there any congenital heart problems?"

"No."

"Diabetes?"

"No."

"Seizure disorders?"

"No."

"Is he on any medication?"

"None that we know of."

"Does he use cocaine?"

"I don't think so. Marijuana sometimes."

A nurse said, "Blood pressure's dropping."

An alarm sounded on one of the machines, like the hang-up tone on a dangling telephone.

The doctor shouted, "This guy's coding! Page code blue!" He made a fist and delivered a tremendous blow to Randy's sternum.

Bess winced and placed one hand over her mouth. She stared, caught in a horror beyond anything she'd imagined, while her son lay on the gurney dying and a medical team fought a scene such as she'd witnessed only on television.

More staff came running, two more nurses, one who started a flowchart, a lab technician to help monitor the vital signs, a radiology technician who watched the monitors, an anesthetist who inserted a pair of nasal prongs into Randy's nose, another doctor who began administering CPR. "Grease the paddles!" he ordered. "We have to defibrillate!" With stacked hands, he thrust at Randy's chest.

Bess and Michael's interlocked knuckles turned white.

A nurse turned on a machine that set up a high electrical whine. She grabbed two paddles on curled cords and smeared them with gel. The doctor ordered, "Stand back!" Everyone backed away from the metal gurney as the nurse flattened the paddles to the left side of Randy's chest.

"Hit him!"

The nurse pushed two buttons at once.

Randy grunted. His body arched. His arms and legs stiffened, then fell limp.

Bess uttered a soft cry and turned her face against Michael's shoulder.

Someone said, "Good, he responded."

Through her tears and her terror, Bess looked back at the table, little understanding why these methods were used. Electrical current, zapping through her son's body, making it jerk and flop, that precious body she'd once carried within her own. *Please don't! Don't do that to him again!*

The room fell silent. All eyes riveted on a green screen and its flat, flat line.

Dear God, they've killed him! He's dead! There is no heartbeat!

"Come on, come on . . ." someone whispered urgently—the doctor, who'd made a tight fist and pushed it into the gurney mattress as he stared at the monitor. "Beat, damn it . . "

The line stayed flat.

Bess and Michael stared with the others, linked by wills and hands, in near shock themselves from this quick plunge into disaster.

Tears leaked down Bess's face. "What is it? What's happening?" Bess whispered but no one responded.

The green line squiggled.

It squiggled again, lifting to form a tiny hillock on that deadly, unbroken horizon. And suddenly it picked up, became regular. Everyone in the room sighed and let their shoulders sag.

"All right, way to go, Randy," one of the medical team said.

Randy was still unconscious.

The lab technician, in a businesslike tone, with his eyes locked on the screen, reported, "We're back to an organized rhythm . . . eighty beats per minute now." The nurse with the clipboard checked the clock and made a note.

Bess looked up at Michael and her face sagged, as if made of wet newsprint. His eyes were dry and burning. He put both arms around her shoulders and hauled her close, cleaving to keep his knees from buckling while Randy began to regain consciousness.

"Randy, can you hear me?" Again a doctor was leaning over him.

He made a wordless sound, still groggy.

"Do you know where you are, Randy?"

He opened his eyes fully, looked around at the ring of faces and abruptly grew belligerent. He tried to sit up. "What the hell, let me outa—"

"Whoa, there." Hands pressed him down. "Not much oxygen getting to that brain yet. He's still light-headed. Randy, did you take anything? Did you take any cocaine?"

A nurse informed the doctor, "The cardiologist is on his way over from the clinic."

The doctor repeated to Randy, "Did you take any cocaine?"

Randy wagged his head and tried to lift one arm. The doctor held it down, encumbered as it was by the blood pressure cuff and the lead-in for an IV.

"Randy, we're not the police. Nobody is going to get in trouble if you tell us but we have to know so we can help you and keep your heart beating regularly. Was it cocaine, Randy?"

Randy fixed his eyes on the doctor's clothing and mumbled, "It was my first time, Doc, honest."

"How did you take it?"

No answer.

"Did you shoot up?"

No answer.

"Snort it?"

Randy nodded.

The doc touched his shoulder. "Okay, no need to get scared. Just relax." He lifted Randy's eyelids again, peered down, held up an index finger and said, "Follow my finger with your eyes." To the recording nurse he said,

"No vertical nystagmus. No dilation." To Randy, "Are any of your muscles twitching?"

"No."

"Good. I'm going to tell you what happened. The cocaine increased your heartbeat to the point where there wasn't enough time during each beat for it to properly fill with oxygenated blood. Consequently not enough oxygen was getting to your brain so at first you probably felt a little light-headed, and finally you fell off your stool. After you got here to the hospital your heart stopped beating completely but we started it again. There's a cardiologist on his way over from the clinic right now. He'll probably give you some medication to keep your heartbeat regular, okay?"

At that moment the cardiologist swept in, moving directly to the gurney in brisk steps. The physician speaking said, "Randy, this is Dr. Mortenson."

While the specialist took over, the other doctor approached Bess and Michael. "I'm Dr. Fenton," he said, extending his hand to each of them in turn. He had grand gray eyebrows and a caring manner. "I imagine you both feel like you're going to be next on that table. Let's step out into the hall, where we can talk privately."

In the hall, Dr. Fenton took a second glance at Bess and said, "Are you feeling faint, Mrs. Curran?"

"No . . . no, I'm all right."

"There's no need to be heroic. You've just been through a stressful ordeal. Let's sit down over here." He indicated a line of hard chairs across from the emergency-room desk. Michael put his arm around Bess and helped her to one, where she sank down gratefully. When they were all seated, Fenton said, "I know you have a lot of questions, so let me fill you in. I think you heard what I was saying to Randy in there—he snorted some cocaine, which can do a lot of nasty things to the human body. This time it caused an abnormally high heart rate—ventricular tachycardia, we call it. When the paramedics answered the call, Randy had been playing the drums and had fallen off his stool. That's because there wasn't enough oxygen getting to his brain. When you saw him arrest, there was so much electrostimulus going through his heart it wasn't actually beating anymore, it was only quivering. When a heart does that we have to bring it to a complete standstill so its normal rhythmicity can return. That's why I struck his chest, and that's what we did when we defibrillated him. Once you do that the normal electrical pathway can take over again, which is what's happened now.

"You saw how Randy got a little belligerent when he was coming awake. That often happens when the oxygen is returning to the brain but he should rest easier now.

"I have to warn you, though, that this can happen again during the next several hours, either from the drugs or from the heart itself, which is very irritable after all it's been through. My guess is Dr. Mortenson will prescribe some medication to prevent fibrillation from recurring. The problem with cocaine is that we can't go in there and get it out like we could poison, for example. We can only offer supportive care and wait for the effects of the drug to wear off. It stays in the system long after the high is gone."

Michael said, "So what you're saying is, there's still a chance that he could die?"

"I'm afraid so. The next six hours will be critical. But his youth is a plus. And if he does go into a fast rate, chances are we can control it with the drugs."

The cardiologist appeared at that moment. "Mr. and Mrs. Curran?"

"Yes, sir?"

Michael and Bess both stood.

"I'm Dr. Mortenson." He had steel-gray hair, rimless silver glasses and thick hands with a generous peppering of black hair on them. His handshake was hearty and firm. "Randy will be in my charge for a while yet. His heartbeat has leveled off now—a little rapid but we've administered inderal, which should help stabilize his heartbeat. If we can keep it reasonably steady for—oh, say twenty-four hours or so—he'll be totally out of the woods. Right now the lab people are drawing his blood gases. Our toxologist will do a drug screen and we'll be running a routine battery of other tests as well—blood sugar, electrolytes—standard procedure where cocaine is involved. We'll monitor him here in the ER for a while, then in a half hour or so he'll be transferred to Intensive Care. He's actually very alert now and asking if his mother is here."

"May we see him?" Bess asked.

"Of course."

She gave a timorous smile. "Thank you, Doctor."

Michael thought to ask, "Are there legalities involved, Doctor?"

"No. As I told Randy, we're not the police, neither do we report these cases to the police. Because he's admitted to using cocaine, however, he'll be referred for counseling, and a social worker will more than likely get involved."

"I heard him say he's never used it before. Is that possible?"

"Absolutely. You recall the death of the young basketball player, Len Bias, a couple of years ago? Sadly enough it was his first time, too, but what he didn't know was that he had a heart defect, a weakness too great to endure the effects of the cocaine. That's the trouble with this damned stuff. It can kill you half a dozen different ways, even the first time you let it in your body. That's why we have to educate these kids *before* they try it."

"Yes . . . thank you, Doctor."

The ER medical staff was still watching Randy's monitors as Bess approached the gurney, with Michael lingering several steps behind. A nurse in a traditional white uniform and cap was filling a syringe with blood from Randy's arm. She snapped a piece of rubber tubing off his biceps and said to him, "You've got nice veins." She sent him a smile, which he returned halfheartedly, then closed his eyes.

Bess stood watching, willing her eyes to remain dry. The lab nurse finished drawing her samples and left, pushing a tray containing rows of glass test tubes that clinked like wind chimes as she moved away. Michael hung back while Bess moved to the bed and bent over their son. He looked ghastly, sickly white, his eye sockets gaunt and his nostrils occupied by the oxygen prongs. The leads from his chest draped away to the monitors. She remembered when he was one and two years old how deathly afraid he'd been of doctors, how he'd cried and clung to her whenever she took him into the clinic. Again she struggled against tears.

"Randy?" she said softly.

He opened his eyes and immediately they filled. "Mom . . ." he managed in a croaky voice as the tears made tracks down his temples. She leaned down and put her cheek to his, found his hand at his hip and took it gingerly, avoiding the IV lead-in taped to its back.

"Oh, Randy, darling, thank God they got you here in time."

She felt his chest heave as he held sobs inside, smelled smoke in his hair and shaving lotion on his cheek, and felt his warm tears mingling with her own.

"I'm sorry," he whispered.

"I'm sorry, too. I should have been there for you, talked to you more, found out what was bothering you."

"No, it's not your fault, it's mine. I'm such a rotten bastard."

She looked into his eyes, so like his father's. "Don't you ever use that word." She wiped the tears from his temples but they continued to run. "You're our son and we love you very much."

"How can you love me? All I've ever been is trouble."

"Oh, no . . . no . . ." She smoothed his hair as if he were two years old again, then braved a wobbly smile. "Well, yes, sometimes you were. But when you have babies you don't say I want them only when they're good.

You take them knowing that sometimes they'll be less than perfect, and that's when you find out how much you love them. Because when you've struggled through it, everybody comes out stronger. And that's how this is going to be—you'll see."

He tried to wipe his eyes but she did it for him, with a corner of the sheet, then kissed his forehead and moved back so Michael could take her place.

He moved into Randy's line of vision and said simply, "Hi, Randy."

Randy stared at his father while his eyes filled once again. He swallowed hard and said, "Dad . . . ?"

Michael braced a hand on Randy's far side, bent over and kissed his left cheek. Randy's arms went around his father's back and clung, trailing IV cords and blood pressure paraphernalia. He hauled Michael down as a sob broke forth, then another. Michael held him as fiercely as possible while attempting to keep his weight off the electronic leads taped to Randy's chest. For a long time they embraced in silence, only an occasional telltale sniffle giving away the difficulty they were having holding their weeping inside.

"Dad, I'm so sorry . . ."

"I know . . . I know . . . so am I."

Ah, sweet, sweet healing. Ah, welcome love. When they had filled both their hearts, Michael drew back, sat on one hip and rested an elbow alongside Randy's head. He put his hand on Randy's hair, looking down into his brimming eyes. "But this is the end of all that, huh? You and I have some time to make up for, and we're going to do it. Everything Mom just said goes double for me. I love you. I hurt you. I'm sorry and we're going to work on it, starting today."

Just don't die. Please don't die when I've just gotten you back again.

"I can't believe you're here when I treated you so shitty."

"Aw, listen . . . we just didn't know how to get past our own hurt, so we shut each other out. But from now on we're going to talk, right?"

"Right," Randy croaked. He sniffed and tried to run the edge of one hand beside his eyes.

"Let me help you. Bess, is there a Kleenex over there?" She brought some and passed a handful to Michael and watched as he ministered to his son much as he had when Randy was a toddler, drying his eyes, helping him blow his nose. The sight of the two of them, close and loving again, brought back fresh tears to her eyes.

At last Michael sat back. "Now listen . . ." he said to Randy. "Your mother has something to tell you." He stood and reached for Bess's hand, his eyes saying, *Just in case he doesn't make it through the next twenty-four hours.* He drew Bess forward and stood behind her, his hands resting on her shoulders. She slipped her palm under Randy's and told him quietly, "Your dad and I are going to get married again."

He said nothing. His eyes locked on hers for some time, then shifted to Michael's.

Michael broke the silence. "Well, what do you think?"

"My God, you've got guts."

Michael squeezed Bess's shoulders. "I guess you'd see it that way. We think we've grown up a lot in the last six years."

Bess added, "And besides that, we fell in love again."

A nurse interrupted. "We're going to move Randy to Intensive Care now. Then I think we'd better let him rest for a while."

"Yes, of course. Well, we just wanted you to know, darling. We'll be outside." Bess kissed Randy. "We'll talk about it more when you're out of here. I love you."

Michael, too, kissed Randy. "Rest. I love you."

Together they went out to the ICU waiting room to face the long vigil that would either take or give them back their son.

chapter 19

During his critical twenty-four hours, time passed for Randy as phantasm. He would sleep as if for aeons and awaken to find the clock had moved a mere ten minutes. Faint sounds interposed themselves between sound sleep and full consciousness like a background score for his dreams. The *beep, beep, beep* of the blood pressure monitor announcing its new reading became his drumsticks on the rim of his Pearls, beginning a new song. The tinkle of test tubes when the lab technician returned became Tom Little's keyboards. The dim squish of rubber soles on hard floors became a rush of tail feathers on a woman who was dancing through his dream, dressed like a Las Vegas chorus girl in a bright pink flamingo costume while he played backup music with the band. She whirled and he caught sight of her face: it was Maryann Padgett. Somewhere in the room rubber wheels rolled across the floor and through his dream sped a skateboard and on it, the kid Trotter, going faster and faster, on a collision course with Maryann. Randy tried to call out, *Trotter, don't hit her!* but Trotter was watching his high-top tennies, jumping black electrical cables, unaware that he was going to wipe out and take her right along with him.

"Trotter, look out!"

Randy opened his eyes. His own voice had awakened him. His heart was thudding in fear for Maryann.

Lisa was standing beside his bed, holding a baby in her arms.

He smiled blearily.

"Hi," she said quietly.

"Hi," he tried but it came out so croaky he had to try again. "Hi. What are you doing here?"

"Came to show you your new niece."

"Yeah?" He managed a weak grin. Lisa wore her smug Ali McGraw smile, the one with the hard edge that scolded while telling him beyond a doubt how much she loved him.

So I'm going to die, Randy thought.

The realization brought little fear, only an incredible sense of well-being, of giving up the fight at last and doing so content in the knowledge that he was surrounded by love. There was no doubt in his mind he was right, otherwise they wouldn't have let Lisa bring that newborn baby in here.

He grinned and thought he said, "I'd hold her but I'd probably electrocute her with all these damned wires."

Lisa showed him the baby's face. "She's a beaut, huh? Say hi to your uncle Randy, Natalie."

"Hi, Natalie," Randy whispered. Jeez, he was tired . . . such effort to get words out . . . cute baby . . . Lisa must have made Mom and Dad so happy . . . Lisa always did. He, as usual, had screwed up again. "Hey, listen . . . sorry I didn't come to see you."

"Oh, that's okay. I had about eight midwives as it was."

His eyelids grew too heavy to keep open. When they dropped he felt Lisa kiss his forehead. He felt the baby blanket brush his cheek. He opened his eyes as she straightened and saw her tears glimmering and knew undoubtedly he was dying.

The next time he woke up Grandma Stella was there, in her eyes the same soulful expression as in Lisa's.

Then his mom and dad again, looking haggard and worried.

And then—too unreal to believe—Maryann, which made no sense at all, unless, of course, he'd already died and this was heaven. She was smiling, dressed in aqua blue. Did angels wear aqua blue?

"Maryann?" he said.

"I was here visiting Lisa, and she asked me to come down and see you."

Virgin mother Mary, she spoke. She was real.

He told her, "I'd pretty much given up on you." To his own ears his voice sounded as if he was in a tunnel.

"I'd given up on you, too. Maybe now you'll get some help. Will you?"

She wasn't an easy woman; rather, an exacting one, a throwback to a time when parents taught their daughters to seek a man who was pure in heart and mind. The crazy thing was, he wanted to be that kind of man for her. He didn't understand it but there it was. Lying on his hospital bed, dying, he promised himself that if by some miracle he was wrong and he got out of here, he'd smoked his last joint and screwed his last groupie and snorted his last coke.

"I guess it's time," he answered and closed his eyes because he was so tired not even Maryann Padgett's presence could keep him awake. "Hey, listen," he said from the pleasant darkness behind his closed eyelids, "you'll be hearing from me when I get my act together. Meanwhile, don't go falling in love or anything, will you?"

When Maryann Padgett returned to the ICU waiting room, his entire family was there. She went straight to Lisa.

"How is he?" Lisa asked.

"Weak but making jokes."

Worry sketched drooping lines down Lisa's face. "I got too involved in my new married life and stopped calling him."

"No," Maryann whispered, embracing her friend. "You mustn't blame yourself."

But at one point or another during their vigil, recriminations fell from everyone's lips.

Michael said, "I should have tried harder to get him to talk to me."

Bess said, "I shouldn't have encouraged him to audition all the time."

Gil Harwood said, "I shouldn't have put him in touch with that damn band."

Stella said, "I shouldn't have given him the money for that van."

By ten o'clock that night, everyone was exhausted. Randy's condition seemed stable, his heartbeat regular, though he remained in Intensive Care, where five-minute visits were allowed only once an hour. Michael said, "Why don't you all go home and get some rest."

"What about you?" Bess said.

"I'll stay here and nap in the waiting room."

"But, Michael—"

"No buts. You do as I say. Get some rest and I'll see you in the morning. Stella, Gil, you too, please. I'll be here and I'll call you if anything changes."

Reluctantly they went.

A nurse brought Michael a pillow and blanket and he lay down in the family lounge with the reassurance that they'd wake him if Randy showed the slightest change. He awakened after what seemed a very brief time, drew his arm from beneath the blanket and lurched up when his watch showed 5:35 A.M. He sat up, rubbed his face, finger-combed his hair, stood and folded the blanket.

At the nurses' station he asked about Randy.

"He had a very good night, slept straight through, and there was no sign of any more problems with his heart."

Less than twelve hours to go before he was totally out of the woods. Michael shrugged and stretched and went to find a bathroom. He splashed cold water on his face, rinsed out his mouth, combed his hair and tucked his shirt in. He'd had these same clothes on since yesterday afternoon. It seemed half a lifetime ago since he'd donned them and come up to the hospital, smiling, to meet Bess and to visit Lisa and the new baby. He wondered how they were. Poor Lisa had had a shock, learning about Randy, but she'd handled it like a trooper, getting permission to bring the baby down here to show Randy in case he died. Nobody'd said as much but they all knew that was the reason.

He stood in the doorway of Randy's room, watching him sleep.

Ten more hours. Just ten more.

He walked to the window and stared out, standing with both hands on the small of his back. What irony, both of his children in the same hospital, one bringing in a new life, the other with his life in the balance.

He thought about it as dawn lifted over the St. Croix valley and lit the river and the boats at anchor and the thick maples that rimmed the water and the dozen church steeples of Stillwater. Sunday morning in late August, and the townspeople would soon be rising and dressing for worship services, and the tourists would soon be flooding in to shop for antiques and buy ice-cream cones and walk the waterfront. And the boat owners would be awakening in their cabin cruisers and stepping out onto their decks and watching the mist rise off the St. Croix and deciding at which restaurant they'd eat brunch. At noon Mark would come to the hospital and take Lisa and Natalie home.

And four hours after that—please, God—Bess and I will do the same thing with Randy.

As if the thought penetrated his sleep, Randy opened his eyes and found his father standing at the window.

"Dad?"

Michael whirled and moved directly to the bed, taking Randy's hand.

"I made it."

"Yeah," his father said, his voice breaking with emotion. If Randy didn't know he needed ten more hours to be out of the woods, Michael wasn't going to disillusion him.

"You been there all night?"

"I slept some."

"You've been here all night."

Moving his thumb across the back of Randy's hand, Michael gave a quarter smile.

"You all thought I'd die, right? That's why Lisa brought the baby for me to see, and why Grandma came, and Maryann."

"That was a possibility."

"I'm sorry I put you through that."

"Yeah, well, sometimes that's what we do to people who love us—we put them through things without really meaning to."

They took a while to study each other and to reaffirm silently that they were done trying to put each other through anything and were ready to take the next step toward a wholesome relationship with one another.

"Where's Mom?"

"I made her go home and get some sleep."

"So you two are getting married again."

"Is that okay with you?"

"You guys in love?"

"Absolutely."

"Then it's okay."

"We'll have some things to work out."

"Like?"

"Getting you well again. Deciding where we'll live."

"I can live anyplace."

You'll live with us, Michael vowed silently, realizing his and Bess's plans to cut Randy free would have to be waylaid for a while. The idea brought him great hope and a sense of impending peace. "Just so you know—we're not abandoning you. Not this time."

"You didn't abandon me before. That was all in my head but the shrinks here are going to get my head on straight again."

Michael bent low over his son, looking into his eyes. "We'll be there for you. Whatever you need, whatever it takes. But now, I'd better go. Five minutes is up and that's my limit. Anyway, I need a shower and a shave and a change of clothes." Michael stood. "I'll call your mother, then take a run home. But I'll be back in a couple of hours, okay?"

Randy looked up at his tired father, whose rumpled clothes and shadowy growth of whiskers bore witness to his night's vigil. It struck Randy in that moment how damned hard it must be to be a parent, and how little he'd considered the fact until now. *I must be growing up,* he thought. It made him feel expansive, and a little scared, taken in the light of the events of the past twelve hours. *What if I have a kid someday and he puts me through this?*

"Dad?" he said.

Michael sensed whatever was coming would be of import. He waited silently.

"You didn't give me hell for using the cocaine."

"Oh, yes I did. A dozen times while you were fighting for your life. I just didn't say it out loud."

"I won't do it again, I promise. I want to get well and be happy."

Michael put his hand on Randy's hair. "That's what we all want, son." Then he leaned over and kissed Randy's cheek and told him, "I'll be back soon. I love you."

"I love you, too," Randy said.

And with those words another fragment of pain dissolved. Another window of hope opened. Another beam of sunlight radiated into their future as Michael leaned down to hug his son before leaving.

Randy was released from the hospital shortly before suppertime that day. His mother and father walked him out into the sunshine of late afternoon, into a setting crowned by a cobalt-blue sky and a world where people moved about their pursuits with reassuring normality. Down at the public beach on Lily Lake some families were lighting barbecues and calling to their kids to be careful in the water. At the ball diamond across the street, a group of little boys were playing kittenball. A couple of blocks north, on Greeley Street, Nelson's Ice Cream Parlor was doing its usual landmark business, lining the concrete step out front with a row of lickers of all ages. Out on the river the drawbridge was raised, backing up traffic clear up to the top of Houlton Hill. The day-trippers were pulling their boats behind their packed cars, heading back toward the city, and the residents of Stillwater were sighing, looking forward to winter, when the streets would once again become their own.

"Where to?" Michael asked, sitting behind the wheel of his Cadillac Seville.

"I'm starved," Bess replied. "Would anyone like to pick up some sandwiches and eat them down by the river?"

Michael turned to glance at Randy in the backseat.

"Sounds fine with me," Randy said.

And so they took the next halting step in their journey back to familyhood.

Six weeks later, on an Indian summer's day in mid-October, Bess and Michael Curran were married in a simple service in the rectory of St. Mary's Catholic Church. The ceremony was performed by the same priest who'd married them twenty-two years before.

When he'd kissed his stole and draped it around his neck, Father Moore opened his prayer book to the correct page, smiled at the bride and groom and said, "So . . . here we are again."

His remark brought smiles to the assembled faces. To Bess's, which shone with happiness. To Michael's, which radiated hope. To Lisa's, which might have been touched ever so slightly by smugness. To Stella's, which seemed to say, It's about time. To Randy's, which held a promise. And even to Natalie's as she lay on her daddy's arm and studied the glistening silver frames on the eyeglasses of Gil Harwood.

When the priest asked, "Who gives this woman?" Lisa and Randy answered, "We do," bringing another round of smiles.

When the bride and groom repeated the words ". . . until death do us part," their eyes shone with sincerity that had depth far beyond the first time they'd spoken the words.

When Father Moore said, "I now pronounce you man and wife," Lisa and Randy exchanged a glance and a smile.

When their mother and father kissed, Lisa reached over for Randy's hand and gave it a hard squeeze.

The small wedding party went to dinner afterward at Kozlak'a Royal Oaks, overlooking a beautiful walled garden decorated with pumpkins, cornshocks and scarecrows. The personalized matchbooks awaiting them at their table and reserving it for them said *Mr. and Mrs. Curran.*

Spying them, after he'd seated Bess and was taking a chair himself, Michael picked up one of the books and folded it into her hand, saying, "Damn right, once and for all." Then he kissed her lightly on the lips and smiled into her eyes.

There were, as in all relationships that matter most, wrinkles that needed smoothing for all of them in that bittersweet autumn. There was Randy's intense counseling, his loss of a way of life, of friends, of drug-dependency, and his search for inner strength and positive relationships. There was family therapy, and the painful resurrection and obliteration of past guilts, fears and mistakes. There was Lisa's anger when she learned her mother and father were selling the family house. There was Michael and Bess's frequent frustration at living with an adult son when in truth they were impatient to have total privacy. There were Michael and Bess themselves, the husband and wife, readjusting to married life and its constant demands for compromise.

Ah, but there were blessings.

There was Randy, coming home one day and bringing a new friend named Steve, whom he'd met in therapy and who wanted to start a band that would be drug-free and would play for school kids to spread the message "Say no!" There was Michael, turning one day from the kitchen stove as Randy asked, "Hey, Dad, think you could teach me how to make that?" There were suppers for three, with three alternate cooks, and Randy eating healthily at last. And days when Lisa and Mark would come breezing in with the baby, calling, "Yo, Grampa and Grandma and Uncle Randy!" And the simpler homely joys of Bess shouting, "All right, who put my sweatshirt in the dryer and shrunk it!" And of Michael, breaking a radiator hose on his way home from work and calling home to hear Randy volunteer, "Hang on, Dad, I'll come and get you." And of Randy learning to change his niece's diapers and describing what he found inside them in phrases that had the entire family in stitches. And one day when Randy finally announced, "I got a job at Schmitt's Music selling instruments and giving drum lessons to little kids. Pay sucks but the fringe benefits are great—sitting around jamming whenever the place isn't busy."

And one day Bess went out to the County Seat and bought herself a pair of blue jeans.

She had them on when Michael came home from work and found her in the kitchen making Parmesan cream sauce for tortellini—it was her turn to cook. The pasta was boiling, the roux was bubbling, and she was mincing garlic as he stopped in the kitchen doorway and tossed his car keys onto the cabinet top.

"Well, lookit here . . ." he said in wonder, ". . . what my bride is wearing."

She smiled back over her shoulder and twitched her hips.

"How 'bout that. I did it."

He ambled toward her, dressed in a winter trench coat, cocked one hip against the edge of the cabinet and perused her lower half. "Looks good, too."

"Y' know what?" she said. "I really don't care if they do or not. They *feel* good."

"They do, huh?" He boosted himself away from the cabinet and put both hands on her, splayed and inquisitive. "Let's see . . ." He rubbed her, back and front, all over her tight blue jeans, kissed her over her shoulder and murmured against her mouth, "You're right . . . feels very good."

Giggling, she said, "Michael, I'm cutting up garlic here."

"Yeah, I can smell it. Stinks like hell." He turned her fully around and caught her against himself with a two-handed grip on her buttocks. Her arms crossed behind his neck, the paring knife still in her right hand.

"How was your day?" she asked, when they'd shared a nice long kiss.

"Pretty good. How was yours?"

"Crappy. This is the best part of it so far."

"Well, good," he said. "I can make it even better if you'd care to turn off those burners and put down that paring knife."

"Mmm . . ." she murmured against his lips, dropping the paring knife on the floor, reaching out blindly to the side, groping for the control knobs on the stove.

At the other end of the condo the door opened.

Michael dropped his head back and said quietly, "Oh, shit."

"Now, now," she chided gently, "you wanted him back, didn't you?"

"But not when I have a hard-on in the middle of the kitchen at suppertime."

She giggled again. "Just keep your coat buttoned awhile," she whispered at the same moment Randy stepped to the kitchen doorway.

"Mom, Dad . . . hi. Hope we're not disturbing anything. I brought someone home for supper." He drew her forward by a hand, a pretty young woman with dark hair and a smile that had put a boyish look of eagerness on Randy's face. "You remember Maryann, don't you?"

Two parents turned, joy on their faces, their embrace dissolving as they reached out to welcome her.

HARDY'S VISION OF MAN

Thomas Hardy. Pencil by William Strang, 1919.

HARDY'S VISION OF MAN

By

F. R. SOUTHERINGTON

BARNES & NOBLE, Inc.
NEW YORK
PUBLISHERS & BOOKSELLERS SINCE 1873

Published by
Chatto and Windus Ltd
40 William IV Street
London W.C. 2

First published in the United States of America, 1971
by Barnes & Noble, Inc.

ISBN 389 04080 0

Printed in Great Britain

For
Kerstin and for Monica
and in recognition of
Lois Deacon

NOTE

The abbreviations used in footnotes are few: *Life* for Mrs F. E. Hardy's *The Life of Thomas Hardy*; C.P. for the *Collected Poems of Thomas Hardy*; *Notebooks* for Evelyn Hardy's edition of *Thomas Hardy's Notebooks*; and Beaminster for monographs from the series of *Monographs on the Life, Times, and Works of Thomas Hardy*, edited by J. Stevens Cox. The monographs have, for convenience, been listed separately in the Bibliography, under the numbers given to them by the publisher.

ACKNOWLEDGEMENTS

The holders of manuscript and published copyright material used in this book have been uniformly generous, and the following acknowledgements are due:

For the use of manuscript material: Lloyds Bank and the Trustees of the Hardy Estate; the Trustees of the Dorset County Museum and the Hardy Memorial Collection; The National Library of Scotland; the Brotherton Library, University of Leeds; Mr H. P. R. Hoare and the National Trust; Colby College Library; the Henry W. and Albert A. Berg Collection of the New York Public Library, Astor, Lennox, and Tilden Foundations.

For published material: Edward Arnold Ltd and Harcourt, Brace and World Inc. for E. M. Forster's *Aspects of the Novel*; and Edward Arnold Ltd for Douglas Brown's *The Mayor of Casterbridge* (Studies in English Literature, 7); the University of California Press for John Paterson's *The Making of the Return of the Native*, and for Clarice Short's 'In Defense of *Ethelberta*' (*Nineteenth Century Fiction*, XIII, 1); Doubleday and Company Inc. and Heinemann Educational Books for William Barrett's *Irrational Man* (© 1958 by William Barrett); Faber and Faber Ltd for T. S. Eliot's *After Strange Gods*; Evelyn Hardy and Russell and Russell for Evelyn Hardy's *Thomas Hardy, A Critical Biography*; the Hutchinson Publishing Group for Lois Deacon's and Terry Coleman's *Providence and Mr Hardy*; Louisiana State University Press for Donald Davidson's 'The Traditional Basis of Thomas Hardy's Fiction'; Macmillan and Co. Ltd and the Macmillan Company for Hardy's published works; the University of North Carolina Press for Samuel Hynes's *The Pattern of Hardy's Poetry*; the University of Malaya Press and Oxford University Press for Roy Morrell's *Thomas Hardy—The Will and the Way*; the Purdue Research Foundation and Richard C. Carpenter for 'Hardy's "Gurgoyles" ' (*Modern Fiction Studies*, VI, 3); Laurence Pollinger Ltd and the Estate of the late Mrs Frieda Lawrence for D. H. Lawrence's *Study of Thomas Hardy*; Simon and Schuster Inc. for the Maude translation of Tolstoy's *War and Peace*; the Toucan Press and the Dorset Natural History and Archaeological Society for my use of the Beaminster pamphlets.

The frontispiece is reproduced by permission of the National Portrait Gallery.

CONTENTS

ILLUSTRATIONS

INTRODUCTION

WHEN I first began these pages I did so in the belief that Thomas Hardy's works, prose and verse, possessed a strong vein of thought which in any other author would have been described as optimistic. I believed *The Dynasts*, despite its forbidding appearance, to be more a cry of hope than of despair, and it seemed that the term 'Fate' as applied to Hardy was of little value unless rigorously and carefully defined. I believed that in the epic and elsewhere Hardy gave to his characters a small measure of freedom and a large measure of responsibility, and I felt convinced that in this light the novels stand before *The Dynasts* in time as a logical prelude to his mature thought.

To some extent that belief has been justified. What I had made no allowance for, however, was the presence of autobiographical features embedded deep in the fabric of the novels. I was aware, of course, that some events in the novels could be closely compared to events in Hardy's career, and that a large number of ideas attributed to his characters could be regarded as Hardy's own opinions. I was not aware of the degree of subjective emotional commitment involved in the later novels, nor did I consider whas the effect of that commitment might be. To this extent these paget have taken a course somewhat different from my first anticipations.

This has affected the relative proportions of the work, about which something should be said. The general outline of Hardy's career is well known, and I have not felt it necessary to repeat established biographical information. On the other hand, new biographical knowledge, some of it established but some falling short of certainty, has had to be included if the comparison made between the earlier and the later works is to be clear; and I have also felt it necessary to suggest, at least, the temperament which lay behind the works. The opening section of this book, therefore, consists of a sketch in which I have tried to indicate certain aspects of events or of the environment which contributed most strongly to Hardy's personality. But even though I have generally followed a chronological pattern, neither the opening section nor the book as a whole purports to be a detailed biography. The chief purpose of this book is criticism and such biography as I have included is intended as an aid to criticism. Even here, however, a qualification needs to be made: Hardy's liaison with Tryphena Sparks and his response to the ancestral past of his family were both strongly influential, and both have become matters for controversy and speculation. My general text refers to both, but a detailed analysis of them would not simply unbalance the biographical sketch but might also give them a disproportionate significance. The two appendices will, I hope, compensate for what may seem from my text a too easy acceptance of disputed material; while the text itself will, I believe, explain the relevance of the appendices.

Wherever possible I have tried to gather primary material rather than rely on published sources. Occasionally this has led to surprising results, and I am aware that some of the judgements I have made will not accord with popular views of Thomas Hardy, in particular of Hardy the private citizen. I can only say, as Hardy himself once said, I am sorry but cannot help it. My judgements are based upon letters on both sides of the Atlantic, and on official and local records. If the results cause any surprise whatever that will only reinforce my plea for the early and complete publication of the letters of Hardy and his two wives. I cannot tell whether these letters have been closely read by Hardy's biographers, although I would hope and imagine that they must have been; and yet they have made curiously little impression upon the standard works of criticism and biography. At the very least, the almost universally sympathetic approach to Hardy at the expense of his two wives (especially the first) deserves to be reviewed; while, so far as the local records are concerned, there is little evidence that they had ever been examined until Lois Deacon, J. O. Bailey and myself began an almost simultaneous search a few years ago.

Where this book is concerned with Hardy's ideas, I have taken the risk of repetitiveness, particularly in the last two sections. This is due entirely to my wish for the consistency and seriousness of Hardy's vision to be appreciated and I hope that the risk has been successfully avoided.

The amount of help I have received is enormous, but I owe very special debts to Professor Dame Helen Gardner, and Professor H. W. Donner of Uppsala, Sweden. Without their generous support, in the first instance academic, in the second academic and financial, it would have been impossible for me to write this book.

Among Hardy scholars I have received kindness which in several happy instances has led to friendship: most especially from Professor J. O. Bailey of the University of North Carolina at Chapel Hill, and Miss Lois Deacon, whose work in this field has been widely underestimated. Miss Deacon and Mr J. Stevens Cox have given me access to otherwise unavailable material, always freely and spontaneously.

To the staff of a number of institutions I offer my thanks: the Berg Collection, New York Public Library; the Library of Colby College, Waterville, Maine; the Library of Congress, Washington, D.C.; Mr F. B. Adams, Director of the Pierpont-Morgan Library, New York; and the Library of the University of North Carolina at Chapel Hill, and of Mary Baldwin College, Staunton, Virginia. On this side of the Atlantic: the National Library of Scotland; the Brotherton Library, University of Leeds; the Bodleian Library, Oxford, and the Fitzwilliam Museum, Cambridge; the library of Queen's College, Oxford; the Curator of the Dorset County Museum, and the Dorset County Archivist; Mr H. P. R. Hoare and the National Trust, for permission to consult the Stourhead Papers in the Wiltshire Archives; the British Museum Manuscripts Room; the Literary Department at Somerset House, and the office of the Registrar-General; the Public Records Office. I owe a special debt, too, to the staff of the library of Åbo Akademi, Finland, who took care to obtain for me materials not readily available in Scandinavia.

Among individuals I owe gratitude to Miss A. M. D. Ashley, Principal of the College of Sarum St Michael, Salisbury; Mr John Antell; Mr E. D. Blackford and the Managers of Puddletown primary school; Mrs Eleanor Bowden; Mr E. G. B. Moore; Mr Peter Millward; Mr Barry Watkins; Mr Patrick Quinlivan; Lektor Tony Lurcock; Lektor Malcolm Hardy; Mrs Carl J. Weber; Professor Jack Salzman; and Miss Robin Spence.

Some debts of special importance, debts of affection and support which can never be repaid, are due to Hélène Wikström-Southerington, to Clara Andersson, Tarja Salmi, and the dedicatees of this book. How they have tolerated the years of its production is a mystery which I shall never know. My assistants at Mary Baldwin College, Hallie Wallace, Helen Delgado, and Bryce Oliver, remain tolerant even as these words are being written.

Staunton, Virginia, 1969

THE MAN

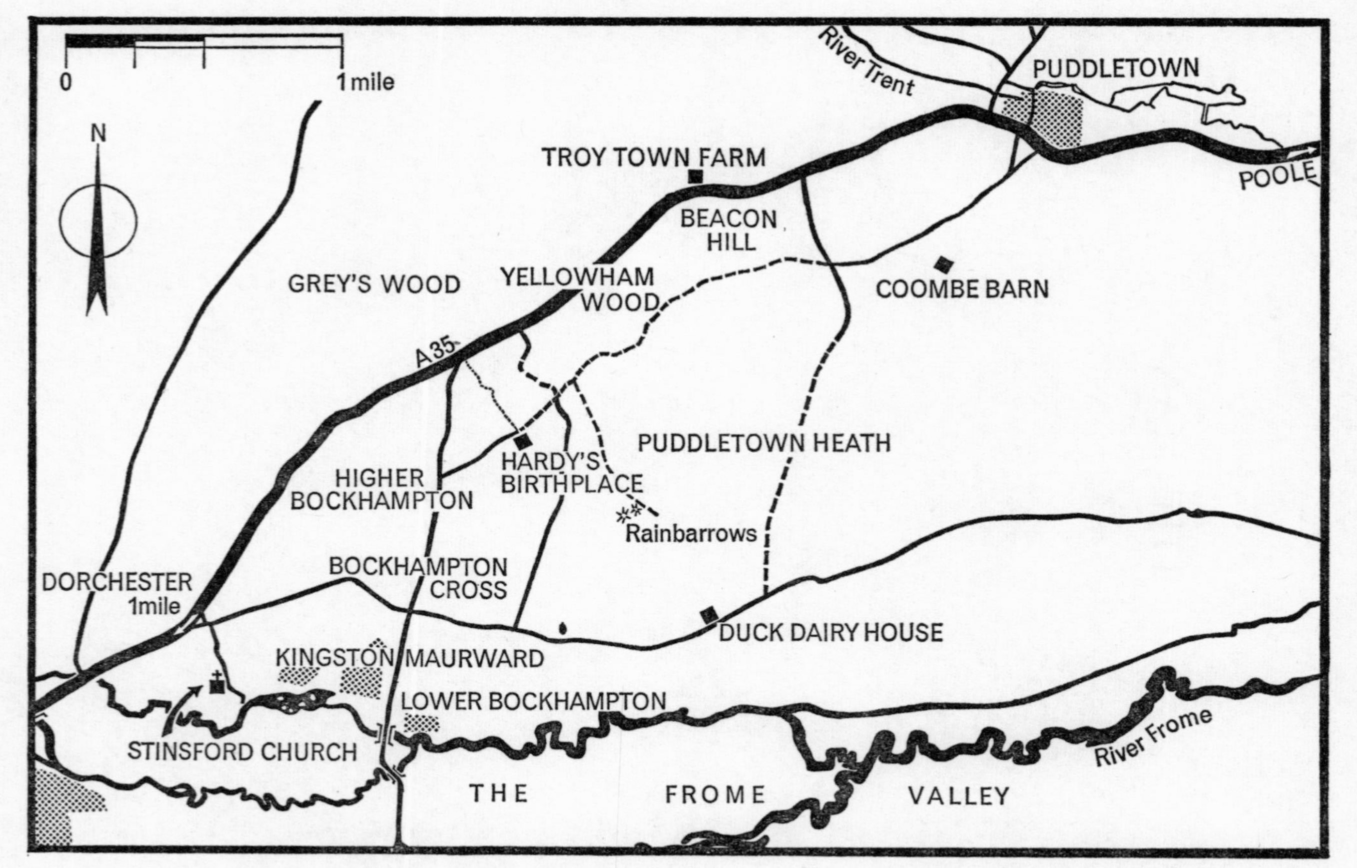
0
1 mile
N
River Trent
PUDDLETOWN
POOLE
TROY TOWN FARM
BEACON HILL
GREY'S WOOD
YELLOWHAM WOOD
COOMBE BARN
A35
PUDDLETOWN HEATH
HIGHER BOCKHAMPTON
HARDY'S BIRTHPLACE
Rainbarrows
BOCKHAMPTON CROSS
DORCHESTER 1mile
DUCK DAIRY HOUSE
KINGSTON MAURWARD
LOWER BOCKHAMPTON
STINSFORD CHURCH
River Frome
THE FROME VALLEY

I

Too fragrant was Life's early bloom,
Too tart the fruit it brought!

C.P. 201

IN the summer of 1840 a certain Mr Firth of Dorchester in the county of Dorset complained loudly to the Governors of the town Grammar School, drawing attention to a statement of grievances signed by himself and his fellow-townsmen. The Governors could do little to satisfy him. The Grammar School was old and short of money: so short, indeed, that it maintained no usher, and the Master, with grievances of his own, was compelled to remain in his position because the three hundred and fifty pounds owing to him from the Governors could not yet be paid. Legal opinions were taken, and some means of modernising the ancient school were sought, but the lawyers were of little help. Since the school was a 'free' school it could not charge fees for the tuition of local children unless it taught subjects other than Latin or Greek; fees might be charged for children from further afield, but the great days of the eighteenth century, when, as 'a seminary of excellence and repute', the school had attracted pupils from well beyond the county boundaries, were long since past. Moreover, since it was also a 'grammar' school there were no terms under its charter which allowed it to teach any other subjects. Only through modernisation could the school's fortunes be revived, and modernisation was apparently barred by a hair-splitting legal interpretation of originally liberal intentions. When, in 1579, Thomas Hardye of Frampton had endowed the school which the townsmen had refounded ten years earlier, it had been a noble and far-sighted gesture. His nineteenth-century successors waited for forty years before State intervention could re-create that early, pious gift.

Yet this was the Dorset of 1840: remote, poor, its present composed of memories, its future of uncertainties. The countryside was emptying, though those who found dirt and degradation in the cities were often leaving rural conditions which were also far from idyllic. Village sanitation was non-existent, and the streams were open sewers. Large families lived in small cottages, often in only two rooms, and incest and illegitimacy were commonplace. Food was scarce, and on a wage of no more than seven shillings a week the countryman was compelled to live on a diet of bread and vegetables only rarely supplemented with meat. During the Irish troubles of 1846 a full inquiry conducted by *The Times* convinced a reluctant House of Commons that there was distress in Dorset equal to that to be found in Ireland. And yet the modern notion of Dorset as a sleepy, backward area is almost entirely a nineteenth-century legacy. It was not a sleepy or an out-of-the-way place for George III, and had played its part in earlier history. King John had his hunting-lodges in the county; Charles II remembered it with affection. Off the southern coast of Dorset the Armada had been battered by the English men-of-war, and a large number of loyal Dorset ships sailed from the harbours to join the fight, Sir Christopher Hatton's son rushing from Corfe Castle to take the lead. Eight hundred years earlier King Alfred had seen the Danish fleet slowly destroyed in these same stormy waters, as a monument at Swanage recalls. Everywhere there were reminders of the past, from the Celtic tumuli and the mighty hill-forts—including Maiden Castle and Badbury, perhaps the lost Mount Badon—to the Regency fronts, elegant and prosperous, gazing impassively across Weymouth Bay. Even in the nineteenth century the independent spirit which had made the Dorset Club Men rise up against *both* sides in the Civil War was not dead: in 1833 six men from the decaying village of Puddletown were transported as criminals from Britain, but left their names behind them in one of the most honoured early phases of the Trades Union movement.

It was, as it has always been, a county of great contrasts, material and spiritual. Shaped like a diamond, and in prosperous times a very jewel among the English counties, its chalk, clay, and gravel had been moulded into swelling downs, low, well-watered valleys, and sombre heath. On the east coast superb chalk cliffs fell sheer into the sea; in the west the long marvel of the Chesil Bank stretched itself from Portland to Lyme Regis, its pebbles so finely sorted by the tides that on the darkest midnight smugglers could identify their landfall by the size of the stones in their hands. On one side of Portland lay King George's watering-place; on the other the troubled waters of Dead Man's Bay picked the bones among the wreckage of generations of sailing-ships unable to round the Bill in south-west gales, while on the Chesil Bank the fishermen themselves might light a vessel to its destruction, plundering its battered timbers. At sea and inland there were records of cruelty and violence, even judicial violence. The legend of Judge Jeffreys, who sentenced ninety-four men of Dorset to the gallows, is still not dead. In Maumbury Rings, the Roman amphitheatre of Dorchester, Mary Channing was first strangled and then burnt before an audience of thousands one fine spring day in 1705; and one section of the Roman ring remains damaged to this day by the trampling of men and horses round the gallows. When, later, executions were transferred to the comparative secrecy of the prison, the crowds would stand knee-deep in the waters of the Frome to catch a glimpse of the hanging man. Bear-baiting and cock-fighting had their appointed place behind the Town Hall, and their traces were still visible in the first half of the nineteenth century; and into modern times fox-hunting has remained, a cruel, if colourful, sport.

Other, more occult, pastimes still lingered. Witchcraft survived, and perhaps still does. The pinning and roasting of an effigy, beliefs in hag-ridden horses, the evil eye, and the more benevolent powers of the local prophet or weatherman, were a powerful rival to Christian enlightenment. Gentler charms were used to guarantee the future, and on the coast the fishermen of Abbotsbury tossed garlands off the Chesil Bank as a gesture of propitiation to the sea, just as the local children do today; and in the same village only twenty years ago a local prophet—in all ways a respectable and respected citizen—responded with a rhyming couplet of wisdom to the children's cries of:

> Mr Morley,
> Tell us a story.

Mr Morley was simply a late counterpart of the Planet-Ruler of Melbury Osmund, Conjuror Minterne of Batcombe, or the famous Conjuror of the Blackmore Vale.[1] Superstition and Christian acceptance flourished side by side, with little incongruity. In the figure of the Devil the powers of black magic were absorbed into a Christian terminology, but they were absorbed only, not destroyed, and the symbols of the Church itself often represented forms of white magic, as indeed they still do in the ritual of exorcism. Nor were ancient customs combined only with the symbols of the Church, for the hierarchy of the saints was adapted to local purposes:

> St Catherine, St Catherine,
> Lend me thine aid,
> Granting that I do not die an old maid.

A husband, St Catherine,
A good one, St Catherine,
But arn-a-one better than narn-a-one.
Please, St Catherine,
Soon, St Catherine . . .

sang the local maidens, with their fingers placed in a hand-mark miraculously preserved in the wall of St Catherine's Chapel.

The communities in which these beliefs and superstitions flourished were small, tightly knit, and innately conservative. Sometimes gathered around a big house, they were often scattered in remote hamlets, untouched by the outside world and suspicious of its ambassadors. A journey to the county town was an adventure, the inhabitants 'foreign'. Incoming families remained new for two or three generations, and in most of the villages, even now, the population is dominated by half a dozen families whose intermarriages over several centuries form the most bewildering—and perhaps disturbing—pedigrees. Often the inhabitants of a single village may still be identified by their features as easily as the members of a single family; and the families themselves bear the stamp of men who three or four centuries ago were powerful figures in the land: the Daubeneys, the Trenchards, the Churchills, the Nappers—and more colourfully still, the Virgins and the Bastards. These names still figure in Dorset, and carry memories of their knighted and illustrious origins.

But the pattern of decline in 1840 was not universal, and it was deceptive. Sheep-farming, for which Dorset was famous, was certainly disappearing. Though the position is again improving, it is still possible to drive across modern Dorset without seeing a single flock; in 1862 the sheep and wool markets here were more than double the value of those of any corresponding area of England. Mechanical aids and new methods of cultivation were slowly being introduced. The water-meadows along the Frome yielded fine grazing land, the Downs were steadily being furrowed and improved by the use of artificial fertilisers, and even the large tracts of heathland were gradually yielding to the plough. Yet wages, high in some areas, were generally low; and practical improvements on the land had only just begun. Rick-burning and machine-breaking were not yet past, though they were dying, and the farm-workers themselves slowly learning to gather with their masters to discuss methods of improving their conditions and their products. Dorset was in a state of transition, edging itself slowly, perhaps reluctantly, into the modern world. As the railways broke through they quickened, though they did not ease, the process; and perhaps it is not entirely finished yet.

It was into this world of transition that Thomas Hardy was born on June 2, 1840. Transition was, in part, his birthright. Though his family escaped the harsher realities of poverty, they were barely prosperous. Hardy's father owned a brickyard and a few cottages, but his was not an ambitious character, and the parish records, which refer to him variously as 'mason' and 'bricklayer' may reveal a genuine uncertainty about his social status. Yet the Hardys were no strangers to the district, and after John le Hardye left Jersey for Dorset in 1488 they had become prominent among the dwellers in the Frome valley. Thomas Hardye of Frampton had been Knight Marshal for Elizabeth I, and had endowed the Grammar School of Dorchester in 1579; in the early years of William and Mary a Thomas Hardy had been Sheriff of the County; and little more than thirty years before the novelist's birth Captain Thomas Hardy had held the dying Nelson in his arms, and had taken place as chief mourner in the splendid London funeral. It was a past of which any family might be proud: yet there are hints that all had not been well. Internal disputes and hot-blooded feuds disrupted the family and its estates, and although the county records give an incomplete picture of this passionate family blood, Hardy knew enough to write of their 'dark doings each against each', and regarded even his more immediate ancestors as 'expert / In the law-lacking passions of life'.[2]

His ancestry was to exercise its influence on his thoughts and on his work. Though, throughout his mature years, he struggled to achieve a rational vision of existence, the imaginative ties which bound him to the Wessex scene bound him too to the actions of his kin, and his vision was troubled by an obscure consciousness of guilt and doubt. In his life and in theirs there were inconsistencies and hidden secrets; and, as he probed the records of his family past, flashes of intelligence would gleam from the musty pages of church and legal records. On both sides of the family there were traces of illegitimacy, over-hasty marriages, and barely suppressed dissension; and these found their way into his work. The rustic background of Hardy's novels is not simply a background of place, but is founded, too, on a personal kinship with the unpretentious rural poor, whose experience was shared by himself and his forebears. Yet there is, too, a sense of separateness, a personal isolation which enabled Hardy to be the detached critic and observer, so that the kinship with Wessex is a kinship of environment but not a kinship of values. The hasty marriage of Hardy's parents—they were married five and a half months before his birth—was no violation of the rural code; yet it troubled Hardy himself. So much so that his attitude towards his parents was strangely ambivalent. Writing of the decline of his family, he adopted a curious disguise for his disillusion:

> The decline and fall of the Hardys much in evidence hereabout. An instance: Becky S.'s mother's sister married one of the Hardys of this branch, who was considered to have bemeaned himself by the marriage. 'All Woolcombe and Froom Quintin belonged to them at one time,' Becky used to say proudly. She might have added Up-Sydling and Toller Welme. This particular couple had an enormous lot of children. I remember when young seeing the man—tall and thin—walking beside a horse and common spring trap, and my mother pointing him out to me and saying he represented what was once the leading branch of the family. So we go down, down, down.[3]

'The man' in this instance is Thomas Hardy's father. There is only one 'Becky S.' connected to the Hardys by marriage: Rebecca Sparks, of Puddletown, whose mother's sister was Jemima Hardy, Hardy's mother. The man's stature and his children are either pure invention, or they have been imported from another branch of the family to strengthen the disguise. Apart from Jemima's 'lapse' which hastened her marriage, what was there about her or her family which could be considered to 'bemean' her husband? Her influence over her son was strong, her character powerful: more powerful, indeed, than that of her easy-going husband. Yet for some reason Hardy felt uneasy about her, and it may be that her energy, which he described as 'capable of incalculable issues', provided one of the many strands which later emerged in the character of Tess.

Hardy's work develops a fairly consistent vision; yet its detachment and objectivity could be broken by emotional responses which can be related directly to his family and his past. His sense of place, however, provides a counteracting weight and stability. To the townsman it may seem dull enough to be born and bred on the outer perimeter of a heath: for a young and sensitive child this sombre tract of land was a continual mystery. The changing voices of the trees, the variety of flora and fauna, and above all the almost unbroken solitude of this region of conifers, ferns, and open sandy ledges where lizards and snakes lay basking during the summer months—all these made an impression so vivid that it was never forgotten, and evoked extraordinary powers of observation. The Egdon heath of a modern imagination is almost entirely Hardy's creation: but that should not blind us to the reality of the heath as it is, and still more as it was more than a century ago. The railway which bisects Egdon, the nuclear research station which stands on its southern fringe, the military training centre, the tank ranges, and the steady encroachment of modern agriculture, have all acted to destroy the landscape; yet there are vales still which throb beneath a burning sun, regions in which the reddleman would come as no surprise, and pools which spring into a short but uninterrupted life with the ingress of each year. In these vales, and not least behind Hardy's own birthplace, one can still recapture the mood which dominated the mind of Hardy as a child and led his footsteps through his life to Egdon as the fountain of his inspiration.

A precocious child, he was also deeply sensitive. The sound of music could bring tears to his eyes almost before he could distinguish between tunes. His father, the genial and unambitious stone-mason, gave him an accordion at the age of four, and later a violin. Soon he was sufficiently master of this instrument to play for local dances, feeling his blood thrill with the excitement of the rhythm, and watching young men and maidens grow passionate and cadaverous as the hours advanced. From both sides of his family he inherited a strong love of music, and this, too, in his later years, was to emerge as a powerful influence on his art, and was perhaps his salvation as a poet. His mastery of rhythm in verse was never so sure as when some deeply hidden and remembered melody surged up within him to control his pen. Nor was it only a memory. In 1918, at the age of seventy-seven, dissatisfied with the dancing in a local production of the dramatised *Mellstock Quire*, 'he took a lady as his partner and . . . nimbly demonstrated to the assembled company the correct steps and positions'. Then, 'borrowing the violin, he played in a lively manner all the required tunes from memory'.[4] Yet his recollections from childhood were not always pleasant, for he had slowly been made aware of the cruelty in man and nature. Once his father threw a stone at a bird, 'possibly meaning not to hit it'; but the bird fell dead. The feel of the cold, starved creature in his hand never left him, and he recalled the sensation even on his deathbed. With his own eyes he witnessed death by starvation, and from his father learned of floggings by the Town Pump at Dorchester. Once, on a visit to relatives at Puddletown, he saw a man sitting in the stocks, and admired his own bravery in talking to him. On another, terrible occasion he watched a transported poacher say farewell to his wife and family. Worst of all, there were the hangings. Looking towards Dorchester one day, he focused his father's telescope on the grim prison that overlooks the Frome: as the building came into sight he saw a victim drop, and crept homewards, 'feeling himself alone on the heath with the hanged man'. Yet there must have been a fascination: in 1856, at the age of 16, Hardy watched the hanging of Martha Brown, executed at Dorchester for the murder of her husband. Seventy years later he recalled 'what a fine figure she showed against the sky as she hung in the misty rain, and how the tight black silk gown set off her shape as she wheeled half-round and back'.[5] Early critics of *A Pair of Blue Eyes* objected to Hardy's allusion to Elfride's rain-soaked figure (Chapter XXII) as if it were suggestive; it seems more likely that this childhood experience forced its way into his imagination. For these were moments when the pressure of living seemed too great a burden for his frame, times when all around him 'there seemed to be something glaring, garish, rattling, and the noises and glares hit upon the little cell called your life, and shook it, and warped it'.* At times like this he was afraid of growing up.

Yet growing up was part of life, and life, as it slowly unfolded, was a series of 'fallings from us, vanishings'. While he was yet in his second year the Mellstock Quire, that small body of dedicated local musicians who had served Stinsford Church for three generations, was dissolved, and even the gallery in which they had performed was dismantled and destroyed. A few years later Hardy began to learn for the first time of the losses suffered by his family, and to reflect upon the injustices which he saw among men and in nature. He could raise no song of thanksgiving for the loss of childhood innocence, and his early observations prepared him for deep disillusion. To this his mother may have contributed, accepting their lot as she did in a spirit of fatalism, and seeing life as a series of pleasurable prospects from which humanity was hurled back by some malignant power.[6] Sometimes her understanding of life could be a puzzle to the boy. When he was six years old a man was hanged for murder: said his mother dogmati-

* *Jude the Obscure*, I-ii. The passage is autobiographical: Cf. *Life*, pp. 15-16, C.P. 825 and C.P. 846.

cally, 'the governess hanged him', and he wondered continually how a governess could hang an able-bodied man. From her, too, he learned the gentler legend of the animals kneeling on Christmas Eve,* and she was an invaluable source of reminiscence, both of his own family and of the legends of the countryside. Her stern outlook on life does not seem to have spoiled her sense of fun, and even in her old age, deliberately defying the protests of her more sedate daughters, she insisted on sitting by the side of the road and waving vigorously with her handkerchief as a party of her famous son's guests whirled in their carriages up the hill towards London. She planted very early in him the love of good books, presenting him with Dryden's *Virgil*, *Rasselas*, and *Paul and Virginia*. In his exploration of the home he came across a history of the Napoleonic wars, brightly and dramatically illustrated, a book which led his mind to the study of Napoleon, and which eventually found re-birth in *The Trumpet-Major* and *The Dynasts*. Still more important, her tales of local life and tragedy gave him a continuous source of inspiration, and the vivid rural legends she passed down to him became immortalised in the long sequence of the Wessex novels.

Whether she also taught him to read and write is uncertain. She was long believed to have done so, but Evelyn Hardy's publication of Hardy's letters from Julia Augusta Martin in 1955, showed that Mrs Martin may have taken at least some hand in this. Hardy was five years old when the Martins came to live at Kingston Maurward House, and he may well have been able to read by this time. If Mrs Martin took him further he owed her a double debt, for when he finally entered the village school at the age of six he was the first pupil to join the school endowed by his patroness. His learning there was presumably as good as he would have acquired at any other country school, but his parents may not have thought so, for a few years later, when he appeared to have overcome his childish frailty, he was sent to Isaac Last's day-school in Dorchester, much to Mrs Martin's disappointment. There seems to have been some estrangement between the Hardys and the Martins at this time, for 'shortly before or after' Hardy's removal from the school—in other words, not as a direct consequence of it—the building work necessary for the Kingston estate was taken out of the hands of Hardy's

* 'It was, of course, his mother who told him the legend of the oxen kneeling in their stables at midnight on Christmas Eve'—Florence Hardy to Lady Hoare, January 7, 1916. (Stourhead Papers, Wiltshire Archives; by permission of Mr H. P. R. Hoare and the National Trust.)

father, who, either through bad feeling or loss of business, even considered leaving the area for good—a particularly rash move for an established businessman whose home was secure for the duration of his lifetime. Just how the estrangement was caused we cannot tell,* but it was regretted by Julia Augusta herself, and by Hardy. But although Mrs Martin was to remain in the parish for three more years, they did not meet again until Hardy was a young man and in London.

Though he was reluctant to leave the Bockhampton school, there is no doubt that in Isaac Last Hardy found a first-class schoolmaster, and Last's attention to his new pupil over the years gives the lie to any suggestion that Hardy was an uncouth, ill-lettered, peasant author. How much of his deeply inquiring nature was already present when he came to Last's school we shall never know, but it would be surprising indeed if Last made no contribution to it, and he performed the most vital of a teacher's tasks in drawing out a native curiosity, and breathing in a lively spirit of criticism. In another Dorchester school the poet William Barnes performed the same task, as many of his pupils later testified, but Barnes's influence on Hardy, though very far from negligible, came too late to have planted the earliest seeds. Last recognised the aptness of his pupil, and began to teach him Latin, a subject outside the normal curriculum though taught at times as an extra. For some the age of twelve would have seemed late to begin the study of the classics (though scarcely later than that of a grammar school boy today), but in Dorchester Hardy was fortunate to have had the chance at all; the Grammar School was still far from reputable,† and all the other schools, perhaps forewarned by the obvious reluctance of local parents to support a strictly classical institution, were more concerned to teach the 'practical' subjects of mathematics, geography, and perhaps history. A country education, related strictly to the countryman's needs, was what was now demanded, and that, for the most part, was what the budding citizens of Dorchester were now given.

* Deacon and Coleman have an interesting discussion of the estrangement. See *Providence and Mr. Hardy*, Ch. 20.

† In 1871 there were no boarders, few dayboys, and the Master derived an extra four hundred pounds a year for the care of a lunatic patient (*Ministry of Education Files*). Not until State intervention in the 1880's, followed by the great headmastership of R. W. Hill (1927-55) did Hardye's School fully come into its own once more. To this Hardy made his own contribution as a Governor for almost twenty years.

But in truth Hardy tells us little about his earlier academic prowess, and he was, with reason, more concerned to recall his emotional development. The pages of the *Life* revive the various childish loves which inspired him from time to time. He records in one instance, 'he was more than a week getting over this desperate attachment'. There would be little to remark in these boyish loves, were it not for the clarity with which his passions were recalled in later years, and for the fact that he deliberately omitted the most important instance from the biography. He remembered the features of the girls, and as Edmund Blunden recalled,[7] 'it was as though he could paint their portraits for himself, and house them quietly and gladly within his heart'. The figures of Lizbie Brown, the daughter of a gamekeeper, and the farmer's daughter 'Louisa in the Lane' were revived long after in his poems.* Lizbie, older than himself, despised him; and the only words he ever heard from Louisa's lips were 'good-night' one evening on the Stinsford road; later she gave him a shy smile, but that was all. The passing of these figures in their maturer years was like the passing of old friends, and the *Life* records 'Louisa lies under a nameless mound in "Mellstock" churchyard'. So did little Fanny Hurd, the frail fellow-pupil from Bockhampton school, whose course seemed to end with her early death but who returned to the sunlight in 'Voices Growing from a Churchyard'. Hardy preserved the past as few authors have done, yet the preservation of these childhood figures could lead him into strange fantasies. The *Life* admits a strong attachment to Julia Augusta Martin, but one remarkable passage of the manuscript was omitted, and shows how curiously Hardy came to regard his friendship for a woman thirty years his senior:

> . . . though their eyes never met again after his call on her in London, nor their lips from the time when she had held him in her arms, who can say that both occurrences might not have been in the order of things, if he had developed their reacquaintance earlier, now that she was in her widowhood with nothing to hinder her mind from rolling back upon the past.[8]

Much of the reality of Hardy's life has been taken from us, and

* Louisa was Louisa Harding of Stinsford and Dorchester, who died unmarried on September 12, 1913, aged seventy-two. Her death was recorded in the *Dorset County Chronicle* of September 18, 1913, and she was buried at Stinsford the day previously (*Stinsford registers*).

some was wilfully kept back by the author himself; yet there is still more than we have ever realised to be recaptured in the pages of the poems and the novels. The smallest incident could begin a train of thought which, though it lay buried for years, carried him forwards towards a rural tragic theme. Watching a drowned boy being taken from Shadwater Weir, he was convinced, by a curious trick of light, that it was the body of a girl. Many years afterwards he told Mrs Gertrude Bugler that 'it was this incident which started the train of thought which led him to write *The Return of the Native*'.[9] Perhaps the writing of a single sentence—'it was not, as he had expected, a woman, but a man'[10] —found Thomas Hardy gazing back across the years to that moment of his youth.

His days were not, on the whole, difficult. He seems to have honoured both his parents, and the frailty which almost caused his death at birth rapidly disappeared as he grew older, and was banished entirely by the long and regular walks to and from his school in Dorchester. But he retained the childish sensitivity which at times made even the ordinary experiences of life an ordeal. Like the friend of his old age, T. E. Lawrence, he could not bear the touch of others—'Hardy, how is it that you do not like us to touch you?' was the frank inquiry of a Dorchester playmate—and to the end of his days he returned only the limpest and hastiest of handshakes. He would walk alone, frightened by the presences which haunted the dark lanes around Bockhampton, but none the less happy in his solitude; he would avoid human contact and find, with an introspective faculty dangerously beyond his years, sufficient refuge in his own thoughts and the sights and sounds of nature. As he grew to maturity and old age experience was to increase his wish to stand alone: at the personal level he would lose the gift of giving,* and find, in the remembered circumstances of his early life, a world of the past which, for all its broken promises, he would feel compelled to inhabit; perhaps the only world which ever had, for him, the truly hopeful prospect of serenity and achievement in life. Yet, perhaps because its promise was doomed to failure, this world's ultimate bitterness was concealed from others when he recalled his early life, even though it was here, and only here, that he was, habitually, at home.

* In view of the sympathy evident throughout Hardy's works this judgement may seem unfounded: it is based, however, on the letters of his two wives, and on reports from Max Gate employees.

The world had seemed to offer innocence, mental and emotional. The first inroads into this childish state were made when he entered formally into a career. One day, while restoring Woodsford Castle, a thatched and fortified manor house six miles east of Dorchester, Hardy's father took the boy along to watch. Though the young Hardy had no experience of architectural work except that gained by observation of his father's methods, the architect, John Hicks, offered to take him as a pupil. The expense of an apprenticeship was large but, through the shrewd efforts of Jemima Hardy, Hicks accepted a fee of forty pounds in place of the usual hundred.[11] So, stifling whatever ideas he might have had of entering the Church—a possibility that had more than once occurred to him—the boy entered the architect's office in South Street, Dorchester, and began his professional career.

Hardy, by his own admission, remained a bookworm, and in Hicks he found a master worthy of his tastes. Hicks's father, a country rector, had been a classical scholar and the architect himself possessed a smattering of Greek and Hebrew, though, says Hardy, 'he was less at home in Latin'. At all events, he left Hardy and his fellow-pupil Robert Bastow enough free time to follow their own courses, perhaps seeing in each of them something more than architectural promise. Hardy had learnt enough at school to wish to develop his own knowledge—and what greater reward can a teacher ask for?—and he continued to read Virgil, Horace, and Ovid in his spare time, as well as to embark on the totally fresh study of Greek. Home, school, and friends had all combined to make a scholar of him, and he repaid that interest in good earnest. If this is to be self-taught then Hardy was self-taught; for myself, I cannot see that the mental discipline required in a boy of sixteen to embark on such a course can be derived from any other source than the most strenuous cultivation of whatever natural talents the boy possessed. He had every reason to be grateful to his elders; and had he never achieved a later triumph they would have had every reason to be proud of the immediate result of their labours. Hicks himself, though standing in a different relationship to the boy, would enter into the labours of his pupils, excelling them in Greek, but often forced to confess his inferior ability in Latin. The architect's office must have presented an unusual face to the outside world when its master, 'cornered and proved wrong', admitted that his apprentices were surpassing him in their knowledge of the classics. When there were doubts one or other of the apprentices would run next door to appeal to the judgement of William Barnes. It almost seemed that architecture was in second place.

The time spent in Hicks's office, however, had a more important outcome for the future novelist. Bastow, who had been bred a Baptist, introduced a note of controversy into Hardy's life, and may have planted the first seeds of a religious doubt that was never to disappear. His immediate impression on Hardy was just the reverse, for Hardy was always ready to give his admiration to anyone who seemed worthy of respect, and the young Bastow, fervently arguing the merits of adult baptism, had an influence which was strong enough to send Hardy to the local priest to discover whether he ought in conscience to be baptised again. The vicar was sincere enough, but puzzled, and eventually recommended Hooker's *Ecclesiastical Polity* as a better course than baptism—an action which seems to have left Hardy more puzzled than the priest. But he decided, perhaps against his conscience, to hold to his High Church principles, and began to battle earnestly with his colleague, and later with the sons of the local Baptist minister. Whether he out-debated Bastow or not, he found his match in the Perkins brothers, who, armed with a knowledge of the Greek testament, could quote chapter and verse for their case, and what was more, could quote them in the original. With a conscientiousness which perhaps seems strange to modern views, Hardy began his own study of the Greek texts, and found himself appalled at the apparent feebleness of argument which lay behind his opponents' views and, one suspects, his own. The disputes soon died a natural death, but the lesson was not forgotten. If, as we may guess, he grew tired of religious debate, he never failed to remember that his beliefs stood in need of proof; nor, on the other hand, did he ever slight the sincerity and piety of the Perkins family. From them he acquired a taste for simple living which he never lost, and just as he gained a questioning spirit which was later to undermine his entire faith, so he gained an admiration for virtuous simplicity which he was later to regard as the most precious gift of true Christianity.

With Bastow's departure from his apprenticeship, first for London and later for Tasmania, Hardy was forced to apply himself more intensely to architecture than at any time hitherto. Though he was already stretching his wings as a poet,* he cannot have failed to enjoy the work in hand, for his sketching and surveying of old churches took him deep into the Dorsetshire

* The poem 'Domicilium', *Life*, p. 4, was written at about this time.

countryside, and he began to know the fields and lanes of other areas as well as he had come to know his own. This had the immediate practical effect of counteracting the weakening result of long and private study, and in his own account of the period he draws attention to the three modes of life which were normal to him at this time, 'the professional life, the scholar's life, and the rustic life, combined in the twenty-four hours of the day'. In the early mornings he would study, by eight he would be plodding along the avenue to Dorchester, and in the evenings he would rush with his violin to play the country-dances at some rustic festival. It was an intense life, but varied, and it served his inner spirit as effectively as it maintained his health. A growing friendship with the Moule family at Fordington Rectory kept him in touch with some of the finest spirits ever to serve the Church in Dorset, and had the secondary effect of encouraging him to continue in his study of the classics, though eventually, when he requested their advice, they gave him the common-sense opinion that a fuller application to architecture would be of more value than the most detailed knowledge of the Greek tragedians.

By the time Hardy reached his twentieth year he had still no fully predetermined course before him. His earlier leanings towards the Church were still alive, and had been whetted, as well as potentially undermined, by religious debate. His apprenticeship as an architect was perhaps a logical outcome of his father's profession, yet his devotion to it, though adequate, was certainly not complete. His ambition as a poet was still in its infancy. Everything pointed to an undramatic but competent career as an architect, and the slow decline of his other interests. Yet at this stage the crucial influence of Horace Moule began to make itself felt. It was Moule, a reviewer and member of Queens' College, Cambridge, who had advised Hardy to abandon his study of the Greek tragedians a year or two before; now it was Moule again who introduced Hardy to the newly published *Essays and Reviews* in 1860, and it may also have been through him that Hardy first came across Darwin's *Origin of Species*. Certainly both books were read by Hardy at this time, and both continued the undermining of his faith, although he was yet to make formal inquiries about the qualifications required for ordination.[12] None the less, it eventually became clear to him that his beliefs could not be reconciled with the preaching of the Christian faith. The insistent demands for rational examination of the Biblical texts which had been put forward by the 'Seven Against Christ' fell on ears already more than half-prepared for their message; while the sombre evidence of Darwin made it impossible for Hardy to accept the Christian idea of a personal God. But there was no sudden break, and eventually the pressure of personal experience may have had as much to do with his ultimate denial of Christianity as the intellectual inquiry which began in 1860. Moule himself, and perhaps Moule's family, seem more than likely to have argued against the rejection of Christianity, and Hardy would be reluctant to ignore Moule's advice. Later he was to send him analyses of style, and accepted that Moule would lecture him on his findings and his plans for writing.[13]

These years, too, marked a change in Hardy's material fortunes. In 1862 his apprenticeship with Hicks was at an end, and though he remained with him for a while, living for the most part in Dorchester and visiting Bockhampton only at weekends, he soon began to consider moving further afield. He had visited London only once before, at the age of eight or nine, and he had no knowledge of the capital; none the less, on Thursday, April 17, 1862, he set out. He carried with him two letters of introduction, but was apparently unconvinced of their value, for he bought a return ticket valid for six months, intending, if the worst should happen, to keep a clear line of retreat while his pocket still enabled him to do so; a trivial example, but showing that even as a young man the policy of planning for the least hopeful of several possible situations, set out in most of the novels, was important to Hardy's personal behaviour. In one instance Hardy thought his scepticism was justified, for on the first inquiry the gentleman 'was civil . . . remembered his father, promised every assistance; and there the matter ended'. However, the 'gentleman' had very little time in which to act, for John Norton, practising as an architect in Old Bond Street, offered every kindness, and even—though he did not need assistance—let Hardy earn a little money by preparing drawings for his office until some permanent opening should appear. Within a week, again thanks to Norton's generous recommendation, he had met Arthur Blomfield, who required a Gothic draughtsman to restore country churches and rectories, and by May 5 Hardy had found his niche in London. In the eyes of some his years in the capital were years of hardship and misery; there is no real evidence of this, and the ease with which he gained and kept his first appointment suggests that materially, at least, he was very fortunate. Nor had his spiritual life yet reached its crisis, though that was slowly approaching; and he seems, indeed, to have thrown himself into the new sights and sounds of a great, dirty, and still old-fashioned city with considerable enjoyment. His countryman's instincts were not yet offended by what he saw, nor his physical well-being undermined by the loss of country air.

He remained in London for five years, with only occasional visits to his home, and like five years in any man's life they were years of successes and reverses. From 1863 onwards he began to send his poetry to periodicals, and though each poem was returned unpublished many of them were kept and only slightly altered for publication half a century later. These rebuffs may have injured him, for by 1865 he can write 'The world does not despise us; it only neglects us'[14]; but such a comment, while it accords with his feelings in later years, may be an inspiration of the mind rather than of the soul. For in that same year he was able to publish his light-hearted prose effort 'How I Built Myself a House' in *Chambers's Journal*. As before, his life was a mixture, and Blomfield's office was scarcely more restrained than Hicks's. Blomfield himself was a tolerant and friendly employer, with a fund of anecdotes about his career and a blind eye to the misdemeanours of his staff. Outside the office there was plenty to see: the Thames embankment was being built, and Charing Cross Bridge gradually stretching itself across the river; Dickens was still giving public readings, and on one occasion Hardy sat beside him in a coffee-shop and listened to him fussing about his bill[15]; there was dancing at Almack's, there were theatre and opera. Hardy visited the Exhibition as frequently as possible, and spent many more hours in the reading-room of the Kensington museum; his head was read by a phrenologist, who gave an ominous report; and once, after gazing at it for weeks, Hardy saved enough to buy an ancient violin which he kept until his death.

Intellectually he continued to move forward. Still alive to the possibility of a future in the Church, he visited the Abbey frequently, and once, with Horace Moule, visited a Roman Catholic service which he found beautiful and moving. He still read at every available opportunity, including the classics once more in his personal curriculum, and he enrolled himself at King's College, London, though his close reading of English literature, and particularly of English poetry, could have left him little time for the study of French for which he had enrolled. And his mind was one day cast back to his childhood reading of Napoleonic history when he visited the House of Commons and heard one of the last speeches of Lord Palmerston. A few weeks later the old statesman was dead, and Hardy watched the burial from a seat high up in Westminster Abbey.

Even in the great city there were elements of the grotesque. The gradual extension of the railways meant the destruction of several old burial-grounds, and more than once Blomfield had been called upon to supervise the removal of the bodies for burial elsewhere. Once, before Hardy's arrival, the bodies had been taken from their places but never, so far as Blomfield could discover, re-interred elsewhere. There were rumours of bones being taken to the bone-mills, which brought the grim remark from Blomfield, 'I believe these people are all ground up!' Hardy himself, working by night to avoid disturbance, supervised on later occasions, and watched the older coffins fall apart as they were brought to the surface. From one fell a skeleton with two skulls, and the watchers drew their own macabre conclusions. At home, and in more conventional surroundings, Blomfield ran a choir, enlisting Hardy's aid; and even, at a later date, allowed Hardy to lecture to his fellow-architects on English literature and poetry. On his side, Hardy seems to have been an able assistant: able enough, at least, to win a medal for an architectural essay—though the judges may have considered its style more impressive than its content.

Of romance he tells us little, though with his temperament he must have been fired with more than one temporary passion. That it was on his mind is certain: no young bachelor lives for five years in London without the wish, at least, to form some lasting attachment, and certainly not a bachelor who has proposed and been rejected at the age of twenty-two.* On his twenty-fifth birthday, feeling dejected and older than he was, he wrote 'wondering what woman, if any, I should be thinking about in five years' time'. He was soon to know.

Five years in London slowly sapped Hardy's strength; feeling mentally and physically exhausted, he was glad to leave the city for a while, and in July 1867 he returned to Dorset. His relatives were shocked by his appearance, though a few weeks in the countryside were enough to restore his vigour. Yet his term in London had not been unproductive. His architectural progress had been satisfactory; he had experienced a style of life unknown to Dorset, though its result may have been only to sharpen his appreciation of the country; through continued visits to the museum and exhibitions of South Kensington he had kept abreast of modern scientific knowledge; and above all, he had

* In 1862 Hardy proposed to a girl named Mary Waight, daughter of a Dorchester printer and bookseller. See Beaminster, 11.

taken his first steps as a poet. From London he brought a collection of manuscripts, most of them afterwards destroyed but some preserved and published many years later, when a tardy recognition of his poetic gift was at last within his grasp.

Most of the surviving poems are not of a very high order, and even one that was ultimately published was labelled in the final manuscript 'To be thrown out'.[16] Yet this very poem is remarkable for the distinctly personal style in which it is written:

> 'Thwart my wistful way did a damsel saunter,
> Fair, albeit unformed to be all-eclipsing;
> 'Maiden meet', held I, 'till arise my forefelt
> Wonder of women'.

The distorted syntax, the mixture of dialect, archaic, and common English, and the occasional coinages which mark this poem were never to disappear, though their relative proportions might be varied. Others of this early group show only one clear influence: the oppressive influence of Shakespeare's sonnets. Yet the quality of his verse at this stage matters little: for him they were his first attempts to find a distinctive personal voice, and seen in this light they reveal a considerable measure of success, the personal idiom triumphing over Hardy's borrowings.

Without setting aside his frequently repeated warning that many of his poems are dramatic, even when they appear to be personal, it is possible to distinguish certain patterns of his own thought which were to become permanent features of his poetry. The first thing we discover is that Hardy's disillusion with life is already setting in. Some of the poems have a facile quality which might suggest that they are derived as much from the spirit of the times as from personal experience—'Young Man's Epigram on Existence' is a case in point; but others suggest that all the time personal experience is pushing the author towards a fuller acceptance of the spirit of inquiry and doubt which was widespread, and which no avid follower of the discussion of religion and the Darwinian theory could have avoided. Disillusion might, too, have been a natural reaction to life in London, where Hardy may have been lonely, and where he certainly felt much of his work to be monotonous and mechanical.[17] An attempt to escape from this monotony led him to toy with the idea of writing blank-verse dramas, and he even approached stage circles in the hope of practical experience, appearing in a pantomime, *The Forty Thieves*, and visiting the theatre frequently as a self-appointed observer. But, as he says, 'the first moment of his sight of stage realities disinclined him to push further in that direction'.[18] One would like to know more about this theatrical experience, just as one would like to know more about the occasions which he shared in London with Horace Moule, whom he saw frequently. Yet Hardy remained surprisingly reticent, and the details of his London career may be lost to us for ever. Perhaps the most that we can say is that a natural melancholy was reinforced by experience, but had not yet been turned into incipient bitterness.

The next few years in Dorset were to bring about that transformation. The Hardy who returned to Dorset was capable of beginning a gay and lyrical idyll, *Under The Greenwood Tree*; yet even while that book was being written Hardy was undergoing the experiences which were, many years later, to produce the bitter pessimism of *Jude the Obscure*. On returning to Dorset in 1867 Hardy fell in love with and became engaged to his cousin, Tryphena Sparks of Puddletown, despite the fact that she was only sixteen, eleven years his junior. The character of Tryphena is now, of course, extremely difficult to assess, but there can be little doubt that she was talented, strong-willed, and probably capricious. The surviving photographs of her show a woman of good carriage and mobile features, capable of varying degrees of attractiveness, and at times of a very real beauty. Her influence upon Hardy's work and personality were crucial, and it is scarcely an exaggeration to say that each of Hardy's works contains her portrait. Fancy Day of *Under the Greenwood Tree* and Sue Bridehead of *Jude the Obscure* may well be very detailed portraits, and the difference in tone between those two books is a measure of the change which his years with her brought upon him.

The engagement failed; and it appears probable that a good deal of rashness marked its course. In the summer of 1868 Tryphena, having previously been dismissed from her post as a student-teacher at the Puddletown village school, gave birth to Hardy's son—a son who remained unacknowledged publicly, and who was brought up by Tryphena's sister, Rebecca Sparks.* It was a somewhat bizarre arrangement: despite her dismissal from Puddletown, Tryphena was accepted as a student in a London teachers' training college, did well, and in January 1872 took up her duties as headmistress of the girls' section of a Plymouth school. At Christmas that same year Rebecca was married to Frederick Paine, a saddler of Puddletown, only to leave him

* For a detailed discussion of this see Appendix B.

immediately to take up residence in Plymouth. One can only guess that, arriving as 'Mrs Paine', she found the presence of a child as easy to explain as the absence of a husband, and the marriage appears to have been contracted solely for Tryphena's convenience. At the least, it enabled her to be near her son.

Hardy's part in these arrangements is unknown. In 1870 he had met Emma Lavinia Gifford in Cornwall, and was clearly attracted to her, though it was not until 1872 that Tryphena returned their engagement ring—a ring which Emma Lavinia later wore. For a time, indeed, Hardy appears to have been uncertain of his relationship with either woman, and it is not impossible that behind his liaison with Tryphena there lay the lurking fear of incest. Tryphena may have been his niece.

Hardy's very silence about these years indicates the deeply traumatic effect they had upon him. Nor is this silence apparent only in the *Life*: his own record of his family, though drawn up in considerable detail,[19] totally omits Tryphena and her nearest kin, just as the Sparks family records totally omit the Hardys, even though the families lived within a few miles of one another and had been on visiting terms in Hardy's childhood. Yet despite these omissions, the reminiscences of Tryphena in the novels, culminating in the violence of *Jude*, show that for Hardy she was a very present factor in his life. In the earlier works it is possible to see a fairly consistent intellectual concern with the problems of human choice and responsibility, in which autobiographical concerns are of minor importance only. But the autobiographical elements ultimately cloud the intellectual issues. As Hardy's works proceed we find him circling around his personal obsessions, obviously aware of their force, and perhaps afraid to bring them into the open. It is only with Tryphena's death in 1890 that personal inhibitions are thrown completely aside, and Hardy's well-nigh neurotic obsession with his own and his family's past comes close to ruining the last great novel.

The reasons for the collapse of the engagement remain to some extent obscure,* but by 1871 it was obvious that it was going badly. On the return—but not the rejection—of the manuscript of *Under the Greenwood Tree* in the summer of 1871 he 'threw the MS into a box with his old poems, being quite sick of all such', and when he was approached by Tinsley a year later he 'didn't know what had become of the MS, and *did not care*'. He had not merely abandoned the *Greenwood Tree* but had given up all ideas

* See Appendix B.

of writing; it is to the credit of Emma Lavinia Gifford that she encouraged him to change his mind.

That Hardy found Emma attractive is beyond doubt; that he formed any early intention to marry her, or that he fell in love with her and abandoned Tryphena for her sake, is less likely. Nor is it convincing to regard *A Pair of Blue Eyes* as a portrait of events in Cornwall, however imaginative: Rutland has shown that some sections of the book were probably written well before Hardy met Emma Lavinia, and Lois Deacon has taken this suggestion further, with considerable weight.[20] It seems clear, indeed, that the initial moves of 'the Cornish romance' were taken by Emma herself, despite the hostility of some members of her family. None the less, Hardy did marry her. His frame of mind at the time of their marriage is difficult to guess, but it is unlikely to have been particularly gay. The wedding itself, which took place in London in September 1874, bore some of the characteristics of an elopement; Tryphena was in Devon and courted by another man; while a year before Hardy had been shattered by the news of the suicide at Cambridge of his friend and mentor Horace Moule. In addition there was an obscure consciousness, which became stronger with the years, of some 'ancestral curse' among his own family which could wreck marriages and lives. None the less, for a brief period the marriage worked. Hardy used to say that the quality which he admired most in Emma Lavinia was the *life* that she possessed; she also had considerable confidence and pride in her husband's abilities as a writer. But as the years went by more and more of that living quality was to disappear. It is too easy to describe her as snobbish, but there is no doubt that she enjoyed social and society life and that she expected, as the wife of an architect, to find more opportunities for it than were ever possible at St Juliot. As Hardy became an established author she must have expected it even more. In some respects she found it. As Hardy's reputation grew he became more and more socially desirable and socially acceptable: the flaw was that much of his social success was based on a literary success which Emma could not share. Even before their marriage she had written:

> My work, unlike your work of writing, does not occupy my true mind much. . . . Your novel seems sometimes like a child, all your own and none of me.[21]

Yet she encouraged him to write, and was for many years a constant and willing assistant in the task of preparing copy for the publishers. It may or may not be true that she snubbed Hardy in public—such stories are based largely on gossip which is difficult to verify—but even without a sense of superiority over her husband she would have found, as the years passed, sufficient reason for discomfort in her marriage. Hardy himself had written 'I feel that a bad marriage is one of the direst things on earth, & one of the cruellest things',[22] but it is too often forgotten that if Hardy was ill at ease, his wife was also; and his wry observations on the married state, which begin with some vein of humour but which rapidly sour, must have seemed to her a public criticism as tactless and outrageous as anything that could be charged against her. She may well have shared her husband's grief at their continued childlessness—'We hear that Jane, our late servant, is soon to have a baby. Yet never a sign of one is there for us'[23]—and this may have contributed largely to their troubles. She disliked the move to Dorchester—Florence Hardy, too, was depressed by Max Gate*—and most of all she felt increasingly at odds with Hardy's agnosticism. Her own religious views were fanciful, even fantastic, in a childish fashion, and little likely ever to have appealed to Hardy at any time of his life; and each year saw them travelling further in opposite directions, she becoming more and more visionary, he more and more rationalistic. When his views were finally expressed in the unequivocal form of *Tess* and *Jude* their marriage was at an end in everything but name. Her own attempts to obtain the suppression of *Jude the Obscure*, though they have become notorious, are understandable; but they brought with them a further exclusion from her husband's affairs:

> My husband's books have not the same kind of interest for me, as for others. I knew every word of the first Edition—in MS sitting by his side—etc, etc—so long ago, & so much endured since in this town in which I have been *unhappy*, that they are bound to be different to me! I had expected always to live in London with occasional visits to the country. (I love the country however)—Perhaps you may *understand*—and perhaps not, that *only authorship* seldom causes the trouble that undesirable proximity does! . . . I would rather go to the seaside—a quiet, forgotten kind of one—than to London just yet.

* See, for example, Florence Hardy to Charlotte Mew, October 1924 (no day given): '. . . the trees that hem us round & make some of our rooms so dark & depressing'. (Berg Collection, New York Public Library.)

> I am ensconcing myself in the study in *his* big chair foraging —he keeps me *out* usually—as *never* formerly—ah well! I have my private opinion of men in general & him in particular—grand brains—much power—but too often, lacking in judgement of ordinary matters—opposed to *un*selfishness—as regards them*selves*—utterly useless & dangerous as magistrates! & such offices & to be put up with until a new order of the universe arrives (*it will*).[24]

The last years of Emma's life were clouded by some form of mental unbalance which appears to date from the period immediately following *Jude the Obscure*, and there is no doubt that that book alone did more to devastate Hardy's marriage than any other of his works, and than any act of personal unkindness. They were perhaps naturally incompatible, but the coldness which broke out between Hardy and his wife after 1890 was closer to enmity than indifference. Emma withdrew to an attic at the top of Max Gate, eating and living apart,[25] writing of it 'my boudoir is my sweet refuge and solace—not a sound scarcely penetrates hither'.[26] In the year of their silver wedding she could write of her husband, 'the *thorn* is in my side still',[27] and a few years later 'my eminent partner will have a softening of the brain if he goes on as he does & the rest of the world does'.[28] For his part, Hardy became increasingly restless, moving his study from room to room[29]; he forgot Emma's birthday every year,[30] and avoided so much as the mention of her name in his letters—'I should think about the 9th or 10th Sept would suit, if we come. But I would leave it to her, for the date makes little difference to me. I believe she is going to sit to my sister for her portrait sometime in September or October, which would necessitate her being here for a week or fortnight.'[31] Not even the words 'my wife' appear in this particular letter.

To apportion blame for this tragic marriage is neither feasible nor relevant, except in so far as it throws light on the spirit in which Hardy's works were written. It should be said, however, that although Hardy scholars in general appear to show little sympathy for Emma, the surviving letters show her in a more sympathetic light than Hardy. His treatment of his second wife lacked charity, and on those grounds we may believe that Emma's complaints were not without justification. Frequently she mentions her own shyness, and this may have made it harder for her to express her unhappiness in terms which would evoke any kindly response; but unhappy she certainly was. Hardy was primarily a dreamer, and the realm in which he dwelt was the dream-world of his own stormy past. He saw this past in terms of absolute good or bad, idealising happiness, as he later idealised Emma herself, and overstressing his unhappiness. Moreover, he approached happiness and unhappiness in different ways: happiness was a series of precise and identifiable events, unhappiness a frame of mind, a screen of melancholy through which life, including its lighter moments, was seen. His views were strongly conditioned by his beliefs, and his beliefs strongly conditioned by his prevailing mood. He could show impatience of the optimism of others, and incredulity in the face of strong Christian beliefs expressed in even moderately fundamentalist terms. In fact he was more intolerant of the faith of others than his works would lead us to guess. He could, on the other hand, accord his fullest respect to the ways of life which faith inspired, and contempt for ways of life which he believed to be hypocritical. His admiration for the Perkins brothers, or for the poet-priest William Barnes, was never hindered by disagreement with their religious opinions, and for the Christian ethic in its purest simplicity he retained a love that was all the greater because he could not share the beliefs involved. When Christianity appeared to him to verge on the superstitious—and Emma's no doubt struck him as doing just that—he could become angry. Of his humility there is no doubt; but it was a complex humility, subject to great strain, and at times a sadness for what he had lost, both spiritually and materially, could express itself in bitter criticism. Once, during his second marriage, Florence Hardy was late home, apparently at a Christian Science meeting with friends from Athelhampton Hall. On discovering that she had not returned Hardy's bitter comment was, 'I suppose she is still down there dabbling with that rubbish'.[32] At other times his attitude towards the supernatural was a reluctant scepticism, but Florence Hardy was unfortunate enough to belong to the realm of the living. Emma Hardy had already taken her revenge: after her death in 1912 Hardy discovered her diaries and a manuscript entitled 'What I Think of my Husband'. As Newman Flower wrote later, 'the core of their tragedy lay in these written sheets'.[33] Hardy burnt the papers, but was overwhelmed with remorse, a remorse which found expression in the poems of 1912-13, and in apparently endless visits to search for the Gifford family graves. His remorse was so strong that he forgot his obligations to his second wife, and she can hardly have enjoyed such expeditions at the opening of her marriage to him. She was almost forty years younger than him, and their marriage had been a marriage of convenience contracted chiefly for his benefit,[34] yet she was never allowed to invite friends to stay at Max Gate.[35] Hardy himself grew increasingly reluctant to leave the house, and resented it if she did so,[36] he offered her no marriage settlement,[37] and kept her short of money, even for substantial medical expenses.[38] His charity was for the dead, not for the living, and he could write of Emma after her death:

> In later years an unfortunate mental aberration altered her much, & made her cold in correspondence with friends and relatives, but this was contrary to her real nature, & I myself quite disregard it in thinking of her.[39]

—though in fact Emma's surviving letters to her friends are anything but cold. But as he had mourned over Tryphena once she was inaccessible to him, so now he mourned over Emma; to such an extent that Florence Hardy was provoked into exclaiming 'All the poems about her are a fiction, but a fiction in which their author has now come to believe'.[40] Hardy's habitual melancholy became infectious, to such an extent that Florence was burdened by a sense of her failure to ease what she saw as depression and world weariness.[41] She was not so far wrong. In 1887 he wrote to Edmund Gosse:

> As to despondency I have known the very depths of it. You would be quite shocked if I were to tell you how many weeks and months in byegone years I have gone to bed wishing never to see daylight again.[42]

And once he told T. P. O'Connor that 'he did not care if every book he had ever written were burned and never seen or heard of again'.[43]

It would be easy to condemn the 'drab little man' of Hardy's old age, and it is not difficult to see that the characteristics which marked him then were already strongly present in early manhood. Yet the picture I have suggested here is that of a man who deserves pity more than condemnation. His experience with Tryphena, his marriage to Emma, and his sensitive, self-protective response to it, meant that rightly or wrongly Hardy felt his life to be a failure: against a background of rich tradition and rural fatality, he could see his own career as emotionally soured, and insignificant; in terms of theological belief he was conscious of what had gone, even though he never ceased to search for some replacement for his lost faith. And in terms of literary endeavour he felt, despite a steady flow of public honours in later life, that his chief merits as a poet were ignored, and his purposes as a novelist misunderstood. The picture is a depressing one.

Yet the sympathetic response to suffering and pain presented in the novels, in the *Life*, and in some of the letters; the genuine acceptance of responsibility for the failure of his first marriage; the deep admiration accorded to him by younger people, literary and unliterary—all these suggest that the picture is inadequate. And all of them are real. During his eighties Hardy visited Sturminster Newton, the earliest of his homes with Emma, and recaptured the experience:

> I planted that tree when I came here. It was then a small thing not so high as my shoulder. . . . I suppose that was a long time ago. I brought my first wife here after our honeymoon. . . . She had long golden hair. . . . How that tree has grown! But that was in 1876. . . . How it has changed. . . . Time changes everything except something within us which is always surprised by change.[44]

His writings, his response to the past, and his deep compassion were real and unchanging, however much they might be obscured in day-to-day personal relations. The passionate side of his nature and the puritan appear to have been widely separated in him, and his self-distrust led to an overwhelming shyness which too often stood in the way of generous and easy intercourse with his fellow-men. It accounts for some of the deceptions in the *Life*, whereas the cloak of fiction in his novels allowed him to throw off his reticence. Moreover, beneath his reticence there was a warm and humane spirit, as the evidence of those who did enjoy his friendship shows. There is Mrs Gertrude Bugler, for example, Hardy's choice for the part of Tess in the London and Dorset production of the dramatised novel, and a woman whom Hardy loved in his old age[45]:

> A great deal has been said and written both during his lifetime and since his death, of the sad philosophy and pessimistic attitude to life of Thomas Hardy, but to us he was not the grim, cynical man often pictured, and if he sometimes emphasised the darker side of life, he never forgot the sunshine of laughter. I can still hear him laugh. . . .[46]

To T. E. Lawrence, with whom he had much in common, he was unchangingly an object of reverence,[47] and to Edmund Blunden 'a sort of dynast in disguise', a 'prophetic' figure.[48] Most revealing of all is the testimony of his second wife, who bore the brunt of his self-enclosure, sensitivity, and the irritableness of old age:

> I am full of joy to see how my husband finds himself in his true environment here. He went off just now in his cap and gown—very, *very* pleased with his adornments—to dine in his college (Magdalene) & he loves being Dr Hardy. He is really just like a boy—or a nice child. He hates wearing his Order of Merit—but he is tremendously proud of his cap and gown. . . . I often wonder how many people realise the simplicity of his nature. He told me the other day that he thought he had never grown up. . . .[49]
>
> . . . Of course I do know he has a tender protective affection for me—as a father for a child—as he has always had—a feeling quite apart from passion. And I feel towards him, sometimes, as a mother towards a child with whom things have somehow gone wrong—a child who needs comforting—to be treated gently & with all the love possible.[50]

Against such a background Hardy emerges as a contradictory figure, passionate and reticent, charitable but with a strong degree of self-centredness, humble but with strongly held and powerfully expressed personal opinions. He has been presented to us as a gentle, frail, essentially simple man: but simplicity is of a strange nature, and Hardy's simplicity had been buffeted too much to remain intact. I can only see him as a figure of great and complex power, whose complexity penetrates his works, and for whom the works were an escape from his own nature.

Emma Lavinia Hardy

Florence Emily Hardy

THE NOVELS

II

> From his work I get few of the meanings, pessimistic or otherwise, that are commonly ascribed to him. His purpose seems to have been to tell about human life in the terms that would present it as most recognisably, and validly, and completely human.[1]

MOST of us do not read Hardy for his ideas, and many do not share his opinions; yet we cannot ignore them. Hardy's indignation at critical interpretations of his opinions is well known, but not entirely justified: he writes with a set of more or less established moral principles—or at least moral attitudes—in mind, and he introduces them frequently into the mouths of his characters and his commentary upon them; they affect our response to the work, and the manner and regularity with which they are introduced are often cited as Hardy's principal weakness. The nature of the controversy can be easily stated: it has been almost unanimously agreed that Hardy's works are tragedies of Fate rather than tragedies of character, but there is less unanimity about the extent to which this supposed emphasis damages the artistic validity of Hardy's work. The most extreme statement hostile to Hardy came from J. S. Smart in 1922:

> [Hardy] insists upon the external causes of disaster, the strange perversities of Nature, Fate, and Chance. His characters are brought to ruin by events over which they have no control, suffer for the sins of others, become the playthings of a blind, irresponsible power. . . . The mystery of the world may not be solved by a belief in a divine guidance which visibly brings out all things for good. But neither is it solved by postulating an all-powerful being endowed with the baser human passions, who turns everything to evil, and rejoices in the mischief he has wrought.[2]

This criticism goes beyond the question of artistic validity and into the realm of personal opinion, and Hardy was right to explain that Smart's views were 'ludicrous'.[3] He refuted such interpretations throughout his career, even introducing his refutation in the dialogue of *Jude*:

'We must conform!' she said mournfully. 'All the ancient wrath of the Power above us has been vented upon us, His poor creatures, and we must submit. There is no choice. We must. It is no use fighting against God!'

'It is only against man and senseless circumstance', said Jude.

'True!' she murmured. 'What have I been thinking of! I am getting as superstitious as a savage! . . .'[4]

Yet no point of view which sees Hardy's characters as *wholly* responsible matches our experience of them, because, patently and systematically, he sets out to portray a world which, in its laws or tendencies, is indifferent or hostile to men. The question which remains is whether that world is one whose limitations on human action are only partial, as Hardy the man seems to have believed; or whether Hardy the novelist presented characters without freedom. This is not merely speculative questioning: on the answers depends a just appreciation of his work. Hardy's style may demand from us some degree of adjustment, possibly the kind of adjustment which E. M. Forster could not make but which Miss Barbara Hardy can. Forster believed Hardy's stress on causality to be detrimental to his characterisation:

> Hardy arranges his events with emphasis on causality, the ground plan is a plot, and the characters are altered to acquiesce in its requirements. . . . They are finally bound hand and foot, there is ceaseless emphasis on fate, and yet, for all the sacrifices made to it, we never see the action as a living thing. . . . The characters have been required to contribute too much to the plot; except in their rustic humours, their vitality has been impoverished, they have gone dry and thin. This, so far as I can make out, is the flaw running through Hardy's novels: he has emphasised causality more strongly than his medium permits.[5]

There is a very real concern here for character, for the 'philosophy'—perhaps we should merely say the ground-plan—of the novels, and for the medium. But if the interpretation of that 'philosophy' is wrong, then any judgements about the medium are difficult to make. That the characters 'are *finally* bound hand and foot' may be generally true, and may possibly be established from the texts; it is much more difficult to establish that they are bound by 'fate', unless 'fate' includes a considerable display of free will and choice. Moreover, the medium 'permits' whatever it can convey without distortion; Hardy's medium certainly will not permit the kind of situation outlined by Forster, but neither does it try to: and to read the novels in this way is to compel oneself to distort a medium which is designed to fulfil other purposes. In *The Appropriate Form* Barbara Hardy shows the same concern for meaning and medium, but comes to a very different conclusion:

> Hardy . . . succeeds in combining animated and realistic psychology with ideological pattern. His story also depends on an arrangement of an action which reflects his general conclusions about the universe. This is the world without a Providence, where there is no malignant President of the Immortals, but conditions in nature and society which, in the absence of Providence, work together to frustrate energy and intelligence. Those who best serve the life-force, like Arabella, prosper best, but those who have imagination and aspiration meet with the frustration of nature's blind biological purpose and society's conventional restrictions.[6]

This offers a very sensible definition of 'fate' in the novels, perhaps because, as Barbara Hardy indicates in a footnote, she shares 'Hardy's metaphysical beliefs'. It is all the more suggestive, therefore, that *Jude the Obscure*, the very novel which she praises for its animated and realistic psychology, is also the novel which Mr Forster and others regard as a failure. The whole question of the characters' freedom of action, and the significance or lack of significance of their moral qualities, is thus disputed ground; and the dispute to a very large extent involves the appropriateness of Hardy's chosen form.

It will be obvious to any reader of Hardy that his form relies on the author's voice, the so-called 'intrusion' which enables him to generalise from events, or to interpret actions for us. The generalisations discuss the moral order against which the plot is set—the most famous being the 'Aeschylean phrase' of *Tess of the D'Urbervilles*. Are these intrusions in fact concerned with causality, or are they intended in some way to illuminate the characters more fully? Generally we have assumed that causality is their concern, the 'ceaseless emphasis on fate' of Mr Forster, but this makes little sense to me. My own recollection, at least, of the novels is always in terms of *people*, and of scenes with people in them; surely Hardy's concern is the same? The character of Gabriel Oak is easier to recall than the plot of *Far From the Madding Crowd*; again, why, in three of his major works, does

Hardy choose *names* for his titles: Jude, Tess, the Mayor, each of them given some relationship with their natural, social, or hereditary environment? The situations are present, certainly, but it is the figures which haunt our imagination long after the precise details of their careers have disappeared from memory. Hardy even adds sub-titles—'A Man of Character', 'A Pure Woman'—as if to focus our attention on the figures and their moral qualities. So we are compelled to say that Hardy succeeds in creating archetypal figures *in spite of* his intrusions. But this is impossible: those intrusions are deeply-woven into the fabric of the novels, they are mostly centred on individuals and their reactions, and we are forced to concede that they are more subtle and pertinent in their effect than we generally care to admit.

The real issue was touched upon by Dorothy Van Ghent when she wrote that 'with the "Aeschylean phrase" on the sport of the gods we feel again that intrusion of commentary which belongs to another order of discourse'[7]; but she boldly presupposes that we already have a clear understanding of the 'order of discourse' which is Hardy's habitual medium. Such an understanding is not easily come by, but it becomes even more difficult to reach if we insist on ignoring a major feature of Hardy's style. The voice is essential: through it we find a continually changing perspective, guided at times to identification with the characters, more frequently finding ourselves pushed towards detachment. The very lack of consistency, sometimes within a single work, about Hardy's generalisations should warn us against too easy acceptance of them as his personal point of view; should warn us still more that there may be no single attitude which we must necessarily adopt at the author's instructions. The elements which contribute towards this variety, which is essentially a means of distancing, are numerous: there is that side of Hardy's art which we call 'primitive' in the best sense—his reliance on traditional themes, the close kinship between his stories and the ballad, and his stress on the function of the novelist as a 'mere tale-teller',* only justified in adopting his role if he has an unusual and striking story to relate. There is the importation of the language of science and philosophy into an ancient structure, and the viewing of the old ballad themes through eyes conditioned by Darwinism, agnosticism, and modern scientific theory. And between these two extremes there is the voice of the local historian, recording the landscape, and at times the actual people and histories of Wessex.

* See Hardy's note on fiction, *Life*, p. 252.

The reliance on traditional forms accounts for certain features which may be regarded as strengths or weaknesses—and just which seems to depend largely on the critic's point of view. A point of view which *demands* developing characters, for example, might look upon Hardy's work with disfavour; whereas a critic like Donald Davidson sees in the 'fixed' characters a powerful source of Hardy's strength.[8] Similarly, the reliance on vigorous action, with little stress on analysis or psychological motivation, and a greater stress on vigour than on probability, may also derive from traditional sources. 'The miraculous, or nearly miraculous, is what makes a story a story, in the old way.'[9] It is from this 'miraculous' base that Hardy's stories derive their weight, appealing to traditions of story and legend which are familiar and pleasing to most readers. Sometimes they have caused difficulty, but I am at a loss to know why. Morton Dauwen Zabel writes that they are 'likely to make the suspension of disbelief a resentful ordeal', and cites the wife-selling in *The Mayor of Casterbridge* as an example.[10] This seems to me to betray a great deal of over-sophistication and, as happens in this case, a reluctance even to believe facts. A critic of Hardy should not be so ignorant of the background of the novels that he is unaware that wife-sales are an attested fact of nineteenth-century history, and were very far from uncommon.* It is more important that this scepticism is based upon a complete misreading of Hardy's method: it is pertinent to remind ourselves that *any* mythical tale may establish itself on facts beyond natural experience or beyond the everyday, and mythical and fabular elements are crucial to Hardy's art. He did not attempt to write along realistic lines, and he has said so:

> The real, if unavowed, purpose of fiction is to give pleasure by gratifying the love of the uncommon in human experience, mental or corporeal . . . human nature must never be made abnormal, which is introducing incredibility. The uncommonness must be in the events. . . .[11]

He added that it was the writer's task to make the uncommon credible—which in *The Mayor* he did—but his stress is clear to see; and the terms in which he defines fiction are quite plainly

* See, for example, *The Ladies Companion*, 1805, and *The Times*, March 4, 1833. Further examples are adduced in *Notes and Queries*, February 17, 1951, and in seven subsequent issues (indexed).

not the terms in which Zabel defines it. Hardy's tales are not the tales of a realist, but are fabular in conception, underpinned by the use of local superstition, folk-lore, and magic, and a world is created which, just as it is only a little removed in time from Hardy's own day, is also removed from the 'real' world of every-day. Different, removed, imaginative rather than realistic—however recognisable this world of Hardy's may be, it represents an idiom which is different not merely from our own, but from that of Hardy's contemporaries also.

It is his extension of this world which is the true source of the difficulties facing modern critics as they approach him, but it is also a source of strength. Had he confined himself solely to the rewriting of traditional tales—and his own testimony is that he used narratives which were related to him or which had been current in his own family*—it is doubtful whether he would ever have been more than a romantic provincial dealing in stock reconstructions. What lends sympathy and understanding to his creation of character is just the refusal to treat his figures only as imaginative revivals. He injects into the older world a vein of realism and rationalism, setting modern ideas and sentiments beside the old-world traditional landscape and its people. It is as if the conflict between the rationalism he wished to hold and the nostalgia for a lost past which he had wished to retain had both been placed side by side in the works, and the conflict within the man exploited for artistic purposes: for there is a tension between sympathy for the old life and thought, and respect for and assent to the new 'rationalism' based on evolutionary principles. This emerges partly through characterisation, the placing of fixed, undeveloping characters, whose fortunes leave them unchanged, beside the developing changeable characters of the new world: the obvious example of Henchard set beside the 'modern' Farfrae springs to mind. It is important to see Hardy's characters in juxtaposition with one another, for even at this level, the stage-managing of characters, Hardy is adopting an 'order of discourse' which is paralleled in the poems: an order which, if it is to be clearly expressive, demands a dialogue or a conflict between two different modes of existence. The commentary reflects Hardy's attempt to subject older ways to a rigorous examination and to

* See, for example, *Black and White*, August 27, 1892: 'I suppose . . . all of your characters are drawn from life?'—'Oh yes, almost all of them. Tess, Mr. Clare, . . . Shepherd Oak . . . Bathsheba Everdene . .. Joseph Poorgrass, Eustacia, . . . Susan Nonsuch . . .'

present his readers with several different perspectives, and we should perhaps expect a tension to be established between the neutrality of the ballad tale and the deliberate absence of neutrality often implied in the author's voice. The device is effective: simply-observed passages—say, Joan Durbeyfield's ' 'tis nater, after all, and what do please God'—which are not subjected to immediate or direct comment, nevertheless become representative of the relaxed attitude of a way of life which can no longer meet and withstand the greater pressures of a moral order placing responsibility solely upon man's alertness.

Nevertheless, we are still entitled to demand that an author's statements be true, not to his opinions or to our own, but to the tale he is telling; and sometimes Hardy's attitude is not entirely clear. At the sociological level, for example, there is the question of sexual morality. The seduction of Tess, 'but for the world's opinion . . . would have been simply a liberal education';[12] Hardy is at pains to stress Tess's kinship with the oozing fertility of the Frome valley; yet Alec d'Urberville is seen and judged largely through the eyes of the world's opinion, even though (or perhaps because) Hardy may have intended to show no more than the anonymous seducer of the traditional ballad.* A similarly ambiguous approach is to be found in *Jude the Obscure*. Hardy clearly states the nature of the kinship between Jude and Arabella:

> . . . there was a momentary flash of intelligence, a dumb announcement of affinity *in posse*, between herself and him, which, so far as Jude Fawley was concerned, had no sort of premeditation in it. She saw that he had singled her out from the three . . . for no reasoned purpose of further acquaintance, but in commonplace obedience to conjunctive orders from headquarters, unconsciously received by unfortunate men when the last intention of their lives is to be occupied with the feminine.[13]

The statement is clear and unequivocal; yet Arabella is more harshly treated by her creator than any other of Hardy's characters—or is she? Critics have seen in her the most odious of Hardy's women, and there are some indications that he agreed with them. Yet he makes Sue, for whom his sympathies are strong, feel an instinctive liking for her.[14] Is there a real ambiguity here, or has it been merely inferred by critics who themselves represent the

* For fuller discussion of Tess, see below, pp. 123-35.

opinion of 'the world'? Or, finally, is Hardy himself torn between the wish to display the instinctual power of sexuality, and his own conditioning by the world? The case seems to me less clear than with Alec d'Urberville, where there appears to be a breakdown of communication between the commentary and the tale, but the question does arise.

Yet when there is no failure of communication the commentary can be extremely effective. As long as we regard it as an exploration of the human environment, and attempt to relate it integrally with the tale Hardy is telling, we have a standard which can be applied to the tale, to the symbolism, and to the use of his traditional material. At their best we find Hardy's novels to be working as a complete organism in which social standards and conventions are judged according to their ability to co-exist with and offset the difficulties inherent in the environment. The rejection of social standards evident in *Tess* and *Jude* is made because society's ways fail to correspond with the natural environment and yet bring no comfort to it; and conduct may be judged according to the same standard. The function of the commentary is to explore the relation between society or individuals and Hardy's universe, and it stands at one extreme from the ballad tale. Between the extremes we look to Hardy's symbolism as the power which fuses tale and commentary, and a clear illustration of this is to be found in *Tess*. At the time of Tess's seduction Hardy introduces the notions of heredity and retribution, and he does so in his own voice:

> Why it was that upon this beautiful feminine tissue, sensitive as gossamer, and practically blank as snow as yet, there should have been traced such a coarse pattern as it was doomed to receive; why so often the coarse appropriates the finer thus, the wrong man the woman, the wrong woman the man, many thousand years of analytical philosophy have failed to explain to our sense of order. One may, indeed, admit the possibility of a retribution lurking in the present catastrophe. Doubtless some of Tess d'Urberville's mailed ancestors rollicking home from a fray had dealt the same measure even more ruthlessly towards peasant girls of their time. But though to visit the sins of the father upon the children may be a morality good enough for divinities, it is scorned by average human nature; and it therefore does not mend the matter.
>
> As Tess's own people down in those retreats never tired of

> saying among each other in their fatalistic way: 'It was to be'. There lay the pity of it. . . .[15]

There is a great deal of complexity here, as indeed there is in the whole episode of Tess's seduction; but for the moment it is enough to note that considerations of heredity, already present in the novel, are again brought into the foreground. When one recalls that Tess's companions at the dairy include at least one other scion of a formerly noble family, it is easy to say that the past greatness of Tess's race is a mere red herring, a useful piece of machinery for the plot and no more. But Hardy does not do things so casually; and the suggestion that her instincts are as much the property of her race as of herself is decisively put in Chapter XLVII:

> Her face had been rising to a dull crimson fire while he spoke; but she did not answer.
>
> 'You have been the cause of my backsliding,' he continued, stretching his arm towards her waist; 'you should be willing to share it, and leave that mule you call husband for ever.'
>
> One of her leather gloves, which she had taken off to eat her skimmer-cake, lay in her lap, and without the slightest warning she passionately swung the glove by the gauntlet directly in his face. It was heavy and thick as a warrior's, and it struck him flat on the mouth. Fancy might have regarded the act as the recrudescence of a trick in which her armed progenitors were not unpractised. Alec fiercely started up from his reclining position. A scarlet oozing appeared where her blow had alighted, and in a moment the blood began dropping from his mouth upon the straw. But he soon controlled himself, calmly drew his handkerchief from his pocket, and mopped his bleeding lips.
>
> She too had sprung up, but she sank down again.
>
> 'Now, punish me!', she said, turning up her eyes to him with the hopeless defiance of the sparrow's gaze before its captor twists its neck. 'Whip me, crush me; you need not mind those people under the rick! I shall not cry out. Once victim, always victim—that's the law!'

The passage is extraordinarily effective, not least because it combines the violence and the passivity of Tess's nature, both of which have been stressed before and after this scene, and because the shedding of blood bringing strangulation as its outcome point us towards the conclusion of the tale. At this moment only 'Fancy' suggests in her action the actions of her forebears—a notable example of Hardy's tact in handling an episode of this sort—yet later, after the blood has been shed and strangulation as a victim of the law is imminent, Angel Clare wonders 'what obscure strain in the d'Urberville blood had led to this aberration—if it were an aberration. There momentarily flashed through his mind that the family tradition of the coach and murder might have arisen because the d'Urbervilles had been known to do these things'.[16] Yet it is not merely the hereditary strain in Tess which is underlined. The change in the social prestige of her race is—again tactfully—stressed also: the leather gloves, once the symbol of might and now only the protection against heavy labour, temporarily removed while she ate her skimmer-cake—a dumpling made of surplus dough,[17] and hardly the ancient fare of the d'Urbervilles. The trapped birds who more than once are paralleled with Tess's fate make their re-appearance in her 'hopeless defiance', her role as victim placed in astonishing juxtaposition with the violence we have just witnessed. The juxtaposition is also stressed in Hardy's commentary, this time in relation to the eviction of the Durbeyfield family:

> . . . Thus the Durbeyfields, once d'Urbervilles, saw descending upon them the destiny which, no doubt, when they were among the Olympians of the county, they had caused to descend many a time, and severely enough, upon the heads of such landless ones as they themselves were now. So do flux and reflux—the rhythm of change—alternate and persist in everything under the sky.[18]

The point which underlies these instances, of course, is that at its best Hardy's commentary is as much a part of the story as the plot; parallel to it, it stresses the broader implications of the theme, without distracting from that theme or blurring the bold lines in which the ballad tale is sketched. The symbolism provides the link between the ballad tale and its modern implications: the complexly-woven details of Tess's character and role ultimately raise questions about the nature of her fate and, for this reader at least, it is more satisfying to meet those questions head-on in the commentary: more satisfying because they are not the only questions raised, and the book affords a series of perspectives too heavy in their irony and ambiguity for the ballad tale to weigh. An approach of this kind explains, though it does not justify, even such passages as Tess's remark that this world is one of the blighted planets*; a remark which is out of place because it is inappropriate, not to this tale, but to this speaker. The question of whether or not it is the author's opinion is irrelevant. Similarly, the question whether the successful passages represent his opinion is irrelevant also: what matters is the degree to which they conform to the vision we have been shown. The 'Aeschylean phrase' may be regarded as a blatant expression of authorial opinion, but what is really important is that in its irony it calls into question the social judgement which pronounces Tess guilty; in its equally ironic association of the President of the Immortals with society's verdict it offers judgement not on any abstract conception of some higher ruling power, but on those who would assign Tess's fortunes to intervention, guidance, or sheer impassiveness on the part of such malignancy. The phrase is certainly ambiguous but, since this is often a quality of irony, so is much of Hardy's art: his purpose is not to explain but to question, and we do him wrong—as he himself so frequently maintained—if we read simple solutions when he has none to offer.

* *Tess*, IV; see below, p. 222.

III

William Dewy, Tranter Reuben, Farmer Ledlow late at plough,
Robert's kin, and John's, and Ned's,
And the Squire, and Lady Susan, lie in Mellstock churchyard now!

C.P. 52

THE ambiguity present in the commentary is to be found throughout the early novels, affecting Hardy's treatment of his tale, his treatment of nature, and the response of his characters. Of *Desperate Remedies* we shall say little at this point. It is a strange work, and it deserves attention; but those qualities in it which are most remarkable are all foreshadowings of later techniques, and they are best seen in relation to the later prose. Moreover, in *Under the Greenwood Tree* we have an early work which displays an assurance which Hardy scarcely equalled in his later works. The concern with change, with the natural environment, and with feminine sexuality and passivity are all present; but they carry with them a mastery of prose which was scarcely intimated in *Desperate Remedies*. Undistorted by irrelevant generalisation, free from self-conscious literary references, and using its few symbols discreetly and naturally, it marks a consistency of sensibility never again equalled in Hardy. It is Hardy at his lightest, but in many senses it is Hardy at his best too. That the treatment of the rustics is occasionally patronising or facetious is admitted; yet such passages play a minor part in the novel and I do not propose to do more with them than note that they are there. It seems more fruitful to point to the qualities of proportion which belie the critical judgement that this is a slight work—a judgement which Hardy regrettably seems to have accepted without demur.

It is no surprise to learn that this was the work of a happy man. Most, probably all, was written during Hardy's courtship of Tryphena Sparks. Yet the book was written, too, after the years in London and after Hardy's loss of faith; so that it is not surprising to find that the book is not all sweetness and light. Its very excellence, in fact, arises because in telling a nostalgic tale of the decay of rustic life, Hardy infuses his theme with an idyllic delicacy which stresses the dignity of the disappearing way. He strikes a balance between awareness of the value of the past and awareness that decline has, in fact, occurred. Landscape plays its part in this balance, since the rural sights and sounds which are Hardy's *métier* are not only closely allied with the human activity which goes on amidst them, but are also lovingly and precisely handled. The tiny rural community is given its home and natural environment with tact and the minimum of self-consciousness, and we see rural life as being in itself a delicate and coherent organism:

> The breeze had gone down, and the rustle of their feet and tones of their speech echoed with an alert rebound from every post, boundary-stone, and ancient wall they passed, even where the distance of the echo's origin was less than a few yards. Beyond their own slight noises nothing was to be heard save the occasional bark of foxes in the direction of Yalbury Wood, or the brush of a rabbit among the grass now and then as it scampered out of their way.[1]

The posts, boundary-stones, and ancient walls mark silently the kinship of these people with the village past: they are men at home in their historical setting and as much a part of the environment as the plants and animals that surround them. Nature itself is ever-present, but its processes are taken for granted, introduced naturally and casually ('. . . and bunches of nuts could not be distinguished from *the leaves which nourished them*'[2]), and man is set in intimate proximity with and relationship to it. Sometimes this can be mildly disconcerting, as Enoch discovers, 'shaking out another emmet that had run merrily up his thigh',[3] but natural processes *are* the environment, and must be worked with. Mr Day's bee-keeping is the most natural thing in the world, literally, and the swarming of Dick Dewey's bees, quite apart from its favourable portent for his marriage,* stresses his community with the local society and environment.

But of course that environment is insecure, and it is the insecurity which is Hardy's theme. For however idyllic Mellstock may be, it is not Arcady, and the impermanence of the ways of life is gently underlined, even as the community is presented to us. As the characters are introduced they are given an air of unreality, and we are reminded that what we see is no more than a *picture* of the past, a loving reconstruction of ways now dead and gone. The sub-title, 'A Rural Painting of the Dutch School', is

* See Firor, *Folkways in Thomas Hardy*, p. 2.

intended to convey more than an impression of a homely, unpretentious narrative: it stands just as much for the basic unreality of the incidents. Our first meeting with Dick Dewey is in a wood where 'all was dark as the grave', and it is truly a voice from the grave that we hear. That voice, it is true, breaks into ancient song, recalling the kinship between human life and the seasons whose movement the book follows:

> . . . with the rose and the lily
> And the daffodowndilly
> The lads and the lasses a-sheep-shearing go,

but when Dick actually appears this living, vigorous presentation which the song conveys is momentarily abandoned, and he appears 'on the light background *like the portrait of a gentleman in black cardboard*'. We are no longer meeting a man, but a representation of something whose reality is past. The same is true of the Mellstock Quire, disbanded in reality in Hardy's earliest years:

> They, too, had lost their rotundity with the daylight, and advanced against the sky in flat outlines, which suggested some processional design on Greek or Etruscan pottery.[4]

Yet if they are no longer real in the flesh, they have their own kind of permanence, for the image of Greek and Etruscan pottery is double-edged. The choir may no longer possess its own reality, yet it does achieve immortality. The tale is invested with its own sense of the timeless, its nostalgia appeals to the immortalising powers of memory and legend, and in the integrity of the Mellstock Quire the survival of its members is sure. We are told so, directly on our first entry into the gallery of the ancient church:

> In the pauses of conversation there could be heard through the floor overhead a little world of undertones and creaks from the halting clockwork, which never spread further than the tower they were born in, and raised in the more meditative minds a fancy that here lay the direct pathway of Time.[5]

The sounds of the clock are metaphorically allied to the members of the choir in the phrase 'which never spread further than the tower they were born in'. Time functions in this book in its traditional roles of preserver and destroyer. It is the progress of

Time which threatens the existence of ancient ways and customs, just as it enshrines them. It is Time which Fancy brings into the village with her new ways, her astonishment at rustic habits and speech, and her reluctant realliance with them.

Yet Time is not the only force that threatens Arcady. As in *Desperate Remedies*, the heroine is invested with as much sexuality as the book allows. Her physical appearance, particularly at the dance in the tranter's home, is carefully indicated, and indeed enhanced by the sweaty neighbours who foot it with her. Her coquettishness, which she acknowledges and to some extent delights in, is a potentially subversive force, and in this and her possession of a secret which she is reluctant to reveal she foreshadows the later heroines. That last cool phrase—'and thought of a secret she would never tell'—carries in it the tragic germ of later plots, and with the benefit of hindsight we may see Fancy Day the coquette as the predecessor of Sue Bridehead, however different this idyll may be from *Jude the Obscure* in other respects.* This is no more than biographical accident, for Fancy is almost certainly modelled on Tryphena Sparks. Like Tryphena, and like Sue Bridehead, she is educated outside her normal environment, and brings into it destructive forces; she is a Queen's Scholar and endowed with considerable intelligence. She has a child-like quality which is nowhere more stressed than in a single verb—'O, O, O, Dick! she cried, *trotting* after him like a pet lamb'[6]—a verb which recurs in *A Pair of Blue Eyes*, but which is most notably and consistently applied to Sue in the last great novel. She occasionally suffers from the passivity common to so many of Hardy's women—'she felt that she was in a measure captured and made a prisoner'[7]—and in her coquetry she utters a sentence which might easily have been the property of Sue:

> 'Dick, I always believe in flattery *if possible*—and it was possible then. Now there's an open confession of weakness. But I showed no consciousness of it'.[8]
>
> 'I like to hear you praise me in that way, Dick', she said, smiling archly, 'It is meat and drink to a woman.'[9]

There are individual scenes, most notably the conversation from the schoolroom window, which parallel Sue's later relationship with Jude. These parallels in no way detract from Fancy's reality: they merely stress that Hardy's comparative failure in the portrait

* There are also some interesting parallels with *The Woodlanders*.

of Cytherea Graye in *Desperate Remedies* has been overcome, almost certainly through closer knowledge of his living model; Hardy is already on the path to the portraits of his maturity. That Fancy, unlike Sue, is ultimately reconciled to the society from which she drew her being is a measure of the degree of alienation which overtakes Hardy's heroes and heroines as he proceeds along his path as a novelist.

Fancy, of course, never reaches the point where her indiscretions can result in catastrophe: but the threat is there. There are other reminders, too, that we are not in Arcady. The natural environment surrounding the community is natural in all its ways, and not all its ways are good:

> . . . the stillness was disturbed only by some small bird that was being killed by an owl in the adjoining wood, whose cry passed into the silence without mingling with it.[10]

Other passages might easily be taken from Hardy's description of the much less idyllic setting of *The Woodlanders*, and possess equal maturity of approach:

> A single vast gray cloud covered the country, from which the small rain and mist had just begun to blow down in wavy sheets, alternately thick and thin. The trees of the fields and plantations writhed like miserable men as the air wound its way swiftly among them: the lowest portions of their trunks, that had hardly ever been known to move, were visibly rocked by the fiercer gusts, distressing the mind by its painful unwontedness, as when a strong man is seen to shed tears. Low-hanging boughs went up and down; high and erect boughs went to and fro; the blasts being so irregular, and divided into so many cross-currents, that neighbouring branches of the same tree swept the skies in independent motions, crossed each other, or became entangled. Across the open spaces flew flocks of green and yellowish leaves, which, after travelling a long distance from their parent trees, reached the ground and lay there with their undersides upward . . .'

Under the Greenwood Tree is characteristic of the later novels in other respects, too, and subtly so. The apparent incompatibility between the old world and the new is already obvious: the very fact that Fancy Day must make a choice suggests that it is not possible for the two worlds to live side by side permanently, and this is again suggested by the interview between the choir and the young vicar. Faced with each other's difficulties, and understanding them, each party is none the less embarrassed and finds itself inadequate to meet the situation. The apparent failure caused by Hardy's introduction of Thomas Leaf into the discussion seems to me to be more of a screening device, allowing Hardy to present the mutual discomfort but sheltering him from the deeper perceptions involved. The mutual uneasiness is there: anything deeper would have marred the book as we have it, and to demand an alternative treatment at this point is, I believe, to demand a very different book.

There is, too, the real but lightly-handled knowledge of the inadequacies of the old rural life. Here Hardy's attention is centred on the 'witch', Elizabeth Endorfield, whose pretence to common sense is so much mistaken and wrongly valued by the community. Hardy's comment here is instructive:

> It may be stated that Elizabeth belonged to a class of suspects who were gradually losing their mysterious characteristics under the administration of the young vicar; though during the long reign of Mr Grinham the parish of Mellstock had proved extremely favourable to the growth of witches.[12]

Here is village superstition: the clumsiness in much village life is apparent during the party at the tranter's, at Dick's meeting with Fancy, and in the inscription on Dick's business-card, presented just as he is about to carry off Fancy in marriage—'Live and dead stock removed to any distance on the shortest notice'.[13] The nostalgia for ancient ways is not uncritical, nor naïve.

But it is not unreal, either. The essential integrity of Mellstock is captured chiefly in the figure of old William, who exercises a humane discipline over the choir, who is throughout plainly the object of the author's sympathy, and whose immortality is suggested openly and directly:

> Some of the youthful sparkle that used to reside there animated William's eye as he uttered the words, and a certain nobility of aspect was also imparted to him by the setting sun, which gave him a Titanic shadow at least thirty feet in length, stretching away to the east in outlines of imposing magnitude, his head finally terminating upon the trunk of a grand old oak-tree.[14]

The essential balance of the book is suggested at its close. The wedding-feast held with rustic simplicity in the open air, sheltered by a firm and ancient tree, and full of the reminders of birth and maturity in the natural world surrounding the bride. The omens appear fair; yet at the same time they are overshadowed by other presences. The tree itself has 'quaint tufts of fungi' in the forks of its branches, as if the old is already preparing for decay; Fancy's attention to dress and her concern lest older customs should seem unfitting, together with her insistence that the tranter should wear an ill-fitting pair of gloves on his awkward hands; and Enoch, the absent guest who refuses the invitation to the wedding, are all enough to shadow the end of this quiet tale, without throwing over it a disproportionate gloom. The last chapter, like the book, is a pleasing and delicate achievement. Hardy's home, his family, fiancée, and their neighbours, are preserved in a gently-dappled light, as yet unembittered by reflection or personal experience.[15]

The delicacy of this work, however, may perhaps mask for us its unity with Hardy's later novels. If this is so, it is because greater stress is laid on the disappearance of the old way than on the plot *per se*, and it is Hardy's sympathetic handling of the theme of rural decline that most seizes our attention. Not, obviously, that the theme is absent from the later works, but that it is more to the forefront here, the lovers representing the old and new ways respectively: their significance for the work lies primarily in their relation to the community, and character as such plays a lesser part than in many of the books. We watch the community as eagerly as we watch individuals, though both are grappling with the problem of adaptation. At this point it is primarily adaptation to the man-made environment, to new, human, ideas of 'progress'. Though the darker side of the natural environment is present, it is not stressed, and in general the community is in harmony with it, Hardy depicting, even at this early stage of his career, the organic unity which his notes discuss. However, the plot—stated simply in terms of a young woman's choice between two men—is the staple of the greater number of the Wessex novels; and it is substantially influential in *A Pair of Blue Eyes*. Where the crisis occurs it occurs because a choice has to be made. For Fancy Day the choice is made easier than for any other of Hardy's heroines, and her recognition of personal responsibility towards Dick Dewey comes with little difficulty, partly aided by Dick's meeting with the vicar, partly because hers is a choice between love and social status, rather than between an old love and a new. The choice for Elfride Swancourt is harder, both in itself—Knight is in many ways superior to Stephen Smith, and Elfride's attachment to him is made to appear more powerful and instinctive than Fancy's brief flirtation with Mr Maybold —and because of the circumstances which surround it. One may freely admit the presence of too many coincidences in *A Pair of Blue Eyes* (H. C. Webster counted thirty-seven 'major' coincidences[16]), yet the crux of the book is still Elfride's decision and, to a lesser extent, the powers of decision in Knight and Stephen Smith. In this *A Pair of Blue Eyes* resembles *Desperate Remedies*: there the whole book turns on the 'accident' of a fire which burns down a valuable group of cottages; but the fire could, and should, have been avoided by greater foresight on the part of Farmer Springrove; and the consequences of the fire could, and should, have been avoided by a more urgent attention to the insurance policies which guarded the gutted row of buildings. No amount of coincidence affects the characters of *Desperate Remedies* as much as these two failures on the part of one man. Similarly, it is true that Elfride Swancourt is powerless against Henry Knight's selfish intolerance; but it is also true that but for her own actions with Stephen Smith, Knight's intractability would not have shown itself in such a disastrous form. And her decision to attempt an elopement with Stephen is based on a frivolity of behaviour that outweighs any interference by Chance. Here the author's attitude is openly expressed.[17] Elfride, 'as if unconsciously' changes her purpose as she rides towards St Launce's, only to change again and resume her ride. Eventually, 'overwrought and trembling' she '*vowed she would be led whither the horse would take her*', and, for reasons which Hardy fully explains (the prospect of more nourishing food at St Launce's), the horse continues its progress away from home. Hardy's direct comment on this pattern of behaviour is made quite explicit: Elfride's is a 'rash action', the result of an 'inane vow' followed at the command of a 'dreamy fancy'. His indirect commentary suggests the same verdict. As Elfride gazed into a road-side pool she contrasts its placidity to the turbulence of her own feelings: but the insects upon it are noted for their 'idle motions', the vegetation waves placidly in the wind—and Elfride, by resigning her powers of choice is equally idle and equally at the mercy of the winds of chance and circumstance and of cause and effect. Elfride does no more than align herself with lower orders of life, and the leaf-skeletons at the bottom of the pool may be intended to suggest the tragic result of just such a refusal to decide.

Certainly there is a quality of innocence and inexperience about Elfride which may tend to disarm one's judgement of her—Hardy tells us that she knew 'no more about the stings of evil report than the native wild-fowl knew of the effects of Crusoe's first shot';[18] but we are also given some clues to Elfride's character which force our judgement in the opposite direction. Elfride's 'capacity for being wounded was only surpassed by her capacity for healing, which rightly or wrongly is by some considered an index of transientness of feeling in general';[19] 'She dismissed the sense of sin in her past actions, and was automatic in the intoxication of the moment';[20] 'She never alluded to even a knowledge of Knight's friend';[21] 'Her natural honesty invited her to confide in Knight. But she put it off';[22] 'Her resolution . . . had been to tell the whole truth, and now the moment had come. . . . The moment had been too much for her'.[23] And later, with much irony, 'It was a particular pleasure for her to be able to do a little honesty without fear'.[24] I believe we are asked to recognise her action, or lack of action, as a piece of gratuitous folly. For Elfride is *not* innocent: she has already experienced the consequence of rashly encouraging a man in the past, and her former encouragement played its part in her eventual rejection by Knight. The young Jethway makes his influence felt very early in the book, and widow Jethway returns at vital intervals to sway the action. The machinery is clumsy, but the point is made: Elfride, whether she had deliberately encouraged young Jethway or not, has led him to think he was being encouraged. In this she may not have been culpable: in her knowledge of the consequences, and her refusal or inability to learn from them, she was.

Her abandonment of Stephen is, of course, another matter. All the effects of the cliff-rescue and the emotional shock which follows it make her transition from one lover to another now inevitable. But even here the moment of decision is already past:

> There before her lay the deposit-receipt for the two hundred pounds, and beside it the elegant present of Knight. . . . She almost feared to let the two articles lie in juxtaposition: so antagonistic were the interests they represented that a miraculous repulsion of one by the other was almost to be expected. . . . By the evening she had come to a resolution, and acted upon it. The packet was sealed up—with a tear of regret as she closed the case upon the pretty forms it contained—directed, and placed upon the writing-table in Knight's room. And

> a letter was written to Stephen stating that as yet she hardly understood her position with regard to the money sent; but declaring that she was ready to fulfil her promise to marry him. After this letter had been written *she delayed posting it—although never ceasing to feel strenuously that the deed must be done.*
>
> Several days passed . . .[25]

Hardy notes her steadfastness 'in her opinion that honour compelled her to meet' Stephen, but goes on, 'for she was markedly one of those who sigh for the unattainable—to whom, superlatively, a hope is pleasing because not a possession', and she begins to see her projected renunciation of Knight as a virtue of self-sacrifice upon the altar of duty. There can be no question, of course, of Hardy believing that she *should* sacrifice herself to 'honour'—indeed, on the question of what she ought to do he is markedly reticent. The only implication which seems to be drawn is that having allowed her power of decision to become atrophied in one instance, she has now opened up a pattern of consequence which any further abdication of judgement will only aggravate. The dilemna he isolates is perfectly clear: marriage with Stephen is unlikely to prove ideal after her love for Knight, but a refusal to marry Stephen at this stage must lead inevitably not only to the loss of Stephen himself but also to the loss of Henry Knight.

Decisions are not formed in a vacuum, however, and Elfride is not solely responsible for her fate. Whatever she decides is judged in a context which includes others, and most notably the two men who love her. Hardy's execution here is so inferior to his idea that the conflict of personalities is scarcely realised, if at all: Stephen Smith is a nonentity, and with Elfride's rejection of him his importance for the novel is virtually at an end. Yet in one respect he shows superiority over his rival: he at least accepts Elfride for what she is, and there is no vain attempt to force her to his wishes; 'his tact in avoiding catastrophes was the chief quality which made him intellectually respectable, in which quality he far transcended Knight'.[26] Knight, on the other hand, is obviously a first draft for Angel Clare, and in his idealisation of his own dreams, and his refusal to accept Elfride when she falls below his ideal, he bears more responsibility than any other figure. Here, too, Hardy is quite explicit:

> It is a melancholy thought that men who at first will not allow the verdict of perfection they pronounce upon their

sweethearts or wives to be disturbed by God's own testimony to the contrary, will, once suspecting their purity, morally hang them upon evidence they would be ashamed to admit in judging a dog.[27]

The moral rightness of this man's life was worthy of all praise; but in spite of some intellectual acumen, Knight had in him a modicum of that wrong-headedness which is mostly found in scrupulously honest people. With him, truth seemed too clean and pure an abstraction to be so hopelessly churned in with error as practical persons find it. Having now seen himself mistaken in supposing Elfride to be peerless, nothing on earth could make him believe she was not so very bad after all.[28]

Knight is inconsistent: he condemns Elfride's love of adornment, but feels a sense of triumph in buying her the very ear-rings he professes to despise. He shows Stephen the surging mass of humanity living and working below his London office; but in his idealism he betrays an ignorance of real life, and demands the placid life of the fish-tank which decorates the interior of his room. He is no sooner saved from the cliff-fall by Elfride than he is conscious of the power of 'a thorough drenching for reducing the protuberances of clothes, . . . Elfride's seemed to cling to her like a glove':[29]—like Angel Clare, his motives are underlaid by a repressed sexuality, hidden even from himself. This, together with the attraction of her 'inexperienced state', puts the morality of his behaviour on a more questionable level, not because his sexuality is reprehensible, but because he treats Elfride not as a person, but as a thing. Her plea, 'Am I such a mere characterless toy?' is made with good reason: 'Haven't I brains? . . . Have I not some beauty? . . . Yet all these together are so much rubbish because I—accidentally saw a man before you!'[30]

It is difficult not to believe that there are autobiographical forces at work here. *A Pair of Blue Eyes* was first published in serial form in 1872, just about the time—perhaps a little after—that Tryphena returned Hardy's ring; but the work was plotted and partly-written well before this date. Clearly some of the circumstances of the book reflect Hardy's visits to St Juliot, yet the book's origin was not to be found there:

The character and appearance of Elfride have points in common with those of Mrs Hardy in quite young womanhood, a few years before Hardy met her (though her eyes would have

> been described as deep grey, not as blue); moreover, like Elfride, the moment she was on a horse she was part of the animal. But this is all that can be asserted, the plot of the story being one that he had thought of and written down long before he knew her.[31]

It is striking, in fact, that the two works written most nearly at the same time as Hardy's association with Tryphena, *Under the Greenwood Tree* and *A Pair of Blue Eyes,* should be so closely parallel in theme, incident, and character as the two books written immediately after her death: *Tess of the D'Urbervilles* and *Jude the Obscure.* Lois Deacon and Terry Coleman defined the plot of *A Pair of Blue Eyes* and *Tess* as 'a pure woman, hunted by circumstances, . . . destroyed by two men'.[32] The same may obviously be applied to a lesser extent to *Jude the Obscure* (Sue's character and the presence of Arabella complicate matters), but it would be less complex to define *Jude* as a work whose heroine destroys two men—Jude himself and the unnamed leader-writer—with perhaps a third potential victim (Phillotson) barely escaping, and only by becoming a destructive force himself. Some elements of this pattern are present in *Under the Greenwood Tree*: the nature of the book is very different, the tone even more so, but it is none the less true that Fancy Day is in a position to destroy Dick Dewey and Parson Maybold. What we seem to witness in these four books are various approaches to the Tryphena theme, each different in stress or mood, and none so explicit as *Jude the Obscure.* If this is indeed true, Lois Deacon's theory that Horace Moule was somehow involved receives a certain amount of support: the closest parallels between *A Pair of Blue Eyes* and *Tess* are to be found in the details of characterisation of Henry Knight and Angel Clare. Knight is a reviewer for a London journal, Clare is the son of a devout country priest. Moule was both of these things, and old parson Clare of the later book is known to have been modelled closely on Moule's father. This may, of course, be nothing but coincidence—Hardy believed that there were as many coincidences in life as there are in his works, and if we choose to share his belief I suppose we cannot be blamed. Personally, however, I do not.

None the less, *A Pair of Blue Eyes* is not simply an autobiographical novel. The issues raised already show that it contains a remarkably keen, sometimes merciless, examination of human motives: an examination all the more remarkable in that Hardy can condemn his characters without losing sympathy for them.

Yet Knight's judgement over Elfride's grave suggests a sympathy based on other grounds:

> 'Can we call her ambitious? No. Circumstance has, as usual, overpowered her purposes—fragile and delicate as she—liable to be overthrown in a moment by the coarse elements of accident.'[33]

This can only be read as deliberate irony of the author's part: Knight's role in Elfride's destruction is considerably more important than any played by Chance.

This is not to suggest that Circumstance plays no part in the novel. With the pattern of coincidence that permeates the book we need concern ourselves little: but it is there, and it affects the course of the action. Yet it does not affect the responses of any major character at moments of decision, except to reinforce decisions already taken. Hardy himself points to the major coincidence of the book:

> That Knight should have been thus constituted: that Elfride's second lover should not have been one of the great mass of bustling mankind, little given to introspection, whose good-nature might have compensated for any lack of appreciativeness, was the chance of things. That her throbbing, self-confounding, indiscreet heart should have to defend itself unaided against the keen scrutiny and logical power which Knight, now that his suspicions were awakened, would sooner or later be sure to exercise against her, was her misfortune. A miserable incongruity was apparent in the circumstances of a strong mind practising its unerring archery upon a heart which the owner of that mind loved better than his own.[34]

As Hardy suggests,[35] in this sense every meeting of two persons is attributable to circumstance. The point still remains that Elfride could not have been subjected to Knight's 'unerring archery' had she not herself first given a hostage to fortune by resigning her own will to the instincts of a horse—a ludicrous abdication of responsibility which opens the door to the forces of cause and effect. As for Knight, he is so concerned with his 'dignity'[36] that he loses all sense of proportion and sympathy. These are not accidents, but regions in which human responsibility can reasonably be expected to play a part.

Lest this should seem an unduly harsh judgement of Hardy's

characters, and one contrary to Hardy's intention, we should pause to consider the much-praised description of the accident on the Cliff Without a Name.[37] This is long, and it is self-consciously executed. But its length has a purely mechanical purpose—the simple purpose of creating suspense, in which it is not particularly successful—and its self-consciousness is perhaps the inevitable result of Hardy's close attention to the implications of his scene. It is sometimes read as an account of man's insignificance in the process of evolution: *yet what it says is exactly the opposite*. Knight, hanging on the cliff, finds himself face to face with 'one of the early crustaceans called Trilobites', 'the single instance within reach of his vision of anything that had ever been alive and had had a body to save, as he himself had now'. But the trilobite had not been saved. Its extinction is accounted for in terms which have an obvious relevance to man:

> The creature represented but a low type of animal existence, for never in their vernal years had the plains indicated by those numberless slaty layers been traversed by an intelligence worthy of the name.

And immediately after:

> The immense lapses of time each formation represented had known nothing of the dignity of man.

If we accept that this scene shows us the insignificance of man, this sentence becomes a piece of gratuitous irony; and surely its point is that it is man's intelligence which gives him dignity, and Knight is here an illustration of it. He clings to the cliff 'not with the frenzied hold of despair, but with a dogged determination to make the most of every jot of endurance, and so give the longest possible scope to Elfride's intentions, whatever they might be'. The cliff itself becomes a symbol of circumstance, and the conditions of Knight's struggle are openly paralleled with the condition of man:

> To those musing weather-beaten West-country folk who pass the greater part of their days and nights out of doors, Nature seems to have moods in other than a poetical sense: predilections for certain deeds at certain times, without any apparent law to govern or season to account for them. She is read as a person with a curious temper; as one who does not scatter

> kindnesses and cruelties alternately, impartially, and in order, but heartless severities or overwhelming generosities in lawless caprice. Man's case is always that of the prodigal's favourite or the miser's pensioner. In her unfriendly moments there seems a feline fun in her tricks, begotten by a foretaste of her pleasure in swallowing the victim.
>
> Such a way of thinking had been absurd to Knight, but he began to adopt it now. . . . We are mostly accustomed to look upon all opposition which is not animate as that of the stolid, inexorable hand of indifference, which wears out the patience more than the strength. Here, at any rate, hostility did not assume that slow and sickening form. It was a cosmic agency, active, lashing, eager for conquest: determination; not an insensate standing in the way.

The transition here is important: West-country people feel this way: Knight began to feel this; then the agency *is* 'lashing, eager for conquest'. Yet that this is obviously only Knight's train of thought, a result of extreme stress, we are told: the elements themselves seem more than usually angry, although the 'rain was quite ordinary in quantity; the air in temperature'. Finally, Hardy writes:

> A fancy some people hold, when in a bitter mood, is that inexorable circumstance only tries to prevent what intelligence attempts.

As Knight's trust in Elfride's ingenuity recedes so he becomes consciously more and more convinced of the cosmic agencies hostile to man, and the whole tenor of the second half of the passage is to reinforce the view that whatever is desired by man is withheld from him in a deliberate effort by Nature to tantalise him. But Knight is wrong: his ability to hold on to the cliff for so long has been due to his trust in Elfride; and as his resolution reaches its end he is given new determination because Elfride does act. With presence of mind, forming the rope from her knotted underclothes, she shows how intelligence may overcome circumstance, and Knight grasps her lesson quickly:

> 'Now,' said Knight, who, watching the proceedings intently, had by this time not only grasped her scheme, but reasoned further on, 'I can hold three minutes longer yet. And do you use the time in testing the strength of the knots, one by one.'

> She at once obeyed, testing each singly by putting her foot on the rope between each knot, and pulling with her hands. One of the knots slipped.
>
> 'O think!, it would have broken but for your forethought!,' Elfride exclaimed apprehensively.

So we have a novel in which there is continual stress on circumstance and the power of accident, but which can be read as an illustration of false choice; and at the heart of the novel as its most dramatic incident, we have a scene which stresses man's place in the evolutionary pattern, the power of the elements, and the power of circumstance—and yet places its final stress on the defeat of those forces by human ingenuity.

There are many aspects which have been ignored. There is, for example, a tentative attempt to establish a pattern of imagery and symbol which would reinforce the 'circumstance motif' if it were successful, and in particular there are the beginnings of a scheme of proleptic imagery foreshadowing Elfride's eventual decline and death. In the greater novels, where its success is more apparent, we cannot ignore it—in *Tess* above all. Much of the schematic pattern attempted in *A Pair of Blue Eyes* would lend weight to those who believe that Hardy's characters are without a defence against circumstance; but if read in this way it would make little sense of the action of the book, concerned as much as it is with motivation and relationships between one person and another. *A Pair of Blue Eyes*, seen alone or in common with the later novels, shows the superiority of the human intelligence in the evolutionary pattern, and attempts to show the strength of the forces which intelligence can, at its best, defeat. Elfride's tragedy is that her intelligence serves her only at a physical crisis, and then on behalf of the man who is primarily responsible for her defeat. In moral crises she has no intelligence at all.

IV

Part is mine of the general Will,
Cannot my share in the sum of sources
Bend a digit the poise of forces,
And a fair desire fulfil?

C.P. 479

EACH of Hardy's earlier novels had been written under special circumstances which occasionally interfered with success, and which certainly justify us in regarding them as experimental works. *Desperate Remedies* was a reaction against the first, unpublished work, *The Poor Man and the Lady*; and its adherence to the advice of George Meredith, with the consequent debt to Wilkie Collins's sensational works, is not much to its advantage. *Under the Greenwood Tree* is successful because Hardy was not drawn too deeply into an analysis of rural decline, nor did he become too morbidly involved with his own personal affairs.* In a *Pair of Blue Eyes* autobiographical elements are again present, the young Tryphena Sparks disguised under the features of Hardy's first wife, for example, and Cornwall selected as the setting. Even here, though, Hardy's chief problem was not personal, but was one of expression and setting: his feeling for the Cornish landscape, whatever it may have become *after* the death of his first wife, does not appear to be very deeply engaged, while his search for a way of expressing his conclusions about human conduct and choice is hampered because he is still dogged by a youthful conception of Chance and Coincidence, and has not yet absorbed it into a larger scheme. Against all this, *Far From the Madding Crowd* marks the end of an apprenticeship, and it has rightly been seen as the 'most characteristic' of Hardy's successful novels.[1] It has all the ingredients of a ballad tale, it strikes a balance between rural strength and rural weaknesses, its lovers are the three stock types—the staunch, rejected lover, the passionately unstable man, and the philanderer; and in its attention to the great consequences of trivial beginnings it focuses most

* I accept Lois Deacon's view that the emotional relationships between Hardy, Tryphena, and Horace Moule form the basis for this early work. See *Providence and Mr Hardy*, Ch. 9.

clearly upon one of the central preoccupations of Hardy's novels. If the book lacks the power of some of Hardy's later work, this may be because his perspective here is more consistently maintained. Neither autobiographical matter nor ideological matter is allowed to dominate the tale. It is true that one of Hardy's aunts, Martha Sharpe, was the model for Bathsheba;[2] it is true that the novel possesses a strongly marked point of view about the meaning of 'good', i.e. beneficially productive, conduct. Yet these considerations are not allowed to affect the proportions of the novel, and indeed, it is to the moral point of view and to Hardy's success in finding a correlation between individuals and the environment that the book owes its coherence. Although so strongly rooted in the 'ballad' tradition, *Far From the Madding Crowd* is a moral work.

This said, we may do well to counter, firstly, the specific objection made by Henry James that the book is essentially a tale made inordinately long by superfluous padding;[3] and, secondly, it is instructive to discuss the general objections to Hardy's work made by T. S. Eliot.[4]

James, in failing to see the organic nature of Hardy's rural society, failed to see the relevance of many of the rustic scenes, commenting:

> Mr Hardy's novel is very long, but his subject is very short and simple, and the work has been distended to rather formidable dimensions by the infusion of a large amount of conversational and descriptive padding, and the use of an ingeniously verbose and redundant style. It is inordinately diffuse, and as a piece of narrative singularly inartistic. The author has little sense of proportion, and almost none of composition.[5]

I take the term *inartistic* to imply substantially the same as a lack of proportion or composition; and as I understand James's criticism he is almost wholly concerned with the demands of the tale and the treatment given to it. Yet in general terms James had agreed with Walter Besant that fiction should have a 'conscious moral purpose',[6] and the proportions of Hardy's novel are wholly dictated by such a purpose. He is not entirely successful in this—the closing stages of Fanny Robin's career seem to be dwelt upon excessively—but he is more successful than James has noted—if, indeed, James noticed the moral purpose at all.

For *Far From the Madding Crowd* is a study of personal equilibrium within a specific, named society. It discusses the nature of equilibrium, and the effect of a disturbance of equilibrium on individuals and society. Without seeing Weatherbury as a total organism I doubt whether one can make much sense of the work except at the ballad level: *then*, indeed, it appears inordinately padded. But Hardy appears to be fulfilling two of the very requirements which James himself had laid down for the novel: he is recording an 'impression of life', and in doing so he attempts to give an 'air of reality (solidity of specification)' to his work.* The rural society which Hardy shows is in a state of equilibrium which retains much that is valuable in the old tradition. Yet equilibrium, which Hardy defines as 'the perfect balance of enormous antagonistic forces',[7] is not a permanent state: it can be destroyed, for better or worse, by a violent alteration of the balance, or for the worse only, by a slow decay of the forces which maintain it. Weatherbury is approaching the latter state, and some positive impetus is necessary before any wholesome balance, let alone any progress, may be re-established. That impetus is provided by the entry of Gabriel Oak into Weatherbury society; while a negative impetus is also provided by the influence of Sergeant Troy. Since much of Oak's significance lies in his role as a restorer and preserver of society, it is difficult to see how Hardy can escape a full discussion of the rural environment. Troy's case is perhaps less obvious, but his disruptive force is apparent, and not only in such incidents as the corruption of local labour and the consequent danger to Bathsheba's ricks.† Troy appears primarily as a lover, and the eventual husband to Bathsheba; and in his danger to Bathsheba lies his danger to the community. For of all Bathsheba's workmen, only Oak possesses and retains independence. Excepting him, the whole of Weatherbury Farm revolves around and depends upon Bathsheba's person. It is a simple question of economic dependence, but such questions are frequently vital to Hardy's plots, and in this instance the 'mean bread-and-cheese question' is at the root of a

* 'The Art of Fiction', p. 54: 'A novel is, in its broadest definition, a direct impression of life; that, to begin with, constitutes its value, which is more or less according to the intensity of the impression'. See also p. 57: 'the air of reality (solidity of specification) seems to me to be the supreme virtue of a novel'.

† Ch. XXXVI. The angelic qualities of Gabriel's name and the 'Satanic symbolism' which surrounds Sergeant Troy suggest the roles that Hardy had in mind. See J. O. Bailey, 'Hardy's "Mephistophelian Visitants" ', *PMLA*, LXI, pp. 1146-84.

rural order whose survival is closely-knit with the moral survival of its principal members. Indeed, the inter-relationship between environmental stability, economic stability, and moral stability is one of Hardy's most subtle and valuable perceptions.

That one aspect of the book is concerned wholly with the material well-being of its characters is implied by the praise which Hardy bestows on the great barn.[8] The barn, Hardy's composite of the great tithe barns of Cerne Abbas and Abbotsbury, represents rural continuity at its best, and its permanence is attributed directly to its purpose:

> Standing before this abraded pile, the eye regarded its present usage, the mind dwelt upon its past history, with a satisfied sense of functional continuity throughout—a feeling almost of gratitude, and quite of pride, at the permanence of the idea which had heaped it up. The fact that four centuries had neither proved it to be founded on a mistake, inspired any hatred of its purpose, nor given rise to any reaction that had battered it down, invested this simple grey effort of old minds with a repose, if not a grandeur, which a too curious reflection was apt to disturb in its ecclesiastical and military compeers. For once mediaevalism and modernism had a common standpoint. The lanceolate windows, the time-eaten arch-stones and chamfers, the orientation of the axis, the misty chestnut work of the rafters, referred to no exploded fortifying art or worn-out religious creed. The defence and salvation of the body by daily bread is still a study, a religion, and a desire.

Yet when Hardy adds, 'So the barn was natural to the shearers, and the shearers were in harmony with the barn', I doubt whether we are asked to see an order which is somehow inevitable for the countryside. His choice of words here is important: it is *the barn*, and what it stands for, that is natural. That the shearers are in harmony with it, that their purpose too is the defence and salvation of the body by daily bread' is the result only of Oak's civilising influence—the same men are equally capable of leaving the ricks to soak and rot in the storm. Some have seen *Far From the Madding Crowd* as the portrayal of a struggle between rural, or natural, surroundings, and urban or civilised values;[9] this is a misleading simplification, perhaps caused by an irony (of which Hardy seems to have been unaware) in the title of the book. If the world 'natural' is taken to mean simply 'unaffected by civilisation, unsophisticated', then the nature, i.e. the human nature, of Weatherbury folk is seen to be not merely unsophisticated, but inadequate and partially corrupt. On Oak's first arrival at Weatherbury the local folk reveal themselves as 'belonging to the class of society which casts its thoughts into the form of feeling, and its feeling into the form of commotion';[10] and it is Oak who saves the ricks from fire. Oak's superior position on Bathsheba's farm is due largely to the dismissal of a thieving bailiff; his attempt to prevent Bathsheba from gaining early knowledge of Fanny Robin's child is foiled by the local predilection for tippling; his second salvation of the ricks is almost foiled by the same weakness, this time aggravated by Troy's corruption; Bathsheba's sheep would have been destroyed but for Oak's skill, the locals remaining ignorant of the finer techniques even of their own world. Everywhere it is the skill of Oak which must be called upon to defend Bathsheba's property, which often takes 'the divinest form that money can wear—that of necessary food for man and beast'. What we see demonstrated is that rural values, indeed any values, can only be maintained through a continued and skilful adaptation to new circumstances.

The point is, of course, not that Oak represents the natural world—he does not—but that he understands it. Howard Babb sees nature as a sympathetic, even a moral force;[11] Gabriel Oak does not. Nature is a-moral, generous with her gifts but wasteful of them too. Just as one of Gabriel's earlier tasks is to save Bathsheba's ricks from destruction through man's negligence, so later he has to battle against nature to save them from nature's own profligate waste. Learning through his ill-fortune and personal negligence (his dead flock were not insured, his half-trained dog had been fed on raw mutton) he becomes the guardian of Weatherbury society precisely because of his understanding of nature as a force to be used or outwitted, but never to be trusted alone for the material salvation of man. To an understanding of nature must be added the skills of man; then, and only then, can there be some opportunity for existence independent of the environment.

The rural environment is thus stressed, but in relation to a society whose resources are of themselves inadequate, just as human nature itself is inadequate without the benefits of self-control, and self-discipline. The barn, symbol of the chief vocation of rural folk, is man-made, an attempt to ward off the hazards threatened by nature, a refuge and a defence, and a testimony of past competence in the rural world. But now the security of rural life is threatened not only by the shortcomings of the workfolk, but also the hazards faced by their mistress; and just as Gabriel guards the community, renewing its equilibrium and reinvigorating it, so he guards Bathsheba. Around him all the social and individual concerns are centred: he redresses the balance of the community by the preservation of the old skills (thatching the ricks) and the introduction of new (curing the sheep), and the personal equilibrium which he possesses and which allows him to do this is our touchstone for Hardy's treatment of the remaining figures.

For the equilibrium of society is matched and partly maintained by a personal balance, also delicate, also in permanent need of renewal. Oak's is well-nigh destroyed by the loss of his flock, and is only regained by rigid self-control. So far from possessing only 'natural' virtues, Oak is governed by self-taught, acquired qualities which subordinate the natural man to the needs of others. He is clearly Hardy's hero, and the nature of his heroism has never been better stated than by T. S. Eliot. Since Eliot was *condemning* Hardy's work it is as well to record his view at some length:

> It is only, indeed, in their emotional paroxysms that most of Hardy's characters come alive. This extreme emotionalism seems to me a symptom of decadence; it is a cardinal point of faith in a romantic age, to believe that there is something admirable in violent emotion for its own sake, whatever the emotion or whatever its object. But it is by no means self-evident that human beings are most real when most violently excited; violent physical passions do not in themselves differentiate men from each other; but rather tend to reduce them to the same state; and the passion has significance only in relation to the character and behaviour of the man at other moments of his life and in other contexts. Furthermore, strong passion is only interesting in strong men; those who abandon themselves without resistance to excitements which tend to deprive them of reason, become merely instruments of feeling and lose their humanity; and unless there is moral resistance there is no meaning.[12]

These remarks, one suspects, are the direct consequence of the manner in which Hardy's works were once read, and there is a good deal of criticism sympathetic to Hardy which would appear to justify Eliot's hostile view. Yet, carefully read, Hardy can be seen to be putting forward a case which is identical to Eliot's. Certainly I know of no better exposition of the moral purpose of

Far From the Madding Crowd than this passage from *After Strange Gods*. Oak's whole meaning is in terms of moral resistance; Boldwood's passionate love for Bathsheba 'has significance only in relation to the character and behaviour of the man at other moments in his life and in other contexts', especially in the context of his relationship to Gabriel; he becomes an 'instrument of feeling'—'vane of passion' is the phrase which Hardy uses[13]—and he abandons himself without resistance to an excitement which literally tends to deprive him of his reason. Of himself he has no significance in the work: set against Gabriel Oak he becomes supremely important as a warning which might be couched exactly in Eliot's terms. Bathsheba, too, might easily have fallen in the same way, for her illusions about Sergeant Troy, though of shorter length, are of the same nature as Boldwood's illusions about her.[14] She has more internal strength, perhaps; more important, she has Oak as a continual reminder of the nature of reality. There is in her, too, a capacity for learning from experience which Boldwood patently does not possess: he is forty, and not inexperienced—'it was possible to form guesses concerning his wild capacities from old floodmarks faintly visible'[15]—yet he has learnt nothing. And it is for Boldwood that Hardy explicitly introduces the notion of equilibrium:

> The phases of Boldwood's life were ordinary enough, but his was not an ordinary nature. That stillness, which struck casual observers more than anything else in his character and habit, and seemed so precisely like the rest of inanition, may have been the perfect balance of enormous antagonistic forces—positives and negatives in fine adjustment. His equilibrium disturbed, he was in extremity at once. If an emotion possessed him at all, it ruled him; a feeling not mastering him was entirely latent. Stagnant or rapid, he was never slow. He was always hit mortally, or he was missed.[16]

Hardy's unnecessary reiteration suggests how deeply he wished to stress this point. And it is interesting to note that all the major characters are introduced in similar terms, and we can see to what degree they have been able to achieve complete balance. 'Oak's intellect and emotions were clearly separated', his moral colour is 'a kind of pepper-and-salt mixture'; a man without extremes of temperament, the most even his friends or enemies can say about him is 'rather a good man' or 'rather a bad man'.[17] Bathsheba has 'elasticity in her firmness',[18] which bodes well for her future in a Hardyan world; but we are also told that she is a 'woman of good sense *in reasoning on subjects where her heart was not involved*', which bodes less well;[19] and her whole course of action is explained by the statements: 'Many of her thoughts were perfect syllogisms; unluckily they always remained thoughts. Only a few were irrational assumptions: but, unfortunately, they were the ones which most frequently grew into deeds.'[20] The clearest statements of all, however, are reserved for Troy:

> His reason and his propensities had seldom any reciprocating influence, having separated by mutual consent long ago. . . . He had a quick comprehension and considerable force of character; but, being without the power to combine them, the comprehension became engaged with trivialities whilst waiting for the will to direct it, and the force wasted itself in useless grooves through unheeding the comprehension.[21]

It seems perfectly accurate to say that Hardy does not take sides with his characters: but to say that he does not *judge* them is a different thing, and is refuted by the text. Judgement is made frequently, and in the same terms: to what extent is there control of the emotions by reason or by the will? To what extent do characters comply with nature, to what extent do they resist, and on what degree of understanding is their choice to comply or resist founded? To what extent is choice taken deliberately and with forethought? Finally, to what extent are human skills used for the benefit of man and the improvement of the conditions in which man lives? These are the questions posed in *Far From the Madding Crowd*, and they are asked of society as well as of individuals. The notion of equilibrium is common to both, and Hardy's detailed study of the rural environment is not thus an attempt merely to create a solid social background for his plot; 'solidity of specification' here does have that function, of course, but it also stresses the communal effects of individual effort, and the part which even one individual may play in the reinvigoration of society. The 'mere padding' which James saw is in fact one of the principal features which give proportion to the work, because it establishes the mutual relationship between the nature of man and the nature of the environment in which he lives and works. The moral lesson which Eliot drew from Hardy's heroes is the positive moral lesson of Hardy's book, for in the answers which he gives to his questioning of man and society he shows us his idea of moral and effective conduct.

The progress of society and the conduct of the individual depend largely on the nature of human choice, and choice is affected by all the questions we have named above. The rural community, like Bathsheba herself, is offered a choice between Gabriel Oak and Sergeant Troy. The nature of the two men is suggested in terms closely akin to the values of rural life: survival through continuity, predictability, and slow adaptation. When Oak first enters the farm he does so as a stranger, but a stranger whose origins are known and respected—'That's never Gable Oak's grandson over at Norwood—never!'[22] In contrast, Troy's uncertain ancestry is not merely a melodramatic flourish: we are asked to set it beside the sturdy continuity which Oak represents. Similarly, we are asked to compare the reactions of the two men at moments of despair. Oak's grief over his flock takes place in a setting where everything appears to invite death:

> Oak raised his head, and wondering what he could do, listlessly surveyed the scene. By the outer margin of the pit was an oval pond, and over it hung the attenuated skeleton of a chrome-yellow moon, which had only a few days to last—the morning star dogging her on the left hand. The pool glittered like a dead man's eye, and as the world awoke a breeze blew, shaking and elongating the reflection of the moon without breaking it, and turning the image of the star to a phosphoric streak upon the water. All this Oak saw and remembered.[23]

—*wondering what he could do:* every suggestion points towards suicide, but before long Oak earns the cost of an evening meal by playing 'Jockey to the Fair' in the streets of Casterbridge.[24] Troy in despair is similarly harassed by the environment: the gurgoyle at Weatherbury church appears to mock his first, tentative attempts at reform. Like Oak, he is free to ignore the suggestions of the environment: unlike Oak, 'he simply threw up his cards and foreswore his game for that time and always'.* Troy's dexterity with the sword is contrasted with Oak's dexterity with the sheep-lance; and on the only occasion on which Gabriel becomes a warrior it is against the elements, his weapons a thatching-beetle and a lance used as a lightning-conductor.[25] Troy's facility

* Ch. XLVI. The notion that Hardy regards the gurgoyle's works as evidence of a malign Providence is silly: the paragraph begins 'he stood and meditated', and the notion is Troy's alone. Hardy's disapproval of Troy's response is clear from the terms chosen for the narrative at this point. These are wholly negative, showing what Troy did *not* do, but could have done.

of speech—'to women he lied like a Cretan'[26]—is contrasted with Oak's cumbrous but dignified honesty; and so on. It is between these two men that the community must choose, and sometimes it makes the wrong choice. ' 'Tis as well to humour the man' is the measure of their weakness on this point. Oak leaves Troy to his tippling in the barn, the others remain, and the consequence is that a fortune's-worth of food is in danger. Even when Troy's danger to others is self-evident they cannot make a firm decision to warn Bathsheba of his presence.[27] Postponement of decision is one danger. Foolish decision is another. Bathsheba's journey to Bath to break off her engagement to Troy is an act of self-deception and folly—a woman does not fly to her lover to break with him.[28] Boldwood's decision to believe in the reality of Troy's death is easily understood: his decision to treat Bathsheba's promises as fixed and real is not. Bathsheba avoids a decision about the valentine by the equal folly of entrusting decision to the fall of a hymn-book, 'idly and unreflectingly' as Hardy says.[29] Decision is not compelled by the environment, as we have seen in the comparisons between Troy and Oak; nor is it compelled by the views or strength of others, as we see in Oak's refusal to treat Bathsheba's rank-blown sheep,[30] or his later refusal to leave Bathsheba's employment.[31] It rests only on honesty and straight dealing: in some works the position is more complicated, but in *Far From the Madding Crowd* it is completely clear.

In seeing nature as an organism which includes man, society, and animate and inanimate states of existence, Hardy sees also a series of parallels or correspondences between different levels of the organism. The parallel between equilibrium in society and in the individual is only one aspect of this organic unity, and his treatment of the environment must be seen in the same framework. Certain features of landscape, for example, may parallel certain features of character. At their most elementary they do no more than illustrate the recurring irony of Hardy's world: the irony that man, though evolved with and through the rest of nature, has none the less a consciousness which isolates and distinguishes him. If we read Hardy's system of nature as a modern re-writing of the Great Chain of Being of earlier times, we can see the special position which he assigns to man as in some ways similar to Pope's 'middle state'—except that Hardy's man has 'too much knowledge' for anything *but* 'the sceptic side', and to become a

> Chaos of thought and passion, all confused

is, in Hardy's world, to invite disaster. The comparison is not a fanciful one: just as earlier ages saw the hand of Providence in everything, so Hardy reads in everything the absence of Providence, a complete lack of design. Had he also been able to see a lack of *law* he might even have been able to derive a crumb of comfort from the fact: instead he saw a pattern which left only limited scope for freedom of action among men. Yet limited scope is not absence of scope, and the parallels between man and nature can, if carelessly read, cause confusion, since a willing creature appears to be equated with will-less existence. However, apart from man's possession of consciousness, Hardy saw the whole created universe in the same terms, subject to suffering under immutable law. This was to influence his language, in prose and poetry, to a marked degree, and it enabled him to transfer the language of one environment or state to another. This is most notably true when the subjects of death or decay arise, as they often do since Hardy sees death and decay as inherent in the frame of things. In *The Woodlanders* trees have 'jackets of lichen and stockings of moss',[32] and rotten tree-stumps protrude from the ground 'like black teeth from green gums'.[33] The planets in *Tess* are like apples on a tree, 'most of them splendid and sound—a few blighted'.* In the same novel the evening sun 'became ugly to Tess like a great inflamed wound in the sky';[34] in *A Pair of Blue Eyes* it is 'a red face looking on with a drunken leer'.[35] In *Jude* the decaying colleges of Christminster assume reptilian personalities:

> Cruelties, insults, had, he perceived, been inflicted on the aged erections . . . several moved him as he would have been moved by maimed sentient beings. They were wounded, broken, sloughing off their outer shape in the deadly struggle against years, weather, and man.[36]

One can amass a number of similar examples from the novels, and many more from the poems. Hardy is conscious of the innumerable parallels between one state of existence and another, and in practice he draws up a new chain of being whose correspondences are as elaborate as those of its earlier counterpart. In *Far From the Madding Crowd* these correspondences first emerge as a general and systematic pattern, but they had already made their appearance in earlier novels, including the first, *Desperate Remedies*.

* Tess, Ch. IV. See also below, p. 222.

Such correspondences perform several functions, but often, as in a passage noted earlier from *A Pair of Blue Eyes*,* their purpose is not merely to stress the parallels between man and nature, but also to stress man's isolation in nature and the responsibility which the possession of consciousness brings with it. Often, in fact, such passages judge the determination with which a given character faces that responsibility.

The earliest major example in Hardy's work is Manston's wooing of Cytherea in *Desperate Remedies*, where the stillness of the landscape oppresses Cytherea and 'reduced her to mere passivity':

> There was the fragment of a hedge—all that remained of a 'wet old garden'—standing in the middle of the mead, without a definite beginning or ending, purposeless and valueless. It was overgrown, and choked with mandrakes, and she could almost fancy she heard their shrieks. . . . Should she withdraw her hand? No, she could not withdraw it now; it was too late, the act would not imply refusal. She felt as one in a boat without oars, drifting with closed eyes down a river—she knew not whither.[37]

This whole passage is extraordinary, and in context illuminating. It would be easy to read it merely as an illustration of the effect of landscape upon temperament, but that is not what it sets out to be. Earlier Manston had gazed into a water-butt at 'hundreds of thousands of minute living creatures, sporting and tumbling in the water, and he had reflected, 'Why shouldn't I be happy through my little day too?' It is easy to see that it is Manston's temperament which is illuminated here, not the effect of the environment upon it. Similarly, in the passage partially quoted above, landscape is used to indicate the temperament of Cytherea and, again, Manston. The leaves, 'the sensuous natures of the vegetable world', are clearly paralleled with Manston himself; the stillness and passivity of the landscape parallels Cytherea's own passivity. Even the mandrakes, which might be read as a proleptic image, are no more than a comment on the potential inherent, not in the situation alone, but in Manston's character.†

* See above, pp. 57-9.

* The passage may deliberately create an ironic ambiguity: mandrakes are said to be nourished beneath the gallows, but are also powerful as love-potions (Firor, pp. 113-14); Manston's attraction and the outcome of it may be combined here. The image is not entirely successful, but it does seem to be a bold attempt to fuse two potential situations.

It seems that what has sometimes been seen as proleptic imagery, indicating a predetermined sequence of events, may rather be read in terms of character-judgement, or assessments of a frame of mind. It may be that an existing mood is strengthened by its parallel in nature, but there is no evidence that Hardy assumes that man should follow the parallel, and more evidence that he believes he should not. The contrast noted above between Oak and Troy would suggest this, and we shall note further instances in which the subordination of human wills to moods of nature leads only to unhappiness, and sometimes to disaster. That man may be misled—not by nature, which is indifferent, but by his own trust in nature—is suggested powerfully in *Tess*, but there are already illustrations of this in *Far From the Madding Crowd*. After Bathsheba had discovered the existence of Fanny Robin's child, she spends a night in the open, sheltered by a brake of fern:

> From her feet, and between the beautiful yellowing ferns with their feathery arms, the ground sloped downwards to a hollow, in which was a species of swamp, dotted with fungi. A morning mist hung over it now—a fulsome yet magnificent silvery veil, full of light from the sun, yet semi-opaque—the hedge behind it being in some measure hidden by its hazy luminousness. Up the sides of this depression grew sheaves of the common rush, and here and there a peculiar species of flag, the blades of which glistened in the emerging sun, like scythes. But the general aspect of the swamp was malignant. From its moist and poisonous coat seemed to be exhaled the essences of evil things in the earth, and in the waters under the earth. The fungi grew in all manner of positions from rotting leaves and tree stumps, some exhibiting to her listless gaze their clammy tops, others their oozing gills. Some were marked with great splotches, red as arterial blood, others were saffron yellow, and others tall and attenuated, with stems like macaroni. Some were leathery and of richest browns. The hollow seemed a nursery of pestilences small and great, in the immediate neighbourhood of comfort and health, and Bathsheba arose with a tremor at the thought of having passed a night on the brink of so dismal a place.[38]

The swamp may be the symbol of the despair into which Bathsheba had so nearly fallen: none the less, the symbolism goes deeper than that. It occurs to Bathsheba 'that she had seen the place on some previous occasion, and that what appeared like an impassable thicket was in reality a brake of fern now withering fast'. And of course the swamp is that same 'hollow amid the ferns' in which only months before she was prepared to be captivated by Troy's demonstration of sword-play.[39] Then the ferns had been 'soft feathery arms caressing her up to her shoulders', the swamp at her feet 'a belt of verdure . . . floored with a thick flossy carpet of moss and grass intermingled, so yielding that the foot was half-buried in it'. The difference between the hollow's two states is not merely a difference between two states of mind: it represents the likely, almost inevitable, outcome of a union between two characters so different morally as Troy and Bathsheba, a union which Bathsheba entered voluntarily and whose implications have at last become clear to her. The 'artificial red' of Troy's cloak finds its counterpart in 'great splotches, red as arterial blood'; the sword which had reproduced the actions of 'sowing, hedging, reaping, and threshing' appears again in 'a peculiar species of flag, the blades of which glistened in the emerging sun like scythes'; the beams of light which had 'well-nigh shut out earth and heaven' now form a 'fulsome yet magnificent silvery veil', shutting out the hedge. On that earlier occasion Bathsheba had cried, 'Why, it is magic!'; and now, in her flight from Troy, she and nature are fused as the leaves rush away in the breeze 'like ghosts from an enchanter fleeing'. But perhaps all that one needs to point to to illustrate the relationship between the two scenes are the ferns, 'plump and diaphanous from recent rapid growth' at first, and now 'withering fast'.

What Hardy has done successfuly here, and what he was to do again, is to find a satisfactory correlative in nature for the phases of the human mind and emotions. Interior monologue or straightforward description of inner thoughts and feelings are abandoned for a method more appropriate to Hardy's views about the general pattern of nature. Here the contrast between the magnetism of flamboyant sexuality and the waste caused by a response to sexuality divorced from reality, is complete. The method gains in subtlety and maturity as Hardy's work matures, but we already find the full correlation between nature and humanity: so complete, indeed, that while one can point to the existence of such passages, and describe their components, one merely emphasises rather than adds to one's knowledge of the situation.

Such passages are not concerned with any predetermined

sequence of incidents, as Holloway suggests,[40] and while they point to a system of parallels in nature they do not indicate a straitjacket of conduct and choice which is inescapable. For example, Bathsheba, before entering the hollow for the first time, actually decides to go home again, and then weakens.[41] They do indicate judgements of character or illuminate states of mind. Moreover, to see them in these terms is to avoid the difficulty indicated by Morrell,[42] who noted that some 'proleptic' images are not in the event fulfilled and therefore cannot be said to foretell a sequence of events. In *Far From the Madding Crowd* there is no prolepsis, nor could there be: Hardy's stress is on the nature of choice and on man's responsibility for events.

The use of landscape, then, serves two purposes in these passages. Firstly, Hardy's treatment underlines the organic unity of man and his social and natural environment, so that we begin to perceive certain systematic tendencies in nature of which man is only a minor part; and secondly, man is *distinguished* from this system by his possession of consciousness: his states of mind may have their parallels in nature, but he is by no means obliged to be led or misled by nature, and when he deliberately misleads himself he is to be condemned. R. C. Carpenter, commenting on the moment in *Desperate Remedies* when Manston looks at the insects in the water-butt, writes:

> This is not the stuff of most action stories but rather one of those moments when we look into the depths, not of a still pool only, but also of reality. Here also is the parallelism or reflection between human affairs and those of the animal world, made ironic and faintly gruesome by the implied comparison of man's life with mindless and miniscule water-snakes.[43]

This misses the point, drawing, in fact, precisely the same conclusion as Manston, though Carpenter's use of the word 'ironic' suggests that he feels something to be wrong here. There is in fact *no* parallel between man and nature here, and Manston, in choosing to draw one, damns himself. Like Troy with the gurgoyle, Manston uses the water-butt subjectively as a justification for actions which he knows to be indefensible; like Elfride, who also gazed into a pool,* Manston allies himself with lower forms of life and in doing so abdicates from the human responsibility

* See above, p. 51.

with which he has been endowed. The fact that Hardy uses the environment as evidence of an organic system and as a means of characterisation does demand care from the reader, but the technique is consistent and coherent, and rarely do we have an excuse for reading it wrongly. Nor, when we understand what Hardy is doing, need we accept Eliot's view that Hardy uses landscape because it is highly suited to an author 'interested not at all in men's minds, but only in their emotions; and perhaps only in men as vehicles for emotions'.[44] Landscape is used, more often than not, to indicate the tragic *failure* of mind, the dominance of emotion over reason, at crucial points in the human career. If it is true that the description of Norcombe Hill in Chapter II is intended as a keynote to Gabriel Oak's character—and I think it is*—then we have a scene where the principal stress is laid on human resistance, sensitivity, and perceptiveness, not at all on emotion. Similarly, the unnatural features of the landscape in Chapter XV reflect Boldwood's rejection of reason in favour of romance in terms which make it obvious that such a course leads only to unbalance and possible disaster.

Far From the Madding Crowd is the first of Hardy's works to make a claim to greatness. The basis for its claim is its treatment of an abiding moral problem, man's relation to his environment and to others; and the claim may be respected, and finally conceded, on the grounds that an old philosophy of the necessity of the dominance of reason over passion is not merely re-stated, but is renewed in terms of a modern vision of nature in which the role of man is reduced, but his significance enhanced.

* Howard Babb, *op. cit.*, overstresses the relationship between the natural backcloth and the characterisation—his comments on Troy, for example, are unconvincing—but in general terms his article is soundly based.

V

Sense-sealed I have wrought, without a guess
That I evolved a Consciousness
To ask for reasons why.

C.P. 260

'THE real cause of its failure was that Hardy was not by nature a social satirist', writes Evelyn Hardy of *The Hand of Ethelberta*, citing Rutland with approval.[1] Without wishing to defend the book against the charge of failure, one can only say that this judgement is wrong: *The Hand of Ethelberta* is not primarily a social satire. It reflects Hardy's further attempt to analyse problems already raised in *Far From the Madding Crowd*, and as an attempt, albeit an unsuccessful one, at a more subtle analysis of the nature of human reason and the emotions, it deserves an important place in any study of Hardy's work. Had Hardy shown more awareness of his own developing attitude to the problems he was facing it might even have played a vital part in our understanding of him, and been a turning-point in his achievement; whereas we are compelled by its failure to see it only as a faltering step towards ideas which he carried out more successfully elsewhere.

Ethelberta is a problem novel. Its theme would appear to be clear enough: the problem lies in the attitudes which underlie it. Like *Far From the Madding Crowd*, *The Hand of Ethelberta* is concerned with the respective roles of reason and emotion. Its 'comic' element consists simply of a satire on the use of reason for paltry and inadequate ends. Leslie Stephen was so anxious that the point should be put across that he suppressed the subtitle, 'A Comedy in Chapters', from the serial edition for fear that his readers might expect a farce.[2] There is no difficulty, faced with the complete text, in accepting the sub-title, and perhaps it is enough to read *Ethelberta* simply as if, in stressing that reason is too valuable to be frivolously used, it made the same point as *Far From the Madding Crowd*. Yet this I cannot do. Hardy's humour is never of the rollicking kind: when it is purely rustic it usually involves some kind of comment upon the central action; when it is satiric it usually possesses a sour, even a bitter edge. And it appears to me that we must approach *Ethelberta* in the frame of mind one adopts when approaching the 'Satires of Circumstance'; in other words, we must not expect a detached, dispassionate satire. Whether this is so or not, Hardy's failure in this work is more closely related to a growing dissatisfaction with the attitudes of *Far From the Madding Crowd*, to a consciousness that the problems treated there are more complex than he had allowed for and, one suspects, to a confusion in the face of new problems.

There are still, it is true, instances when his attitude is quite unambiguous, when he sees the powerful influence of the passions as dangerous to human stability and self-determination. Christopher Julian says at one point,[3] 'I have a feeling of being moved about like a puppet in the hands of a person who legally can be nothing to me', and his sister soliloquises:

> Ethelberta, having already become an influence in Christopher's system, might soon become more—an indestructible fascination—to drag him about, turn his soul inside out, harrow him, twist him, and otherwise torment him, according to the stereotyped form of such processes.[4]

Against the impressionable Christopher, Ethelberta ought to be a heroine of self-controlled restraint. When her emotions come into play, as they do frequently, they are repressed. Yet the achievement won by her restraint is a highly dubious one, and this not merely because her aims are dubious. She does not even succeed in her initial plan 'not meanly to ensnare a husband just to provide incomes for herself and her family, but to find some man she might respect, who would maintain her in such a stage of comfort as should . . . enable her to further organise her talent, and provide incomes for them herself'. Her ultimate marriage to Mountclere, in the light of such an aim, is laughable, and Hardy's ironic twist of plot whereby Ethelberta herself is trapped by a lascivious old man exposes Ethelberta, and not the society in which she moves, to ridicule.

There is no reason to believe that this may not have been Hardy's intention, though it does raise problems about his motives in writing the book. Before dealing with these, however, we must face the basic reason for his failure, which can best be approached by way of an analogy with *Tess of the D'Urbervilles*. Evelyn Hardy noted that the moral issues of the books were similar,[5] and it is possible to go even further, and to point to similarities between the characters of each novel. The butler, Chickerel, is not more than a more sophisticated John Durbeyfield, relying on his daughter to maintain the family fortunes, while Ethelberta herself is a Tess who *is* ready to prostitute herself to offset her father's inadequacy, and in a sense her character complements that of Tess. Without Tess's 'purity' (whose implications we may examine only later) she yet possesses a forthright honesty which Tess fails to show. Ethelberta's secret is disclosed to Mountclere with little hesitation: and Mountclere's honesty in seeing that her birth is irrelevant to her virtues is enough to eclipse Angel Clare's priggish chastity. Hardy himself pinpoints the problem at the end of Chapter XXXVI: 'Was the moral incline up or down?' and Evelyn Hardy summarises it nicely in the words, 'Is it good and right that a woman should benefit others, to whom she is bound by ties of blood and affection, by sacrificing her chastity and her heart?'[6] As Evelyn Hardy notes, neither Ethelberta nor Hardy can solve the problem. But it is one to which he will return.

Possibly Hardy could not solve it because he could not state it in a convincing form. His failure here is fundamental. Any inadequacy in drawing polite society—and Hardy's incompetence in this field has always seemed to me over-rated—is irrelevant beside such an integral flaw. Whether he had properly defined the book's moral terms for himself seems doubtful: in any case, he could not present them, simply because he could not provide a suitably convincing plot. The moral problem arises only if Ethelberta has a real responsibility towards her family: in *Tess* the shiftless father, his ill health, and death, are crucial to the family; in Ethelberta the father is possessed of a good job, a home to live in while he pursues it, and, one would infer, sufficient means to support his family. Nor is that family wholly dependent on the father's earnings: Picotee is a schoolteacher, two brothers are at work. So far from being destitute, the family would appear to be moderately comfortable. Ethelberta herself is content to leave them in obscurity rather than offend the elder Lady Petherwin by leaving her society: and her decision to do so cannot be defended on the grounds that it is for her family's good, since her ultimate ambition is to raise them out of the social (or at least the financial) class to which they belong. Hardy remarks at the opening of the first chapter that 'a bear may be taught to dance', and Ethelberta's aim seems merely to achieve some greater degree of sophistication for her relatives. This is not an unpraiseworthy aim: but neither does it present a moral issue. The ultimate responsibility does not lie on Ethelberta, but on her father.*

Despite this basic flaw, the book remains interesting as a step in Hardy's career. Clarice Short saw it as important chiefly as a contrast to Hardy's view of tragedy:

> If in Hardy's view comedy is the triumph of reason over emotion, the victory of the individual will, rather than the victory of time, chance, passion, and social convention, Ethelberta is a consistently portrayed heroine of comedy.[7]

But this is not enough: we have seen that *Far From the Madding Crowd* was as much concerned as Ethelberta with the triumph of reason over passion. What distinguishes Ethelberta is the light in which that triumph is portrayed. Ethelberta as a heroine possesses honesty, passion, and sensitivity; in the course of her career she strips herself of all these, except perhaps her honesty. In doing so she becomes alienated from herself until she becomes identifiable by little more than her function as the seeker of a rich husband and maintainer, or rather social improver, of a large number of dependants. It is in this slight sketch of self-alienation that the importance of *Ethelberta* lies, for it suggests that, of feeling and reason, it is feeling which is the richer for the pursuit of life.

This is a judgement which cannot be defended on the basis of this book alone, and which appears to be doubtful if one takes into account Hardy's previous work. Yet a change, of which Hardy himself appears to have been unaware at first, is making itself felt, and will exercise its domination still more in *The Return of the Native*. It is substantially a change of vision, and its nature was noticed acutely by D. H. Lawrence in his *Study of Thomas Hardy*,[8] and so far as I know has been noticed nowhere else:

> *The Hand of Ethelberta* is the one almost cynical comedy. It marks the zenith of a certain feeling in the Wessex novels, . . . the feeling that the best thing to do is to kick out the craving for 'Love' and substitute common sense, leaving sentiment to the minor characters.
>
> This novel is a shrug of the shoulders, and a last taunt to hope, it is the end of the happy endings, except where

* That Hardy doubted the sense even of raising a family from one social class to another seems likely, since he satirises not only the upper classes but the aspirations of the lower, as well as the inverted snobbery of the lower classes.

> sanity and a little cynicism again appear in *The Trumpet-Major*, to bless where they despise. It is the hard, resistant, ironical announcement of personal failure, resistant and half-grinning. It gives way to violent, angry passions and real tragedy, real killing of beloved people, self-killing. Till now, only Elfride among the beloved, has been killed; the good men have always come out on top.

It is always difficult to go all the way with Lawrence, and it is so here: but as so often in his comments on Hardy he has seized the central point, and these few remarks, almost all that he wrote on *Ethelberta*, are probably the most fruitful words ever written about that novel. Because there is a feeling of personal failure, quite apart from the book's artistic failure; and it seems to stem from an awareness that the balance expressed so neatly in Gabriel Oak may not always be adequate to prevent human desiccation. The real beginnings of an exploration of the balance between reason and the emotions has not yet begun, but it is significant that in *The Hand of Ethelberta* Hardy satirises what he has formerly praised. It is also significant that the one exception among the later books which Lawrence notes, *The Trumpet-Major*, marks the end of a period in which Hardy appears to have had no clear understanding of what was happening to him, no clear understanding of his slowly changing attitude. *The Hand of Ethelberta* marks the beginning of the process of change, *The Trumpet-Major* its final stages: while in *The Return of the Native* and its revisions over a period of years, Hardy became aware of, and began to express fully, the dilemma which faced him.

That he was not at first conscious of what he was doing in *The Return of the Native*—that in fact he intended a 're-write' of *Far From the Madding Crowd*—has been fully established by John Paterson in *The Making of The Return of the Native*.* Eustacia Vye's position in the book, for example, was to have been quite different from that which she finally assumed—she was, indeed, to have been more a 'Mephistophelian visitant' than Diggory Venn, and local opinions that she was a witch were to have been given stronger foundation than mere suspicion.[9] In fact, as Eustacia's character began to assert itself Hardy began a drastic re-appraisal of his task; so that we are now faced with a novel which defines,

* California, 1960. '. . . *The Return of the Native* had its inception in a novel not so different in subject and treatment from *Far From the Madding Crowd* . . .', p. 164.

more clearly than *Ethelberta*, a problem which Hardy could not solve. The book is not a total success, and contains some serious elements of failure: that its impact is none the less impressive is due entirely to Hardy's handling of problematic material.

The failure, as in *Ethelberta*, is caused by a mishandling of the plot, and as such is a failure to convince. This faulty approach is in itself a mark of Hardy's uncertainty of aim, since there is some doubt in the novel as to where the principal stress should lie. Paterson points out[10] that the strength of the leading role is diffused by the struggle for dominance between Eustacia, Clym, and Mrs Yeobright, and rather surprisingly he also sees Thomasin as a contender for the heroine's place. This may well have been true of Hardy's earlier conception of the novel, but Thomasin is hardly a contender in its final form. However, there is a further, and more important, fragmenting of emphasis. Hardy's plot would seem to stress that the catastrophe is caused by the consequences of personal failure among the principal characters. Eustacia, for example, could have totally averted the catastrophe by waking Clym after his mother's call, or, when he awoke, by telling him of it; or alternatively she could herself have made an active search of the heath immediately after her failure to open the door (Hardy says that Mrs Yeobright did not follow the path, but she could hardly have gone far). That Eustacia was unable to do these things is directly attributable to her own consciousness of a guilty past with Wildeve; but this, too, is a consequence of her own inadequacies and actions. That the catastrophe need never have occurred does not appear to me to be a criticism of Hardy's art: rather it would appear that Hardy himself would have taken the same view, making the point, as he made it in *Far From the Madding Crowd*, that we may bind our future by our present actions, and that consequence is the most powerful force in depriving us of our freedom. Nor, as Morrell shows,[11] are Eustacia and Damon Wildeve essentially different from Hardy's other wayward heroes and heroines:

> These romantic natures in *The Return of the Native* are almost incapable of choice, because they can choose resolutely and wholeheartedly only what they think they have lost. Eustacia's love for Wildeve varies inversely with his accessibility, and the degree of her commitment to him. When she thinks she has won him, her affections at once cool. . . .

They are no different from Elfride, sighing for the unattainable, and in placing their propensities before their reason they resemble Troy or the early Bathsheba.

As in the earlier novels, too, Hardy is concerned to show the nature of the environment's effect upon character, and in a striking example he illustrates once more that the influence of the environment does not alter men's responsibility for decision, but does throw light on their state of mind. Indeed, in *The Return of the Native* he repeats, almost word for word, a passage from *Desperate Remedies* to imply that Clym Yeobright, after his proposal of marriage and its acceptance by Eustacia, is conscious of having taken an unwise step. As we have seen,* Cytherea Graye's indecisiveness before making a choice which she distrusted had the effect of making her particularly sensitive to the surroundings, whose 'helpless flatness' oppressed her. This is immediately followed by Manston's further approach which, had he pressed it, would certainly have brought about Cytherea's consent. In *The Return of the Native* we find Clym and Eustacia alone on the heath:

> They stood still and prepared to bid each other farewell. Everything before them was on a perfect level. The sun, resting on the horizon line, streamed across the ground from between copper-coloured and lilac clouds, stretched out in flats beneath a sky of pale soft green. All dark objects on the earth that lay towards the sun were overspread by a purple haze, against which groups of wailing gnats shone out, rising upwards and dancing about like sparks of fire.†

This is immediately followed by Eustacia's whisper, 'O! this leaving you is too hard to bear!', and the decision to marry. Less than fifty lines later we find:

> As he watched, the dead flat of the scenery overpowered him, though he was fully alive to the beauty of that untarnished early summer green which was worn for the nonce by the poorest blade. There was something in its oppressive horizontality which too much reminded him of the arena of life; it gave him a sense of bare equality with, and no superiority to, a single living thing under the sun.

* See above, p. 71.

† III, 5. Compare this and the subsequent passage with *Desperate Remedies*, Ch. XII, 6.

As if to stress how conscious Clym has become of the rash nature of his action Hardy adds: 'Now that he had reached a cooler moment he would have preferred a less hasty marriage; but the card was laid, and he determined to abide by the game'. And there is almost a note of incredulousness, even in the author's voice, as he concludes the chapter: 'Whether Eustacia was to add one other to the list of those who love too hotly to love long and well, the forthcoming event was certainly a ready way of proving.'

What happens, both to Clym and Cytherea, is that they experience a failure of nerve, not at the force exerted by the environment but by the utter refusal of the environment to take responsibility for their actions. Cytherea eventually accepts Manston, as Clym adheres to his proposal to Eustacia, under the pressure of their knowledge that they are alone with their decision, and because they realise the weight of the decision they must take. This is implicit in *Desperate Remedies* and in the first part of *The Return of the Native*, but before Hardy has finished with Clym he reminds us of Clym's failure of nerve, and attributes it directly to his sense of the 'vast impassivity' around him:

> A consciousness of a vast impassivity in all which lay around him took possession even of Yeobright in his wild walk towards Alderworth. He had once before felt in his own person this overpowering of the fervid by the inanimate; but then it had tended to enervate a passion far sweeter than that which at present pervaded him. It was once when he stood parting from Eustacia in the moist still levels beyond the hills.[12]

This has a point which Hardy has made before and will make again: against the impassivity of nature, and situated in an unconscious universe, the only responsibility which can possibly exist is man's. The destructive figures of his work are characters who make decisions rashly and hold to them, even when there is time to withdraw, in the illusion that life is a game and that a card once played cannot be withdrawn; characters who are blinded by romance, until they are deprived of choice, or characters who deliberately postpone choice, form the agents of Hardy's plots. Clym postpones visiting his mother until it is too late; in precisely the same way, he says of his wife 'I will wait for a day or two longer—not longer than two days certainly; and if she does not send to me in that time I will send to her'.[13] When he eventually does send for her there might still, just, be time: but

Eustacia's grandfather postpones delivery of the letter just as Clym has postponed writing it. Hardy does not strain credibility here: he always provides reasons for vacillation; but beneath all the vacillations the reasons for action are stronger. There are also characters who refuse to blame themselves, and who incur the author's disapproval by doing so:

> Having resolved on flight Eustacia at times seemed anxious that something should happen to thwart her own intention. . . .[14]

> She had certainly believed that Clym was awake, and the excuse would be an honest one as far as it went; but nothing could save her from censure in refusing to answer at the first knock. Yet, instead of blaming herself for the issue she laid the fault upon the shoulders of some indistinct, colossal Prince of the World, who had framed her situation and ruled her lot.[15]

In all of these instances—and they are duplicated again and again—Hardy is concerned with individual reactions to a specific situation; and he makes it clear that the responsibility for those reactions always rests upon the figures themselves. In this respect he is wholly consistent with a definition of tragedy which he drew up shortly after the completion of the serial version of the novel:

> A Plot, or Tragedy, should arise from the gradual closing in of a situation that comes of ordinary human passions, prejudices, and ambitions, by reason of the characters taking no trouble to ward off the disastrous events produced by the said passions, prejudices, and ambitions.[16]

It is just because of his consistency in observing this definition that the greater inconsistency of the book becomes apparent.

Had *The Return of the Native* been a drama of human incompetence, and nothing more, Hardy's point would have been made, and allusions to the influence of 'Fate' over the characters would have had the same relevance as they have for *Far From the Madding Crowd*—in other words, 'Fate' interpreted in terms comparable to Eustacia's 'Prince of the World' is an invention intended as self-excuse by romantic characters. But in laying so much stress on the Promethean myth, and in attempting to write a novel in some ways parallel with Greek tragedy,* Hardy was appealing

* The evidence for this is embodied in Paterson's study.

to a grander notion than that of mere human incompetence, setting his figures against a cosmic background which would ennoble them despite their weaknesses. That this does, to some extent, happen is due to factors other than plot and setting: and the only two characters to whom it even begins to happen are Clym and Eustacia. The remaining figures are in no sense in rebellion against a cosmic order, or even protesting against a cosmic disorder: they are the victims of human inadequacies and personal resentments.

This ought to condemn the book as a total failure: yet one is immediately conscious that, for the sympathetic reader, *The Return of the Native* is impressive. Often the stature of the book is explained vaguely in terms of 'Egdon Heath', or the more thoughtful approach which Paterson adopted:

> By a virtually systematic accumulation of classical allusions, [Hardy] evoked the atmosphere or background of Greek tragedy and, by so doing, framed and transfigured, as he had not done in *Far From the Madding Crowd* and as he would not do in *The Woodlanders*, his purely pastoral narrative. By a perceptibly cumulative movement that began with the decision to incorporate certain formal features of classical drama, that continued with the proliferation of such classical allusions as those to Parian marble, Sappho, and Oedipus, and that culminated in Eustacia's designation . . . as the lineal descendant of Homeric kings, Hardy created the illusion of a world larger than Wessex, a world capable of . . . epic-tragic dimensions. He evoked, furthermore, by a proliferation of the imagery of fire, the major theme of the Prometheus legend and thereby gave to the substance of the novel a still more specific and significant frame.[17]

I would not dispute the powerful cumulative effect of such allusions and images, least of all the effectiveness of the Promethean metaphor, which Paterson establishes well. This is invoked very early in the work:

> . . . to light a fire is the instinctive and resistant act of man when, at the winter ingress, the curfew is sounded throughout Nature. It indicates a spontaneous, Promethean rebelliousness against the fiat that this recurrent season shall bring foul times, cold darkness, misery and death. Black chaos comes, and the fettered gods of the earth say, Let there be light.[18]

It subsequently returns in a highly-intelligent series of cross-references, most strikingly in the passages describing Mrs Yeobright's exhaustion on the heath, and Clym Yeobright's face. The first is made more striking by being associated with a 'vision' of the normal routines of the earthly life and the life of man's aspirations, and each returns to the notion of man as a chained divinity:

> In front of her a colony of ants had established a thoroughfare across the way, where they toiled a never-ending and heavy-laden throng. To look down upon them was like observing a city street from the top of a tower. . . . She leant back to obtain more thorough rest, and the soft eastern portion of the sky was as great a relief to her eyes as the thyme was to her head. While she looked a heron arose on that side of the sky and flew on with his face towards the sun. He had come dripping wet from some pool in the valleys, and as he flew the edges and lining of his wings, his thighs, and his breast were so caught by the bright sunbeams that he appeared as if formed of burnished silver. Up in the zenith where he was seemed a free and happy place, *away from all contact with the earthly ball to which she was pinioned;* and she wished that she could arise uncrushed from its surface and fly as he flew then.*

> . . . it was a natural cheerfulness striving against depression from without, and not quite succeeding. The look suggested isolation, but it revealed something more. As is usual with bright natures, *the deity that lies ignominously chained within an ephemeral human carcase* shone out of him like a ray.[19]

That the Prometheus myth forms an integral part of the treatment is suggested by these examples, but their relevance to any of the figures who live and struggle in the work is scarcely apparent. So far from strengthening the work, they would be a fundamental blemish if we were to attempt to interpret the plot in terms of human rebellion against an unjust god or gods. The rebellion, in fact, is not rebellion on the part of Hardy's characters, but on the part of Hardy himself. And what he rebels

* Ch. IV, 6. The passage is indebted to a note in Hardy's first Literary Notebook (see below, pp. 219-20) which Hardy made from G. J. Wood, *Ants*: 'Many suggestive generations of ants continue to use the same track they have once taken to. I have been shown ant-roads by old men who state that they have been familiar with these from their earliest recollections.'

against is not God or the gods, since he has abandoned any notion of either, but an objectified metaphor for views which he feels compelled to accept, but can only accept with reluctance. Nor is this apparent 'intrusion' of Hardy's damaging. It is in fact the chief source of strength, for the mating of Clym and Eustacia on remote Egdon provided him with a satisfactory 'objective correlative' for his resentment, and, indeed, justified some of the less credible sections of the plot.

In his dramatisation of the roles of reason and passion Hardy has taken a major step since *Far From the Madding Crowd*. There, and at one level of *The Return of the Native*, Hardy gives reason a superior moral position, and indeed comes very close to implying that the act of rational decision is a natural function which it is our duty to exercise. In the later work, however, reason and passion are on more even terms: there is still, because of the force of Hardy's earlier notions, a tendency to give greater moral superiority to reason (the failure of his characters to choose rationally is clearly indicated) but Hardy is more preoccupied with the mutual destructiveness of reason and passion. And it may be that he had in mind a further development of those ideas. For *The Return of the Native* recognises that reason itself is a product of evolution, and it is possible, at least, that Hardy wondered on what moral basis the superiority of reason could rest if deprived of its supposedly divine origin. Certainly even the step which he directly expressed implies a recognition which modern philosophy takes very seriously indeed. A popular work on existentialism sums up the point:

> Steeped as our age is in the ideas of evolution, we have not yet become accustomed to the idea that consciousness itself is something that has evolved through long centuries, and that even to-day, with us, is still evolving. Only in this century, through modern psychology, have we learned how precarious a hold consciousness may exert upon life, and we are more acutely aware, therefore, what a precious deal of history, and of effort, was required for this elaboration, and what creative leaps were necessary at certain times to extend it beyond its habitual territory.[20]

'Only in this century'?—yet in 1878 we have Hardy adumbrating precisely this idea (and later developing it until the whole conception of *The Dynasts* emerges from it) and doing so in very much his own characteristic mood:

> The truth seems to be that a long line of disillusive centuries has permanently displaced the Hellenic idea of life, or whatever it might be called. What the Greeks only suspected we know well; what their Aeschylus imagined our nursery children feel. That old-fashioned revelling in the general situation grows less and less possible as we uncover the defects of natural laws, and see the quandary that man is in by their operation.[21]

The notion is a modern one, and Hardy's response to it is deeply personal, seeing his own personal moods as a product of history, generalising from his own experiences to create a melancholy view of the mood of his own age. That this view of reason made a powerful impression upon Hardy, and that it belongs among the deepest of the 'personal impressions or seemings' which made up the fabric of his beliefs, is proved by the frequency with which he repeated the idea elsewhere. In the preface to *The Dynasts* he speaks of modern man 'unhappily perplexed by—

> Riddles of Death Thebes never knew . . .'

and the poems provide numerous other instances:

> When you slowly emerged from the den of Time,
> And gained percipience as you grew . . .[22]

> Sense-sealed I have wrought without a guess
> That I evolved a Consciousness . . .[23]

> Man's mounting of mindsight I checked not,
>   Till range of his vision
> Now tops my intent . . .[24]

> . . . the ancient faith's rejection
> Under the sure, unhasting, steady stress
> Of Reason's movement . . .[25]

In the poems, too, we find an expression of the effects on man of this growth of perception:

>   A time there was—as one may guess
> And as, indeed, earth's testimonies tell—
>   Before the birth of consciousness
>   When all went well.

None suffered sickness, love, or loss,
None knew regret, starved hope, or heart-burnings,
None cared, whatever crash or cross
Brought wrack to things.

If something ceased, no tongue bewailed,
If something winced, no heart was wrung;
If brightness dimmed, and dark prevailed,
No sense was stung.

But the disease of feeling germed,
And primal rightness took the tinct of wrong;
Ere nescience shall be re-affirmed
How long, how long?[26]

Some of these references are, of course, concerned not only with reason but with consciousness itself, every kind of perception. Yet I think it is clear that Hardy has in mind primarily man's ability to reason out his situation in a godless and disorderly world, and the effects which this may have upon his perception.

This is certainly true of *The Return of the Native,* where there is a remarkably strong focus upon modes of perception. One key passage discusses the change in terms of aesthetic responses:

> Indeed, it is a question if the exclusive reign of this orthodox beauty is not approaching its last quarter. The new Vale of Tempe may be a gaunt waste in Thule: human souls may find themselves in closer and closer harmony with external things wearing a sombreness distasteful to our race when it was young. The time seems near, if it has not actually arrived, when the chastened sublimity of a moor, a sea, or a mountain will be all of nature that is absolutely in keeping with the moods of the more thinking among mankind. And ultimately, to the commonest tourist, spots like Iceland may become what the vineyards and myrtle-gardens of South Europe are to him now; and Heidelberg and Baden be passed unheeded as he hastens from the Alps to the sand-dunes of Scheveningen.[27]

The notion, too, that the evolution of reason is a continuing process, a process of becoming rather than of being, is clearly stated:

> In Clym Yeobright's face could be dimly seen the typical countenance of the future. Should there be a classic period to art hereafter, its Pheidias may produce such faces. The

> view of life as a thing to be put up with, replacing that zest for existence which was so intense in early civilizations, must ultimately enter so thoroughly into the constitution of the advanced races that its facial expression will become accepted as a new artistic departure. People already feel that a man who lives without disturbing a curve of feature, or setting a mark of mental concern anywhere upon himself, is too far removed from modern perceptiveness to be a modern type.*

Finally, we should note that Hardy sees the development in *The Return*, as well as in the poems, as a tragic development:

> He already showed that thought is a disease of flesh, and indirectly bore evidence that ideal physical beauty is incompatible with emotional development and a full recognition of the coil of things. Mental luminousness must be fed with the oil of life, even though there is already a physical demand for it; and the pitiful sight of two demands on one supply was just showing itself here.[28]

I have devoted some time to illustrating Hardy's preoccupation with the growth of consciousness and reason because *The Return of the Native* makes no sense unless one takes it into account as a major feature of the novel. It is this, and not some ill-defined need to create a Greek drama of chance and fate, which determined Hardy's drastic re-organisation of the book, and it is this which ultimately saves it from failure. For *The Return of the Native* is an imaginative, and in some senses allegorical, study of the 'mutually destructive interdependence of spirit and flesh'. Seen in these terms the relative failure to transform local gentility into figures of Promethean grandeur matters less: Thomasin, Mrs Yeobright, Wildeve, Diggory Venn, all lose significance, it is true, because they are scarcely adequate to the framework which Hardy depicts. But if we look for a tragedy of chance and fate then Eustacia and Clym sink into insignificance also (in seeing Eustacia as a good matron in a boarding-school Clym, indeed, is

* Ch. III, 1. The notion is repeated in Ch. I of *A Laodicean*: 'A youthfulness about the mobile features, a mature forehead—though not exactly what the world has been familiar with in past ages—is now growing common; and with the advance of juvenile introspection it probably must grow commoner still. Briefly, he had more of the beauty—if beauty it ought to be called—of the future human type than of the past. . . .'

almost half-witted, and Eustacia's belief that he will take her to Paris is scarcely more credible). But if we look for a drama of the spirit and the flesh, in the terms I have suggested, then Clym and Eustacia not merely gain enormously, they also become vitally integrated with the author's personal observations. The lengthy discursive passages imbedded in the description of the heath, and the portraits of Clym's face, also take on a new freshness and significance for the work.

The Return of the Native is concerned with Time, and the evolution of consciousness within Time. It is concerned with the demands of the mind and the spirit, and the incompatible demands of the flesh. And Hardy's method of dramatising this is notably close to his method in the poem 'The Convergence of the Twain',[29] where concrete realities, the 'Titanic' and the iceberg, signify cosmic abstractions. The realities of *The Return of the Native* are Egdon, Clym, and Eustacia. Without wishing to schematise the plot too rigidly, it is none the less possible—indeed, essential—to regard the heath as representative of the background of Space and Time, and Clym and Eustacia are representative of different phases of existence within Time—Clym representing the 'modern type', Eustacia representing 'that zest for existence which was so intense in early civilizations'. One is, of course, aware of what actually *happens* to Eustacia, and so far from weakening this case her fate strengthens it. John Paterson claimed that '*The Return of the Native* dramatizes the predestined failure of consciousness in an unconscious universe'[30]—in fact, it dramatises the inevitable collapse of outdated views of existence at a time when those views have become visibly incompatible with the coil of things; and I would prefer to say that at one level, at least, it dramatises the vital *necessity* of consciousness in an unconscious universe. Eustacia is certainly the tragic heroine, but she is so because she objectifies Hardy's resentment or regret at the destruction, on the personal level, of his own 'zest for existence', and on a universal level the inevitable destruction of the romantic view of life which failed to take the facts into account. The book marks a major stage in Hardy's thought: a stage which may very well be wholly pessimistic, but it is none the less Hardy's first attempt to take 'a full look at the Worst'[31] in the hope that amelioration might come that way:

> . . . would men look at true things,
> And unilluded view things,
> And count to bear undue things,

> The real might mend the seeming,
> Facts better their foredeeming,
> And Life its disesteeming.[32]

This view of the book is wholly consistent with the terms in which Clym and Eustacia are drawn, and the relationships which exist between these terms and the description of Egdon Heath. Egdon, while it possesses 'an ancient permanence which the sea cannot claim', and sums up in its past the geological and historical past of mankind, is also representative of modern man in its essentially modern appeal. This modern appeal is set against the 'youthful zest for existence' of earlier times by direct statement, and indeed by direct contrast with the objects of Eustacia's passion for escape, symbolised first of all by Budmouth:

> Budmouth, if truly mirrored in the minds of the heath-folk, must have combined in a charming and indescribable manner, a Carthaginian bustle of building with a Tarentine luxuriousness and Baian health and beauty.[33]

Egdon and Budmouth represent two extremes of aesthetic perception; between them, and accounting for them, comes the whole history of man's emotional and spiritual development, and the test of modern man's ability to survive lies in his ability to see and respond to Egdon for what it is: not merely a geographical background, or even a representative only of historical time, but a norm of perception against which one's perception of the modern world may be gauged. 'The number of their years', Hardy writes, may have adequately summed up Jared, Mahalaleel, and the rest of the antediluvians, but the age of a modern man is to be measured by the intensity of his experience',[34] and in man's perception of Egdon is expressed his perception of experience. Hardy does not deny the reality of Budmouth, Paris, or the Mediterranean south, but he does deny their validity as representatives of the modern mood.[35] The 'Hellenic idea of life', the 'old-fashioned revelling in the general situation' is dead, or 'grows less and less possible as we uncover the defects of natural laws, and see the quandary man is in by their situation'.

It is not surprising then that in Eustacia's rejection of the heath we should see her as representative of an immature, an essentially unreal, mode of perception. At the most straightforward level she shows her inability to face an existing situation; at a deeper level she shows her inability to survive. Hardy might have written of her, as he writes of the reddleman, that she fills a place in the world which 'the dodo occupied in the world of animals . . . a curious, interesting, and nearly perished link between obsolete forms of life and those which now prevail'.[36] We thus find that he most commonly identifies her with images of fire, and that Promethean rebellion which Clym has specifically rejected, or with images of the Hellenic, romantic, or escapist ideal. Sometimes the fire-imagery is dramatic in its use, more often it is unobtrusive*: the most striking is her use of fire as a principal instrument in her rebellion against her situation, when she summons Wildeve to the bonfire before her father's cottage; and perhaps we may see her as a victim of the fire which Susan Nonsuch uses for the burning of her effigy. In her rejection of what she imagines to be an ill-deserved fate she is willing to rebel against the gods, blaming heaven, some colossal Prince of the World, and the cruel obstructiveness of all around her, and in this, too, she is out of tune with a time that demands the maximum awareness of man's responsibility and his potential. At the same time Hardy heaps upon her beauty a series of historical and classical allusions, identifying her with the glories of past civilisations, the beauty of exotic (and thus outdated) landscapes, and the nature of rebellious and romantic women. She is compared to Artemis, Athena, and Hera, she might have been a fitting divinity for Olympus, 'one had fancied that such lip-curves were mostly lurking underground in the South as fragments of forgotten marbles', her skin is like Parian marble, her presence reminds one of Bourbon roses and rubies, and Hardy even endows her with a nobility of birth, linking her with an ancient English, as well as a classical Mediterranean ancestry. There can be little wonder that Egdon is her Hades, or that its sublimity can be compared to the façade of a prison. Eustacia is, too, identified with older practices: partly by association, as by the crude local superstition which regards her as a witch, and more directly and dramatically through the genuine Satanic attributes she is given: the hour-glass, traditionally a property of Satan,[37] and her wish to exult over Wildeve by calling him up as 'the Witch of Endor called up Samuel'.[38]

Yet against all this splendour, it is Clym who survives in the modern world, and the terms in which he is presented are surely an attempt to indicate greater realism of approach. Almost no

* In the Library Edition such images occur on pp. 71, 75, 79, 104, 107, 137, 215, 216, to select only some.

imagery is bestowed upon him: he identifies with Oedipus, blinded and apparently guilty of a crime against his mother; he is a John the Baptist who takes ennoblement rather than repentance for his text; and in his blindness and his revival after near-drowning he is compared to Lazarus. These images are all relevant only to their immediate situation, and one can only feel that they are deliberately deprived of the wider resonance of the images applied to Eustacia. For the greater part Clym is cut off from the traditions which Eustacia represents, both in his situation in the modern world (which Eustacia shares without sharing his perception of it) and by his own choice in deliberately rejecting the world of romance and unreality for which Eustacia longs. Like the heath, his face is 'overlaid with legible meanings' more relevant to his own experience than to an alien civilisation; he is 'wild and ascetic'; his kinship with the heath is continually stressed until, in his garb as a furze-cutter, he becomes absorbed by it. Most strikingly of all, it is he who assumes Eustacia's dominant position at the summit of Rainbarrow:

> On the Sunday evening . . . an unusual sight was to be seen on Rainbarrow. From a distance there simply appeared to be a motionless figure standing on the top of the tumulus, just as Eustacia had stood on that lonely summit some two years and a half before.[39]

Given the symbolic associations of Rainbarrow as 'the pole and axis of this heathery world', and that Hardy sees the figure of man at its summit as 'so perfect, delicate, and necessary . . . that it seemed to be the only obvious justification' of its outline, I think we have little choice but to regard this final metaphor of the work as symbolic of the place of the new consciousness in Nature. Hardy certainly appears to regard the death of the old as tragic; but that he believes the new consciousness to have its own morality is implicit in his equation of Rainbarrow with the Mount of Olives, and his view of Clym's addresses as 'a series of moral lectures or Sermons on the Mount'.

The Return of the Native thus dramatises the death of older forms of perception in the struggle for survival in the modern world. It dramatises the evolution of consciousness and if there are moments when that evolution appears to be a tragic process, it is so not of itself but because of the nature of the perception that it brings. It is because they objectify these abstractions that Clym and Eustacia achieve grandeur, and it is this additional and systematically contrived stratum of the book that gives impressiveness to the novel. Despite crudities in dialogue (one thinks particularly of the quarrel in V, 3), despite weaknesses of characterisation (Thomasin and Wildeve especially), the ambitious structure of the book, and the careful attention to the Promethean and classical allusions, are justified because Hardy has chosen a modern theme whose grandeur approaches, if it cannot equal, the inquiries of his classical forebears.

VI

Years whiled. He aged, sank, sickened; and was not.
And it was said, 'A man intractable
And curst is gone.'

C.P. 140

IF *The Return of the Native* marks a new departure, so too does *The Mayor of Casterbridge.* Of all Hardy's works it is probably the most individual, and it stands in contrast to the other novels, where he attempts to give a partial explanation of his characters, either in terms of environment or of heredity, or of both. Thus Clym may be partly understood as a product of his upbringing on Egdon Heath, Eustacia by her Mediterranean ancestry; the same sort of explanations occur in *Tess* and *Jude.* In these works not only does the environment affect the events in which the characters are involved, but the very nature of the characters derives in part from their environment. Yet when we first meet Michael Henchard, and in all our subsequent dealings with him, we find a hero who is rootless, scarcely integrated—if at all—with the social environment, and totally without antecedents. Certainly his environment influences the events of his career, but his character is none the less a given entity, and remains unexplained however much it may be explored. Despite the indication that the action takes place 'before the nineteenth century had reached one-third of its span', the opening of the book possesses a deliberately-rendered timelessness: the scene is one that 'might have been matched at almost any spot in any county in England at this time of year', the road is featureless, 'neither straight nor crooked, neither level nor hilly', and the only sounds are the murmur of mother and child and 'the voice of a weak bird singing a trite old evening song that might doubtless have been heard on the same hill at the same hour, and with the self-same trills, quavers, and breves, at any sunset of that season for centuries untold'. In this detached objective opening one senses Hardy's warning that whatever may take place in this work, and whatever social forces operate, we are to study a character in isolation, not only from others but from himself, not only from his own time but from any time. And the structure of the opening of the novel, with its swift dramatic prologue to an action of twenty years later, implies that the laws of cause, effect, and retribution may also play a major part.

For though his character remains unexplained, the social, moral, and spiritual isolation of Henchard are revealed to be the consequences of his own actions, and even more of his own nature. In his frequent stress on heredity and environment Hardy faces the mystery behind the formation of human personality: and the fact that he so clearly *chooses* not to attempt an explanation here, as he partly attempts it in his other works, suggests that his purpose is more than an analysis of character. Indeed, we find an analysis of the influence of character upon events, and of the slowly strengthening hold of Consequence over character. In a very real sense the theme of this work is closely related to the theme of *The Dynasts*, and despite its attention to a specific individual in a specific, named and localised society, it is also a study of human history whose conclusions match the conclusions of *The Dynasts* in several major respects.

That the novel possesses very real social preoccupations would not, I think, be challenged by any reader. They are implicit in the title, which significantly names not a man but an office, and the society in which that office is held. The pattern of rural change which flows as a powerful undercurrent has received much critical attention, most strikingly from Douglas Brown.[1] Yet my own view that the recent stress on the social background results, despite its excellence, in a disproportioning of the novel that Hardy actually wrote may be seen from the fact that many, probably including Brown, would disagree with my reference to the social theme as an 'undercurrent'. Perhaps I can clarify the matter by quoting Brown on a point where, fundamentally, I find myself in agreement with him:

> Nor does the study of the novel, in my experience, deepen or increase our appreciation of the personalities there. I have read that Henchard represents a subtle intuitive projection of 'the great 19th-century myth of the isolated, damned, and self-destructive individualist', a pre-Freudian exploration of the pathology of punishment. But this is not at all the experience of reading Hardy's novel itself; such hints as we do find pointing in the psychological direction seem (once found) to dry up, to take us no further. Guerard's is a different novel about Henchard, not the one Hardy created. Hardy's psychology has the essential truth and penetration of provincial wisdom, wide reading, tradition; but not creative insight into

> the human spirit. So we need still to refer the question back: why this sketch (that's what we have) of the lonely Promethean figure blindly stumbling to his own defeat? What pressures are at work? Isn't the figure we meet in the pages of the novel rather legendary than psychological?[2]

The answer to this last question is, of course, yes. The analogies between *The Mayor* and the Oedipus myth, the first book of Samuel, or the legend of Faust, establish very clearly the archetypal qualities of Henchard's experience, and it seems reasonably clear, though not certainly so, that the parallels that can be drawn are the result of an instinctive literary sympathy rather than of self-conscious imitation of the past. But all this merely refers us still further back to the question: what was it that impelled Hardy to re-create this archetypal pattern?

One of the peculiar features of Hardy's novels is that they possess either a personal or an ideological basis, and sometimes they possess both. We have seen some instances of the personal basis in stories whose germ may be found in the history of Hardy's family or of Hardy himself, and we shall have occasion to revert to the subject again: in contrast, *Far From the Madding Crowd* and *The Return of the Native*, though they are not free of possibly autobiographical elements, may be fruitfully discussed chiefly in terms of their ideological content. *The Mayor* deserves to be grouped with them, for in it the discussion of personal and social equilibrium which appears in *Far From the Madding Crowd* and the broad historical preoccupation of *The Return of the Native* find their meeting-place. The question of personal and social equilibrium as it affects Michael Henchard is possibly the more obvious, and I shall turn directly to the second, historical preoccupation. The ideological content of *The Mayor of Casterbridge* may be defined as a treatment of Necessity, taking as our definition of Necessity:

> Constraint or compulsion having its basis in the natural constitution of things, *esp.* such constraint conceived as a law prevailing throughout the material universe and within the sphere of human action.[3]

For Hardy the constraint is not total, though it is well defined. He comments on *The Dynasts* that 'neither Chance nor Purpose governs the Universe, but Necessity',[4] and he makes clear that 'the will of man is neither wholly free, nor wholly unfree'[5]—a theme which, as we shall see, *The Dynasts* illustrates and which is present in a number of poems. That we have an approach to this view in *The Mayor* is, I believe, made clear by an image-parallel which may or may not have been deliberate,* but which seems to be clear and which can be justified by the sequence of events in the novel.

As Henchard prepares to sell his wife the company is distracted by 'a swallow, one among the last of the season, which had by chance found its way through an opening into the upper tent. . . . In watching the bird till it made its escape the assembled company neglected to respond to the workman's offer, and the subject dropped.' Here, at least, Henchard is afforded an opportunity to avoid an action whose consequences will later enmesh him. At the end of the novel[6] he brings Elizabeth-Jane a caged bird, which like him dies. We have here a symbolic link, and it is not difficult to see Henchard as a creature, initially free, but now caged by the consequences of his own deeds, a pattern of consequence which appears (unusually for Hardy's novels) to possess its own necessary justice. The caged bird, dying, is like Henchard a sacrifice to Elizabeth-Jane's happiness; and its sentimentalism does not outweigh its symbolic effect, the image of freedom transformed to the image of captivity and death. Nor is it difficult to discover the source of the symbol. Hardy is known to have read Carlyle's essay on Goethe's *Helena*—indeed he quotes it in *The Mayor*. Carlyle's subsequent comments may also lie behind Hardy's portrait. The passage quoted by him reads in full:

> Thus Faust is a man who has quitted the ways of vulgar men without light to guide him on a better way. No longer restricted by the sympathies, the common interests and persuasions by which the mass of mortals, each individually ignorant, nay, it may be, stolid and altogether blind as to the proper aims of life, are yet held together, and, like stones in the channel of a torrent, by their very multitude and mutual collision, are made to move with some regularity,—he is still but a slave; the slave of impulses, which are stronger, not truer or better, and the more unsafe that they are solitary.[7]

Some four pages earlier Carlyle commented:

> . . . the Soul of Man still fights with the dark influences of Ignorance, Misery, and Sin; *still lacerates itself, like a captive*

* Probably not, since the second use was temporarily withdrawn from the novel.

> *bird, against the iron limits which Necessity has drawn around it;* still follows False Shows, seeking peace and good where no peace or good is to be found.[8]

With or without this source, it seems clear that the Necessity which binds Henchard at the end of his career was not so compulsive at its beginning, and that Henchard's self-destruction is also self-laceration against the limits imposed upon him by himself. Necessity, in fact, implies no more than the need to face the inevitable sequence of cause and effect. It does not imply lack of choice—Henchard chooses freely and repeatedly—for it governs situations and not, primarily, actions—though clearly it may *limit* action.

If one is right to see this as primarily a book about Necessity, and Henchard's conduct as an abuse of limited freewill (an abuse because his choice is not based upon an accurate reading of his situation) then our way of looking at the novel may be changed. Douglas Brown's stimulating and persuasive essay, for example, may appear to be misguided, since it stresses social change at the expense of character; it is difficult to see that Brown views Henchard as more than the creature of agricultural and social transition. 'Henchard cannot live on the terms which the new order proposes', he writes[9]—but could Henchard have lived on the terms proposed by any social order? His offence is not social, but moral. Social change is an instrument, no more, and it is difficult to believe that Henchard could fit into any society, changing or stable. It is true that his initial strength in Casterbridge is that by journeying further west than Weydon Priors he is able to defy change a little longer, and to benefit from skills which elsewhere are growing outdated. But it is also true that as change begins to affect Casterbridge we find Henchard ready to face it, and no more at the mercy of it than Farfrae. Farfrae has the skills, but it is Henchard who has the power, and it is Henchard who persuades Farfrae to abandon his plan for emigration. As Casterbridge responds to change the credit is given to both men:

> . . . the great corn and hay traffic *conducted by* Henchard throve under *the management of Donald Farfrae* as it had never thriven before . . . as in all such cases of advance, the rugged picturesqueness of the old method disappeared with its inconveniences.[10]

The paragraph is nicely weighed between its objective comment on the present, and its nostalgia for the past—the chief source of Hardy's sympathy for Henchard—but the point is still made. Change brings success to a business which is still conducted by Henchard, and the agent of change is Farfrae, which is perfectly proper, for what are managers for? Hardy specifically mentions Henchard's respect for Farfrae's brain,[11] and the use of originality and skill in others is as effective an instrument for social advance as is the development of those skills. The recognition of Farfrae's merit is as much to Henchard's credit as his dismissal of Farfrae is to his blame.

Of course the social background is important, and of course the Mayor's prosperity depends upon his contribution to it. But his exile from society may be traced to purely personal factors—his treatment of Susan, Elizabeth-Jane, Farfrae, Abel Whittle, and his fellow town councillors who had smarted so often under his heavy sarcasm. And I doubt whether we should see Henchard in terms of his environment unless we can see him in contrast to it: he is totally alien. Casterbridge is a town which, though in the throes of change, manifestly adapts itself to change, and builds on its past. 'Casterbridge announced old Rome in every street, alley, and precinct',[12] but for all that it is not a Roman fortress, not a ruin, not empty. It occupies, indeed, very much the position of the barn in *Far From the Madding Crowd*, as the living symbol of productive, everyday life. That it is prepared to be progressive when shown is revealed by Farfrae's comment on the seed-drill:

> 'Is the machine yours?' Lucetta asked Farfrae.
> 'O no, madam', said he, '. . . I merely recommended that it should be got.'[13]

As he says, 'the machines are very common in the East and North of England', and Casterbridge, later perhaps but conclusively, is following the pattern of progress which will 'revolutionize sowing', the chief source of the town's stability. Henchard's ridicule indicates his unwillingness to adapt, but that unwillingness is not primarily instinctive or natural to him—he had not objected to Farfrae's new methods in his own barns—but merely the result of a personal dislike:

> '. . . 'Twas brought here by one of our machinists on the recommendation of a jumped-up jackanapes of a fellow. . . .'[14]

Henchard's problem, in brief, is that after twenty years he remains the same man, having learnt nothing from experience. Personal contact has been denied. Once he is outcast he certainly finds himself in a changed world, but Hardy states that this is not his problem:

> And thus Henchard found himself again on the precise standing which he had occupied a quarter of a century before. Externally there was nothing to hinder his making another start on the upward slope, and by his new lights achieving higher things than his soul in its half-formed state had been able to accomplish. But the ingenious machinery contrived by the Gods for reducing human possibilities of amelioration to a minimum—which arranges that wisdom to do shall come *pari passu* with the departure of zest for doing—stood in the way of all that. He had no wish to make an arena a second time of a world that had become a mere painted scene to him.[15]

He has work, the very work he had undertaken in his youth, but stripped of social dignity, of personal affection, and of self-respect, a future becomes pointless, and personal contacts impossible because he himself has destroyed them.

Yet this moral nakedness is a natural descent for Henchard. Until the end of his career he is totally unable to make contact with people, because he lacks consistent generosity; he cannot communicate because he lacks any sense of community. Society is an instrument for his temperamental and acquisitive instincts, and it is in terms of self that he looks at the world. His downfall is a transfiguration only in that his self-abasement leads him, for the very first time, to consider the needs of Elizabeth-Jane above his own. He receives—and deserves—admiration, because through his own criminal and irresponsible actions he moves through a range of qualities from, on the one hand, a choleric enmity or irresponsible perversity to, on the other, a self-castigating contrition. But even in repentance there is no balance in the man—'it was part of his nature to extenuate nothing, and live on as one of his worst accusers'[16]—and in the Henchard who sold his wife there never could be balance, simply because in that act he unleashed the forces of imbalance against himself. And here one touches upon the most difficult question of all: for if *The Mayor* implies some moral order involving retribution and justice, *what* is the moral order, and whence does it flow?

That Hardy is thinking in deliberately restricted terms here is obvious. Had it been his intention to arraign or justify 'the Gods' in Henchard's career he would presumably have carried his terms of reference further; but, as we have noted, he deliberately excludes such problems as the origin of personality, and concentrates only on the given character of Henchard, without much speculation on the severity of the justice to which Henchard is forced to submit. The closest he comes to such an arraignment is in his observation that 'wisdom to do shall come *pari passu* with the departure of zest for doing', in which 'the Gods' functions as no more than a metaphor on which to hang the obvious, but none the less important, statement that experience is perforce accompanied by age, and frequently by disillusionment. Instead we see Hardy deliberately explaining that Henchard's exertions are the cause, self-willed, of his disaster:

> Misery taught him nothing more than defiant endurance of it. His wife was dead, and the first impulse for revenge died with the thought that she was beyond him. He looked out at the night as at a fiend. Henchard, like all his kind, was superstitious, and he could not help thinking that the concatenation of events this evening had produced was the scheme of some sinister intelligence bent on punishing him. Yet they had developed naturally. If he had not revealed his past history to Elizabeth he would not have searched the drawer for papers, and so on. The mockery was, that he should have no sooner taught a girl to claim the shelter of his paternity than he discovered her to have no kinship with him.[17]

The idea is repeated elsewhere:

> . . . if anything should be called curious in concatenations of phenomena wherein each is known to have its accounting cause.[18]

Hardy is doing no more than repeat what he had noted sympathetically from J. A. Symonds several years previously:

> Each act, as it has had innumerable antecedents, will be fruitful of immeasurable consequents.[19]

Henchard at least escapes Eustacia's fault, in that he does not blame some 'colossal Prince of the World', but he is tragically slow to *learn*—'Misery taught him nothing more than defiant endurance of it', writes Hardy, and the negative framing of the sentence is important, and parallels the judgement of Sergeant Troy: 'he did not attempt to fill up the hole, replace the flowers, or do anything at all. He merely threw up his cards and foreswore his game for this time and always.'[20] To say that a man did *not* do or that he 'learnt nothing more than' is to imply that he has within his grasp the power to do or to learn. The recurring tragedy of Hardy's heroes and heroines is their failure to learn, and within this framework *The Mayor* is firmly established.

The moral order which enables Hardy to make his judgements has no divine or eternal sanction, but is the morality of which perhaps Henchard receives a glimmering before his death. Seeing himself as a disruptive element he withdraws, and his progress from moral chaos to moral understanding may be said to parallel the progress of man as Hardy saw it. For it is man-made morality which is applied, and the laws of that morality are the laws of survival in the organism of society. It is easy to see that Henchard is in revolt, against his social environment, but perhaps it is less easy to see that his revolt, even while it chafes at universal conditions, none the less parallels universal conditions: the universe is itself blind, instinctive, unpurposive, and each of these terms, except just possibly the last, may be applied to Henchard himself. Society, on the other hand, at least attempts to be rational, controlled, and purposive, adapting itself to conditions which it cannot avoid, but attempting throughout to place less and less dependence on the mercy of these blind forces. The rejection of Henchard is the triumph of society, triumph over a man who has violently broken the closest social link that he can form.

In this pattern, too, lies the tragedy of the work, and the foundation for Henchard's archetypal qualities. For in a sense he *is* man, and exemplifies the progress and the limitations of man. Bound as he is by the only abstract laws which exist, the laws of Chance and Consequence and Time, he is also subject to the evolved laws of consciousness, and in Henchard's suffering passage towards self-awareness we can read the sufferings of an entire species in its struggles to master, crudely and ignorantly, a destiny which demands the subjection of powerful instinctive forces. The compassion extended towards him is Hardy's compassion for all men who, to survive, must suppress their strongest and most vigorous instincts for the good of the social commonwealth. Typically, however, Hardy's sympathy is also extended to Elizabeth-Jane, whose wisdom is the subject of a final paragraph which has been widely misunderstood:

> . . . she did not cease to wonder at the persistence of the unforeseen, when the one to whom such unbroken tranquillity had been accorded in the adult stage was she whose youth had seemed to teach that happiness was but the occasional episode in a general drama of pain.

This teaches that tranquillity can be achieved: but only by the recognition that man belongs to a social organism from which all disruptive elements must be excluded; and the tragedy behind this is that in excluding his disruptive energies man must exclude a dynamic part of his own being.

VII

I am the family face;
Flesh perishes, I live on . . .
C.P. 407

IN *The Return of the Native* Hardy had dramatised the role of two modes of perception in the modern world, and *The Mayor of Casterbridge* is capable of similar 'allegorical' interpretation; but it should be noted that in these works his representative types are creatures of high sensitivity. In *The Trumpet-Major* and *A Laodicean* Hardy's concern with Time and the role of man in Time is still present, although his power is muted, and *The Trumpet-Major* confines itself specifically to the past, a past seen through a veil of nostalgia but none the less positive and productive. *A Laodicean* is concerned with both the past and the future, and it expands its concern by introducing a new type to contrast with the sensitivity of Clym, Eustacia, and their kind. Potentially it is a greater book than *The Trumpet-Major*, yet it is more subjective and negative in its approach, and for this reason, as well as through Hardy's serious illness of 1880-81, when the book was written, it seems an irretrievable failure. In some senses both novels are about Hardy himself: the attitudes expressed are his, and they illustrate his perplexity at his position as the last scion of a noble but decayed stock.

There may be a danger here of seeing these works out of focus, of selecting features of the work which are marginal, and of neglecting the stories themselves. But I think the danger is more apparent than real. In the case of *The Trumpet-Major*, for instance, the fact that Hardy could introduce Nelson's Hardy into the tale was, one suspects, a powerful attraction for him, and even if it were not, the story of Mrs Garland, the Miller, and their families was the stuff of common life in Dorset during the Napoleonic era. Hardy was writing of country life as he and his immediate ancestors knew it, and in selecting the Napoleonic age rather than his own he was in fact getting closer to his own roots, and handling traditions which had been his spiritual nourishment. It is a mistake to see *The Trumpet-Major* as a precursor of *The Dynasts*: the later work is an objective study; the first, in its origins at least, derives from an emotional or spiritual need.

A Laodicean is an even clearer case. The circumstances in which it was written—most of it dictated to Mrs Hardy from the author's sick-bed—have made it a worse novel, but have given us a Hardy whose defences were down. It is customary to see the early discussion of paedo-baptism, for instance, as the desperate gatherings of a man who is compelled to provide magazine copy at considerable cost to his own health, and whose only resource is his earlier experience. Certainly these pages are no longer easy reading, if indeed they ever were; but the fact that they are there should be an indication that, for whatever reason, Hardy is reaching towards some of the most fundamental preoccupations of his earlier career. I am not here referring to the Tryphena episode (though that had been reflected in the cousin-relationship between Clym and Thomasin, and I believe it is also present in the relationships between Paula, Somerset, and de Stancy, and it also affects the portrait of Paula), but to problems which on the face of it are purely intellectual but which the books reveal to have a powerful emotional content for the author himself. The intellectual advance present in *Far From the Madding Crowd* and dictating the very structure of *The Return of the Native* is abandoned. In *The Trumpet-Major* it probably had no place; but in *A Laodicean* it could have been fundamental. In some senses the book prefigures a powerful theme of Forster's *Howard's End*, for in contrasting the decaying de Stancys with the 'progressive' industrial Powers, Hardy is simply posing the question 'Who shall inherit the earth?' The roles of the dynamic, forward-looking men of the new generation and the sensitive but ineffective aristocracy of the old could—and one is almost tempted to say should—have provided Hardy with one of his richest themes. That theme never emerges clearly, and I cannot believe that it would have done so even if Hardy had been in good health (though he approached it in the far richer texture of *The Mayor of Casterbridge*). A more limited treatment might have emerged more clearly than it does, along the lines of a note written on February 17, 1881:

> Conservatism is not estimable in itself, nor is Change, or Radicalism. To conserve the existing good, to supplant the existing bad by good, is to act on a true political principle, which is neither Conservative nor Radical.[1]

There are shadows of this in *A Laodicean*; but they are only shadows.

What we have, in fact, is a novel in which several related

themes are adumbrated, but none fully developed. Occasionally, for instance, the question 'Who shall inherit the earth?' is raised, and Hardy appears to answer very firmly that his sympathies are with the 'new' generation:

> '. . . I wish I had a well-known line of ancestors.'
>
> 'You have. Archimedes, Newcomen, Watt, Telford, Stephenson, those are your father's direct ancestors. Have you forgotten them? Have you forgotten your father, and the railways he made over half Europe, and his great energy and skill, and all connected with him, as if he had never lived?'[2]

Along with this we may set the view of the railway cutting as an object of beauty,[3] the telegraph wire as symbolic of 'cosmopolitan views and the intellectual and moral kinship of all mankind',[4] or the new and shining clock of Stancy Castle, proudly declaring that times have changed and a new era in being.[5] But none of these apparent tributes to the modern is unambiguous. The beautiful railway-cutting only requires a change of mood to become a 'dreary gulf',[6] the telegraph wire is also significant of 'the modern fever and fret which consumes people before they can grow old',[7] and the proud new clock may signify the same:

> 'It tells the seconds, but the old one, which my very great grandfather erected in the eighteenth century, only told the hours. Paula says that time, being so much more valuable now, must of course be cut into smaller pieces.[8]

Even an apparent hostility to the ugliness of modernism is ambiguous: Somerset's first reaction to the hideous chapel erected by John Power is modified by the thought that the chapel has 'a living human interest that the numerous minsters and churches knee-deep in fresh green grass, visited by him during the foregoing week, had often lacked.'[9]

Hardy's attitude to the modern need cause no difficulty. Here, as elsewhere, he shows a belief in progress, but a strictly pragmatic belief which has as its first foundation the usefulness of progress in furthering human welfare. That he saw his novel—which, perhaps significantly, is not a tragedy—as arising from 'the changing of the old order' he declared in his preface. And in a letter to H. Rider Haggard, while regretting many features caused by the decline of rural life, he still shows that 'things are different now':

> [the labourer's] life is almost without exception one of comfort, if the most ordinary thrift be observed. I could take you to the cottage of a shepherd not many miles from here that has a carpet and brass-rods to the staircase, and from the open door of which you hear a piano strumming within. . . . The son of another labourer I know takes dancing-lessons at a quadrille-class in the neighbouring town. Well, why not?[10]

Hardy's most significant comment on modern progress and its uses, however, is made in the noble 'Apology' to *Late Lyrics and Earlier*. This, perhaps the most compressed statement of Hardy's attitude, is not an optimistic essay, foreshadowing as it does the threat of 'a new Dark Age', but in his plea for a firm look at the evils of the world Hardy adds that a vital need if the lot of the 'human and kindred animals' is to be improved is the diminution of pain by 'loving-kindness, *operating through scientific knowledge*, and actuated by the modicum of free-will conjecturally possessed by organic life. . . .' This seems to me to be a qualified but precise statement of the need for progress through human endeavour.

But if Hardy's attitude to the modern is clear, his attitude to the past is much less so. 'You cannot spoil what is past', says Paula,[11] but the question is not whether the past can be spoiled, but whether it is relevant. In *The Trumpet-Major* the past is there, untouchable and valued in itself, nourishing the present; and the throbbing human life from one generation to the next is more vital to the book than the historical frame which surrounds it:

> . . . though Bob Loveday had been all over the world from Cape Horn to Pekin, and from India's coral strand to the White Sea, the most conspicuous of all the marks that he had brought back with him was an increased resemblance to his mother, who had lain all the time beneath Overcombe church wall.[12]

The words are simple, but they ache with compassion for the humble affections of humanity, and against them Hardy's judgement of Napoleon as 'less than human in feeling, more than human in will' is a stern condemnation. It is difficult to find this degree of compassion in *A Laodicean*, and yet the transmission of life and features from one generation to the next is present as a major theme. It may be that the explanation of the difference is indicated by a single passage. Paula has met Captain de Stancy for the first time, and listens to his well-rehearsed comments on the portraits of his ancestors:

> In a short time he had drawn near to the painting of the ancestor whom he so greatly resembled. When her quick eye noted the speck on the face, indicative of inherited traits strongly pronounced, a new and romantic feeling that the de Stancys had stretched out a tentacle from their genealogical tree to seize her by the hand and drawn her in to their mass took possession of Paula.[13]

'New and romantic', perhaps; but a *tentacle*, *seized*, 'to draw her into their mass'—these terms are cruel in their impassive inhumanity, and it is difficult not to believe that something of Hardy's attitude towards his own ancestry is unconsciously expressing itself here. In 'The Pedigree', written long after *A Laodicean*, in 1916, the family tree becomes a 'seared and cynic face' controlling the poet's own actions; 'Family Portraits' refers to the 'blood's tendence' which is to shape his life,* and later in *Tess* and *Jude* heredity is to play a major part in the tragedy. However 'new and romantic' the feeling may be for Paula, the implications of her insight for de Stancy are sinister. The 'spent social energies' of the Hardys are transferred to the de Stancys, and Captain de Stancy utters a thought which had more than once crossed Hardy's mind:

> '. . . I acquire a general sense of my own family's want of merit through seeing how meritorious the people are around me. I see them happy and thriving without any necessity for me at all; and then I regard these canvas grandfathers and grandmothers, and ask, 'Why was a line so antiquated and out of date prolonged till now?'[14]

One has only to compare the undated poem 'Night in the Old Home'[15] to see the relevance of this to Hardy:

> When the wasting embers redden the chimney-breast,
> And Life's bare pathway looms like a desert track to me,
> And from hall and parlour the living have gone to their rest,
> My perished people who housed them here come back to me.
>
> They come and seat them around in their mouldy places,
> Now and then bending towards me a glance of wistfulness,
> A strange upbraiding smile upon all their faces,
> And in the bearing of each a passive tristfulness.

* See above, pp. 7-8, and Appendix A.

'Do you uphold me, lingering and languishing here,
A pale late plant of your once strong stock?' I say to them;
'A thinker of crooked thoughts upon Life in the sere,
And on That which consigns men to night after showing the
day to them?'

'—O let be the Wherefore! We fevered our years not thus:
Take of Life what it grants, without question!' they answer
me seemingly.
'Enjoy, suffer, wait: spread the table here freely like us,
And satisfied, placid, unfretting, watch Time away beamingly!'

Hardy had always been conscious of heredity, but it may be that he brooded over it increasingly after his note of July 1877, a few years before *A Laodicean*:

> We hear that Jane, our late servant, is soon to have a baby. Yet never a sign of one is there for us.[16]

The suggestion is reinforced by 'She, I, and They',[17] a poem written in 1916, the same year as 'The Pedigree', and thus suggesting that childlessness was associated in Hardy's mind with the decay of his race. The portraits of his ancestors are heard to sigh:

Half in dreaming,
'Then its meaning',
Said we, 'must surely be this; that they repine
That we should be the last
Of stocks once unsurpassed,
And unable to keep up their sturdy line.

There is an indication, too, that Hardy intended to strengthen still more the stress on heredity which we find in this novel. In Chapter III-v, Somerset visits his bank to investigate his own pedigree. Apart from allowing him to overhear Paula's visit to the bank the incident has no relevance to the novel as it now stands: and we can only assume that it was at first intended to play a more significant part.

My attention to what I believe to be purely personal and subjective features in this novel is not merely perverse, nor is it fanciful. *The Hand of Ethelberta* used material which was probably derived from Hardy's mother's experience in London,* and there are autobiographical elements in *Under the Greenwood Tree*

* See Appendix A.

and *A Pair of Blue Eyes*. Their full relevance will only be completely clear when seen in relation to *Tess of the D'Urbervilles* and *Jude the Obscure*. In these novels it will be apparent that throughout his career as a novelist Hardy more and more frequently touched upon personal issues which finally grew into obsessions, and which destroyed his artistic objectivity. *Tess* survives, but *Jude* is very close to being wrecked as a work of art, though it remained a powerful personal document. In a sense it represents Hardy's complete disintegration as a novelist, though perhaps as a thinker it may have been his salvation. After *Jude* he shows himself capable of clear and objective thought, and the intellectual strands of the novels, shorn of disturbing and personal influences, are gathered into a finely-woven thread of argument, which subtly and artistically presents the role of humanity in an environment of Time and Chance. My point here is that *A Laodicean*, perhaps because of Hardy's severe illness, foreshadows that disintegration. The influence of heredity, though powerful, is never followed through to any conclusion. Nor, ultimately, is it more than a side-issue in the resolution of the plot. The marriage of Paula and Somerset, neither of whom has a clear pedigree—Somerset's is never produced, and Paula is untypical of hers—simply relegates to the background a conflict of old and new which has been dominant throughout the book. Two creatures, of moderate but not outstanding sensitivity, settle for life in a new house, 'eclectic in style', for the rest of their lives. The design, I think, is apparent: both Somerset and Paula may be said to be of 'mixed ancestry', and their house, borrowing from various styles, may represent the most sensible course for men of the future—a judicious selection of beliefs, tastes, and modes of conduct from the past. Possibly even the title, often taken as an ironic comment on the nature of Paula, may indicate that strong loyalties to the past are less healthy than a lukewarm allegiance. Yet though apparent, the design is not clear: our perceptions are muddied by a lack of balance in the book, and on the issue of the degree to which ancestry affects our conduct the book suggests much, yet avoids a conclusion. The symbolical structure of the book—I think Morrell is correct in regarding de Stancy and Dare as 'doomsters', the figures of Time and Chance who almost wrest Paula from Somerset's hands[18]—is crudely expressed, and the continual wandering through Europe, again based on Hardy's experience, is merely tiresome. It is a bad book; but it could have been a good one.

Biographical elements are also present in *Two on a Tower*,

though they contribute little to its failure, which is simply due to the farcical nature of the plot. Lady Constantine would appear to owe something to Julia Augusta Martin, Hardy's childhood benefactress from the Kingston Maurward estate. In the 1895 preface, written two years after Julia Augusta's death, Hardy wrote of the 'pathos, misery, long-suffering, and divine tenderness which in real life frequently accompany the passion of such women as Viviette for a lover several years her junior', and we have already noted the odd reference to her which was deleted from the *Life*:

> . . . though their eyes never met again after his call on her in London, nor their lips from the time when she had held him in her arms, who can say that both occurrences might not have been in the order of things, if he had developed their reacquaintance earlier, now that she was in her widowhood, with nothing to hinder her mind from rolling back upon the past.*

That she was somewhere in his mind while writing the book would appear to be confirmed by the naming of Swithin's grandmother. Yet old Mrs Martin, so far as she derives from any real figure, is not Julia Augusta Martin, but Mary Head, Hardy's maternal grandmother. 'You should not have waited up for me, granny', says Swithin, returning late one evening; and she replies:

> ' 'Tis of no account, my child. I've had a nap while sitting here. Yes, I've had a nap, and went straight back into my old county again as usual. The place was as natural as when I left it,—e'en just three-score years ago! All the folks and my old aunt were there, as when I was a child. . . .[19]

Swithin's maternal grandmother, she is closely described:

> This woman of eighty, in a large mob cap, under which she wore a little cap to keep the other clean, retained faculties but little blunted. She was gazing into the flames, with her hands upon her knees, quietly re-enacting in her brain certain of the long chain of episodes, pathetic, tragical, and humorous, which had constituted the parish history for the last sixty years.[20]

* See above, p. 13, and Appendix A.

Hardy's memorial poem for Mary Head shows the old lady recalling the incidents of her childhood life in the 'old county', at Fawley, Berkshire:

With cap-framed face and long gaze into the embers—
  We seated around her knees—
She would dwell on such dead themes, not as one remembers,
  But rather as one who sees.[21]

Then there is Mrs Martin's reference to her 'old aunt', and one recalls that in *Jude the Obscure*, set in Fawley, Jude, an orphan like Mary Head herself, lives with his great-aunt Drusilla Fawley. There may, too, be a recollection of Tryphena Sparks—the name of Tabitha Lark seems a scarcely-veiled synonym. These are all marginal points, but they indicate that in this work, too, Hardy is gently probing his knowledge of his own and his family's past, and that in all of these central works Julia Augusta Martin, Mary Head, Tryphena, and the notion of hereditary influence are all present, and apparently related.

Yet Hardy's memories are not dominant in *Two On a Tower*. In 1881, a year before the book's publication, Hardy had written in his journal:

> *May 9*. After trying to reconcile a scientific view of life with the emotional and spiritual, so that they may not be interdestructive, I come to the following:
>
> General Principles. Law has produced in man a child who cannot but constantly reproach its parent for doing much and yet not all, and constantly say to such parent that it would have been better never to have begun doing than to have *over*done so indecisively; that is, than to have created so far beyond all apparent first intention (on the emotional side), without mending matters by a second intent and execution, to eliminate the evils of the blunder of overdoing. The emotions have no place in a world of defect, and it is a cruel injustice that they should have developed in it.
>
> If Law itself had consciousness, how the aspect of its creatures would terrify it, fill it with remorse![22]

Yet *Two on a Tower*, while it shows the human environment in a hideous light, yet demonstrates the triumph of emotion over circumstances and the environment. In his second literary notebook Hardy transcribed a comment from John Oliver Hobbes's

Robert Orange, published in 1900, which in spite of its late date would seem to be appropriate to the novel:

> *The passion of love* invariably drives men and women to an extreme step in one direction or another. It will send some to the cloister, some to the Tribune, some to the stage, some to heroism, some to crime, and all to their natural calling.

By any standard, Viviette expresses a natural heroism and self-sacrifice, qualities which are not unusual among Hardy's women, but which are rarely shown by him to such beneficial effect. In his aim to 'set the emotional history of two infinitesimal lives against the stupendous background of the stellar universe, and to show that the smaller scale might be the more important', Hardy failed; but his purpose is clear enough, and the stress which he places on love and loving-kindness in this book ought not to be overlooked. Viviette's act in releasing Swithin from his 'obligation' to marry her is an illustration of foresight and charity which is infrequent in Hardy's women.

Hardy's lapse is not in his presentation of the environment. All his consciousness of the tininess of the human frame emerges from Swithin's description of stellar space, and this, though self-conscious, pleased Hardy so much that he was later to versify it, with greater effect, in *The Dynasts*:

> . . . horrid monsters lie up there waiting to be discovered by any moderately penetrating mind—monsters to which those of the oceans bear no sort of comparison. . . . Impersonal monsters, namely, Immensities. Until a person has thought out the stars and their interspaces, he has hardly learnt that there are things much more terrible than monsters of shape, namely, monsters of magnitude without known shape. . . . Look, for instance, at those pieces of darkness in the Milky Way. . . . You see that dark opening in it near the Swan? There is a still more remarkable one south of the equator, called the Coal Sack, as a sort of nickname that has a farcical force from its very inadequacy. In these our sight plunges quite beyond any twinkler we have yet visited. Those are deep wells for the human mind to let itself down into, leave alone the human body! . . . to add a new weirdness to what the sky possesses in its size and formlessness, there is involved the quality of decay. . . .[23]

Yet but one flimsy riband of Its web
Have we here watched in weaving—web Enorm,
Whose furthest hem and selvage may extend
To where the roars and plashings of the flames
Of earth-invisible suns swell noisily,
And onwards into ghastly gulfs of sky,
Where hideous presences churn through the dark—
Monsters of magnitude without a shape,
Hanging amid deep wells of nothingness.

(After-scene)

Against such a background the obvious question of what *use* human endeavour can have becomes urgent. *The Dynasts* appears at first sight to state that it has no use at all, and some have seen Hardy's reading of the universe as a statement of the futility of human action. Yet this is not what he actually says:

Yet seems this vast and singular confection
Wherein our scenery glints of scantest size,
Inutile all—so far as reasonings tell.

(After-scene)

> . . . whatever the stars were made for, they were not made to please our eyes. It is just the same in everything; nothing is made for man.[24]

Both these statements, as concise as any Hardy made, are interesting for their common assumption: so far from dismissing the idea of human value, they assert it; for the universal environment is judged by its ability to serve man, and to have some place in a universal scheme possessed of divine or human significance. Man is the judge, and the horror of the universe is that in its size and formlessness human values are neglected, and indeed, appear totally irrelevant. There is no pessimism in this, only a stark realism; and the interest of both *The Dynasts* and *Two on a Tower* is that they re-assert the worth of human values even against a valueless and planless cosmic setting. The passage above compares very appropriately with the cliff-sequence in *A Pair of Blue Eyes*: just as Henry Knight's vision of man's primeval past is a re-assertion of the values of human consciousness and endeavour, so Swithin's vision of the universe helps to focus the one bright spot in the frame of things—the superior consciousness and sensitivity of men. It would be foolish to deny that there are moments when Hardy despairs, when he looks upon consciousness as a blight in nature, and sensitivity as a curse—there are too many poems and prose passages which present just such a view. But it would be equally foolish to deny what almost every serious reader has experienced from Hardy's works—a sense of man's worth and the essential seriousness of his values. Even those who have seen his characters as the victims of a malign Fate have referred to their triumph over Fate, and I think one must see in this something more than stoical acceptance.

It is certainly not stoical acceptance which emerges from *Two on a Tower*. Hardy's note of 1881 suggests strongly that at the outset of his work on this book he intended to produce a work in which despair was more marked ('the emotions have no place in a world of defect'), and for just this reason it is interesting to see why the book failed. For the imbalance of the work arises precisely because the cosmic background is irrelevant to the problems faced by Swithin and Lady Constantine. I doubt if Hardy could ever have successfully removed the imbalance: for the whole pressure of his sympathies led him to assert that, of the cosmic background and the human state, it is the cosmic background which is meaningless. The universe, in this book, is there to be dismissed, while the basic problems emerge from human passions and from simple chance (the ill-luck which brought a premature announcement of Sir Blount Constantine's death in Africa) in which one can again see a comment on the blind formlessness of man's environment. But the basic triumph emerges as a triumph over Chance, in Lady Constantine's generosity to Swithin when she learns that their marriage is invalid. Chance is used, and an unexpected opportunity to show loving-kindness is exploited. Passion, too, is conquered:

> . . . she laboured, with a generosity more worthy even than its object, to sink her love for her own decorum in devotion to the world in general, and to Swithin in particular. To counsel her activities by her understanding, rather than by her emotions as usual, was hard work for a tender woman; but she strove hard, and made advance. . . . It may unhesitatingly be affirmed that the only ignoble reason which might have dictated such a step was non-existent; that is to say, a serious decline in her affection. Tenderly she had loved the youth at first, and tenderly she loved him now, as time and her after-conduct proved.[25]

It is perhaps significant that Hardy attributes this self-effacing conduct to an older woman: his younger heroines are usually charming and flirtatious, but at least potentially irresponsible. Yet the notion of loving-kindness as stronger and nobler than love is present throughout Hardy's works, though it is rarely as central and explicit as here, and only infrequently attributed to a woman. Lady Constantine's simple act of charity is of more significance for man than the external universe can ever be, and although Hardy's theme is badly spoilt by the presence of the melodramatic brother Louis, the silly complications over Viviette's jewellery, and the farcical role of the Bishop, it has at its heart the burden of a passage which meant much to Hardy, more indeed than any other:

> Charity suffereth long and is kind; charity envieth not; charity vaunteth not itself, is not puffed up, doth not behave itself unseemly, seeketh not her own . . .

It was a theme to which he was to return with strengthened powers, and whose greatness was to lift him once and for all above the crudities of *Two on a Tower*. And it is a belief which is impossible for a man to whom human life is an insignificant masquerade.

VIII

Would that your Causer, ere knoll your knell
For this riot of passion, might deign to tell
  Why, since It made you
  Sound in the germ,
  It sent a worm
To madden Its handiwork, . . .

C.P. 741

IT is extremely difficult to take *The Woodlanders* seriously if we regard it as Hardy appears to ask us to regard it, a drama of 'grandeur and unity truly Sophoclean'. The death of Giles, the essential pettiness of Grace Melbury's tastes, and the melodrama centring on Fitzpiers, Felice Charmond, and the gentleman from South Carolina, are all distractions, and unconvincing. Sometimes, indeed, there is a note of cynicism in the author's treatment of his plot, most especially in the reunion of Grace and her erring husband, and it is a cynicism which Hardy confirmed in his comments to Rebekah Owen:

> . . . I spoke of Marty's very beautiful character, of her being called by many the one truly noble and womanly woman in his novels. He said, 'Ah, well! She did not *get* Giles, you see; very likely if she had it would have been a different matter' (He never wrote anything more cynical than this). He further said that he could not make the end as clear as he should have done & perhaps would do in a revised edition: he found that people (I among them) did not see that he means that Fitzpiers goes on all his life in his bad way, & that in returning to him Grace meets her retribution 'for not sticking to Giles'. Her father hints at it in one sentence, or forebodes it, but the matter is not made manifest.[1]

The plot, indeed, is little more than a repetition of the plot of *Under the Greenwood Tree*—the country girl 'corrupted' by contact with a more sophisticated environment, who returns to face a conflict of loyalties—with melodramatic additions from the later works. The book was, apparently, Hardy's favourite among his works, but it is a weak performance whose chief abiding interest lies in its connections with *Tess of the D'Urbervilles* and its treatment of more or less abstract ideas.

That interest, however, is a strong one. More openly than in any previous work Hardy establishes a sense of the organic unity between man and nature, in terms which question the possibility of happiness within any human or natural society. The novel is the most overtly Darwinian of Hardy's books, and a pattern of struggle throughout nature is applied to man and his environment. Hardy frequently uses the same terminology for man and for his surroundings: just as the branches of the woodland trees disfigure each other, or hollow oaks become afflicted with tumours, so time brings in its strains and spasms for men, 'hiding ill-results when they could be guarded against for greater effect when they could not'.[2] The eternal presence of decay and the purely temporary nature of the recuperative powers is made ironic by human insistence on those recuperative powers. 'Even among the moodiest the tendency to be cheered is stronger than the tendency to be cast down' writes Hardy,[3] and it is a theme which he pursues more rigorously in *Tess*. Yet this ironic delusion is one of the few which Hardy appears to regard as beneficial in its effects. His reading of von Hartmann (which appears to have taken place at the time of *The Woodlanders* or soon after) would have confirmed for him that this recuperative spirit is present throughout nature, and so long as it affords some comfort it can be viewed as a source of strength.[4] But this position carries within itself two destructive elements: in the first place, the irony may sooner or later be perceived; and secondly, disillusion may result in the destruction of the very will to live. This is not a theme which *The Woodlanders* directly states, but it may lie beneath the almost carelessly cynical approach which Hardy takes towards his plot, and it seems certain that ideas expressed more directly in *Tess* and *Jude* are already moving beneath the surface.

The most obvious kinship of themes between this story and its successors is of course that provided by the discussion of marriage. The preface to the work shows that this theme is quite deliberately introduced, and the course of the entire action confirms that Hardy believed that a marriage should be dissolvable on the consent of each contracting party, although he might not have put it in such direct terms. He wrote to Sir George Douglas in 1895:

> I feel that a bad marriage is one of the direst things on earth, & one of the cruellest things, but beyond that my opinions on the subject are vague enough.[5]

This concern with social institutions is not new in Hardy, though it had never been so clearly stated by him; and it is not a concern which can consistently be held by one who believes that man's actions are bound and his future necessarily doomed. Hardy has been accused of inconsistency, because in his aim to show that tragedy may be created 'by an opposing environment, either of things inherent in the universe, or of human institutions' he neglects the fact that 'if man is "inherent in the universe", so are his institutions'.[6] Yet there is no inconsistency here: one of the qualities of man is his ability to create, and to change what he creates, and man's social laws and institutions are neither more nor less inherent in the universe than the reforms which may be brought about in them. A major burden of Hardy's work up to the time of *The Woodlanders* had been that man possesses an adaptability in the face of his environment. This is why his works are fundamentally meliorist in their outlook. Certain things cannot be avoided: there is the 'destiny' which decides that Marty South shall be born to labour, or that Fitzpiers shall possess sexual charm; there is the struggle for survival waged at all levels of creation: and there is the unforeseeable intervention of Chance. All of these things are unalterable. But man's possession of reason enables him to free his social codes so that they best enable him to withstand these forces, or adapt to them. Hardy writes of Melbury that he

> perhaps was an unlucky man in having the sentiment which could make him wander out in the night to regard the imprint of a daughter's footstep. Nature does not carry on her government with a view to such feelings . . .[7]

—but there is no logic which insists that because Nature ignores man's finer feelings, man should do so also. Hardy's view of the constructive marriage is a tribute to man's ability to use sentiment for positive ends:

> In truth, her ante-nuptial regard for Fitzpiers had been rather of the quality of awe towards a superior being than of tender solicitude for a lover. It had been based upon mystery and strangeness—the mystery of his past, of his knowledge, of his professional skill, of his beliefs. When this structure of ideals was demolished by the intimacy of common life, and she found him as merely human as the Hintock people themselves, a new foundation was in demand for an enduring and staunch

> affection—a sympathetic interdependence, wherein mutual weaknesses are made the grounds of a defensive alliance. Fitzpiers had furnished nothing of that single-minded confidence and truth out of which alone such a second union could spring. . . .[8]

Loving-kindness and truth are the values which consciousness can supply; and to abandon them is to court disaster. Melbury's attitude towards Fitzpiers had been one of 'confidential candour' but it was displaced by a 'feline stealth' which, Hardy tells us, 'did injury to his every action, thought, and mood'.[9] The moves of Fitzpiers and Felice, though none of them constitute deliberate intention, are none the less all against judgement.[10] In each case a refusal to use the mind causes hardship to mind and body.

We are faced again with the point of view that has met us all along in Hardy's work: the view that sets man in contrast to the natural world, and distinguished from it. The view that man's consciousness and foresight are the well-springs of a tentative hope. One cannot deny that *The Woodlanders* places more stress on the hostility of man's natural and social environment than any of the previous novels; there is indeed a darkening of the vision. But the basic principles on which it is written are unchanged.

The darkening appears to result from an insight into the challenge of irrational sexual impulses. The fascination of sexual appeal had certainly been present in Hardy's heroines, particularly, since the beginning of his career; but a parallel between the struggle for survival and the struggle for natural selection in man, implied strongly in *The Woodlanders*, had previously been muted. For the first time Hardy acknowledges clearly that sexual selection may take place independently of men's wishes, and may possibly be beyond their control. The values of Giles Winterborne, however morally great they may be, are shown to be fundamentally irrelevant to the struggle for Grace; while Grace's position is less clearly her own responsibility than, to draw the closest earlier parallel, had been the case with Bathsheba Everdene. Grace may be tricked into marriage by a lie (Fitzpiers deceives her with Suke Damson even before marriage), and she may also possess the feeling that Fitzpiers's fascination is an unreal thing so long as Fitzpiers is not with her. But when he is with her the fascination is very real indeed, and at no time does Grace submit herself to the whims of a horse (Elfride) or the fall of a hymn-book (Bathsheba). The 'handsome, coercive, irresistible Fitzpiers' is genuinely handsome, coercive and irresistible.

Here, indeed, Hardy's judgement shows signs of confusion. Marty South's sale of her hair is a voluntary abandonment of the one weapon she possesses in the sexual struggle; and the implication appears to be that naturalness is the chief basis for sexual success. A similar stress on naturalness occurs when John South's death is caused by the removal of a tree which has been associated with his life since its planting. There may be some kind of parallel to be drawn between these instances of a rejection of natural qualities or the natural environment, and Grace's sophisticated education. 'She had fallen from the good old Hintock ways' writes Hardy,[11] who emphasises her false sense of superiority over the rural community. If this plea for naturalness is indeed a note struck by the book, the rejection of social forms is logical, since social patterns of marriage and divorce virtually ignore the sexual drive as an instinctive, a-social force, imposing penalties where no penalty can be due. Hardy's view that if Grace 'would have done a really self-abandoned thing (gone off with Giles) he could have made a fine tragic ending of the book'[12] implies the same conflict between natural conduct and social restraint. Yet this conflict never takes life in the work. Hardy was too embarrassed by his public, too trammelled by the conventions of his medium, or too confused in his thinking at this point; for whatever reason, a degree of condemnation is reserved for the sexual exploits of Fitzpiers, and to perhaps a lesser extent of Mrs Charmond. The conflict is never adequately resolved. Giles dies, and his death is a direct result of social and conventional attitudes, an indirect result of sexual drives which ignore moral values; Mrs Charmond is shot by her lover, in whom the passions are crudely—and conveniently—dominant; Grace and Fitzpiers suffer the mutual burdensomeness of their marriage—he for too much self-indulgence, she for too little; and the only 'triumphant' character of the work is Marty South, in whom the extinction of sexuality is so marked that it appears as an impracticable recommendation from the author.

The same conflict appears in a more drastic and potentially more damaging form in *Tess of the D'Urbervilles*, a work which appears to me to present the most crucial critical problem raised by Hardy's novels. It is a great book. Yet as a work of art it falls more clearly into two levels than any of his novels: the ballad tale of the maiden seduced by the dashing young squire forms the basis for the book; this basis is overlaid by a sombre moral commentary which cannot be ignored. Hardy's sub-title makes a moral claim for the heroine, and his appeals to our judgement in the text make the same claim from varying points of view. What Hardy had to say in self-extenuation after the work was published is directly relevant only to the ballad tale:

> . . . I still maintain that her innate purity remained intact to the very last; though I frankly own that a certain outward purity left her on her last fall. I regarded her then as being in the hands of circumstances, not morally responsible, a mere corpse drifting with the current to her end.[13]

This much is evident from the narrative proper; the commentary, on the other hand, involves not only a statement of Tess's moral condition but also an analysis of the reasons which lie behind it. Hardy is not concerned primarily with the mechanics of Tess's fate, but with its cause and the moral justification for it. The issues may be clarified by his treatment of Tess's seduction:

> 'Tess!' said d'Urberville.
>
> There was no answer. The obscurity was now so great that he could see absolutely nothing but a pale nebulousness at his feet, which represented the white muslin figure he had left upon the dead leaves. Everything else was blackness alike. D'Urberville stooped; and heard a gentle regular breathing. He knelt and bent lower, till her breath warmed his face, and in a moment his cheek was in contact with hers. She was sleeping soundly, and upon her eyelashes there lingered tears.
>
> Darkness and silence ruled everywhere around. Above them rose the primeval yews and oaks of The Chase, in which were poised gentle roosting birds in their last nap; and about them stole the hopping rabbits and hares. But, might some say, where was Tess's guardian angel? where was the providence of her simple faith? Perhaps, like that other god of whom the ironical Tishbite spoke, he was talking, or he was pursuing, or he was in a journey, or he was sleeping and not to be awaked.
>
> Why it was that upon this beautiful feminine tissue, sensitive as gossamer, and practically blank as snow as yet, there should have been traced such a coarse pattern as it was doomed to receive; why so often the coarse appropriates the finer thus, the wrong man the woman, the wrong woman the man, many thousand years of analytical philosophy have failed to explain to our sense of order. One may, indeed, admit the possibility of a retribution lurking in the present

catastrophe. Doubtless some of Tess d'Urberville's mailed ancestors rollicking home from a fray had dealt the same measure even more ruthlessly towards peasant girls of their time. But though to visit the sins of the fathers upon the children may be a morality good enough for divinities, it is scorned by average human nature; and it therefore does not mend the matter.

As Tess's own people down in those retreats are never tired of saying among each other in their fatalistic way: 'It was to be'. There lay the pity of it. An immeasurable social chasm was to divide our heroine's personality thereafter from that previous self of hers who stepped from her mother's door to try her fortune at Trantridge poultry-farm.[14]

In attempting to assess the effect of this passage one must, I think, discard any discussion of 'intrusion', 'order of discourse', etc.* In *Tess of the D'Urbervilles* the moral commentary is an integral part of the order of discourse, which imposes upon us a standard of judgement through which we are obliged to see the heroine. We may like it or we may dislike it: to pretend that it is there only as an excrescence is a piece of critical sleight-of-hand which conveniently abandons a full attempt to relate the moral comment to the work. The only questions which arise from it are its truths to the tale that is told, the degree of coherence it embodies, and the artistic justification, if any, for any lack of coherence. What is most striking in this passage is the speed at which varying attitudes towards Tess's fate are reviewed: it is seen in its natural environment as a normal process of nature, a lapse on the part of divine providence, a pattern of 'coarse' moral fibre (though in what sense it is coarse remains variously defined), an act of ancestral retribution, and a malign stroke of fate. These responses are clearly not compatible. Equally clearly, since they are so closely juxtaposed, and because they reach out towards other contradictions in the moral comment, they are not presented for their compatibility. Hardy draws attention to a number of causes for Tess's fate, and a number of possible responses to it. The passage appears to embody some of that personal confusion which later allowed him to 'rise up in the arable land of Wessex and shake his fist at his Creator',[15] but it embodies much else. Whatever reasons impelled him to introduce confusion at this point, it affects our judgement of character to such an extent that, even

* See above, pp. 34-43.

at the ballad level, the tale is affected by it. *Tess* is in danger of being undermined as a work of art since some of the judgements are false to the tale that is told; yet there are few who would question its stature. Somehow, the contradictions have been fused.

Before they may be reviewed an even more fundamental question demands an answer: what precisely *happens*? Are we faced with a rape, a seduction, or a surrender to which Tess herself materially contributes? Any notion of the morality of her actions, or d'Urberville's, must start from this point, as must any general moral to be drawn from the event.

Everything suggests that Tess herself contributes to her union with Alec, that she does so consciously and half-willingly. There are extenuating circumstances: her tiredness after a day's work and the long evening at Chaseborough, and the cumulative effect of d'Urberville's persistent wooing. Allowing for these, however, Tess's nature is passionate, as we are shown in the periodic violence of her responses, the dedication of her love for Angel Clare, and the parallels drawn between her 'luxuriant' figure and the oozing fertility of nature—especially the passage which describes Tess in the overgrown garden, her dress stained by the blights from plants.[16] One moment of the passage above seems to denote physical action: '. . . her breath warmed his face, and *in a moment* his cheek was in contact with hers'. Perhaps it is subjective to regard the natural quickening of the prose at this point as indicating Alec's change from a kneeling to a prostrate position beside Tess; at least it is no more fanciful than to believe that she remains asleep throughout, as the passage would otherwise appear to suggest. And presumably, if this movement exists, it also marks the moment of Tess's awakening. If no consent were given at this point there seems little reason why Tess should have remained at Trantridge after this evening, yet she remains for a further two months.* She admits that d'Urberville has 'mastered' her;[17] she admits, too, that she hates and loathes herself for her weakness.[18] And her awakening to her position seems to have occurred some time after the evening in the Chase:

> She had never wholly cared for him, she did not at all care for him now. She had dreaded him, winced before him, succumbed to adroit advantages he took of her helplessness; *then*,

* The visit to Chaseborough takes place in her second or early third month at Trantridge; at her departure she is Alec's 'four-months' cousin'.

> *temporarily blinded by his ardent manners, had been stirred to confused surrender awhile: had suddenly despised and disliked him, and had run away. That was all.*[19]

Her temporary blindness before Alec's 'ardent manners', causing the fear of, perhaps the wish for, surrender accounts in full for the tears upon her cheeks before her fall.

We may leave aside for a moment the question, In what sense, if any, this is the conduct of a 'pure' woman? Tess's conduct is natural, and that is enough: the natural setting of the Chase, the kinship between Tess's instincts and the fertility of nature, the continual stress on the discrepancy between natural values and social values, all point to a freedom from sin which remains intact when Tess herself is no longer so. The obtuseness, not to say criminality, of Clare's treatment of Tess, arises because of his blindness to this very purity.

But if Tess's response to sexual desire is natural, so then, is Alec's. His role in the story is melodramatically villainous, and this works at the ballad level. Yet in terms of morality, even conventional morality, his treatment of Tess and her family is more generous than any single act of Angel Clare. The 'coarse pattern' traced upon Tess's feminine tissue cannot be regarded as coarse if it is true that 'she had been made to break an accepted social law, but no law known to the environment in which she fancied herself such an anomaly'.[20] Joan Durbeyfield's comment, ' 'Tis nater, after all, and what do please God' becomes literally correct. If d'Urberville sins against Tess at all he does so in terms of the social contract, and, in the first instance, because he treats her as an object with scant regard for the person she is. Socially, he knows the consequences of an illicit union, he is in a position to guess Tess's ignorance, and he takes advantage of it. But the tenor of much of the commentary is to attack the very social principles on which this judgement is founded; take away these and much of d'Urberville's liability is removed. Nor is his social offence of long duration, if Hardy is to be believed: 'women do, as a rule, live through such humiliations, and regain their spirits, and again look about them with an interested eye';[21] 'She might have seen that what bowed her head so profoundly—the thought of the world's concern at her situation—was founded upon an illusion'.[22] Tess recovers, and the most direct consequence of her fall, her rejection by Angel Clare, is the responsibility of Clare himself, who bases his reactions on just those social values which Hardy appears determined to reject.

Almost; but not quite. For there is a level at which Hardy cannot reject social values. We may assume—although it is questionable—that he himself had been liberated from the relics of an orthodox moral training; but Tess has not. Much of the work is an analysis of states of consciousness, and the central consciousness is always Tess's: 'Upon her sensations the whole world depended to Tess; through her existence all her fellow-creatures existed, to her. The universe itself only came into being for Tess on the particular day in the particular year in which she was born'.[23] Between this localised sense of existence and the broad perspectives from which at times Hardy views the story, the narrative varies its focus. No single judgement, as Robert C. Schweik has observed,[24] may certainly be attributed to Hardy as a belief, or to Tess as a permanent state of mind. Only one set of judgements would appear to be an exception to this:

> Men are too often harsh with women they love or have loved; women with men. And yet these harshnesses are tenderness itself when compared with the universal harshness out of which they grow; the harshness of the position towards the temperament, of the means towards the aims, of to-day towards yesterday, of hereafter towards to-day.[25]

These clauses cover a range of situations which may be expressed approximately in terms of the novel. Sexuality of temperament is in conflict with a hostile social environment. Aspirations may be limited by character, as in the case of Angel Clare, over whom hung 'the shade of his own limitations',[26] or by circumstances of birth, descent, or social rank. Past guilt, or the sense of it, may be set cripplingly against the reality of present hopes, now destroyed by consequence. There is little doubt that Hardy's condemnation of social pressures is genuine, but only of social pressures seen in the context of a universal environment; there is no doubt that he recognised that even with control of events man might still, by the force of consequence, find himself in a situation where events had passed beyond his control. Wherever these themes are present in the novel they carry a total conviction which is relevant to every word that Hardy ever wrote. Other judgements, however, must be taken in perspective, weighed against these and other opposing ideas, and the balance accepted.

In this sense, d'Urberville's moral 'coarseness' may be clear. His sin is not a social sin, as such, but a sin against the individuality of Tess's existence, since, for her, as a given person in a given situation, social pressures are meaningful. Given Hardy's stress on personal loving-kindness, it should come as no surprise to find that sin is seen solely in terms of inter-personal relations, and no nonsense is involved by stating that Alec is both innocent and guilty. Against any broad perspective his conduct towards Tess has no meaning. Even Tess's experience is directly meaningful only to herself, and there are moments when the focus of the narrative is adjusted to show that her total meaning in universal terms is non-existent. Tess herself realises this at one point:

> . . . what's the use of learning that I am one of a long row only—finding out that there is set down in some old book somebody just like me, and to know that I shall only act her part; making me sad, that's all. The best is not to remember that your nature and your past doings have been just like thousands' and thousands', and that your coming life and doings'll be like thousands' and thousands'.[27]

The narrative makes the same point. Tess, treated so closely and humanely at times, at others becomes merely a feature of the landscape or a product of nature, and her experience is paralleled by theirs:

> Another year's instalment of flowers, leaves, nightingales, thrushes, finches, and such ephemeral creatures, took up their positions where only a year ago others had stood in their place when these were nothing more than germs and inorganic particles.[28]

Both her grief and her pleasure have their analogies in nature:

> She was, for one thing, physically and mentally suited among these new surroundings. The sapling which had rooted down to a poisonous stratum on the spot of its sowing had been transplanted to a deeper soil.[29]

> She had consented. She might as well have agreed at first. The 'appetite for joy' which pervades all creation, that tremendous force which sways humanity to its purpose, *as the tide sways the helpless weed*, was not to be controlled by vague lucubrations over the social rubric.[30]

There are also times when Tess's significance may be reduced by direct statement, and she becomes like 'a fly on a billiard-table of indefinite length, and of no more consequence to the surroundings than that fly'.[31] Against such backgrounds as these there can be no broad moral code against which either Tess or Alec may be judged. However, these backgrounds represent only one extreme in the range of Hardy's narrative. A paragraph which dismisses as 'ephemeral' such creatures as 'flowers, leaves, nightingales, thrushes, finches', embodies its own protest, since these words carry strong value-associations for most readers. Such values are based on a purely subjective approach to material objects, but it is in the realm of such subjective approaches that most human experience lies. In a paragraph which appears, at its outset, to affirm Tess's unimportance, Hardy reverses his order of priorities, and material objects become real only in terms of Tess's experience:

> At times her whimsical fancy would intensify natural processes around her till they seemed a part of her own story. Rather they became a part of it; for the world is only a psychological phenomenon, and what they seemed they were. The midnight airs and gusts, moaning amongst the tightly-wrapped buds and barks of the winter twigs, were formulae of bitter reproach. A wet day was the expression of irremediable grief at her weakness in the mind of some vague ethical being whom she could not class definitely as the God of her childhood, and could not comprehend as any other.[32]

The same process can be joyful as well as melancholy, and the narrative preserves its faithfulness to Tess's 'vague ethical' belief:

> She heard a pleasant voice in every breeze, and in every bird's note seemed to lurk a joy . . . recollecting the psalter that her eyes had so often wandered over of a Sunday morning before she had eaten of the tree of knowledge, she chanted: 'O ye Sun and Moon . . . O ye Stars . . . O ye Green Things upon the Earth. . . .[33]

In the context of a narrative whose focus is variable, religious belief becomes meaningful if it is seen as an expression of personality, and irrelevant if it is seen as a crippling social restraint ill-adapted to the conditions of existence. Neither religion nor philosophy, the creations of men's subjective faculties, can solve the 'problem' of Tess's fall; and, once invoked, set themselves before her as obstructions on the path towards a new life. The naïveté of Tess's responses to her situation (if one accepts a knowledge of Wordsworth as probable in a Sixth Standard pupil) is realistic in its very inadequacy. 'Alone on a desert island would she have been wretched?' reasons Tess,[34] and her reasoning has more than once been regarded as comic. It is certainly ludicrous, for that is its function. In a society whose scale of values matched the terms imposed by the environment Tess would be as little wretched in her social setting as in isolation; her reaction at this point is a childish rejection of values which she can already see to be false. Ultimately it is society which is ludicrous, and not Tess's reasoning. For the code imposed by society is based upon beliefs which are inconsistent with an un-ordered, blind universe in which human beings have no significance; at the same time it ignores the significance of the individual when viewed purely in terms of human consciousness and awareness by imposing arbitrary laws which do not correspond to human experience.

Tess of the D'Urbervilles is based, as was *The Return of the Native*, on a knowledge of an inevitable conflict in nature: the conflict between sentient man and insentient forces. But it steps beyond that knowledge to question the appropriateness of social institutions and social concepts as weapons in that conflict. Hardy uses a set of irreconcilables to point to parallel irreconcilables in nature. A social code which regards sexuality as in itself evil, and holds men and women responsible for impulses for which they hold no responsibility is contrasted with a view of sexuality as an instinctive, irresistible force. In this sense *Tess* is a work about determinism. Sexuality is neither condemned nor praised; it is merely accepted. There are times when the 'appetite for joy' appears to be synonymous with sexuality; there are moments, too, when the 'well-judged plan' of the mating of men and women is described as 'ill-judged' in its execution.[35] These conflicting attitudes are unreconciled. Nor is it clear to what extent Hardy regards sexuality as uncontrollable:

> Latterly [Clare] had seen only Life, felt only the great passionate pulse of existence, unwarped, uncontorted, untrammelled by those creeds which futilely attempt to check what wisdom would be content to regulate.[36]

One could wish for greater clarity here, since the degree to which man can or cannot regulate sexual passions is relevant to our judgement of the characters in *Tess*. The basic discrepancy, however, between social laws and natural conduct is drawn clearly enough. So too is the parallel discrepancy between a universe in which man is irrelevant, and a consciousness through which he becomes the centre of that universe. Tess's tragedy is that her consciousness is trapped by its growing awareness of the irrelevance of social ordinances, and the mastering influence of her natural being.

For, in addition to sexual determinism, this work goes far to postulate hereditary determinism also. Speaking after the publication of the novel Hardy commented:

> The murder that Tess commits is the hereditary quality, to which I more than once allude, working out in this impoverished descendant of a once noble family. That is logical. And again, it is but a simple transcription of the obvious that she should make reparation by death for her sin. . . . . You ask why Tess should not have gone off with Clare and 'lived happily ever after'. Do you not see that under *any* circumstances they were doomed to unhappiness? A sensitive man like Angel Clare could never have been happy with her. After the first few months he would inevitably have thrown her failings in her face.[37]

This is more than a statement that the murder reflects qualities inherent in Tess's character; it is a statement of natural limitations in both characters. Just as much as Tess's hereditary qualities, Clare's are stressed in the portrait of Parson Clare. Yet that same portrait comments:

> His creed of determinism was such that it almost amounted to a vice, and quite amounted, on its negative side, to a renunciative philosophy which had cousinship with that of Schopenhauer and Leopardi.[38]

We may fairly expect, then, that *Tess of the D'Urbervilles* rejects determinism as a creed. Yet it is the work in which 'proleptic' images are most consistently fulfilled, one in which little chance appears to be offered to either Tess or Clare, and a novel in which the illusion of inevitability is most clearly maintained. The only real opportunity which is given to Tess to escape from the trap in which she is caught is ruined by the loss of courage which hinders her from appealing to Clare's parents. The remaining opportunities are negated by innate qualities; so too, however, are our judgements of the failings of both Tess and Clare. One may fairly say that if Tess's career is not predestined, it certainly appears so. To search for causes, however, is to come once more face to face with Hardy's search as he narrates the details of the evening of Tess's fall. And to face this is to realise that Tess's eventual fate is caused solely by ill-adapted social ordinances: only an 'illicit' union and the birth of an 'illegitimate' child condemn Tess, and the words 'illicit' and 'illegitimate' each reflect the religious or ethical misunderstandings of men. So long as social codes fail to take account of reality, for so long does man expose himself obtusely to tragic possibilities. Heredity, economic forces, Time, Chance, and Consequence shape Tess's career and bring about her downfall. Only social convention *causes* it.

Tess, therefore, remains sexually pure, since 'unchastity' cannot be said to be unnatural. She remains morally pure because the murder of d'Urberville, even as the product of hereditary passions, is brought to being by a situation for which Tess is not morally responsible. As Hardy penned his last paragraph to the work his ironic appeal to 'Justice' spoke its plea to his readers to examine the social code which could both cause and condemn, and the religious code which could deny human responsibility even as it punished. In parts *Tess of the D'Urbervilles* fails to balance its narrative against its commentary; in parts the commentary appears querulous and ill-judged. But in its portrait of an innocent sensibility violated by social ignorance it becomes a passionate appeal for sanity in a difficult and confusing world.

It is also something more. For *Tess of the D'Urbervilles* embodies those autobiographical elements which had increasingly troubled Hardy's mature consciousness. They had been present in *The Woodlanders*, whose setting, the Hintocks, represents the area around Melbury Osmund, Jemima Hardy's early home. The comment on intermarriages, in particular, is instructive:

> As in most villages so secluded as this, intermarriages were of Hapsburgian frequency, and there were hardly two houses in Little Hintock unrelated by some matrimonial tie or other.[39]

Cousinship had again been present on the fringes of the novel: we are told that Giles's father had married a member of Marty South's family.[40] There may be a recollection of Julia Augusta Martin in the portrait of Felice Charmond—the lady of the local great house has almost become a stock figure for Hardy's fiction —and Hardy may have seen something of his own temperament in Fitzpiers's capacity for several concurrent infatuations.[41] These minor elements, and some major ones, are repeated in *Tess*. Mrs Martin appears as Clare's godmother, Mrs Pitney, 'the Squire's wife'[42] (Julia Augusta had married Francis Pitney Martin); there is at least a reminiscence of cousinship in the false family relationship between Tess and Alec d'Urberville; and there is especially the notion of heredity, a fundamental theme of the work. Hardy's family is once directly named, and ideas familiar to us from the poems make their appearance:

> There's the Billetts and the Drenkhards and the Greys and the St. Quentins and the Hardys and the Goulds, who used to own the lands for miles down this valley; you could buy 'em all up now for an old song a'most.[43]

> There is something very sad in the extinction of a family of renown, even if it was fierce, dominating, feudal renown.[44]

> I cannot help associating your decline as a family with this other fact—of your want of firmness. Decrepit families imply decrepit wills, decrepit conduct.[45]

Most of all, there are the reminiscences of Tryphena Sparks. Some of them are casual, like the mention of a chicken named Phena,[46] or the fact that Tess belongs to a large rural family. More striking is the description of Tess as a child, which carries with it the flavour of remembered knowledge:

> In those early days she had been much loved by others of her own sex and age, and had used to be seen about the village as one of three—all nearly of the same year—walking home from school side by side; Tess the middle one—in a pink print pinafore, of a finely reticulated pattern, worn over a stuff frock that had lost its original colour for a nondescript tertiary—marching on upon long stalky legs, in tight stockings which had little ladder-like holes at the knees, torn by kneeling in the roads and banks in search of vegetable and mineral treasures; her then earth-coloured hair hanging like pot-hooks; the arms of the two outside girls resting round the waist of Tess; her arms on the shoulders of the two supporters.[47]

Part of the force of this novel stems from this quality of real knowledge, and some attempt has been made by the author to preserve it. 'The name of the eclipsing girl, whatever it was, has not been handed down' he writes of Clare's first dancing-partner;[48] and most suggestively there is the reference to 'the stopt-diapason note which her voice acquired when her heart was in her speech, and which will never be forgotten by those who knew her'.[49] Tess's voice and her hair, though not her figure, correspond to these of Sue Bridehead, who can be much more closely associated with Tryphena; but Tess also undergoes the experience of pregnancy in her seventeenth year, and she begins a recovery from it in her twentieth, at the same age as Tryphena left Dorset for London. The phrase 'it was a fault which time would cure', used in reference to Tess's mature figure, recalls a similar remark made by Tryphena during her interview for her post in the Plymouth school:

> When she went to Plymouth for an interview the chairman of the school board remarked that she was very young.
>
> 'Well, sir,' she said, 'that is a thing that time will cure.'
>
> She was appointed headmistress.[50]

And just as in Puddletown after Tryphena's removal from her post as pupil-teacher, the headmistress had lectured her girls on the meaning of the Seventh Commandment, so Tess, on leaving Trantridge, flees from the sight of the commandment written on a five-barred gate. Parson Clare was modelled on Horace Moule's father; and in the dripping of the blood after the murder of Alec d'Urberville we may catch a reminiscence of the inquest report upon Moule's death. These are small details, but they have their own cumulative effect: and it is difficult not to believe that Hardy was consciously recalling some aspects of his earlier career. With *Jude the Obscure* the suspicion that he did so becomes a certainty.

IX

Thus do I but the phantom retain
Of the maiden of yore . . .
C.P. 55

FOR Thomas Hardy 1890 and the years immediately following were years of emotional turmoil. The reasons for this were not entirely domestic. The reception of *Tess of the D'Urbervilles* was not uniformly friendly, to say the least, and Hardy was alarmed at the degree of hostility aroused in some quarters. In a cancelled passage of the *Life* he gave a startling revelation of his feelings:

> The subtitle of the book, added as a casual afterthought, seemed to be especially exasperating. All this would have been amusing if it had not revealed such antagonism at the back of it, such distortion of truth bearing evidence, as Hardy used to say, 'of that absolute want of principle in a reviewer which gives one a start of fear as to a possible crime he may commit against one's person, such as a stab or a shot in a dark lane for righteousness' sake'. Such critics, however, 'who differing from an author of a work purely artistic, in sociological views, politics, or theology, cunningly disguised that illegitimate reason for antagonism by attacking his work on a point of art itself,' were not numerous or effectual in this case. And, as has been stated, they were overpowered by the current of dumb opinion.[1]

There were domestic sadnesses also. A number of relatives died, including his father on July 20, 1892. His marriage was clearly not going well—though the final estrangement caused by *Jude the Obscure* was still to come—and his thoughts reverted, as they had clearly done in the preparation of *Tess*, to Tryphena Sparks. It is probable, though not certain, that Hardy had had no contact with Tryphena since his marriage, although his friend Eden Philpotts, who later wrote a novel called *Tryphena*,* lived close

* London, 1928. Philpotts's Tryphena is the illegitimate daughter of a local squire. See *Providence and Mr Hardy*, pp. 180-1.

Tryphena Sparks

Randal, son of Hardy
and Tryphena Sparks.

to the Gale home at Topsham. None the less, in a train bound for London, on March 13, 1890, Hardy began a poem to Tryphena, 'Thoughts of Phena', though he completed only the first few lines at that time. In the *Life* he describes this as a 'curious instance of sympathetic telepathy'—the quality he describes as existing between Jude and Sue. Six days later, on Monday, March 19, Tryphena died. Among the mourners at her funeral was her son Randal.* Hardy did not attend, but in the following July he cycled from Dorchester with his brother Henry, leaving a wreath on her grave bearing the message 'In Loving Memory. Tom Hardy'. The occasion was recalled by Tryphena's daughter:

> . . . when I first saw Thomas Hardy it was after my Mother died and I was thirteen years old. It was a lovely hot day and Hardy and Henry called in at our home to see us and say they had been to the cemetery and taken a wreath and put it on Tryphena's grave with Tom's name and card and it stayed there for years. I wish I had saved it now. I gave them lunch, they were cycling and going back to Dorchester. Henry looked at me and said 'You are exactly like your Mother' but his brother did not say much. Henry said 'I must kiss you' and we all laughed and said Goodbye.[2]

For Hardy the visit was a poignant one. Mrs Bromell described how he winced when Henry Hardy kissed her; and his feelings are suggested in the poem 'To A Motherless Child':

> Ah, child, thou art but half thy darling mother's;
> Hers couldst thou wholly be,
> My light in thee would outglow all in others;
> She would relive to me.[3]

The thought is found in Chapter I-viii of *Jude*, where Jude projects his mind into the future to see Sue surrounded by her children; and it clearly underlies *The Well-Beloved*.

Tryphena's death exercised an effect on Hardy's work comparable with that of the death of Emma Lavinia Hardy in 1912. Even the manuscript revisions indicate how strongly she had become present in Hardy's mind. It is clear that in the early form of the manuscript Sue Bridehead was to have been a major factor in the novel from the beginning, while a considerably more subordinate place was to have been occupied by Phillotson.

* See Appendix B.

It is difficult to see how Hardy's earliest plans for Sue—she was to have been a recent resident of Marygreen, leaving there after being adopted by the Provost of Cloister College, Christminster, and before Jude's arrival in the village—would have left it open for Hardy to pursue the theme of academic frustration, since presumably such a friendly College principal would have been equally interested in the fortunes of another and related young talent. None the less, the initial plan was there, and Hardy's own indication in the preface that the story was partly occasioned by the death of a woman in 1890 is a strong indication that in Sue Bridehead we have a great deal of Tryphena Sparks. Moreover, the original use of the surnames *Hand* and *Head* for Jude's and Sue's ancestors indicates that the theme of a malign heredity, strong in *Tess* and *Jude* and apparent in even such a minor work as *A Laodicean*—all three books bearing traces of Tryphena's influence—suggest that the Tryphena story was in some way connected with Hardy's own ancestral broodings.* So, too, does the connection apparently established in the book between the fortunes of Hardy and Tryphena and those of Hardy's paternal grandmother, Mary Head of Fawley. For not only is her name reproduced in the forms *Mary*green and Bride*head*, and Jude's surname taken from Mary's birthplace, but the manuscript shows that one original possibility was *Hopeson*: certainly an appropriate enough name for Jude, but also a derivative of the maiden name of Mary Head's mother, whose fortunes in Berkshire were inauspicious.† Nor are these the only autobiographical associations to be made with the novel. Strands of past history flooded into Hardy's mind. Not only did he recall his courtship of Tryphena, but also the wooing of his sister Mary by a cousin: one exploit of Mary Hardy, when she escaped from Salisbury Training College at night, was revived in Sue's escape from the Melchester Normal College, based upon Mary's old school. Horace Moule may be present in the portrait of Phillotson: the gap between his age and Tryphena's and that between Phillotson and Sue is identical, while in Hardy's memorial poem to Moule he has Moule ask:

> Since you agreed, unurged and full-advised,
> And let warmth grow without discouragement,
> Why do you bear you now as if surprised,
> When what has come was clearly consequent?[4]

* See Appendix A. *The Jude* MS. is in the Fitzwilliam Museum, Cambridge.

† See Appendix A.

In *Jude the Obscure* the same pattern—which appears to be some encouragement by the younger man of the older to let an attachment develop—is bitterly noticed by Jude, as Phillotson places his arm about Sue's waist:

> The ironical clinch to his sorrow was given by the thought that the intimacy between his cousin and the schoolmaster had been brought about entirely by himself.[5]

The academic frustrations of Moule's career and the vocational frustrations of Hardy's were each given their place in the novel, as was Hardy's childhood wish not to grow up, his childhood reading, his very birthplace 'at Mellstock, down in South Wessex', which is assigned to Jude. In fact no one who cares to study the Hardy family history, and Hardy's response to it, can avoid the conclusion that this work is, to a major degree, autobiographical. It is not even impossible that some of Hardy's tortured vision of Tryphena in later years may have crept into the portrait of Arabella: Tryphena's husband kept a Topsham hotel, in which Tryphena herself sometimes assisted, and the poem, 'My Cicely', suggests fairly plainly that at moments, at least, Hardy saw his ex-fiancée, with 'liquor-fired face'.* Not all the events, clearly, nor all the characters, are direct transcripts from Hardy's career; but the book represents his emotional history from 1868 until 1890. Hardy denied it, as have some critics since. That denial cannot stand against the evidence. Nor should this be surprising: the most influential period of Hardy's career was marked by a love-affair with a girl ostensibly his cousin, the birth of a child, the death of Horace Moule, and by a steadily-growing obsession with hereditary influence, based in part on his observations of his own family. There are traces of these years throughout the novels, but only in the three named above are all these elements of major importance to the plot. Of these *A Laodicean* was written during a serious illness which compelled Hardy to draw on his emotional attitudes more directly than usual, and both *Tess* and *Jude* were written within the years immediately following Tryphena's death. Of the other books, two have a distinct relationship to this group: *Under the Greenwood Tree*, written while Hardy's association with Tryphena was still in being, and *The Well-Beloved*, written partly under the influence

* For a discussion of 'My Cicely' and Tryphena, see *Providence* . . ., pp. 122-3.

of Hardy's visit to Tryphena's home at Topsham. Lois Deacon and Terry Coleman have convincingly shown that the earlier versions of *The Well-Beloved* are remarkably close to *Jude the Obscure*, and they justify their description of it as a 'Jude-sketch'.[6] Of the remaining works, the closest in time to Hardy's association with Tryphena is *A Pair of Blue Eyes*—and that, as we have seen, is in many respects to be associated with *Tess*. It is difficult to avoid Lois Deacon's conclusion that Tryphena Sparks was the principal inspiration behind Hardy's works, despite the number of other influences during his mature years; nor does that conclusion depend upon a reading from the works to the life. It rests simply on the comparison of known facts with the known works of fiction.

To search for objective comment in *Jude the Obscure* thus becomes an almost vain attempt. Hardy was not writing objectively; he was pouring his heart's blood into the work. When *Jude* was complete there were no more novels to write, for the almost obsessional reflections of the previous years found their fulfilment. This final summary of his experience with Tryphena—for that is what it is—was also the last expression in prose of a passion which became stronger, not weaker, during the years of separation. If the poems of 1912-13 are a monument to Emma Lavinia Gifford, *Jude* is the living memorial to Tryphena Sparks. Its effect is startling. Few novels in the English language have a more powerful impact, yet few major works are so ill-defined in their aims. *Jude* is almost wrecked by its subjective elements; yet were they absent *Jude* could not exist.

What is the theme of *Jude the Obscure*? Hardy himself defined it in his preface as:

> . . . the fret and fever, derision and disaster, that may press in the wake of the strongest passion known to humanity, . . . a deadly war waged between flesh and spirit; . . . the tragedy of unfulfilled aims . . .

It is difficult to apply all three ideas consistently to the novel. The love between Jude and Sue is complicated by two factors: the epicene quality of Sue; and the ancestral curse which hangs over their family. Neither of these complications is a fundamental cause of their tragedy, even though they loom large in the text. They enjoy, indeed, several years of happiness together, and it is the chance of ill health which first undermines their contentment—'we gave up all ambition', says Sue to Arabella, 'and were never so happy in our lives till his illness came'.[7] A parallel is drawn between the misfortunes of their ancestors and their own lives, but it is a parallel which is never fulfilled. Neither of these factors is introduced into the story primarily for the story's sake—indeed, it is only in *Tess* that heredity is raised as a crucial issue. They are there for subjective reasons, adding perspective to the story, certainly, but no more. Nor is it their love or its consequences which accounts for their separation.

Similarly, the 'war between flesh and spirit' is a concept which has only superficial connection with the work. Jude's first marriage, it is true, lends colour to the belief that he is over-sexed, a victim to his own sexual passions—until one recalls that it is not until he is nineteen that he even looks at a woman as an object of sexual desire; and Hardy's text makes it clear that his passions are perfectly normal. His life with Sue before she eventually yields to him is more remarkable, and shows that he has firm control over himself; and, despite her eventual submission to him, there is little to suggest that their love was damaged by his self-control, or that he would have broken down. Arabella's contribution to the plot is partly artistic—she contributes vitally to the cyclical movement of the narrative—and partly as a contrast to Sue. If, indeed, she represents the flesh as Sue represents the spirit, one could perhaps construct an allegorical or morality pattern for the work; but such a pattern would add little to the impact of the book if applied, and nothing to its significance.

The tragedy of unfulfilled aims? Jude's aims are scholastic, and though his marriage to Arabella is a practical hindrance and his parentage of bastard children a social one, neither plays any part in his failure to achieve an academic career. For such as Jude, as the title implies and the book shows, an academic career was a practical impossibility. He acknowledges this himself—'it was my poverty and not my will that consented to be beaten'.[8] However, it is this theme of the work that is the most fundamental, and Hardy was, in a sense, justified in maintaining that the discussion of the marriage laws was simply machinery on which to construct his tale. Jude's rejection by Christminster, and the idealistic longing which survives it, are materially relevant to the rupture between Jude and Sue. It should be clear, however, that social injustices and the exclusion of Jude are only partly responsible: Jude's careless neglect is also a major cause. The rejection of his academic hopes, the social ordinance which brands illegitimacy, and the domestic attitudes which lead to a refusal of lodgings to a pregnant woman play their part. But

Jude's refusal to make practical inquiries about methods of admission to a college, the self-deception which prevents him from seeing the blemishes of Christminster at first sight ('when he passed objects out of harmony with its general expression he allowed his eyes to slip over them as if he did not see them'[9]) are reflected in his eagerness to watch the Christminster processions when he should have been searching for rooms. He postpones this task until even Sue is aware that his frustrated idealism has not served them well:

> She thought of the strange operation of a simple-minded man's ruling passion, that it should have led Jude, who loved her and the children so tenderly, to place them in this depressing purlieu, because he was still haunted by his dream. Even now he did not distinctly hear the freezing negative that those scholared walls echoed to his desire.[10]

Jude's career is a career of consistent failure, with the exception of a few brief years of happiness with Sue. This much is clear. Yet no one formula explains that failure. Social barriers and social attitudes, endowed personal characteristics, and occasional carelessness all contribute. But it is perhaps *Jude*'s greatest merit that it cannot be reduced to a formula. For it is in its portrait of two struggling and sensitive souls against a whole range of obstacles that the success of *Jude the Obscure* lies. Despite its apparent fragmentation of themes the book is saved by its contrast, at times explicit, between man's aspirations and his opportunities. The sexual and scholarly sides of Jude's nature are linked by a parallel between his ambition for learning and his love for Sue. Christminster is an ambition for subjective reasons only:

> It had been the yearning of his heart to find something to anchor on, to cling to—for some place which he could call admirable. Should he find that place in this city if he could get there?[11]

His approach to Sue is identical:

> To an impressionable and lonely young man the consciousness of having at last found anchorage for his thoughts which promised to supply both social and spiritual possibilities, was like the dew of Hermon. . . .[12]

In each case the anchorage is unsafe. Christminster is unsafe partly because it is unattainable, even more because it is no longer relevant. The mediaevalism of its architecture, 'dead as a fern-leaf in a lump of coal', represents the mediaevalism of approach which makes it 'a nest of commonplace schoolmasters whose characteristic is timid obsequiousness to tradition'.[13] Sue is unsafe because her principal ideal, for all her 'modern' notions, is 'a return to Greek joyousness' which is no longer possible. Indeed, Jude and Sue stand in relations very similar to those of Clym Yeobright and Eustacia Vye, the men representing an adjustment to the modern environment, the women a tradition which can no longer survive. That Jude adjusts slowly, and only with self-knowledge, and that that self-knowledge involves virtual self-annihilation, is the measure of Hardy's development—if that is the right word—since *The Return of the Native*. In *Jude* all that a consciousness of the modern environment can lead to is 'the universal wish not to live'.

Discussion of Hardy's debt to Schopenhauer and von Hartmann would suggest that this is a logical development of Hardy's thought, and that the evolutionary meliorism which he came to adopt is a partial and inadequate answer to pessimistic notions to which he was more deeply committed. The evidence is against such a view. There is no doubt that his reading of philosophy influenced Hardy, just as there can be little doubt that the Parnell divorce case and subsequent Press comment had their effect.[14] Hardy did not live in isolation from current events, and he read deeply and seriously. But his responses, as his literary notebooks, the comments in the *Life*, and the surviving letters all suggest, were conditioned by mood and subjectivity. Hardy was a feeler first, only secondarily a thinker, and his reading was often an attempt to confirm impressions already formed. Nor did he claim otherwise. *Jude the Obscure* is an almost total negation of the message of Hardy's other work. It would be difficult, to say the least, to make a case for *Jude* as optimistic or melioristic philosophy; it is equally difficult to make a case for it as philosophy at all. More than anything else he wrote, this work, despite philosophical asides—many fewer than in *Tess*—is an 'impression', a 'seeming', highly subjective, highly emotional, even unbalanced. The suicide of Little Father Time and the murder of the children are the neurotic expression of something whose analysis defied even Hardy himself; and it can only be glimpsed remotely even now. The loss of Tryphena, the suicide of Moule, the birth of the child, the failure of a marriage, the frustration of a vocation for the ministry, and the subsequent loss of faith—who can gauge adequately the effect of these upon a sensitive and brooding spirit whose inspiration had been consistently derived from the past? I have seen no adequate estimate of the power of *Jude the Obscure*, and certainly I cannot offer one. The most that I can say is that the answer lies here, in the life and soul of Thomas Hardy, and not in the source-books of European philosophy, or the English divorce-courts. If there is a death-wish in *Jude the Obscure* it may even be true to say that it represents a longing for death even in Hardy's soul—the kind of longing expressed in such a poem as 'Her Immortality', illustrated in *Wessex Poems* by a sketch of Coombe Eweleaze, where Hardy had spent much of his courtship with Tryphena:

> I said: 'My days are lonely here;
> I need thy smile alway:
> I'll use this night my ball or blade,
> And join thee ere the day'.
> A tremor stirred her tender lips,
> Which parted to dissuade:
> 'That cannot be, my friend,' she cried;
> 'Think, I am but a Shade!
> 'A Shade but in its mindful ones
> Has immortality;
> By living, me you keep alive,
> By dying you slay me . . .[15]

Hardy's previous works, while accepting the intimidating nature of the universal environment, had none the less shown a refusal to be intimidated. The following works, *The Dynasts* above all, explore methods of resisting irrevocable universal forces. *Jude*, and *Jude* alone, appears to admit wholly negative impressions.

Superficially, Jude, like Tess, is at the mercy of social disadvantages; yet one is hard put to see Jude content in any society. The breakdown of his marriage and his life with Sue are so clearly, even if incompletely, paralleled with the turbulent lives of their common ancestors that they cannot be seen as purely local and temporary features: there is something fundamental here, a force possessed by the blood alone. This force is never clearly explained, and Hardy, as his poems show, did not know the explanation himself. He may have derived something from Weismann's *Essays on Heredity*, but he had no need to explore authorities to find the notion of a family curse. That he should have associated Mary Head and her family with his tale, without, so far as one can tell, knowing the full details of her story (though 'One We Knew' suggests that he knew more than we do, particularly of the hanged ancestor who appears in *Jude* and the gibbet of the poem), is sufficient evidence that his motives here as elsewhere were chiefly personal. Nor did he need wholly to invent the reactions of a lonely, sensitive, and impassioned man to a capricious and tantalising woman. None of the letters between Hardy and Tryphena survive, if they ever existed, and it is obviously difficult, even dangerous, to make hasty assertions about her character as a young girl. But the fact that Fancy Day of the early 1870's and Sue Bridehead of the 1890's bear so many clear resemblances should make us think. Each of these periods of Hardy's life was one in which Tryphena was dominant. Some have seen in Sue a closer reflection of Florence Henniker, who had become Hardy's close friend at this time. That friendship certainly existed and was important; but it survived the publication of *Jude*, which seems more than a little surprising if Hardy had made such a detailed analysis of Mrs Henniker's sexual responses. I discount Mrs Henniker entirely. But however much of Hardy is in Jude, however much of Tryphena is in Sue (and, perhaps, in Arabella), nothing can alter the fact that Hardy successfully brought to life the psychology of his characters to a degree surpassing any of his previous attempts. Sue Bridehead is perhaps the most remarkable feminine portrait in the English novel. There is a restraint in characterisation in this book which is new and impressive, and it is perhaps seen most clearly in Sue's grief over her failure to respond to Phillotson:

> 'I have only been married a month or two!' she went on, still remaining bent upon the table, and sobbing into her hands. 'And it is said that what a woman shrinks from in the early days of her marriage—she shakes down to with comfortable indifference in half-a-dozen years. But that is much like saying that the amputation of a limb is no affliction since a person gets comfortably accustomed to the use of a wooden leg or arm in the course of time!'
>
> '. . . there is nothing wrong except my own wickedness, I suppose you'd call it—a repugnance on my part, for a reason I cannot disclose, and what would not be admitted as one by the world in general! . . . What tortures me is the necessity of being responsive to this man whenever he wishes, good as he is morally!—the dreadful contract to feel in a

> particular way in a matter whose essence is in its voluntariness! . . .[16]

Nor are the grounds for these feelings ever given. Perhaps this is simply a reflection of Hardy's caution towards his audience, but it is pleasant to think that it reflects a natural delicacy, not about sex—he is deliberately and forcibly indelicate at times—but about art. The flamboyant parading of sexual motives and physiological causes of the twentieth century is tactless for reasons which have nothing to do with propriety: and no author, including Lawrence, has so sensitively and perceptively observed a woman's reactions. The same is true throughout his portrait of Sue. He can quietly criticise her—'tears of pity for Jude's approaching sufferings at her hands mingled with those which had surged up in pity for herself'[17]—yet he conveys always the sheer nervous vibrancy of her nature, the fear of emotional commitment, and the desperate longing for love without sexual or psychic danger. Jude's comment on Sue is perhaps truer of her psychology than of her body:

> You were a distinct type—a refined creature, intended by Nature to be left intact. But I couldn't leave you alone.[18]

—except that it is not Jude's passion which has violated Sue, but her predicament as a mobile, sensitive consciousness in an unconscious universe. Sue's morality, until the end, is complete: only the sexual attractiveness she has been given, and the sexual impulses which lead her to an enticing capriciousness are expressions of the a-moral. And over these she has no control. 'Sue, Sue, you are not worth a man's love', Jude cries: there is little evidence that Hardy agreed with him. Nor, to speak subjectively, could I. The unfailing compassion which penetrates this work is the greatest justification for Hardy's 'descent' into naturalism, since against man's nobler aspirations nature is crude, even coarse, in its blind disregard. Neither Sue, nor Jude, nor Arabella is condemned (the latter perhaps locally, but scarcely in the full context of the work), while Phillotson's conduct emerges as heroic. Where he fails, and his rigid self-control as he regains sexual dominion over Sue approaches a failure of compassion, his motives are given and they are human. Each of the characters is compelled to bow before a force which is stronger than they, even though each of them acquires some understanding of what that force means. Phillotson retreats into social approval, Arabella preserves her gift for animal enjoyment—in other words, she abandons herself happily to the life-force—Sue is broken, and Jude stumbles bitterly and cynically towards his death. If this were all this book might be impressive, yet its power could hardly be called tragic. One paragraph alone sums up the strongest mitigating force in the work, again an expression of Hardy's personal attitudes:

> 'Don't think me hard because I have acted on conviction. Your generous devotion to me is unparallelled, Jude! Your worldly failure, if you have failed, is to your credit rather than to your blame. Remember that the best and greatest among mankind are those who do themselves no worldly good. Every successful man is more or less a selfish man. The devoted fail . . . 'Charity seeketh not her own'.
>
> 'In that chapter we are at one, ever beloved darling, and on it we'll part friends. Its verses will stand when all the rest that you call religion has passed away.'[19]

That, despite the book's grimness, is its final impression. But it is scarcely implicit in the action. Like the grimness itself, it springs from motives deep in the author himself, conditions his attitudes to his characters, and gives nobility both to him and to them.

THE DYNASTS

X

O Innocents, can ye forget
That things to be were shaped and set
Ere mortals and this planet met?
III, vi, 3

HARDY'S poetry has had a curious history. In the first place much of it, though written early in the poet's lifetime, lay unpublished until he was nearly sixty years old. As early as 1870 Emma Lavinia Gifford noticed a manuscript sticking from the author's pocket, while poems to Tryphena and others were written even before that time. Yet most of these early attempts were, if submitted, rejected by the magazines, and none appeared in book form until the close of the century. *Wessex Poems* was published in 1898, *Poems of the Past and the Present* in 1902, both volumes including material written before 1870. They were greeted with interest rather than enthusiasm. The critics were a little puzzled, though generally not unkind. Hardy's reception as a novelist had for the most part been respectful, sometimes even more, and the controversies caused by *Tess* and *Jude* certainly did not damage their popularity; they may, of course, have damaged Hardy. It is difficult to know how much credence to attach to his statement that the reception of *Jude* entirely cured him of novel-writing,[1] but his highly personal reaction to criticism of the work may have been because so much of himself was in it that he felt the attacks to be personal also. However, it seems more likely that Hardy's fundamental sources of energy for the novel were now exhausted. These had been two-fold, intellectual and emotional. *Jude the Obscure* very effectively expressed the stratum of embittered emotion which had been present throughout Hardy's career as a novelist; while he may well have felt that his intellectual inquiry would better be expressed in verse. The mild reception accorded to his first volumes of poetry must have convinced him that he was right (though Swinburne's experience in the sixties with *Poems and Ballads* might have given him pause). Even so, Hardy did not always feel that his poetry was justly reviewed, but there are no outbursts like that originally intended for the *Life*, but subsequently deleted:

> The dear old marionettes that critics love, and the dear old waxen hero, and the heroine with the glued-on hair! This cowardly time can stand no other.[2]

Hardy's change was perhaps the thing that puzzled the critics most. The *Times Literary Supplement* was especially perplexed by the First Part of *The Dynasts*:

> Mr Thomas Hardy's long silence has been broken at last with the first volume of a drama of the Napoleonic wars, in three parts, nineteen acts, and one hundred and thirty scenes. His interest in the period, particularly as it affected his own now doubly-famous Wessex, is a matter of common knowledge, and his admirers have long expected and hoped that he would treat it on a large scale. It is as well to say at once that this is not the book we expected or desired. Why should Thomas Hardy, a master of prose narrative, have chosen to hamper himself with the dramatic form?[3]

Such discomfort is typical of much of the early criticism of *The Dynasts*—though as Parts Second and Third appeared the chorus of admiration grew stronger—and it was caused less by the choice of dramatic form than by the abandonment of prose narrative. The 'long silence' was non-existent; during the previous eight years there had been two novels and two major books of verse, but it had been possible to discount the verse in a way in which it was not possible to discount *The Dynasts*. In the subsequent years the second and third parts of the drama appeared, to be followed by six volumes of verse and *The Queen of Cornwall*. Even excluding the novels, we have a vast corpus of work representing every period of Hardy's life from his twenties to his last year, when he was eighty-seven. In our own time he has been accepted as one of the major poets of the century, and with some critics, at least, his novels have been forced to take second place.

Hardy's regular appearance in the anthologies, the steady sale of his verse, and the success of Hardy readings at the Dorchester Hardy Festival, might all lead us to assume that his position in the first rank of our poets was a matter of unqualified assent. This apparent popularity may be misleading, particularly in the case of *The Dynasts* which may be the least-read great poem in the English language—yet *The Dynasts* is a touchstone of Hardy's stature. A central body of shorter poems aside, there is a remarkable lack of consensus on the kind and value of his poetry. Moreover, lukewarm critics have so often been able to convict him of grave faults of form, diction, and content—faults which his admirers have felt bound to confess—that forty years after his death his reputation as a poet still rests on the same central core of verses.

In some ways he may have seemed a difficult poet. His language is often particularly idiosyncratic, though we may now be more prepared to accept such idiosyncrasies in our authors; while the so-called 'philosophy' of the poems has been thought repellent by some and exaggerated by others. Yet his language and meaning go hand in hand: the meaning is often uncomfortable, harsh, and jagged, and the vision sometimes confused; the style is often knotted and the diction twisted accordingly. Even to talk of a 'meaning' or a 'philosophy' may be a mistake: these poems are frequently explorations towards a meaning, part of the same search for spiritual fulfilment which had been present in Hardy's youth and onwards. We listen to the authentic voice of doubt, a voice which is often scarcely addressed to us at all. From the novels the perspective has changed. Instead of men against a universal background the poems show, almost exclusively, details of behaviour and mood. Only *The Dynasts* attempts to fuse these different perspectives, with humanity and the background against which their scene is played being fully studied and integrated. *The Dynasts* stands as the major statement of Hardy's impressions of existence, although it is in the poems that we are as close as we shall ever be to Hardy the man, and are guided by the musings of an individual, introspective voice.

Perhaps the epic-drama becomes of supreme importance just because that voice is absent. For in framing his work upon a conflict of ideas, represented on the one hand by the Spirit of the Years and on the other by the Spirit of the Pities, Hardy was able to objectify his own personal responses within the basic structure of his drama, and he allowed free play both to ideas which commanded his grudging intellectual assent, or at least consideration, and to his emotional responses to human pain and suffering. *The Dynasts* has been seen as an epic of determinism, and would thus stand in direct opposition to the patterns of choice and responsibility indicated by the novels; in fact those patterns are as much Hardy's concern in the epic as they had previously been. Only the change of method has obscured this fact.

We can be quite clear that *The Dynasts* is a historical drama; we can also be quite clear that it is a philosophical poem. What is not immediately clear is to which of these we should give precedence, and whether the two forms are satisfactorily united—there is little point in using two forms in one work if they are not intended to cohere, and Hardy's first uncertainties over the form suggest that he was looking for a method which would unite both elements of his conception. The danger is obvious, and at first sight it looks as if Hardy failed to overcome it: *The Dynasts* appears to be as discrete as any work in the language. A first reading of it is invariably disappointing, and the slow reception of the work is understandable, if not excusable. For the discreteness is an illusion, fostered by Hardy for the simplest and profoundest of reasons: what he depicts appears to be discrete too. To him it seemed that a careful study of all the apparently separate human actions revealed their essential unity; and, for his readers, a careful study of this apparently discrete work reveals *its* essential unity. One thinks, indeed, of Hardy's citation from Myers's article on the human personality, entered in his first commonplace book:

> . . . the cells of my body are mine in the sense that for their own comfort and security they have agreed to do a great many things at the bidding of my brain. But they are servants with a life of their own. . . . Does my consciousness testify that I am a single entity? That only means that a stable *coenesthesia* exists in me just now; a sufficient number of my nervous centres are acting in unison. I am being governed by a good working majority. Give me a blow on the head which silences some leading centres, and the rest will split into 'parliamentary groups' and brawl in delirium or madness.*

In *The Dynasts* this idea, and that of an essentially *organic* creation, are developed, and so far from watching an all-powerful Will ruthlessly exerting its pressures we see a combination of wills struggling towards the achievement of some common aim. This is, of course, a radical over-simplification of a complex meaning. Only a study of the methods of the poem can illustrate its basic accuracy.

In January 1887, at a time when he had already begun to consider the theme and nature of his epic, Hardy made the following note on the visual arts:

> After looking at the landscape ascribed to Bonington in our

* See below, pp. 221-30.

> drawing-room I feel that Nature is played out as a Beauty, but not as a Mystery. I don't want to see landscapes, i.e., scenic paintings of them, because I don't want to see the original realities—as optical effects, that is. I want to see the deeper reality underlying the scenic, the expression of what are sometimes called abstract imaginings.
>
> The 'simply natural' is interesting no longer. The much decried, mad, late-Turner rendering is now necessary to create my interest. The exact truth as to material fact ceases to be of importance in art—it is a student's style—the style of a period when the mind is serene and unawakened to the tragical mysteries of life; when it does not bring anything to the object that coalesces with it and translates the quantities that are already there,—half hidden, it may be—and the two united are depicted as the All.[4]

In the following month we find this:

> *Feb 13th.* I was thinking a night or two ago that people are somnambulists—that the material is not the real—only the visible, the real being invisible optically. That it is because we are in a somnambulistic hallucination that we think the real to be what we see as real.[5]

The concern for a vision reflecting a new awareness of man's predicament, expressed in the novels most clearly in *The Return of the Native*,* is now given a practical realisation in *The Dynasts*, which we may see as an attempt to break out of the 'somnambulistic hallucination' to find a 'mad, late-Turner rendering' of the facts of human choice and existence. Hardy's Overworld, and the visions it creates, represent the deeper reality behind the human, scenic, action. Yet this underlying reality exists not at the expense of the scenic, but in conjunction with it. The human scene is presented graphically and clearly, although it is compressed to give rapidity to the whole—indeed, this compression is one of the immediate causes of the apparent discreteness of the work: the spirits have no sooner visited one area of the human scene than they are off to another. Yet the manuscript revisions suggest that compression was exactly what Hardy was aiming to achieve—fully-realised actions fleeting enough to be conceived as mere threads or pulsations of the Will. Speed of action in the human scenes is one method of suggesting the fleeting nature of

* See above, pp. 87-95.

the scene. One can see clearly the effectiveness of Hardy's plan by comparing, say, III, i, iv, with its source. The procession of French warriors past the portrait of the young King of Rome is set in brief but effective contrast with the procession of the Russian clergy:

> . . . a portrait of the young King of Rome playing at cup-and-ball, the ball being represented as the globe. The officers standing near are attracted round, and then the officers and soldiers further back begin running up, till there is a great crowd. . . . The Old Guard is summoned, and marches past surveying the picture; then other regiments . . . NAPOLEON watches. The Russian ecclesiastics pass through the regiments, which are under arms, bearing the icon and other religious insignia. The Russian soldiers kneel before it.

The two scenes occupy twenty-six lines in all, while Tolstoy, in the corresponding passage of *War and Peace*,[6] deals with the French and Russian scenes separately and at some length. One cannot compare the two passages qualitatively, their purpose and technique being so different, but it is significant that Hardy is prepared to devote so little space to an ironical situation—the type of situation which in his shorter poems appeals to him more than any other. The very presence of such conciseness should give us pause in our assessments of the work: if its effect is to destroy the unity of the work then *The Dynasts* is a failure—but if there is an over-riding unity such conciseness may be essential. And in the face of Hardy's deliberate exclusion at so many points we are compelled to seek some explanation less simple than downright failure.

To some extent we have to seek it in ourselves. *The Dynasts*, though cast in dramatic form, is essentially a *poem*, and demands the same sensitivity of response as one would apply to any complex poetic text. At the most obvious level, the reader himself is asked to visualise the action for himself, since there are no actors and no stage for him to look at. He is also asked to follow the guides embedded in the text until the twin actions of the drama, the human and the spirit-world, achieve their own unity of purpose; the task of synthesis, indeed, is a task imposed by the text upon the reader. The Overworld, the human action, and the language, all offer pointers to the way in which that unity may be achieved, but there can be no final unity without the reader's aid. Hardy himself insists within the preface that we cannot read his work without previous knowledge of the historical events: we also have to supply the perceptions required to mould these into an artistic whole. For, despite the apparent explicitness of the work, it is essentially an Impressionist achievement, if by Impressionism we understand the 'literary presentation of salient features, done in a few strokes'.[7] Hardy's salient features are quite explicit, and are given through the structure of both language and action. It is to the language that we first turn our attention.

The structural contrast found throughout Hardy's shorter poetry[8] is also to be found in *The Dynasts*: to talk of apparently separate actions, the one 'scenic', the other 'real', is at once to talk of two contrasting, indeed contradictory, impressions. The epic can only be interpreted or assessed when the meaning of this contradictory structure has been grasped, and particularly when the ambiguity resulting from that structure has been explored.

Edward Wright, a reviewer for the *Quarterly Review*, focused on the key principle in Hardy's construction of poetic terms when he wrote, on May 18, 1907:

> I intend to discuss your drama as an expression of one phase of the philosophy of Will. My only quarrel with you will be that 'unconscious Will', at least to me, implies a kind of enlightened action: action enlightened by an idea or directed, so to speak, by a frame of mind. But this is only a question of words. I, for instance, should prefer 'Unconscious Impulse'.[9]

Questions of words, of course, are questions of meaning: and Hardy's reply indicates that he had taken some pains to analyse his description of the Immanent Will, and that he had aimed at conciseness, though he admitted shortcomings:

> I quite agree with you in holding that the word 'Will' does not perfectly fit the idea to be conveyed—a vague thrusting movement in no predetermined direction—But the word you suggest—Impulse—seems to me to imply a driving power behind it; also a spasmodic movement unlike that of, say, the tendency of an ape to become a man, and other such processes.[10]

First of all, then, we should be prepared to have to supplement the descriptions of *The Dynasts* with some recognition that language does not allow the picture of the Will to be summed up in a single term. But we may fairly claim that the *total* picture should be as consistent as possible, and if we find ambiguity or contradiction in Hardy's picture we must decide whether this is a serious limitation in Hardy's art, or the result of a deliberate process of poetic composition. He may ask us to supply the unifying details to an Impressionistic formula, but we should not be asked to supply the salient features as well.

Ambiguity there certainly is: but this ambiguity differs in no way from Hardy's general descriptive method. And reduced to its outline, the ambiguity here is this: the image of the Will seems to be the image of an unconscious force, and the descriptions of It often contain lesser, supporting images of automatic or mechanistic content; but against that supporting imagery runs a parallel series of images which are only applicable to consciousness, and are taken from organic matter, often from human organisms but also from the rhythms and processes of nature. So that images of clockwork machines, the dance, puppetry—in short, images of automatic processes—are set against images drawn from the natural processes of growth, fruition, decay, and death. This marriage of opposites results in a strangely tense descriptive medium, threatening to dissolve at any moment, yet never actually doing so. Such a pattern parallels exactly the situation Hardy was attempting to describe: a compact, interdependent universe, full of contradictions.

Nor is this pattern confined only to the imagery: it lies behind the connotations of apparently the most ordinary words. The first two lines of *The Dynasts* reveal the pattern we may expect:

> *What of the Immanent Will and Its designs?—*
> *—It works unconsciously, as heretofore . . .*

The key words are *designs* and *unconsciously*. The questioner, the Shade of the Earth, has as much experience of the processes of the Will as anyone except the Spirit of the Years, yet she still credits It with *designs*—that is, with pre-set plans deliberately and consciously evolved in a manner that can be predicted (if they can *not* be predicted there is no point in asking the question). But the reply—*It works unconsciously*—is a denial of everything implied in the question. Is this apparent confusion an accident? Just Hardy's clumsy method of introducing the Will as the principal character in the drama?

The answer to such questions lies in the lines which follow:

CHORUS OF THE PITIES (aerial music)

Still thus? Still thus?
Ever unconscious!
An automatic sense
Unweeting why or whence?
Be, then, the inevitable, as of old,
Although that SO it be we dare not hold!

SPIRIT OF THE YEARS

Hold what ye list, fond unbelieving Sprites,
You cannot swerve the pulsion of the Byss,
Which thinking on, yet weighing not Its thought,
Unchecks Its clock-like laws.

This brief passage is characteristic of the conversation of the Spirits concerning the Will: a constant debate which is, in Hardy's term, an *antilogy*, a contradiction in terms. We have here an implicit war or debate between nouns and verbs on the one hand, and adverbs and adjectives on the other. An 'active' or 'organic' verb is allied to a passive or mechanistic adverb, or *vice-versa*: and the nouns stand in the same relation to their adjectives. Thus in lines 1-2:

What of the Immanent Will and Its designs?—
—It works unconsciously, as heretofore . . .

the noun and the verb (*designs*, *works*) are 'conscious' terms; the adverb (*unconsciously*) is a denial of consciousness. Similarly, in line 5:

Seem in themselves Its single listless aim

the Will has an *aim*, a purpose; but the aim is *listless*, an adjective which deprives the noun of much of its content: the aim lacks a sense of direction. *Automatic sense* is what Edward Wright would have called a misuse of terms—*sense* implies feeling, consciousness, responsiveness, everything that *automatic* denies. *Thinking* implies reason and judgement applied to responsiveness; yet *weighing not Its thought* at once denies these implications, and reinforces the denial with the mechanistic epithet *clock-like*. So we are given two parallel views of the Will, the first suggesting some positive direction of affairs, using words with which one senses that someone or something is in control of the actions of the human characters of the drama, the second denying that such control is possible.

And the speeches of the Spirit of the Pities and the Spirit of the Years demonstrate and underline the paradox at length: the Pities consider the possibility that consciousness may be an attribute of the Will: Years denies it.

This difficult, self-contradictory language is repeated again and again in the language of the Spirits, and since it never under any circumstances occurs in the human dialogue we may be quite sure that it is the deliberate intention of the author. The first effect is to set up a number of responses which are qualified by a number of alternative and incompatible responses. Opposites cannot be forced together without strain, and this strain of attempting to reconcile irreconcilable linguistic forms indicates at once the conflict which Hardy sees in his universe. Language becomes a metaphor for Hardy's vision of the world: the evolution of consciousness against an unconscious background is as much the theme of *The Dynasts* as of the novels—indeed, it is *the* theme.

Again, just as in the poems, the conflict is embraced by the imagery. *The Dynasts* as a whole shows that the Will includes the totality of all actions in the universe, including even what we think of as the physical, non-sentient world. We need not be surprised at this extension of the metaphor: Hardy has often invested inanimate objects with voices and souls, even remarking 'In spite of myself I cannot help noticing countenances and tempers in objects of scenery, *e.g.* trees, hills, houses'.[11] The complainings of the Shade of the Earth, and the imagery and personifications of the Overworld are a logical development of this. And when we look at this totality of actions we see that however much It may possess the habits of an automaton, Its composition is that of an organic body: It, too, has been invested with personality. To restrict his action to comprehensible terms Hardy makes his European scene symbolic of the totality: and one of the earliest stage-directions shows the continent in organic terms:

> The nether sky opens, and Europe is disclosed as a prone and emaciated figure, the Alps shaping like a backbone, and the branching mountain-chain like ribs, the peninsular plateau of Spain forming a head. Broad and lengthy lowlands stretch from the north of France across Russia like a grey-green garment hemmed by the Ural mountains and the glistening Arctic Ocean.
>
> The point of view then sinks downwards through space, and

> draws near to the surface of the perturbed countries, where the peoples, distressed by events which they did not cause, are seen writhing, crawling, heaving, and vibrating in their various cities and nationalities.
>
> . . . A new and penetrating light descends on the spectacle, enduing men and things with a seeming transparency, and exhibiting as one organism the anatomy of life and movement in all humanity and vitalized matter included in the display.[12]

Europe—an organism whose anatomy we are shown. The way in which that anatomy is described is particularly suggestive. The organism has recognisably human delineations: Europe is seen in anthropomorphic terms. On its body are human masses described as *writhing*, *crawling*, *heaving*, *and vibrating*, a list of activities not primarily applicable to humanity. Part of the purpose behind the selection of these terms is, obviously, to give the reader a sense of detachment and distance, and the suggestion is that what we are watching is not a mass of people but a mass of insect or similar creatures. They are running across a body described as 'emaciated'; and what we are asked to envisage is a large-scale portrait of physical decay. If the body is not dead already, it has the seeds of death within it, and the fecundity of life upon it suggests that putrefaction has already set in. The human body of Europe carries on it a life which is in itself a symptom of something wrong, something which is diseased and dying.

The relevance of this is not immediately obvious, although such an interpretation is entirely consistent with the ideas Hardy expresses elsewhere in his work, and with his almost obsessive preoccupation with death as the principal manifestation of change. But, along with death, decay and the fact of human consciousness seem to be linked in Hardy's mind. That death is a recurrent theme in Hardy's writings is a commonplace; yet the emphasis which he places upon decay and the fact of consciousness is even stronger. Sometimes it is the decay after death which seizes Hardy's imagination, though this is usually the excuse for a simple, detached observation—'I shall rot here' begins one poem[13] whose theme is not death but the separation which death brings. Sometimes it is the death of ideas whose subsequent decay produces further corruption in nature:

> I lit upon the graveyard of dead creeds
> In wistful wanderings through old wastes of thought,
> Where bristled fennish fungi, fruiting nought,
> Amid the sepulchres begirt with weeds . . .[14]

—though in this poem, eventually, the creeds are seen as bringing forth more potent living ideas; and of course decay can bring forth new growth too:

Soon will be growing
  Green blades from her mound,
And daisies be showing
  Like stars on the ground,
Till she form part of them—
Ay—the sweet heart of them—
Loved beyond measure
  With a child's pleasure
All her life's round.[15]

The decay of the body may be mocked and emphasised by the continuing vitality of the faculties, as in the poem 'I Looked Into My Glass'.[16] And most of all, it is the decay of human feelings which the poems mourn:

. . . they will fade till old,
And their loves grow numbed ere death, by the cark of care.[17]

In the novels, the most extensive meditation on the subject of decay is probably that in *Two on A Tower*, where what we see is not even the ancient doctrine of mutability, but one of complete extinction.[18]

If we are asked to see this same picture of universal decay in *The Dynasts*, we are also given a hint of its cause. The Earth is always female, always passive, always subject to events whose cause is the working of the Will. And these events are described as *births*, and their consequences as *pangs*. The Shade of the Earth warns that she is

but the ineffectual Shade
Of her the Travailler, herself a thrall
To It.[19]

—a *travailler* is one who gives birth. The Earth, a thrall, is subject to the Immanent Will: what we are asked to visualise is a mismarriage of the conscious and the unconscious, a gigantic rape of the conscious Earth by the unconscious Will, an unnatural union resulting in the unnatural offspring of human events and activities, activities themselves so unnatural that they can only be viewed in terms of decay, and that decay arising, perhaps, from the death or extreme agony of the mother herself. Again, it is an idea which is common in Hardy. The principal difference in its presentation in *The Dynasts* and its presentation elsewhere is that in the drama it is the Mother who is conscious; in the poems it is she who remains unconscious, to be questioned by her conscious children:

> 'O Time, whence comes the Mother's moody look amid her labours,
> As of one who all unwittingly has wounded where she loves?
> Why weaves she not her world-webs to according lutes and tabors,
> With nevermore this too remorseful air upon her face,
> As of angel fallen from grace? . . .
>
> And how explains thy Ancient Mind her crimes upon her creatures,
> These fallings from her fair beginnings, woundings where she loves,
> Into her would-be perfect motions, modes, effects, and features
> Admitting cramps, black humours, wan decay, and baleful blights,
> Distress into delights?'
>
> —'Ah! Knowest thou not her secret yet, her vainly veiled deficience,
> Whence it comes that all unwittingly she wounds the lives she loves?
> That sightless are those orbs of hers?—which bar to her omniscience
> Brings those fearful unfulfilments, that red ravage through her zones
> Whereat all creation groans . . .'[20]

The Dynasts, by providing a Sire as well as a Mother, makes the image more coherent, perhaps, but the consequences are the same —'cramps, black humours, wan decay'.

The decay which so oppresses Hardy's mind, and the apparently unconscious forces which govern the universe, are seen to be linked and fundamental to his work. Decay seems to be the consequence of a paradox: and *The Dynasts* itself is chiefly an illustration of this paradox, the conflict between the unconsciousness of blind forces and the consciousness of the subjects of those forces. We, who are thinking, feeling, perceptive creatures, are subject to elemental and apparently irresistible forces which are without values, neither hostile nor benevolent. That is the sickness from which Hardy's universe suffers, and it is that same disease which afflicts the Europe of *The Dynasts*. When Hardy tells us that the Will 'connotes the Everywhere'[21] we begin to understand why his language is constructed as it is: everything is part of the Will, men and Spirits, as well as unconscious being, and Hardy is obliged to present the Will in terms which will be sufficiently comprehensive to illustrate this *and* to illustrate the basic conflict. If the Will is anti-logical, if It is a contradiction in terms, then the language in which It is presented must be self-contradictory as well. In his imagery Hardy makes the organic living world correspond to his conscious protagonists, and the automatic, mechanistic world corresponds to his unconscious protagonists. Thus *The Dynasts* is, in a sense, not about Napoleon at all: Hardy could as well have illustrated his conception from the Punic or any other wars. The battles in Europe are only the external symptoms of the disease from which the Will-organism is suffering; or, in a different metaphor, only the outcome of a fatal union; or, finally, a mere sideshow of a greater battle. Napoleon is the hero in the sense that it is his career upon which the action hangs; yet that career itself is summarised in a passage which displays all the conscious and unconscious elements which have been described:

You'll mark the twitchings of this Bonaparte
As he with other figures foots his reel,
Until he twitch him into his lonely grave:
Also regard the frail ones that his flings
Have made gyrate like animalcula
In tepid pools.[22]

The imagery proceeds from a composite image—*twitch*—suggesting both puppetry and the irritation of physical disease, to a mechanistic image—the dance—*as he with other figures foots his reel* (it is worth observing that the reel, being highly rhythmic and stylised, is especially mechanised in its nature)—to a simile which brings us back to the organic world, and strangely close to the world of organic decay—*like animalcula in tepid pools*.

Consciousness and unconsciousness united in one creation, and the result a process of decay—that is our central theme. Since it has been drawn chiefly from implicit features of the language there is a danger that one's reactions and conclusions may be purely subjective. Yet the treatment is not so radically different from that which we have already seen to operate in *The Return of the Native*; and there are, moreover, quite explicit statements of the same idea. One, indeed, is from the novel:

> He already showed that thought is a disease of flesh, and indirectly bore evidence that ideal physical beauty is incompatible with emotional development and a full recognition of the coil of things. Mental luminousness must be fed with the oil of life, even though there is already a physical need for it; and the pitiful sight of two demands on one supply was just showing itself here.
>
> When standing before certain men the philosopher regrets that thinkers are but perishable tissue, the artist that perishable tissue has to think. Thus to deplore, each from his point of view, the mutually destructive interdependence of spirit and flesh would have been instinctive with these in critically observing Yeobright.[23]

The poem 'Before Life and After' takes up the same idea:

> A time there was—as one may guess
> And as, indeed, earth's testimonies tell—
> Before the birth of consciousness,
> When all went well.
>
> None suffered sickness, love, or loss,
> None knew regret, starved hope, or heart-burnings;
> None cared whatever crash or cross
> Brought wrack to things . . .
>
> But the disease of feeling germed,
> And primal rightness took the tinct of wrong;
> Ere nescience shall be re-affirmed
> How long, how long?[24]

'The mutually destructive interdependence of spirit and flesh'—consciousness, or mind, allied with unconsciousness or matter, resulting in disease or decay of the flesh. *The Dynasts*, like much of Hardy's work, shows that whatever happens to man is neither better nor worse than what happens to the rest of creation, organic or inorganic; and instead of a struggle merely between spirit and flesh, we are given a struggle engaging the whole of creation:

> Looked out of doors just before twelve, and was confronted by the toneless white of the snow spread in front, against which stood the row of pines breathing out: ' 'Tis no better with us than with the rest of creation, you see!'[25]

Man is differentiated only by his possession of consciousness—the ability to *know* his situation. This may lead to frustration or bewilderment, but not to a difference of experience. Hardy's imagery takes up the same theme: Europe is like a decaying mortal, while, on Egdon Heath, fungi become like the 'decaying liver and lungs of some colossal animal'.[26] The imagery of all states of being is interchangeable, since all states are subjected alike: men are like insects, insignificant in the total Will, and the stars themselves are subjected to the same influence of decay as man. Nothing is exempted from this fierce union of irreconcilables. The greatest irony of all, however, must be that these irreconcilables *do* cohere, even if their union produces a turbulent and dying state of affairs. The consciousness of man embraces a knowledge of his situation and of the suffering environment in which he is bound.

This is not an easy theme to display, particularly within the dramatic form, and our satisfaction with *The Dynasts* must depend upon an understanding of Hardy's method. We have already noticed the paradoxical references to the Will. These in combination form a coherent though anti-logical image; and they are reinforced by extended images which deal either with the Will as an organic body, or with It as a mechanistic body. First of all the Will is displayed as something wholly organic:

> . . . there is again beheld as it were the interior of a brain.[27]

and this brain-image is a constant one in the stage-directions and in the verse-descriptions:

> *These are the Prime Volitions,—fibrils, veins,*
> *Will-tissues, nerves, and pulses of the Cause,*
> *That heave throughout the Earth's compositure.*
> *Their sum is like the lobule of a Brain*
> *Evolving always that It wots not of;*
> *A Brain whose whole connotes the Everywhere,*
> *And whose procedure may but be discerned*
> *By phantom eyes like ours.*[28]

Then the Will is described as a mechanism: many of Its actions are the actions of a *knitter drowsed*,[29] with *webs* and *threads* in Its anatomy. Everything, men and nature, is subject to Its mechanical dictates:

Thus doth the Great Foresightless mechanize
In blank entrancement now as evermore
Its ceaseless artistries in Circumstance
Of curious stuff and braid, as just forthshown.
  Yet but one flimsy riband of Its web
Have we here watched in weaving—web Enorm,
Whose furthest hem and selvage may extend
To where the roars and plashings of the flames
Of earth-invisible suns swell noisily,
And onwards into ghastly gulfs of sky,
Where hideous presences churn through the dark—
Monsters of magnitude without a shape,
Hanging amid deep wells of nothingness.[30]

We have, then, a conflict between single terms reinforced by these extended metaphors, a conflict which stresses the dual nature of the Will, part conscious and part unconscious. The Will's conscious element is clearly representative of the consciousness of sentient beings; Its unconsciousness represents the forces to which those beings are subject. It should be plain, therefore, that a study of the human action will reveal men's behaviour both as subject and as conscious beings: if the Overworld represents the 'real' state of affairs, the Earth Itself offers a display of the 'scenic' which overlays the real. In other words, *The Dynasts* is given coherence not only in the verse, but by actual demonstration of the Will as expressed through human action. Within that action we find that characterisation and motive have a place, although Hardy's choice of form and subject determines that neither can be expressed with more than a degree of realism. The limitations of the Will, and the nature of human action—by which one understands the degree to which it is free—are the principal concerns of *The Dynasts*.

XI

Part is mine of the general Will,
Cannot my share in the sum of sources
Bend a digit the poise of forces,
And a fair desire fulfil?

C.P. 479

HARDY'S descriptions of the Immanent Will exploit a tense, contradictory style; and the language indicates that at least two elements, the conscious and the unconscious, organic and inorganic, constitute the Will. It would also seem obvious that the Will is regarded as a vital force, possibly as a thing-in-itself, and at least as a phenomenon greater than Man, since It expresses Itself partly through Man. In this Hardy is very close to Schopenhauer:

> He will recognise this will of which we are speaking not only in those phenomenal existences which exactly resemble his own, but the course of his reflection will lead him to recognise the force through which the crystal is formed, that by which the magnet turns to the North Pole, the force whose shock he experiences from the contact of two different kinds of metals, the force which operates in the elective affinities of matter as repulsion and attraction, decomposition and combination, and lastly, even gravitation . . . all these . . . he will recognise as different only in their phenomenal existence, but in their inner nature as identical, as that which is directly known to him so intimately and so much better than anything else, and which in its most direct manifestation is called *will*.[1]

Hardy's entire attitude to the natural world, in which plants and animals are engaged in the ruthless struggle of evolution, suggests that he accepts this interpretation of the frame of things, or one very much like it; and sometimes he explicitly states that this is so:

> They went noiselessly over mats of starry moss, rustled through interspersed tracts of leaves, skirted trunks with spreading roots whose mossed rinds made them like hands wearing green gloves; elbowed old elms and ashes with great forks, in which

> stood pools of water that overflowed on rainy days and ran down their stems in green cascades. On older trees still than these huge lobes of fungi grew like lungs. Here, as everywhere, the Unfulfilled Intention, which makes life what it is, was as obvious as it could be among the depraved crowds of a city slum. The leaf was deformed, the curve was crippled, the taper was interrupted; the lichen ate the vigour of the stalk, and the ivy slowly strangled to death the promising sapling.[2]

This, too, adds extra point to remarks like that in *The Woodlanders* when Grace Melbury notices the ground coated with acorns, some unsound, and wonders 'if there were one world in the universe where the fruit had no worm, and marriage no sorrow'.[3] This is not an idle parallel but a reference to two effects of the same sad blight.

Yet if Hardy goes this far with, or parallel to, Schopenhauer, there is a further step which he will not take, and which is contrary to the spirit of *The Dynasts*, however much the epic may appear, superficially, to subscribe to it:

> . . . it is not the individual, but only the species that Nature cares for, and for the preservation of which she earnestly strives . . . she is always ready to let the individual fall, and hence it is not only exposed to destruction in a thousand different ways, but originally destined for it, and conducted towards it by Nature herself from the moment it has served its end of maintaining the species.[4]

There are, obviously, some passages of the epic which echo this; but such a point of view, however awful it may be, is none the less a point of view which sees some kind of order in creation. It may be an order hostile to man, but it *is* an order. *The Dynasts*, on the other hand, laments lack of order:

> *But out of tune the Mode, and meritless*
> *That quickens sense in shapes whom, thou hast said,*
> *Necessitation sways! . . .*
> . . . *Things mechanized*
> *By coils and pivots set to foreframed codes*
> *Would, in a thorough-sphered melodic rule,*
> *And governance of sweet consistency,*
> *Be cessed no pain, whose burnings would abide*
> *With That Which holds responsibility,*
> *Or inexist.*[5]

The 'quickening of sense in shapes' is Hardy's indictment of the frame of things, and it is Chance which is directly responsible for this flaw:

The cognizance ye mourn, Life's doom to feel,
If I report it meetly, came unmeant,
Emerging with blind gropes from impercipience
By listless sequence—luckless, tragic Chance,
In your more human tongue.[6]

Yet this fortuitous situation, in which not pain but the consciousness of pain is the tragic flaw, is not completely unalterable. While *The Dynasts* completely accepts the supremacy of Chance, it does not accept the Will as an unalterable thing-in-itself. Consciousness of pain cannot be changed except by death, natural or self-sought; but the widespread prevalence of pain may be alterable. Hardy's characters are given *some* influence, though not complete control, over their fortunes, and it is the abuse of their influence which *The Dynasts*, at the human level mourns. We are shown men acting in a way which so far from diminishing pain actually increases it. Men themselves, by an abuse of freewill, contribute to the disease of the Will. They are not wholly, nor even chiefly, responsible for it, as the poem emphasises, but because it is only their part of the frame of things which is alterable by conscious effort it is on them that the epic focuses attention.

There is no escaping the blind force of accident, the 'crass Casualty' of the early poems; no escaping the possibility, even, of a conflict of wills through Chance, for *The Dynasts* is based squarely on the acceptance of the theory of evolution through Chance, just as the poems are. Hardy sees the struggle between human wills in exactly the same way as he sees the struggle in Nature:

> From the other window all she could see were more trees, in jackets of lichen and stockings of moss. At their roots were stemless yellow fungi like lemons and apricots, and tall fungi with more stem than stool. Next were more trees close together, wrestling for existence, their branches disfigured with wounds resulting from their mutual rubbings and blows. It was the struggle between these neighbours that she had heard in the night. Beneath them were the rotting stumps of those of the group that had been vanquished long ago, rising from their mossy setting like black teeth from green gums.[7]

The *struggling, vanquishing, wrestling,* is no more an accidental or figurative intrusion here than is the general mixture of organic and inorganic imagery. Like Nature, man is engaged in the struggle for existence, a struggle which can become as ruthless as that of the natural world. But accepting what can happen, and accepting the theory of evolution through Chance, is not in itself pessimism. What Hardy is doing is taking that 'full look at the Worst' which he himself recommended. Human beings have a consciousness which is denied to the rest of the creation, and because that consciousness is capable of crying out against the violence of struggle in which men engage themselves, there is at least a chance that knowledge will give the opportunity to adjust themselves more capably to events and the environment. The parallel to evolution suggests that just such an adjustment must be made: the struggle in which men are engaged is seen to be wholly destructive, as the Will-imagery underlines, and if survival is to be possible that struggle, wherever it is wilful and deliberate, must be abandoned. So far from being a pessimistic work, Hardy's epic shows the slow development of sanity among his human characters, a development hindered by blindness and marked by pain and disillusionment, but none the less real. His characterisation is based not on man's inferiority before the Will, but on his ability to comprehend events and surroundings, and his talent for self-adaptation. 'Write a history', Hardy wrote in 1882,

> of human automatism, or impulsion—*viz.*, an account of human action in spite of human knowledge, *showing how very far conduct lags behind the knowledge that should really guide it.*[8]

The Dynasts is that account, and consequently the human figure at its centre becomes vitally important, not merely for the dramatic shape of the human action, but also for our understanding of the Will. At the centre of the action Napoleon does not stand out as very heroic; but he is not intended to be an epic hero. He is dwarfed by events precisely because he has once understood them but has allowed himself to abandon the lesson he once learned; his conduct lags behind the knowledge that should guide it, whereas the knowledge of the 'poor, panting peoples' develops slowly until their conduct overthrows him as a wholly destructive force. The nations themselves are the heroes of this epic, though their understanding is limited and fitful. Napoleon has been referred to as a puppet, but what is tragic about the downfall of a puppet? And if he and the other characters *are* puppets, why does Hardy begin his Preface to the work by talking of 'the great Historical Calamity, or Clash of Peoples, *artificially brought about* some hundred years ago'? Despite this clear indication to the contrary we continue to treat this work as a display of human puppetry, even as the epitome of Hardy's supposedly pessimistic viewpoint. *The Dynasts* is the reverse of pessimistic, an almost impassioned appeal to men *not* to behave like puppets and a lament because it is so easy for them to do so. Hardy makes his attitude clear in a poem written in 1906 while he was still at work on the epic-drama:

> Mankind, you dismay me . . .
> Acting like puppets
> Under Time's buffets;
> In superstitions
> And ambitions
> Moved by no wisdom,
> Far-sight, or system,
> Led by sheer senselessness
> And presciencelessness
> Into unreason
> And hideous self-treason . . .[9]

The parallel scenes of the Russian clergy worshipping their icons while the French troops 'worship' the portrait of Napoleon's son (III, i, 4) are at once suggestive of the superstitions and ambitions in which men are led to act as if they had no control. Napoleon, mocking at the Russian devotions, grunts 'Better they'd wake up old Kutuzov', yet he himself, in allowing his men to file reverently past the portrait of the King of Rome, shows an ambition equally foolish and considerably more selfish. In this effective, swift contrast Hardy has pointed to Napoleon's blinding fault: the keen worship of his own personality, embodied in his wish to perpetuate it in an heir. Common sense and self-purposed action have become absorbed in this imperial selfishness.

Lack of wisdom and lack of foresight are the chief faults this poem condemns; and by implication some of the men's misfortunes may be redressed through the possession of these qualities. But the poem was written before the First World War, which, it has been said, turned Hardy from his hope of 'evolutionary meliorism' to complete pessimism. Yet after the war, in 1922,

Hardy published his 'Apology' to *Late Lyrics and Earlier*, and repeated his belief in the possibilities open to humanity. The Apology is completely consistent with both the poems and *The Dynasts*. He accepts that the First World War has taken place; he still accepts the idea of evolution through Chance; but these things merely make his message the more urgent:

> Happily there are some who feel . . . that comment on where the world stands is very much the reverse of needless in these disordered years of our prematurely afflicted century: that amendment and not madness lies that way. And looking down the future these few hold fast to the same: that whether the human and kindred animal races survive till the exhaustion or destruction of the globe, or whether these races perish and are succeeded by others before that conclusion comes, pain to all upon it, tongued or dumb, shall be kept down to a minimum by loving-kindness, operating through scientific knowledge, and actuated by the modicum of free will conjecturally possessed by organic life when the mighty necessitating forces—unconscious or other—that have 'the balancing of the clouds', happen to be in equilibrium, which may or may not be often.

The notion of equilibrium, of course, was the product of a slowly-matured process of thought, reflected in Hardy's commonplace books and in the poems.* 'He Wonders About Himself', written in 1893, shows that already the idea had been accepted, and that the poet was wondering to what extent one individual will might influence or alter the course of events. The 'Apology' to *Late Lyrics and Earlier* implies that it is possible, while the novels very clearly show not simply that action is free, but that it carries responsibility. A letter to Edward Wright states Hardy's view succinctly:

> The will of man is . . . neither wholly free nor wholly unfree. When swayed by the Universal Will (as he mostly must be, as a subservient part of it) he is not individually free; but whenever it happens that all the rest of the Great Will is in equilibrium the minute portion called one person's will is free, just as a performer's fingers are free to go on playing the

* See below, pp. 223-33.

> pianoforte of themselves when he talks or thinks of something else and the head does not rule them.[10]

The Dynasts may thus be seen to be a discussion of the wrong use of limited freewill, and of the helplessness of the man who allows himself to be absorbed by the Great Will through the folly of identifying with It without displaying an adequate awareness of Its mechanism. The state of equilibrium seems to be a state in which the conflict of human wills has for the moment ceased, and it is at that moment that the application of loving-kindness can do most good—or that hate can do most harm. And *The Dynasts*, apart from showing the state of the Immanent Will when It lacks equilibrium also shows the results of such a lack of balance; suggesting, by contrast, the picture of equilibrium as a desirable state, since it is only then that amelioration can be furthered. Finally it shows us the full force of the Will exerted to end the chaos which Its first impetus had caused.

This is not a contradiction: it merely indicates a change of purpose among the nations involved, and individual changes of mind are visible around each one of us at all times. On the level of human action Hardy is concerned only with the sum of all individual human decisions. In 1914 he writes:

> The nature of the determination embraced in the theory is that of a collective will; so that there is a proportion of the total will in each part of the whole, and each part has therefore, in strictness, *some* freedom, which would, in fact, be operative as such whenever the remaining great mass of will in the universe should happen to be in equilibrium.[11]

Hardy in fact never allows us to see the whole Will in equilibrium, though he does show parts of It in this state. To do this he would seem to have adopted an idea comparable to one from Tolstoy's *War and Peace*. There is in the Russian novel the same appearance of voluntary and spontaneous action, underlined by the assertion that for the most part actions are *not* voluntary and spontaneous. The principal actors are seen as mere instruments without will of their own:

> They were moved by fear or vanity, rejoiced or were indignant, reasoned, imagining that they knew what they were doing and did it of their own free will, but they were all involuntary tools of history, carrying on a work concealed from them but comprehensible to us. Such is the inevitable

> fate of men of action, and the higher they stand in the social hierarchy the less are they free.*

Hardy would certainly have agreed with this, except, possibly, with the notion that events become more comprehensible as they recede into the past. But Tolstoy goes further, and very much closer to the ideas that were eventually incorporated as fundamental to *The Dynasts*:

> To the question of what causes historic events another answer presents itself, namely, that the course of human events is predetermined from on high—depends on the *coincidence of the wills of all who take part* in the events, and that a Napoleon's influence on the course of these events is purely external and fictitious.
>
> . . .
>
> The actions of Napoleon and Alexander, on whose words the event seemed to hang, were as little voluntary as the actions of any soldier who was drawn into the campaign by lot or by conscription. This could not be otherwise, for in order that the will of Napoleon and Alexander (on whom the event seemed to depend) should be carried out, the concurrence of innumerable circumstances was needed without any one of which the event could not have taken place. It was necessary that millions of men in whose hands lay the real power—the soldiers who fired, or transported provisions and guns—should consent to carry out the will of these weak individuals, and should have been induced to do so by an infinite number of diverse and complex causes.
>
> We are forced to fall back on fatalism as an explanation of irrational events. . . . The more we try to explain such events in history reasonably, the more unreasonable and incomprehensible do they become to us. . . .
>
> There are two sides to the life of every man, his individual life, which is the more free the more abstract its interests, and his elemental hive life in which he inevitably obeys laws laid down for him.[12]

* Tolstoy, X, i, p. 761. More than one critic has claimed that Hardy had not read Tolstoy when he wrote *The Dynasts*, and their claim emanates from Hardy himself. In fact the draft MS. of Part Third (Dorset County Museum) includes a number of direct quotations from *War and Peace*, and acknowledges their source.

Here, too, we have two states of men, the one free, the other unfree, and we have the notion of men acting subject to Providence, Fate, or History—Tolstoy seems to use the terms synonymously.* If Hardy differs greatly from the Russian it is because he takes a rather different view of the swarm-life: Hardy's rustics, though acting within a severely restricted sphere, exhibit a freedom derived from acceptance of their social and environmental roles. Within their limited sphere they can contrive to avoid difficulties imposed by accident or circumstance:

> 'And here's a mouthful of bread and bacon that miss'ess have sent, shepherd. The cider will go down better with a bit of victuals. Don't ye chaw quite close, shepherd, for I let the bacon fall in the road outside as I was bringing it along, and may be 'tis rather gritty. There, 'tis clane dirt; and we all know what that is, as you say, and you baint a particular man we see, shepherd.'
>
> 'True, true—not at all,' said the friendly Oak.
>
> 'Don't let you teeth quite meet, and you won't feel the sandiness at all. Ah! 'tis wonderful what can be done by contrivance!'[13]

Very often such contrivances are negative, taken deliberately as defensive or evasive actions. Yet that they can be positive is shown by Oak's makeshift erection of a lightning-conductor to protect himself, and through self-protection, to protect Bathsheba's harvest,† or by Knight's and Elfride's stratagem on the Cliff without a Name.‡ Here it is the doing, rather than the refraining, which becomes significant. Man's immediate environment may be in some respects unalterable; but his response to it is not, and it is in humanity's response to its environment that freewill lies. The point seems to be that when equilibrium allows some exercise of the will, the consequences of decision may well destroy the very state which made decision possible: if the response is wrong the decision and its consequences may be awful. The pattern is no different from that shown in the novels: Bathsheba's caprice and vanity are an inadequate response to her role as the mistress of a compact rural society; Jude's refusal to search for lodgings instead of watching the Christminster procession stems from an

* To judge from translations alone.

† *Ibid.*, Ch. XXXVII. See above, p. 68.

‡ See above, pp. 58-9.

inadequate assessment of his own shattered ideals—and all the disasters of the close of *Jude the Obscure* are derived from that refusal.*

The Dynasts opens with a situation of precarious balance: Napoleon's offer of peace is friendly, and may be genuine, yet it is rejected by the British government as 'an act of shameless presumption'. The more profitable approach is voiced but dismissed: 'he must be taken for what he is, not for what he was'. The Spirits, as always, indicate the alternative consequences of decision at this point:

SPIRIT OF THE PITIES

Ill chanced it that the English monarch George
Did not respond to the said Emperor!

SPIRIT SINISTER

I saw good sport therein, and paean'd the Will
To unimpel so stultifying a move!
Which would have marred the European broil,
And sheathed all swords, and silenced every gun
That riddles human flesh.[14]

As it is, the decision is made, and there is no turning back: the European broil is now inevitable, and cannot cease without the capitulation of one of the major parties. Hardy's concern with the consequences of decision is illustrated in caricature, as well as in the major action:

> 'Mr Pitt made the war, and the war made us want sailors; and Uncle John went for a walk down Wapping High Street to talk to the pretty ladies one evening; and there was a press all along the river that night—a regular hot one—and Uncle John was carried on board a man-of-war to fight under Nelson; and nobody minded Uncle John's parrot, and it talked itself to death. So Mr Pitt killed Uncle John's parrot; see it, sir?'[15]

Tolstoy's viewpoint is that events cannot take place without the contribution of each minute will, and that without the conjunction of personal volitions in support of the decisions taken by statesmen no dynastic tragedy could have occurred. This, as we

* See above, pp. 140-42.

have suggested, is one of the principles by which Hardy's Will acts:

> *Thus do the mindless minions of the spell*
> *In mechanized enchantment sway and show*
> *A Will that wills above the will of each*
> *Yet but the will of all conjunctively;*
> *A fabric of excitement, web of rage,*
> *That permeates as one stuff the weltering whole.*[16]

The minions are *mindless* in at least two senses: firstly they are unconscious or unheedful of the processes to which they are subject; secondly their wills are ineffective unless combined with the wills of others—mindless, in fact, seems to mean both *unknowing* and *unpurposive*. While they are in this state they are absorbed in the Great Will. In human terms, they are simply carried along by events, without knowing how or why they are so involved.

Yet they are not totally captive. In the general Preface to the work Hardy suggested:

> a monotonic delivery of speeches, with dreamy conventional gestures, something in the manner traditionally maintained by the old Christmas mummers, the curiously hypnotizing impressiveness of whose automatic style—that of persons who spoke by no will of their own—may be remembered by all who ever experienced it.

But throughout the drama there are lines which could not possibly be spoken in this way, whose vigour and earth represent natural and living dialogue, and Hardy admitted that there were variations:

> In December (1887) he quotes from Addison: 'In the description of Paradise the poet [Milton] has observed Aristotle's rule of lavishing all the ornaments of diction on the weak, inactive parts of the fable'. And although Hardy did not slavishly adopt this rule in *The Dynasts*, it is apparent that he had it in mind in concentrating the 'ornaments of diction' in particular places, thus following Coleridge in holding that a long poem should not attempt to be poetical all through.[17]

The actual distribution of Hardy's 'ornaments of diction' is interesting. In fact the language of the epic-drama is built upon a set of contrasting speech-conventions which indicate the status of the characters before the Will.

There are three obvious types of speech. Firstly, the inhabitants of the Overworld speak a language rich in imagery, distorted in syntax, and built on paradox. In contrast, the dynasts—the statesmen who 'govern' affairs—speak a flat, undistinguished blank verse, devoid of character. This is inevitable: the dynasts are necessarily part of events, and as such they are for the most part completely subject to the Will. They, above the others, lend themselves to the dreamy monotonic manner which Hardy suggested—lacking vision, they cannot speak the visionary style. But there *are* characters, in the full sense of the word, among the rustic and anonymous figures who crowd so many of the scenes. These people speak a racy, convincing prose, full of vigour, and often with humour. We may regard this, in its freedom and conviction, as the language of equilibrium.

The opening of the play, the Forescene, is completely in verse, some of it quoted above to reveal its paradoxical content. Among the Spirits there is room for characterisation of a limited sort. The eldest of them all, Years, speaks in an authoritative, detached manner, indifferent to events but compelled to witness them:

> . . . *In the Foretime, even to the germ of Being,*
> *Nothing appears of shape to indicate*
> *That cognizance has marshalled things terrene,*
> *Or will (such is my thinking) in my span.*
> *Rather they show that, like a knitter drowsed,*
> *Whose fingers play in skilled unmindfulness,*
> *The Will has woven with an absent heed*
> *Since life first was; and ever will so weave.*

The detachment of Years is increased simply because so many of the mechanistic descriptions of the Will are attributed to him, and at times he seems almost to be endowed with some of the raptness of what he describes. At the opposite extreme is the language of the Pities, plaintive, wistful, compassionate, 'the Universal Sympathy of human nature'.* Almost all of the Pities' speeches may be assigned at once to their rightful speaker on the grounds of style alone:

* Schlegel; quoted by Hardy in the Preface.

We would establish those of kindlier build,
In fair Compassions skilled,
Men of deep art in life-development;
Watchers and warders of thy varied lands,
Men surfeited of laying heavy hands
Upon the innocent,
The mild, the fragile, the obscure content
Among the myriads of thy family.
Those, too, who love the true, the excellent,
And make their daily moves a melody.

Between these two extremes comes the language of the other spirits: the Earth, as we have seen, female, and suffering; Sinister and Ironic, both melodramatic, and almost as emotionally involved in events as the Pities, though from different motives; and the Recording Angels and Spirits of Rumour, whose style is considerably flatter than that of the other spirits, toned down for narrative to something altogether closer to the style of the dynasts, though often breaking into a song-like metre alien to the other spirits:

O woven-winged squadrons of Toulon
And fellows of Rochefort,
Wait, wait for a wind, and draw westward
Ere Nelson be near!

The Pities, of course, have their songs; but whereas the urgent plaintive songs of the Pities express an emotional response to the general situation, the urgency of the Recording Angels is the immediate urgency of affairs as felt by the men involved.

All these variations are included in our first style, a style altogether richer than that of the dynasts. For them Hardy has often simply recast into verse the existing historical records. Such is Pitt's speech to the House of Commons:

Not one on this side but appreciates
Those mental gems and airy pleasantries
Flashed by the honourable gentleman,
Who shines in them by birthright. Each device
Of drollery he has laboured to outshape,
(Or treasured up from others who have shaped it,)
Displays that are the conjurings of the moment,
(Or mellowed and matured by sleeping on)—

Dry hoardings in his book of commonplace,
Stored without stint of toil through days and months—
He heaps into one mass, and lights and fans
As fuel for his flaming eloquence,
Mouthed and maintained without a thought or care
If germane to the theme, or not at all.[18]

—which is an adequate versification and précis of Pitt's actual words of March 6, 1805:

> The honourable gentleman seldom condescends to favour us with a display of his extraordinary powers of imitation and fancy; but when he does come forward we are prepared for a grand performance. No subject, however remote from the question before the house, comes amiss to him. All that his fancy suggests at the moment, or that he has collected from others—all that he has slept on and matured—are combined and produced for our entertainment. All his hoarded repartees —all his matured jests—the full contents of his commonplace book—all his severe invectives—all that he has been treasuring up for days, weeks, and months, he collects into one mass, and out it comes altogether, whether it has any relation to the subject in debate or not.[19]

The speech as a whole is a dramatised composite of those made in the House of Commons on March 6 and 23, and July 22, 1805. This and similar speeches are often treated harshly by Hardy's critics, but without good reason: they are poetically flatter than the language of the spirits, without the vitality of the prose passages: but they represent the dynastic formal style, a mode of utterance which demands flatness (Pitt's lines are, of course, the language of a statesman making a set parliamentary speech, and consequently may be regarded as naturally a little remote from normal everyday existence). But the dynastic style alters little. In the battle-scenes it sometimes springs into sudden life (Uxbridge's 'I have lost my leg, by God!' at Waterloo[20]) but the pattern is more likely to follow the speech of the Prussian lady in II, i, 6:

Is this what men call conquest? Must it close
As historied conquests do, or be annulled
By modern reason and urbaner sense?—
Such issue none would venture to predict,
Yet folly 'twere to nourish foreshaped fears
And suffer in conjecture and in deed.

Or Captain Hardy's at Trafalgar:

> My lord, each humblest sojourner on the seas,
> Dock-labourer, lame longshore-man, bowed bargee,
> Sees it as policy to shield his life
> For those dependent on him. Much more, then,
> Should one upon whose priceless presence here
> Such issues hang, so many strivers lean,
> Use average circumspection at an hour
> So critical for us all.[21]

We can safely recognise the Shakespearean echoes and the 'Dock-labourer, lame longshore-man, bowed bargee' as characteristic of twentieth-century Thomas Hardy, but there is no special reason why they should be regarded as characteristic of his nineteenth-century namesake. The Captain here is given no special role beyond that of spokesman for a general opinion, and as such is assigned the dynastic style.

The rustic and anonymous figures form the third, sharply-distinctive group, whose ancestry is in places clearly the Wessex novels. Little of any extended passage comparable to those quoted above could be mistaken for part of an individual poem, but many of the prose passages could be mistaken for part of a novel:

> . . . there's no honesty left in Wessex folk nowadays at all! 'Boney's going to be burned on Durnover Green tonight,'—that was what a pa'cel of chaps said to me out Stourcastle way, and I thought, to be sure I did, that he'd been catched sailing from his islant and landed at Budmouth and brought to Casterbridge Jail, the natural retreat of malefactors!—False deceivers!—making me lose a quarter who can ill afford it; and all for nothing! . . . Durnover folk have never had the highest of Christian characters, come to that.[22]

Not all the prose is used for humour, but there is little without vigour.

Each of these types of diction is clearly defined, and is allotted to a clearly-defined group of figures in the drama. The spirits are above events, the dynasts are clearly involved and possess little will of their own, while the remaining rustic and similar figures are merely on the fringe of events, or are not involved at all. These distinctions are clearly maintained throughout most of the text. It is therefore especially striking to find some sudden change of style in a context where there is no reason for it on grounds of characterisation. Either Hardy is to blame for poor dramatic sense, or he has a specific aim which can only be achieved by some sudden switch from one style to another.

If we look at III, iii, 6, for example, we find that half the scene is in prose: a dialogue between Wellington and his officers, who are attempting to explain the listlessness of the French fighting at the Battle of Nivelle. But Wellington's French guests, officers captured during the battle, enter the scene, and from that moment it proceeds in verse. Whatever Hardy's motives were in changing the mode of speech at this point, they were not accidental: in manuscript the scene is in prose throughout. To understand the change we have to examine the content of the scene.

Explaining the difference between the spirit-language and the language of the dynasts, Samuel Hynes points out that the human actors perceive things-as-things, whereas the spirits perceive relationships and consequently talk in metaphor: 'Metaphor is a mode of knowing, and since man cannot know, he can only speak in flat, discursive, unmetaphorical language'.[23] Knowledge, or the lack of it, is often the key to changes of style in *The Dynasts*. So far from seeing things-as-things at the opening of III, iii, 6, Wellington and his men are expressing ignorance and uncertainty: there is no action since they lack the information on which to act. Neither can they relate the details of the battle. But Wellington's guests *can* give the details, and the scene at once breaks into verse. Moreover, Wellington and his officers also begin to speak verse as soon as they receive knowledge: and quite clearly the significance of this change is that without knowledge of events they cannot plan their future actions; once they possess such knowledge their plans begin once more. Broadly speaking, we might say that prose in *The Dynasts* is a symbol of ignorance—in the case of the rustics it might even be blissful ignorance—verse is a symbol of knowledge, and metaphorical verse a symbol of knowledge with added perception. Such a distinction of styles is certainly approximate, and there is no reason to assume that Hardy worked out this pattern with conscious precision and attention to detail (although the broader patterning has clearly been planned); but the application of this pattern does lend a coherence to changes which would otherwise remain unexplained, and the pattern itself is supported by the underlying theme of the work. Changes in the manuscript also suggest that sudden lapses into prose or elevations into verse were carefully planned, and all the evidence of craftsmanship that Hardy shows elsewhere suggests that some definite pattern was in his mind. Certainly in this scene the diction takes on an added point through its abrupt change: for the first half of the scene Wellington momentarily ceases to be a part of the Will, and is in a position to make an unfettered—because uninformed—decision. His estimate of the French strength is a high one—'I don't quite see why we should have beaten them!'—and he is faced with the problem of future action. By the end of the scene, with renewed knowledge of events, he is able to make his decisions in the light of an unexpected French weakness, and his will again becomes involved in the purposes of men and leaders throughout the continent. His last words in this scene emphasise its significance:

> I count to meet
> The Allies upon the cobblestones of Paris
> Before another half-year's suns have shone.
> —But there's some work for us to do here yet:
> The dawn must find us fording the Nivelle!

Which contrasts strongly with the uncertainty of the scene's opening speech:

> It is strange that they did not hold their grand position more tenaciously against us today. By God, I don't quite see why we should have beaten them!

The verse-speech is a declaration of purpose, long-term and short-term—Wellington's pledge to the Will bringing him back into his normal dynastic style.

The narrative style of the Recording Angels and Spirits of Rumour is one which is also frequently usurped by mortals. Among mortals, however, there are signs that Hardy attempted to use it with care and discrimination. It is never, for example, used in matters of conjecture: when Napoleon, who of all people might be expected to speak verse throughout, speculates in II, i, 8, on what might have happened had he yielded to the Queen of Prussia's appeal for the return of Magdeburg, he breaks into the only prose passage of the scene:

> My God, it was touch-and-go that time, Talleyrand! She was within an ace of getting over me. . . . Had she come sooner with those sweet, beseeching blue eyes of hers, who knows

what might not have happened! But she didn't come sooner, and I have kept in my right mind.

When, however, some definite information is to be passed on, prose is abandoned for the style of the Recording Spirits. This is sufficiently close to the dynastic style to be introduced without much violence. On one striking occasion, however, there is a very marked change. In I, vi, 7, there is a conversation between the Spirit of Rumour and a street-woman of Paris. The Spirit's speech is characteristic at least of a spirit, if not of the young beau whose disguise he adopts:

What man is this, whose might thou blazonest so—
Who makes the earth to tremble, shakes old thrones,
And turns the plains to wilderness?

As spirit-language the one objection to this is an obtrusive reminiscence of the Psalms—though even this may be intended to be a suggestive and ironical comment upon Napoleon's claims and ambitions. But what are we to make of the prostitute's replies?

In courtesies have haughty monarchs vied
Towards the Conqueror! who, with men-at-arms
One quarter theirs, has vanquished by his nerve
Vast musterings four-hundred-thousand strong,
And given new tactics to the art of war
Unparallelled in Europe's history!

. . . .

Well, learn in small the Emperor's chronicle,
As gleaned from what my soldier-husbands say:—
Some five-and-forty standards of his foes
Are brought to Paris, borne triumphantly
In proud procession through the surging streets,
Ever as brands of fame to shine aloft
In dim-lit senate-halls and city aisles.

This may be defended in part on the grounds that Hardy is using the woman as a mouthpiece to give necessary information. Certainly she is that. But Hardy has no need to fall into this kind of rhetoric when he gives similar pieces of information elsewhere; dumb-shows, spirit-narratives, or plain prose description do the trick equally well. But the woman has a further significance: Paris as a whole in 1805-6 has become increasingly aware of the way the tide of events is flowing, and of the apparent invincibility of Napoleon. And it is more fruitful for the reader to treat this as a scene of symbolic, rather than realistic, value: the woman stands for the people of Paris in 1805-6, just as the servants who don Bourbon colours in the Empress's chamber later in the play symbolise the Paris of 1815 (III, iv, 3). The prostitute is an appropriate and perhaps fully-intended symbol of the public will: she changes masters as readily as Paris, and she does have access to the sources of information which she claims. What we are witnessing here is a complete lack of equilibrium, a whole populace caught up in the splendours of the moment with little heed for the ultimate consequences. We are not witnessing an individual decision, but a symbolic gesture indicating a fresh burst of energy for the Will. Nor should we shy away from treating such scenes as symbolic rather than realistic in content: throughout *The Dynasts* the juxtaposition of contrasting scenes immediately gives them symbolic as well as realistic moment, while the whole device of the spirit-world is merely a symbolic representation of men's own faculties:

Our incorporeal sense,
Our overseeings, our supernal state,
Our readings Why and Whence,
Are but the flower of Man's intelligence . . .[24]

How far Hardy intended shifts of diction to illustrate his meaning is an open question, but not a particularly fruitful one. He certainly had some such purpose: and if we extend this purpose beyond his original intentions all that matters is that by doing so, and by following those shifts perceptively, we can gain some further insight into the motivation of his characters.

XII

—Not a creature cares in Lodi
How Napoleon swept each arch . . .
C.P. 97

MOTIVATION there obviously is, even in cases where men have been caught up in circumstance. Freewill, limited or not, implies the power of choice and decision, and the characters in *The Dynasts*, like those in life, act continually as if they possessed such freedom. Hardy is not attempting to show that men do not make decisions, nor even to show that apparent spontaneity of choice is in fact predestined action. He accepts that there are certain limitations of freedom, social, economic, and hereditary, as well as the less calculable forces of circumstance, but within those limitations he is concerned with the nature of decisions actually taken, and with man's responsibility: 'write a history . . . showing how very far human conduct lags behind the knowledge that should guide it'. Uninformed or unheeding decision on the one hand, and the slow growth of maturity on the other, determine the dramatic plan of *The Dynasts*.

Napoleon's central role has been widely acknowledged, and is, of course, indisputable. But Napoleon *alone* at the centre of the action does not make sense. He cannot act in a vacuum, and his decisions and their consequences are related to the human background of his time. The fall of the Emperor accords with the old tragic pattern of a fall from prosperity to misfortune, and

it is a grete disese
Whereas men han been in greet welthe and ese,
To heeren of hire sodeyn fal, allas!

But on the other hand

the contrarie is joy and greet solas,
As whan a man hath been in povre estaat,
And clymbeth up and wexeth fortunat . . .[1]

The Dynasts presents two such parallel changes of fortune. It is not only the epic tale of the fall of Napoleon, with a metaphysical analysis added, but a careful study in which the fall of Napoleon is seen as the corollary and outcome of a slowly-evolving maturity among the nations. The nations, seen collectively as a character, slowly clamber up from poor estate to wax fortunate. There is something strongly prophetic in this, comparable to the vision of Isaiah or, even, of Karl Marx. *The Dynasts* puts forward, tentatively, and with some contradiction, the notion of men in an unfriendly or indifferent universe, men whose only hope lies in the elimination of self-division. There is, too, the suggestion that it is through the dynamic of history that men's actions are determined; and if there is in any sense a ruling hand of Fate in this epic, it is Fate seen in terms of historical determinism—a concept not far removed from that which Hardy had already employed in *The Mayor of Casterbridge*. The concept has about it no theological overtones whatever. *The Dynasts*, then, is a powerfully humanist work, implicitly against what Marx would have called 'tsarism', and passionately opposed to war carried on for the sake of dynastic interests. This is not to suggest any kind of Marxist influence: it is unlikely that Hardy had read anything of Marx's ideas when he wrote the epic, nor is there any evidence that he did so later. It is only to point to some indications of Hardy's deep concern for humanity, and for the betterment of the human condition. Napoleon presents an instance of a self-divided man, a man of genius, talented in the art of self-adaptation, and one conscious of his role in history; and also a man prostituting his talents in the name of ambition and self-centredness. The nations, if we treat them collectively as a single character, are similarly self-divided: in the early pages that self-division is expressed simply enough—and indeed as it had to be—as a patriotic and political division between the English and the French. At the conclusion, although Hardy is forced to take into account the historical realities—the restored Bourbons do, after all, represent the 'mouldy thrones'—there is a very strong indication that mature knowledge has overtaken the popular consciousness, healing the divisions; and the downfall of Napoleon is seen to be caused by that very growth of knowledge.

This is an approach to *The Dynasts* which has, I believe, been neglected; but it explains the whole notion of the Will slowly evolving into consciousness, and if properly followed it is an approach which substantiates to the full Hardy's decision to end the epic on a note of hope. Nor is it an approach which excludes the unforeseen elements in the Will's workings. The probability that the Will as a whole may evolve can be seen logically to follow from the fact that It is an organism, a portion of which has evolved to conscious being.

Hardy speaks of these wars in his Preface, referring to them as the 'Clash of Peoples': if we substitute the word *wills* for *peoples* we have one of the major themes of *The Dynasts*—explaining why the clash of peoples is 'artificially' brought about—and, indeed, of the novels. Not one of them depends on Chance alone: all spring from conflicting interests and selfishness whose resultant difficulties are aggravated by Chance. Thus love itself, because it is so often expressed by the will of one person attempting to influence or dominate another, is almost always a destructive force in Hardy. Almost the only major character in the novels who does not fail is Gabriel Oak, whose love is patient, strong, able to wait without hope. Against him Boldwood and Troy, both more dynamic characters, stand out as types of personal selfishness, as indeed does Bathsheba for the greater part of *Far From The Madding Crowd*. Similarly in *The Dynasts* Napoleon fails because he too is obsessed by selfishness and by his attempt to mould events to his own will with complete indifference to the will of others. Nowhere in the epic is there an indication that Napoleon cares a fig for the fate of France, as Hardy stresses by his decision to give a chronicle beginning in 1805 instead of 1789, as he at first intended.[2] We are not confronted by the young adventurer who could turn events to his own advantage, and who captured popular support by his championship of liberty, but by the older dictator who has become flushed with victory to the point where he becomes not 'Destiny's man', a devoted follower merely, but a 'man of Destiny', controlling or attempting to control, instead of seizing the opportunities given to him. The Pities indicate this change of character at the outset of the drama:

> *'Twere better far*
> *Such deeds were nulled, and this strange man's career*
> *Wound up, as making inharmonious jars*
> *In her creation whose meek wraith we know.*
> *The more that he, turned man of mere traditions,*
> *Now profits naught. For the large potencies*
> *Instilled into his idiosyncrasy—*
> *To throne fair Liberty in Privilege' room—*
> *Are taking taint, and sink to common plots*
> *For his own gain.*[3]

None the less, we are offered some few remnants of the earlier Napoleon, aided partly by his own skill—which Hardy never denies—and partly by the 'feeble-framed dull unresolve, unresourcefulness' of Britain and her allies. Napoleon can resolve and he is resourceful: we are shown the energy of the French as they prepare the invasion barges at Boulogne (I, i, 4) and the contrasting lack of energy in England. The First Part also illustrates Napoleon's realism: after the Battle of Trafalgar he speaks moodily of the English success:

By luck their Nelson's gone, but gone withal
Are twenty thousand prisoners, taken off
To gnaw their finger-nails in British hulks.
Of our vast squadrons of the summer-time
But rags and splintered remnants now remain.[4]

But what after all is Napoleon doing here but 'taking the full look at the Worst'? He rapidly assesses his chances, finds them still not unfavourable, speaks hopefully of victory at Austerlitz as a counterpoise to defeat at Trafalgar, and already has his new plans formulated:

I'll bid all states of Europe shut their ports
To England's arrogant bottoms, slowly starve
Her bloated revenues and monstrous trade,
Till all her hulks lie sodden in their docks,
And her grey island eyes in vain shall seek
One jack of hers upon the ocean plains.

Nor is there any false optimism about the forthcoming struggle: 'even here Pitt's guineas are the foes'—he credits all his misfortune to the greater power of Pitt's will:

'Tis all a duel 'twixt this Pitt and me;
And, more than Russia's host, and Austria's flower,
I everywhere tonight around me feel
As from an unseen monster haunting nigh
His country's hostile breath!

To some extent the Emperor is right; but his personalisation of the struggle is too easy a solution. Very soon Pitt is dead; Fox in his turn is hustled from the scene. But the source of their power is made obvious from the start:

Once more doth Pitt deem the land crying loud to him.—
Frail though and spent, and an-hungred for restfulness
Once more responds he, dead fervours to energize,
Aims to concentre, slack efforts to bind.[5]

The role of the individual in history is here: effort and individual aims must be harnessed and 'dead fervours' brought to life; but the individual plays this role because of a general realisation of a need for him, a popular appeal whose extent is stressed in the very first lines of the first human scene:

Hark now, and gather how the martial mood
Stirs England's humblest hearts!

At this point Hardy is not questioning the public mood, although there is evidence that he might condemn it: the mood is embodied in the figure of the King, and it is the King's obstinacy and pride which accounts for the fresh outbreak of the European struggle. But if it is the case that Hardy regarded King George as responsible at this point, there is a later point which stands in marked contrast to the later portraits of the Emperor:

O fearful price for victory! Add thereto
All those I lost at Walcheren.—A crime
Lay there! . . . I stood on Chatham's being sent:
It wears on me, till I am unfit to live![6]

But at this opening point of the drama the emphasis is placed not on personal responsibility in England, but on collective responsibility expressing itself in faith in a leader whose explicit concern is for Britain to 'save Europe by her example'.

That this is not a pious and chauvinistic piece of glossing over is made apparent by the first scene in which Napoleon appears in person. Against the display of a leader called to office by popular demand Hardy has set the Milan coronation of the Emperor, and, through the Pities, he stresses the personal and ambitious nature of this act:

Thus are the self-styled servants of the Highest
Constrained by earthly duress to embrace
Mighty imperiousness as it were choice,
And hand the Italian sceptre unto one
Who, with a saturnine, sour-humoured grin,

Professed at first to flout antiquity,
Scorn limp conventions, smile at mouldy thrones,
And level dynasts down to journeymen!—
Yet he, advancing swiftly on that track
Whereby his active soul, fair Freedom's child,
Makes strange decline, now labours to achieve
The thing it overthrew.[7]

The Pities stress, too, the effect of this action not only on the people of France, who are tacitly assumed to support it, but on the other nations, reminding us that it cannot be isolated from its consequences. The 'vulgar stroke of vauntery' alienates Austria and the other continental lands and joins them to Britain in defiance of the Emperor. The very splendour of the scene is reduced to the splendour of a merely local cult,

A local cult called Christianity,
Which the wild dramas of the wheeling spheres
Include, with divers other such, in dim
Pathetical and brief parentheses,
Beyond whose span, uninfluenced, unconcerned,
The systems of the suns go sweeping on . . .

This is the beginning of Napoleon's role in the drama, an 'unhealthy splendour' which, even in such a local sphere, marks a 'rash hour' and superficial success. And what follows? The three books contain the picture of success muted and slowly overcome by English persistence and doggedness, eventually so powerful that even Napoleon's personal support begins to waver. In a sense, *The Dynasts*, for all its appearance of detachment and universality, is a patriotic work, and it is, like Wessex, at once both local and universal. If we ask ourselves what the earlier scenes lead us to expect from the action we find our answer in the mistaken coronation-scene on the one hand, and on the other in the picture of a parliament 'insular, empiric, unideal'—and it is the empiric quality which is important. The war in Spain is described at the opening as 'an error giving vast delight to France', but it is an error which eventually leads to Napoleon's downfall, and it throws up the general who is to defeat him. As Napoleon's fortunes decline Wellington's increase: in Part I the Duke does not even appear; in Part II he appears but remains mute; only in Part III does he emerge as a dominating figure as his personal encounter with Napoleon draws nearer. England is, as it were, the Gabriel Oak of *The Dynasts*, adjusting, waiting, often injured, but waiting still.

Yet it is not merely Napoleon's misjudgement of his foes which brings him down, but his abuse of his own role as a liberator, and his indifference to the fortunes of France. These traits in his character are summed up not on the battlefields but in the domestic scenes concerned with his divorce and remarriage. If he is in any sense a tragic hero, there is also a strong element of the Fool about him. What mesmerises Napoleon is not the Will, but his *own* will, which leads him to follow a disastrous course. The central point of the action, both structurally and dramatically, is II, v, 2, in which he not only abandons Josephine but incurs Russian enmity as well by abandoning the Russian princess Anne in favour of the Austrian Marie Louise. Even if he were right in pressing his own need for an heir, his marriage to Marie Louise is a deliberate attempt at personal aggrandisement, and his chief justification for it is his 'sense of my own dignity', which is affronted at the slowness of the Russian diplomatic machine. The marriage itself is surrounded by forebodings: in a piece of grim comedy the bride mistakes her husband for a highwayman at their first encounter; the Italian cardinals boycott the wedding; and Marie Louise's acceptance and marriage are haunted by the spirit of Marie Antoinette, the last Austrian bride to come so fatefully to France. There is nothing of success about these scenes, in which the women concerned act against their own judgement and, as they see it, without a will of their own, and which are followed by disaster in Spain and the long retreat from Moscow to Waterloo.

Napoleon's abandonment of Josephine and of the princess Anne occur simply because he has personalised his sense of his own destiny: the insight which first made him recognise his own part in history becomes corrupted until he descends from adjusting his own destiny to that of France to an attempt to adjust France's destiny to his own career. The cause of his second marriage, he exclaims to Hortense, his step-daughter, is:

> no personal caprice of mine
> But policy most painful,—forced on me
> By the necessities of this country's charge.[8]

Josephine herself knows the hollowness of his explanation:

> But why this craze for home-made manikins
> And lineage mere of flesh? You have said yourself

It mattered not. Great Caesar, you declared,
Sank sonless to his rest; was greater deemed
Even for the isolation. Frederick
Saw, too, no heir. It is the fate of such,
Often, to be denied the common hope
As fine for fulness in the rarer gifts
That Nature yields them. O my husband long,
Will you not purge your soul to value best
That high heredity from brain to brain
Which supersedes mere sequences of blood, . . .
Napoleon's offspring in his like must be;
The second of his line be he who shows
Napoleon's soul in later bodiment,
The household father happening as he may![9]

Napoleon admits that at one time he would have listened to such a plea. But the context of the whole work makes clear that he insists on deceiving himself, substituting now the notion of destiny for what is in reality the *personal* need to establish his own dynasty and secure his permanent fame. As if to press the point home by an effective and ironic contrast, Josephine herself laments her lack of freewill—'no free-will's left in me'—but hers is, as she knows and says, a will fettered not by any supernatural agency, but by the insistence of a single man. Selfishness and greed, Hardy seems to say, are powerful enough to limit not only our own freewill, but that of those around us.

Napoleon's appeal to the force of destiny is no more than a routine defence-mechanism to justify his own actions to others, and possibly even to himself. That he is at heart an opportunist is clear on every page of the work, and there are reminders of it even when his fortunes are deteriorating. Perhaps the most suggestive demonstration occurs after the fall of Paris when Napoleon's hopes are dashed, at least temporarily:

NAPOLEON

. . . Yes—all is lost in Europe for me now!

BERTRAND

I fear so, sire.

NAPOLEON (after some moments)

But Asia waits a man,
And—who can tell?[10]

It is a very light, almost a passing touch, but it crystallises very effectively the wide-ranging mind of the professional gambler with fortune. And it is as a gambler with fortune and other people's lives that Napoleon is presented. His supposed helplessness before the Will is shown in its true colours in a subtle commentary in the Second Book: the Queen of Prussia begs for the return of Magdeburg and receives in response the gift of a rose, a piece of superfluous gallantry. In the face of further appeals Napoleon replies:

> Know you, my Fair
> That I,—ay, I—in this deserve your pity.—
> Some force within me, baffling mine intent,
> Harries me onward, whether I will or no.
> My star, my star is what's to blame—not I.
> It is unswervable!
>
> . . . SPIRIT OF THE YEARS
>
> *He spoke thus at the Bridge of Lodi. Strange,*
> *He's of the few in Europe who discern*
> *The working of the Will.*
>
> SPIRIT OF THE PITIES
>
> *If that be so,*
> *Better for Europe lacked he such discerning!*[11]

It is not merely that the reader may well agree with the Pities which matters here: the point is that the discernment discussed by the Spirits does not exist. Napoleon's comments to Talleyrand indicate that he was merely playing with the Queen, and his reply was a frivolous one:

> My God, it was touch-and-go that time, Talleyrand! She was within an ace of getting over me. . . . Ha-ha, well; a miss is as good as a mile. Had she come sooner with those sweet, beseeching blue eyes of hers, who knows what might not have happened! But she didn't come sooner, and I have kept in my right mind.

This argues policy and expediency, and not a state of helplessness before destiny. As the Pities remark elsewhere:

So he fulfils the inhuman antickings
*He thinks imposed upon him . . .**

As *The Dynasts* constantly repeats, the difference between what a man thinks is so and what actually is so may be very great indeed. In Napoleon's case the tragedy is partly one of ignorance, and partly one of knowledge unheeded. He knows the power of decision at the right moment, he knows the power of his own personality; but he also knows the consequences of his actions in terms of blood, and he is indifferent to them. He grows blind to the course of his own career, and is unable to see or appreciate the tide of human will that is slowly turning against him.

Napoleon's true scale of values is seen clearly in the way he ignores the personal considerations of others. Josephine complains of a lack of freewill; Marie Louise in childbirth complains that she is 'but a means to an end'; and after the birth of his son the Emperor's only reaction to the news of defeat in Spain is:

O well—no matter:
Why should I linger on these haps of war
Now that I have a son![12]

The enormous egotism of this is immediately heightened by the swift movement of the action: the following scene shows us the field of Albuera, and we see just what it is that has become so meaningless to Napoleon:

> . . . the ghastly climax of the strife is reached; the combatants are seen to be firing grape and canister at speaking distance, and discharging musketry in each other's faces when so close that their complexions may be recognized. Hot corpses, their mouths blackened by cartridge-biting, and surrounded by cast-away knapsacks, firelocks, hats, stocks, flint-boxes, and priming-horns, together with red and blue rags of clothing, gaiters, epaulettes, limbs, and viscera, accumulate on the slopes, increasing from twos and threes to half-dozens, and from half-dozens to heaps, which steam with their own warmth as the spring rain falls gently upon them.[13]

* III, i, 5. In the draft MS. the source from Tolstoy is quoted: 'He begins to fulfil that trying & inhuman role which was imposed on him'. Hardy then suggested: 'So he fulfils the inhuman antickings imposed on him—*or chosen*'. The final text makes his reservations clear.

If we read this drama prepared for such contrasts we cannot find a more bitter and angry comment than this upon the ambition of a single man.

The beginnings of Napoleon's indifference are shown in the early pages, when he is wilfully blind to the real state of Villeneuve's fleet, and blames his admiral for the failure of the invasion plans.[14] By the opening of Part III those beginnings have become the dominant trait of the Emperor's character. In Part II it is Spain to which he is indifferent; in Part III it is Russia and the Grand Army:

MARIE LOUISE

And where is the Grand Army?

NAPOLEON

Oh—that's gone . . .
. . . layers of bleaching bones
'Twixt here and Moscow. . . . I have been subdued;
But by the elements; and them alone.
Not Russia, but God's sky has conquered me!
(With an appalled look she sits beside him)
From the sublime to the ridiculous
There's but a step!—I have been saying it
All through the leagues of my long journey home—
And that step has been passed in this affair! . . .
Yes, briefly, it is quite ridiculous,
Whichever way you look at it.—Ha-ha!

MARIE LOUISE (simply)

But those six hundred thousand throbbing throats
That cheered me deaf at Dresden, marching east
So full of youth and spirits—all bleached bones—
Ridiculous? Can it be so, dear, to—
Their mothers, say?

NAPOLEON (with a twitch of displeasure)

You scarcely understand.
I meant the enterprise, and not its stuff . . .
I had no wish to fight, nor Alexander,
But circumstance impaled us each on each;
The Genius which outshapes my destinies
Did all the rest! Had I but hit success,
Imperial splendour would have worn a crown
Unmatched in long-scrolled Time![15]

'Had I but hit success'—there is the real motive behind the Emperor's callous indifference, and the little tribute to destiny is again no more than lip-service. He is blind to the realities of war, blind to the perilousness of his situation, and, worst of all, contemptuous of the public to whom he is ultimately responsible. 'Ah, but we loved you true' sings the mad soldier as he freezes to death on the Russian plains,[16] yet the beloved leader's response to such unnecessary death is:

> . . . to gild the dome of the Invalides
> In best gold leaf, and on a novel pattern.
> . . . To give them something
> To think about. They'll take to it like children,
> And argue in the cafés right and left
> On its artistic points.—So they'll forget
> The woes of Moscow.[17]

His contempt is ill-justified: all across Europe the tide is turning rapidly against him. His one-time allies unite in the last thrust to overthrow him, at Leipzig large sections of his foreign troops desert him, Marie Louise flees from Paris with their son, and finally their servants don the Bourbon colours. Only Josephine, whom he himself has deserted, remains loyal to him. On the battlefield Marmont and his troops abandon the imperial cause—and this time the deserting forces are French. In the streets

> The Paris folk are flaked with white cockades;
> Tricolours choke the kennels. Rapturously
> They clamour for the Bourbons and for peace . . .

Napoleon cannot pretend that he did not know all this. Perhaps the most detailed and important analysis of his character, illustrating the deeply personal nature of his motives, occurs in II, v, I. This paves the way for his marriage to an Austrian princess, and suggests very powerfully the strengthening opposition to his rule:

> The trustless, timorous lease of human life
> Warns me to hedge in my diplomacy.
> The sooner, then, the safer! Ay, this eve,
> This very night, will I take steps to rid
> My morrows of the weird contingencies
> That vision round and make one hollow-eyed . . .
> The unexpected, lurid death of Lannes—

Rigid as iron, reaped down like a straw—
Tiptoed Assassination haunting round
In unthought thoroughfares, the near success
Of Staps the madman, argue to forbid
The riskful blood of my previsioned line
And potence for dynastic empery
To linger vialled in my veins alone.
Perhaps within this very house and hour,
Under the innocent mask of Love and Hope,
Some enemy queues my ways to coffin me . . .
When at the first clash of the late campaign,
A bold belief in Austria's star prevailed,
There pulsed quick pants of expectation round
Among the cowering kings, that too well told
What would have fared had I been overthrown!
So; I must send down shoots to future time
Who'll plant my standard and my story there;
And a way opens.—Better I had not
Bespoke a wife from Alexander's house.
Not there now lies my look.

And a little later in the same scene:

Children are needful to my dynasty,
And if one woman cannot mould them for me,
Why, then, another must.

Later, after his return from Elba, Napoleon claims that he comes to save France from 'ancient abuses, feudal tyranny—From which I once of old delivered them', which is a claim striking enough in itself to make us turn back to the earlier pages of the work. In them, and in the soliloquy above, we see merely the upstart dictator joining his line to the oldest feudal tyranny in Europe, and anxious for an heir simply to assure his own fame. His self-analysis before his second marriage is accurate enough; but ironically so, since the diplomatic marriage which he hopes will safeguard his line and perhaps guarantee peace alienates his closest and most powerful ally, and leaves him and his soldiers at the mercy of a Russian winter. *The Dynasts* opens with his abandonment of the role of an adventurer for Liberty, its central point is this hope to establish a personal dynasty, and his final soliloquy shows him still lagging behind his own knowledge in self-occupied reverie:

I should have scored
A vast repute, scarce paralleled in time.
. . . My only course
To make good showance to posterity
Was to implant my line upon the throne.
And how shape that, if now extinction nears?[18]

We cannot, of course, ignore the alternative suggestions put forward by the spirits, and simply reason as if

A self-formed force had urged his loud career[19]

—in other words we cannot forget that there are other forces that work with him, demanding an heir and the establishment of a personal dynasty. Yet these forces are only popular forces, the total of wills like his own. His access to power was through their will as much as, indeed, more than, through his own; and the need for continuity of authority inevitably generates further support for his actions—as the 'web-like' descriptions of the Will suggest, there is a whole network of conflicting forces, and it is because Napoleon cannot adjust fully to them that he fails. He fails to appreciate the power of hostility abroad; and at home he cannot see the needs of any but himself. In consequence his popular support becomes a wasting asset. In III, iv, 4, he remarks 'I could give Paris peace as well as they' (the Bourbons). But as Ney remarks:

Well, sire, you did not. And I should assume
They have judged the future by the accustomed past.
. . . They see the brooks of blood that have flowed forth;
They feel their own bereavements . . .

It has hardly been observed that this supports in full Hardy's belief in human responsibility. It is, after all, a comment on the mature, if belated, judgement of an entire nation; a comment that stresses that ultimately it is *their* Will and not Napoleon's which is decisive. As the Pities later remarks:

Yet it is but Napoleon who has failed.
The pale pathetic peoples still plod on
Through hoodwinkings to light.[20]

Nor can we forget the Shade of the Earth's references to 'puppetry'—but we have to balance them against the statements of the other spirits, and against the action as a whole. Each viewpoint is expressed in the Choruses, and we have to form our impression of the Will not from individual statements but from a balanced synthesis of all the statements. When we do so we are left in no doubt as to what kind of Will it is that has brought Napoleon to his final downfall. If there should still be a doubt the very title of the work should be a reminder of Hardy's central theme: *καθεῖλε ΔΥΝΆΣΤΑΣ ἀπὸ θρόνων*—'He hath put down the mighty from their seats; and hath exalted the humble and meek'.*

Once we realise that we are watching the slow tightening around Napoleon of a net of conflicting interests and wills, one of the most serious criticisms of *The Dynasts* falls away. A gifted and distinguished Hardy critic has written†:

> If it were a question of making the point in the first few lines, then I would agree with you that *The Dynasts* did not differ from *Paradise Lost*: in both the theme is stated before it is, as it were, illustrated in action . . . in *The Dynasts* the theme is stated, illustrated in the Trafalgar campaign, and then all over again in the subsequent campaigns of Napoleon. I cannot feel that the passages about the Peninsular War, the Russian campaigns, and the Hundred Days, add anything to the general significance of the theme. The work would be just as much a whole if it ended at Trafalgar, whereas it would be impossible to end *Paradise Lost* half-way through.

If we take *The Dynasts* to be only an illustration of the Immanent Will as expressed by the Overworld, and if we regard the Will as a separate entity, a thing-in-itself, then there is no answer to such a criticism. But it is not possible for us to do so: firstly we should have to ignore such passages in the spirit-commentary as:

> *A Will that wills above the will of each,*
> *Yet but the will of all conjunctively.*

Secondly we should have to ignore the entire human action. The spirits tell us that we will 'watch the twitchings of this Bonaparte/Until he twitch him into a narrow grave'; we certainly do not do that in Part I. On the contrary, Part I ends with the deaths of Nelson and of Pitt, Napoleon's principal adversaries. After

* Hardy quotes this passage from the Magnificat in the After Scene.

† In a letter to the present author.

Trafalgar comes Austerlitz, and Part I ends with Napoleon looking hopefully to the future. The human scene—specifically offered to us as a demonstration of the Will in action—is about the fall of Napoleon, not his rise: the spirit-commentary itself is *only* a commentary, it is not itself action, and we must therefore look to the human scene for a resolved dramatic pattern. And, as we have suggested, that pattern is based upon the exaltation of the 'humble and meek', however temporarily and inadequately that exaltation may be achieved.

The real test of the unity of this work is to see whether the fall of Napoleon corresponds with a continued deterioration in his character from its early condition as 'fair Freedom's child'. His ambition is central throughout, but at least his judgement is not totally impaired by it during the earlier scenes. Towards the conclusion, on the other hand, that judgement is most seriously impaired, as we can see merely by examining the Emperor's conduct before Austerlitz and comparing it with his preparations for the disastrous battle of Leipzig.[21] Before Austerlitz Napoleon assesses his chances, and finds his marshals in agreement with him:

> Even as we understood, Sire, and have ordered.
> Nought lags but day to light our victory!

Before Leipzig, however, their assessments differ. Napoleon enters buoyantly, full of confidence:

> Comrades, the outlook promises us well:

—only to be greeted drily by Murat:

> Right glad are we you tongue such tidings, sire,
> To us the stars have visaged differently . . .

The process which began with Napoleon's refusal to accept Villeneuve's assessment of the battle-fleet in 1805 has now extended to obliterate judgement even on land, and he cannot believe in anything but his own success. He counters his general's fears coldly:

> The enemy vexes not your vanward posts;
> You are mistaken.

—which is nothing more informed than wishful thinking. He falls into irritated recriminations against the 'atmosphere of scopeless apathy' which surrounds him, without troubling to discover the source of such apathy:

> Would that you showed the steeled fidelity
> You used to show! Except me, all are slack!
> (*To Murat*) Why, even you yourself, my brother-in-law,
> Have been inclining to abandon me!

We are not dealing with the Napoleon of Part I, but with a querulous man whose will is now attempting to force success despite lack of opportunity, rather than snatching at success when opportunity offered. This development of Napoleon's character is an essential aspect of the drama, as essential as the Will itself, simply because Napoleon is part of the Will, the slow decline of his fortunes being the very medium through which the Will is shown to us. The most deceptive thing about *The Dynasts* is the force with which the Will is revealed in the metaphysical passages; perhaps the emphasis there is too strong, overweighing the human action. But it is admittedly difficult to see how Hardy could have kept a coherent picture without disturbing the balance too much in the opposite direction, and the unity and progression *are* clear. His mortals have to be shown struggling against a power which is often too strong for them; but equally that power has to be seen to stem in part from their own voluntary actions. And in the end, despite all intermediate sufferings, those voluntary actions are modified by the sequence of cause and effect until Napoleon is overthrown.

The Dynasts, then, demonstrates how human wills can form a totality which is capable of over-riding individual wills, and which leads them on once it has captured them: if it had ended with Part I we would have seen the totality without having seen its full effects—in fact, we should have the statement without the full illustration. The Overworld gives us the statement at once, but the development of the human action requires the full scope of the work. In the end the disease of Europe is not cured: the After Scene shows that Europe is still 'prone and emaciated'. But the slow evolution of sanity among the peoples has been demonstrated, and the united determination to end war has been successful. Perhaps only for the moment; but evolution is a slow process, and at the mercy of some forces beyond the control of humanity. With all his stress on the human role, Hardy does not forget these other, darker, powers.

XIII

Ere nescience shall be re-affirmed
How long? How long?

C.P. 260

SEVERAL aspects of the Will, and Hardy's methods of displaying it, have now become clear. We have, firstly, a display of Europe in terms suggestive of a body diseased or dying; Hardy then confirms that this body is indeed a single organism, in the 'seeming transparency which exhibits as one organism the anatomy of life and movement'; and with this description, repeated throughout *The Dynasts*, he couples the commentary of the Overworld, which reveals that the organism is ravaged by internal conflict, and this conflict is the cause of the decay. We may regard these three points as comprising Hardy's initial statement of the Will.

With the statement come three illustrations. The first is purely linguistic: Hardy demonstrates in his language the tension caused by a fusion of irreconcilables, the powerful unconscious and the weaker conscious elements: and he shows in his imagery that reconciliation can be made, but only at the cost of life and decay. The conflict of consciousness and unconsciousness thus illustrated has as its outcome a series of catastrophic and uncontrollable events to which all men are subject in some way, and from which they can only begin to escape when they do not lend their wills to the 'Will that wills above the will of each'.

His second illustration, underlined by the diction, shows the mortal states: men lending their wills to the Will, and men in equilibrium. Where men cause or contribute to events, their diction is dynastic and they are uncomprehending; where they are merely victims or beyond the scope of events their diction is the diction of equilibrium, racy, characteristic prose. It is also true, however, that the state of equilibrium represents an ironic opportunity: the opportunity to remain withdrawn from events, or to contribute to them in a positive way—thus again losing control of the sequence of cause and effect, but, hopefully, for beneficial ends.

Finally, he shows us the Will in action, and reveals through that action that the decay revealed by the language—the 'rape of the conscious Earth by the unconscious Will'*—is the result of the combined actions of men, men acting without sympathy and loving-kindness, men acting without comprehension; and he takes as his type the figure of a man obsessed by his own ambition and indifferent to the results for others.

This vision of the Will as a single organism, divided in Itself, is shown not on a naturalistic but on an Impressionistic plane. The salient features of Hardy's Impressionism are: first, swift and concise action, without detailed analysis, and presented as a series of contrasting scenes; next, the commentary of the Overworld, with its powerful suggestion that the Will as evinced in human action is the total of men's individual volitions; and thirdly the language, repeating the antinomial pattern of creation as Hardy saw it and, through the diction of the human figures, suggesting the characteristic styles of people subject to or partially free of the Will. These three features can be combined to give the impression of a single organism whose self-division is the result only of the divisions among men; and, if this were all, would not only describe the disease but would also, by implication, suggest the cure.

Such an impression, however, can be based only on a synthesis which excludes some of the most powerful elements of the Spirit-commentary. For there are some descriptions which flatly contradict the notion that the Will consists simply of the combined volitions of all men involved in events. And in any complete synthesis we find it impossible to claim that the Will is *just* combined volitions, even though we have to allow this notion considerable influence in our decisions about the Will's nature. First of all, there is the notion that the Will Itself may gradually evolve into consciousness, just as men have done:

> The assumption of unconsciousness in the driving force is, of course, not new. But I think the view of the unconscious force as gradually *becoming* conscious: i.e. that consciousness is creeping further and further back towards the origin of force, had never (so far as I know) been advanced before *The Dynasts* appeared. But being only a mere impressionist I must not pretend to be a philosopher. . . .[1]

This is a notion which can be explained entirely in terms of a growing consciousness among men: if the force which controls men's action is indeed a form of historical determinism, in which

* See above, p. 162.

men's actions are governed by a web of consequences from the past and from the actions of others, then the growing determination among men towards any given end—and the ending of war is the chief hope of *The Dynasts*—may breed its own fruitful and positive consequences. To put such an interpretation in crude and simplistic terms, the state of equilibrium might involve a man in a position between conflicting tides of opinion analogous to that of the chairman who must make the casting vote. Yet, even allowing for the vast complications of tides of opinion on national and global scales, to say nothing of tides of passions, resentments, prejudices, and self-seeking, Hardy's note seems to refer to something more complex still than this. Moreover, an entirely 'rational' explanation in terms of human motivation offers no place to a being

> *Loveless, Hateless!—past the sense*
> *Of kindly-eyed benevolence*[2]. . .

This is something outside humanity; in its perception, indeed, inferior to humanity. And Hardy's impressions cannot be synthesised adequately unless, taking this aspect of the Will into account, we treat It as a dichotomy. If we can do this all the conflicting components of the language and action fall into place.

The pattern of the language is entirely compatible with the notion of a dichotomous Will: we have seen how it mixes conscious and unconscious elements. The unconscious elements have their equivalent in the human action when men are portrayed as subject to the Will, as automatons, even though the source of their automatism may lie in their own actions' consequences. But while the conscious and organic terms are underlining the belief that human beings are *not* puppets and *have* consciousness which it is in their power to use—in short, while the conscious elements suggest that men can break out of their automatism—the unconscious elements powerfully contradict such a view. The significance of the human action, with conscious humanity offering at least some prospect of amelioration, is only one aspect of the Will: the unconscious protagonists suggested by the language include not only men acting without comprehension but other elements less easily disposed of. If the only conflict were between human blindness and human perception, the cure for Europe's disease might be presented in purely human terms: the very terms, indeed, of Hardy's poem:

Part is mine of the general Will,
Cannot my share of the sum of sources
Bend a digit the poise of forces
And a fair desire fulfil?

But the notion of

A Will that wills above the will of each
Yet but the will of all conjunctively,

while it is vitally important to our understanding of *The Dynasts*, is not our immediate response to the Will. Our immediate conception of It is one of an all-powerful, all-controlling force. Even the Spirit of the Pities comes near to accepting the doctrine of the Spirit of the Years at one point, and denies the power of men to influence events:

SPIRIT OF THE PITIES

It irks me that they thus should Yea and Nay
As though a power lay in their oraclings,
If each decision work unconsciously
And would be operant though unloosened were
A single lip!

SPIRIT OF RUMOURS

There may react on things
Some influence from these, indefinitely,
And even on That, whose outcome we all are.

SPIRIT OF THE YEARS

Hypotheses! . . .[3]

The Dynasts is full of such hypotheses. But there are moments when none of them help, when neither men themselves nor the Will can bear responsibility for events. One such scene is II, vi, 5, where George III is shown in his madness and attended by his doctors. The first half of the scene is in prose, but there is one section in verse: a pitiful speech of the King is followed by the Spirit of the Pities with:

The tears that lie about this plightful scene
Of heavy travail in a suffering soul,
Mocked with the forms and feints of royalty
While scarified by briery Circumstance,

Might drive Compassion past her patiency
To hold that some mean, monstrous ironist
Had built this mistimed fabric of the Spheres
To watch the throbbing of its captive lives,
(The which may Truth forfend), and not thy said
Unmaliced, unimpassioned, nescient Will!

This is almost an affirmation of the nescience of the Will, an expression of the frequent bewilderment of human sympathy when confronted with unnecessary and inexplicable pain; but it is even more an affirmation of 'briery Circumstance'. Moreover, as the scene develops we find that our synthesis stands in need of revision: the King is informed that he has won a victory in Spain:

He says I have won a battle? But I thought
I was a poor afflicted captive here,
In darkness lingering out my lonely days,
Beset with terror of these myrmidons
That suck my blood like vampires! Ay, ay, ay!—
No aims left me but to quicken death
To quicklier please my son!—And yet he says
That I have won a battle! Oh God, curse, damn!
When will the speech of the world accord with truth,
And men's tongues roll sincerely!

GENTLEMAN (aside)

Faith, 'twould seem
As if the madman were the sanest here!

After which the Pities cry:

Something within me aches to pray
To some Great Heart, to take away
This evil day, this evil day!

CHORUS IRONIC

Ha-ha! That's good. Thou'lt pray to It:—
But where do Its compassions sit?
Yea, where abides the heart of It?

Is it where sky-fires flame and flit,
Or solar craters spew and spit,
Or ultra-stellar night-webs knit?

What is Its shape? Man's counterfeit?
That turns in some far sphere unlit
The Wheel which drives the Infinite?

This 'It' is something very different from the 'will of all conjunctively'. What we have in this scene is the open acceptance of something which is outside the scope of the Will, as we have seen It so far, and for which men are not responsible. The King's madness is seen as the result of Chance, a terrifying evil which exists, just as disease exists among the plant and animal worlds. Hardy does not deny the existence of this evil; nor, generally, does he blame the 'purblind doomsters' for it either. He merely accepts that it is there, and that it is an unconscious part of the frame of things.

What is worse is that this evil, unconscious itself, can make even consciousness seem evil in its turn. Hardy, in taking his 'full look at the Worst' cannot escape the tentative conclusion that if things are as they are, it might be better for us to exist in a state of nescience, since it is through consciousness that we are aware of the ill-effects of Chance. In the poems the notion is stated most clearly in 'Before Life and After',[4] and it is re-stated in *The Dynasts*:

SPIRIT OF THE YEARS

The cognizance ye mourn, Life's doom to feel,
If I report it meetly, came unmeant,
Emerging with blind gropes from impercipience
By listless sequence—luckless, tragic Chance,
In your more human tongue.

SPIRIT OF THE PITIES

And hence unneeded
In the economy of Vitality,
Which might have ever kept a sealed cognition
As doth the Will Itself.[5]

Nothing could be more terrifying than this idea of 'primal rightness',[6]—but all that it implies is an order of things in which grief and perception of grief do not exist. In this context one recalls the comment in *Tess*:

> Upon her sensations the whole world depended to Tess; through her existence all her fellow-creatures existed, to her.

> The universe itself only came into being for Tess on the particular day in the particular year in which she was born.[7]

It is through consciousness that we are aware of events; and it is through that awareness that we come to recognise evil. Good and evil are central to Hardy's work, and it is difficult to resist the impression that for him the capacity for good lies, perhaps exclusively, in the hands of man, while evil, though found in man, exists also in a region beyond human control. Even so, *The Dynasts* does not reject the desirability of consciousness, and seems ultimately to suggest that while evil is inevitably in the frame of things, there is no reason why men should contribute to it. Simply because it is 'primal' Hardy faces the fact that it is there: he knows that the forces of Chance are usually more powerful than the forces of men; and he knows, too, that even the best motives of men may fail:

> How arrives it joy lies slain,
> And why unblooms the best hope ever sown?
> —Crass Casualty obstructs the sun and rain . . .[8]

As it is, we do not live in a state of nescience, and must therefore discover if a 'way to the Better there be'. The whole tragedy of human blindness is that it is often self-imposed, and it takes away man's one opportunity to withstand the blindness in the frame of things. Hardy regards this as all-important: like man's environment, consciousness is there, and must be *used.*

His difficulty in this work is that the Will has to stand on two levels: firstly, as the product of the combined volitions of men; secondly, as an entity greater than men's volitions, though including them, and Itself subject to Chance. The Will cannot, therefore, stand as an image for the Prime Cause, though there are moments in the drama when it effectively seems to do just that. It can only stand for the frame of things, a representation of things-as-they-are rather than of the source of things. In this the Immanent Will differs from the Prime Force of some of the earlier poems, and represents a change of attitude on Hardy's part. In those poems he is often concerned not only with the frame of things, man's environment, but also with the source. With the passing of any hope of belief in God came the recognition that human reason offered no way to a discovery of the origin of things. For some this recognition may open the way to acceptance of faith: for Hardy this was impossible. But his response, so far from being negative, hopeless or frustrated, was one of inquiry: at least conditions as they are could be examined. That his own inquiry was imaginative rather than rational does not detract from its value.

So, at Its second level, the Will stands as a separate entity, indifferent to men, and existing as a vehicle for Chance though It is Itself subject to Chance. This very subjection offers a gleam of hope. The Will as a single organism may be affected by the movements of Its parts, just as men's volitions may be guided by the expression of a single will. And if a part has evolved consciousness through Chance, why not all?

. . . a stirring thrills the air
Like to sound of joyance there
That the rages
Of the ages
Shall be cancelled, and deliverance offered from the darts that were,
Consciousness the Will informing, till It fashion all things fair![9]

This is not just a hopeful tag to end the work: the same idea is presented, and coupled with the idea of influential human decision, in the earliest pages of the epic, after the casting of votes in the House of Commons:

There may react on things
Some influence from these, indefinitely,
And even on That, whose outcome we all are.[10]

The concept of the Will as an organic body within an evolutionary framework lends itself easily to this belief in a spreading of consciousness, and the notion is further reinforced by the stress Hardy places on human influence and human responsibility for decision. His hope is that through responsibility a new sanity may evolve in which the self-division of mankind will disappear. Hardy is in fact asking for positive action to speed the process of evolution throughout the Will-organism. The disease of that body is illustrated by its symptoms, the wars which scar Europe, and those wars are in large part the creation of men: if men can remove their own divisions the most obvious signs of the Will's disease may be removed, and the extension of sanity may 'react on things, indefinitely'. *The Dynasts* might thus be read as a massive extension of the poem 'The Sick Battle-God', which equally stresses human sanity:

. . . new light spread. That god's gold nim
And blazon have waned dimmer and more dim;
Even his flushed form begins to fade,
Till but a shade is left of him.

That modern meditation broke
His spell, that penman's pleadings dealt a stroke,
Say some; and some that crimes too dire
Did much to mire his crimson cloak.

Yea, seeds of crescent sympathy
Were sewn by those more excellent than he,
Long known, though long contemned till then—
The gods of men in amity.

Souls have grown seers, and thought outbrings
The mournful many-sidedness of things
With foes as friends, enfeebling ires
And fury-fires by gaingivings! . . .

Let men rejoice, let men deplore,
The lurid Deity of heretofore
Succumbs to one of saner nod;
The Battle-God is god no more.[11]

The reference to the 'penman's pleading' indicates Hardy's view of his own role in the Immanent Will as an advocate of sympathy and loving-kindness among men. Perhaps it is not fanciful to believe that the growth of internationalism in the task of peace-making would have been regarded by him as a sign of the human evolution he desired, and perhaps, even, his own influence 'in-definitely' made its contribution. His deep concern is also with the manysidedness of things, the ramifications and consequences which hinder man's objectivity and make sanity more difficult, so that *The Dynasts*, apart from its treatment of human values, Chance, and Circumstance, is also vitally concerned with decision itself. His vision of equilibrium as the state or moment at which 'the modicum of freewill conjecturally possessed by organic life' may be exercised is another important element in the complex fabric of the epic.

Hypotheses! snorts the Spirit of the Years: and of course he is correct. *The Dynasts* does not resolve any problems whatever. But Hardy does not see himself as solving problems, only examining such problems as exist, and presenting them impressionistically:

> Yes: I left off on a note of hope. It was just as well that the Pities should have the last word, since, like *Paradise Lost*, *The Dynasts* proves nothing.[12]

But even if it proves nothing, *The Dynasts* seems to ask: if the creation of which men form a part is bound to involve pain and grief, why should men add to such evils? If contributing wills combine to form one vast Will, why should they be evil in their intent? Not all of the poems nor even all of *The Dynasts* accept this, obviously: some of them contradict it, and seem to assert that men *are* puppets. But Hardy has given his own warning:

> The pieces are in a large degree dramatic and personative... and this even where they are not obviously so.[13]

The warning, from his first volume of verse, was repeated in the volumes which followed, and the larger question was taken up at length in *Late Lyrics and Earlier*:

> It is true . . . that some grave, positive, stark, delineations are interspersed among those of the passive, lighter, and traditional sort presumably nearer to stereotyped tastes. For —while I am quite aware that a thinker is not expected, and, indeed, is scarcely allowed . . . to state all that crosses his mind concerning existence in this universe, in his attempts to explain or excuse the presence of evil and the incongruity of penalizing the irresponsible—it must be obvious to open intelligences that, without denying the beauty and faithful service of certain venerable cults, such disallowance of 'obstinate' questionings and 'blank misgivings' tends to a paralysed intellectual stalemate. Heine observed nearly a hundred years ago that the soul has her eternal rights; that she will not be darkened by statutes, nor lullabied by the music of bells. And what is today, in allusions to the present author's pages, alleged to be 'pessimism' is, in truth, only such 'questionings' in the exploration of reality, and is the first step towards the soul's betterment, and the body's also.
>
> If I may be forgiven for quoting my own old words, let me repeat what I printed in this relation more than twenty years ago, and wrote much earlier, in a poem entitled 'In Tenebris':
>
> > If way to the Better there be, it exacts a full look at the
> > Worst:

> that is to say, by the exploration of reality, and its frank recognition stage by stage along the survey, with an eye to the best consummation possible: briefly, evolutionary meliorism. But it is called pessimism nevertheless; under which word, expressed with condemnatory emphasis, it is regarded by many as some pernicious new thing (though so old as to underlie the Gospel scheme, and even to permeate the Greek drama)....

Then follows the noble passage pleading that 'pain to all . . . shall be kept down to a minimum by loving-kindness'.

We must read *The Dynasts* tentatively, realising that its fabric is made up of hypotheses, sometimes of deliberately conflicting hypotheses. We will find that the poem stresses human values, not only in the unfolding of the Will but in the scenes of immense human interest which fill its pages. Blind, mad King George provides one, but we look for the most part to the rustic scenes or the scenes of human misery during the Spanish campaigns or the Moscow retreat. Despite all the talk of the Will, there is a great deal more about man's inhumanity to man. In the last analysis, that, more than any other issue, dominates Hardy's view of nineteenth- and twentieth-century Europe.

CONCLUSION

XIV

'I do not promise overmuch,
  Child; overmuch;
Just neutral-tinted haps and such'
  You said to minds like mine.
Wise warning for your credit's sake!
Which I for one failed not to take,
And hence could stem such strain and ache
  As each year might assign.

C.P. 846

THE pattern of ideas which emerges in the novels and reaches its affirmation in *The Dynasts* was the result of many years of deep reading and thought, a diligent personal inquiry. We know from the *Life* that Hardy read widely in philosophy, in an attempt to find some belief based on purely rational premises which would match the facts as he saw them: however, the facts which he saw were very much the product of a personal mood, and Hardy's eventual beliefs owed more to his frame of mind than his frame of mind owed to his beliefs. Even as a child he was affected by a prevailing melancholy. Lying on the grass, wishing he might never grow up, was an experience he never forgot, and which he recalled in the *Life*, in *Jude*, and in at least two poems.[1] Possibly as a result of the rural changes he saw and the spiritual changes which he underwent, he grew to interpret life in terms of change and decay, and this interpretation expressed itself powerfully in his writing; it may even be that the value which he set upon the past had its source in the unchangeability of the past in memory. Perhaps the most powerful influence of all, however, was that of Darwin: it is not certain that Hardy accepted all the implications of Darwin's theory, but the notion of life as a perpetual struggle for survival, with the downtreading of the weak or incapable, affected his outlook to such an extent that it contributed powerfully to the death in him of Christianity, and made it impossible for him to accept any vision in which that struggle was not a dominant feature. Such a morality inherent in the frame of things was totally opposed to an apparently man-made ethic based on compassion and understanding. And from this observation grew the notion that the human environment was unworthy of the creature that had evolved within it. It seemed illogical that a blind, instinctive process should be the rule, and that men should be subject to it, when men themselves possessed reason and foresight. It seemed not merely illogical, but unjust, that men should possess a sensibility which caused them to suffer from a dispensation which they apparently could not change. It was Hardy's purpose to find some area in which meaningful change might be caused by human endeavour.

Earlier ages had discerned a natural order in the universe which, if it did not always explain suffering and evil, at least gave reassurance by asserting that there *was* an explanation. The Great Chain of Being of the mediaeval world, which found expression in Shakespeare's notion of order and harmony inherent in the universe, or in Pope's view that

> whatever wrong we call
> May, must be right, as relative to all

had, despite Pope's confidence, weakened over the centuries, and it became impossible for many in the age of Darwin. Some clung all the more to their old faith as a refuge (and Victorian faith is not a thing to be despised); others were able to learn to suspend judgement, welcoming a spirit of inquiry without regret. Hardy could do neither of these things: there is no doubt that he felt rational inquiry was to be welcomed, but he was disturbed by the lack of order which appeared to be Nature's rule, and he may have felt with J. A. Symonds:

> Give a man . . . one creed, throw him a mustard seed of faith, and he will move mountains. It does not much matter what a man believes; but for power and happiness he must believe something.[2]

For Hardy the position was complicated because his needs were not primarily rational: the power of instinct and the appeal of the supernatural, though dismissed by his mind, were seized by his spirit with a deep yearning; what he wished to do was to satisfy his spiritual and emotional needs on a rational basis:

> I am most anxious to believe in what, roughly speaking, we may call the supernatural—but I find no evidence for it! People accuse me of scepticism, materialism, and so forth; but, if the accusation is just at all, it is quite against my will. For instance, I seriously assure you that I would give ten years of

> my life—well, perhaps that offer is rather beyond my means—but when I was younger I would cheerfully have given ten years of my life to see a ghost—an authentic, indubitable spectre . . . my will to believe is perfect. If ever a ghost wanted to manifest himself, I am the very man he should apply to. But no—the spirits don't seem to see it!*

Hardy's deepest wish was to impose order upon experience and nature; any order, but preferably some system that would match the facts of experience by justifying reason and sensibility, and by giving some purpose to human existence. I believe that in the end he failed, because the order which he discerned could not satisfy his emotional needs. But he did discern an order.

That there was a conscious effort to replace his faith he made clear himself:

> After reading various philosophic systems, and being struck with their contradictions and futilities, I have come to this: *Let every man make a philosophy for himself out of his own experience.* He will not be able to escape using terms and phraseology from earlier philosophers, but let him avoid adopting their theories if he values his own mental life. Let him remember the fate of Coleridge, and save years of labour by working out his own views as given him by his surroundings.[3]

That Hardy did in fact do this is suggested clearly enough by the novels; but there is also the evidence of his commonplace books, which contain a large collection of literary notes taken from a wide range of contemporaries. The preoccupations of the novels and especially of *The Dynasts* are clearly evident in these selections. The two notebooks, housed in the Dorset County Museum, can be roughly dated by their extracts from periodicals, the first

* William Archer, 'Real Conversations', *Pall Mall Magazine*, XXIII, 1901, pp. 527-37. Interestingly enough, Hardy did see a ghost in his later years: 'He saw a ghost in Stinsford Churchyard on Christmas Eve, and his sister Kate says it must have been their grandfather upon whose grave T. H. had just placed a sprig of holly—the first time he had ever done so. The ghost said: "A green Christmas"—and T. H. replied "I like a green Christmas". Then the ghost went into the church, and being full of curiosity, T. followed to see who this strange man in eighteenth-century dress might be—and found no one. That is quite true—a real Christmas ghost-story.' Florence Hardy to Sydney Cockerell, quoted in *Friends of A Lifetime*.

book beginning in 1867 and taking us up to the beginning of 1887 or 1888, the second running from 1888 to at least 1921, and possibly containing all the extracts of this type up to Hardy's death. They thus cover a very large part of his life, and probably the whole of his literary career. It is therefore surprising that the range of subjects they embrace is limited, and it appears that Hardy has noted only those ideas which correspond or seemed likely to contribute to his own—that in fact these jottings are marginalia to his own spiritual search. Of course, the ideas he evolved during his reading were tentative, and he was frequently at pains, especially with reference to *The Dynasts*, to deny that he had established any system. In this he was overstating the case, but none the less his mind remained open—just because, one may guess, his needs were not fully met—and it should be remarked that what may be stated here as a firm belief was in reality held by Hardy himself as a working hypothesis only.

The two notebooks show that although Hardy's reading among the major philosophers was wide,[4] he was more persuaded by the thinkers of his own time, and often by those writers who are now regarded as representatives only of Victorian thought, and not as contributors to the main stream of philosophy. They illustrate very clearly the extent to which he belonged to his age and shared the most obvious ideas of the Victorians. Any limitations that this may imply are misleading: the Victorians were commonly involved in the crisis of faith which followed the prolonged genesis of Darwin's theory, and it is in the impact of evolution upon man that Hardy's interest chiefly lay. The passages of which he took special note, though rarely his direct sources, have their parallels in the views which gradually emerge as Hardy pursues his career as a novelist.

As might be expected, then, these passages are primarily concerned with the nature of human conduct, and with the role of human conduct within an evolutionary setting. Occasionally a phrase attracts the attention as the source of a line or a paragraph, and where this happens we may often see how Hardy's mind was working. One such passage, which discusses the nature of order in the universe, is taken from J. A. Symonds's *The Greek Poets*,[5] which Hardy read closely:

> *Greek morality* . . . leaned on a faith or belief in the order of the universe . . . Man is answerable only to its order for his conduct . . .. If disease and affliction fall upon us we must remember that we are limbs and organs of the whole, and that

> our suffering is necessary for its well-being. We are thus citizens of a vast estate, members of the universal economy. . . . Humanity is part of the universal whole. . . . Nature [Man's] with all its imperfections in the physical and moral orders . . . must be accepted as the best possible, and that which was intended to be so.[6]

That Hardy saw man as belonging to a single organism is readily apparent in *The Dynasts*, but can also be seen as early as *Under The Greenwood Tree*, and is directly relevant to *Far From the Madding Crowd*; yet in each of these early instances the organism is as much metaphorical as real, a ready way of focusing our attention upon the interaction between man and man and event and event. In *The Dynasts* that notion is extended in terms well outside the social context, to embrace cosmic as well as individual consciousness. However, Symonds's passage defines attitudes enjoyed in a state of Hellenic consciousness, which, as we have seen, is no longer relevant or meaningful. For Hardy it was difficult to recognise any morality in the universal estate—yet he wished to believe that the universe was moral. When a fragment of this passage re-emerged in the epic it stated the problem succinctly:

SPIRIT OF THE YEARS

The cognizance ye mourn, Life's doom to feel,
If I report it meetly, came unmeant,
Emerging with blind gropes from impercipience
By listless sequence,—luckless, tragic Chance,
In your more human tongue.

SPIRIT OF THE PITIES

And hence unneeded
In the economy of Vitality,
Which might have ever kept a sealed cognition
As doth the Will Itself. (I, v, 4)

This is no solution to the problem, only a statement of it: the unhappy contrast between the consciousness of men and the unconsciousness of the forces inherent in the universe. With the recognition that of itself that setting could not alter came the idea that an apparent deficiency in man—consciousness and foresight—might be turned to an advantage if through it some amelioration of men's physical and spiritual condition might be obtained. He grasped readily at the idea—present in Symonds but probably not derived from him—that the universal whole was an organism in which we are 'limbs and organs', on the grounds that organisms are not static but must evolve. A number of the passages he selected repeat this view, and stress the similarities of predicament at different levels of the natural world, as seen through post-Darwinian eyes. A passage from *Jude the Obscure*, noted above,* refers to 'the little cell called your life', and the organic term is certainly not accidental—whether the organism whose cells we are be the family, society, the realm of animal life, or the entire cosmic frame. But although Hardy could accept this, he felt compelled to accept, too, the evidence of universal corruption. The imagery of his work, verse and prose, shows a profound awareness of the universality of change and decay, and when he found a concise statement of this he recorded it:

> *Galton on the defects, evil, and apparent waste on our globe:*—'We perceive around us a countless number of abortive seeds and germs; we find out of any group of a thousand men selected at random, some who are crippled, insane, idiotic, or otherwise incurably imperfect in body or mind, and it is possible that this world may rank among other worlds as one of these.[7]

The idea made a deep impression on Hardy, and became the source for a passage of *Tess of the D'Urbervilles*:

> 'Did you say the stars were worlds, Tess?'
> 'Yes.'
> 'All like ours?'
> 'I don't know; but I think so. They sometimes seem to me like the apples on our stubbard-tree. Most of them splendid and sound—a few blighted.'
> 'Which do we live on—a splendid one or a blighted one?'
> 'A blighted one.'[8]

There is no evidence that Hardy did not continue to accept this judgement, but his development did not stop at this point. Writing of Leslie Stephen, Hardy said that his 'philosophy was to influence his own for many years, indeed more than that of any other contemporary';[9] and from Stephen he quoted, and particularly marked, one passage:

* See above, p. 10.

> By Darwinism we are no longer forced to choose between a fixed order imposed by supernatural sanction and accidental combination capable of instantaneous and arbitrary reconstruction, but recognise in society, as in individuals, the development of an *organic structure*, by slow secular processes.[10]

We are faced, simply, with a quasi-metaphysical extension of the doctrine of progress; an extension which led to the hope that Darwinism, which had done so much to wreck one faith, might yet point towards a new meaning. If the universal order were not supernaturally imposed, and if it were not dependent on 'instantaneous and arbitrary factors', then possibly it might not merely develop but might *be* developed. Such a development, as *The Dynasts* shows and as had already been implicit in *Far From the Madding Crowd*, could only be the result of combined human effort, since only human beings possessed the required knowledge combined with foresight and perceptiveness. It seems to have been through a process of thought similar to this that Hardy reached the notion of equilibrium, a state in which mortals might influence the development of their environment. He noted an instance of equilibrium as it affected the universal order:

> The universe, it may be said, consists of a multiplicity of independent beings who gradually come to settle down into a stable equilibrium—atoms or molecules making as it were a permanent social contract with one another. The world would then be the 'best of all possible worlds' in the sense that it is the arrangement best fitted to survive. Such a view undoubtedly agrees with much that is commonly said about evolution.[11]

And he noted, further, a passage from F. W. H. Myers which sees stability within one man's consciousness, and in the consciousness of many, as the result of the same kind of social contract; a passage which may suggest how he came to regard the effects of the criminal or disruptive individual on the social order:

> *The unity of an individual organism*—'a unity aggregated from multiplicity'—the cells of my body are mine in the sense that for their own comfort and security they have agreed to do a great many things at the bidding of my brain. But they are servants with a life of their own; they can get themselves hypertrophied, so to speak, in the kitchen, without my being

> able to stop them. Does my consciousness testify that I am a single entity? That only means that a stable *coenesthesia* exists in me just now; a sufficient number of my nervous centres are acting in unison. I am being governed by a good working majority. Give me a blow on the head which silences some leading centres, and the rest will split up into 'parliamentary groups' and brawl in delirium or madness.[12]

It is a straightforward step to transfer this notion of physical equilibrium into a view of society as a single organism consisting of numerous potentially stable or discordant elements, and it is that step which Hardy took in *The Dynasts*, and which he appears to have been working towards for some years. The idea is present as early as *Far From the Madding Crowd*, which, like *The Dynasts*, reveals the dissolution of one state of equilibrium and the gradual re-establishment of another.* This was a logical culmination of Hardy's thought, and the passages cited above are chosen chiefly because they illustrate his interest—only rarely may we say that they are themselves his source-material.

In a note made in 1880 he refers to 'the organism, Society',[13] and in 1890 he writes:

> Altruism, or the Golden Rule, or whatever 'Love your Neighbour as Yourself' may be called, will ultimately be brought about I think by the pain we see in others reacting on ourselves, as if we and they were a part of one body. Mankind, in fact, may be and possibly will be viewed as members of one corporeal frame.[14]

Together with this mention of altruism we should perhaps remind ourselves of Hardy's comment on the principal figure of *The Dynasts*, Napoleon himself, as

> the man who finished the Revolution with a 'whiff of grapeshot', and so crushed not only its final horrors but all the worthy aspirations of its earlier time, made them as if they had never been, and threw back human altruism scores, perhaps hundreds of years.[15]

The Dynasts presents Napoleon as a betrayer of the human cause. Hardy does not deny him his original good intentions, but sees

* See above, pp. 60-75.

him much as he sees Gabriel Oak's dog, whose good intentions lead only to the destruction of the sheep he had been supposed to guard.* Yet to write in these terms Hardy must have had some belief in the effectiveness of human action, and his comments on history, so far as they are present in the *Life*, suggest the same. So, too, does a letter written a year and a half before his death:

> I fear that rational religion does not make much way at present. Indeed the movement of thought seems to have entered a back current in the opposite direction. These however are not uncommon in human history.[16]

In general, his approach seems to be that it is possible for human acts to sway events, providing that certain features of his environment are recognised: firstly, that unrelenting change is inherent in the universe and is part of the nature of all things; secondly, that human action can only alter the course of change, it cannot obstruct it. What certainly is not clear is the *extent* to which human endeavour may be effective, or to what extent it may be consciously and voluntarily undertaken. The passages which Hardy cites on this point—like many that could be cited from Hardy himself—all suggest that the degree of voluntary action available to us is extremely limited. Firstly we will be bound by the actions of our predecessors:

> *Our actions:*—Each act, as it has had immeasurable antecedents, will be fruitful of immeasurable consequents; for the web of the world is for ever weaving.[17]

This, which has an obvious relevance to 'the great web of human doings' of *The Woodlanders*,[18] is immediately followed by the observation from Symonds that 'always and everywhere men have been more and more ruled by the whole body of their predecessors'. Again, *The Dynasts* provides us with specific examples. After Napoleon has been crowned at Milan the Spirit of the Pities immediately draws attention to the consequences of his action, consequences which will affect the whole continent;[19] and later in the notebook Hardy quotes a passage from Auberon Herbert which was reshaped in *The Dynasts* and which takes up the same question:

* *Madding Crowd*, Ch. V. The dog is described standing on the edge of the quarry, 'dark and motionless as Napoleon at St Helena'.

> In politics so much the largest part of what we do is only clever adaptation to meet opinions which are not really our own. . . . In all that seething multitude of men and women . . . was there a thought, or feeling, or habit, or a ceremony that, like the tracings on a chestnut leaf, had not been formed in its smallest detail by the infinite succession of touchings and retouchings too many and delicate to be imagined.[20]

This illustrates very clearly what Hardy had in mind when he penned the Spirit of the Years' final comment on Napoleon. The phrase 'tracings on a chestnut leaf' lodged itself in Hardy's brain and re-appeared, much changed, but identifiable:

> *Such men as thou, who wade across the world*
> *To make an epoch, bless, confuse, appal,*
> *Are in the elemental ages' chart*
> *Like meanest insects on obscurest leaves*
> *But incidents and grooves of Earth's unfolding.*
> (III, vii, 9)

The 'tracings' on the leaf have now become 'incidents and grooves of Earth's unfolding', a metamorphosis whose course can be seen clearly, but there is the same notion of minute and continuous adjustments affecting Napoleon's course. The remainder of Herbert's passage, which Hardy obviously read but does not cite, elaborates the idea, and draws conclusions which were not foreign to some of Hardy's moods:

> Was there a thought or a feeling, a habit or a ceremony amongst them all, that, like the tracings on a chestnut leaf, had not been formed in its smallest detail by the infinite succession of touchings and retouchings, too many and too delicate to be imagined, which had fallen upon it from that marvellous and eternal surrounding of matter wedded to force, of which indeed all these things were creatures, and yet of which, when once called into existence, they themselves became a living and reacting part? And as he thought of the never-ceasing conflict, of the destroying and escaping, of the ever-revolving machinery, of the endless chain beginning where no eye could follow it, his brain turned sick, and thinking itself became a weariness to him, until at last he broke into the same complaint that so many others have done before him. 'What can a man do, except merely creep through

> it all as best he may? It is all too terrible and too large. It is best not to think. Who dreams that he can alter or shape the great forces as they carry him along their unknown path?'[21]

Any reader of *The Dynasts* may quickly observe that men's actions there, though they certainly are governed by consequence, and by mute opinion—which several of Hardy's notes in the *Life* treat very seriously indeed—are also at the mercy of other forces. History, or the universe itself, possesses its own dynamic force, and man's consciousness is not only partly controlled by this, but has actually emerged through it—it is this notion which allows Hardy to entertain the idea that consciousness may spread until it affects the Source itself. To some extent Hardy has adapted or inverted the theory of the Unconscious to explain this dynamism. He quotes von Hartmann:

> In all combinations of circumstances which by their nature occur but seldom, or where for other reasons a mechanism can only be constructed with difficulty, the direct activity of the Unconscious must display itself . . . e.g. the inclusion of the Unconscious in human brains which determine and guide the course of history . . . in the direction intended by the Unconscious.[22]

Hardy then adds a personal comment:

> [the practical philosophy of the whole] is the complete devotion of the personality to the world-process for the sake of its goal, the general world-redemption: otherwise expressed: To make the ends of the Unconscious ends of our own Consciousness.
>
> *The goal:*—The world redemption from the misery of volition (i.e. life), a condition being that the yearning after annihilation attains resistless authority as a practical motive.

This 'yearning after annihilation' is an idea about which Hardy remained undecided. His reading of Schopenhauer[23] had brought him face to face with a definition of tragedy, which he noted, as a development of the intellect until it reaches a stage where 'the vanity of all effort is manifest, and the will proceeds to an act of self-annulment',[24] but we have also seen that the notion of equilibrium in the social consciousness had its appeal; and so far from believing that we should make 'the ends of the Unconscious ends of our own Consciousness' Hardy asserted that the

Unconscious had *no* ends, and that we should use our own consciousness to direct the course of events.

Earlier he had selected a passage from Myers's article on personality, quoted above, and added his own note to it:

> *Lowest form of life*—'the single cell of protoplasm, endowed with reflex irritability'—'*a more complex organism*'—'mere juxtaposition of cells, attaining to what is styled a 'colonial consciousness', where the group of organisms is for locomotive purposes a single complexly acting individual, though when united action is not required each polyp in the colony is master of his simple self.
>
> The drift of the article [adds Hardy] is that beings have a *multiplex* nature, human as others; that what we suppose to be choice is reflex action only—that by implanting impulses in hypnotic states they can be made part of the character. There seems reason in this, for physical developments, e.g. of the hand—can be produced in other ways (by labour say) as well as hereditarily.[25]

The state of equilibrium thus appears to correspond to a hypnotic state of this kind, but it is the organism, and not the individual, which is seen to be hypnotised into a trance; a trance in which impulses may be implanted and the course of affairs altered by cause and effect thereafter. Hardy returned to the idea more than once. In the poem 'He Wonders About Himself',[26] for instance, he would write in 1893 of his own 'share in the sum of sources', while the 'Apology' to *Late Lyrics and Earlier* makes specific reference to human contributions made possible by equilibrium.

This notion appears to have been gathered from a number of sources, including Leslie Stephen, whose influence Hardy regarded as crucial. Yet his own view was formulated on premises which were different from Stephen's. In *The Science of Ethics* Stephen had maintained that pain and pleasure were the motives for action, and he went on:

> . . . in all cases pain as pain represents tension, a state of feeling, that is, from which there is a tendency to change; pleasure represents so far equilibrium or a state in which there is a tendency to persist.[27]

Hardy, while recognising the importance of pleasure and pain in determining motives, regards the *intellect* as the most fruitful source of change. His own definition, whose 'rather vague import' he admits, is not opposed to Stephen's, but its stress is different:

> Discover for how many years, and on how many occasions, the organism, Society, has been standing, lying, etc, in varied positions, as if it were a tree or a man hit by vicissitudes.

There would be found these periods:

1. Upright, normal or healthy periods.
2. Oblique or cramped periods.
3. Prostrate periods (intellect counterpoised by ignorance or narrowness, producing stagnation).
4. Drooping periods.
5. Inverted periods.[28]

It is difficult to make much sense of all these categories, and especially the last; but the third, in which intellect is 'counterpoised by ignorance or narrowness' would seem to represent the state of equilibrium. And if this is true we can see that for Hardy equilibrium was a negative state, whereas for Stephen it appears to have been positive. Hardy's equilibrium is clearly a balance of motives as much as of conditions; it is also a balance which can be eroded by change. One may imagine that the 'drooping' and 'inverted' periods are those during which ignorance or apathy are stronger than the forces of intellect, and the failure to use the intellect at a point of equilibrium will be as effective as a negative choice in producing these periods. The periods which are 'upright' represent those in which intellect achieves its greatest strength. Clearly to move up in the scale requires effort; to move down one may simply remain still, without initiative. The third period, being transitional, represents the one state in which human initiative may be decisive and the delicate counterbalance may be destroyed, in man's favour, by conscious positive action. The same stress is present in the 'Apology' to *Late Lyrics and Earlier*: Hardy's appeal for an end to pain is based upon intellect and loving-kindness 'operating through scientific knowledge'. And the same stress is to be seen in *The Dynasts* and the novels, where, in differing degrees, we find revealed the superiority of the intellect over ignorance, apathy, or 'narrowness', this last taking many forms. It may be the narrowness of Napoleon, blinded by his vision of a personal destiny, or the narrowness of Michael Henchard, blinded by a mercenary self-centredness and by the powerful forces of his own instincts. In *The Dynasts* intellect is the property of the nations of Europe, who struggle, consciously if imperfectly, towards some kind of personal freedom; in *The Mayor* it is the property of Farfrae and Elizabeth-Jane, who attempt to adjust their own skills and attitudes to their fortunes and the changing community about them.

For it is in adjustment, and the recognition that change is inevitable, that intelligence lies. Again, the root of the perception is from Darwin, but its blossoming may be due to Leslie Stephen:

> . . . the theory of evolution brings out the fact that every organism, whether social or individual, represents the product of an infinite series of adjustments between the organism and its environment. In other words, that every being or collection of beings which forms a race or a society is a product of the continuous play of a number of forces constantly shifting and re-arranging themselves in the effort to maintain the general equilibrium.[29]

The question of freewill in Hardy may, in the light of these points, be seen to resolve somewhat. Firstly, we may find actions whose course is determined solely by what one may call the historical environment: by the consequences of actions already undertaken and of present action undertaken deliberately in such a way as to disturb the equilibrium. The *effectiveness* of actions is another question: their effectiveness will be determined entirely by the extent to which they are in accord with the environment, historical or natural. Many of Henchard's actions are self-willed and voluntary, but cannot succeed because they are opposed to his environment. Farfrae, on the other hand, makes himself a part of the changes affecting society, and an instrument of them; and it is because of this that he succeeds where Henchard fails. The attitude to be taken may be illustrated by a personal example: I once asked a Finn whether his country was independent, in view of the fact that many of her policies are dominated by the presence of her Russian neighbour; he replied seriously, 'You must not mistake limited independence for lack of independence'. In the same way, we should not mistake the limited freewill of Hardy's characters for lack of freewill. As J. O. Bailey has written, 'Conscious reflection allows man to choose on the basis of reason instead of impulse. Since there are two bases for action . . . (1) impulses of the Immanent Will and (2) reflection of the mind upon sensations from the external world, some freedom of the will is possible'.[30] It should be added, of course, that the forces of Chance and Change, not strictly forces of the Will (since they affect It), also complicate man's position, making foresight at best a tentative instrument.

The pattern is revealed fully in *The Dynasts*. Hardy appears to see the Revolution as an enlightened attempt to disturb the prevailing equilibrium, and to force events in the direction away from stagnation. Without being blind to the consequences of revolution—he admits, for instance, that Napoleon 'crushed its final horrors'—he none the less recognises it as a genuine expression of human aspirations, and condemns Napoleon for his failure to adapt himself to those aspirations. Napoleon's career is presented as falling into two phases, one positive, the other totally negative and destructive:

> *. . . 'twere better far*
> *Such deeds were nulled, and this strange man's career*
> *Wound up . . . For the large potencies*
> *Instilled into his idiosyncrasy—*
> *To throne fair Liberty in Privilege' room—*
> *Are taking taint, and sink to common plots*
> *For his own gain.* (Fore-scene)

The historical environment in which Napoleon finds himself is represented in terms of a historical determinism based upon consequence, and upon united action:

> *Thus do the mindless minions of the spell*
> *In mechanized enchantment sway and show*
> *A Will that wills above the will of each,*
> Yet but the will of all conjunctively . . . (III, i, 5)

The minions are *mindless* at this point because they are unaware of the nature of the forces that grip them; in no way is it implied that they are not responsible for those forces. Later, when Napoleon is overthrown, his downfall is explicitly shown to be the outcome of a conscious wish:

> *Yea, the dull peoples and the Dynasts both,*
> *Those counter-castes not oft adjustable,*
> *Interests antagonistic, proud and poor,*
> *Have for the nonce been bonded by a wish*
> *To overthrow thee.* (III, vii, 9)

Earlier Ney warns Napoleon that his people have

judged the future by the accustomed past . . .
They see the brooks of blood that have flowed forth;
They feel their own bereavements . . . (III, iv, 4)

The irony of *The Dynasts*, of course, is that the people are hoodwinked in their efforts: the 'mouldy thrones' are restored. But it is a poem about human development within an evolutionary frame, and evolution is a sickeningly slow process: the peoples must 'still plod on/Through hoodwinkings to light' (III, iv, 4). Other poems, most notably 'The Sick Battle-God' and 'A Plaint to Man',[31] make it clear that at the heart of Hardy's hopes for the future was a belief in the influence of human reason over the evolution of mankind and the organism of which each individual is a part. It is essentially a hope for collectivist action, which in turn must be based upon individual perception. He held to this view even after the crisis of the First World War, and expressed it in a letter to J. H. Morgan in 1924:

> . . . there is in my opinion a real hope that the League of Nations may result in something—for a reason which apparently (I say it with great deference) neither Lord M[orley] nor yourself perceived, or at least cared to consider—the self-interest of mankind. Principalities & powers will discern more & more clearly that each personality in them stands himself to lose by war, notwithstanding a promise of gain at first, & this thought will damp prime movers down to moderators.[32]

What, then, of the 'longing for annihilation' which we have briefly noted above? It would appear to fit some of Hardy's characters: possibly Henchard, possibly Jude. Is there any conflict of ideas here?

I believe there is. Hardy recognised the necessity of adaptation to the human environment, and at the same time admired the strength of those who attempted to break through the limitations of necessity. He recorded a review of Carlyle from *The Spectator* which presented life in just such terms:

> Carlyle showed us how small a proportion of our life we can realize in thought; how small a proportion of our thoughts we can figure forth in words . . . how vast the forces around which the human spirit struggles for its little modicum of purpose . . . how, in spite of this array of immensities, the Spirit whose command brings us into being requires of us the kind of life which defies necessity.[33]

The tragedy, often, in Hardy is the destruction of personal aspirations because they arise in an environment which is unsuited to their fulfilment, and the tragic action consists of the struggle to escape from the necessity of adaptation. In 1885 Hardy stated that tragedy 'exhibits a state of things in the life of an individual which unavoidably causes some natural aim or desire of his to end in catastrophe when carried out',[34] and in 1895 he expressed this idea still more explicitly:

> Tragedy may be created by an opposing environment either of things inherent in the universe, or of human institutions. If the former be the means exhibited and deplored, the writer is regarded as impious; if the latter, as subversive and dangerous; when all the while he may never have questioned the necessity or urged the non-necessity of either.[35]

His normal method, and this is of course especially true of the later novels, is to present a character encompassed by both social and universal obstacles. As far as the social obstacles are concerned, the personal plea which ends the note is somewhat ingenuous: it is highly unlikely that any reader of *Tess* or *Jude* will accept that Hardy had no strong views on the necessity of social change, and the non-necessity of some existing social institutions. And even against the charge of impiety Hardy was, perhaps, on weak ground. In abandoning the Divine Order he chose to attempt to discover another which seemed truer to the facts of existence: and he virtually re-created a scientific Chain of Being in which every tiny link contributed to the whole. The biggest difference between the old order and the new natural order which he saw was that the new possessed no special significance or purpose, and that man, so far from being an instrument of purpose, was now responsible for creating a sense of direction and an aim.

If the term 'Fate' means anything in relation to Hardy's work, then, we may see it as representing a combination of different forces. The first of these is the inherent nature of the universe: its dependence upon evolution as a means of change, and the necessity of change in all things; the passage of time, bringing with it the processes of decay and, among human beings, the impossibility of retrieving lost opportunities. In this intellectual generalisation Hardy could obviously apply his own personal experiences. Secondly, we can discern historical necessity, the inevitable limitations imposed upon human actions by consequence, and the inevitability of a future dependent in the same way upon the consequences of present actions. Thirdly, the requirement that, to be effective, human actions must be adapted to the environment, and the certainty that actions which refuse to take the environment into account are doomed to failure. The human resources which may be set against these limitations are consciousness and the gift of foresight, however imperfect; the opportunity afforded by the state of equilibrium to channel events into a new course; and the gift of the human intellect, making it possible to develop new methods of coping with, and even of altering, man's environment. It is no easy way which Hardy offers. Writing of Nietzsche he comments:

> He assumes throughout the great worth intrinsically of human masterfulness. The universe is to him a perfect machine which only requires thorough handling to work wonders. He forgets that the universe is an imperfect machine, and that to do good with an ill-working instrument requires endless adjustments and compromise.[36]

But at least the personal will *is* an instrument, and humanity must make the best possible use of it. Setting aside all the natural limitations imposed upon human behaviour, there remain only the self-imposed limitations of which Hardy wrote in his poem 'Thoughts at Midnight':[37]

> Mankind, you dismay me . . .
> Acting like puppets
> Under Time's buffets;
> In superstitions
> And ambitions
> Moved by no wisdom,
> Far-sight, or system,
> Led by sheer senselessness
> And presciencelessness
> Into unreason
> And hideous self-treason.

The novels deal with these acts of self-treason, as well as with Fate in the terms defined above. Indeed, the writing of these works contributed to the development of Hardy's ideas more powerfully, perhaps, than anything except personal experience. The novels face, too, one aspect of human conduct which appears little in Hardy's notes: but the drive of sexuality and its pressure upon human conduct is a force of which Hardy was aware through his own instincts and experience. The knowledge of sexual necessity, and its place within the evolutionary frame, was not the result of an act of intellectual understanding but of bitter personal troubles.

That, as Hardy's novels proceed, we can discern a change in his approach, is due to a number of causes, some of them purely intellectual in character. *Far From the Madding Crowd* is without doubt the most consistent and balanced of the major novels; in the works immediately following Hardy's attention is captured more and more by the challenge of the individual consciousness and with those who lead 'the kind of life which defies necessity'. His scope widens as his stress narrows: where *Far From the Madding Crowd* restricts itself chiefly to the effects of Troy's and Oak's conduct on Weatherbury society, *The Return of the Native* is preoccupied with attitudes towards Time, and evolutionary development within Time. Clym is a 'modern' figure attempting to avert hopelessness in the face of a higher appreciation of the human predicament, Eustacia a romantic dreamer who suffers through ignorance rather than knowledge. The work ends with a note of hope, though scarcely a hope that is defined in real terms: however, the description of Clym's addresses as Sermons on the Mount suggest that moral values can survive the new awareness. To a degree *The Mayor of Casterbridge* shares the same social and historical preoccupations, but from this point onwards, it seems, Hardy's development ceased, or took a new turn which, in the field of ideas at least, was to be a cul-de-sac, even though it drew upon his deepest sympathies. This is not a judgement on the quality of the novels, but of their kind. And the reason for the change seems to be explicable primarily in biographical terms. Together with this biographical involvement comes a deepening pessimism: a pessimism which is not ignorant of moral values, but which sets those values against a universal background of increasing utility.

Hardy was unable to forget or ignore the pulsing force of the individual, temperament will. The conflict between the individual and the community deepens as the novels proceed, and while Hardy's reasoning leads him towards a system of communal and collective values his sympathies led to an increased identification with the individual. Since that individual was so often a projection of areas of his own being and experience, and since his last novel is derived so crucially from his own life, this is scarcely surprising. In *The Dynasts* the problem was solved in part because the individual is dwarfed in the cosmic setting; still more, perhaps, because *Jude the Obscure* had effectively voiced Hardy's bitterness. Before that time, however, the challenge which Hardy's belief in the community presented to his sympathy had been evident, and it was noticed acutely by D. H. Lawrence:

> This is the theme of novel after novel: remain quite within the convention, and you are good, safe, and happy in the long run, though you never have the vivid pang of sympathy on your side: or, on the other hand, be passionate, individual, wilful, you will find the security of the convention a walled prison, you will escape, and you will die, either of your own lack of strength to bear the isolation and the exposure, or by direct revenge from the community, or from both. . . . The growth and the development of this tragedy, the deeper and deeper realisation of this division and this problem, the coming towards some conclusion, is the one theme of the Wessex novels.[38]

In its general argument this is right: only in its final statement is it at fault. For the Wessex novels of themselves lead to no conclusion. They raise a number of different intellectual and personal issues, at first centring broadly on the conflict between the individual and the community, much in the terms Lawrence used but showing a sensitive awareness of the problems raised by man's understanding of his limited yet responsible role in the community—an awareness which Lawrence totally misses, both in his comments here and in his works. These intellectual issues are treated more or less in isolation, although up to *The Return of the Native* they may be assimilated into a single, developing argument. That argument never reaches a conclusion in the novels, for in place of a primarily rational approach Hardy substitutes personal involvement, not to say personal obsession. At least one major cause for Hardy's sympathy with the rebellious and impassioned individual is that he was rebellious and impassioned himself. There is little about the grand old man of the 1920's to support such a view, certainly; but the novels were not written by the semi-recluse of Max Gate but by the lover, married man, socialite, and the mourner, of the second half of the nineteenth century.

Indeed, there is throughout Hardy's work a strange duality. The poems, like the novels, have a two-fold voice, while *The Dynasts*, although suppressing the personal voice, is built upon a dual vision. In the poems we find a philosophy whose negative quality is shown to be more apparent than real. There is a constant tension, in form and subject, as Hardy tries to reconcile his rationalism with his imaginative pietism:

> If someone said on Christmas Eve,
> 'Come; see the oxen kneel
>
> 'In the lonely barton by yonder coomb
> Our childhood used to know',
> I should go with him in the gloom
> Hoping it might be so.[39]

As usual, Hardy himself is aware of what is happening:

> You must not think me a hard-hearted rationalist. . . . Half my time (particularly when I write verse) I believe—in the modern sense of the word—. . . in spectres, mysterious voices, intuitions, omens, dreams, haunted places, etc., etc.
>
> But then, I do not believe in these in the old sense of belief any more for that. . . .[40]

'I believe; I do not believe'—this is really the true basis for any approach to Hardy: the reader must be prepared to meet 'seemings', 'impressions'—and yet those impressions are remarkably consistent. In the precise, disturbed language of the poems we find the same distinction between the 'scenic' and the real, the same irony pointing towards a failure of vision or a tragic unawareness of the human condition. Whether his subject is war, the failure of love, the collapse of belief, or the simple wish of a milkmaid to receive her new gown in time to win back her lover, there will be found irony; and, too, evidence of Hardy's gentle and humble compassion. In compassion, perhaps, lies the key to the growth of man's higher consciousness, even in the most personal and individual situations:

> You love not me,
> And love alone can lend you loyalty;
> —I know and knew it. But, unto the store
> Of human deeds divine in all but name,
> Was it not worth a little hour or more
> To add yet this: Once you, a woman, came
> To soothe a time-torn man; even though it be
> You love not me?[41]

The poem is reticent, deeply personal, free of reproach; it is also a muted restatement of the comment in *Jude the Obscure*, 'nobody did come, because nobody does'.

His vision, so mature and complex in some ways, was in others almost that of a child, and one can recognise in Florence Hardy's protective tenderness for him a just estimate of one side of his character:

> . . . I feel towards him, sometimes, as a mother towards a child with whom things have somehow gone wrong—a child who needs comforting—to be treated gently with all the love possible.[42]

Yet there is more than a child: there is the shy, sensitive youth who became the passionate wooer of a member of his own family; the scion of a once-noble family and the historian troubled by the personal consequences of his own researches; the simple believer in piety and loving-kindness and the harsh, unsympathetic figure sometimes presented to his wives, or revealed in his personal comments on unsuspecting and occasionally maligned critics; the profound opponent of war, yet capable of writing patriotic and nationalistic—though scarcely bellicose—war poems; the disbeliever in an anthropomorphic God, compelled to address himself to personalised abstractions. These conflicts are present in the works, as they were present in the life. The conflict between the claims of the individual and the community is not a simple confusion, but is grounded upon a humane pity on the one hand, and an attempt, on the other, to express that pity in rationalistic terms.

Observers who knew Hardy in his last years saw in him no fear of death; only a placid resignation which rose to the sublime in the lines of 'Afterwards'.[43] As Edmund Blunden wrote, 'he lived in the still centre'.[44] But it was a hard-won achievement, based upon self-knowledge and knowledge of the world. His intellectual faculties remained alive, as the letters and the *Life* amply testify, while the poems are a tribute to a massive creative energy which appears to have survived almost to the end. His mental flexibility enabled him to overcome the shock given to his long-matured beliefs by the First World War, and he continued to see man, united to his environment by suffering and death, in isolation as the master of his own future. And yet, at the very end, he may, in Blunden's words again, have come to believe 'that the retreat from our furthest point of civilised intelligence and spiritual pilgrimage was imminent because the world was so made, as the mortal span is for individuals'.[45] Certainly his views on change and decay might lead to such a conclusion; but if they did so they would involve an abandonment of his belief in the power of men to achieve at least a limited control. Yet that final retreat from faith seems to have occurred:

> We are getting to an end of visioning
> The impossible within this universe,
> Such as that better whiles may follow worse,
> And that our race may end by reasoning.
>
> We know that even as larks in cages sing
> Unthoughtful of deliverance from the curse
> That holds them lifelong in a latticed hearse,
> We ply spasmodically our pleasuring.
>
> And that when nations set them to lay waste
> Their neighbours' heritage by foot and horse,
> And hack their pleasant plains in festering seams,
> They may again,—not warely, or from taste,
> But tickled mad by some demonic force.—
> Yes. We are getting to the end of dreams.[46]

The direct simplicity of this late poem carries with it the sense of personal conviction; it is perhaps an echo, too, of a frame of mind felt many years before:

> Far be it from my wish to distrust any comforting fantasy, if it can be barely tenable. But . . . pain has been, and pain is: no new sort of morals in Nature can remove pain from the past and make it pleasure for those who are its infallible estimators, the bearers thereof. And no injustice, however slight, can be atoned for by her future generosity, however ample, so long as we consider Nature to be, or to stand for, unlimited power. The exoneration of an omnipotent Mother by her retrospective justice becomes an absurdity when we ask, what made the foregone injustice necessary to her Omnipotence?[47]

The cry is an age-old one, and it remains unanswered. However, the tragic vision of a world in which 'pain has been, and pain is' also embraces the knowledge that pain may be aggravated by human folly, and it embraces an appeal for the sanity and compassion of mankind. In a profound sense, Hardy was a great thinker, but not the creator of a consistently-worked-out philosophy. He was great because of his response to existence, an unflinching courage of mind. His sombre view of life deepened his imaginative response to human aspirations, and is lent its own integrity by the mute, faltering longing for faith and hope, and the sure acceptance of charity. His fellow-poets truly honoured themselves when, in 1921, they wrote:

> In your novels and poems you have given us a tragic vision of life which is informed by your knowledge of character and relieved by the charity of your humour, and sweetened by your sympathy with human suffering and endurance. We have learned from you that the proud heart can subdue the hardest fate, even in submitting to it. . . . In all that you have written you have shown the spirit of man, nourished by tradition and sustained by pride, persisting through defeat. . . .
>
> We thank you, Sir, for all that you have written . . . but most of all, perhaps, for *The Dynasts*.[48]

Hardy was, in his way, a prophet; and he was a bitterly unhappy man.

APPENDIX A

THE 'FAMILY CURSE'

HARDY'S attitude towards his ancestry was, like many other of his attitudes, ambivalent; yet it exerts a considerable influence on his work, and seems to provide the clue to a sense of exhaustion in the man himself—a feeling not merely that human effort is futile and human success transitory, but that the Hardys themselves were an example of futility and transience. His reflection on the family decline and lost lands (see above, pp. 7-8) was carried over into the novels, and in writing of the d'Urbervilles as a family who had 'gone under' Hardy was writing of his own.

Since this preoccupation with decline, transience, and futility runs directly counter to the intellectual 'message' of Hardy's work, it is worth examining its background. Hardy himself collected many details of his family, and subsequent research (the common pool of the efforts of Lois Deacon, J. O. Bailey, and myself) has added many more. The foundation for the 'family curse' motif is not fully clarified by our knowledge, but some of its contributory causes appear.

The first of the family to be traced, Thomas le Hardy, was Rector of the Jersey parish of St Martin in the 1460's, and may have possessed the strain of recklessness which Hardy notes in his more immediate ancestry. For when a French agent, one William Carbonell, was employed to root out all traces of anti-French feeling in the island, Thomas le Hardy was arrested and brought to trial. According to Balleine's *History of the Island of Jersey*, some of the trial records have survived, and show Thomas to have been educated and hospitable, and in the habit of keeping open house after his Sunday sermon. The outcome of the trial is not recorded, but if Hardy was guilty of complicity in anti-French intrigue—and it does not seem unlikely—his weekly hospitality may well have been an effective cloak for less innocent pastimes. But the records, dating from 1463, reveal nothing of his family, nor of his eventual fate. We can picture him riding his parish rounds on a mule; we know that he educated at least one child in his home; but little more.

Standing trial with Thomas was a brave, stocky man of forty-five, Renaud Lempriere, born French but English-speaking, and married to a Dorset girl more than twenty years his junior. His home sheltered a number of young children, including his illegitimate son, 'the bastard of Rozel' and a niece, Guilleme, at that time aged fifteen. Within a few years she would become the foundress of the modern Hardy line when she would marry Clement le Hardy, a man as brave and reckless as his kinsman Thomas. In 1483, after an abortive rising against Richard III and at a time when Jersey was predominately Yorkist in its sympathies, Clement assisted Henry Tudor to escape to France; in return, after Henry's successful assault on the throne in 1485, he received the offices successively of Bailiff and Lieutenant-Governor of the island. His independent spirit seems to have been no respecter of persons, however, and caused his downfall: shortly before his death in 1489 he was dismissed from office for stealing the proceeds of a wreck, rightly the property of the king.

Another branch of the family had already settled in West Dorset, and may have maintained contact with the Jersey cousins. For in 1488 Clement's son, the young John Hardy, adopted the anglicised form of the name and, with the assistance of the powerful Paulet family, settled at Eggardon among Dorset's western hills, only a few miles from the earlier Hardy immigrants. From him we can trace a continuous pedigree of sheriffs, squires, and landed gentry, of whom the most outstanding is Thomas Hardye of Frampton and Melcombe Regis who, as Knight Marshal for Elizabeth I,[1] endowed the ancient Grammar School of Dorchester on August 3, 1579, and was in return acknowledged as its founder (though truly the borough elders, who rescued it from the ruins of monasticism in 1569, equally deserve that honourable title). For the modern novelist the uniformed schoolboys of the town, bearing the Hardy coat-of-arms on their peaked caps, were living reminders of his origins. When, on July 21, 1927, he laid the foundation-stone for new school buildings, he commented on the foresight of his ancestor in terms which make it clear that this, his last official public appearance, was almost a rite for him. In the following months his walks regularly took him to watch the rising walls of the new school, and brought him within sight of the monument to that other Hardy who had held the dying Nelson in his arms. Certainly these visible presences strengthened the poet's already strong roots in his native county, roots which were nourished with a rich pride. But there were other presences too, and pride was mingled with regret, perhaps with fear. Hutchins's *History of Dorset* impartially records: 'the manor of Wolcombe Matravers, and lands in Bagleshay . . . were held by Hardy . . . till about the reign of Charles II',[2] and the same story is repeatedly told of the south and west of the county. There is no record of political involvement bringing the loss of lands as a result of the Civil War: rather there are hints of mishandled estates, family feuds, and marital irregularities. The county law-suits reveal more than one internal dispute, one Robert Hardy, for example, being disinherited and 'sent into Ireland for reasons which it is not fit should be mentioned'.* Hutchins surmises a dispute between two brothers for control of the estate at Up-Sydling; and even the august founder of Hardye's School may have disinherited his daughter for some unrecorded cause, since she figures as an unsuccessful claimant to his property after his death.[3] There is more than one suggestion of hot-bloodedness in the family records, and in Hardy's own scattered comments about his ancestry: he recalls in 'Family Portraits', for example, their 'dark doings each against each', and regards them as 'expert/In the law-lacking passions of life'.[4] The records give an incomplete picture of this family blood, and Hardy himself, though he knew the details, scarcely ever referred to them openly; but there are veiled allusions in *Jude the Obscure*, a novel which contains more family history than Hardy ever cared to recognise publicly or in print. At this distance the full stories are unclear, but some of the details survive.

Among the women of his family there was his paternal grandmother, Mary Head, of Fawley, Berkshire. Hardy rarely refers to her in the *Life*, but he does record that her memories of her childhood home 'were so poignant that she never cared to return to the place after she had left it as a young girl'.[5] The local records show that her mother, formerly Mary Hopson and the wife of James Head of Fawley, had buried her husband on May 6, 1772, five months before the younger Mary was born. In April 1779, Mary Hopson Head gave birth to another child, an illegitimate son who was baptised William, but who died just one week later. The mother died six days after that. No father is named in the records, even though both parents of bastard children are commonly named; and Mary was left an orphan at the age of seven years. These are the bare facts, publicly recorded.[6] At this date it seems impossible to discover the drama that lies behind them, though Hardy's account of Mary Head in 'One We

* Dorset Suits, VI (1646). These records, bound and indexed, are in the Dorset County Museum. Since they were compiled by Hardy's close friend Alfred Pope, Hardy was almost certainly aware of their contents whenever his own family were affected.

Knew'[7] suggests that for the young girl the experience was a traumatic one, and he may have known more than the bare facts. In the summer of 1864, thirty years before *Jude the Obscure*, Hardy visited Fawley, sketched the old church,* and may well have looked through the records. That they contributed to *Jude the Obscure* is certain: Jude's surname is taken from Fawley, and the village rechristened *Mary*green; Sue's surname is Bride*head*, and Jude's, at one stage of the manuscript, was to have been *Hopeson*—appropriate enough to his role in the novel, but clearly a derivative of *Hopson*, the maiden name of Mary's mother. Widow Edlin, who features in the book, carries a name several times recorded in the Fawley registers, and it is tempting to believe, though without evidence, that it was to the Edlin home that the orphan girl was taken. Of the mysterious hanged ancestor referred to in *Jude* there is no sign, although the gallows referred to in the novel and in 'One We Knew' stood barely a mile from Fawley. We cannot tell why Fawley and its events were so important to Hardy, but perhaps we have a hint in a snatch of conversation from the novel:

> 'She said marriage always used to end badly with the Fawleys.'
>
> 'That's strange. My father used to say the same to me of my mother's people.'[8]

The last speaker is Sue, whose mother's family is also Jude's; until page 40 of the manuscript their name is given as *Head*, and in both the manuscript and the book Hardy lays great stress on the common ancestry of Jude and Sue. Since the most formative love affair of Hardy's life was with a cousin who shared his ancestry the relevance to him of Fawley and the fortunes of Mary Head may be more subjective and imaginative than real. We know that Hardy never married his cousin; that his engagement to her was probably condemned by his family; and that in the manuscript of *Jude* a sentence remains undeleted to read:

> 'Jude, my child, don't you ever marry. 'Tisn't for the Heads to take that step any more.'[9]

We have too little material to re-create the events of Mary's earlier years, but the details which we do possess, taken with

* The sketch, signed and dated, is in the Firestone Library, Princeton University, and was brought to my attention by Professor J. O. Bailey.

other autobiographical elements in *Jude* and in the poems, suggest that there is some parallel between the experiences of Mary Head and her family and the experiences of Hardy himself. That he might in some sense be re-enacting the past was a vivid possibility to him, and it troubled him. For he found other mysteries, too. In a pedigree which he drew up and which is now in the Dorset County Museum,[10] he records that the marriage of his maternal grand-parents, George Hand and Elizabeth Swetman, was 'clandestine'; the poem 'In Sherborne Abbey',[11] described as 'a family tradition', would appear to refer to this incident. Yet the marriage was in no sense clandestine. The banns were called regularly in the parish church of Melbury Osmund, despite the opposition of Elizabeth's crusty father, yeoman John Swetman; in a parish of little more than three hundred souls he must have known of the calling of the banns. Moreover, a daughter, Maria Hand, was born just eight days after the wedding, which would have made it difficult, even dangerous, for Elizabeth to elope. Possibly George Hand and his bride-to-be eloped much earlier, returning to marry only when the coming child forced John Swetman to swallow his opposition. However, to complicate the situation even more, Hardy's poem 'Her Late Husband'[12] appears to refer to George Hand and Elizabeth Swetman. The wife asks that her body may in due time be buried under her maiden name and among her own kin; her husband is to be buried near another woman, his wife in the sight of God. The notion that a woman's first lover is her natural husband is of course a common one in Hardy; yet if Elizabeth were within a week of childbirth at the time of her marriage, and if the father were George Hand, she, as much as anyone, was his wife in the sight of God.

Hardy certainly delved into these local records, as the poems and the *Life* reveal; he also heard many accounts from his parents and relatives from which he could fill out the bare bones of the historical summary. He seems to have been genuinely disturbed by what he found, and perhaps still more by what he conjectured. One still faces the details of this family career with the sense that one is on the edge of a consistently tragic family course, yet they are so elusive that it seems impossible to trace any pattern with certainty. Even so, the references to ancestry and heredity scattered through poetry and prose reinforce the view that Hardy himself had traced a pattern, albeit a vague one, and that at times he was obsessed by it, feeling himself bound to repeat the mistakes of his forefathers, his character and conduct ruled by the dead generations. 'Family Portraits' and 'The Pedigree',[13] in particular, repeat this notion, the latter in horror-stricken terms. The notion of ancestral patterns was not an uncommon one among the Victorians, and had Hardy so needed he could have found contemporary scientific opinion to support his view. Writing in the *Fortnightly Review* in 1883 Francis Galton had argued the need for medical family registers which would allow men to foretell 'in a general way, which are the families naturally fated to decay and which to thrive, which are those who will die out and which will be prolific and fill the vacant space'.[14] A year previously, in the same vein, he had commented on the 'surprisingly small margin which seemed to be left to the effects of what we are accustomed to call "free-will" '.[15] Yet it is improbable that Hardy was merely dramatising some of the existing moods of his contemporaries. That these moods had their effect upon him is incontrovertible, but he would not have been so affected as to let them influence even the treatment of his autobiography unless he regarded them as more than imaginative fiction; and his own relationship with a girl who was also a descendant of the Swetmans and Hands seems sufficient reason for him to ponder the implications of an ancestral pattern, particularly when that relationship was ultimately doomed to failure. All the evidence suggests that Hardy had enough facts and suspicions about his own family to convince him that hereditary behaviour patterns not only existed, but were present in his own kin. He was an avid student of local records, and he confessed his own approach to the official genealogies in the preface to *A Group of Noble Dames*: he would compare the dates of births, marriages, and deaths with those of kindred births, marriages, and deaths, and from that comparison would raise images, 'filling into the framework the motives, passions, and personal qualities which would appear to be the single explanation possible of some extraordinary conjunction in times, events, and personages'. If he approached his own family records in this light he may have conjectured too much. For it is a simple fact that the home of Hardy's maternal ancestors lies at the gateway of a great house, that there are odd conjunctions of dates, the most striking being the marriage of Elizabeth Swetman—Elizabeth, owner of thirty gowns and a stock of reading 'of exceptional extent for a yeoman's daughter living in a remote place'[16]—the strange birth of Maria Hand being another. It is a simple fact, too, that Hardy tampered with the early pages of the *Life* to give a sequences of events incompatible with the records, and that the late Earl of Ilchester, one of whose ancestors boasted that he had 'peopled an entire village',[17] was strongly inclined to believe that Ilchester blood ran in the Hardy veins.[18] This is indeed the basis for conjecture, and some would regard it as shocking conjecture. Shocking it may be, but idle it is not. The course of Hardy's career was in part determined by his attitude towards the past; even his attitude towards the degree of freedom possessed by his heroes and heroines was based on a conflict between doctrines which received his intellectual assent, and emotional convictions which swayed, and at times undermined, his intellect.

For a sense of mystery about his ancestors was not confined to only one branch of his family, nor was he untouched by it. He appears, if revisions to the *Life* are an indication, to have been sensitive about the hasty marriage of his parents. He may, too, have been uncertain about his mother's past. The *Life* indirectly reveals that his father was thought to have 'bemeaned' himself by the marriage, and there is a disturbing air of mystery about Jemima Hand. 'Family Portraits' would suggest that Hardy felt the existence of a real parallel between the experiences of his forebears and his own: the poem, with its reference to 'some drama, obscure', a tragic love-match involving one man and two women, appears to refer most directly to his own parents—the only known portraits are of them. Yet the text of the *Life* deepens rather than solves the mystery:

> Among Elizabeth's children there was one, a girl, of unusual ability and judgement, and an energy that might have carried her to incalculable issues. This was the child Jemima, the mother of Thomas Hardy.[19]

He recalls the stressful experiences of her youth, 'of which she could never speak in her maturer years without pain', and one is struck by the similarity of this description to that of Mary Head.[20] We know too little of the career of either to be sure of the force of this parallel, but it may not be too fanciful to believe that in this 'energy that might have led to incalculable issues' we have one of the many strands which later emerged in the character of Tess.

For Hardy was not prepared to tell the truth about Jemima. In particular he did not care to admit that his birth, on June 2, 1840, occurred only five and a half months after his parents' marriage at Melbury Osmund on December 22, 1839.[21] When preparing his wife for the production of a posthumous autobiography he appears to have toyed with the idea of obscuring the dates completely. A manuscript draft for the *Life* contains the following remarkable statement:

> 1848. Thomas Hardy, the third child, was rather fragile . . .[22]

—even though Florence Hardy, as she typed these notes, must have been as well aware as the author of the relative ages of Hardy and his family. Either Hardy was attempting to tamper with the facts, or Jemima was already the mother of two children.* Another cancelled passage mingles probable fact with certain fiction:

> . . . his mother learned tambouring, and was a skilful embroiderer of kid gloves; but her eyes being weakened she formed the idea of becoming a club-house cook and, it is believed, applied to Henry 2nd Earl of Ilchester, to assist her. It appears that he sent her to his brother, the Hon. Charles Fox-Strangways, where she became a a skilful cook, accompanying the family to London. Here she meant to take a further stride, but on returning met her future husband, and was married to him at the age of five-and-twenty.
>
> The club-house idea was, however, not abandoned by her, and in a few months she proposed to leave her husband in the country and seek such a post. To this he objected, & the birth of children gave the death-blow to this rather adventurous scheme.

This account can be reconciled neither with the facts, nor with the account subsequently published in the *Life*; both accounts are deliberately inaccurate, but it may have been because some of the facts were ultimately verifiable with ease that Hardy or his wife eliminated such confusions from the final text. Even so, Hardy did attempt to tamper with the dating, for the *Life* retains the statement that his mother married at the age of five-and-twenty. Born in 1813, and baptised on September 20 of that year, she would have been twenty-five in 1838, almost eighteen months before her son's birth; but as we have seen, her marriage took place at Christmas, 1839. It appears to be true that she worked in London for some years, though this detail, too, is modified in

* Thomas was christened July 1, 1840; Mary, January 23, 1842; Henry, August 24, 1851; Katharine, October 26, 1856 (Stinsford registers). Lois Deacon is convinced that Rebecca Sparks was also the child of Thomas and Jemima Hardy. See Appendix B.

the *Life*: 'She resolved to be a cook in a London club-house, but . . . met her future husband', which implies that she never carried out her resolve. It also very effectively suppresses any connection with the Fox-Strangways family. If she did indeed work for Charles Fox-Strangways, her employment would have ceased in 1836, for in that year he died. However, she appears to have been employed at the Kingston Maurward estate from about that year,[23] and Hardy's suggested date for the first meeting of his parents, '*circa* 1835',[24] may be fairly accurate.

Jemima is to be closely associated with three of her son's works. That she was the model for Mrs Yeobright of *The Return of the Native* is well known. She has, however, a connection with two very different books, *The Hand of Ethelberta* and *Tess of the D'Urbervilles*. The germ of the first of these seems to have been provided by her experiences in London and after. If we are to believe Hardy's suppressed note and accept that she considered leaving her husband and family in Dorset while she pursued her London career, the course of Chickerel, Ethelberta's father, offers an interesting parallel. There is, of course, no known or guessed parallel between Ethelberta's stories and anything in Jemima's life; but Ethelberta's role as the virtual provider for a large number of dependants may be closer to fact—George Hand, Jemima's father, had died in 1822, and although Jemima was far from being the youngest child it is not impossible that the need to contribute to the claims of a numerous and fatherless family may have dictated her departure from Dorset. These are marginal connections, but there may be a stronger one. Hardy writes in Chapter VII of *Ethelberta*:

> One of them actually said that you must be fifty to have got such an experience. Her guess was a very shrewd one in the bottom of it, . . . for it was grounded upon the way you use those experiences of mine in the society that I tell you of, and dress them up as if they were yours. . . .

Just as Ethelberta derived from her parent the material stories of London society, so Hardy may have relied upon Jemima.

However, it seems more striking to record that, if the connection with *Ethelberta* exists, Hardy associated his mother with a work whose fundamental question, despite the superficial and ill-executed comedy, is a moral question: to what extent should a woman sacrifice herself for the welfare of her family? That question is also fundamental to *Tess of the D'Urbervilles*, and we find that there, too, Jemima is associated with the story, or at least with the subjective notions that led Hardy to his theme. Just as Hardy concealed the details of Jemima's London career, so he disguised the fact that his reflections about his mother and the decline of his family were closely linked:

> The decline and fall of the Hardys much in evidence hereabout. An instance: Becky S.'s mother's sister married one of the Hardys of this branch, who was considered to have bemeaned himself by the marriage. . . . I remember when young seeing the man—tall and thin—walking beside a horse and common spring trap, and my mother pointing him out to me and saying he represented what was once the leading branch of the family. So we go down, down, down.[25]

This is taken from the *Life*; it would be better placed in one of the novels, since much of it is fiction. The only 'Becky S.' connected by marriage with the Hardys was Rebecca Sparks of Puddletown, whose mother, Maria Sparks, was that very Maria Hand born just eight days after her parents' marriage. 'Becky S.'s mother's sister' is, more simply stated, Jemima Hand, later Jemima Hardy. Hardy's father did represent the leading branch of the family, although he was not 'tall and thin'; nor, unless the records are far more discreet than they seem, did they have an awful lot of children. The passage is an almost grotesque confession of Hardy's dissatisfaction with his parents, the stranger because there is no doubt that his respect and love for them was genuine. It is difficult to see why Hardy's father had 'bemeaned' himself by the marriage: the registers state that George Hand, Jemima's father, was a 'servant' to the Earl of Ilchester; some family traditions maintain that he was a shepherd. On the other hand, Jemima's mother, Elizabeth Swetman, was the daughter of a yeoman, and could claim a status at least comparable to that now enjoyed by the Hardys. Moreover she came from a family which seemed to be considerably more literate and bookish, and Hardy's intellectual gifts probably owed more to Elizabeth than to the long line of Hardys.

We are again in a position where there is room for conjecture, but almost none for stated fact. Jemima seems to be closely associated with the imaginative springs of two of the novels (London on the one hand; family decline on the other) in which the principal question is one of morality. We also know that Hardy and several of his family stated firmly that the adventures of Tess had actually happened to a relative of theirs. Was she Jemima? Or, more probably, were Jemima's experiences, whatever they were, combined with the distressful experiences of several members of the family through several generations? We cannot tell —and the problem in examining Hardy's forebears, and his own conflicting and confused account of them, is that we are able to tell less and less the longer we stare at the available facts. All we can say is that Hardy was aware of them; and was aware, too, that he was successfully confusing the issue for posterity.

The message conveyed by this confused pattern is threefold: firstly, it suggests that confusion which Hardy himself was facing, and the reasons for his apparent fear of it; it indicates his sensitivity to its implications—a sensitivity which may account in part for the reticence and shyness which marked his whole career; and finally, it calls into question the reliability of the *Life* as source-material for any accurate biography of Hardy. Some years ago Lois Deacon and Terry Coleman published *Providence and Mr Hardy*; freely admitting that some of their work was conjecture, they offered a new interpretation of the early years, and produced new information about Hardy's career. In the critical uproar which followed one vital fact was overlooked: Deacon and Coleman had read the documentary records; I am afraid their critics had only read the *Life*.

APPENDIX B

HARDY AND TRYPHENA

THE fact of Hardy's engagement to Tryphena Sparks was first made public by Miss Lois Deacon in a Toucan Press monograph in 1962, and discussed in greater detail by Deacon and Coleman in *Providence and Mr Hardy* (London, 1966). My own knowledge of Tryphena, derived from a study of the ancestry, gave me little reason to believe the case expounded in 1966, but a subsequent study of the records, including Miss Deacon's own papers, letters, and research notes, has caused me to modify my position considerably.

The evidence for the engagement was derived principally from Tryphena's daughter, Mrs Eleanor Tryphena Bromell (1878-1965), whose letters and recollections written between 1959 and her death repeat that Hardy and Tryphena were engaged, and that the engagement began after Hardy's return from London in 1867. It was continued during Tryphena's training at Stockwell College, South London, and during her first years as headmistress of the Girls' Section of the Coburg Street School, Plymouth:

> When she came out of college, 1871, & went to Plymouth, Tom gave her a ring. He was 'tacking after her' while she was in college, & he in London training for architect.
>
> (Mrs Bromell's recollections).[1]

The detail of the ring was later corroborated by Miss Irene Cooper Willis, co-executor of the Hardy estate, who had been told by Florence Hardy that the ring given to Hardy's first wife had been intended for a Dorset girl.[2] This is one indication that, despite her age, Mrs Bromell's recollections of her mother's conversations were reliable. It is also true that when she was questioned about Tryphena's childhood home at Puddletown, which she had never seen but had heard her mother discuss, her descriptions of it were accurate. Hardy's poetry for this period, as well as the reference to Tryphena in the preface to *Jude the Obscure*, make it fairly clear that Mrs Bromell's story of the engagement was the truth.

In Mrs Bromell's possession was an album of photographs, formerly the property of Tryphena. The most interesting of its contents was the portrait of an unidentified young boy. Mrs Bromell was first shown this photograph by Lois Deacon, accompanied by one of her literary trustees, on September 9, 1960—i.e. four and a half years before her death. At that time Mrs Bromell offered no conclusive identification of the child: in answer to Lois Deacon's question 'Who is that?' she replied: 'Oh, that's just a little boy who used to come to see Tryphena.' She volunteered no name for the child, and no background; but clearly any identification of the photograph has to take account of this statement, made when Mrs Bromell was clearly in command of her faculties. In her last years, and especially in her last months, when she was eighty-six, she was weak, and sometimes confused. Thus her statements at this time must be treated with caution. Yet she could accurately identify photographs of the young Hardy and of Tryphena as a girl, and her memory seemed generally unimpaired. She was not, however, again shown the photograph of the child until she was visibly weakening, sick, and a hospital patient. When she did see the photograph her responses to it were checked by her ability to identify photographs of Hardy and Tryphena. Lois Deacon's account, written a few days before the event, explains the procedure that was adopted:

> . . . I propose to take with me the picture of Tryphena aged eighteen, and of Tom . . . to find out, first of all, whether she still recognises them. Then [a member of the family] would quietly place before Nellie [Mrs Bromell] the picture of 'the small boy', explaining that it was from Tryphena's album, and asking [her] who this was.[3]

This was done for the first time on January 17, 1965. Mrs Bromell stated several times 'That was Hardy's boy', 'Everyone knew it was Hardy's boy'; but she did not know his Christian name, nor did she know the identity of the boy's mother. She described him as 'delicate', 'frail', older than herself, fond of birds, of reading poetry, and of drawing. She also said that he had hurt his hand in a bicycle accident (later she said that it had been scratched by a dog), but she could not say how old he had been when this took place. The portrait of the small boy shows no sign of that injury.

Mrs Bromell went on to say that the boy had attended Tryphena's funeral, but had never revisited the Gales at Topsham after that. Until then, she said, 'he came to see Tryphena'.

Charles Frederick Gale, whom Tryphena had married on December 15, 1877, 'did not like the boy'.

It is perhaps important to state here that several members of the family were present, and Mrs Bromell's daughter asked for the photograph to be produced a second time for the old lady's inspection. The presence of the family, and their clear concern for their mother's welfare, seem a sufficient guarantee against undue pressure on an old and weakened lady; and Miss Deacon's transcripts, together with the letters written to her at this time by Mrs Bromell's relatives, make it clear that not only was such pressure not contemplated, but that no statement was accepted unless it had been witnessed by members of the family. In Miss Deacon's paper several statements were disregarded because they had been unwitnessed.

A further interview in which the same standard of care was shown was held during the following month (February 7, 1965). Shortly before her guests arrived Mrs Bromell had been sufficiently clear in her mind to discuss Hardy's novels with her nurse, and the nurse commented on this before the interview began. The same set of photographs was then produced by Miss Deacon, together with one other, the photograph of a young man aged twenty or twenty-one. This, too, was from Tryphena's album. Miss Deacon also carried with her an autograph album, presented to Tryphena by her pupils on the occasion of her marriage. Two of the pages were decorated with pressed fern leaves and wild flower leaves, arranged in a circlet; at the centre of the circlet on each page were written the words 'He will be our guide, even unto Death'. At the foot of each of these pages was the inscription, apparently in Tryphena's hand:

Ry.
Decr. 1873.

This, too, was eventually shown to Mrs Bromell.[4]

Again, the young boy was identified, without pressure, as 'Hardy's son'. On one occasion Mrs Bromell said 'Hardy's nephew', but she immediately corrected her own words, saying 'Hardy's son . . . I always took it to be Hardy's son. . . .He came to see Tryphena.' When shown the autograph album Mrs Bromell said that the ferns had been picked by her brother, Charlie, and she repeated the statement. Presumably, however, the date in the album, 1873, refers to the day on which the leaves were plucked; Charles Gale the younger was born in 1880, and it is clear that Mrs Bromell's replies were improbable at this point. Miss Deacon then turned to the other photographs, but Mrs Bromell gave no certain indication that the small boy and the young man were the same person. She did, however, look at the right hand of the young man, and remarked 'He hurt his hand.' On a subsequent occasion she said that he was 'Hardy's boy grown up'—though in this instance Lois Deacon recorded that it was impossible to be fully sure of her statement, since she was visibly tired and confused.

We may again take up the question of Mrs Bromell's reliability. Most of the information concerning only Hardy and Tryphena came during the preceding five years. Although Mrs Bromell recognised the photograph as early as September 1960 ('a little boy who used to come to see Tryphena'), her more detailed identification of him came only when she was on her death-bed. And it certainly appears that there was some confusion in her mind: the statement about the fern and flower leaves seems nonsense: flowers cannot be picked by a child who is not yet alive. Were Mrs Bromell's remarks nonsense throughout? Is there, for example, any evidence that the young man had indeed hurt his hand—for if so, Mrs Bromell's mental powers and her memory were clear at this point, and we have reasonable grounds for believing that the two portraits are of the same person.

The photograph of the young man is not clear, especially because the right hand is shielded by the left, and the casual observer might well be shy of forming an opinion. The photograph was therefore subjected to inspection by two competent medical authorities, Dr Rune Wikström, Director of Mösseberg Sanatorium, Sweden, and Dr Y. Raekallio, Professor of Forensic Medicine at the University of Turku, Finland.* Their inspections took place independently of each other, and their conclusions, concisely stated by Professor Raekallio, were identical:

> It is impossible to be sure, but it could be that some of the fingers of the right hand are missing. This is a guess, but something seems to be wrong.[5]

* The reviewer of *Hardy's Child: Fact or Fiction?* for the *Times Literary Supplement*, July 25, 1968, asks 'why these northern countries, unless to promote the shivers?' The answer, of course, as the monograph makes clear, is that I was working in those countries, and went to the nearest qualified authorities. So far as I know, a temperate climate is not an essential requirement for good practice or judgement.

Neither Dr Wikström nor Professor Raekallio had been asked to comment on the hand. The question put to them was simply: 'In your opinion does this photograph show evidence that this man had ever suffered an injury?' The only injury suggested by either doctor was an injury to the right hand.

The implications of this seem to me to be fairly clear. When Mrs Bromell stated that the small boy had hurt his hand she did so from memory, since there is no trace of an injury in the small boy's photograph. Neither, at that time, had she looked at the photograph of the young man. When she did so she commented on an injury which was confirmed by independent medical witnesses who were unaware of the reason for my inquiry. In each case Mrs Bromell appears to have recognised the same person: in other words, the child and the young man appear to be one and the same. To at least one reviewer[6] the resemblance between the photographs was not apparent, but that is scarcely the point: the resemblance was apparent to Mrs Bromell, who was the only living witness who had seen and could recall the subject of these portraits. And her most striking recollection has been confirmed.

Mrs Bromell turned, spontaneously, to look again at the portrait of the boy, and the conversation ran as follows:

> *Lois Deacon:* The boy was some years older than you?
> *Mrs Bromell:* Yes, he was older than me . . . That was Rantie . . . R.A.N.T.I.E., Ranty, Randy. . . .
> It *could* be short of Randolph [*this in response to a question*] . . . He was a Sparks. He was in Bristol most of the time. That's where he lived.

According to Mrs Bromell's subsequent statements, 'Randy' had been brought up at Plymouth by Mrs Rebecca Paine, Tryphena's sister, and later lived at Bristol in the home of Nathaniel Sparks, Tryphena's brother. She stated that he had been trained as an architect, but in a later interview with Lois Deacon alone she said that he had helped Nathaniel Sparks, who was a violin-maker, and that his job had been to assist with the accounts.

This, in brief, is the principal evidence that Hardy was the father of a child, and is the source for the only name we know that child to have borne. But Lois Deacon noted one interesting footnote. Mrs Bromell's granddaughter, on hearing Miss Deacon and the family discuss the old lady's comments, recalled the name: '. . . a friend had a little boy, overseas somewhere. They had nothing to do with Grandma, but we were saying that

"Randy" was a funny name to give a boy, and Grandma said she knew a "Randy".'[7]

Providence and Mr Hardy adduces several literary parallels which the authors believe to be biographical allusions, and many of them are persuasive. But leaving literary parallels aside, the evidence would still appear to be strong. Mrs Bromell did not know who the boy's mother was, certainly; but the photograph was in Tryphena's album. She was certain that Hardy was the boy's father, and she produced, without pressure, a name which corresponds to the 'Ry.' of Tryphena's autograph album. She did *not* say that Randy had picked the pressed leaves, but she did find an impossible alternative candidate. She produced information about the child's upbringing, tastes, and physique; she mentioned an injury which is the strongest link between the two photographs. Moreover, she came very close to identifying Tryphena as the mother when she admitted that 'he was a Sparks'. None of the information volunteered during the last phase of her life conflicts with her comment on the photograph in 1960. If what she said is *not* true then we are faced with what seems a more incredible alternative: that Mrs Bromell, old, sick, and knowing that she was nearing the end of her life, *invented* a non-existent person, gave him a non-existent name (which another member of her family recognised), and foisted him onto Thomas Hardy. A further alternative, that she confused a non-existent Randy with another actual child of the family, seems unlikely, since no living member is able to recall a child who might fit the photograph and the inscription, and no one is able to explain the one alternative proposed by Mrs Bromell herself ('Charlie').

Much has been made of Mrs Bromell's five-year silence on this child, a silence maintained even though she was talking and writing extensively about her memories of Tryphena. If Randy —whose full name, Mrs Bromell revealed, was Randal—were indeed Tryphena's son her silence seems to me to be quite natural, particularly in view of her family's subsequent expressions of outrage at the idea that there might have been an illegitimate birth. (At the 1968 Hardy Festival in Dorchester the Bishop of Salisbury himself was subject to criticism for having publicly endorsed the views put forward by Deacon and Coleman, the *Western Gazette* carrying a front-page report headed 'Hardy's Cousins berate Bishop on alleged slur'.) Moreover, Mrs Bromell gave a direct indication that there were subjects which she did not wish to discuss. An early indication of this may be seen, with the benefit of hindsight, from a letter written to Lois Deacon on August 11, 1960, four and a half years before Mrs Bromell's death. After commending Lois Deacon for having done '"yeoman service" in probing all the past events you have found', Mrs Bromell stated that there was still something which remained to be discovered. She gave no clue as to what this might be, but it certainly could not have been the pattern of illegitimacy which Lois Deacon believed she had traced in the generations preceding Tryphena's birth: only two months later, on October 11, 1960, Mrs Bromell wrote in strong terms reacting against the very idea of illegitimacy in the earlier branches of the family. It seems reasonable to believe that what Miss Deacon had then failed to discover was the existence of Randy; and at that stage Mrs Bromell had no intention of telling her more. It also seems possible—no more—that Mrs Bromell may have had some suspicion though no certain knowledge of her mother's involvement. She knew that the child came to see Tryphena; and in an interview on Christmas Day, 1964, she said repeatedly, and with visible distress, 'Hardy loved her, but they said she was a *whore*.' Miss Deacon was shocked and distressed by what she thought she had heard, and asked for corroboration from a member of the family: it was confirmed that Mrs Bromell's words were as they are quoted here. Mrs Bromell added 'They said she ran around with other men.' These two remarks not only point to the probability that Tryphena was indeed the mother of the child, but they also answer one of the principal criticisms to be directed at this case.

For it is a fact that no one in Puddletown, either members of families distantly connected with the Hardys, or the older inhabitants, can recall hearing any kind of scandal, or gossip about a scandal, in the 1860's. Of course no contemporaries are now alive, but scandals tend to live on in Dorset villages long after the principal actors have died. And members of the family do have knowledge of family affairs which took place before their birth, and have given me valuable information on that basis. Mr John Antell, a descendant of Hardy's mother's sister, is a valuable source of information, and states vigorously that he has no reason to believe in the existence of a Hardy child, and has heard no gossip or rumours about it. None the less, Mrs Bromell's remarks suggest that there had been gossip. If the gossip were muted, this is not surprising: for within a year or two of the child's birth, as the census records show, all members of the Sparks family had left the village, leaving no members or descendants to serve as a focus for gossip. In such circumstances only a whisper could have remained.

And, indeed, a whisper does seem to have lingered into the present century. In 1940 an American scholar, Harold Hoffman, visited England for an investigation into Hardy's life, and spent some time in Puddletown. His contact with Mrs Bromell came very late—indeed too late in his visit for him to talk to her—but before this he had come across traces in Puddletown of a girl related to Hardy who had been baptised as the daughter of her actual grandmother, and as the sister of her actual mother. This is precisely the pattern which Miss Deacon believes she has found surrounding Tryphena's own birth. She claims that Tryphena, although baptised as the daughter of Maria Hand Sparks, was in fact the daughter of her 'elder sister', Rebecca Sparks. It is striking, to say the least, that two independent investigators, separated by a period of twenty years, should none the less both present the same hypothesis. Miss Deacon's reasoning has been presented in her published work; we are not so fortunate with Harold Hoffman. He died in 1940, shortly after his return to the United States, and no effort to trace his papers has yet proved successful. But since nothing appears in the local records to justify his theory one can only assume that he was working on the basis of local gossip. Certainly such cases of concealed illegitimacy are not uncommon, even today, as many an inhabitant of country villages will know. Public records may help, but they are not always more reliable than local knowledge, and sometimes they are considerably less so.

This, of course, is not gossip that Tryphena had borne a child, still less that she had borne Hardy's child. But it does suggest that Tryphena was the subject of gossip, as indeed do the school records: this further indication that she was in trouble must also be taken into account.

Lois Deacon maintained, purely on the basis of her reading of the poems, that the most likely date for Randal's birth was the summer of 1868. One small detail that contributed to this was Hardy's reference to a lost poem, written in February 1868, and called 'A Departure by Train'. The heading under which this entry appears reads:

1868. JANUARY 16 AND ONWARDS.

There seems no reason why the missing poem should be mentioned at all, nor is there an obvious explanation for the minute detail with which the date is specified in the heading—it happens nowhere else in the *Life*. But in August 1967, I received permission from the headmaster of Puddletown school to study the school log for the 1860's, and with the headmaster's assistance found that from November 7, 1866, until January 1868, Tryphena Sparks was employed as a pupil-teacher at the school. There are several references to her work, which seems to have been satisfactory except that she was weak in Geography. Then, in 1868, we find:

> *January 16, 1868.* Reproved pupil teacher for neglect of duty—parents very angry in consequence—determine to withdraw her a month hence. [*My italics*]

In fact Tryphena appears to have left the school almost at once, for on January 20 we read:

> Change of teachers. Frances Dunman being appointed P.T. in T. Sparks's place.

On the same day the log records that the usual lessons were not given, and that Tryphena was transferred to the boys' section of the school; but there is no record of her ever carrying out any duties there. The records are well kept: Tryphena disappears from them on January 20. Nor, beyond 'neglect of duty' and the anger of parents, is any reason offered for her dismissal. Set against her steady work during the previous months, and her later career as a highly competent headmistress, this looks very odd. Stranger still is that on January 22, 1868, just two days after Tryphena's removal from the girls' section, the headmistress 'explained fully to 1st & 2nd classes the 7th commandment. . . .' 'Thou shalt not commit adultery' is unusual fare for a group of young girls in Victorian England (although there are some other recorded instances). The timing of the headmistress's explanation is suggestive, as also is the original decision to remove her to the boys' section: if she had been guilty of neglect of duties among the girls, why should she be more energetic among the boys? On the other hand, it might have been considered less morally dangerous to expose the boys to any dangerous example which Tryphena might have presented.

Mrs Bromell had also said one further word on the subject, not recorded in the published transcript of November 1, 1962 (*Tryphena and Thomas Hardy*, pp. 26-30). In the presence of Mrs Bromell's daughter and Lois Deacon, Mr J. Stevens Cox put a direct question to Mrs Bromell: 'Did Hardy and Tryphena have a child?'

Mrs Bromell: I've told you quite enough. We are not going to wash all our dirty linen in public. You know too much already.

J.S.C.: Of course, of course, but can you say they didn't have a child?

Mrs Bromell: No, I won't say that.

Taking all these details together the evidence for a child of Tryphena and Hardy is persuasive. What is true, however, is that to this date *no* details of the child's subsequent career have been found. No certificates of birth, marriage, or death; no details of his working life, no details of his whereabouts after his removal from Plymouth to Nathaniel Sparks's home. The reason for this is not difficult to seek, but the lack of this evidence imposes a large burden of proof on those who believe Mrs Bromell's statements to have been true.

The principal difficulty is that although Mrs Bromell said 'He was a Sparks', there appear to be no records of any child named Randal Sparks. For final proof of the child's existence the search for such records has to continue; and it is not impossible that the child might have borne some other surname from the family. One of the most likely of these is 'Paine', perhaps spelt 'Pain' or 'Payne'.

On Christmas Day, 1872, Rebecca Sparks was married to Frederick Paine, a saddler of Puddletown. Mrs Bromell told Lois Deacon that Rebecca and Frederick had been 'going around together' for several years, and indeed one hopes so, for Frederick saw very little of his wife once the ceremony was over. Tryphena was a witness to the wedding, and on her return to Plymouth to resume her duties as headmistress she was accompanied by Rebecca, who helped her as her housekeeper, and eventually joined the school staff as a needlework mistress. Mrs Paine, in fact, appears to have been a wife in name only. We have Mrs Bromell's word for it that it was Rebecca, and not Tryphena, who looked after Randal while he lived in Plymouth. If this is so—and again the alternative is that Mrs Bromell invented this bizarre story—Randal could only have passed as Rebecca's son. Indeed, there seems no other explanation for the event. Mrs Bromell, it is true, saw nothing strange in this abrupt abandonment of a husband:

> It was rather hard on him, perhaps, but they were going about together for several years before they were married I

> know, and then Tryphena was left by herself in a house in Plymouth . . . so of course their mother being dead she took pity on her and came to look after her.[8]

The notion that a woman would abandon her husband so soon, simply to become her sister's housekeeper, surpasses belief. Rebecca never returned to Frederick Paine, remaining in the Gale household after Tryphena's marriage, and dying there. All that the husband got from the marriage was sixteen pounds, the remaining value of Rebecca's Post Office book at the time of her death.

If all these details contribute to the probability of Mrs Bromell's statements, so do some of the poems, most particularly 'On A Heath' and 'A Place on the Map',[9] which appear to refer to a pregnancy. These should be read in conjunction with Lois Deacon's discussion on Hardy's replies to Vere H. Collins, when questioned on the phrases 'another looming', 'one stilly blooming', and 'a shade entombing', in the last stanza of 'On A Heath'.[10] It is difficult, with Mrs Bromell's evidence to hand, to read these poems without the conviction that, like many others of the 1860's, 1870's and 1890's, they refer to Tryphena.

Setting aside literary sources, however, it remains true that these conclusions rest primarily on an old lady's memories of conversations which took place in her childhood, and referred to events before her birth. Some would claim that they are therefore unreliable. I would make the opposite claim. No one familiar with the conversations of the very old can fail to be struck by the fact that their recollections of childhood are more reliable and vivid than their recollections of yesterday. For the very aged it is often the case that the past is of infinitely more significance than the present, and remains clear even when some of the faculties have become blunted. There is no doubt about Mrs Bromell's lucidity over most of the five and a half years in which she gave her evidence, and the checks made upon her state of mind as she lay on her death-bed seem to me to have been adequate and responsible. At that time Lois Deacon received praise and encouragement from the family, who believed that her conversations with the old lady were beneficial rather than disturbing. There is no doubt that Mrs Bromell was in a position to gather the evidence: her recollections of her mother were based on a strong affection which would in itself have prompted her to cherish her memories; while, after her mother's death, she learned a great deal more from her father. She also stated once that Nathaniel Sparks was an even more important source of information: she lived in his home while she was a student, and he had, according to her, looked after Randal during Tryphena's marriage. Even before identifying the photographs, she had remembered three young men in Nathaniel's Bristol home, although he had two sons only; and Randal would, moreover, have been her half-brother. On most occasions when she made a statement capable of external confirmation (as, for example, the description of Tryphena's home at Puddletown, which she had never seen) her statements were found to be correct. Her memories of other members of the family were accurate most of the time. Where she is incorrect (as, for example, her statement that Hardy was training as an architect in London, when he was actually practising there) the error is usually slight and understandable. The principal discrepancy, the naming of her brother Charlie as the gatherer of the pressed leaves, is much more serious; but any doubts it throws on her reliability seem to me to be dismissed by her memory of the injured hand, which is not obvious in the photograph, and must have been still less obvious to her weakened eyes.

Mrs Bromell, then, gave an apparently firm identification of the two photographs. The first, that of the small boy, was taken by Daniel Couch, of Union Street, Stonehouse; the second, that of the youth, by J. E. Palmer, also of Union Street. R. F. Dalton, formerly Curator of the Dorset County Museum, accepted Lois Deacon's estimates of the age of the child (about eight and twenty-one years respectively), and proceeded to argue that as town directories show the photographers to have left their Union Street premises, Couch by 1875 and Palmer by 1889 at the latest, Mrs Bromell's identification was wrong. Quite apart from the fact that local directories are notoriously unreliable, Mr Dalton's argument suggests only that it was Miss Deacon who was wrong. And there is no doubt that her assessments of the child's age were mistaken. The Victorians over-dressed their children on every formal occasion, a visit to the photographers being no exception; with the result that the young subjects of early photographs are endowed with a maturity which is not theirs. The small boy of the first portrait is no more than five years old, while the young man is certainly not more than sixteen. Moreover, if Mrs Bromell were indeed wrong in her identification of the photographs, they must represent some other member of her family, or someone close to it. There appears to be no candidate. She herself offered none, and it cannot be Charles Gale, Tryphena's husband, as has been more recently suggested: during his childhood years the collodion process had not been perfected. Neither can it be Charles Gale the younger, since by his fifth and sixteenth years the photographers had indeed gone out of business. To question Mrs Bromell's judgement on this point seems rather silly: she knew her family and its friends; she identified all other photographs accurately; she offered no other name for the subject of these portraits.[11]

Deacon and Coleman, of course, made a number of additional suggestions about the course of Hardy's relations with Tryphena. However, there is one vital difference to be drawn between these and the case outlined above: the case for Randal does not depend upon hypothesis, but upon Mrs Bromell. There are additions, certainly: as we have seen, Mrs Bromell did not say that Tryphena was the mother of the child. None the less, all the circumstances point to this conclusion, and the argument is based upon conjecture only to a limited degree. If Mrs Bromell's evidence is discounted as pure gossip, it is surely remarkable that she could have produced such gossip about a mother whose memory she genuinely loved. If it is discounted as the ramblings of a confused and dying woman, then those ramblings are remarkably consistent. If they were invented, for whatever reason, we must suppose in Mrs Bromell a knowledge of Hardy's works so detailed that a story could be produced, fitted to existing photographs and verifiable recollections, and yet still remain consistent with Hardy's literary preoccupations and some of the recurring themes of his work. I do not believe any of these verdicts to be even remotely tenable. Despite much work remaining to be done, I am convinced that Hardy had a son, that Tryphena was the mother, and that the photographs adduced as evidence are genuine portraits of the child.

Providence and Mr Hardy suggests, however, that Tryphena was illegitimate, that Rebecca Sparks was her mother, and that because Rebecca herself was Hardy's illegitimate sister Tryphena was in fact his niece. Hardy's child would thus be the offspring of an 'incestuous' union (the term is used loosely, since in law it would not have been incest). If this were correct it would certainly explain what Providence had 'done to Mr Hardy', but the difficulty of proving it true is enormous.

Initially, all the evidence is against it. Documentary records, as Miss Deacon acknowledges, help little here: but this is a point against her view, not merely a neutral statement of fact. For it is not true that the local records contain no documentation of incest and illegitimacy. If one confines one's search to the parish records which Hardy knew from his own research into his pedigree—principally, Melbury Osmund, Puddletown, Owermoigne, and Stinsford, all in Dorset; and Fawley and Chaddleworth, Berkshire—one finds numerous cases of illegitimacy, some cases of incest, and a considerable number of cousin-marriages. Such records of the unconventional are continued until very late into the nineteenth century, and it is only with the approach of the twentieth that a modern reticence creeps in. It is true that the earlier records are inconsistently or sporadically maintained, but had there been three generations of illegitimacy, culminating in an incestuous union, it is surprising that no trace at all should appear. Tryphena's own illegitimacy seems the most difficult to prove: the case rests primarily on the fact that at the time of Tryphena's birth Maria Sparks, then forty-six years old, was able to travel to Dorchester and back to register the child, and did so within six days of the delivery. It is also stressed that eight years had passed between the birth of Nathaniel and that of his sister Tryphena. To take the latter point first: it is equally true that there are other similar gaps in the family, and there is also a period of ten years between the birth of Hardy's sister Mary and his brother Henry. Similarly, it is a fact that a large number of Hardy and Hand women gave birth to children in their forties; and none of them found it necessary to travel to Dorchester to register the child. John Cox, the registrar, travelled from parish to parish with a horse and trap, making entries in the register as he went.[12] Indeed, every local record points to the complete legitimacy of Tryphena.

This said, Miss Deacon's views cannot be pushed aside. Although there is no official record of illegitimacy, it is possible that Hardy himself knew Tryphena's birth to be irregular. We have seen that in 1940 Harold Hoffman came across a Hardy relative whose birth-registration had been falsified, and the fact that he wrote to Mrs Bromell inquiring about Tryphena suggests that he knew who she was. Miss Deacon's hypothesis is identical. It has to be stated that public records are now all that we have, and Miss Deacon is not supported by local knowledge. But if one rejects her hypothesis and yet accepts, as I believe one must, that Tryphena bore Hardy's child, then one is compelled to ask why Hardy failed to marry her. Miss Deacon's greatest strength is that she is not reluctant to face this question.

It is true that cousin-marriages were subject to strong social disapproval, and during the passage of the Census Act in 1871 the matter was even raised in the House of Commons.[13] It also appears that Hardy was not the only member of his family to cause bitterness, for his sister Mary was apparently engaged to a cousin for several years, until ultimately the family prevented the marriage[14]—a fact which sheds additional light on Thomasin's situation in *The Return of the Native*. Yet it seems improbable that opposition to the marriage of cousins could have been so strong as to prevent Hardy's legal union with Tryphena once she was pregnant by him. It seems equally unlikely that the objection could have been made on the grounds of Tryphena's illegitimacy, supposing for the moment that she really was illegitimate—Hardy himself had been the cause of a hasty wedding. Nor, for that matter, is one justified in assuming that Hardy simply met Emma Lavinia Gifford in 1870 and abandoned Tryphena for her sake: there is no evidence that Hardy loved Emma Lavinia in 1870.*

Hardy's own approach to official records, both those of his own family and those of the landed families of Dorset, was highly sceptical. And if one adopts the procedure which he outlined in the preface to *A Group of Noble Dames*, comparing dates of births, marriages, and deaths, and drawing one's conclusions from them and not from the records themselves, one comes face to face with the formidable character of Rebecca Sparks. When Rebecca died suddenly in Tryphena's married home at Topsham, on September 3, 1885, an inquest was deemed necessary. Death was due to natural causes, and that fact was entered on the death certificate. So, too, was Rebecca's age, and one may guess, since the death was subject to an official inquiry, that it was entered accurately. According to the certificate, Rebecca was fifty-four. Yet the entry in her own Bible indicates that she was three days short of fifty-six. It is also highly suspect: 'Rebecca Maria was born at P'town: 26th. Sept. 1829'. That is nine months, almost to the day, after the marriage of James and Maria Sparks on Christmas Day, 1828. This is certainly possible, but there are so many attempts to adjust the family records that I do not believe it to be true. Yet if, on the other hand, she were really fifty-four years old her birth would have taken place in 1831; and if that were the case, she cannot have been a member of the Sparks family, since her supposed sister, Emma Sparks, was born on May 26 of that year. Rebecca's Bible is also remarkable in that its record was inscribed in 1868, when Rebecca herself was well over thirty-five

* See below, pp. 269-71.

—it seems a late age to begin a family register, unless some special birth or death took place at that time. It was, indeed, the year of her mother's death; it is also, however, supposed to be the year of Randal's birth. If Miss Deacon's hypothesis is true, i.e. if Rebecca were in fact a Hardy and not a Sparks, the birth of a child to Tryphena would have made it imperative to establish an apparently authoritative record to conceal the facts.

These details were Lois Deacon's starting-point, and together with the circumstantial details given in Chapter 13 of *Providence and Mr Hardy*, particularly details of the relationships which existed between the Hardys and the Martins from the year before Tryphena's birth in 1851, they begin to make a rather more imposing case that has generally been acknowledged. For although Miss Deacon has been widely criticised for her interpretation of events, not one of her critics has faced the fact that *the official record is impossible.* The degree of conjecture involved in her interpretation is, admittedly, enormous; yet I can see no alternative to it. We are faced on the one hand with Miss Deacon's view, apparently unacceptable to Hardy's admirers, and certainly not proven; but, on the other hand, we meet a set of dubious family records compiled in part by the family of an author who showed a marked aptitude for cloaking his own life story, and with a sequence of events which is demonstrably not true. The greatest strength of Miss Deacon's views is that they do provide an explanation for the records and for the events, and they are compatible with Hardy's own expressed fears about his ancestry. If her theories are accepted we must assume that unwitting incest took place; if we refuse to believe that, we have to reckon with a Hardy who wantonly abandoned the cousin who had borne his child, and who apparently refused to acknowledge the child's existence for the rest of his life. I can accept unwitting incest as a probable feature of Hardy's career; I cannot accept that he wrote as he did and lived as he did if his life were based upon a lie.

It would be easy to ignore all this, and to accept the standard biographies of Hardy's life which were authoritative until Lois Deacon's work was published: to write of the dignified elder man of letters and to assume that his character in old age reflected the character and conduct of his youth. Easy, but dishonest. And, moreover, of very little help in explaining the nature of Hardy's work. It is inconceivable that *Jude the Obscure* grew out of a cool, platonic love-idyll between two cousins; inconceivable that Hardy, for whatever reason, failed to marry Tryphena and therefore felt so deeply that there was a 'family curse' to which he himself was subject; and almost inconceivable that Little Father Time and his macabre exploits were simply the diseased products of the imagination of a childless man. The suggestions put forward above are not proved, and may very possibly be wrong; but they are nearer to the truth than the early chapters of the *Life*, and they do more honour to Hardy in that they attempt, at least, to discover and accept the truth.

It will readily be observed that the time-sequence for this conjectural interpretation of events does not fit the time-sequence indicated in the *Life*, so far as the *Life* indicates a time-sequence at all for these years; and most especially it takes no account of Hardy's 'Cornish romance' with Emma Lavinia Gifford in 1870. The reason for this is that all the material available for Hardy's visit to Cornwall is *post hoc* evidence. Very oddly, the account in the *Life* is presented through the eyes of Emma Lavinia, Hardy, by his own admission, having made 'laconic and hurried' notes merely.[15] When he does make a direct comment on this period it is not to be trusted: he wrote of his wooing, for example, as 'without a hitch from beginning to end, and with encouragement from all parties concerned', which is totally at variance with Florence Hardy's view:

> On Thursday he started for Plymouth to find the grave of Mrs H.'s father (—that amiable gentleman who wrote to him as 'a low-born churl who has presumed to marry into my family').[16]

That Hardy found Emma attractive is beyond doubt; that he formed any early intention to marry her, or that he fell in love with her and abandoned Tryphena for her sake, is less likely. Again Florence Hardy, a biased but probably trustworthy source, gives us a more consistent pattern of events:

> . . . I cannot believe that those days in Cornwall—at St Juliot—were really so free & happy. Her father at that time was a bankrupt—and I hear since has been struck off the rolls—another brother had shown signs of insanity—and another was bringing the whole family into disgrace. One sister had married the old clergyman to escape the life of companion to an exacting old lady—and she was trying to marry her youngest sister—the late Mrs T. H.—to any man who would have her. They had nearly secured a farmer

> when T. H. appeared. And she was nearly thirty then. And the sisters had violent quarrels. Of course the whole situation has been much idealized. I expect though the poor girl liked being in the Rectory as it must have been an improvement on her truly horrible home—with the father's drunken ravings—once in Plymouth he chased the mother into the street in her night-gown.[17]

Nor is it convincing to regard *A Pair of Blue Eyes* as a portrait of events in Cornwall, however imaginative: Rutland has shown[18] that some portions of the book may have been written before Hardy met Emma Lavinia, and Lois Deacon has taken the suggestion further, with considerable weight.[19] The legend of the 'Cornish romance' is based primarily on the 1912-13 poems, which suggest that Hardy carefully remembered the incidents of his visits to Cornwall; and indeed, his preservation of memories of his childhood loves would suggest that this would have been in character. In particular one would expect him to recall the laying of the foundation-stone for the restored church of St Juliot, since the ceremony was performed by Emma Lavinia herself. Yet he wrote to the rector of St Juliot in 1913:

> It was a pleasure for me to be able to inscribe upon [the memorial plaque to his wife] that my late wife laid the foundation stone for the rebuilding—a fact that I had forgotten till reminded by an old diary of hers. I can now recall that Mr Holder gave the school children a tea on the occasion, & made a speech to them asking them to remember the event. Some may still be living in the parish who do remember it & remember her.[20]

One is tempted to question whether he was there at all—he subsequently failed to appear for the church's reopening.[21] Hardy's letter is in no sense a recollection of the event, but is a paraphrase of Emma's note:

> Mr Holder made . . . a speech to the young ones to remember the event, and speak of it to their descendants, just as if it had been a world-wide matter of interest. I wonder if they do remember it, and me.[22]

Hardy himself made it clear that the interest which grew up between them was not of rapid growth:

> The second visit being by invitation of Mr Holder, the third and fourth professional, and the later ones entirely personal.[23]

Emma Hardy's recollections also show that even Hardy's precise memories of 1870, as expressed in his poems, were mainly the result of his reading of Emma's notes, and this changes the value of the 1912-13 poems as evidence very considerably.

None the less, Hardy did marry Emma Lavinia Gifford, and he did not marry Tryphena. She had met Charles Frederick Gale in Plymouth, and was eventually persuaded by him to return Hardy's ring. In September 1874, Hardy and Emma were married. Tryphena waited longer, until December 1877, but in that month she married Charles Gale, and her child appears to have been sent to Nathaniel Sparks in Bristol. Whatever the detailed course of events, it seems clear that the blow which struck Hardy during his young manhood struck during these years, and that Tryphena was deeply involved.

So, too, was Horace Moule. There is no record of any meeting between Hardy and Moule between his departure for Cornwall in 1870 and a chance meeting in 1872—Hardy simply says they had not met 'for a long time'. About a year later he dined with Moule in London and five days afterwards visited him at Cambridge, staying in rooms in Queens' College. Three months later, on September 4, 1873, Hardy heard that Moule had committed suicide at Cambridge. The death was particularly appalling: Moule had cut his throat, having left his brother calmly enough half an hour before, and his brother had been aroused by the sound of trickling blood. The inquest revealed no certain cause, Moule had been subject to depression, and had apparently sought refuge in periodic drinking bouts which served only to increase his depression. His academic career, as Deacon and Coleman have shown,[24] was extremely arduous, and it was not until thirteen years after his matriculation at Cambridge—itself following three years at Oxford—that Moule eventually took his B.A. He had been talking of suicide long before his death, and his doctor had feared it for at least thirteen months, i.e. since about August 1873, roughly the time when he met Hardy again after their separation. Hardy records several times in the pages of the *Life* that he himself was 'not in bright spirits', 'in no very grand spirits', etc., during 1870, 1871, and 1872, and there seems some reason to believe that both men were oppressed by the same difficulties. Hardy's memorial poem, 'Standing by the Mantelpiece'[25] suggests that Moule's death was the result of personal difficulties, and one may accept Lois Deacon's view that Hardy had 'let warmth grow without discouragement', and that Moule had some association with Tryphena during her period as a trainee in London. The pattern of *A Pair of Blue Eyes*, in which a younger man loses his fiancée to an older, is repeated through the novels, and may very possibly be founded upon fact. That the pattern is repeated particularly in *Jude the Obscure*, a book acknowledgedly influenced by Tryphena, strengthens the possibility: academic frustration, sexual frustration and betrayal, periodically alleviated by drinking; descriptions in the novel of photographs which accord with some of those found in Tryphena's album[26]—all these strengthen the possibility even more.

All in all, the initial scepticism with which *Providence and Mr Hardy* was greeted—a scepticism which I shared—was ill-justified. In some respects it is a faulty book, but that does not make it a wrong one. And it represents a consistent attempt to see Hardy true, and to discover the mainsprings of his inspiration. His sources were, of course, many and varied: and yet it remains a fact that, throughout his work, the most consistent influence was that of a woman, Tryphena Sparks.

BIBLIOGRAPHY

Abercrombie, Lascelles, *Thomas Hardy, A Critical Study*, London, 1912; New York, 1964.

Allen Walter, *The English Novel*, London, 1954, pp. 232-46.

Andersen, Carol Reed, 'Time, Space, and Perspective in Thomas Hardy', *Nineteenth Century Fiction*, IX, December 1954.

—— 'Hardy's Imbedded Fossil', *Studies in Philology*, XLII, July 1945.

—— 'Hardy's Mephistophelian Visitants', *PMLA*, LXI, December 1946.

Bailey, J. O., *Thomas Hardy and the Cosmic Mind*, Chapel Hill, 1956.

—— 'Hardy's Visions of the Self', *Studies in Philology*, LVI, January 1959.

Baker, Ernest A., *A History of the English Novel*, London, 1938, Vol. IX, pp. 11-96.

Barber, D. F., ed., *Concerning Thomas Hardy*, London, 1968.

Bartlett, Phyllis, 'Seraph of Heaven: A Shelleyan Dream in Hardy's Fiction', *PMLA*, LXX, September 1955.

Beach, Joseph Warren, *The Technique of Thomas Hardy*, Chicago, 1922.

—— 'Bowdlerized Versions of Hardy', *PMLA*, XXXVI, December 1921.

Beatty, C. J. P., *The Architectural Notebook of Thomas Hardy*, Foreword by Sir John Summerson. Dorchester, England, 1966.

Beckman, Richard, 'A Character Typology for Hardy's Novels', *ELH*, 30, March 1963.

Bentley, Phyllis, 'Thomas Hardy as a Regional Novelist', *Fortnightly Review*, CLIII, June 1940.

Berle, Lora Wright, *George Eliot and Thomas Hardy: A Contrast*, London, 1917.

Block, Haskell M., 'James Joyce and Thomas Hardy', *Modern Language Quarterly*, XIX, December 1958.

Blunden, Edmund, *Thomas Hardy*, London, 1942, 1951.

Blunt, Wilfred, *Cockerell*, London, 1964, pp. 212-23.

Braybrooke, Patrick, *Thomas Hardy and His Philosophy*, Philadelphia, 1928; London, 1928.

Brennecke, Ernest, *Thomas Hardy's Universe: A Study of a Poet's Mind*, Boston, 1924.

—— *The Life of Thomas Hardy*, New York, 1925.

Brown, Douglas, *Thomas Hardy*, London, 1954.

Buck, Philo M., *The World's Great Age*, New York, 1936, pp. 331-56.

Carpenter, Richard C., 'Hardy's "Gurgoyle's"', *Modern Fiction Studies*, VI, Autumn 1960.

Cecil, Lord David, *Hardy the Novelist*, London, 1943.

Chapman, Frank, 'Revaluations IV: Hardy the Novelist', *Scrutiny*, III, June 1934.

Chase, Mary Ellen, *Thomas Hardy From Serial to Novel*, Minneapolis, 1927.

Chew, Samuel C., *Thomas Hardy, Poet and Novelist*, New York, 1921.

Child, Harold, *Thomas Hardy*, New York, 1916.

Clifford, Emma, 'The Child, The Circus, and *Jude the Obscure*', *Cambridge Journal*, VII, June 1954.

Cockerell, Sydney C., *Friends of a Lifetime*, ed. Viola Meynell, London, 1940.

Collie, J. M., 'Social Security in Literary Criticism', *Essays in Criticism*, IX, April 1959.

Collins, Vere H., *Talks with Thomas Hardy at Max Gate, 1920-22*, London, 1928.

Conacher, W. M., '*Jude the Obscure*, A Study', *Queen's Quarterly*, XXXV, 1928.

Davidson, Donald, 'The Traditional Basis of Thomas Hardy's Fiction', *Southern Review*, VI, June 1940.

Deacon, Lois, and Coleman, Terry, *Providence and Mr. Hardy*, London, 1966.

Dobree, Bonamy, *The Lamp and the Lute*, Oxford, 1929, pp. 21-44.

Douglas, Sir George, 'Thomas Hardy, Some Recollections', *Hibbert Journal*, XXVI, April 1928.

Duffin, Henry C., *Thomas Hardy, A Study of the Wessex Novels*, Manchester, 1916, 1937.

Eliot, T. S., *After Strange Gods*, London, 1934, pp. 54-8.

Elliott, Albert Pettigrew, *Fatalism in the Works of Thomas Hardy*, Philadelphia, 1935.

Ellis, Havelock, *From Marlowe to Shaw: The Studies, 1876-1936, in English Literature of Havelock Ellis*, ed. John Galsworthy, London, 1950, pp. 230-90.

d'Exideuil, Pierre, *The Human Pair in the Work of Thomas Hardy*, trans. Felix W. Crosse, London, 1930.

Felkin, Elliott, 'Days with Thomas Hardy', *Encounter*, XVIII, April 1962.

Firor, Ruth A., *Folkways in Thomas Hardy*, Philadelphia, 1937; New York, 1962.

Flower, Sir Newman, *Just As It Happened*, London, 1950, pp. 81-108.

Fowler, J. H., *The Novels of Thomas Hardy*, English Assn. pamphlet, No. 71, Oxford, 1928.

Garwood, Helen, *Thomas Hardy, An Illustration of the Philosophy of Schopenhauer*, Philadelphia, 1911.

Goodheart, Eugene, 'Thomas Hardy and the Lyrical Novel', *Nineteenth Century Fiction*, XII, December 1957.

Goldberg, N. A., 'Hardy's Double-Visioned Universe', *Essays in Criticism*, VII, October 1957.

Graves, Robert, *Goodbye To All That*, London, 1929, 1960, pp. 248-51.

Gregor, Ian, 'What Kind of Fiction Did Hardy Write?' *EIC*, XVI, pp. 290-308.

Grimsditch, Herbert B., *Character and Environment in the Novels of Thomas Hardy*, London, 1925.

Guerard, Albert J., *Thomas Hardy, The Novels and the Stories*, Harvard, 1949; New York, 1964.

—— ed., *Hardy, A Collection of Critical Essays*, Englewood Cliffs, 1963.

Hardy, Barbara, *The Appropriate Form*, London, 1964, pp. 51-82.

Hardy, Evelyn, *Thomas Hardy, A Critical Biography*, London, 1954.

—— *Thomas Hardy's Notebooks, and Some Letters from Julia Augusta Martin*, London, 1955.

Hardy, Florence Emily, *The Life of Thomas Hardy*, London 1962 (contains *The Early Life of Thomas Hardy*, 1928, and *The Later Years of Thomas Hardy*, 1930).

Harrison, J. E., 'Hardy's Tragic Synthesis', *Durham University Journal*, XLIII, 1950-51.

Hawkins, Desmond, *Thomas Hardy*, London, 1950.

Heilman, Robert B., 'Hardy's Sue Bridehead', *Nineteenth-Century Fiction*, XX, March, 1966.

Hellstrom, Ward, '*Jude the Obscure* as Pagan Self-Assertion', *Victorian Newsletter*, 29, 1966.

Holland, Clive, *Thomas Hardy, O.M., The Man, His Works, and the Land of Wessex*, London, 1933.

Holland, Norman, '*Jude the Obscure*, Hardy's Symbolic Indictment of Christianity', *Nineteenth Century Fiction*, IX, June 1954.

Holloway, John, *The Victorian Sage, Studies in Argument*, London, 1953, pp. 244-89.

Hoopes, Kathleen R., 'Illusion and Reality in *Jude the Obscure*', *Nineteenth Century Fiction*, XII, September 1957.

Howe, Irving, *Thomas Hardy*, New York, 1967.

Hurley, Robert, 'A Note on Some Emendations in *Jude the Obscure*', *Victorian Newsletter*, 15, Spring 1959.

Hyde, William J., 'Theoretic and Practical Unconventionality in *Jude the Obscure*', *Nineteenth Century Fiction*, 20, September 1965.

Hynes, Samuel, *The Pattern of Hardy's Poetry*, Chapel Hill, 1961.

Johnson, Lionel, *The Art of Thomas Hardy*, London, 1894, rev. 1923.

King, R. W., 'Verse and Prose Parallels in the Works of Thomas Hardy', *RES*, XIII, 49, February 1962.

Klingopulous, G. D., 'Hardy's Tales Ancient and Modern', *From Dickens to Hardy, Pelican Guide to English Literature*, ed. Boris Ford, Vol VI, London, 1958.

Lagarde, Fernand, 'A Propos de la construction de *Jude the Obscure*', *Hommage a Paul Dottin*, Faculté des Lettres et Sciences Humaines de Toulouse, 1966, pp. 185-214.

Larkin, Philip, 'Wanted: Good Hardy Critic', *Critical Quarterly*, VII, 1966.

Lawrence, D. H., 'Study of Thomas Hardy', *Phoenix: The Posthumous Papers of D. H. Lawrence*, ed. Edward MacDonald, London, 1936; reprinted in *D. H. Lawrence: Selected Literary Criticism*, ed. Antony Beal, London, 1961.

Lawyer, W. R., 'Thomas Hardy's *Jude the Obscure*', *Paunch*, 28, February 1967.

Lea, Hermann, *Thomas Hardy's Wessex*, London, 1913.

Leavis, Q. D., 'Thomas Hardy and Criticism', *Scrutiny*, XI, 1943.

Lefner, Lawrence, and Holmstrom, John, *Thomas Hardy and his Readers*, London, 1968.

Lillard, Richard Gordon, 'Irony in Hardy and Conrad', *PMLA*, March 1935.

MacDowell, Arthur, *Thomas Hardy, A Critical Study*, London, 1931.

McDowell, Frederick P. W., 'Hardy's Seemings or Personal Impressions: The Symbolical Use of Image and Contrast in *Jude the Obscure*', *Modern Fiction Studies*, VI, Autumn 1960.

Mizener, Arthur, '*Jude the Obscure* as a Tragedy', *Southern Review*, IV, June 1940.

Morrell, Roy, *Thomas Hardy, The Will and the Way*, Kuala Lumpur/Oxford, 1965.

Muir, Edwin, 'Novels of Thomas Hardy', *Essays on Literature and Society*, London, 1949, pp. 110-19.

Muller, Herbert J., 'The Novels of Hardy Today', *Southern Review*, VI, June 1940.

Murry, J. Middleton, 'Thomas Hardy', *Katherine Mansfield and other Literary Portraits*, London, 1949, pp. 215-29.

Newton, William, 'Chance as Employed by Hardy and the Naturalists', *Philological Quarterly*, XXX, April 1951.

—— 'Hardy and the Naturalists: Their Use of Physiology', *Modern Philology*, XLIX, August 1951.

Nieman, Gilbert, 'Thomas Hardy, Existentialist', *Twentieth Century Literature*, I, January 1965.

—— 'Was Hardy Anthropomorphic?', *Twentieth Century Literature*, II, July 1956.

O'Connor, Frank (Michael O'Donovan), *The Mirror in the Roadway*, New York, 1965, 237-50.

Orel, Harold, *Thomas Hardy's Personal Writings*, Kansas, 1966.

Paterson, John, 'The Genesis of *Jude the Obscure*', *Studies in Philology*, 57, 1960.

—— *The Making of The Return of the Native*, California, 1960.

Philpotts, Eden, *From the Angle of 88*, London, 1951, pp. 68-76.

Pilkington, Frederick, 'Religion in Hardy's Novels', *Contemporary Review*, CLXXXVIII, July 1955.

Pinion, F. B., *A Hardy Companion*, London, 1968.

Porter, Katherine Anne, 'Notes on a Criticism of Thomas Hardy', *Southern Review*, VI, June 1940.

Purdy, Richard L., *Thomas Hardy, A Bibliographical Study*, Oxford, 1954.

Richards, Mary Caroline, 'Thomas Hardy's Ironic Vision', *Nineteenth Century Fiction*, III, March 1949.

Roppen, Georg, 'Darwin and Hardy's Universe', *Evolution and Poetic Belief*, Oxford: Blackwell, 1957, 283-316.

Rutland, W. R., *Thomas Hardy, A Study of His Writings and Their Background*, Oxford: Blackwell, 1938; New York, 1962.

Sankey, Benjamin, *The Major Novels of Thomas Hardy*, Denver, Colorado, 1965.

Schofield, Geoffrey, 'Hardy and the Tragic Sense', *The Humanist*, May 1960.

Scott, James F., 'Spectacle and Symbol in Thomas Hardy's Fiction', *Philological Quarterly*, XLIV, 1965.

Scott, Nathan A., 'The Literary Imagination and the Victorian Crisis of Faith: The Example of Thomas Hardy', *Journal of Religion*, XL, October 1960.

Sherman, G. W., 'Thomas Hardy and the Agricultural Labourer', *Nineteenth Century Fiction*, VII, September 1952.

Slack, Robert C., 'The Text of Hardy's *Jude the Obscure*: A Letter and a Foreword', *Nineteenth Century Fiction*, XI, March 1957.

Smart, Alastair, 'Pictorial Imagery in the Novels of Thomas Hardy', *RES* XII, 47, August 1961.

Smart, J. S. ,'Tragedy', *Essays and Studies*, VIII, 1922.

Spivey, Ted R., 'Thomas Hardy's Tragic Hero', *Nineteenth Century Fiction*, III, September 1949.

Stevenson, Lionel, *Darwin Among the Poets*, Chicago, 1932, pp. 237-97.

Stewart, J. I. M., *Eight Modern Writers*, Oxford, 1963, pp. 19-70.

Tomlinson, May, 'Jude the Obscure', *South Atlantic Quarterly*, I, January 1946.

Van Ghent, Dorothy, *The English Novel: Form and Content*, New York, 1953, pp. 195-209, 418-427.

Weber, Carl J., *Hardy of Wessex, His Life and Literary Career*, New York, 1940, rev. 1965.

—— *Hardy and the Lady From Madison Square*, Waterville, Maine, 1952.

—— *The Letters of Thomas Hardy*, Waterville, Maine, 1954.

—— *'Dearest Emmie': Hardy's Letters to his First Wife*, New York, 1963.

Webster, Harvey C., *On A Darkling Plain: The Art and Thought of Thomas Hardy*, Chicago, 1947.

Woolf, Virginia, 'Novels of Thomas Hardy', *The Second Common Reader*, New York, 1932, pp. 266-80.

Zachrisson, R. E., *Thomas Hardy's Twilight View of Life*, Stockholm, 1931.

—— *Stil och personlighet: Thomas Hardys diktning*, n.d.

BEAMINSTER MONOGRAPHS

Illustrated Monographs on the Life, Times, and Works of Thomas Hardy

General Editor: J. Stevens Cox

1. *Personal Recollection of Thomas Hardy*, by Gertrude Bugler.
2. *Hardy, Tess, and Myself*, N. J. Atkins.
3. *Tryphena and Thomas Hardy*, Lois Deacon.
4. *The Domestic Life of Thomas Hardy*, E. E. Titterington.
5. *Thomas Hardy at the Barber's*, W. G. Mills.
6. *Thomas Hardy in his Garden*, B. N. Stephens.
7. *Motoring With Thomas Hardy*, Harold Voss.
8. *Thomas Hardy: His Secretary Remembers*, May O'Rourke
9. *Young Mr. Thomas Hardy*, May O'Rourke.
10. *Guest of Thomas Hardy*, Edmund Blunden.
11. *Thomas Hardy Proposes to Mary Waight*, Constance M. Oliver.
12. *Memories of Mr. and Mrs. Thomas Hardy*, Dorothy M. Meech.
13. *The Return of Wessex*, Wessex Redivivus.
14. *Hardyana.*
15. *Thomas Hardy as a Musician*, J. Vera Mardon.
16. *The Homes of Thomas Hardy*, Evelyn L. Evans.
17. *My Father Produced Hardy's Plays*, Evelyn L. Evans.
18. *Thomas Hardy and his Two Wives*, Christine Wood Homer.

19. *Florence and Thomas Hardy, A Retrospect*, Joyce Scudamore.
20. *Thomas Hardy Through the Camera's Eye*, Hermann Lea.
21. *Appreciation of Thomas Hardy's Works in Japan*, Professor Saburo Minakawa.
22. *Life in Thomas Hardy's Dorchester*, O. M. Fisher.
23. *Thomas Hardy on Maumbury Rings*, W. M. Parker.
24. *A Visit to Thomas Hardy*, W. M. Parker.
25. *Thomas Hardy and the Birdsmoorgate Murder, 1856*, Lady Pinney.
26. *Some Romano-British Relics Found at Max Gate, Dorchester*, Thomas Hardy.
27. *Paupers, Criminals, and Cholera at Dorchester*, Rev. Henry Moule.
28. *The Early Hardys*, F. R. Southerington.
29. *Poems and Religious Effusions*, Emma Lavinia Hardy, ed. J. O. Bailey.
30. *William Barnes, Friend of Thomas Hardy*, A. T. Davies.
31. *The Chosen by Thomas Hardy, Five Women in Blend*, Lois Deacon.
32. *Annotations by Thomas Hardy in his Bibles and Prayer-Books*, Kenneth Phelps.
33. *Tryphena's Portrait Album and Other Photographs of Hardy Interest*, Lois Deacon.
34. *Hardy's Grandmother, Betsy, and Her Family*, Lois Deacon.
35. *Stinsford (Mellstock): A Hardy Church*, C. J. P. Beatty.
36. *Thomas Hardy's Will and other Wills of his Family.*
37. *A 'Mellstock Quire' Boy's Recollections of Thomas Hardy*, W. G. L. Parsons.
38. *Hardy's Summer Romance, 1867*, Lois Deacon.
39. *Identification of Fictitious Place-Names in Hardy's Works*, J. Stevens Cox.
40. *Memories of the Hardy and Hand Families*, L. M. Farris.
41. *Recollections of a Visit to Thomas Hardy*, R. L. Ball.
42. *Hardy's Child—Fact or Fiction?*, F. R. Southerington.
43. *Thomas Hardy at Cattistock*, D. Stickland.
44. *Memories of Thomas Hardy as a Schoolboy*, Charles Lacy.
45. *Letters from Eden Philpotts to Mrs. F. E. Hardy.*
46. *Thomas Hardy's Sturminster Home*, Olive Knott.
47. *The Moules and Thomas Hardy*, Lois Deacon.
48. *Dorchester in 1851.*

NOTES

CHAPTER I

1. *Notebooks*, pp. 40-1.
2. C.P. 878.
3. *Life*, pp. 214-15.
4. Beaminster, 15.
5. Beaminster, 25.
6. *Notebooks*, p. 32.
7. Blunden, *Thomas Hardy*, pp. 11-12.
8. Quoted in *Providence* . . . , p. 163.
9. Beaminster, 1 (quoted by permission of the Dorset Natural History and Archaeological Society).
10. *Return*, V-ix.
11. The terms are quoted from the unpublished notes for the *Life*, Dorset County Museum.
12. Dr. Elsie Smith, Librarian of the Cathedral Library at Salisbury, has publicly stated that she has documentary evidence of this, though she has not yet published her source.
13. See, for example, Moule's letter of July 2, 1863 (Dorset County Museum), quoted in *Providence* . . ., p. 98.
14. *Life*, p. 48.
15. Newman Flower, *Just As It Happened*, New York, 1950, pp. 88-9.
16. C.P. 5; Purdy, p. 97.
17. *Life*, pp. 46-7.
18. *Ibid.*, p. 54.
19. Dorset County Museum; reproduced in Evelyn Hardy, *Thomas Hardy, A Critical Biography*, facing p. 224.
20. Rutland, pp. 124, 128; *Providence* . . . , Ch. 9.
21. *Notebooks*, p. 48.
22. Thomas Hardy to Sir George Douglas, November 20, 1895 (National Library of Scotland).
23. *Life*, p. 116.
24. Emma Hardy to Lady Hoare, April 24, 1910 (Stourhead Collection, Wiltshire Archives; by permission of Mr H. P. R. Hoare and the National Trust).
25. See Emma Hardy to Rebekah Owen, February 2, 1899 and April 24, 1910 (Colby College, Waterville, Maine).
26. Emma Hardy to Rebekah Owen, April 24, 1899 (Colby).
27. *Ibid.*
28. Emma Hardy to Rebekah Owen, May 20, 1908 (Colby).
29. Emma Hardy to Rebekah Owen, February 19, 1897 (Colby).
30. Florence Hardy to Sydney Cockerell, November 11, 1922. Quoted in *Friends of a Lifetime*.
31. Thomas Hardy to Edward Clodd, August 5, 1910 (Berg Collection, New York Public Library).
32. Beaminster, 4.
33. *Just As It Happened*, p. 96.
34. Florence Hardy to Rebekah Owen, February 9, 1914 (Colby).
35. Florence Hardy to Rebekah Owen, July 17, 1915 and December 3, 1915 (Colby).
36. Florence Hardy to Violet Hunt, December 23, 1925 (Berg Collection, New York Public Library).
37. Florence Hardy to Rebekah Owen, December 30, 1915 (Colby).
38. Florence Hardy to Rebekah Owen, June 7, 1915 (Colby).
39. *Essays and Studies*, 1966, p. 117.
40. Quoted in *Cockerell*, p. 223.
41. Florence Hardy to Lady Hoare, December 6, 1914 (Stourhead Papers, Wiltshire Archives).
42. Quoted by Irene Cooper Willis, 'Thomas Hardy', an unpub-

lished typescript in the Colby College Library, dated 1940, p. 11.
43. *Daily Telegraph*, January 13, 1928.
44. *Just As It Happened*, p. 97.
45. See *Cockerell*, pp. 214-16.
46. Beaminster, 1; by permission of the Dorset Natural History and Archaeological Society.
47. See David Garnett, *Letters of T. E. Lawrence*, London, 1964, p. 592.
48. Beaminster, 10.
49. Florence Hardy to Lady Hoare, April 7, 1914 (Stourhead Papers).
50. Florence Hardy to Lady Hoare, December 9, 1914 (Stourhead Papers).

CHAPTER II

1. Donald Davidson, 'The Traditional Basis of Thomas Hardy's Fiction', collected in *Hardy: A Collection of Critical Essays*, ed. A. G. Guerard, Englewood Cliffs, 1963, pp. 10-24.
2. *Essays and Studies*, VII, 1922.
3. *Life*, pp. 243-4.
4. *Jude*, VI-iii.
5. *Aspects of the Novel*, London (Penguin), 1962, pp. 100-1.
6. *The Appropriate Form*, London, 1964, pp. 70-1.
7. 'On Tess of the D'Urbervilles', collected in Guerard, *Hardy, A Collection of Critical Essays*, pp. 77-90.
8. Davidson, *op. cit.*
9. Davidson, p. 17.
10. Guerard, *Hardy, A Collection . . .*, pp. 38-9.
11. *Life*, p. 150.
12. *Tess*, XV.
13. *Jude*, I-vi.
14. *Jude*, V-iii.
15. *Tess*, XI.
16. *Tess*, LVII.
17. *English Dialect Dictionary.*
18. *Tess*, L.

CHAPTER III

1. I-iv.
2. IV-i.
3. IV-iv.
4. I-i.
5. I-v.
6. III-iii.
7. III-i.
8. III-ii.
9. IV-iv.
10. IV-ii.
11. IV-iii.
12. V-iii.
13. IV-vii.
14. II-ii.
15. For the reference to Hardy's neighbours, see Beaminster, 51.
16. *On A Darkling Plain*, Chicago, 1947; reprint 1962, p. 104.
17. XI, my italics.
18. XII.
19. *Ibid.*
20. XXVII.
21. *Ibid.*
22. *Ibid.*
23. XXVIII.
24. *Ibid.*
25. XX, my italics.
26. XXVII.
27. XXXIV.
28. XXXV.
29. XXII.
30. XXXII.
31. *Life*, p. 74.
32. *Providence . . .*, p. 108.
33. XL.
34. XXX.
35. XIII.
36. XXX.
37. XXII.

CHAPTER IV

1. See Roy Morrell, *Thomas Hardy, The Will and the Way*, Kuala Lumpur/Oxford, 1965, pp. 59-72.
2. *Notebooks*, p. 48.
3. James's review is reprinted in *Literary Reviews and Essays by Henry James*, ed. A. Mordell, New York, 1957, pp. 201-7.
4. *After Strange Gods*, London, 1934, pp. 54-8.
5. *Op. cit.*, p. 294.
6. See 'The Art of Fiction' in *Henry James, Selected Literary Criticism*, ed. M. Shapiro, London, 1963, pp. 49-67.
7. Ch. XVIII.
8. Ch. XXII.
9. See especially Howard Babb, 'Setting and Theme in *Far From the Madding Crowd*', *ELH*, 30, 2, 1963, pp. 147-61.
10. Ch. VI.
11. *Op. cit.*, p. 149.
12. *After Strange Gods*, p. 55.
13. Ch. XXXI.
14. Morrell, *op. cit.*, p. 60.
15. Ch. XVIII.
16. Ch. XVIII.
17. Ch. I.
18. Ch. XII.
19. Ch. XVII. My italics.
20. Ch. XX.
21. Ch. XXV.
22. Ch. VIII.
23. Ch. V.
24. See also Morrell, *op. cit.*, p. 12.
25. Ch. XXXVI-XXXVII.
26. Ch. XXV.
27. Ch. LIII.
28. Ch. XXXVII.
29. Ch. XIII.
30. Ch. XXI
31. Ch. XXIX.
32. *Woodlanders*, Ch. XLII.
33. *Ibid.*
34. *Tess*, Ch. XXI.
35. *Blue Eyes*, Ch. XXII.
36. *Jude*, Ch. II-ii.
37. *Desperate Remedies*, Ch. XII-vi.
38. Ch. XLIV.
39. Ch. XXVIII.
40. *The Victorian Sage*, London, 1962, pp. 268-9.
41. Ch. XXVIII.
42. *Op. cit.*, Ch. I.
43. 'Hardy's "Gurgoyle's"', *Modern Fiction Studies*, 6, 3, 1960, p. 225.
44. *After Strange Gods*, p. 55.

CHAPTER V

1. Evelyn Hardy, *Thomas Hardy*, p. 154; Rutland, p. 176.
2. *Life*, p. 104.
3. Ch. IV.
4. Ch. V.
5. *Op. cit.*, pp. 150-1.
6. *Ibid.*
7. 'In Defence of *Ethelberta*', *Nineteenth-Century Fiction*, June 1958.
8. *Phoenix*, London, 1936 and 1961; also in *D. H. Lawrence: Selected Literary Criticism*, ed. Antony Beal, London, 1961.
9. *Op. cit.*, esp. Ch. 2.
10. *Op. cit.*, p. 166.
11. Morrell, *op. cit.*, p. 145.
12. Ch. V 3.
13. Ch. V, 6.
14. Ch. V, 7.
15. Ch. IV, 8.
16. *Life*, p. 120.
17. *Op. cit.*, p. 167.
18. Ch. I, 3.
19. Ch. II, 6. My italics.
20. William Barrett, *Irrational Man*, New York, 1962, p. 82.
21. Ch. III, 1.
22. 'A Plaint to Man', C.P. 306.
23. 'New Year's Eve', C.P. 260.
24. 'The Mother Mourns', C.P. 101.
25. 'A Cathedral Façade at Midnight', C.P. 666.
26. 'Before Life and After', C.P. 260.
27. Ch. I, 1.

28. Ch. II, 6.
29. C.P. 288.
30. *Op. cit.*, p. 125.
31. C.P. 154.
32. C.P. 262.
33. Ch. I, 10.
34. Ch. II, 6.
35. See M. A. Goldberg, 'Hardy's Double-Visioned Universe', *Essays in Criticism*, VII, 1957, pp. 374-82.
36. Ch. I, 2.
37. Firor, pp. 46, 48.
38. Ch. I, 6.
39. Ch. VI, 4.

CHAPTER VI

1. Douglas Brown, *The Mayor of Casterbridge*, London, 1962.
2. *Op. cit.*, p. 38.
3. NED, Necessity, 2nd entry.
4. *Life*, p. 337.
5. *Ibid.*, p. 335 (where Hardy uses the word in its absolute sense) and p. 449.
6. Ch. XLIV.
7. Carlyle, *Miscellaneous Essays*, London, 1872, Vol. I, pp. 137-8.
8. *Ibid.*, p. 133, my italics.
9. *Op. cit.*, p. 43.
10. Ch. XIV.
11. Ch. XIV.
12. Ch. XI.
13. Ch. XXIV.
14. Ch. XXIV.
15. Ch. XLIV.
16. Ch. XLV.
17. Ch. XIX.
18. Ch. XXIX.
19. J. A. Symonds, *The Greek Poets*, quoted in Literary Notebook I (see pp. 219-22), presumably in 1876, since other entries at this point are from periodicals of that year.
20. *Madding Crowd*, Ch. XLIV.

CHAPTER VII

1. *Life*, p. 148.
2. Ch. I-xiv.
3. Ch. I-xii.
4. Ch. I-ii.
5. Ch. I-iii.
6. Ch. I-xii.
7. Ch. I-ii.
8. Ch. I-iv.
9. Ch. I-ii.
10. *Life*, p. 312.
11. Ch. I-xiv.
12. *Trumpet-Major*, Ch. XV.
13. Ch. III-ii.
14. Ch. III-iii.
15. C.P. 253.
16. *Life*, p. 116.
17. C.P. 408.
18. Morrell, *op. cit.*, p. 174.
19. Ch. II.
20. *Ibid.*
21. C.P. 257.
22. *Life*, pp. 148-9.
23. Ch. IV.
24. Ch. IV.
25. Ch. XXXV.

CHAPTER VIII

1. Transcribed from Rebekah Owen's copy of *The Woodlanders*, Colby College, Waterville, Maine. Also quoted by Weber, *Hardy and the Lady From Madison Square*.
2. Ch. IV.
3. *Ibid.*
4. E. von Hartmann, *Philosophy of the Unconscious*, trans. W. C. Coupland, London, 1884, Vol. I, Ch. VI.
5. Thomas Hardy to Sir George Douglas, November 20, 1895. Original in the National Library of Scotland, Edinburgh.

6. Webster, *On A Darkling Plain*, p. 170.
7. Ch. III.
8. Ch. XXVIII.
9. Ch. XXX.
10. Ch. XXXI.
11. Ch. VI.
12. Inscription in Rebekah Owen's copy of the novel.
13. *Black and White*, August 27, 1892, p. 240.
14. Ch. XI.
15. Review by Edmund Gosse, *Cosmopolis*, January 1896.
16. Ch. XIX. See David Lodge, *Language of Fiction*, London, 1966, Ch. II, 4.
17. Ch. XII.
18. *Ibid.*
19. *Ibid.*
20. Ch. XIII.
21. Ch. XVI.
22. Ch. XIV.
23. Ch. XXV.
24. R. C. Schweik, 'Moral Perspective in *Tess of the D'Urbervilles*', *College English*, Vol. 24, 2, October 1962, p. 15.
25. Ch. XLIX.
26. Ch. XXXIX.
27. Ch. XIX.
28. Ch. XX.
29. *Ibid.*
30. Ch. XXX. My italics.
31. Ch. XVI.
32. Ch. XIII.
33. Ch. XVI.
34. Ch. XIV.
35. Ch. V.
36. Ch. XXV.
37. *Black and White*, August 27, 1892, p. 238.
38. Ch. XXV.
39. Ch. IV.
40. *Ibid.*
41. Ch. XXIX.
42. Ch. XXXIV.
43. Ch. XIX.
44. Ch. XXX.
45. Ch. XXXV.
46. Ch. IX.
47. Ch. V.
48. Ch. II .
49. Ch. XIV.
50. *Providence and Mr. Hardy*, p. 40.

CHAPTER IX

1. Florence Hardy's 'Notes for the Life of Thomas Hardy', Dorset County Museum.
2. Mrs Bromell's Recollections.
3. C.P. 58.
4. C.P. 846.
5. *Jude*, II-v.
6. *Providence* . . ., Ch. 10.
7. V-vii.
8. VI-i.
9. II-i.
10. VI-ii.
11. I-iii.
12. II-iii.
13. V-iii.
14. See Rutland, p. 250.
15. C.P. 48.
16. IV-ii.
17. IV-iii.
18. VI-iii.
19. VI-iv.

CHAPTER X

1. *Life*, p. 286.
2. Florence Hardy's 'Notes' for the *Life*, Dorset County Museum.
3. *TLS*, January 15, 1904.
4. *Life*, p. 185.
5. *Life*, p. 186.
6. *War and Peace*, tr. L. & A. Maude, New York, 1942, X, 21 and 26.
7. *Shorter Oxford Dictionary*.
8. See Samuel Hynes, *The Pattern of Hardy's Poetry*, Chapel Hill, 1961.

9. Edward Wright to Thomas Hardy, May 18, 1907. Dorset County Museum.
10. Hardy to Wright, June 2, 1907. Quoted, *Life*, p. 334, with some alterations.
11. *Life*, p. 285.
12. Forescene.
13. C.P. 301.
14. C.P. 687.
15. C.P. 321.
16. C.P. 72.
17. C.P. 484.
18. *Two On A Tower*, Ch. iv.
19. Forescene.
20. C.P. 106.
21. Forescene.
22. Forescene.
23. *Return*, II, vi.
24. C.P. 260.
25. *Life*, p. 231.
26. *Return*, V, vii.
27. I, i, 6.
28. Forescene.
29. Forescene.
30. After-scene.

CHAPTER XI

1. Schopenhauer, I, 142.
2. *Woodlanders*, VII.
3. *Ibid*, XXVIII.
4. Schopenhauer, I, 356.
5. I, v, 4.
6. *Ibid.*
7. *Woodlanders*, XLII.
8. *Life*, p. 152. My italics.
9. C.P. 798.
10. Dorset County Museum; also quoted in *Life*, p. 335.
11. *Life*, p. 449.
12. *Ibid*, X, xxviii, p. 875 (my italics) and IX, i, pp. 669-70.
13. *Madding Crowd*, Ch. VIII.
14. I, i, 1.
15. I, v, 5.
16. III, i, 5.
17. *Life*, p. 203.
18. I, i, 3.
19. Hansard, March 6, 1805.
20. III, vii, 8.
21. I, v, 2.
22. III, v, 6.
23. *The Pattern of Hardy's Poetry*, p. 166.
24. I, vi, 8.

CHAPTER XII

1. Chaucer, Prologue to *The Nun's Priest's Tale*.
2. See Hardy's note of June 1875, *Life*, p. 106.
3. Forescene.
4. I, vi, 1.
5. I, i, 3.
6. II, vi, 5.
7. I, i, 6.
8. II, v, 2.
9. II, ii, 6.
10. III, iv, 6.
11. II, i, 8.
12. II, vi, 3.
13. II, vi, 4.
14. I, ii, 2 and I, iii, 1.
15. III, i, 12.
16. III, i, 11.
17. III, i, 12.
18. III, vii, 9.
19. I, i, 6.
20. III, iv, 4.
21. I, vi, 1, and III, iii, 1.

CHAPTER XIII

1. *Life*, p. 449.
2. After-scene.
3. I, i, 3.
4. C.P. 260.
5. I, v, 4.
6. C.P. 260.
7. *Tess*, Ch. XXV.
8. C.P. 7.
9. After-scene.
10. I, i, 3.
11. C.P. 88.
12. *Life*, p. 454.
13. Preface to *Wessex Poems*.

CHAPTER XIV

1. *Life*, pp. 15-16, *Jude*, I-ii, C.P. 825 & 846.
2. Quoted in W. E. Houghton, *The Victorian Frame of Mind*, Yale and London, 1957, p. 98.
3. *Life*, p. 310.
4. Hardy's reading is treated extensively in Rutland, *Thomas Hardy, A Study of His Writing and Their Background*, Oxford, 1938, New York, 1962; and Bailey, *Thomas Hardy and the Cosmic Mind*, Chapel Hill, 1956.
5. J. A. Symonds, *Studies in the Greek Poets*, 2 series, London, 1873-6.
6. First literary notebooks. The addition in square brackets is Hardy's.
7. Literary Notebook I.
8. Tess, IV.
9. *Life*, p. 100.
10. Literary Notebook I. The italics are Hardy's. Source: 'An Attempted Philosophy of History', *Fortnightly Review*, 27, January-June 1880, p. 679.
11. Literary Notebook II. Source: D. G. Ritchie, *Philosophical Studies*, London, 1905.
12. Literary Notebook I. Source: F. W. H. Myers, 'Human Personality', *Contemporary Review*, February 1885.
13. *Life*, p. 146.
14. *Life*, p. 224.
15. *Life*, p. 436.
16. Thomas Hardy to Edward Clodd, July 1, 1926. Berg Collection, New York Public Library.
17. Symonds, *Greek Poets*, quoted in Literary Notebook I.
18. *Woodlanders*, Ch. iii.
19. *Dynasts*, I, i, 6.
20. Literary Notebook I. Auberon Herbert, 'A Politician in Trouble', *Fortnightly Review*, 34, July-December 1883, pp. 361, 370.
21. *Op. cit.*, p. 370. Hardy's punctuation of his transcript of the earlier lines varies from that of the original.
22. Literary Notebook II. *Philosophy of the Unconscious*, III, xiv. The best discussion of Hardy's Reading of von Hartmann is Bailey, *Thomas Hardy and the Cosmic Mind.*
23. See Rutland, p. 93ff.; and Garwood, *Thomas Hardy, An Illustration of the Philosophy of Schopenhauer*, Philadelphia, 1911.
24. Literary Notebook II. Source cited by Hardy as '*Studies in Pessimism*, Schopenhauer (May 13 '91). 69'.
25. Literary Notebook I.
26. C.P. 479.
27. London, 1882, p. 51.
28. *Life*, p. 146.
29. *Science of Ethics*, pp. 33-4.
30. *Op. cit.* p. 162.
31. C.P. 88 and 306 respectively.
32. Thomas Hardy to John Hartman Morgan, April 21, 1924. Berg Collection, New York Public Library.
33. Literary Notebook I. Source: *Spectator*, April 8, 1862.
34. *Life*, p. 176.
35. *Life*, p. 274.
36. *Life*, p. 364.
37. C.P. 798.
38. D. H. Lawrence, *Selected Literary Criticism*, p. 168.
39. C.P. 439.
40. *Life*, pp. 450-1.
41. C.P. 124.
42. Florence Hardy to Lady Hoare, December 9, 1914 (Stourhead Papers, Wiltshire Archives).
43. C.P. 521.
44. Blunden, p. 173.
45. Blunden, p. 279.
46. C.P. 886.
47. *Life*, p. 315.
48. *Life*, pp. 412-13.

APPENDIX A

1. Calendar of State Papers, Domestic 1547-80, p. 127.
2. Hutchins, 3rd ed., IV, p. 433.
3. Hutchins, IV, p. 502; Somerset House, Administration Books, 1599, 1605. See also Beaminster 28.
4. C.P. 878.
5. *Life*, p. 420.
6. Fawley parish registers.
7. C.P. 257.
8. *Jude*, III, vi.
9. *Jude* MS., Fitzwilliam Museum, Cambridge.
10. Reproduced in Evelyn Hardy, *Thomas Hardy, A Critical Biography*, facing p. 224.
11. C.P. 721.
12. C.P. 151; Melbury parish registers.
13. C.P 878 and 431.
14. *FR.*, Vol. 34, July-December 1883, pp. 244-50.
15. *FR.*, Vol. 31, January-June 1882, pp. 332-8.
16. *Life*, p. 7.
17. Papers of Rebekah Owen, Colby College Library, Waterville, Maine.
18. Papers of Lois Deacon.
19. *Life*, pp. 7-8.
20. *Ibid.* p. 420.
21. *Ibid.* p. 1; and Melbury parish registers.
22. 'Notes of Thomas Hardy's Life, by Florence Hardy (taken down in conversations, etc.)'—Dorset County Museum.
23. Beaminster, 44.
24. See 'A Church Romance', C.P. 236.
25. *Life*, p. 214.

APPENDIX B

1. Three MSS. in the possession of Lois Deacon, dated June 25, 1959, July 8, 1959, and July 1959; each written by Mrs Bromell alone, and sent through the mail to Miss Deacon.
2. Beaminster, 3, pp. 18-19.
3. Lois Deacon to Terry Coleman, January 14, 1965.
4. Sources at this point are the letters of Lois Deacon to Terry Coleman and other correspondents, copies of which are in Miss Deacon's possession.
5. Statement to the author, October 22, 1967.
6. *Times Literary Supplement*, July 25, 1968.
7. Deacon correspondence.
8. Mrs Bromell to Lois Deacon, February 18, 1960.
9. C.P. 441 and 302 respectively.
10. *Providence and Mr. Hardy*, pp. 184-186.
11. For Dalton's article, see the *Bridport News*, July 12, 1968.
12. Information from Mr John Antell, confirmed by the Dorset Registrar's Office, Dorchester.
13. See G. H. Darwin, 'Marriages Between First Cousins', *Fortnightly Review*, 18, July-December 1875.
14. Information from Mr John Antell, related to both the Hardy and the Sparks families.
15. *Life*, p. 74.
16. Florence Hardy to Edward Clodd, March 7, 1913 (Brotherton Library, University of Leeds).
17. Florence Hardy to Rebekah Owen, October 24, 1915 (Colby College Library, Waterville, Maine).
18. Rutland, pp. 124, 128.
19. *Providence* . . ., Ch. 9.
20. Thomas Hardy to the Rev. J. H. Dickinson, June 1, 1913 (Berg Collection, New York Public Library).
21. *Some Recollections*, p. 59.
22. *Ibid.*, p. 56.
23. *Ibid.*, p. 56.
24. *Providence* . . ., pp. 95-6.
25. C.P. 846.
26. See Beaminster, 33.

INDEX